Penny Vincenzi, who died in 2018, was one of the UK's best-loved and most popular authors. Since her first book, *Old Sins*, was first published in 1989, she went on to write sixteen more bestselling novels and two collections of stories. She began her career as a junior secretary for *Vogue* magazine and went on to work at *The Daily Mirror*, *Tatler*, and later as a Fashion and Beauty Editor on magazines such as *Woman's Own*, *Nova* and *Honey*, before becoming a Deputy Editor of *Options* and Contributing Editor of *Cosmopolitan*. Over seven million copies of Penny's books have been sold worldwide and she is universally held to be the 'doyenne of the modern blockbuster' (*Glamour*).

Praise for A *Question of Trust*:

'The queen of the posh blockbuster returns with another chunky decade-spanning saga' *Sunday Mirror*

'This magnificent doorstep of a book contains everything we expect from Vincenzi – glamour, passionate affairs, secrets and betrayals. Another winner' *Sunday Express*

'With a rich cast of characters buffeted by love, betrayal and loyalty, glamour and conflict, this is Vincenzi at her best' *Woman & Home*

'This author never lets you down – her latest novel is superb' *Sun*

'[A] hugely enjoyable romantic drama . . . lots of the period characters [that] Vincenzi does so well' *Daily Mail*

'A Sunday afternoon in autumn, a pot of tea, a round of toast and a new Penny Vincenzi novel – I know of no finer way to while away a few hours' *Red*, Best Books of the Month

'Glamorous, escapist and gloriously enjoyable, this decade-spanning novel is rich in detail' *Best*

*By Penny Vincenzi*

Old Sins
Wicked Pleasures
An Outrageous Affair
Another Woman
Forbidden Places
The Dilemma
The Glimpses (short stories)
Windfall
Almost a Crime
No Angel
Something Dangerous
Into Temptation
Sheer Abandon
An Absolute Scandal
The Best of Times
The Decision
Love in the Afternoon and Other Delights (short stories)
A Perfect Heritage
A Question of Trust

# PENNY VINCENZI

## THE NO.1 BESTSELLER

*A Question of Trust*

REVIEW

First published in Great Britain in 2017 by Headline Review
An imprint of HEADLINE PUBLISHING GROUP

First published in paperback in 2018
by HEADLINE REVIEW

6

Cataloguing in Publication Data is available from the British Library

ISBN (A-Format) 978 0 7553 7765 7
ISBN (B-Format) 978 0 7553 7764 0

Offset in 10.34/13.24 pt New Caledonia by Jouve (UK), Milton Keynes

Printed and bound in Great Britain by Clays Ltd, Elcograf S.p.A

HEADLINE PUBLISHING GROUP
An Hachette UK Company
Carmelite House
50 Victoria Embankment
London EC4Y 0DZ

www.headline.co.uk
www.hachette.co.uk

For the Magnificent Nine: William, Jemima, Ollie, Honor, Grace, Ellie, Niamh, Samuel and Beth: my grandchildren.

# Character List

Tom Knelston, *a young left-wing solicitor, with political ambitions*

Jack Knelston, *his father, the postman in West Hilton, a small Hampshire village where Tom has grown up*

Mary Knelston, *his mother*

Colin and Arthur Knelston, *his brothers*

Jess Knelston, *his eldest sister*

Isobel Parsons, *Tom's godmother*

Alan Parsons, *her husband and heir to Parsons, a large department store in Hilchester, the nearby town*

Miss Rivers, *Tom's teacher at primary school*

Tristram Sherrin, *history master at the grammar school*

Angela Smithers, *Tom's first girlfriend, a salesgirl at Parsons*

Pemberton & Marchant, *firm of solicitors where Tom works as a trainee*

Gordon Pemberton and Basil Marchant, *the two partners there*

Nigel Pemberton, *Gordon's son, also a trainee*

Betty Foxton, *secretary to the two partners*

Mr Roberts, *chairman of the Hilchester branch of the Labour Party*

Ted Moore, *Labour Party member and Tom's champion there*

Laura Leonard, *a teacher and staunch member of the Labour Party*

Edith, *her mother*

Babs, *her sister*

Brigadier Sir Gerald Southcott, *local grandee, living at West Hilton Manor*
Caroline, *his wife*
Diana, *their beautiful, spoilt daughter*
Michael, *their elder son, a medical student*
Richard, *their younger son*

Ned Welles, *a fellow medical student and friend of Michael Southcott*
Sir James Welles, *his surgeon father, a consultant at St Peter's, Ned's first hospital*
Sir Neil Lawson, *chairman of the board of governors of St Luke's, Ned's second hospital*
Sir Digby Harrington, *on the board of governors of St Luke's*
Phillip Harrington, *his son and a registrar*
Jennifer, *Ned's secretary at his private practice*
Persephone Welles, *Ned's beautiful mother who ran away with an artist when Ned was very young*
George Tilbury, *a boyfriend of Persephone's*
Susan Mills, *a young patient of Ned's*

The Hon Johnathan Gunning, *who Diana marries*
Jamie, *their son*
Sir Hilary and Lady Vanessa Gunning, *his parents*
Piers and Timothy Gunning, *Johnathan's brothers*
Catherine, *a girlfriend of Johnathan's*

Sir Harold Morton, *Diana's obstetrician*
Hugh Harding, *her solicitor*

Wendelien Bellinger, *a socialite and Diana's best friend*
Ian Bellinger, *her husband*
Ludo Manners, *good friend to Ned Welles and part of the Bellingers' set*

Cecily Manners, *his wife*

Betsey Southcott, *married to Michael after the war, also one of the Bellingers' set*

Donald Herbert, *a rich and successful businessman, and important power behind the throne of the Labour Party*

Christine Herbert, *his long-suffering wife*

Robert Herbert, *his brother, Islington solicitor, and Tom's employer*

Colin Davidson, *Tom's constituency agent*

Alice Miller, *a young nurse at St Thomas' Hospital*

Alec and Jean Miller, *her parents*

Philip Jordan, *a doctor, her boyfriend*

Kit, Lucy and Charlie, *Alice and Tom's children*

Mrs Hartley, *Tom and Alice's kindly neighbour*

Dr Redmond, *their GP*

Jillie Curtis, *Alice's best friend at boarding school, and a medical student*

Geraldine and Peter Curtis, *her rich and well connected left-wing parents*

William Curtis, *her uncle, a prominent obstetrician*

Mrs Hemmings, *cook and housekeeper to Jillie's parents*

Eleanor (Nell) Henderson, *a young novelist*

Julius Noble, *her fiancé*

Seth Gilbert, *editor at Eleanor's publishers*

Patrick Brownlow, *suitor of Jillie's*

Harry Campbell, *the editor of the* Daily News

Jarvis McIntyre, *the proprietor*

Clive Bedford, *the political editor*

Josh Curtis, *his assistant and cousin of Jillie*

Philippa Parry, *the women's editor*

Blanche Ellis Brown, *fashion editor of* Style *magazine*
Esmé, *Diana's agent when she becomes a model*
Freddie Bateman, *an American photographer*

Miss Dickens, *the editor of* American Fashion
Ottilie, *her fashion editor*

Leo Bennett, *the diary editor of the* Dispatch *newspaper*
His brother Marcus, *a garden designer*
Mark Drummond, *proprietor of the* Dispatch
Fiona Jenkins, *a journalist on the* Dispatch
Ricky Barnes, *a keen young trainee reporter on the* Daily Sketch
  *newspaper*

Christian Greenfell, *a vicar*

# Chapter 1

## 1936

Tom Knelston was very fond of saying that the first time he met Diana Southcott he had been up to his waist in shit.

And it was literally true; he had indeed been standing waist deep in a blocked drain outside his parents' cottage and she had come riding up the lane on the rather fine bay mare she had just acquired and was putting through her paces before taking her out next time she rode to hounds.

'Oh,' she said, pulling the mare up. 'Hello. That looks fun.'

Tom had looked up, trying to muster a smile in response to what she undoubtedly thought was a joke, thinking at one and the same time how beautiful she was – and how enragingly pleased with herself – and said, 'Yes, it is. Want to join me? I could do with some help.'

'I'd love to, but unfortunately I'd be late for luncheon. Good luck with it, though.' And she pressed her heels into the mare's sides and trotted on up the lane.

Tom looked after her for a moment – at her gleaming dark hair tucked neatly under her riding hat, at her perfectly cut hacking jacket, at her long slender legs encased in cream jodhpurs which, despite being spattered with mud, looked somehow immaculate – and returned to the drain.

He knew who she was: the only daughter of Brigadier Sir Gerald Southcott who lived at the Big House – officially West Hilton

1

Manor – in the village where Tom's family lived. He had seen her before many times, in church, at the village fete, at the Christmas concert in the village hall, together with her two elder brothers and her parents, all so clearly aware of their position and of doing their duty by the village.

Sir Gerald, who disappeared three days a week up to London where he worked in the City, spent the remainder of the week engaged in hunting, shooting and other country pursuits, and Lady Southcott was on the board of the village school, the cottage hospital and the orphanage which West Hilton shared with East Hilton and Hilton Common, a cluster of small Hampshire villages just south of Winchester. She was also one of the few women still to ride side-saddle – and look magnificent while doing so – when out hunting.

In short, they were the perfect First Family of the village, popular but slightly distant. Tom, whose father was the village postman, and who was already discovering rather egalitarian principles nurtured by his grammar-school education, regarded them with less awe than most of the village and was rather satisfied by his exchange with Diana. His mother he knew would have quite possibly made a small bob and his father – perhaps slightly grudgingly – raised his cap as she passed them by.

It was many years before he spoke to her again.

Tom was the golden boy, set bang in the middle of five siblings, with two elder sisters and two younger brothers. His sisters alternately adored him and resented the adoration showered upon him by their parents, being the longed-for first boy, and his little brothers looked up to him and considered him the fount not only of all wisdom, but pretty much every other quality as well. He was certainly the cleverest of them – Jack and Mary Knelston were conscious of that – and at parents' evenings Miss Rivers, his teacher at the village school, reported favourably upon his exceptional reading skills; while most of the children were still struggling with the simplest of stories, Tom, at six, was reading real books – *Babar the Elephant* being his favourite, with its illustrations and thick cardboard covers – and at eight venturing into such glories as *Huckleberry Finn*, which resulted in him making his own raft and setting sail across the stream at the bottom of the village, soon to sink in a morass of water weeds. His favourite present every Christmas was *The Monster Story Book for Boys*, which silenced him for several days.

When Tom was ten, Miss Rivers asked Jack and Mary to come and see her. In her view, Tom was exceptionally bright – grammar-school material. She would like to enter him for the scholarship.

Jack and Mary felt panicked. They couldn't possibly afford school fees, they said – they were at least £5 a year – and why should Tom rise to the unimaginable heights of a grammar-school education and not the other children? It wouldn't be fair.

Miss Rivers explained that there wouldn't be any fees, that a third of grammar-school places were free to children from elementary schools, provided by way of the scholarship examination; the only cost would be his uniform.

There was a silence and then she continued, 'I really do think Tom is an exceptional child; it would be wrong to deny him this chance.'

Whereupon Mary said, with the look on her face that Jack knew there was no escape from, that if Tom passed the scholarship they would find the money for the uniform somehow.

Miss Rivers was delighted and said she would enter Tom along with two other boys and one girl in their class – since 1922 girls had been considered worthy of free education – and that the examination would be held in the early spring.

Words were exchanged as the Knelstons walked home; Mary told Jack he had heard what Miss Rivers said, it would be wrong to deny Tom this chance, and if she had to take in washing to pay for the uniform she would. After a brief struggle, Jack gave in.

'But none of the others'd better want it,' he said, 'or you'll be doing the washing for the whole village.'

When they told Tom he went pink with pleasure. He'd often looked at the grammar-school boys as they got off their school bus in their uniforms and thought how lucky they were. He'd never dreamed he'd have a chance to join them.

'Why lucky exactly, lad?' Jack asked, genuinely intrigued.

'Because they get to know so much,' said Tom simply, and it was this that swung Jack round wholeheartedly. If it was knowledge that above all mattered to Tom, then Jack could sympathise; he had had to leave school at twelve and found the education he was enjoying stopped for ever. He'd embarked on a correspondence course for a while in geography, always his favourite subject, but once marriage and babies overwhelmed him, he gave up. He was, however, genuinely worried that Tom might be lost to the family as he grew older; but he told himself that he hadn't sat the exam yet, and might not even pass it. Miss Rivers's idea of exceptional might not be the same as the examiners'.

Tom did pass the scholarship, though, and with very high marks. Mary was about to advertise herself as a washing resource when Tom's godmother, Isobel, stepped in and said she would like to pay for the uniform. Isobel was a rather glamorous figure; she had gone to school with Mary but married well – to the heir to Parsons, the big department store in Hilchester, the nearest proper town. She and the heir, one Alan, lived in a red-brick villa on the edge of Hilchester and had the unimaginable luxury of a housemaid. They also had help in the garden.

Isobel had remained close to Mary and, being childless, became involved in Mary's large family and was particularly fond of Tom. When he heard what she was going to do for him he went into Hilchester on the bus to thank her personally. Isobel was very touched and celebrated by giving him chocolate eclairs for tea and trouncing him at draughts.

Tom was very happy at the grammar school. Tall and well built, good at games as well as lessons, he was never in danger of being bullied; there was a genuine cross section of class in the school and the sons of local farm workers, jobbing builders and tradespeople were taught alongside those of businessmen, teachers and doctors. Tom particularly attracted the attention of the history master, a rather flamboyant character called Tristram Sherrin; he was a brilliant, inspiring teacher, and had sent many boys on to read history at university. He ran a chess club after school, which Tom joined, after which he would sit and chat with the boys and talk about their futures and their aspirations. Tom told him that what he really wanted to do was become a barrister: 'The law really interests me, and I'd love to stand and argue people's cases in court.' Sherrin said this was an admirable ambition, but a university degree was essential, adding tactfully that he feared this would not be an option for Tom on financial grounds. However, Tom might become a solicitor, by way of taking articles, and this too was fascinating work. 'Not as glamorous, perhaps, but I think you'd enjoy it. I have a friend who is a solicitor; if you're interested when the time comes, we can have a further conversation.'

Tom said he would be very grateful and challenged him to another game of chess which he won. Sherrin looked after him as he left the room and marked him down as a boy to watch.

As Tom reached sixteen and faced the School Certificate, there was certainly no sign of him developing the dreaded ideas above his station. He was as devoted a son as could be wished for and by the time of the chance meeting in the lane with Diana Southcott, he was also becoming extraordinarily good-looking.

# Chapter 2

## 1937

The Southcotts were not proper aristocracy – Diana's father had been knighted after the war, rather than inheriting his title, but that was a detail that both he and Lady Southcott considered of little importance. The Manor House in West Hilton had been bought by Sir Gerald's father, a rich industrialist who had raised his eldest son to consider himself landed gentry. Sir Gerald and his family moved into the house after he died, thereby cementing their impression of themselves, and indeed the impression of everyone else in the area.

Lady Southcott took her duties as Lady of the Manor very seriously, and devoted herself to her charities, and to the local community, most assiduously. She produced an heir (and a spare) to the dynasty, Michael and Richard, and had then offered a final flourish, Diana, who would be presented at court in the next London Season.

That summer of 1937, Diana was seventeen years old, beautiful, accomplished, supremely self-confident, and waiting impatiently for her season in the sun – or at least in London and planning her own dance, to be held in May at West Hilton Manor, at the end of which she would quite possibly have found herself several rich and suitable young men as suitors, one of whom (ideally titled) would, fairly swiftly, become first her fiancé and then her husband. Such was the ordered and indeed expected rite of passage for girls of her class and upbringing.

Diana's dance – actually her whole season – was a great success. Held on one of the loveliest nights of the year, early in June, at Hilton

6

Manor in a marquee filled with white roses and studded, like the garden, with starry lights, it was a fairy-tale occasion, as several of the society pages chose to call it. A hundred and fifty young people attended, the girls all sweet faced, the boys well behaved, the band fashionable. The food – a small dinner beforehand and a breakfast at dawn – was splendid, the champagne vintage. Sir Gerald had been budgeting for the occasion for years, knowing his daughter's future could very well depend upon it.

Diana had serious work to do, and only a short time in which to do it; this had been none too subtly impressed upon her by her mother, who had been reading aloud from the engagement column in *The Times* over breakfast for several months now, exclaiming at the felicity of one girl's choice and the inopportuneness of another's. Putting the paper down when she had finished, she would smile at Diana and say, 'Well, darling, this time next year, who knows?' Or words to that effect.

Had Diana had more of an education she might have baulked at her role in this drama. As it was, she accepted it excitedly, and entered into preparations for it with great enthusiasm. And as she danced the night away and a seemingly endless procession of suitable young men told her how beautiful she was, many of them adding that they would hope to see her again very soon, she realised the fulfilment of her – and her mother's – ambitions were to be achieved without undue difficulty. To love, at this stage, she gave little consideration.


Tom left the grammar school with several credits in his Higher School Certificate, and Tristram Sherrin kept his promise to introduce him to Gordon Pemberton, a local solicitor, who was looking for an articled clerk. He was impressed by Tom and took him on. There was a little difficulty over the fee of £300 required for articles; once again, the admirable Isobel was happy to advance this. Tom, deeply grateful, assured her he regarded it as a loan, and that as soon as he was earning anything at all substantial, he would repay it.

He was fairly happy during his first two years at Pemberton & Marchant. It was a very quiet life. The firm was a small one, with just two partners: Pemberton himself and Basil Marchant, both in their early fifties; then there were two senior clerks, with two secretaries, one for each partner, and Gordon Pemberton's son, Nigel, studying for his articles like Tom.

Tom's favourite member of staff was Basil's secretary, Betty Foxton. She was fifty and a widow, bosomy, rosy and very cheerful. She behaved in a motherly way towards her 'boys' as she called them, often bringing them in a cake she had baked, and always interested in what they had done at the weekends.

The work was almost entirely conveyancing, with some probate thrown in, but Tom's dream of becoming a solicitor made him feel that whatever he was doing was important.

'It does have its moments,' he told Angela Smithers, with whom he had been going out for six months. Angela was a salesgirl at Parsons, and he had met her through his godmother. She was very pretty, endowed with blonde hair and big blue eyes but not a great brain; she had high hopes of her relationship with Tom Knelston even though he was, as her mother pointed out, 'only a postman's son'. Angela, a spirited girl, retorted that she couldn't see much difference between that and being a motor mechanic's daughter.

Tom had no hopes, high or otherwise, of his relationship with Angela, except to kiss her more often and perhaps more excitingly, and in six months they had certainly progressed beyond the peck on the cheek, the dry kiss on the lips, to quite exploratory activities, usually in the back row of the cinema – she had even once or twice allowed him to stroke one of her breasts (very briefly). He could see he was never going to get beyond that stage without certain commitments which he was most assuredly not prepared to make. For the time being, she was fun and they enjoyed one another's company.

Mr Pemberton didn't often praise Tom or even speak to him, but at the end of his first six months, he said, 'I'm pleased with you, Tom, very pleased. You've worked hard and done well. I hope you're happy here.'

Tom told Mr Pemberton that he was. Mr Pemberton nodded and said he hoped he and Nigel were getting along, and Tom said, yes, of course, Nigel was extremely pleasant to work with.

This was absolutely true as far as it went: Nigel had never been remotely unpleasant to him, always nodded to him in the morning and said goodnight to him at night and occasionally commented on the weather; that was about it. Tom put this down initially to the fact that he was indeed rather in awe of Nigel who was older than him and had been to university. At Pemberton & Marchant, he was the heir apparent – Basil Marchant had only daughters. Nevertheless, they were the youngest people in the office by a country mile, as Betty would say, and it would have been good to make a real pal of him. Tom once tried, suggesting they went to the cinema together when the much-vaunted film *Lost Horizon* came to Hilchester, but Nigel said he was busy on Saturday night.

'Doesn't have to be Saturday,' Tom said. 'Friday, maybe, or if it arrives Thursday we could go then.'

'No, thanks,' said Nigel. 'Not really my bag.'

Tom shrugged, tried again once with a different film, and then gave up.

They had really nothing in common apart from their work. Nigel was a keen golf player, went on holiday to places like Eastbourne and Cornwall with a crowd of friends, and from time to time up to London. Tom would learn of these activities through Nigel's answers to Betty's questions. She was insatiably curious about both boys' leisure activities and Nigel didn't seem to regard this with anything but good-natured amusement. It was as if he came from another country, speaking another language and with terms of reference Tom couldn't understand. It puzzled him at first, but gradually it dawned on him: he was from a totally different class. The Pembertons lived in a big house on the outskirts of Hilchester, with a family car and servants; and apart from the cachet of having been to university, Nigel had also gone to public school. He had an easy confidence bordering on arrogance, simply by virtue of this, or so it seemed to Tom. He occasionally, very politely, asked about life at the grammar school and seemed surprised when he was told some pupils went to university.

Some of the differences were created purely by money: Nigel could afford to belong to the local tennis and golf clubs, to go to concerts and the theatre, and he and his father were often to be heard discussing some book or other they had bought, rather than borrowed from the library. Money – Nigel's possession of it, his own lack of it, and the difference that must make – Tom could understand.

Class, that was different. Apart from the Southcotts, the village grandees, as his father called them contemptuously, were clearly from another world so alien it might have been Mars. It hadn't occurred to him that some perfectly ordinary people, going about their business, whatever that might be, might consider themselves superior to other perfectly ordinary people, purely by virtue of what their fathers did and, to a degree, how they spoke. Tom was aware that the grammar school had taught him to speak differently from his parents, but that had been a result of hearing what was called Received Pronunciation all day long. He had made no conscious effort to change his accent, and would have been astounded if anyone had suggested he might. Having become aware of the class thing, Tom became first irritated, then annoyed, and finally slightly disturbed by it. It seemed genuinely regrettable to him, this yawning chasm between him and someone of his own age, doing the same job. For the first time he properly understood his father's hostility to his own tacit ambitions of leaving his class behind.

The other yawning gap between him and Nigel was their clothes. Nigel had at least three winter suits and three summer ones and many ties. Tom knew it was absurd to care, but he couldn't help it, and as his cheap work suit grew shiny on the seat and his two ties increasingly worn, he became acutely self-conscious about the whole thing and asked Isobel for money for clothes when she enquired what he would like for Christmas. Isobel realised what the problem was, having risen in the social firmament herself, and duly provided the wherewithal for several ties and a pair of new shoes, offering to take him shopping for a new suit when it was his birthday.

In the office, Tom was rather lonely, despite loving the work; he missed the camaraderie of school, the genuine sense of friendship and shared endeavour that had constituted life there. He did see some of his old friends at the weekends, but they too were divided. The cleverest had gone to university – one to the unimaginable heights of Oxford – and others into their father's businesses, some to do quite menial jobs or to work on farms.

But Tom had very little money to spend; apart from taking Angela to the cinema, he could only manage occasional nights at the King's Head in West Hilton with his mates. And his father kept him busy at the weekends, demanding rather than requesting his assistance with the endless tasks in the house and garden; it was his way of reminding Tom where he belonged, and maintaining his own dignity against the fact that his eldest son was marking out a path so different from his own.

Mary was inordinately proud of him and never stopped talking about how well he was doing; but Jack's primary emotion on the subject seemed closer to distaste. Tom found this, as he said to Angela, hurtful. Angela, surprisingly sensitive over such matters, kissed him and told him Jack was probably just jealous, which Tom conceded. But he would still have greatly preferred his father to speak as proudly of him as he did of his brothers, Colin and Arthur, who were both apprenticed to local builders.

# Chapter 3

## 1938

'Michael's asked if he can bring someone called Edward Welles down this weekend.' Lady Southcott smiled at Diana across the breakfast table. 'He's a new friend from the medical school at Barts. I don't know anything more about him, except that we are to call him Ned and his father's a famous surgeon. But I'm sure he's very nice – Michael's friends always are.'

This was a bit of a sweeping statement, Diana thought, and quite untrue. Some of them were ghastly, loud, blustering and over-confident, but anything would be better than the stultifying boredom of another weekend alone with her parents.

Michael had finished his three years at Oxford and gained an Upper Second in his first MB; he was now at St Bartholomew's Hospital in London to do his clinical training. He loved it and was extremely happy.

Diana envied him desperately. She was finding the autumn and the ending of the season very dull and disappointing after a whirl-wind summer; and until the winter party season began, almost every invitation seemed to be to an engagement party, some for girls in her year. Diana found these hugely irritating; it wasn't that she actually wanted to be engaged (and indeed was quite vocal on the subject) but she liked to shine, and seeing diamond rings flashing on the fingers of other girls, while her own left hand remained indisputably bare, clearly made this difficult.

'Well – let's hope,' was all she said now.

'Darling, don't be negative,' Caroline said. 'Now, I had thought we could do a dinner party, but Michael said they'd rather keep it just family. He and Ned have had a very heavy few weeks and they don't even want to go hunting; Ned's not a horseman apparently. So it'll just be the five of us for dinner on Saturday. Unless you want to invite a girlfriend, darling. Suki, perhaps – we still owe her for her cocktail party.'

Diana didn't. If Ned Welles was even half attractive, the thought of anyone amongst her girlfriends vying for his attention was not a happy one. On the other hand, she didn't want him to think she had nothing else to do for a whole weekend.

'No,' she said firmly. 'No, she'd be bored. She's a party girl and this is family, you said so yourself.'

Caroline looked at her with a sweet expression. 'Well, I realise it would make the weekend a bit man-heavy, but what about inviting Johnathan Gunning? He's such a sweet man, and you get on rather well. He's a bit stuck in London at weekends, with his people living up in Yorkshire. He told me last time I saw him how much he loved hunting.'

'I thought Ned didn't want to hunt,' said Diana.

'Darling, Ned is Michael's friend and responsibility, not yours, so you could give Johnathan a day's hunting.'

She looked at Diana hopefully. Johnathan Gunning's family was not only rich but titled. He was the third son of Sir Hilary Gunning, Bart, and thus an Hon. The extra h in his name was a family idiosyncrasy and Diana rather liked it; you couldn't hear it, of course, but written down, especially with the Hon. in front, it made it look rather special. He had grown up in considerable grandeur in the family seat, Guildford Park in Yorkshire, and was training to be a stockbroker in his uncle's office.

Although he wasn't exactly handsome, he was very nice looking, with light brown hair and dark eyes, and more of a chin than so many of his compatriots. He was charming, if in a slightly quiet way. He lived in a flat in Knightsbridge belonging to his mother, where Diana had been to a couple of dinner parties. The flat was quite grand in an old-fashioned way, and it seemed to her to symbolise unimaginable grown-upness and independence.

He was in many ways a considerable catch and at nearly twenty-four the right age for her. The catching was a distinct possibility and her mother was very excited by the idea. He clearly liked Diana and as well as the dinner parties had escorted her both to Ladies' Day at Ascot and to Goodwood, and to the theatre a couple of times. The only thing was, she found him rather dull. He was certainly very clever – he had a First in Classics – and he loved going to the theatre – the proper theatre, not musicals, but Shakespeare and Restoration comedy (which had seemed extremely unamusing to her); he also liked to talk about politics and the situation in Europe. Of course, that was extremely important and worrying (her father never stopped talking about it either) but again not exactly fun over dinner.

So, with the season over, they had rather drifted apart; Johnathan worked very hard in London, she was very much back in the country, and there were few opportunities for them to meet. Maybe this weekend would be a chance to make quite sure it wasn't worth trying. Hunting would be fun, and with him sitting next to her at dinner Ned Welles was more likely to find her attractive and interesting.

'That's a good idea,' she said. 'Why don't you ring him up, see if he's free? Only do make clear it's for the hunting, won't you? I don't want him to think I'm chasing him.'

'Darling, of course I will. Now dinner – pheasant do you think, or some good old-fashioned beef?'

Diana hardly heard her mother chattering on. She was worrying now that she had done the wrong thing, encouraging Johnathan, muddying the possible waters with Ned Welles. Oh, for goodness' sake, she thought, he was probably short, with pimples. She decided to go for a ride. It wasn't quite raining and it would pass the morning.

It was pathetic to be leading the life of little more than a child when she was nearly eighteen, she thought, turning her horse towards the Downs. She occasionally thought about getting a job in London, but then what on earth could she do? She had no skills or qualifications. It was how things were, so it wasn't her fault. You had to wait until you were married and then you were busy, running a house and entertaining and having babies. Maybe when she saw Johnathan this weekend she would find him more, well, more what she wanted.

But . . . she just didn't find him attractive. There was no spark there, he just wasn't sexy. She had been kissed enough by sexy boys to know what that felt like. Being kissed by Johnathan was perfectly pleasant, but it didn't create that hot churning feeling inside her that some of the other boys' kisses did. She had a fairly clear idea of what sex might be like, and a few of her more daring girlfriends had actually Done It – Suki Riley-Smith amongst them, which was another reason for not letting her near Ned Welles at dinner – and reported varying degrees of satisfaction, ranging from 'rather thrilling' to 'absolutely amazing, impossible to imagine'.

Diana, however, had no intention of sampling the pleasures; she adhered to the old-fashioned view, heavily stressed by her mother, that your virginity was something best saved for your future husband, and if it wasn't, you risked losing respect and gaining an unsavoury reputation.

As she rode back, still with a sense of restless depression about herself and her situation, she passed the cottage where she had had the encounter with Tom Knelston as he dug out his parents' drain. The meeting came back to her with great clarity. Now he was *really* attractive, absurdly good-looking with his dark auburn hair and wonderful green eyes, and quite – well, *very* – sexy, his eyes moving over her, half in appreciation, half in a sort of mocking disapproval. His whole demeanour, in fact, had disturbed her even then, when she was sixteen. He was a year younger, or so Michael told her; he had played in the village cricket match against him for the last two years, and pronounced him a bloody good player for a village boy. She had seen him occasionally at church, cycling through the village on his way to school, occasionally helping his father deliver the post at Christmas, growing ever taller and more handsome.

She was sure Tom Knelston had quite a lot of experience of Doing It.

Tom, greatly to his regret, still had no experience whatsoever of Doing It; Angela was determined to preserve her virginity at all costs, and if those costs included losing Tom, then that was a small price to pay.

15

Tom knew this; and he was sufficiently fond of Angela to put up with it. She was slowly allowing a slackening of her rules, and he was now permitted to stroke and even fondle her breasts to his heart's content, given the opportunity, but the moment his hands drifted downwards she emitted a stern reprimand. It was all very frustrating; she was so pretty and so sweet to him, and always looked extremely nice. She had very little money for clothes, but she was clever at sewing, and made most of her dresses out of discounted materials from Parsons, using the free patterns that came with *Woman's Own* or *My Weekly*, her favourite magazines. By the summer of their courtship, in 1938, they managed to save up enough money to buy bicycles, second-hand but beautifully restored by Angela's father. They set off every Sunday, unless it was absolutely pouring with rain, with picnics laden into their bicycle baskets: sandwiches, hard-boiled eggs, slices of delicious cake baked by Angela herself and cold lemonade in the Thermos flask (or tea for the chillier days). Looking back from much later in his life, Tom remembered those days, pedalling through the countryside, challenging Angela to races, picnicking in fields and woods and arriving home sated with fresh air and sunshine, as some of the happiest in his life.

They would talk of Angela's life at the store, or of Tom's life at Pemberton's, and when, if ever, he might become a fully fledged solicitor, but they also discussed – to Tom's surprise that she should be interested, and even modestly well informed – the growing threat from Hitler's Germany. It was not an unusual topic, of course; everyone was worried and aware of the dangers, although of differing opinions. Angela's father was a great appeaser, claiming that there was some good in what Hitler said and was doing: 'Say what you like, he's turned that country round.' Jack took the opposing view, reinforced by the appalling behaviour of the fascist Oswald Mosley's Blackshirts; Mary kept silent about her views, but she nursed a silent passion for the wildly romantic Duke of Windsor and he was clearly of a mind to go along with Hitler – and why not, if it meant there would be no war? With three sons under threat, war was to her a nightmare of dreadful proportions.

'I suppose you'd have to go and fight if there was a war?' Angela asked one day as they lay back in the long grass, and Tom said, yes, of course, any right-minded man would, and then found himself distracted, as he so often was, by more personal considerations. Angela had made herself one of the new divided short skirts for their cycling, finishing just above her knees and revealing more of her legs than he had ever dreamed he would be privy to. Tentatively he put out a hand and stroked one of her calves, then moved upward above her knee, expecting to be slapped down any moment. But she merely looked at him and laughed and said, 'Oh, go on then,' adding, 'No higher than that, mind,' as he reached mid-thigh. But that was enough happiness for now as he started to kiss her, and the war and Mr Hitler were of as little consequence as the skylarks flying high above them in the blue sky. Yes, it was the happiest time.

And then he met Laura.


'Well,' Caroline Southcott said happily, as they waved off first Michael and Ned and then Johnathan after a rather extended Sunday luncheon, 'what a lovely two days. Ned is such a sweetie, and Johnathan is an absolute charmer. I like him so much and so does Daddy. They had the most wonderful conversation about Hitler and his goings-on after dinner last night.'

'Yes, I know,' said Diana shortly. She had found the conversation hugely irritating as it consumed Johnathan's attention for at least an hour. At first she had been quite pleased, thinking this was her chance to concentrate on Ned and indeed get him to concentrate on her. For Ned was quite something. Not short, not pimply, but tall, with dark floppy hair and what she could only describe as burning dark eyes, which he turned on her with great intensity as they were introduced. He was amusing too, and, she discovered after supper, a very good jazz pianist.

'So,' said Caroline. 'Have you been exposed to patients already?'

'Good Lord, no. Kept well away from them, poor souls,' said Ned, laughing. 'We're taught entirely in the medical school. It's just across Charterhouse Square from the hospital.'

'I believe your father is a surgeon. Is his hospital Barts?' said Johnathan, who had been very quiet until then; he had arrived much later than the others, only just in time for dinner.

'No, no, thank God,' said Ned, and although he laughed, Diana had a feeling he meant it. 'He's at St Peter's Chelsea. Orthopaedics, real old sawbones he is. Literally. Sorry,' he added, seeing Caroline's face. 'Not ideal dinner-table subject. Trouble with growing up in a medical household, you're a bit insensitive. He's terribly disappointed I'm not in a surgical firm—'

'Firm?'

'Yes, that's how we're divided up,' said Michael. 'Medical and surgical. Apprenticed to a team of doctors, headed by a consultant, whole thing called a firm. Of course, you do both in the end. We medical chaps are called clerks, the surgical students are dressers. As in dressing wounds. Oh, dear, perhaps we'd better change the subject.'

'Yes, I think we had,' said Caroline, laughing. 'Johnathan, how is the City these days?'

And they were off. Diana almost pleaded a headache, but didn't want to appear feeble – although she did leave the table first, saying she wanted an early night, with a day's hunting ahead.


'I don't know who's enjoyed it more, us or them,' said Jonathan. They were leaning on the gate of the paddock, watching their weary horses cropping at the grass.

'I'm glad we could offer you such a good day,' said Diana. 'Perfect weather. The horses love it, being part of a herd, and—'

'And we love it for the same reason.'

'Oh, dear,' she said. 'I'm not sure I quite want to be part of that herd. They're a bit . . .'

'What? Two-dimensional?'

'Well, yes. I suppose so. Present company excepted, of course,' she added quickly.

'Of course. But I don't think you're right, actually,' he said slowly. 'My parents both adore it, but they're two very different people; my father is far more thoughtful than my mother, intellectual I suppose you would say.'

'Like you,' she said, smiling at him.

'Oh, he makes me look a complete philistine.'

'Good heavens. And your mother?'

'She *is* a complete philistine,' he said, laughing. 'But fearless – no fence could daunt her. Whereas he's actually almost sick with fear the morning before a day out. But once out there, he's perfectly happy. Wouldn't miss it for the world. Says he becomes someone else.'

'That's brave, still to do it when you're terrified. I'm more like your mother, I just love it, don't think about the consequences.'

Johnathan looked at Diana and smiled. 'Good,' he said. It was an odd response. She felt she had learned more about him in that one conversation than during the whole summer: and liked him better too.

He still wasn't exciting though. She sat between him and Ned at dinner, but it was difficult not to concentrate entirely on Ned. If she was honest, she didn't seem to be entirely captivating him. He chatted away, easily and amusingly enough, but seemed to be as interested in her mother and Michael as he was in her. She was an accomplished flirt, and used to getting any man she fancied, but it wasn't working with Ned. It irritated her, and she turned back to Johnathan, but he was already engrossed in another deep conversation with her father about Europe and the likelihood of war.

After dinner, Michael said he and Ned were going to have a game of billiards. They invited her to join them, and she accepted but she was off form – usually she was rather good – and she became so irritated with herself that she said she was going to find Johnathan and left them to it. Johnathan was by this time sitting with her mother, listening to the radiogram. Caroline had bought a new recording of Beethoven's 'Pastoral' Symphony, eight records dropping painfully slowly, one by one, onto the turntable, and as they were only halfway through, Diana had a long wait, flicking through the pages of *Vogue* and *Tatler* to relieve the boredom. When the music was finally over, she suggested a game of gin rummy, hoping it would liven things up, but Johnathan said he was hopeless at card games and actually pretty tired after the hunting and would they forgive him if he went to bed.

At this point, Michael and Ned reappeared and said they were going to have a quick nightcap. Ned smiled at Diana and said perhaps they could play billiards again some time, he could see she was actually jolly good. 'You looked pretty happy on that horse of yours as well this morning. Do you enjoy hunting?'

'Yes, I love it,' said Diana and was about to launch into a description of the day, but then remembered her mother saying there was nothing more boring to non-hunting people than hearing it discussed and so she asked instead if Ned ever hunted.

'No,' he said. 'No, I don't. I actually think it's rather cruel.'

'Really?'

'Well, yes. You must be able to see that, however much you enjoy it.'

'I – I never really thought about it,' she said, truthfully. And indeed, she had not; from her very first day out when she was blooded as quite a small girl, aged nine or ten, she had loved it, the speed, the challenge of keeping up with the field, the adrenalin rush of facing the fences and the gates, the increasing excitement. She'd never questioned the rectitude of the thinking behind it.

'It keeps down foxes,' she added, rather feebly, 'and they are the most cruel, awful animals.'

'But I have heard some hunts actually import foxes into an area, so there are more to chase. That doesn't exactly meet the claim about keeping them down, does it?'

'Oh, I'm sure that's not true,' she said, although she had heard this too and chosen to ignore it. 'It's probably just a myth. We can certainly agree that foxes are beastly animals. Oh, hello, Michael.'

She accepted a small brandy from Michael as he joined them and sat back, hoping they would start talking about their student lives which always amused her. To her great disappointment, they returned to the subject of Europe and Hitler's persecution of the Gypsies, and after a very short while she excused herself and went, greatly disappointed, to bed.

Next morning it was pouring with rain, and Ned, Michael and her father read the papers for what seemed for ever, first over the breakfast table and then in the drawing room, and then launched into still further discussion until Caroline joined them for pre-lunch G and Ts, then it was lunchtime and a lot of excellent red wine was drunk, and then Michael and Ned drove off.

Diana hoped most fervently that she would be able to meet Ned again. He might not have shown a great interest in her – or actually the slightest, if she was honest – but she felt instinctively that she could rectify that. And the weekend had served one very important purpose, confirming her view that Johnathan Gunning, for all his money and apparent suitability, was not remotely right for her.

# Chapter 4

## 1938

'You what?' Jack's voice was stern, defensive, not in the least the delighted welcoming reaction Tom had hoped for – even expected. God, he was hard to please. He'd thought his father would like the fact that he wanted to join him at the Labour Party meetings, events that were, for him, sacred affairs, akin to going to church; it seemed instead to be inspiring yet more resentment and hostility.

'I do, Dad. I really would like to come. Do you have any objections?'

'Well – no. I suppose not. As long as you're coming in the right state of mind. I don't want them to think you're some would-be toff, looking to put them through their paces.'

'Dad! I am not a would-be toff. I genuinely want to join the party – I've thought about it long and hard. I think it's more important than ever, with the state the country's in, war almost certainly on its way, and that idiot in charge. I mean, I don't want war – who does – but it's better than lying down and just taking whatever Hitler doles out, which is what Chamberlain seems to have brought us to. It scares me, I tell you.'

Jack stared at his son; his expression was thoughtful. Then he smiled, his rare, rather grudging smile.

'In that case come. It'll be good to have your company.'

It was a moment that Tom never forgot, marking not only the beginning of his lifelong commitment to the Labour Party, but almost more importantly, the sense that, at last, he had found a way to win his father's approval.

The meeting was at seven, in the Methodist church hall, Hilchester. They met early. 'That'll give you a chance to meet some of the members before start of business. Can't promise you much excitement, just one of the councillors speaking, Alan Broadburn, but he's very sound.'

There were fewer there than Tom had expected, but they all knew Jack. They had clearly dressed for the occasion, as if for church, many of the suits as shiny as Tom's own (he deliberately hadn't worn his new, birthday-present one) and were for the most part middle-aged, the youngest being at least thirty. There were even, to his astonishment, a few women, mostly middle-aged too, but a couple of young ones, rather depressingly dressed, in drab too-long skirts, and shapeless cardigans over equally shapeless jumpers. Angela would not have admired their style, he thought.

Jack introduced him to a few of the men. He clearly regarded the women as not worthy of his attention. They were all friendly; Jack had told him he wasn't to make a great song and dance about what he did for a living, but a couple of them asked Tom and he wasn't going to lie. They seemed impressed, and then to Tom's absolute astonishment, Jack said, 'Oh, he's a bright lad, all right. Went to the grammar school, you know, did his Higher. Three Distinctions, wasn't it, Tom?'

It was the first time Tom could ever remember his father boasting about, or even admitting to, his academic success.

'By heavens, you must be a clever one,' said one of the men. He held out his hand to shake Tom's. 'Ted Moore. Very glad to welcome you, Tom. We need some young blood, especially of your calibre.' He smiled at him. 'I hope you'll decide to join the party.'

'I already have,' said Tom.

At seven, the committee took their places on the platform, and the minutes of the last meeting were read and signed. Then came Any Other Business, mostly such matters as whether the two failed street lights on the High Road had yet been given the attention of the council, and who should represent the branch at the forthcoming Remembrance Day parade.

At eight o'clock, tea was served by the ladies, together with some very dried-up cheese sandwiches and extremely soggy biscuits. In the middle of this, Alan Broadburn, the evening's speaker, arrived, flustered and red in the face. He had been held up at the town hall. 'By the mayor. I did tell him of course that I had this meeting to attend, but he wanted my opinion on something rather important.'

Tom wondered what the important matter was, but he guessed it was more likely to be about street lights or dustbins than any matter of national concern. He made a note that at the next meeting – not this one; Jack would be horrified at his drawing attention to himself so early – he would raise the matter of the possible need for public air-raid shelters. If it took months to get street lamps mended, how on earth would any shelters get dug before the war was a distant memory?

The chairman, Councillor Roberts, clapped his hands and asked everyone to return to their seats as Councillor Broadburn would now give his talk on 'Challenges in Education in Hilchester' adding rather peremptorily, 'And perhaps the ladies would clear the things away?'

The ladies were clearly going to miss at least the beginning of the talk, which seemed very unfair to Tom. He half rose to offer help, but Jack tugged at his jacket and shook his head at him in disapproval.

'Let them do it,' he said, his voice low, looking anxiously about him lest anyone should have noticed. 'That's their job, they expect it.'

Councillor Broadburn rose to his feet and cleared his throat, pulling out a sheaf of notes from his large, shabby briefcase. Tom was rather pleased by the subject, clearly an advance on street lighting, despite his concern about the ladies. Then, just as the talk began, the door burst open and a girl came in. She had clearly been running as she was out of breath, her face flushed. It was a very pretty face, Tom noted, crowned by brown curls, with big brown eyes and what one of Angela's magazines would have described as a rosebud mouth. 'Sorry,' she said. 'So sorry. I missed the bus.'

'Councillor Broadburn is only just starting his talk,' the chairman said. 'The other ladies are washing up. Perhaps you could go and give them a hand before you sit down.'

This was clearly designed as a reprimand, but the girl was not to be put in any place except a chair in front of Mr Broadburn.

'No,' she said firmly. 'I've come to hear the talk. It's of great interest to me as I'm a teacher and I don't want to miss any of it. I'm happy to wash up afterwards.'

Her brown eyes met the chairman's defiantly; he could hardly insist without causing a scene. The talk began.

If Tom had expected to hear a debate on standards of education, or the relative merits of the state and private schools in Hilchester, he was to be disappointed; it was an elongated and very boring rant about the conditions in the schools: leaking roofs, constantly failing heating systems, cracked windows, and most important of all, a shortage of basic stationery, not just paper, but pens and pencils. 'Shocking, it is, quite shocking. And of course it's all down to lack of funds, and has this government helped? Of course they haven't. The education budget is a disgrace. Totally insufficient, but why should they care, their children are all in the private school, no worn blackboards or leaking roofs at Eton, we can be sure of that . . .'

There was a loud 'hear, hear'.

The late-arrival girl put her hand up.

The chairman shook his head at her disapprovingly

'Questions at the end, if you please, Miss – Miss –?'

'Leonard,' she said, 'Laura Leonard.' She seemed undeterred by the reprimand. 'I just wanted to say—'

'There will be plenty of time for questions at the end,' said the chairman firmly.

'Well, at least he has all the right ideas,' said Laura Leonard, uncrushed, 'and we must be thankful for that at least. But I simply wanted to add my experience to raise another matter, closer to the matter under discussion.'

'Miss – er – Leonard, I did say "questions at the end",' said the chairman rather feebly but Councillor Broadburn invited Miss Leonard to make her point.

'Well, one problem at my school, St Joseph's Hilchester Primary, East Hilton, is that—'

'Position there?' said the chairman, determined not to allow her the floor uninterrupted.

'Deputy Headmistress,' she said with a look that could only be described as smug, 'and my problem is lack of books. They're in really bad condition some of them, pages missing, that sort of thing. And I have to say, it's getting worse. The children mistreat the books—'

'Mistreat them? I find that very shocking. That seems to me to smack of a lack of discipline, Miss – er –'

'Leonard,' said Laura Leonard, her eyes brilliant, clearly fired up for battle. 'I do assure you, we do our very best with discipline, in every area of school life, but why should children treat carefully a book with half the pages falling out? I spend quite a lot of time glueing them back each evening. But is it so surprising the boys decide to make darts with them?'

'I'd have thought,' said the chairman, seizing revenge, 'well-disciplined children would do nothing of the sort. Perhaps those in your care—'

'With respect, sir,' said Laura Leonard, 'there are thirty-seven children in my class. I do my very best, we all do, but some children are undisciplined at home and therefore disruptive at school. Without doubling the staff at our disposal, it is virtually impossible to keep order all the time. Perhaps you would like to make a visit to St Joseph's one day and see for yourself?'

'I would obviously be delighted,' said Roberts, 'but I am a very busy man.'

'Well, you will have to take my word for it then. And they have water fights, filling their water pistols from the buckets in the toilets, put there for catching the rain—'

'Are they allowed to bring water pistols to school? Surely not!'

'Of course they're not. But they do. And short of searching them all every morning, pockets, lunch bags – which we don't have time for – well, again I can only say, Mr Roberts, you should try stopping them.'

'So what is your question?'

'Not a question! Merely an observation. Adding to Councillor Broadburn's own plea for bigger budgets. But I would propose that before the next election, we add that to our manifesto—'

'Yes, well, we could consider that and then possibly vote on putting it forward,' said Roberts. 'Now—'

'And there's something else,' said Laura. 'Something different. But it's all linked and might help if it could be addressed. It is that we are one school governor short and it's extremely difficult to recruit them. I thought if I brought this to your attention, you might be able to help.'

The committee looked at one another, spoke under their collective breath and then Councillor Roberts said, 'Well, you're right, it is difficult to find people willing to give the time and expertise. I consider it a position of utmost importance. More so with secondary schools, of course. Unfortunately, I am governor of a secondary school in Hilchester, so I can't take another one on.'

'Of course not,' said Laura Leonard, and Tom could see her struggling to disguise her horror at the possibility that the councillor might join her team. 'I – I wouldn't dream of asking you. But there might be a – a person known to some of you gentlemen . . .'

There was a silence; then Mr Roberts wound up his speech.

'I would like to propose a vote of thanks to Councillor Broadburn for sparing his valuable time to give us a most thought-provoking talk.'

Subdued applause followed; and then the chairman closed the meeting.

Tom stood up, winding his scarf round his neck; he had no overcoat and it was getting very cold. He caught Laura Leonard's eye and smiled at her; she smiled back, and they stood there, two bright, promising young people among the dingy middle age of the meeting.

'Come along, lad,' said Jack. 'We've a bus to catch.' Tom turned obediently, to be intercepted by Ted Moore.

'You know what, young Tom,' he said, 'you might consider that governor's position yourself. You're young, of course, but you've got the education and the energy, I'd guess. We could go and ask the young woman. I liked her – mind of her own. What do you say?'

'Oh, I don't know,' said Tom, embarrassed. 'I've no idea what school governors do.'

'As much or as little as they're prepared to. It can't be hard, I've done it myself. Bit of fundraising, support to the staff in various ways, that sort of thing. But the right person can bring a lot to a school. Come along, let's have a word with her. Miss Leonard – a moment of your time, please?'

And thus it was that Tom Knelston, aged only nineteen, became a governor of St Joseph's Hilchester Primary, East Hilton, and, as a consequence, rather good friends with its feisty young deputy headmistress.

# Chapter 5

## 1939

*The engagement is announced between the Hon. Johnathan Gunning, youngest son of Sir Hilary Gunning, of Guildford Park, Yorkshire, and Diana, only daughter of Sir Gerald and Lady Southcott, of the Manor House, West Hilton, Hampshire.*

So she'd done it. Well, it wasn't surprising, Ned supposed. She had clearly been compelled to get her life sorted, or as near as was possible in this bloody awful world they were in at the moment. Everyone was doing that to an extent, rushing into all sorts of arrangements and liaisons. Hers was an entirely personal need, of course, nothing to do with the impending war.

He did feel a certain responsibility, though; he had to a degree, albeit hopefully a small one, driven her to it. He was sure she didn't love the bloke, just needed a ring on her finger. If he'd responded to her more enthusiastically that night at the Savoy, both guests at a dinner dance, given by a friend of her brothers . . . but he hadn't. He'd rejected a pretty blatant overture, with as much charm as he could manage. It wasn't charm she'd wanted, it was sex, and with him, Ned Welles, not Johnathan Gunning. She'd been very drunk, worked every trick in the book on him, teasing, flirting, tempting, her lovely body pressed against him as she pulled him onto the dance floor, her mouth briefly on his, her eyes naked and hungry. She'd been so angry, clearly felt completely humiliated when he took her

29

back to the table, thanked her, bowed slightly and asked to be excused. She wasn't used to rejection, beautiful as she was, amusing and self-assured. And sexy, so sexy.

Anyway, Gunning had been there too, and she'd gone straight into his more than welcoming arms; he'd never seen any girl working on a man with such determination. It was a lesson in, well, women, he supposed. The expression in her eyes as she looked over her shoulder at him and waltzed off with Johnathan was of absolute triumph. I don't want you, that look said, never did, I was just fooling around. That had been mid-December, this was mid-February. He'd put money on the wedding being pretty soon, almost certainly this summer.

Well, he really couldn't worry about it any more. She was nineteen, not a child, and Diana Southcott was most assuredly not his responsibility. He had more immediate concerns. He was having dinner with his father at the Reform and he knew exactly why the invitation had been issued. Sir James was not convinced Ned was working hard enough; he wanted to check on that and also make sure that surgery would be his ultimate discipline. He was haunted by the notion that Ned would choose ENT or, God forbid, obstetrics. The first and only time Ned had voiced his interest in that, a casual listener might have thought a career in organised crime had just been mooted.

Well, he could tell his father he was set on surgery and had rather gone off the obstetric notion, though specialising in paediatrics seemed interesting. He wondered what the reaction might be to that. He could do with a good dinner; he'd blown his allowance for the month in two weeks, mostly on drink. It helped, pushed the nightmare away a bit.

Crossing London by bus, in the direction of Pall Mall, he looked out at the trenches dug in the great parks, offering shelter for people caught in any possible air raids; he couldn't see they would be of enormous help, but at least they were there. Otherwise London seemed determined to ignore any imminent danger.

Most people held the view that war simply couldn't happen again, that no politician would be foolish enough to allow it, after the horrifying lessons of a mere twenty years earlier.

Ned could still hear his father's voice raging about the iniquity of what had come to be known as the Munich crisis the previous September. 'Bloody disgraceful load of pacifists in charge of the country! They should all be strung up, Chamberlain first, allowing Germany to annex whatever it likes. Why can't they get out there and face the bastards down?'

There had been a few pockets of action immediately after Munich; huge barrage balloons appeared over London to protect it from German bombers, but swiftly disappeared again, deemed more trouble than they were worth. One had been caught in electric cables, five immediately broke adrift. There were calls from Herbert Morrison, leader of the London County Council, for volunteers to the Auxiliary Fire Service, but only a handful of people had turned up: in response to the assumption that three thousand firefighting appliances would be required, it transpired that to date only ninety-nine were available. And when the Canon of Westminster decided he should set an example by attending lectures on a first-aid course, the better to care for the thousands of casualties that would clearly result after a German attack, the initial talk was on the treatment of snake bites.

The country needed his father, Ned thought, or rather, someone like him, dragging buried heads from the sand, forcing a realistic appraisal of what was happening. The nearest anybody seemed to have got to seriously defending the realm and its inhabitants at this stage had been in the issuing of gas masks. It was generally felt, learning from the lessons of the Great War, that the greatest danger would be from poisonous gas and roughly ninety per cent of the population of London had been given them: the shortest expedition to the corner shop was not supposed to be undertaken without one.

Well, there was nothing he could do about it; except continue to listen to his father. That would be his war effort for the time being. If war was declared, then he wasn't sure what he would want to do.

The announcement looked so extremely splendid there on the court pages of *The Times* and the *Telegraph*; Diana still couldn't quite believe it had happened. She kept smiling at the ring on her finger, which had been there for nearly a week, but she still hadn't got used to the look of it, the feel of it, even. It was very beautiful, a row of five diamonds, catching and reflecting the light every time she moved her hand. Johnathan had had it in his pocket and he'd produced it after she'd said yes. It was all very romantic. He said he was sorry it wasn't a family heirloom – with his being the third son they'd run out of those – so he'd chosen it and he hoped so much she'd like it. If she didn't, they could change it; the shop in Hatton Garden had agreed to that and they could choose another. She didn't want that, she loved the way he'd chosen it, it was so romantic, a bit unlike him really, and she told him it was perfect and she loved it and she loved him, which she did of course, so very much. She couldn't imagine now how she could ever have thought she didn't.

She knew when she had actually fallen in love with him. Looking back, it was that day they first went hunting together, the first weekend he'd been to stay, and thank goodness her mother had thought of asking him, otherwise she'd have been stuck with Ned Welles, and what a pain he'd turned out to be. Good-looking, and very amusing, of course, but far too pleased with himself. That father of his was just a joke – no wonder Ned's mother, with her really ridiculous name, Persephone, had run away. It was quite a story, that: he was an artist who was painting her and she fell in love with him and Sir James was – or so Ned said – more upset about him taking the painting, which had cost the earth, than his wife.

Diana'd often wondered if Ned, who was spectacularly good-looking, took after the wicked and beautiful Persephone. She asked Michael if Ned ever saw his mother, and Michael said only about once a year, that Ned was still terribly hurt and couldn't forgive her for abandoning him. It was no wonder really he wasn't like any of the other men she knew, with that sort of thing in his background.

She wondered if he'd seen the announcement and what he'd thought. Not that she cared, of course. He just wasn't her type, never had been, right from the beginning, and she'd been so happy when Johnathan told her he was in love with her.

Now they were engaged, officially, and his parents were coming down to stay with her parents to discuss Things with a capital T. They had decided already that it mustn't be a long engagement, because of the state of the world, but if war was declared – and her father seemed to think it was inevitable – Johnathan would want to join his father's old regiment. If he was going to do that and leave her and go away to France, she wanted a home of her own in London. She could decorate it to her own taste, and she and Johnathan could give smart parties and she could have her own life at last. Well, shared with him, of course. She couldn't wait to be a good wife, look after him, and she thought she would learn to cook and entertain his clients and—

'Diana, darling!' It was her mother. 'Telephone. Johnathan.'

He rang a lot at the moment; it was lovely. He kept telling her how much he enjoyed just talking to her and they were going to start house-hunting next week. Oh, it was all so exciting.

She ran out to the hall, picked up the telephone.

'Hello, darling,' Diana said. 'How are you today? Have you seen the announcement – isn't it all too exciting?'


'Come on, come on, pass pass pass – Rory, not down there, look out, come on, now, run run – Callum, that's good, go on, Mick, you too.'

Tom stood still for a moment, looked at the football pitch covered with little boys, who were in their turn covered with mud, and thought how very happy he was. It was a good moment. Very good.

Becoming a school governor had expanded into being football coach on Saturday afternoons. He would have liked to do so after school as well, but he couldn't get away from Pemberton's early enough. It didn't seem to matter; he was a good coach, and the boys loved him. Him and the sessions. He had changed football at St Joseph's Primary from being little better than an excuse for the boys to run up and down into a game that was to be given serious consideration and effort.

'Don't come and waste my time – I don't mind about yours,' he said to them after the very first session. The boys took it seriously, worked hard, and now were divided into two teams who played each other, and winning a game was a prize worthy of exaltation. Tom's next ambition was to form a school team and set up a competition between other primary schools; this happened at secondary-school level, but not enough at primary, and he was trying to convince governors and masters from other schools in the district. It wasn't easy, but he was making progress and a couple of fixtures were set towards the end of term.

He had expanded the role of a school governor into being the lover of the deputy headmistress. This had proved easier than setting up the football league. Laura was one of the new breed of women; a couple of decades earlier, she would have been a suffragette. As well as belonging to the Labour Party, she was heavily involved in the local branch of the Co-operative Women's Guild (motto 'Of a whole heart cometh hope') and held passionate views on female equality. She believed that women had the right not only to equal opportunities and equal pay, but equal lives; and that, in her view, meant taking sexual pleasure for themselves should they desire it while refusing to cooperate on demand with their husbands. Men should give the time and attention to wooing their wives in bed each and every time they wanted them, being sensitive to their needs and generally behaving in a way to which they were not accustomed, or even prepared to be accustomed.

Tom had not had the opportunity before to behave either sensitively or insensitively in bed and was an enthusiastic pupil, which meant doing exactly what she wanted – at first, anyway.

It had been a complete shock the first time she had made clear her availability to him; nice girls, he had always been told – primarily by Angela, but also his parents, by implication, and by the joshing confidences shared with his friends – didn't go to bed with men until they had rings on their fingers. Not only was it hugely dangerous, in that they might become pregnant; it also meant they were cheap, their most precious possession given away to be talked, boasted and even sniggered about by the recipient, the right to a respectable life, a white wedding, an honourable husband gone for ever.

So it was that sitting by the fire one night, quite early on in their relationship – which had moved swiftly from the purely professional to the personal, cool friendship, to warm interest, to attraction, and thence to a mutual desire – and after an excellent supper cooked by Laura, in the tiny flat she rented, she suddenly removed his hand from her thigh (a new development) and proposed that they might actually go next door to her bedroom and into her bed. Tom was fairly shocked, completely terrified and absolutely overwhelmed.

'Well,' she said, 'come along. Or don't you want to?'

'Yes, of course I do!' he said.

'Well, then. We don't want to go off the boil, do we?'

'No. No, we don't. But—'

'Oh, I know you haven't done it before,' she said, standing up, plumping the cushions and carrying the coffee cups over to the sink, for all the world as if he would now kiss her goodnight and start on the long cycle ride home. 'Never mind, I have. And don't worry about getting me in the family way either, I can deal with that. Oh, come on, Tom Knelston,' she added impatiently. 'You're the most gorgeous man I've ever set eyes on and I can't quite believe my luck, so you can't let me down now.'

And he didn't.


Laura was like no one he had ever known. She and her younger sister, Babs, had been brought up virtually single-handed by their mother, a formidable woman, also a teacher. Her husband was unable to work after losing a leg in the First World War, depression overtaking him entirely, his pension pitifully inadequate. She worked all the hours God sent her, putting Laura in charge of the household from the age of eight, when Mr Leonard's feeble efforts at caring for it and the girls failed altogether and he took to his bed for the remaining five years of his life. She never gave up on him; she had an understanding of mental illness that was decades before her time and brought the girls up to be of the same persuasion. Babs married young and already had two children, but Laura was her mother reborn, tough, determined and idealistic, with an equal capacity for hard work. Nothing fazed her; she drove through obstacles scarcely acknowledging them. She had risen from junior teacher to deputy headmistress in three years, seizing opportunities when they arose and then doing whatever was necessary to capitalise on them. Her pupils loved her, for she inspired as well as taught them; she had already inaugurated an annual storytelling prize among all the schools in the area, against the wishes of many of the headmasters, who said it would be too much work. She looked at them witheringly and told them she was prepared to do whatever was necessary herself if they were not. She was pretty, charming – and very sexy. If Tom had been asked to create his perfect woman, it would have been Laura Leonard who stood before him, holding out her hand and inviting him into her bed.

But it wasn't just the sex; their interests and passions – mostly political – bound them as closely. Deeply socialist, horrified by the long years of unemployment endured by the working class during the dreadful recession of the thirties, they listened in an agony of disbelief to Laura's little wireless breaking the news that the Tory candidate, one Quintin Hogg, had won the first by-election after Munich.

Tom, largely as a result of a talk held at one of the Labour Party meetings, was becoming fiercely and angrily focused on the lack of medical provision for the poor and the constant dread of illness in the millions of families who simply could not afford a doctor. He told Laura of a dreadful night when his little brother Arthur had developed a temperature of a hundred and four. Scarlet fever was feared, with its inevitable hospitalisation and high death rate; the family weren't on the panel of the local GP (whereby a small weekly fee ensured treatment if genuinely required) and were afraid to call him. Many long hours of spongeing down and homespun medicines saw him through; but it had been a night that had burrowed deep into Tom's soul.

All these things and more bound him and Laura together in fierce and crusading zeal; they would see things put right, they told one another, they would work for justice and equality and rights for all. They weren't sure how, except via the somewhat unsatisfactory aegis of the local Labour Party – although the Women's Guild provided a more satisfactory outlet for Laura's energies and ideals – but they were absolutely united in the clear vision of what should be done. It was a strong tie.

Ending the relationship with Angela had been awful; she had cried and cried. Tom had done the honourable thing, and not let things drag on.

'But I don't see what I've done wrong,' she kept saying. 'We're always so happy together.'

Useless to say that the happiness had been a counterfeit, the togetherness no more than a sweet illusion; she would not have understood. And simpler, if crueller, to say he had found someone else and he could not therefore carry on seeing Angela, and he was very, very sorry and it had been wonderful, but it would be wrong of him to allow things to continue.

Once she had stopped crying, she became angry, telling him he was a rotter, that he had no business to abandon her after all she had done for him, 'listening to you going on and on about your work, it was so boring, and sitting through films I hated, and cycling out when it was almost raining, and coming back early from outings so you could listen to the six o'clock news with my father, and those picnics, all those picnics I made. You enjoyed them, didn't you?'

Tom said she had indeed been the perfect girlfriend, and he was sorry he'd bored her and the picnics had been wonderful, but it had to end now.

It had taken Angela a long time to get over it. She was not to be seen at village dances, or the cinema, or indeed anywhere at all, apart from Parsons; and this made Tom feel truly terrible. Then his godmother told him that Angela had taken up with the head of Home Furnishings and was very taken with him, and he with her, and Tom relaxed and was able to fully enjoy Laura – in every sense of the word – and contemplate from such unlikely places as muddy football pitches how extremely happy he was. If it hadn't been for the shadow of war hanging over everything, he would have said he was perfectly happy. If war was declared, which everybody said it wouldn't be – even the politicians couldn't be that stupid – he would clearly go and fight, along with all his friends and colleagues. Meanwhile, they could all only wait and trust and pray they were in good hands.

Then, at the dentist one evening, nursing a nasty toothache, he picked up a rather dog-eared copy of *The Times*; it was open at the Court Circular and he was about to turn it over quickly, in search of some news that mattered, when he saw a familiar name and learned that Diana Southcott had become engaged to some titled creature from Yorkshire. No doubt they deserved one another: two toffs with a single purpose – to breed more toffs. While not wishing Diana ill, but remembering the way she'd looked down on him, literally as well as figuratively, as he stood in the drain, he couldn't wish her well either. She was very beautiful though, no one could deny that, and sexy too, even at sixteen.

'Mr Knelston, do come in, the dentist will see you now.' And all thoughts of Diana Southcott, her beauty and her sexiness, were wiped out by half an hour of excruciating pain followed by an evening of excruciating pleasure with Laura Leonard.

# Chapter 6

## 1940

He should have gone into the Air Force, Johnathan thought. It would have eased the guilt he felt to have risked that almost certain death. A lot of his friends had chosen that path, and many, many of them were gone, their planes shot down. Piers, his beloved eldest brother, so handsome, so dashing, had been one of them, one of the Few, the fighter pilots taking to the skies in their crazily tiny Spitfire planes, and into open warfare with the German Luftwaffe. 'Never,' said Winston Churchill – now, thank God, in charge of the country and the war – his rumbling, roaring tones spilling out of the wireless, 'was so much owed by so many to so few.' And Piers had been among them, grinning out of photographs taken before he was sent up, complete with the statutory accessories of dangling cigarette, fur-collared flying jacket and parachute. They were the bravest of the brave, all of them: it was like facing a firing squad, day after day, going up, coming back, seemingly inviolate.

Only finally Piers wasn't; stalking one German plane he was spotted by another which opened fire on him and his plane went down into the sea. Everyone said death must have been instant, but Johnathan was very much of the opinion that everyone could be wrong; there was the hell of being engulfed in flames, the terror, the waiting for the end as he plunged down. Nothing very instant about any of it.

The pain of losing Piers was appalling. He tried to find comfort in Diana but although she made an effort to console him, he sensed that her emotions lacked substance. She had not known Piers very well, and Johnathan tried to make excuses for her on that basis, but that was not the point; it was his grief that he expected her to understand, and she did not. She had never experienced any serious loss herself and seemed incapable of imagining it. He was discovering, not for the first time, that she lacked emotional imagination.

He finally despaired when she said that of course it was dreadful, but it had been a hero's death and he must be so proud of Piers, as if that made the loss less savage. Angry with her, and trying to conceal it, he went to see his parents and his brother Timothy without her. They were all devastated, their father particularly so. His mother had somehow prepared herself for it, and Timothy was distracted from the worst excesses of his grief by an imminent naval posting to Norway, but Sir Hilary seemed completely inconsolable. He wandered around the house like a shadow, and could often be heard weeping behind closed doors. Years later he explained to Johnathan that it had been made far worse by having seen so many young men die in the trenches in the First World War, but for now he withdrew into himself, unable to share how he felt even with his wife. Piers had been his firstborn and his heir, the love of his life to a great extent. Hilary had married Vanessa out of duty, pressed by his own father to continue the line. He was fond of her, of course, and she was a wonderful consort, but in no way was she a soulmate and never less of one than now. Johnathan, recognising Diana's failure in this regard, only to a far lesser degree, realised that his father, like him, felt absolutely alone. He was just a little able to convey this to him, and could see it was some kind of comfort.

He stayed at Guildford Park for longer than he had planned; two weeks went past, and he would have extended them had he not been ordered back to his regiment. He had joined the Welsh Guards, his father and grandfather's regiment, without waiting for call-up as had his brothers. His regiment was still in training in Scotland and he went straight up there without going to see Diana. She was living with her parents in Hampshire again, since London was so dangerous, and he had no desire to see them, without being quite sure why. A psychiatrist could have told him it was in part at least because both their sons were still unscathed and on a subconscious level he saw this as a piece of injustice. The fact that it could change any moment didn't help very much. Michael was at Barts, caring nightly for the casualties of the Blitz, and Richard, the younger boy, had joined his father's regiment and was, like Johnathan, awaiting a posting.

Diana had never been so bored, or so miserable. A year into the war, the excitement and happiness of the first four months of marriage seemed like a distant memory. Her father was deeply disgruntled, having failed to obtain a job at the War Office, and dissipated his energies by berating just about everyone who came into his orbit; and her mother had joined the WVS, partly to keep out of the house and her husband's way. She urged Diana to join too but spoilt as she was by amusing London society, the bossy and overbearing ladies of the county were not Diana's idea of desirable companions. So, like her father, she moped about the house, rode a lot and fretted over Johnathan, both his safety and the fact that she had failed him with his grief over Piers. It was not the only way she had failed him, she knew, reflecting rather sadly on the first year of her marriage. She was not his intellectual equal in any way; and her scanty education had been no preparation for his sophisticated range of interests. Yes, they had lots of fun together, but he also loved to read, liked going to art galleries, adored music and opera was his great love.

Not much of this had emerged during their courtship, and Diana felt, with a completely illogical resentment, that he should have made it all clearer. She supposed, since most of the time they spent together that first year had been taken up either with the events of the London Season, then the engagement, meeting Johnathan's vast circle of friends and visiting his family, that the opportunity for such leisurely occupations hardly arose.

They bought a pretty little mews house in Knightsbridge, exactly what she had dreamed of, and she had the greatest fun decorating and furnishing it and then settled into what seemed at first a perfect life as London continued to ignore the fact that there was a war on. She enjoyed looking after Johnathan and being a good wife; she ran the house beautifully, was a wonderful hostess, entertaining his clients as well as their friends, never overspent on her admittedly generous household budget, and even cooked some simple meals herself when they were alone at home, which he liked very much.

But gradually she had to face the fact that they didn't have very much in common. His mind was far more serious and analytical than hers and she was horribly aware that very often her responses to his observations and indeed conversations were a disappointment to him. The only time she really felt at one with him was when they were in the country, either at her parents' home or at Guildford Park, riding, hunting, accompanying him on shoots.

Then there was the worst thing: sex. She did not enjoy sex. It was a shock, for she had been easily aroused before they were married, as he kissed and held her close to him, but their wedding night had been a disappointment and they both knew it. She was, of course, a virgin, and there was a certain amount of discomfort and anxiety involved, but neither of them worried too much about it, assuming things would swiftly improve. They did not, although she pretended to him that they had and that she was enjoying it, but actually she found it an increasing chore and was relieved when she had the curse as an excuse.

Her lack of enjoyment distressed her and he seemed to have very little awareness of what she wanted; on the rare occasions when something pleasurable did begin to happen, he would suddenly have his orgasm and roll off her, thanking her dutifully and leaving her close to tears of frustration and disappointment.

There was no one she could talk to about it. Her mother had said, unusually frankly, when they had what she called a little chat one day shortly before the wedding, that it was all rather nice and she hoped Diana would enjoy it as much as she did. So confessing to her mother that she didn't in the very least would make Diana feel even more of a failure. Maybe, when they were consciously making babies, it would be more fun – although she couldn't quite think why. They had agreed that babies must wait. Neither of them wanted her left alone with a child while Johnathan was away for months at a time or worse.

'Time to reproduce ourselves when the war is over,' Johnathan said, kissing her, 'and that will be wonderful, won't it, lots of jolly little things running about.'

Diana said very wonderful, and indeed she liked children, was already a godmother several times over. She found children fun, loved reading to them and playing games like Snakes and Ladders and Ludo, and invented the most wonderful games herself. But that was rather different from full-time care of a baby; they were, from her observation, demanding, exhausting and frequently smelly. So it was as well, she thought, that for now there would be no question of having one – although such was her boredom that she occasionally thought wistfully that the decision might have been a mistake. At least it would have given her something to do.

Ned was throwing up. He threw up relentlessly, day after day; he tried to think of it as something nobler than run-of-the-mill seasickness, as his war effort, but that didn't help. He had thought he would get used to it, get used to the sea and its horrors – it was always said you did and it was wrong. It was awful. Someone had described the progress of one of the Motor Torpedo Boats – the MTBs as they were known – as being like driving a sports car with no springs along a bumpy road while being shot at. These had been his chosen vessels, once he had obtained his commission, but he was beginning to doubt the wisdom of it.

He thought, as he tried uselessly to control the vomiting, of how he could have been on dry land, very dry land, on the wards at Barts. Still useful, possibly in less danger – although that was dubious as long as the Blitz endured. Why had he done this insane thing, leaving a reserved occupation? It had made his father angrier than he had ever seen him – although beneath the rage was a fierce pride – putting himself literally into the firing line. And of course he knew. He knew that it wasn't so much courage as buying off fate, of keeping people from finding out, or even suspecting; it was brave beyond anything, what he had so unnecessarily done. He would probably have been called up anyway, for he would have been qualified, no longer a student, and the exemption had only been on the grounds of his student status.

He had joined the Y Scheme, which took public-school boys – and some of them were literally straight from school, nineteen years old – the idea being that after six months on the lower deck as an ordinary seaman, you progressed automatically into the officer class and training.

He left London with great bravado, seen off by a huge drinking session with his fellow medics, and arrived at the barracks in Portsmouth with a sinking heart and a rising sense of terror. He was right; it was one of the worst periods of his life. The petty officers loathed and tormented him and Crispin Steele, his only compatriot in the Y Scheme, and did and said everything they could to make their lives as difficult as possible. Well, who could blame them, he kept telling himself, as he tried to find some comfort and explanation for their behaviour; a pair of toffee-accented lads, wet behind the ears, being trained to rise to become, theoretically, their superiors.

Ned had looked at Crispin with misgivings when he met him for the first time: a pretty boy with brown curls, a history graduate, who looked as if he might burst into tears any moment. He would greatly increase the chances of their both being labelled as mummy's boys, probably fairies. At least, Ned thought, feeling a rare stab of gratitude towards his parents, he had a sensible name. Crispin, for God's sake.

It was evening when they arrived, and they were given their kit and sent below, away from the danger of the constant bombing of the docks, where, allotted bunks, they were told to get undressed. Crispin, Ned was grateful to see, was on the other side of the room.

He had just removed his trousers when a huge tattooed man appeared at his side and said, 'Well, who the fucking hell are you? What's your fucking name?' He pushed his face into Ned's, then studied his almost naked lower half, his expression a sniggering leer. Ned felt he was probably about to be raped.

'Well, come on, posh boy. Lost yer tongue?'

'Welles,' said Ned, trying to keep his voice strong and steady, 'Ned Welles.' The man stood back, and after a short silence, spat on the ground and then laughed.

'Welles,' he said. 'What a fucking stupid name.'

And he moved on.

Ned got into bed; he was longing for a pee, but he was too frightened to leave the comparative safety of his own area. Hours later, when the petty officers had gone, with cheery promises that all forty of them would soon wish profoundly never to have been born, he managed to locate the toilet block. As he left, Crispin Steele came in; clearly he had been crying. Ned pretended not to have noticed, nodded to him briefly and hurried back to his bunk. He felt ashamed of that moment for the rest of his life.

After a couple of days they were moved in the middle of an air raid to Collingwood, a naval training base near Portsmouth; the next six weeks were spent square bashing, climbing ladders and ropes to terrifying heights – and even worse a huge mast – the petty officers shouting abuse at them from below. It was a nightmare. As he lay in his bunk at night, exhausted, sickened by the brutality, the ceaseless profanity, Ned marvelled at his stupidity in subjecting himself to this misery. Sometimes he was actually frightened by the sheer vindictiveness of the whole thing.

'You want to watch it,' his first tattooed tormentor, who turned out to be a butcher in civilian life, warned him one night. 'You annoy somebody once too often, you could go overboard in the middle of the night. No one would ever know – we'll get rid of you and good riddance, you fucking filthy poncey snob.'

There was no apparent reason for this threat. Ned had committed no crime, had neither said nor done anything to offend anyone; the only possible response was silence. Once, when he was loading up shells, his hands raw with cold and bleeding, he was made to continue for a double shift; there was no redress, no hope of reprieve. The only thing was to endure it and survive it – although he was not sure what for.

After a few weeks they were transferred to a newly built destroyer; he had hoped it might be better than the endless square bashing but it was worse. Crispin got pneumonia, nearly died, and was finally shipped home to hospital, never to return. Ned envied him from the bottom of his heart. He, however remained stubbornly healthy; and the destroyer was sent to the North Atlantic on the Murmansk Run, taking supplies to Russia, one of Churchill's obsessions at this stage. And then, finally, it was over and he was posted for officer training at Hove.

It was truly, he often said afterwards, like finding yourself in heaven after a very long spell in hell.

'Hello, Mr Pemberton.'

Mr Pemberton looked up, failing just for a moment to recognise Tom: a different, thinner, more grown-up-looking Tom, in uniform. Then he smiled: a tired, delighted smile.

'Tom,' he said. 'How very nice to see you. Do come in and sit down – Mrs Foxton, look, it's Tom Knelston, come to pay us a visit. Cup of tea, Tom?'

'Oh, yes, please.'

'My word, you've grown up,' said Betty, beaming at Tom. 'Suits you, though, you look like a real man. And more handsome than ever. Like a piece of cake with your tea? Looks like you could do with some feeding up.'

'Thank you,' said Tom. 'That'd be lovely.'

She disappeared; Gordon Pemberton sat back and studied Tom.

'So – Royal Engineers, eh? You enjoying it?'

'Yes, very much. I can drive now – well, I can drive a jeep. And build a Bailey bridge.'

'Can you now? Well done. That'll stand you in good stead when this is all over. You got a posting yet?'

'Yes,' said Tom, 'yes, I have. Somewhere very exciting. But we're not supposed to tell you where. Off at the end of the week. I'm on my way home, but we were dropped off here, so I thought I'd come and see you.'

'That's very good of you.' Gordon Pemberton was clearly genuinely touched. 'I'm delighted you did. You know Nigel's somewhere overseas now?'

'Well, I assumed so,' said Tom. 'What regiment is he in?'

'The Royal Artillery,' said Pemberton, and his voice was thick with pride. 'He went straight in as an officer, of course. Second lieutenant. Apparently he could be a captain before very long. His commanding officer thinks the world of him.'

Tom wondered how Mr Pemberton knew, but said, 'Really?' in a tone that he hoped was convincingly awestruck.

'He joined up immediately. Wouldn't hear of waiting. Very brave, my son. But – what am I thinking of? You don't want to hear about him. Let's talk about you.'

'Well,' said Tom, 'I'm a corporal now.'

'Already? Well done. And decent lot of chaps you're with?'

'Very decent, yes. My sergeant's a really nice bloke.'

'Is he? Nigel had a brute while he was doing his basic training. Treated him like some sort of idiot, humiliated him on the parade ground, that sort of thing.'

'They all do that,' said Tom cheerfully. 'That's how they lick us into shape.'

'Well, maybe, but it's most unnecessary. Especially with someone like Nigel. He writes regularly, very brave, cheerful letters. Mind you write to your parents. Makes all the difference.'

'Yes,' said Tom, 'yes, I do. I must go, catch the next bus, or I won't be there for tea. Mum's so excited.'

'I'm sure she is. Well, thank you for coming, Tom. It was very nice of you. It's meant a lot to me, it really has. You take care of yourself. And come back to us . . .'

Laura was away until the next day, at a teachers' training course in Southampton. He didn't know quite how he was going to wait. He had a very small box in his breast pocket, which contained a ring bearing a very, very small diamond; he was going to place it on Laura's finger tomorrow and ask her to marry him.

# Chapter 7

## 1943

Tomorrow, tomorrow, she would see him. It seemed impossible; for not only years, but a complexity of emotions stood between them. The grief of their parting, the aching loneliness, the gnawing ongoing anxiety about his safety, the impatience for letters, all the things she had thought were bad, had been crushed into insignificance over the past few months. The terror at the news of his injuries (brought to her by his mother, waiting white-faced outside the school for her) the struggle to determine exactly what and how bad they were, the dread that he would not recover. These were the new and dreadful demons, increased by lack of news, and when that came, the impatience of his long, slow convalescence. Now at last he was home, still clearly frail, in the military hospital at Aldershot, and she was permitted to visit him. Tomorrow. After three years. It seemed scarcely possible.

He had been extremely ill; stationed with Montgomery's forces at El Alamein, he'd survived two years of it, but then he'd caught a mine. His left leg was badly injured, and he'd also sustained serious damage to his chest; infection set in, turning to pneumonia and septicaemia. He'd very nearly died, but he had survived, written to her from the hospital as soon as he was well enough, making light of it all, praising the American nurses. 'They're fantastic, so kind and so efficient and brave.' He complained only of his frustration at missing the Big Battle, the one that had been such a turning point in the war. Laura could only offer up fervent thanks to the God she didn't believe in that he had.

The thought of seeing Tom, of being physically near to him again, able to touch him, hear him, smile at him, was so extraordinary, so dazzling, that she could only allow her mind to contemplate it occasionally, otherwise she would not have been able to function at all. As it was, she would still find herself struck unawares by it from time to time with a force so strong it made her physically dizzy, and she would stand, smiling foolishly at the children, unable to remember their names, what lesson she had been teaching, even. She had received two letters from him in three days, telling her how he was longing to see her too, begging her not to be late – as if she would be – and warning her that he wasn't looking quite the fellow she'd last seen leaning out of the train window as it pulled out of Southampton. He had told her once again that day, before they left for the station, that he loved her more every day, 'more than you could ever believe possible, Laura Leonard', and the minute the war was over they would get married; she had had to live on that moment with its heart-catching sadness for three years, watching his face grow smaller until it was unrecognisable, and even his waving arm, lost in a forest of other waving arms, stilled with the distance.

It had been truly dreadful; she had gone home and, refusing to cry, had sat staring at the wall of her sitting room, willing him back there by the sheer force of memory, his smile, his eyes, his arms round her, his hands on her, his voice, telling her he loved her and for a very little time that was sufficient, it soothed and eased her, but soon the void he had left, the blankness before her, bore him away more finally than the train and she gave in to grief and wept for hours.

She had heard that when a limb was amputated, you could still feel it, feel pain in it; she felt the same, as if the part of her life he had filled was a huge, savagely painful void.

But while Tom was in deadly danger, day after day, so for much of the time was she, volunteering at weekends under the aegis of the Co-operative Women's Guild, to work in Southampton. During the Blitz the city endured nights as harsh and as cruel as those in London. For fifty-seven nights it went relentlessly on, and the firestorm of the worst of the raids could be seen from France.

In spite of the pacifist doctrines at its heart, and its most famous heritage, the launch of the white poppy campaign, the Guild fought its own particular corner. Attendance at the often rather sparse peacetime meetings soared; women wanted to help, and the Guild helped them to do so, often joining up with the WVS, running canteens, mending and finding clothes for the homeless, helping shocked, terrified people into shelters, and, strictly unofficially, firefighting. All these things Laura hurled herself into; she would walk the streets at night, during raids if she wasn't needed at the canteen or shelter, her tin hat perched jauntily on her curls, looking for people in need of help. Sometimes she stood behind the men as they drove the mighty hoses into the fires, the fires that always threatened to defeat and sometimes did, ushering people away from the scene, and more than once she helped to hold a hose herself, as a man overcome with heat and exhaustion fell.

You lived for each day as it came, everyone looked after everyone else, and you simply didn't have time to think about yourself and the danger you were in.

She also organised teas and concerts for convalescent men in hospital, even the occasional dance, and they were incredibly popular, restoring happiness and hope however briefly, by way of the music of the great Glenn Miller and England's own Henry Hall, and such great dance-floor hits of the time as the Lindy Hop and the Jitterbug, imported mostly by the dashing new arrivals, the GIs. And as well there were such staider home-grown counterparts as the Palais Glide and 'Underneath the Spreading Chestnut Tree', greatly favoured by the King and Queen and the little Princesses. She danced herself if invited, but mostly she was content to stand and watch the girls in their pretty dresses, stocking seams drawn on bare legs with eyebrow pencils, their hair in elaborate Betty Grable curls, flirting and laughing, the men in their best suits, their drawn faces flushed with pleasure. She would often sit with the men who liked to come even if they were in wheelchairs, chatting and sometimes flirting with them, listening to their stories about the girls they had loved and left behind, and who had been to visit them in the hospital or were coming 'any day now'. She worried about the 'any day now's. If Tom had been in hospital over the past three years, she would have been there with him somehow, every weekend. But she would smile at them and admire the battered snapshots that were pulled out of wallets and pockets and they would smile back and when she returned to school on Monday, exhausted, she never complained, never talked much about what she had been doing. For her, as much as it was her war effort, it was also a bargaining with fate, warding off something worse: losing Tom.

And it had worked. Just. She had nearly lost him, but now he was safe, and properly safe for the rest of the war, for he had written to tell her he was no longer required, as he put it with a certain bitterness, but invalided out.

Well, she would disabuse him of the bitterness, the sadness. And they would be together, properly together, perhaps married, before they had dreamed possible, their lives fused, their happiness safe. And in only twenty-four hours that happiness would begin.

Tom lay in his bed in the hospital at Aldershot, focusing on nothing but Laura's arrival, his mind wiped clean of anything but his love for her. He was still in a lot of pain; his breathing was a struggle and his left leg, patched together by a novice field surgeon in an operating theatre lit by a hurricane lamp while a sandstorm raged outside, and now a little shorter than the right one, ached constantly. He slept badly. Normally he dreaded the nights, but this one was a joy, because it gave him time and space to think about Laura. He could conjure her up in his head, the brown curls, the wide brown eyes, the curvily sweet mouth that she hated – 'I look like a soppy girl in a story' – and her small, bustling figure, the full breasts, the frankly plump thighs that she despaired of but he loved. He could hear her voice in his head too, a little deep for a girl, expressive, and capable of roaring across a room and a playground, but he somehow couldn't quite put it all together, conjure her up and imagine her beside him. When he had been really ill and they thought he would die, he had wild, feverish dreams in which she was always on the other side of a door, standing behind him, walking away from him, never standing and smiling in front of him. But today, today he would have her, the real her, there, by his bed, holding his hand, talking to him, listening to him. It was happiness too impossible to believe.

He had been in the hospital for three weeks and now at last Sister, the stern sister who terrified everyone, even the young doctors, had told him he could have a visitor. 'Just one, mind,' she said briskly, only her twinkling eyes giving her away. 'I don't want all your friends and family here.'

The nurses all knew Laura was coming; he had been walked to the bathroom, helped into the bath, clean pyjamas had been found, his hair brushed, even his nails cut by his favourite nurse, Molly she was called, while Sister wasn't looking. She wasn't coming until three, he knew, but by nine he was ready, too excited to eat his breakfast.

'If you don't eat we won't let her in,' Molly said briskly.

Six hours to go: what could he do? He tried reading; he had discovered the works of Rider Haggard and was presently deep into *She*. But even that failed today; it simply could not compete with thoughts of Laura and her arrival. About ten o'clock, having slept so very little, he drifted into something that was half sleep, half memory about his time in the desert, mostly the good – the camaraderie, the sense of adventure, and of knowing that what they were doing was truly vital, of Monty's presence, so strong, so driving, the palpable relief when he arrived to take over from Auchinleck, the sense within days that they were in good hands.

Monty had an incredible rapport with his soldiers: 'Gather round, boys, gather round,' he would say before some briefing of vital information he needed to impart. And the arrival of the tanks, the Sherman tanks, he could remember that so vividly, knowing they were there, knowing how many they had, hundreds more than Rommel. It had been a huge morale boost. The bad was mostly physical; the awful sand, worse in the sandstorm when it stung your face and all you could do was bury your head in your arms; it got in your tea and gave you dysentery. The heat you got used to, but never the sand. And never the lack of water, only enough to clean your teeth for days on end, not to wash – and just enough to drink.

His job was laying mines. They would arrive at some place, as they drove forward through the desert, clear the German ones away and lay their own. He could still remember the one that had done for him and knew he always would; it had gone off a yard or so away, badly injuring his foot and hip and then torn up to his waist and burst again. It hadn't hurt at first and he remembered being furious because he couldn't move, couldn't get on with his work; then he blacked out, and came to being stretchered to an ambulance. After that the pain began. Weeks, months of it, and then the illness, making him so weak he thought quite often he must be dying.

Now he was lying in a cool, clean hospital, with no sand, plenty of water – and Laura on her way to see him. Laura. His love.

The journey had looked fairly simple. A bus into Winchester, then a train to Aldershot. And then another bus to the hospital. She'd allowed twice the time she'd theoretically need, because trains were often cancelled, always late. She didn't mind. She'd have crawled on her hands and knees, willingly, happily, all the way if she'd had to.

She got up at six, so as to have lots of time to get ready, and do things like washing her hair and pressing her skirt. She'd bought a new lipstick, rather extravagantly, and she took the bottle of Yardley Lavender Water her mother and sister had given her for Christmas out of her underwear drawer – you had to store perfume in the dark to keep it fresh – and dabbed it on in all the right places. She'd read somewhere that you should apply perfume to wherever you'd like to be kissed. That was quite good guidance. Not that there'd be much scope for kissing in the hospital ward, but – well, Tom would want her to smell nice. He always noticed that, he said.

It was a horrible day; not that she cared. Wet and windy and cold; a classic February day. She left the house soon after eight, and half ran to the bus stop. She was lucky; the bus was more or less on time and so was the train. It was packed, absolutely packed full, almost entirely with soldiers. Aldershot was a big military town and base. The men were mostly very cheerful and noisy, delighted to be with a pretty girl, chatting her up, asking her where she was going, really interested when she told them; a few of them had mates out in the desert, they told her, and that it was Monty's Desert Rats, as they were called, who were winning the war out there. She felt fiercely proud to be in some way representing them.

Half an hour out of Aldershot the train stopped for almost an hour;

when it started again it crawled jerkily along. The guard fought his way along the train to tell them it was a signal failure. Laura looked at her watch. Only one o'clock – she still had two hours. According to the timetable it was only a half-hour ride.

They arrived in Aldershot at one fifteen. The soldiers said goodbye and made their way towards a fleet of trucks waiting for them. She spotted the bus shelter and found a queue so long she was standing out in the rain. Well, never mind, she had her umbrella. She put it up; but the wind promptly blew it inside out. She decided she'd be better without it, and pulled the hood of her macintosh over her head.

Quarter of an hour passed, half; no sign of the bus. At two o'clock someone arriving at the station on a bicycle called that it had been cancelled. Laura began to panic. She went back into the station, asked the station master how far it was to the hospital; three or four miles, he said, the other side of town. She tried to keep her voice calm, said did he have any idea when the next bus might come. He said he didn't. Laura, most uncharacteristically, burst into tears.

There was one thing he was quite sure of: she wouldn't be late. Not after three years. She'd have left with hours to spare: she had told him she would in her last letter.

*Do you think I would waste one second of the time we'll have?* she wrote. *I will be there, as the clock strikes three. Earlier, if they'll let me in.*

He knew they, or rather Sister, wouldn't. She was unbelievably strict about visiting hours. About everything, of course. Heaven help you if you spilt so much as a drop of tea on your clean sheets, or didn't finish the disgusting food that was supposed to be so good for you, or even asked for painkilling drugs before they were due. Or tried to read under the bedclothes with a torch. He'd done that once, unable to sleep, and one of the probationers had lent him her torch. Sister, doing a late, unexpected round, caught him at it; the probationer was practically asked to leave and he was given very short shrift, told his book would be confiscated if he ever did such a thing again. And with visiting hours – well. On the dot of three, the doors opened, and at half past four they closed again, everyone having been ordered out five minutes previously. No one ever questioned it.

At three Laura would be there. The first through the door, he knew, her large brown eyes looking for him – he had told her where his bed was, five down from the door on the right. And he would watch her, coming towards him, not in his imagination as so often she had been, but for real, the real Laura, *his* Laura, and he would hold out his hands and she would reach him and take them and he dared think no further.

The station master looked at her. Pretty little thing. Her story was a sad one. He'd heard it so often, variations anyway. Small, private, personal sadnesses, frustrations, rage. Part of war, as inevitable as the bombs. Usually he shrugged, said he was sorry, nothing he could do, advised a cup of tea and patience. But somehow, this one – standing there, so pretty, so despairing, crying . . .

'I could lend you a bike, I suppose,' he said slowly. 'Got a couple of spares out the back, case we have to get somewhere quickly, signal failure or something. Long as you promise to bring it back.'

Somehow, the last hour passed: quarter to three, ten to, five to; he sat up, parade-ground straight, his heart beating violently, an odd drumming in his ears. He hardly dared blink lest he might miss a moment of her. Soon, so soon, one minute, thirty seconds . . . he took a deep breath, trying to calm himself, waiting, waiting . . . Now . . .

Three. A nurse opened the door. Agonisingly slowly. At last, at last . . . Laura, Laura . . .

The bike was rusty and the pedals kept sticking. But to Laura, it was perfection: a chariot of fire to take her to Tom, to her love. She rode it a couple of times round the station yard, wobbling at first, then settling into it. The saddle was very wet; she could feel the moisture seeping right through to her knickers. She didn't care. She could do it, she wouldn't be late for him, she couldn't be late for him.

She wasn't the first. Nor the second. Nor even the last. People poured in; but she wasn't among them. She just wasn't there. He felt sick. Angry. Not with her, but with the not-there-ness of her. Where?

Why? Oh, but it was only five minutes. Perhaps she had gone to the wrong ward. The wrong floor. It was a big hospital. If someone could go to find her . . . Near to tears, he called a probationer over.

'Please,' he said. 'Please, Laura hasn't come, she's lost somewhere in the hospital, she must be, she wouldn't be late. Please help me.'

She looked at her watch, then at him, smiled.

'Tom,' she said, 'it's only five past three. That's not late, it's nothing, it's—'

'It's not nothing to me,' he said, 'or to her. She'd be here, if she was all right, I know she would. Could you just see if she's outside in the corridor, looking for the ward? Or maybe upstairs, it's very confusing here, all the floors . . .'

The nurse looked at him. He felt a tear roll down his cheek and brushed it angrily away.

'Please,' he said again.

'All right.'


It was quite a simple journey, all on the main road; she couldn't get lost, and besides, trucks filled with soldiers kept passing her, as if leading her on her way. But it was difficult; and the rain and the wind were driving against her, slowing her down. It was already after three; he would be waiting, waiting: worried, fearful, think she wasn't coming. How could this have happened, how could she be failing him in this way? There was nothing she could do but keep going. She pedalled on. It was turning to dusk now, and the light, the muted regulation light of the bicycle, hardly reached the road. She began to dread each lorry passing her, huge monsters, sucking her towards them, the power of them making the bike wobble. She tried not to think of anything, to save her emotional as well as her physical energy for Tom, for getting to Tom, for not failing Tom. She would get there because she must; there was no alternative.

An animal, a dog or even a cat, ran across her path; she slammed on her brakes but they didn't work, the bike slithering wildly on the wet road. She fell off, climbed back on, battling against tears, against panic. Keep going, Laura, keep going, it couldn't be much further.

She heard the roar of another truck behind her, braced herself for

its passing. There was a stone in the road; she swerved to avoid it . . .
the truck reached her . . .

In the darkness, in the driving rain, on the unlit bicycle she had no
chance.

It was six o'clock when Sister came in and pulled the curtains round
Tom's bed. He did not even turn his head to look at her. He had lain
for hours, white faced, still, staring at the ceiling, trying to make
sense of it all: of his absolute despair, his bewilderment that she could
fail him, his terror that something dreadful had happened to her, his
rage that something, anything, could have robbed him of the happiness that he had waited for so long and had thought that at last he
could reclaim. He had refused food and drink and even to take his
medication, which lay on his bedside locker, seeing no point, no
future in becoming well, or even surviving.

'Well, now,' Sister said, 'I hear you have refused to take your medicine. That won't do, Corporal Knelston, it simply won't do.'

He said nothing.

'You have to take it, and you have to eat and you have to drink.
Otherwise you won't get well.'

He shrugged.

'And you need to get well. It's very important. Corporal Knelston,
look at me, please, when I'm talking to you.'

He ignored her.

'Tom, you heard what I said. Look at me.'

Her authority was irresistible; slowly, almost imperceptibly, Tom
turned his head.

And saw – what did he see? Behind the sternness something else:
something unaccustomed, a softening, almost – no, couldn't be, he
was hallucinating now, but – almost humour, nearly a smile.

'Come along,' she said, moving over to him, 'sit up, make an effort,
that's better.' She adjusted his pillows. 'Now, take these tablets,
please, at once. And I'll give you your injection.'

'I don't want it.'

'Corporal Knelston, you need it. And then you must eat your supper. You have to get well.'

'What for?' he said, his voice almost insolent. 'Why should I get well?'

'You have a job to do.'

'What job?' he said. 'If you mean defending my fucking country, what for, what for, for f—'

'Corporal Knelston, I will not have language like that on my ward. Apologise immediately.'

'I'm – sorry,' said Tom, genuinely shocked at himself. 'I'm so sorry, Sister.'

'Don't do it again. Now roll up your sleeve, please, while I give you your injection. And I'll tell you what for.'

He rolled up his pyjama sleeve, and then looked at her again; and it was there still, the almost-soft expression, the near-smile.

'Right,' she said, as the syringe emptied, and she withdrew it, laid it on its tray and stood back. Then the miracle happened and she did actually smile. 'I'll tell you what you have to get well for.' He stared at her, sitting motionless, frozen in time, fearful, hopeful, bewildered; every moment, every heartbeat, interminable.

'First, so that you can get yourself into that wheelchair,' she said and nodded towards Molly, who had pulled back the curtains and was standing beside the chair, her eyes sparkling; she was smiling broadly, and behind her were two of the other nurses, all of them smiling. 'And then so we can take you to Ward F. There's a young lady down there, with a broken leg, a broken arm, a fractured pelvis and a mild concussion, and she is going to need a great deal of care and help over the next few weeks. And if you promise to eat your supper when you get back, Nurse Davis here –' she gestured at Molly – 'will take you down to see her. I can assure you, from my personal experience, nursing is not something that can be done on an empty stomach. Corporal Knelston, do be careful, you'll fracture your own leg again.'

Tom looked up at her as he collapsed, breathing heavily, into the wheelchair. His eyes were huge and bright in his flushed face, and his smile, a huge, brilliant smile, was oddly unsteady.

'Sister,' he said, 'oh, Sister, I love you.'

Then it was Sister's face that was flushed and almost shocked, but she smiled again as she said, 'I don't think the young lady would quite want to hear such nonsense. Now go along – and mind, they said you could only have ten minutes with her, she's very tired.'

And Tom, dizzy suddenly with shock, lack of food, and exhaustion, slumped back into the wheelchair and was borne by Nurse Molly to Ward F where lay his happiness, his future and his love.

# Chapter 8

## 1944

'There must be something I can do. I'm sick of being treated like a child, stuck away at school, when most girls my age are doing something useful for the war effort, working in factories and stuff like that, joining the forces . . .'

'The forces! At your age! Don't be so ridiculous, Alice. Quite apart from being far too young, you've no idea what life would be like, the sort of people you'd come up against.'

'What do you mean? Oh, you think they're common. For heaven's sake! Even Princess Elizabeth is in the ATS, so it must be all right. Anyway, I don't have to do that – I could work in a factory like I said. Please, please, Mummy. Couldn't you and Daddy just consider letting me leave that stupid place, stuck away in the back of beyond? I hate it, I've always hated it.'

'Of course you don't hate it, Alice.' If Jean Miller's gentle face could have glared it would have done. The best she could manage was a deep frown. Her husband was very good at glaring. And scowling. *And* shouting. He would have dealt with this absurd nonsense. But he had gone to see a client in London – no doubt why Alice had chosen this moment to go on the attack. 'It's one of the best girls' schools in the country, and you're very lucky to be there . . .'

'It's not a fine school, and I'm very unlucky to be there. The girls are all such snobs, and all they think about is who they might marry, and how soon.'

'Well, there are worse things to think about.'

'Mummy! What about getting qualifications, a career? How can a husband compare with that? I want to do something – something useful.'

'Alice, the most useful thing you can do is stay where you are so we don't have to worry about you. And get on with studying for your exams, pass them well. You're not even sixteen yet—'

'I will be in three weeks. Anyway, Granny was married when she was fifteen!'

'That was rather a long time ago. And I thought you despised marriage?' said Jean, seeing a flaw in Alice's argument, and able to make a point.

'No, I despise people who think marrying the right man, by which they mean rich and not common, is the only thing they want to do.'

'Alice, this is turning into a rather silly conversation. The answer's no. Now I'm very busy. If you really want to help, you can sew the Cash's name tapes onto your summer uniform, so that I can get on.'

'With what? Going to the hospital, I suppose, pushing your trolley round. *I'd* quite like to do something like nursing. How old are the probationers? Sixteen? I thought so. But you wouldn't even let me do that, I bet. Oh, it's so unfair.'

'Alice, listen to me. If you're so keen to have a career – and I think nursing is an excellent one for a girl – then you should stay on at school and take your School Certificate and your Higher.'

Whereupon Alice left the room, banging the door behind her.

Her mother sighed. Alice was such a pretty girl, and she and her husband had high hopes for her; talented and popular, she attracted boys effortlessly, and was always the belle of the ball at the junior tennis club dances. The Millers weren't quite in the league of those whose daughters were presented at court, but they moved in a well-heeled middle-class society and Alice's prospects as the wife of a rich and successful man were, they felt, extremely good.

Alice had been born in 1928, shortly after her parents' first wedding anniversary. At thirty-five and thirty-two, Alec and Jean were a little old to be bride and bridegroom; and Jean, who was not a beautiful girl, had expected to remain a spinster. Being both bright and personable, she became a secretary to a firm of solicitors in Ascot. Her boss, one of the partners, who would have been on the brink of retirement had not the Great War removed two of the three younger partners, invited her and her widowed mother to a Christmas party at his home a year after she joined the firm and there she met Alec, his nephew. He was charmed by Jean, having had his heart broken by a girl who had chosen not to wait for his return from the front, and he had embarked on his long-postponed degree course in law at Durham University with a view to never exposing himself to a broken heart again. However, Jean, with her gentle ways and pleasant looks, so clearly the opposite of the girl who had jilted him, won his heart almost against his will. They were married in 1927, Alec taking up a position at his uncle's firm.

They settled in Sunningdale. Which, with its solid, aspirational respectability; large houses, many of them built in the newly fashionable mock-Tudor design; and close proximity to Ascot to lend it further class, suited them very well. With Jean as tireless hostess and a large circle of friends among the Sunningdale wives, very important to an ambitious man, he rose quite quickly to become one of the area's leading solicitors.

They had hoped that Alice would be the first of many children, but that was not to be. They bore their disappointments stoically, although after the fourth miscarriage Jean was so distressed that she told Alec she couldn't face any more. They considered adoption, but neither of them was particularly keen. 'The thing is,' Jean said to her closest friend Mildred, who was the only person in the world she had confided in, 'one never knows quite how the child might turn out. Some of these girls come from very doubtful backgrounds.'

In all other ways, however, things went well for them: when Alec's uncle retired, he became the firm's senior partner. They acquired a larger house (still Tudor style) with a big rhododendron-filled garden, a maid, a part-time gardener and a cook. Jean continued to play the perfect wife; her only failure indeed had been to produce the longed-for boy, but Alec was so proud of his daughter that he managed to overcome his disappointment and his pride in her was enormous. She was a pretty little girl, with shining fair curls, very large blue eyes, amazing dimples and a rosebud mouth; she was also, being sweet natured and generous, very popular with other little girls, and her social life was hectic from her earliest years.

The Millers had at first thought themselves safe from the worst excesses of Mr Hitler's efforts, and in many ways Sunningdale life appeared largely unchanged to the casual observer, apart from an absence of any young men; its older residents continued to run their businesses, and everyone played golf, tennis and bridge as they always had done. The main problem, endlessly bewailed over bridge and supper tables, was that so much of the domestic help was no longer available; the females had gone to work in factories, and the only gardeners to be found were rather elderly and unsuited to heavy work. Food was on the plain side, and making palatable meals from powdered eggs and Spam a challenge, but there was a war on, the women all kept reminding one another, and one had to do one's bit.

There were very few cars on the roads, largely because of petrol rationing, and Alice and her friends could cycle about in perfect safety, often into Bagshot almost five miles away, where they even bought that unimaginable luxury, ice cream. The only serious traffic, and an indication that all was not as it had been, was the long convoys of army tanks and lorries, packed with soldiers who would wave and shout at the children as they travelled to the southern ports to be shipped into war.

But it proved not so safe after all. There was a munitions factory at nearby Longcross, which was a target for bombing, and one after-noon during the summer of 1940, a squadron of bombers had flown over the golf courses and manicured gardens of Sunningdale and been attacked by Spitfires.

The Millers were badly shaken by this, and agreed that while it wasn't dangerous enough for the whole family to move, Alice's life must not be endangered. She was sent to board at a famous cradle for well-bred young ladies, St Catherine's, near Taunton in the depths of Somerset, where she missed home and her friends dreadfully.

* * *

When the war was over, Johnathan read about the Battle of Monte Cassino and marvelled that he was still alive to do so. Fifty thousand men dead; how war diminished the meaning of those numbers.

His greatest fear was of becoming brutalised; and he knew, of course, that to a degree he had been. No one could fight as he had done, see the things he had seen, and emerge unscathed. He knew he was desensitised to a degree, less susceptible, far from the gentle young man he had been. But he had clung to a determination not to be entirely hardened as if to a religion, to believe in the rightness of the cause he was fighting for, and to see that as the justification for all that he had been asked to do. He had to remain true to himself. But it was never easy, and often seemed impossible.

He would never forget, and was glad that he would not, the morning after the bombing of the abbey, crowning as it did the lovely town of Monte Cassino, all reduced to a stark dead rubble. Only about forty people remained in the town: six monks, sheltering in the vaults of the abbey, a handful of tenant farmers, orphaned and abandoned children, and some badly wounded and dying. The old abbot led them down the path, reciting his rosary as they came; Johnathan found it impossible not to weep. That it was a great victory – for the abbey was not an isolated fortress, but part of the great Gustav Line stretching from the mountains to the sea – seemed at that moment irrelevant.

He had arrived in Italy towards the end of 1943 having been heavily involved in the fighting in North Africa; but he had got the sand out of his shoes, as he put it, and had been part of the successful invasion of Sicily. One of his happier memories had been the landing in the Bay of Salerno near Naples. The villagers had treated them with sheer joy, cheering when they saw the Allied flag. It was Christmas time; he ate tinned turkey, and tried not to think about Christmases past at Guildford Park, the vast tree in the hall, the Christmas dinner table laden with goodies – obscenely now, it seemed to him – midnight service in the village church, Boxing Day shoots. Some of his fellow officers, and indeed his men, took comfort from their happy memories; Johnathan found them tantalising and hurtful. He tried and entirely failed to even find any kind of reality in

Diana and her place in his past or his future. That frightened him more than anything.

But there were good things: and one of them was the incredible mishmash of nationalities who formed the Allied troops. Americans, Indians, New Zealanders, Canadians, French and the Gurkhas. Archetypal Englishman that he was, inclined to be awkward when confronted by any foreigner, he found an entirely new form of easy camaraderie: epitomised just before the worst of the fighting began, by a football match, followed by tea parties, a concert, a great deal of wine and a film at the camp cinema. He could never remember afterwards what the film was – some kind of absurd comedy – but the whole day somehow stood out for them all, a beacon of cheerful common sense, shining against the insanity of war.

The run-up to the fighting was incredibly difficult; they could do nothing by day without drawing enemy fire, so resupplying was all done at night; there was a problem with the water and few of the wells contained anything fit to drink, which didn't help.

They were relieved at one point at night by a troop of men from the Royal Fusiliers who moved in silently, boots wrapped in sandbags, the only sound the croaking of frogs. In the marshes. Incredibly, Johnathan found himself at breakfast staring at one of his greatest friends from Eton, found himself greeted with a clap on the back and, 'Good Lord, Gunners, nice to see you. How are you, old chap?' It was almost in the Dr Livingstone league of British understatement.

The bloody, savage fighting finished in victory on 18 May when the long battle was over; exhausted, they learned of the fall of Rome on 4 June.

Now what? he thought.

One thing was settling into firm resolution in his mind: he could not return, if he ever got home, to his rather pointless job in the City. He wanted, indeed needed, to go home to Guildford Park, to work on the farm and the estate, to build a more satisfactory future for himself than one based on the rise in value of the stock exchange, a growing client list, and an annual increase in salary. How Diana would fit into that future, he could not begin to imagine. Or even think about.

\* \* \*

'Just listen to this.' Laura looked up from the *Daily Mirror*. 'Fortnum and Mason are stocking grapes, peaches – at seven and six each, I might say – and chocolates! Oh, it's disgusting. And did you know, the Dorchester is packed every night with its own extra-deep shelter, lest the poor toffs get caught out by an air raid. How can this still be happening? When ordinary people are homeless and often hungry. Oh, it makes me so angry. How can it be allowed?'

Tom said rather feebly he didn't know; in truth, at that moment neither did he care. He was too depressed.

Both of them had finally been released from hospital, Tom invalided out of the army, Laura returning to school part-time until the spring term. They were both living at her little flat, while he tried to come to terms with his new, empty situation and what he might do: even with the small diamond on her finger, this could never have happened before the war, a young couple, unmarried, living under the same roof. Tom's parents were shocked and Laura's headmaster was very vocal on the subject.

'It's a bad example for the children, and the parents won't like it. If the wedding isn't very soon, Laura, I shall have to consider my position.'

Laura knew that his wasn't a strong position, as half the staff had been called up, and she was an excellent deputy headmistress; but just the same it all added to Tom's general unhappiness and sense of uselessness. He sat about a great deal, feeling wretched.

Laura, working extremely hard, finally ran out of sympathy, ordering him one afternoon to go and see Mr Pemberton. 'He'd be pleased anyway and you never know, he might want you back . . .'

'Even if he did, I can't keep a wife on what he pays me, and—'

'Oh, Tom,' said Laura, and her face took on the expression that he knew there was no arguing with. 'Your wife, as you call her, is working, and earning a decent wage, and we can perfectly manage between us, so I don't see the point of not going. In fact, I want you to go and if you don't, I shall be quite annoyed, and you know you don't like that.'

Tom didn't, and so it was that he went to see Mr Pemberton that very afternoon.

Laura walked into the flat to find the table laid, a delicious smell of cooking in the air, and even a bottle of cider chilling in cold water in the sink.

And Tom actually smiling.

'So – what's this about then?' she said, and he told her. Mr Pemberton had indeed been pleased to see him; but Betty had told him the dreadful news before he went in: that Nigel had been killed two years earlier, in action in Italy.

'He's been very down ever since, Tom, can't seem to come to terms with it, and Mrs Pemberton's been quite ill with it, so that must be dreadful for him too.'

'I'm sure it is,' said Tom, 'and don't think I don't feel really sorry for him, Laura – he was so proud of Nigel, and he was going to take over the business, of course.'

'Yes, I know, you've told me many times,' said Laura, taking off her hat and looking at him. She found Tom's admiration for Mr Pemberton and his unquestioning acceptance that Nigel should automatically inherit the business hugely irritating.

'Laura, he'd been shot and they didn't hear for several weeks, imagine how dreadful—'

'Happens to everybody,' said Laura briskly.

'Yes, I know but . . . There was a letter from his commanding officer, saying all the usual things, praising Nigel's courage and his leadership qualities, and assuring them that he had died instantly. He asked me what I thought about that,' Tom added, 'if it was true. He said I'd know, having been in the army, if they all said that. I hadn't an idea, of course, but I said I was sure it was. True, I mean.'

'That was the right thing to say,' said Laura.

'I hope so. "I've found it very difficult to bear, Tom," he said. "At times, I – well, never mind." I knew what he meant – he'd wanted to die himself. And he said, and this was the worst thing, that he'd loved him, more than he'd ever loved anyone. And now he'd gone, the world seemed very empty. Empty and dark, he said. It was so dreadful, Laura, so sad.

'Then he said he wanted to help me as much as he could with passing my article exams and then maybe one day – well, he said, "I'm

67

very fond of you, Tom. I always have been." And then he said that with Nigel gone, and no one else to take his place, if I worked really hard and I became a partner – a partner, me! – who knows what might happen? "I'm not young any more," he said, and then he stopped talking and I don't even dare think what he might have meant.'

'Well, I do,' said Laura. 'He was saying he saw you as his heir. And quite right too. Why not?'

'Anyway,' Tom said. 'I feel pretty overwhelmed by what he's doing for me already. Especially while he's so unhappy.'

'Well,' said Laura slowly, after considering this, 'I think you'll make him feel less unhappy. Which is a wonderful thing.'

'But what this is all leading up to is, Laura Leonard, I can now properly ask you to marry me. Why are you laughing?'

'Because you're so ridiculous. I'm marrying you anyway. You've already asked me, unless I was dreaming and this ring is some kind of apparition.'

'Yes, but I can ask you to marry me now, at once! We can set a date, and I thought New Year's Day – it would make a good start to the year – or as near as we can get. What do you say?'

'I say,' said Laura, 'could we just leave that lovely stew stewing, and that cider getting colder, and could we pop next door to the bedroom just for a bit before supper, so I can show you how wonderful I think you are?'

Diana had finally found a solution to her boredom and sense of use-lessness during the war; she wasn't particularly proud of it, but it was the best she could manage. Johnathan had forbidden so many of the things she would have been prepared to do – but she still felt pro-foundly guilty at her lack of contribution. One of her friends – those drawn from the Johnathan circle as she thought of them – a chic sparky beauty called Wendelien Bellinger ('You pronounce it like Gwendolyn without the G') had set up a fortnightly event at her house in Knightsbridge, which she called a Bring and Give. 'It's sort of like a Bring and Buy, in that we collect all sorts of stuff – clothes, obviously, and blankets, but also books, gramophone records – from people we know mostly, and bring it all here, and then instead of selling it, we take it to people like the WVS Canteens, and the church shelters and so on. You get to see all your chums and have a really jolly afternoon, and it's amazing what we persuade people to part with.'

Diana said she thought Wendelien could have persuaded the chief Beefeater at the Tower to part with the Crown Jewels if she'd put her mind to it.

'Sweet of you to say so, but it really isn't that difficult. The only rule is, we're not allowed to keep anything for ourselves. Absolute agony I went through last week when Tilly Browning brought in the most gorgeous Jacques Fath coat; I longed to keep it, it really suited me, but of course that would be awfully bad form. Anyway, if you think you'd like to help, it would mean coming up to London once a fortnight. It's not so dangerous any more, and we haven't got anyone in your area so you're bound to pick up lots of lovely stuff . . .'

Diana, who found the thought of getting up to London regularly exciting, said she would love to. And indeed, her life changed for ever; not only did she do rather well at the Bringing and Giving, as Wendelien had prophesied, but she also became part of her inner circle.

Anyone reading Wendelien's pocket diary, which was so packed as to be almost illegible, would have found it hard to believe it was being lived out against a background of one of the most appalling wars in history. Dinners and cocktail dates were recorded nightly at the smartest of venues; even more surprisingly, most of the main London couturiers were open for business, encouraged to form an association by the Board of Trade. Wendelien took the bemused Diana on a round one afternoon, of Molyneux, Digby Morton, Norman Hartnell and Worth. Diana, who had been wearing her old clothes for three years, hardly daring to buy so much as a pair of gloves, found temptation beyond endurance there and ordered a suit from Digby Morton.

Wendelien absolutely refused to move from her pretty little house in Knightsbridge. 'I would die if I had to leave it and move to some deathly dull suburb, so I might as well be bumped off by a bomb.'

In spite of her rather flippant protestations, she did display considerable bravery. Her street took a direct hit one night, and most of the surviving residents had moved away, including her neighbours on either side. She remained firm, taking *Vogue*'s advice at the time to offer baths, rather than drinks: *Soap and water are a far more pleasing offer than any amount of gin.*

'I made lots of new friends – you'd be surprised,' she said to Diana, who wasn't at all.

Wendelien's adored and extremely handsome husband was commander of a destroyer in the North Atlantic and living in extreme danger. 'And there's another reason, you see,' Wendelien would say. 'If he gets killed – and let's face it, it is quite likely – I certainly don't want to be left without him, so there's another reason for taking on the bombers. I just know if I did move to the country, his ship would be torpedoed straight away. So much better to stay here, don't you see? And at least I'm having fun, and don't spend all my time with nothing to do except worry.'

Diana didn't see, but she couldn't quite formulate her argument.

Most of Wendelien's evenings were spent at the big hotels; the Dorchester ('the Dorch' to its intimates) was probably the most sought out, and said to have the safest air-raid shelter in London, but the Savoy, Claridge's and the Ritz were packed too.

There were the nightclubs, the Colony Club and the Café de Paris – also supposed to be the safest place in London – where people danced to the music of such luminaries as Snakehips Johnson and Lew Stone.

'There are always a few chums home on leave,' Wendelien said carelessly when Diana asked her who on earth she went with. 'And then there are my parents and their friends – some of them are huge fun, and not too terribly over the hill.'

She was two years older than Diana, and had always moved in the most glittering circles; her mother, equally chic and beautiful, was rumoured to have had an affair with the Prince of Wales, briefly to become Edward VIII, and it was even more wildly rumoured that Wendelien was his child. 'But of course as everyone knows, that's completely impossible,' she said to Diana, over cocktails at the Dorchester one evening.

Diana, excited by such infinite glamour touching her own life, asked why. Wendelien laughed. 'Diana, you're such an innocent. Because he couldn't – you know – just couldn't, everyone knows that.'

'Well, I didn't,' said Diana, slightly crossly. 'And nor did anyone else I know.'

'Well, darling, that's exactly why I couldn't bear to live in the country,' said Wendelien. 'Now don't look like that. Let's have another drink. And then I've just seen Ludo Manners – he must be home on leave. He's just the most handsome man I've ever met, apart from my darling Ian, of course, and such fun, you'd absolutely love him – or do you know him already?'

Of course Diana didn't.

'Well, you must meet him. He didn't get married for ages, and there were lots of people who said he was a fairy, but I never believed it, and he got married just a year before the war. To Cecily Johnson. She was in my year, a very sweet, bit unsophisticated, but terribly pretty, country girl like you. Don't look so cross, I'm only teasing. Come on, let's go over and you can meet him.'

Ludo Manners was indeed charming and, Diana thought, one of the nicest men she'd met. He was, in spite of his unarguably wonderful, blonde look, self-deprecating with beautiful manners, introducing them to his companions – his godfather and his uncle – expressing huge interest in Johnathan's war, and volunteering great admiration for Ian Bellinger's.

'It really is the Senior Service – wish I'd joined them in a way.'

He was home convalescing. 'I got in the way of a bit of shrapnel couple of months ago – so stupid – had to have some surgery on my leg, and then got incredibly lucky and got a couple of weeks at home. Going back next week.'

'So where's Cecily?' asked Wendelien.

'Oh, at home in the country.' Wendelien shot Diana a glance of amused malice, at this. 'We've got one little sprog, expect you heard, born just before the war, jolly little chap, and now there's another on the way, so she doesn't feel quite the thing. I had to come up, get details of my next posting, and – well, what do you do with a spare evening in London? Head for the dear old Dorch.'

# Chapter 9

## 1945

'I can't believe it.'

For the rest of his life, whenever Tom heard those words, he was back in the big shabby office at Pemberton & Marchant, staring at Betty Foxton as she stood in the doorway, her eyes bright, her cheeks flushed, her large bosom heaving.

'It's over,' she said, her voice almost a shout. 'The war's over. I can't believe it, I just can't believe it. My mother just telephoned, said she didn't think Mr Pemberton would mind.'

Tom stared at her. 'Really? Officially?'

'Really. Mr Churchill's just been on the wireless. Oh, I can't believe it.'

'Nor can I,' said Tom. 'Not really. Oh, God. How amazing.' He was silent for a moment, oddly sober, 'Oh, Betty. If only I was still out there with them all. Properly part of it.'

'Now then, we don't want any of that. You did your bit, more than most, so don't go thinking you didn't. Now, where are the other two?'

'They went to lunch very late,' said Tom. 'They won't be long, I'm sure.'

'Oh well, Mr Pemberton, do you think he's heard? Should I go in, do you think? As Miss Forshaw's away today.'

'I – I don't know.' And then, looking at Mr Pemberton's closed door, reflecting on his own regret, contemplating a far greater one, he said, 'Tell you what, Betty, I'll tell him. I've got to go in anyway.'

Tom felt that possibly the last thing Mr Pemberton would welcome at that moment was an overexcited Betty.

Mr Pemberton was sitting at his desk, staring out of the window. He was very pale. He looked at Tom and half smiled.

'Hello, Tom. And yes, I have heard the news. My wife telephoned. My goodness, what a wonderful . . .' And then his voice tailed off, and he looked down at his hands, and when he looked up, his pale blue eyes were very bright. He tried to smile, his mouth oddly distorted; and then a tear rolled down his face. He wiped it away, took out his handkerchief and blew his nose.

'I'm sorry, Tom,' he said, 'sorry, it's – it's –'

And he put his head down on his arms on the desk, and began to sob heavily. And Tom, considering his own regret, considered Mr Pemberton's own, infinitely greater one, considered his embarrassment too, and very quietly left the room.

It was actually something of a fiction that peace exploded that day in May on an unsuspecting public, and especially in London. It had been awaited for months. The Home Guard had been disbanded, celebrated by a parade down Whitehall as early as the autumn of 1944, followed in February by the part-time firefighters. The closure of the public air-raid shelters and the removal of the bunks in the London underground stations caused surprising sadness: of the six thousand people who had slept in them for years, only a quarter of them did so from genuine necessity. They'd just got used to it and they liked it.

'My dear old char loves it down there,' Wendelien said to Diana. 'Says it's home. Now she's got to go and live with her daughter, and she says she's losing lots of friends. They had a high old time in the middle of the war, you know, concert parties used to put on shows and everybody used to sing and dance. Oh, and listen to this, it says in *The Times* there's a run on bunting for when the celebrations really get going.'

Diana and Wendelien had become very close; Diana often stayed with Wendelien, and wondered sometimes what Johnathan would say if he had known that forbidding her to join the WVS or work in a munitions factory had led her into arguably far greater danger. She decided she didn't care.

She had even been at the little house in Knightsbridge through some at least of the Little Blitz. 'Not so little, darling,' Wendelien said, as they took shelter under her heavy dining table one night when St James's came under fire. 'Honestly, to have survived for so long, so annoying to get done for now. Here, pass me the brandy. God, if we survive we'll have hangovers in the morning.' They did survive; and the hangovers were predictably bad.

And then it was over officially: 8 May took off. Perhaps the greatest moment, one Diana would have loved to have experienced, was when Mr Churchill had stood on a balcony in Whitehall. 'This is your victory,' he said to the crowds below. His car was then pushed by them all the way to Buckingham Palace. They had listened to him on the wireless; then contemplated going to the Mall to see him and the Royal Family on the balcony and decided they couldn't face the crowds.

Wendelien gave a party at her house instead. They drank the last of Ian Bellinger's claret, and a magnum of vintage champagne (he had had two, one being kept for his return), and as darkness fell, they all went on to the Ritz, fighting their way through the crowds, clinging to one another, terrified of becoming separated. It was an extraordinary night. London was quite literally heaving, and every so often the women were lifted off their feet. People were singing, dancing, climbing anything there was to climb – lamp posts, pub signs, statues – sitting on upper-storey windowsills, kissing complete strangers. The pubs had run dry by eight p.m. but the Ritz did better.

Now, Diana thought as she fell, swirling headed, into bed in Wendelien's house, now she had to face real life again, make a marriage, be a good wife. And even mother. Which would be wonderful. Wouldn't it?

Alice had won. Just as the British and Mr Churchill had won. In much the same way, really, just doggedly refusing to be beaten. What she'd actually done had been quite clever actually, Alice thought – she'd just threatened to run away, which would mean she'd be expelled anyway, and that would have completely destroyed her parents. And so they'd relented, and she was home in Sunningdale, back at her day school, and today was VE Day and the war was over and she was celebrating with her family at a bonfire party. It was terribly exciting.

There were a lot of bonfires, she'd heard, a symbol of the country's release from the darkness of war. Alice had a strong sense of living in history that day; she could see it was something that would be wonderful to tell her children and her grandchildren about.

They'd all been in lessons in the early afternoon and they'd been summoned into the hall and Miss Thompson, the headmistress, had stood on the platform at her lectern and said, 'Girls, this is a wonderful day and one none of us must ever forget. Mr Churchill has announced on the wireless that there is at last victory in Europe; this long terrible war is over. Against all the odds of the first years, when we stood alone and refused to surrender, we have won. Many sacrifices have been made, many lives have been lost, and I would remind you, even in our joy, that there is scarcely a family in the land, and indeed in this school, that has not lost a member, often several. But right has conquered, with God's help, and I would ask you now to put your hands together in prayer and offer our thanks for the great victory that has been granted us today.'

Silly old bat, Alice thought, she obviously feels she's made some huge contribution herself; but even so, as they all sang the school hymn, she did find a sentiment approaching pride herself. It was awfully special to be British today.

After that they were sent home, Alice accompanied by her best friend, Jillie Curtis, a friendship formed at boarding school, and cemented by their common hatred of the place. 'My parents are raving socialists, I don't know what they're doing sending me here,' Jillie had said.

Alice had looked at her in awe; she'd never met a socialist or anyone related to one before.

Jillie was very clever, and not conventionally pretty, but extremely attractive, tall and very slim, with long straight brown hair and green eyes. She lived in London; her father was at Sotheby's and her mother worked as an art critic, whatever that might mean. 'She goes to endless exhibitions and writes books and articles about art.'

'So who looked after you, when you were little?'

'Oh, a nanny, and now we have a housekeeper who's there and gives me lunch and stuff. Mummy works at home a lot but I get left to my own devices most of the time, don't really mind at all.'

It sounded wonderful to Alice.

'And now,' she said, smiling at Jillie in the darkness, looking at the sparks flying through the air, past the big apple tree, up towards the stars, 'now we can take our Higher Cert and leave school and get on with our lives.'

'What are you going to do, do you think?' asked Jillie.

'I'm going to be a nurse – a really, really good nurse. In a really, really good hospital in London. Probably even become a matron. And nobody is ever going to dare to suggest I've got to marry some stupid rich, important man. In fact, if I do ever get married, I'll be the most important person in the family. How about you?'

'I thought I might be a doctor,' said Jillie.

It was over. Over. All that agony. All over. Ned found it hard even to begin to know what he felt.

He was in Malta on the day itself. The war had been crumbling to an end for months, in the Med at least. He sat in the mess, staring out to sea, listening to his fellow officers whooping, trying to share their excitement – and completely failing. It was the biggest anticlimax of his life. He had seen death and fear and courage and the loss of so much – millions of lives, undreamed-of horrors. And for what? Victory. It should have been enough. But for him at least, it wasn't.

Now he had the peacetime world to face, not the easy escape of war.

He had actually had a successful war, personally. He'd been given command of three vessels, he'd been mentioned in dispatches, he'd fought bravely. But he'd made mistakes. They were what he remembered now, even as he downed one whisky, and then another. Hitting a mine one night, the boat blown up, losing half the crew. Men he'd lived with for over a year, his friends, some of them still alive, wounded in the water. He knew he'd hear their cries for the rest of his life, knowing there was nothing he could do. If there was a hell, he had thought, he had entered it then.

But some of it he'd enjoyed: the camaraderie, a recognition that he was becoming a useful and competent member of the team and its operations, earning the respect of his men. He had always been popular, even at school, but this had been less easily won; it was not enough simply to be charming and amusing. He had not only to be brave and decisive, but also seen to be those things.

There had been time on shore; that had been good. He'd caught a bit of shrapnel in his leg, been sent to Malta to recover. He hadn't been badly injured, but it took a time to heal; hadn't felt too bad, but some of the other chaps were in a really bad way. Seeing it as a mission to cheer them up, he'd organised polo matches in the ward with crutches and other such nonsense. They were an undoubted nuisance and the nurses got pretty browned off, but as a war effort, he felt it was pretty positive.

There was a shout from the bar: 'Hey, Welles! What's the matter with you? Come on over, drinks on the house . . .'

He went, smiling: he would continue to survive. Of course he would.

Johnathan, still in Italy, spent the early part of the day writing to Diana, telling her how much he was longing to come home and be with her again. He made no mention of his decision; that was something too important to trust to paper. He knew she would find it difficult, but he was sure she would make the very best of it and indeed come to love the new life and the glorious countryside of Yorkshire.

Tom and Laura returned home from the celebrations, first at Laura's school, then at the recreation ground in Hilchester (another bonfire). They talked quite soberly about how the ending of the war, which had done so much to rid the country of its dreadful class distinction, must surely see a new dawn for socialism, for fairness, for true equality, and vowed they would do everything in their power to work towards that themselves.

# Chapter 10

## 1945–6

It was such a totally unsuitable setting to receive the news.

She'd just been thinking she really was perfectly happy, that the war years and their long separation had ended exactly how she would have wished, sitting at a table in the River Room at the Savoy, after a marvellous dinner and a lot of very good champagne; a pianist playing Cole Porter and boats going past on the Thames below, their lights shining on the water. It was all so very lovely. He'd only been home a couple of days; gorgeous days they'd been, she'd been so very glad to see him, genuinely so, loving being with him, making him happy. They were actually spending two rather extravagant nights at the Savoy.

But then he'd taken her hand and said he had something very important to tell her. She'd sat, trying not to show her horror as she heard what it was: that he wanted to give up his London life as a stockbroker and go and work on the estate in Yorkshire. His father wasn't well, he said, had never recovered from Piers's death, and his mother and Timothy had been struggling to cope since the end of the war. 'Mother's been amazing, Tim says, but she's not young, and Tim – well, his heart's not in the whole estate thing. He really wants to get back to London and his life as a barrister, and he has a real talent for that, Diana, it's wrong for him to miss out.'

She'd asked, floundering about for some sort of salvation, about Johnathan's life as a stockbroker, and he'd said it seemed to him a rather stupid, vapid life, making rich people richer. Whereas running the estate, the farm, that really appealed to him, seemed an important thing to do. 'I know it's a big thing to ask, but I want to go back to Yorkshire, and make my life there. I'll need you and your support desperately.'

'But Johnathan . . .'

'Darling, I can see it's a bit of a shock, of course it is, and for that very reason you must take time to get used to the idea.'

And if she didn't, she wondered, what then? Clearly, she'd be going anyway.

'I suggest you go and stay with your parents for a few days. I have to go up to Yorkshire tomorrow, to see Mother and Father and talk to them both, with Timothy, put our proposal to them. And then perhaps you'll come up and join us? You've never spent much time there, and it's so beautiful, I know you'll learn to love it . . .'

She waved him off gaily next day, and then went to meet Wendelien. She was truly horrified; horrified and afraid. How could she do it, leave everything and everyone she knew and loved and go to live hundreds of miles away, to that cold, ugly house, set in that harsh, hostile landscape? To live with a man she could see very clearly now she didn't actually love at all. She would be exiled, alone, lost, friendless. She couldn't do it, it was too much to ask, too much for her to give. She would never have agreed to marry Johnathan had she known of this gargantuan condition. She wept many tears, feeling she had been robbed of everything.

Wendelien's response had been very straightforward. 'Just don't go, darling, say you'd be useless and miserable and he shouldn't ask you.' Her parents' response had been quite different, especially her father's. He had told her he was ashamed of her reaction, that Johnathan was a very fine chap, who loved her, and it was her duty as a wife to stand by him and do whatever he wanted. Her mother had said much the same, in a gentler way: 'It's true, darling, you marry the man, not the life—'

'No, you don't,' Diana had said angrily. 'The life is part of the man, and this just isn't fair, not what I was led to expect.'

'Diana, this is real life, not some fairy tale,' her mother had said. 'You were delighted to marry Johnathan, I seem to remember.'

80

'Yes, but—'

'No buts. Not now. I do think, Diana, it's time you grew up a little and realised you don't live in a romantic novel. Marriage isn't all about one person, it's about two.'

Diana had fled to her room and refused to come down for supper. Later Caroline Southcott went up to see her, relented a little, told her she did understand and she hadn't been all that keen to leave London herself as a young bride. 'But that was what your father wanted, and I went along with it.'

Diana didn't even try to explain that Hampshire was very near London, that they still had a lot of very jolly friends, and for a time, a little flat in London. As for Johnathan's mother, Vanessa Gunning was a nightmare, and she would, at first at any rate, be her most constant companion. She didn't like Diana, it had been obvious from the very first meeting; she saw her as a most unsuitable wife for Johnathan. But she listened to her parents and realised she had no option, apart from leaving Johnathan which was clearly unthinkable and so, with the very best grace that she could muster, she told him that of course she would come up to Yorkshire and be as supportive and helpful as she could manage.

He had been touchingly grateful, had said he realised it would be hard for her and not what she had expected. 'But hopefully, darling, there'll be little ones about soon, and they'll be fun and keep you busy, and if there's one thing I can offer you it's a jolly nice house.'

That was true; they would have the Dower House, a seventeenth-century, six-bedroomed, beautifully proportioned place built by an unusually civilised and artistic Gunning for a wife, who had perhaps, Diana thought, been a refugee from the south like herself. It had huge fireplaces, a lovely staircase rising from the stone-flagged hall, and tall shuttered windows: but it was still grey, built of Yorkshire stone, and cold, so cold. Nothing grew up its rather forbidding front-age; it stood there, unadorned, stark and demanding. She could not love it, or even like it at first, but it was hers now and it gave her some-thing to do. She had a talent for houses; she got rid of much of the heavy, seventeenth-century furniture – to Lady Gunning's clear disapproval – and went eighteenth instead, moving some charming sofas and chairs and pretty side tables into the drawing room, and a lovely table for sixteen, with matching chairs for entertaining, into the dining room. She hung heavy curtains in the windows, a protest against the cold as much as the very plain shutters, installed two modern bathrooms upstairs, and even put carpets down in the bedrooms.

Guildford was half a mile from the Dower House; one of Diana's first demands had been for a car of her own, and she bought a pretty little Austin 7 which became her lifeline so she could potter backwards and forwards to the house, down into the village and – she had hoped – to visit friends. But they had proved a bit of a mirage; as had the social life she had hoped for. Johnathan was always busy on the farm and estate, and too exhausted to host dinner parties. So the lovely table remained unused, and the drawing room was deserted as a place for Diana to pursue her (very limited) hobbies. She would sit in the kitchen by the Aga, listening to the radio and devouring any novels she could get her hands on.

She tried; she really tried. She offered to do the paperwork for the farm, knowing that she was efficient and would do it well. Johnathan, initially enthusiastic, consulted his mother and came back to Diana rather shamefaced to say that his mother said she was already doing it perfectly well. She made overtures to the other young women, joined their committees, helped with their charities, but she found no friends among them. She was an outsider, and they did not seem to like her enough to make an effort for her.

Johnathan was also too exhausted to want to have sex with her very often. That was a relief, in its way – it hadn't really got much better – but she couldn't help feeling rejected in another; it also of necessity lessened her chances of becoming pregnant. The first year came and went and she experienced her first Yorkshire winter, which created in her a true hatred of the place, with its violent raw winds, its long grey seemingly endless days, its icy daybreaks, its dreadful silence, devoid of birdsong or sunlight. She couldn't walk, she couldn't ride; it was too hostile, it seemed turned against her. She tried but she would return from some expedition almost before it had begun, defeated, raging silently, angry with Johnathan, and worse, with herself.

Occasionally she went to stay with her mother, in the sweet chill which was what the Hampshire winter seemed, and cried and railed against her fate. Her mother, worried about how thin she had become, how unlike her sparkling self, would allow her to stay an extra day or two, and then found herself insisting she go home again, literally forcing her onto the train.

'Spring is coming, darling,' she would say. She would prepare a parcel for her, packing copies of *Vogue* and *Tatler*, bottles of Dior scent, her favourite Coty make-up, some pretty lace hankies, novels by her favourite authors, Georgette Heyer and Angela Thirkell. Then she would drive home to West Hilton having dropped Diana at the station, weeping all the way. It was a dreadful thing to see your child so helplessly – and she was beginning to fear hopelessly – unhappy.

Laura was marking books when Tom came in. It was something she actually enjoyed, unlike so many of her colleagues. She spent a lot of time and trouble on it, adding comments to her ticks and crosses, even in maths books, so that the children could learn from them, rather than just look for the mark at the bottom of each piece of work, and move on. Like all the best teachers, Laura's desire was to enthuse her pupils and expand their interest in subjects, rather than simply inform them; and although she was not always successful, she knew she did well. She particularly enjoyed the older children's work, the nine- and ten-year-olds. The older pupils were gearing up for their examinations into the grammar schools; and while the subjects didn't include anything more basic than English, arithmetic and the general paper, she knew that a child who had been enthused by a study of how the North Americans lived (other than fighting one another as cowboys and Indians) or was intrigued by how exactly the marriage of Henry VIII had changed the religious character of England was more likely to bring an intelligence and clear-sightedness to the hardest part of the eleven-plus.

Even as she coached her pupils, some considerable part of her fretted over this disparity and wished there could be some more equable solution so that all children might have access to the advantages of the grammar schools and not be cast aside into the limbo of the

Secondary Moderns, failures for all the world, including themselves, to recognise at the age of eleven.

She had already finished one pile and was embarking on history, when Tom appeared. She never failed to be slightly surprised at the way her heart seemed to lift when he returned to her each evening. It wasn't of course that she expected him not to do so, it was that she loved him so much and never felt that things were quite in order until he was there. She often wondered if their relationship was rare in its happiness; listening to her fellow teachers who were married, and her friends as well, come to that, she felt extraordinarily fortunate.

They had married in the little church at West Hilton, just a few friends, their families – rather more of his than hers, of course, but her sister Babs and her husband Dick Carter with their four children were there. And her mother, the redoubtable Edith, now physically frail. It was the prettiest wedding, the church filled with jugs of wild flowers, Laura in a simple blue dress made by her mother. 'Well, I can hardly wear white now, can I?' she said to Tom, laughing. When Tom turned and looked at her as she reached him, and she smiled at him and, rather irregularly it was felt although nobody particularly minded, reached up to kiss him, love seemed to fill the little church, as visible as the flowers and as audible as the strains of 'Love Divine' ringing down from the organ loft.

Later that night, as the guests danced to the Hiltons Village Band, a more than slightly inebriated Jack said to Mary that he'd had his doubts about Laura; she was a bit of a forward piece, and now he had met her mother he could see where it came from. He had to admit, however, that she had her good points and he had come to the opinion that she was going to make Tom very happy.

And indeed she had; and moreover, equally importantly, he made her so. Incredibly, beautifully happy.

This evening, Tom was late, having been to London, dispatched for the day by Mr Pemberton to visit the reference section at the Law Society, and making a detour – without Mr Pemberton's permission or knowledge, but reflecting that what he didn't know wouldn't hurt him – to Transport House to purchase a couple of books, one for himself on the history of trades union law, and one that Laura had requested on the suffragettes. Books were very cheap at Transport House as they considered it immoral to charge any price above what they had paid the publisher or supplier. He had only been there once before and he had loved it, been surprised and impressed by its rather splendid appearance, walking literally, he felt, into the history of all he most cared about.

He was looking quite extraordinarily excited now, his green eyes shining; he was carrying several books and a newspaper – normally agreed by them both to be an extravagance – and a bottle of pale ale.

'My goodness, Tom, whatever's happened? You look as if you've seen a vision.'

'I have,' he said, coming over to her, dropping the books onto the table, and giving her a kiss. 'No, much, much better than a vision. A real person. A man. Well, not just a man. Someone incredibly special.'

'Who?'

'You won't believe it when I tell you. You really won't.'

'Tom, who, for heaven's sake . . . ?' Laura put down her pen and screwed the top onto the ink bottle. This was clearly a serious matter.

'Well. I went into the lift, just for the ride really, and you know it's a great big open thing and you can see who's in it when you decide to get in or not?'

'Yes, I do.'

'And I'd waited because the one before me was a bit crowded and this one came down and – well, oh, Laura he was there, in the lift.'

'Who was?'

'Bevan. Aneurin Bevan. He stood right next to me. Right next to me, there, in the lift. Can you believe that?'

'Oh, my goodness,' said Laura. Bevan was Tom's hero, his god. He saw in him the embodiment of all his dreams and hopes for the new Britain, recovering so slowly from the ravages of war. He and Laura had rejoiced when the Labour Party under Clement Attlee won their victory at the polls in July 1945. They had worked tirelessly for the local branch, delivering leaflets; persuading people to put up posters in their windows; urging them to attend meetings, where they served endless cups of tea, set out and put away chairs, and helped to welcome people at the door. On polling day they helped old people to get to the polling stations, pushing wheelchairs, organising lifts. The party was offering an irresistible promise to a tired and disillusioned nation, of nationalisation of all the major industries, comprehensive national insurance and dearest to Tom's heart, a national health service, health care free to everybody in the country – to be brought to fruition by his idol, Aneurin Bevan, appointed Minister of Health in Attlee's cabinet.

There was little Tom didn't know about Bevan, from his childhood in a mining village where a mother of extraordinary energies raised her large brood in the tiny cottage, turning at night when her other work was done to her own trade as dressmaker and tailoress; and a father of extraordinary grace, who as well as feeding his family by a lifetime underground, toiling in the mines, instilled in them all a love of music and literature and he and Aneurin would sing together for many hours and miles as they walked over the Welsh hills.

He was indeed one of Tom's favourite topics of conversation. He would regale an audience – usually the long-suffering Laura – with the tales that Aneurin was a troublemaker at school, and that, extraordinarily, for so brilliant an orator, he had a very bad stutter which he only with huge difficulty learned to overcome; that he had a passion for comics which his father finally banned, and that he was considered too stupid to try for the eleven-plus – despite his prodigious reading and his talent for writing poetry – that he always spoke without notes, even his early and passionate work for the trades union, and at fourteen went down the pits with his father.

Indeed, Laura had been forced to ban discussion of Mr Bevan at mealtimes, for she said she was extremely weary of the subject. 'If you tell me once more he was chairman of his lodge at nineteen, the youngest ever, I shall throw your supper in the dustbin.'

But this was truly special, Tom being in the lift with him, and even she could not get enough of it. 'What does he really look like? Did you speak to him? What did he say?'

'Laura, how could I speak to him? What would I say?' Tom sounded shocked.

'I would have done. I would have told him how wonderful I thought his plans for the National Health Service were and—'

'Well, maybe, but I'm not you. But Laura, I did smile at him, and he smiled back, in a really friendly way. Imagine, Aneurin Bevan, smiling at me. He's not very tall, and he has this very thick grey hair, and he was wearing what looked like quite an expensive suit, and very well-polished shoes. I did notice that.'

'Well, I hope he polishes them himself and doesn't expect his wife to,' said Laura briskly. 'I'm very happy for you, Tom, really. But I still have lots of work to do, and we have supper to eat, so however wonderful your day has been, and I can see it has, we can't sit here talking about Aneurin Bevan all night. Much as I daresay you'd like to. And did you get the book I wanted, about the suffragettes? Because I'm going to start telling the girls about them in the next history lesson.'

Tom said he had and came slowly back to earth.

# Chapter 11

## 1947

It was in early February that the telegram came – at the heart of the harshest winter in living memory, the snow relentless, day after day, blocking roads, railways, cutting off villages. It found its way, that awful winter, into every corner of society, every life, old and young; there was no one unaffected. Coal, its stocks low after the war, struggled to get through to power stations, many of them shut for lack of fuel. Much of the fuel that was there was stockpiled, stuck for lack of functioning transport. The government was introducing draconian measures, restricting domestic consumption, cutting industrial supplies. Factories were being shut down, and unemployment followed. People were cold, and they were hungry, food also being held up by the same relentless lack of transport. It was a wretched time for a nation already exhausted and demoralised by six years of war.

Tom was making his way home through the driving sleet. He walked carefully, for tonight he was making a speech; it would never do if the speaker fell and broke his leg before he even got there. The speech was on a subject very dear to his heart: the shocking lack of hospital provision for wounded servicemen, and indeed care of any sort. He was looking forward to it, despite being terrified, for he had a far bigger audience than he was used to, including some dignitaries from the council, and two representatives of the board of Hilchester Hospital. The *Hilchester Post* was sending a reporter. It was a seriously important meeting and its success would be down to him. Then, as he rounded the corner, he saw the telegram boy on their doorstep, looking up and down the street, clearly about to leave again.

He waved at him, hurried forward as fast as he dared, took the yellow envelope, opened it with clumsy fearful fingers.

*Dad ill. Pneumonia. Come when you can. Mother.*

Helpless with fear, panic making him indecisive, he asked Laura what to do: should he go at once, or should he stay and give his speech, and go in the morning?

'I just can't tell how bad he is. I don't want to let all these people down tonight, it's so important. But he must be bad for Mother to send a telegram. Suppose he died and I wasn't there? I'll never get there anyway, tonight. Tell me what to do, Laura, please.'

And Laura, as always the embodiment of calm and common sense, told him not to go tonight. 'There's more snow forecast, none of the buses are running. You can go in the morning. We'll send a telegram to your mother first thing, so she knows you're coming.'

'But she'll be waiting for me, hoping I'll come tonight. I need to make contact with her She'll be so frightened and—'

'She has the girls,' said Laura, 'she won't be alone. And Arthur too, he lives in the village. He'll be with her. Do you know anyone in the village with a telephone? Anyone at all.'

'The vicar,' said Tom. 'But then he'd have to walk down to the cottage, and—'

'If he has any goodness in him, which he most certainly should have, he will walk down to your parents' cottage. It's not exactly far. Now, let's go to the phone box and ring him. He might even know how your father is.'

So Tom spoke to the vicar, who not only showed that he did have some goodness in him, and said of course he would go down to the Knelstons' cottage, but added that he had called in that afternoon and Mr Knelston hadn't seemed too bad, although obviously not at all well, and the doctor had been and was coming again in the morning. 'Don't think of coming tonight, Tom. It's starting to snow really hard and none of the buses are running.'

'There,' said Laura when he passed this information on. 'You see.

Not so bad. Now, come on, you're going to be late for your speech if you don't get a move on.'

'Laura I – I don't know if—'

'Tom,' said Laura firmly. 'I think I know what you were going to say and if I'm right, then you mustn't even think it. Do you think your Mr Bevan would not give a speech he had promised, however worried he was about something else?'

Thus it was that Tom Knelston gave a speech of such passion, increased by his own distress, that the women in the audience were moved to tears, and even a few of the men blew their noses quite hard. 'These men gave their youth, their health, their future, for this country and now they have been abandoned, it seems, many of them, despite the best efforts of the Disability Employment Act, left literally on the streets to beg. Some of them, you'll have seen them, legless, with rubber tyres on their knees so they can shuffle along, and other poor souls, airmen, with their dreadfully burnt faces, so bad that people turn away from them, no hope of getting work ever. There is help out there, but not enough; not for many of them, with false legs or arms, nor with their chronic bronchitis caused by lungs damaged by shellfire. Nor with their permanent pain from bones improperly set in the field hospitals. They should be a top priority, yet they have been sent to the back of the queue, by the medical profession and the government, and it's shocking that it should be our government, our Labour government, to whom we entrusted our hopes and our future. They should be ashamed, discarding these men like so much litter not fit for their consideration. Not the heroes they were, fighting so bravely and so selflessly.'

They heard him out in utter silence, and when he had finally finished, flushed, exhausted, close to tears himself, they rose and applauded. The reporter from the *Hilchester Post*, who had indeed come, rushed to speak to Tom to get further quotes and said he would make it his lead story that Saturday, and the two board members from the hospital, looking rather shamefaced, said they would do everything in their power to bring the plight of the soldiers to the attention of the regional board.

'Now when – and please God it will be soon – Mr Bevan's National

Health Service comes in, we shall see a change, of course. They have promised rehabilitation services and not only to the war wounded, but those injured in industrial accidents. Then everyone will get the medical care they deserve,' said Tom fervently. 'But we have to be vigilant, we cannot afford to be complacent, to leave it to the government and the NHS. With the best will in the world, their efforts may not be enough – the problem is too great.' The reporter made a note and resolved to make it an important feature of his article.

'You were wonderful,' said Laura when finally they got back to the flat. 'Wonderful. I was so proud of you. Now, you must go straight to bed. I'll bring you some cocoa to help you sleep – I'm afraid you're going to have a terribly long and difficult day tomorrow.'

She shooed him off to bed, but in spite of the cocoa, Tom hardly slept; he felt exalted by what he had done that night, held the room in his hand, taken hold of its consciousness and moulded it to his will; it was heady, astonishing stuff, and he could hardly believe it had been possible. Then, as the adrenalin slowly left him, fear for his father and remorse that he had not at least tried to get to him that night took over.

It was also the first time his professional and his personal life had been in any kind of conflict. He had experienced a shot of regret, swiftly crushed but there nonetheless, that he might miss the chance to make his mark if he set off for West Hilton. He was to look back on that night, down the years, recognising it as a kind of watershed.

'Mummy! Mummy, come up here quickly, please. Look, look –'

Diana was standing in her bedroom, white with fear, a pool of liquid at her feet. 'It's – is it? Oh, it can't be, surely, not my waters breaking? It's three weeks early – suppose something's wrong? Oh, God, suppose I hadn't come in time?'

'Well, you did, and darling, try to keep calm. Panicking won't help. It's a perfectly normal start to labour, it happened to me with Michael.'

'We must get up to London at once, now, please go and ring Sir Harold.'

'Diana – darling –' Caroline hesitated. 'Darling, I don't think it's remotely possible for you to get to London tonight. The snow is really deep, all the trains have been cancelled.'

'Then we must drive.'

'I'm afraid that's out of the question. Half the roads are blocked. We'd never get there – you'd end up having your baby in a snowdrift.'

'But – but we've got to. Just got to. I can't have this baby without Sir Harold. Maybe he can get here.'

'Of course he can't. If we can't get there.'

'Oh, God,' Diana tensed suddenly, gripping her stomach. 'God, it's a pain, it hurts, it hurts. Oh, Mummy, it's starting, what are we going to do?'

'First, you must lie down and try to relax. I'll go and phone Dr Parker, he'll be able to get here.'

'No, no, don't leave me – and not Dr Parker, don't be ridiculous. What does he know about childbirth?'

'Quite a lot,' said Caroline briskly. 'He delivers at least two or three every month – sometimes, so he told me, in cottage bedrooms so small he can hardly move. He'll look after you.'

'He can't, he can't!' Diana's voice rose in a wail. 'I can't have this baby here, with Dr Parker. I'll die!'

'Diana, you will not die. Please try to calm down, you're being ridiculous.'

'But what about the pain? Sir Harold told me he had this stuff, he promised me, gas and air, it stops the pain. I have to get to him, Mummy, please. Oh, God, there's another pain coming. Oh, it's so bad, so bad.'

Dr Parker said he would come later, of course, when Mrs Gunning was further advanced in her labour, but it was quite a walk through the snow, and he had at least two other visits to make, so meanwhile he would send for Nurse Timmings, who was a qualified midwife.

'I don't suppose Nurse Timmings has a gas and air machine?' said Caroline. 'Diana is, well, very nervous, and her London obstetrician had assured her she could have it.'

'Yes, yes, of course she does,' said Dr Parker, and there was an

92

edge to his voice. 'We may not have rooms in Harley Street, Lady Southcott, but we are not quite in the Dark Ages. You'd be surprised, we seldom deliver babies in ditches . . .'

'No, no, of course not,' said Caroline, apologetically. 'I just – well, thank you so much, Dr Parker. I'll be very pleased to see Nurse Timmings, and even more pleased to see you. I—' She was interrupted by another wail from upstairs. 'I think Diana's labour might be progressing faster than usual for a first baby. I hope Nurse Timmings will be here in time and I don't have to deliver it myself.'

'Most unlikely,' said Dr Parker. 'But yes, I'll ring her straight away. And I'll see you later.'

Diana had finally become pregnant in the early summer, when even she found Yorkshire suddenly beautiful; when the farm was alive again, the fields filled for miles and miles with tentative shoots of bright green; when lambs, hundreds of the pretty playful things, filled the fields near the house; when the sun shone, and the wind grew warmer, and the trees in the orchards were covered in flowers; and she took out her horse, her southern-bred horse, as pleased with the improved weather as she was. She rode through the countryside, smiling at last, and discovered its lovely secrets, its steep rocky foaming waterfalls, its sudden woods and pools, its low stone walls studding the countryside like so many pictures in a child's book; where she could gallop for miles across the huge rolling sheets of land that were the moors, rich with brilliant gorse and where, when she stopped, she could hear bees, working in that gorse, and the raw cries of curlews, and the calls of the cuckoo too, that made her feel at home. She would arrive home happily, sweetly tired, and wait for Johnathan's return when twilight fell.

And he, happy at her happiness, just as he had felt despair at her despair, fell freshly, if slightly tentatively, in love with her again, and they would make love, half surprised that they should want to, night after night. And – to both their absolute delight, and even the rather grudging pleasure of Vanessa, she had become pregnant, swiftly and easily.

But there was a shadow over her happiness: a terror of childbirth, induced by finding, at the age of eleven, when she was just becoming aware of such things, a book of her mother's describing the pain, the need for a labouring mother to have a sheet tied to the bed to cling to when the pains were at their height. One sentence in particular had haunted her ever since: *The moment of greatest agony being the birth of the head.* She would look at pregnant women and wonder how they could smile, speak, even. With this inescapable ordeal ahead of her, and the prospect of giving birth to her own child filling her with dread, she had insisted on having the baby in London, in care of the excellent and prominent obstetrician who had delivered her and her brothers. Sir Harold Morton was no longer young, but he was exactly what she needed: reassuring, and calm, but dismissive of her fears, and he had promised her he would personally be with her through her confinement. Lady Gunning was deeply disapproving, having given birth to all three sons in her own bed, but Diana really didn't care. She was booked into Sir Harold's private clinic in Welbeck Street, and Johnathan had agreed that she should move down to stay with her parents until the baby was born. The thought of spending several weeks away from Guildford Park and Lady Gunning, and living in comparatively close proximity to London, almost outweighed her horror of childbirth.

'It was shocking, her behaviour,' Nurse Timmings told one of the other district nurses later. 'The fuss! She screamed, she shouted and she swore. I've never heard anything like the language. She told me I didn't know what I was doing, ordered me to phone every house in the village to find Dr Parker. Well, of course I didn't. She refused to cooperate, wouldn't try to relax, try to breathe properly; she kicked me when I was examining her, told me I was hurting her!'

'Did Dr Parker ever get there?'

'He did. But too late. Baby Gunning had arrived, and then she was all sweetness and light, of course. She apologised for the way she'd behaved, thanked me for everything I'd done.'

'And was the baby a boy or a girl?'

'Boy. Fine little chap, seven and a half pounds. But if she has another, I'm not delivering it!'

'Do you think they're all like that, the aristocracy? You'd think they should set an example.'

'No, I delivered Lady Smithe's baby and she never made a sound all the way through, so brave she was; it was a very long labour, and the baby weighed nine and a half pounds. Now she's what I call a proper lady, but oh, no, this one was in a class of her own. A disgrace. An absolute disgrace.'

'I was a disgrace, wasn't I?' said Diana ruefully, looking at her mother over James Gunning's downy head. 'I really didn't behave very well. Not exactly brave. I'm sorry, Mummy.'

'Oh, darling, don't be silly. I didn't mind,' said Caroline untruthfully, for she had been ashamed of her daughter, in particular with the swearing. She could remember the birth of all her babies, and she had managed to remain silent, and there had been no gas and air then, just a whiff of chloroform towards the very end. 'How are you feeling this morning?'

'Oh – fine. I'm just being lazy. I'll be up soon. This maternity nurse is marvellous. So clever of you to find her so quickly. She just lets me sleep right through, gives Jamie bottles. Three last night – imagine if I'd had to do that, get up and everything, I'd be exhausted.'

'He is very sweet,' said Caroline, smiling down at her grandson. 'Such a shame Johnathan can't get here to see him.'

'I know. But they're completely snowed in. I've described him very carefully. Awful we can't even get some snaps developed to send. Thank goodness I'm here, though – it would be awful if I was up there with only *Her* for company and no escape. It's been so lovely, being with you and Daddy, and we're here for a while longer, I'm afraid. We're lucky, aren't we, Jamie?'

'Well, it's lovely for us. Oh, dear, the milkman had some sad news – wonderful how he's managing to get round most, although we're down to one pint a day now, there's a real shortage – Jack Knelston, the postman, has died, apparently. He was such a nice chap. So reliable. It's the funeral tomorrow. I thought I'd write a note to Mrs Knelston.'

'Oh, yes, he was a nice man. And his son, the oldest one, did rather well, went to the grammar school. Michael said he was very good at cricket.'

She was silent, the image of Tom digging out the drain suddenly vivid in her memory. How good-looking she had thought him, with his wild auburn hair and amazing green eyes. Probably wouldn't look so good to her now, of course. She'd met a few really good-looking men over the past few years.

It had taken Tom almost eight hours to get home to West Hilton. One bus was running, over-packed with people, and the conductor would have refused him had he not explained his desperate need to get home. That took him almost to East Hilton; after that he had to walk. It was only four miles, but it was heavy going; the snow was deep, although the snow plough had cleared it once, only to have it blocked again two days later. He got a lift on a tractor for a couple of miles; the farmer was in despair. 'All the sheep are getting buried in the snow – most of the ones I find are already dead. We're going to lose most of the flock, and that means the lambs too. Don't know how we'll survive this year, I really don't. We're ruined already and it's only just begun. As for the cattle . . .'

Tom said he was very sorry, but could find nothing else to offer by way of sympathy; he was almost relieved when the journey was over and he was back on the road. He had got very cold, sitting on the tractor; at least when he was walking, he got warmer – apart from his feet. He had his stoutest boots on, but they had begun to leak miles back; freezing wet feet didn't make the walking any easier. He reached the cottage at three, opened the door and found himself confronted by a roomful of people – Arthur, Jess his eldest sister, two of her younger children, a couple of neighbours and, coming down the little staircase, Colin.

'Oh,' said Jess, rushing across the room and hugging him. 'Oh, Tom, how good to see you. How wonderful of you to get here – we didn't think it possible. '

'Hello, Tom. It can't have been an easy journey,' said Colin.

'Not exactly, but I'm here. How – how is he? I'm not too late . . . ?'

'No, he's putting up a fight.' It was Jess, white with exhaustion. 'The doctor says he really should be in hospital. But he won't go and anyway, how would we get him there? Oh, Tom, go up and see Mother quickly, she'll be so pleased to see you.'

Mary was; she stared at him in silence for a long moment as if he was an apparition. Then her exhausted face relaxed, smiled even, and she stood up and went into his arms.

'Thank God,' she said. 'Thank God. Thank you, Tom, for coming. I didn't think you would, the snow's so bad . . .'

'Well, of course I came,' he said. 'I'm sorry it wasn't sooner – you should have told us before.'

'He's gone down quite quickly,' she said. 'He's got very frail recently, had funny pains in his chest, and I wouldn't wonder if there wasn't something else as well, but he refused to have any tests, said they were a waste of money. Got the cough that turned to bronchitis, and now – this.'

She turned to Jack, lying on the bed. He was breathing with horrible difficulty, coughing hideously in spasms; but he saw Tom and his face, like Mary's, softened into a smile. He clasped his hand and said, between coughing spasms, 'Hello, Tom. Good to see you.'

'He should be in hospital,' said Mary. 'But he refuses. Says people die in hospital and if he does go, he wants it to be from his own bed.'

Jack's wish was granted, three days later, during which time the snow fell relentlessly, a quiet and peaceful backdrop to the seemingly endless struggle within. Tom was in the room, holding one of his hands, when the moment came, Mary holding the other, both willing the end to come, Colin and Jess at the end of his bed; the others were all downstairs, for there was no room for more. The sudden silence and stillness in the room was a bittersweet relief; his suffering had been horrible to see. The doctor, exhausted himself and generous with his time and indeed his treatment, had done his best, administering what little he had of the only drug that might help, sulphonamide. His stock was small – Jack was not the only pneumonia patient in the village – and he made his decision, as supplies dwindled, that a small boy of four should take priority. Mercifully, the Knelston family did not know this.

Tom had stayed on; in any case, the return journey was by now impossible. He grieved and fretted that Laura could not be with him, or indeed even know what was happening – he'd thought of telephoning the school but the telephone lines were all down; he was truly marooned.

The funeral was bleak and dreadful, although the church was almost full which helped a little; Jack had been popular in the village and many came to bid him farewell. The vicar preached a good sermon, saying how Jack had enriched many lives, both in his work 'so vital to the life of the community' and his other occupations: 'his work for the trades union movement, his lifelong membership of his beloved Labour Party; and perhaps most important of all, his devotion to his wife and family'. Mary sat ramrod straight, silent and dry-eyed, right to the very end, when the organist played 'The Day Thou Gavest, Lord, is Ended' and then she dropped her face into her hands and wept for a long time.

The coffin was left to rest alongside several others under a hastily erected wooden cover, for it was impossible to dig graves in the frozen ground. Tom stayed behind as the others left, Jess and Colin helping the exhausted Mary back to the cottage. He stood staring at the coffin, remembering his father and their difficult relationship.

It had been a real grief in Tom's life, his father's awkward love for him; the clear joy of his welcome as Tom arrived in the cottage at his sickbed was perhaps the clearest manifestation of that love Tom had ever known. That night, when Tom settled for what seemed like the hundredth time under a thin blanket on the couch, he thought he had never been so utterly wretched, not even in the field hospital in the desert; and never had he felt so robbed of anything that might feel hopeful and good to him.

Two days after the funeral, he went for a walk; he was desperate to be out of the sad, shocked house, and so bored, devoid as he was of any books or proper conversation. He took the East Hilton road. Alternately finding himself slipping and sliding along the compacted snow, and plunged into drifts, he suddenly fell hard and found it almost impossible to get up again; but he found a post to cling to and hauled himself upright, and then realised two things: that his weak ankle was excruciatingly painful, and that the post was part of the Manor House fence. As he stood there, shocked and close to tears, so dreadful did everything seem to him, he heard a shout from the house.

'You all right?' Sir Gerald, standing in the open doorway.

'Yes – yes, I think so, thanks. I just fell—'

'I saw. Stay there, I'll come and help you, dug out the drive this morning myself.'

'No, no, I'm all right,' said Tom but his entire demeanour was so exhausted and broken that Sir Gerald, having reached him, said, 'You look all in. Tom, isn't it, Tom Knelston? Sorry to hear about your father. Look, you come inside, have a rest and something to drink. Lean on my arm . . .'

So surprised was Tom to find the bluff Sir Gerald capable of sympathy and generosity, and so exhausted and filled with pain, that he said only, 'That would be very kind, thank you.' He took the proffered arm and somehow, every step on his right leg an agony, managed to get to the house.

The first thing he noticed, as he limped into the hall, was that it was warm: that seemed to him so extraordinary that he thought he must be imagining it; the second that in the doorway to one of the rooms, a roaring fire behind her, and walls literally lined with books, stood Diana Southcott, rather pale to be sure, and perhaps rather less slender, but still immensely beautiful, and smiling at him with nothing but welcome and concern.

'Tom,' she said. 'What have you done? Here, come and sit down by the fire, you look terrible.'

She held out her hand. Simultaneously Sir Gerald released his hold on Tom's arm, and standing became completely impossible. He crumpled and fell onto the hard, stone floor of the hall, a howl of pain escaping him.

'Oh, God,' said Sir Gerald. 'Poor fellow. Caroline, Caroline! Call Rawlings in, he's chopping wood, I think. Diana, don't you try and do anything, for God's sake. Ah, Rawlings, help me get Mr Knelston up, and Caroline, you might ring Dr Parker – oh, no, I suppose the bloody telephone's still out of order. Rawlings, get down to Dr Parker's house in a minute and ask him to come as soon as he can.'

Rawlings and Sir Gerald half carried him into the room where Diana stood and they lowered him into a chair by the fire; he apologised repeatedly about his boots and the state of his trousers, while wincing as he struggled to find a remotely comfortable position and gazing hungrily, almost desperately, at the books, having had nothing to read, he felt, for weeks.

'Here – drink this –' Sir Gerald held out a glass which was half filled with what Tom could smell was brandy; he drank it slowly, the warm seeping into him, easing what seemed to be almost terminal cold, as well as his pain.

'Your poor thing,' Diana said, surveying him from the other side of the fire where she settled herself, sympathy in her dark eyes. 'It obviously hurts like hell. Never mind, hopefully Rawlings can get Dr Parker to come soon. And – and we were sorry about your father, he was such a –' she paused, clearly struggling to find an appropriate phrase – 'such a kind man. He was always so nice to me and my brothers when we were little and it was our birthdays or something, and he had lots of cards and parcels – always said he hoped we'd have a nice day.'

This was a shock to Tom, who would have expected his father to take exception to a surfeit of gifts and goodies arriving at the Manor House. It clearly showed in his face.

'You look surprised,' said Diana.

'Well – I am a bit.'

'That's fathers for you. Daddy was so strict with us, wasn't he, Mummy?' She looked up at her mother who had come into the room, carrying a baby.

'Yes, he was. But he never could refuse you anything, really. Specially you. Now Diana, Jamie needs feeding – shall I take the bottle upstairs? Or will you feed him in the kitchen?"

'No,' said Diana firmly with an expression that was more of the kind that Tom remembered. 'No, bring it in here, please. I'm sure Mr Knelston won't mind. That's all right, isn't it, Tom, if I give the baby his bottle here?'

'Yes – yes, of course,' said Tom, and then, seeing that Lady South-cott was not entirely happy with this idea, added, 'but if you'd rather I – I left . . .'

'Don't be ridiculous, you can't leave,' said Diana. 'You can't move. No, I'll feed the baby here. Thank you, Mummy, so much.'

Lady Southcott handed her the baby and Diana took Jamie and set-tled him with his bottle with a skill that for some reason surprised Tom; Lady Southcott left again, clearly not entirely happy with the situation.

'So sweet isn't he?' Diana said. 'I can't believe he's mine.'

'How – how old is he?' said Tom. All he could see was the top of a head and a tiny hand that had been waving about in its hunger and now entirely relaxed.

'Ten days. He really is heaven, so good. So sad that Johnathan – that's my husband – hasn't seen him, and can't for ages yet, probably. He's in Yorkshire, where we live. It's terribly different from here. It's so cold, freezing cold, even in the summer sometimes, and people say the scenery's lovely, and I suppose it is, but it's awfully wild and bleak. And pretty remote really, where we live. Miles from the nearest town, which is Harrogate, and that's a bit of a dump.'

'And what does your husband do?' asked Tom curiously. It didn't sound the sort of place he would have expected Diana to have chosen to live.

'Oh, he runs the estate,' said Diana. 'He and his mother. His father's really not up to much these days – the war took its toll, their eldest son was killed. So Johnathan gave up his job in London, and went up there. And of course I went with him.' She sighed almost imperceptibly and looked down at the baby, who was now sleeping peacefully, the bottle drained. 'We'll go back when the snow has gone, won't we, Jamie? But not till then.'

'Do you like it up there? Living in that wild place?' asked Tom, and he knew the question was not one he should have asked. She met his eyes with her great dark ones and for a moment he thought she was going to berate him, but she said, 'No, actually. Since you ask – and you are not to tell anyone, of course – I hate it. Absolutely hate it.'

It was an extraordinary confidence to exchange with someone she scarcely knew, who was moreover her social inferior, and it was years before Tom understood why she had done it. It was to create an intimacy, a bond between them, that she should entrust him with this confidence, knowing that he would keep it for her; and also that she was so clearly anxious that he should know she hated it, that she was not happy with her new life.

He sat there, taking it all in, and taking her in too, so very beautiful, still pale and clearly tired by the birth of her son, but softened too, less arrogant, her figure slightly more rounded, her arms holding the baby so surprisingly gentle and confident, where he would not have expected her to be either. And then she smiled, and said, 'It's very nice to be able to talk to you, Tom. How are you feeling now? Oh look, Mummy's brought your tea and some for me, too. Come and join us, Mummy, why don't you?' showing Tom that the intimate part of their conversation was over, and that she trusted him entirely not to reveal any of it.

Lady Southcott said she would, adding that Rawlings had returned and Dr Parker would be up shortly.

'I believe you are married, Mr Knelston? To a schoolteacher, I think your mother said.' Tom said yes, he was, and began to talk about Laura, and that made him miss her so much that combined with his pain and the brandy he found himself close to tears.

Dr Parker fortunately arrived, examined the ankle, and said it wasn't broken, just very badly sprained. He would strap it up and Tom must rest it for at least a week.

'Only I can see that might be difficult in the cottage – you haven't got a proper bed, have you? I remember when I called . . .'

Tom said one of his sisters would be able to offer him a room, and that he hadn't left before because of wanting to be with his mother; and that one of his brothers-in-law and one of his brothers should between them be able to get him home, while wondering precisely how, until Lady Southcott said that their wood cart would make a splendid stretcher on wheels if Tom wouldn't mind. And would he like Rawlings to go down to their respective cottages to summon them?

Tom waited patiently while help was organised, and he watched Diana as she chatted and laughed and winded the baby; Diana with her gleaming dark beauty, and her slightly low-pitched voice with its perfectly honed, clipped accent and her perfect legs, those at least unsullied by childbearing, crossing and uncrossing themselves as she shifted in her chair to re-settle the baby. And seeing, and not being able to help noticing, that those eyes, those incredible dark eyes, quite often and unmistakably met his very directly, in a sort of openness that he did not even dare to reflect upon, while being aware that Lady Southcott's presence was very strong and her eyes on her daughter very intent. Then he took a deep breath, literally, and said he did hope they would not consider he was asking too much of them, but might it be possible to borrow a book? He had nothing to read and there was nothing in his parents' house or his sisters' of any interest to him whatsoever, and the days were going to be very long, and Diana said of course he must borrow a book, more than one, and what sort of book would he like to read, fiction or biography or what, and what were his interests, and he said politics, particularly, but really anything, anything at all.

'Politics!' said Lady Southcott, and her voice was much cooler than it had been before. Tom wondered if he had gone too far, asking to borrow a book. 'How interesting. What do you think of this dreadful new Labour government, poor Mr Churchill being thrown out after he saved the country, almost single-handed at one point.'

Tom sat silent, flushed, partly by emotion, partly by the fire and the brandy, wondering desperately whether he should lie and betray his principles or speak the truth and quite probably find himself thrown out in the snow. Diana jumped up, placing the baby in his grandmother's arms, and said, going over to the bookshelves further down the room, 'Have you ever read any Trollope? I haven't, of course –' she gave him a slightly shamefaced smile – 'but Johnathan absolutely loves them, the Palliser novels. They're just the thing for you and we have a complete set, so take the first two, and then come and change them for the next two if you finish them; just think of us as a library.'

Tom, touched and surprised beyond anything that she should read his needs so well, took the two books she handed him and gazed at them, at the treasure they represented, and thanked her.

Lady Southcott said, rather briskly, that she thought the baby's nappy needed changing, and gave him firmly to Diana. Diana, with an odd look at her mother, said yes, of course, and if the rescue party came for Tom before she came back, she had been so delighted to meet him again, and wished him a swift recovery. Then she was gone and the room died a little – some of its charm, some of its beauty, faded – and the boys arrived to take him to Jess's house, bearing a waterproof horse blanket to cover Tom and protect him from the snow which was falling relentlessly once again.

'Nice young man,' Caroline Southcott said, as Diana walked into the small morning room where she was embroidering some rompers for the baby. 'Rather more socially – what shall I say – confident than I would have expected.'

'Mummy, you are such a snob!' said Diana. 'Why shouldn't he be? He's working for a solicitor, his wife's a teacher, and the war has done away with all that, anyway. I thought he was very interesting.'

'Yes, I could tell that,' said Caroline slightly tartly. 'A little too interesting, Diana, if you don't mind my saying so. I hope you won't be going to visit him or anything silly like that.'

'Of course I won't,' said Diana irritably. 'Although I don't see why you should consider it silly.'

'Well, actually, I'm not sure that I believe you,' said Caroline. 'Diana, please don't, if you have any sense. Johnathan wouldn't like it, and I could see you were unsettling Tom Knelston as well. Now, would you like an omelette for your supper? We have plenty of eggs at least—'

'I'm very tired of omelettes,' said Diana, standing up, her face cold. 'I'll just have a sandwich in my room, and go to bed early – I'm awfully tired. Send Nurse Blake up when she gets here, please, to take Jamie. And don't make judgements about what Johnathan would and wouldn't like, Mummy. I know him a little better than you do. Goodnight.'

She went up to her room, and sat for a long time, staring out at the darkness, holding the baby close to her, angry with her mother for reading her so well, and reflecting that rather than she unsettling Tom Knelston, it was he who had unsettled her.

# Chapter 12

## 1947

Alice could hardly believe that here she was. Her very first day as a probationer, actually at St Thomas' Hospital. She'd done her thirteen weeks at the training school in Godalming and that had been both fun and incredibly interesting; she'd made lots of friends, and it had confirmed what she'd always known, that nursing was for her. And she was for nursing.

She hadn't been able to start immediately after the war ended, as she'd hoped; you had to be nineteen. She'd completed her Higher and got lots of distinctions, and then, because she was still only eighteen, had had to find something else to do; her parents wanted her to go to some terrible finishing school in Paris, but she'd absolutely refused and finally agreed to do a secretarial course. 'Nursing may not work out for you, Alice, or one day you may be married and you may want a part-time job while your children are small. Believe me, you can always get a job as a secretary.'

Alice felt sure she could always get a job as a nurse as well, and one she would enjoy a great deal more than typing some stupid man's letters, but she had learned not to argue with her mother on the subject. It really was a complete waste of time and energy.

She had been interviewed at the hospital, of course, but it hadn't exactly been gruelling. She had travelled with her mother to the great building, on the River Thames right next to Westminster Bridge and facing the Houses of Parliament, and had sat in the office of a lady called Miss Smyth; as far as she could see the only purpose of the interview was to see that she had nice manners, and had had a basic education. Later she was to discover that you had to be recognisably a Thomas' type – you needed to be highly intelligent, not merely well-educated, to display a certain self-confidence and outgoingness and above all to 'speak proper', as she confided, giggling on the phone to Jillie, after she had got through her first week at the training school,

'No common voices at St Thomas', I can tell you,' she said. 'All terribly well spoken, we are. Anyway, I love it. I'm just so happy, I don't know what to do.'

Jillie was now studying medicine, which sounded rather more impressive than Alice's ambitions, but Alice saw nursing as being in no way inferior to Jillie's calling. That was what she had for so long wanted to do and at last she was doing it, and she was perfectly happy.

There were thirty girls at the Godalming training school, divided into three houses; Alice was put into the Clock House.

The first piece of medical equipment she was given was a duster: a nurse's first duty, they were told, was to make sure everything was as tidy and clean as it could possibly be; and her first morning at St Thomas' reinforced this.

They had to be on the ward by seven thirty when the night staff went off duty. There were three of them, Alice, Hazel and Suzanne, in their new purple-and-white striped probationer uniforms, all trembling, even Alice, the most self-confident of them. They stood in the doorway and looked at the new world which they would now inhabit: at a vast room, very light and airy, with thirty beds, fifteen on each side, with their curtains pulled back; at the patients being washed and tidied; at gas fires mounted on pillars, and an area in the middle where stood a large and impressive boiler and sinks.

A steely-eyed, rather forbidding personage walked up to them and announced, 'I'm Staff Nurse and in charge of you at this moment at least. Welcome to Clement. You address me as Staff. Sister, as of course you'll know, is Sister Clement. Let's get you making yourselves useful. Plenty to do. We divide the ward into three – Dayside, Night-side and Thirds. You, nurse –' she pointed at Alice – 'you go onto

Dayside. Which means you work on the left side of the ward and your first duties every day are hot dusting. Take your duster –' she pointed at the boiler area – 'wring it out in hot water from one of the sinks, and do all the surfaces. Along the rails of the beds, the legs and then the lockers, any brass pieces you can see, and of course the wheelchairs. Put a clean pinny on whenever you come onto the ward – don't want you getting your uniforms dirty unnecessarily – you'll find them in the linen cupboard. Now, there's no time to be lost. At eight, you'll hear Big Ben strike – Sister will be in for prayers and by then everything has to be in order.'

At eight o'clock, Big Ben did indeed strike and as predictably and promptly, Sister did come in, proceeded to her desk, knelt and said prayers. Looking anxiously at the others for guidance, Alice saw that some of the nurses stood through this, some knelt. For this at least there was no rule.

After prayers, Sister did her inspection: of the general tidiness and cleanliness of the ward, the state of each patient, and any problems that had cropped up during the night of which she was unaware. The patients, who had to lie completely flat for the duration of the prayers, were then allowed to sit up and eat their breakfast.

Breakfast, or rather its preparation, was one of the probationers' duties: porridge was the standard ration, followed by toast and marmalade and a cup of tea. It was wheeled round on a large trolley, with one of the pros, as they were called, pushing it, and another walking beside her and serving the food. The patients were most polite to them, without exception, and almost as respectful as if they had been, if not Sister herself, at least Staff. They ate everything; rejecting food was simply not an option. 'And anyway,' one of the nurses told Alice over lunch, 'half of them are half starved when they come in, poor things. They think the food is absolutely wonderful.'

Once breakfast was cleared, and the trolley wheeled to the kitchen, they became fractionally more like nurses. All three of them were allotted patients; all three of them became part of a team working under a senior nurse. They had to know everything about each of their patients; their names, of course, but what was wrong with them, how long they had been in hospital, their treatment, their progress.

They suffered from a variety of things, some gynaecological or gastric problems, chest infections, chronic bronchitis, some even pneumonia, severe arthritis. Several were anaemic. They all looked to Alice extremely pale and listless, often more anxious about what might be going on at home than their own conditions, she learned. They were also mostly very thin.

Her first medical duties of the day were taking her patients' temperatures and their pulses; a senior nurse instructed her in the art of taking blood pressure – not easy, but she got the hang of it quickly, to her huge relief, observing from the corner of her eye Hazel, one of her fellow pros, finding it hugely difficult and becoming flustered. There was also the matter of the bedpans: bringing them if required, emptying them in the sluice, asking the delicate twice-daily question about whether they had had their bowels open, which most of the women found desperately embarrassing, especially if the answer was 'No'. All this had to be recorded in the notes at the foot of the bed, making up the important record, including information on the prescribed drugs.

After which came the terrifying procedure of the doctors' round. Sometimes, a consultant would be in the team, trailed by a group of medical students, sometimes a senior registrar. God help any nurse who was asked a question about a patient that she was unable to answer.

It was, however, Sister who was the most important figure in the hierarchy; she greeted the doctors at the ward – and had been known to refuse them entry, even the lofty consultants, if she was engaged on an emergency. Alice found this hugely satisfying to observe. Her mother and indeed her friends tended to regard nursing as a humble secondary career to being a doctor; here on the ward, that was absolutely not the case. The ward was Sister's kingdom and she ruled over it.

And how amazing to work just across the river from one of the most famous and beautiful views in the world, that of the Houses of Parliament and Big Ben, in one of the most famous if not beautiful hospitals in the world. It did have its charms, of course, not least its position, but it had been bombed several times and swift and impressive repairs had nonetheless left it scarred and something of its finer proportions sadly lost.

Oh, she loved it: loved it, and was proud beyond anything to be one of its nurses, its Nightingales (named after its formidable and legendary founder, Florence Nightingale). They were steeped not just in its discipline and its standards, but in the honour of simply being a Nightingale. Admission was not easy, as indeed it was not to any of the great hospitals, Guy's and Barts and the London. It wasn't so much that the academic requirements were high, and the social ones higher, it was that becoming a Nightingale admitted you to an association of legendary distinction and indeed conferred something of that distinction upon you. Being a Nightingale meant you had learned invaluable qualities beyond medical skills: self-discipline, calm, and unquestioning adherence to the highest standards.

She might only be a probationer, Alice reflected, as she lay in bed exhausted each night, after her twelve-hour shift, followed by private study, but she was training in those qualities as well as the medical. She could not imagine being any happier.

Laura could not, for the time being at any rate, imagine being unhappier. She was lying in bed, bleeding, in considerable pain, in the full awareness that she was about to lose the third baby that she and Tom had been so joyfully expecting. Well, perhaps a little less joyfully as she had been extremely anxious as well, but she had got further this time, almost to the magic twelve weeks as the midwife at the surgery called it. She had felt much better too, less sick, not so exhausted. But it had all been a wish, a prayer if she had believed in them, a nothingness. She had to retrace her steps along that misleadingly hopeful road, with its landmarks – the first few days when it didn't happen, each one more hopeful than the one before, then beginning to trust and believe, then telling Tom and seeing his joy, the plans, the looking forward, the sickness even, horrible to be sure, but worth it, the silly conversations about girl or boy, the names – and then suddenly, the shock of the pain, coming out of nowhere, the panic, the instructions from the midwife to take it easy, lying in bed, scarcely daring to move, and then . . . Then the beginning of the end, the bleeding, staring at it in disbelief, the increasing pain, and more blood, sitting and sobbing, crying aloud, clinging to Tom, and when it was over, the grief, the sense of failure, the knowledge of loss.

It hadn't been too bad the first time; most people could tell her of a similar experience, people who now had several children, her sister, her mother. She herself had been hopeful, confident, even, the second time, but it had happened even sooner, before the second-month milestone. That time she felt guilty, had thought she should not have gone on teaching, but stayed at home resting. The midwife said no; there was really nothing she could have done.

'But why? Why does it keep happening?' she had asked this time, her voice deep with the rawness of her grief. The midwife told her nobody knew, it was a mystery. The only thing they were sure of was that miscarried babies usually had something wrong with them, were best not carried to term – it was nature's way of dealing with imperfection.

Laura had nodded, too wretched to argue, but later she began to question this cosy, bland philosophy. In the first place, how did they know? How could they look at the mess that was a miscarriage and say, oh, yes, look, definitely something wrong there. It was ridiculous, and she began to feel angry, that she was being fobbed off with something.

A few days later, still miserable and vengeful but recovering, she made an appointment to see the doctor. He looked at her warily as she told her story, then with scarcely disguised impatience as she made her request for further information, perhaps some treatment for repeated miscarriage.

'Mrs Knelston –' Dr Andrews looked at her over his spectacles – 'miscarriage is a perfectly natural process, nature's way of ridding the body of an imperfect foetus – that is, a baby.'

'I am perfectly aware of what a foetus is, thank you,' said Laura firmly. 'I'm sorry, I don't believe that is the only explanation for what I have had to endure. It seems to me that there may be other reasons, some failure in my reproductive system that could be addressed.'

'Well, the person to talk to is a midwife,' said the doctor. 'She will know everything there is to know about these things . . .'

'I'm afraid I disagree with you,' said Laura firmly. 'She seems to know very little, apart from the progress of an absolutely normal pregnancy. So I want to see a specialist in this field, and I would be grateful if you would recommend one to me.'

'That would involve either a very long wait, or your paying rather a large fee,' said Dr Andrews, in tones that made it clear the latter route was not remotely within Laura's reach. 'These men are highly qualified.'

'I would hope they are,' snapped Laura. 'Are they all men? Could I not see a female gynaecologist? I would greatly prefer that anyway.'

The doctor glared at her, looked at his watch and then told her that there was a hospital, the Elizabeth Garrett Anderson in Bloomsbury, which specialised in enabling poor women – he put a stress on the word 'poor' – to obtain medical help from gynaecologists.

'You would need a letter of referral. And then you would have to make an appointment.'

'I am quite capable of that,' said Laura. 'How and from whom would I obtain this letter of referral?'

'I am too busy to do it now, if that is what you want – you will have to call back for it in a week or ten days.' Dr Andrews sighed.

'Really? So long? To write a letter?' Laura was beginning to feel quite cheered up by this battle with the medical hierarchy, which baffled her greatly at the same time. What was she meant to do? Go home quietly and continue having miscarriages, being told it was nature's way? Was there some reason women were not allowed to seek further help with this miserable problem? She wondered if it would have made a difference if Tom had come with her; she suspected it would. She was fairly sure the doctor would then have belittled her further, would have addressed all his remarks to him.

'Mrs Knelston, I have a great many patients. Yours will not be the only letter I will have to write. Now, a few details quickly, if you please? This is your second miscarriage?'

'Third,' said Laura.

'And had you reached the end of the first trimester?'

Laura knew what he was doing, trying to make her feel stupid

111

because she didn't know what trimester meant. He had clearly taken a great dislike to her.

'Not quite,' she said. 'I had missed two of my monthly periods, and was about halfway through the third month.'

He nodded, looked up at her and said, 'You can come and see if the letter is ready in a week.'

'How kind. Good afternoon,' said Laura. 'And thank you for your help.'

When Tom got home that evening, expecting to find the wretchedly depressed wife he had left that morning, and hoping he had sufficient emotional resilience to meet her needs, he found her quite changed. She made him a cup of tea and said she felt all was not quite lost and that she had been making enquiries and she was hopeful there might be another way out of this unhappiness than simply accepting what had happened to her so far. 'If there isn't, well, at least I shall have tried. What a disgusting creature Dr Andrews is,' she added, sitting down with her own cup of tea.

'Really?' said Tom. 'I've always found him very nice and helpful. And he has a large panel. He's not all bad.'

'You might ask him, next time you have to go and see him, if he's joining your Mr Bevan's National Health Service,' said Laura. 'He might be a bit less nice and helpful after that.'

'Of course I will,' said Tom. 'I'm sure we shall be able to have a very interesting conversation about it.'

'Now, let me tell you about the Elizabeth Garrett Anderson Hospital in London. It's where I plan to go as soon as your nice and helpful Dr Andrews will give me a letter. Oh, and I can make an appointment, of course. There's quite a long waiting list. Don't look so suspicious – it's specifically for poor women to get help. I'm sure your Mr Bevan would approve.'

'I wish you wouldn't keep calling him that,' said Tom and then, because she seemed so much more cheerful, he told Laura he had been invited to give his speech about the lack of medical provision for ex-servicemen at a big meeting in Winchester. It had seemed wrong to think hopeful thoughts of his own, when Laura's situation was beginning to seem so fruitless, but he was beginning to feel he really had something to contribute to not just this but many other causes.

'Ned, darling, hello, how lovely to see you. It's been much too long. How are you, and what are you doing here?'

'Same as you, I daresay,' said Ned, smiling with genuine pleasure at Wendelien, as she approached him at a fast trot across the marbled, art deco foyer of Claridge's Hotel. 'Having a jolly evening. You look marvellous, Wendelien.'

'Thank you. I so love these clothes. You know they put dreary old Stafford Cripps into a frightful rage, said there should be a law against them. Such a relief after those skimpy short skirts we've been wearing for ever.'

She was dressed, like all fashionable women of the time, in Christian Dior's New Look, a full-skirted, almost-ankle-length dress: this one in dark red taffeta, with long tight sleeves, and a swathe of black lace round her shoulders, her gleaming dark hair pulled back in a chignon.

'Thank you. If we can't have a jolly evening here, there's not much hope for us at all. So lovely, isn't it?'

'It is indeed. And I so loved them giving the penthouse to poor Mr Churchill after he lost the election, to stay as long as he wanted.'

'My favourite story is him making it Yugoslavian territory, so that Crown Prince Alexander could be born on his own country's soil.'

'I know, wonderful. Anyway, how are you, Ned? Who are you meeting?'

'I'm very well, thank you. I'm meeting Ludo and Cecily Manners. And—'

'Love him, so bored by her,' said Wendelien, interrupting him. 'Every baby's made her duller. And as he's now got four . . .'

'Wendelien, one of these days that tongue of yours will get you into real trouble,' said Ned. 'So unkind to poor Cecily.'

'No, just truthful. I'm very nice to her face, of course. Oh look, there they are. And there's Michael Southcott and lovely Betsey. Look, why don't we all have a drink first before dinner? Michael, Betsey, over here, look who I've found . . .'

'Ned, my dear old chap, what a treat,' said Michael, slapping him on the back.

'Darling Ned,' said Betsey, kissing him repeatedly. 'How are you? It's been much too long.'

'Well, we've all been working much too hard,' said Ned. 'That's the truth of it. I especially had a lot of time to make up after the war. My father breathes fire and brimstone about getting me an honorary at Pete's –' this referred to St Peter's Chelsea – 'unless I pass every single one of my papers with distinction.'

'Well, you'll do that easily,' Michael said. 'You always were brilliant. And still keen on doing the old paediatrics, are you?'

'Yes, absolutely,' said Ned. 'It's something that really fascinates me. Father is still hoping I'll do general surgery, but I think specialisation is the big thing, especially with all these reforms coming up.'

'What, bloody Bevan's?' said Michael.

'Yes. Not that I think they'll make that much difference to us. In the hospitals, I mean. The hospitals were all nationalised during the war – we're already giving our services free to them.'

'Ned! Didn't think you were a pinko. Of course it'll make a difference. We'll lose our independence before you can say "scalpel". Get told what to do, how long to work, how to do it, quite possibly.'

'Oh, nonsense,' said Ned, 'and I'm not a socialist, of course I'm not. But he's been pretty generous to us, old Bevan. You heard what he said, he was going to stuff our throats with gold. And he is. And we'll still have our consulting rooms, to do our own work—'

'Oh, stop, stop it,' cried Betsey. 'God, am I tired of the subject of the National Health Service. Let's find a lovely corner and order some cocktails.'

'All right,' said Ned, 'that'd be fun.'

'So when are you and Michael getting married?' Ned asked Betsey, as they settled at a table.

'In the spring. We thought of sooner, but Princess Elizabeth would steal our thunder a bit, we think. Goodness, now there's a handsome man, that Philip. So attractive. I met him briefly at a ball at the Docklands Settlement – you see, we do do our bit for the working class – and, well, the old knees went quite weak. Michael's been quite

114

boring about sticking to the knife-before-wife rule, but now it's over, I'm quite pleased – it's been worth the wait. He's got some marvellous rooms in Welbeck Street, he's an honorary at the London and we've bought just the dearest little house in Kensington.'

'Kensington?'

'Yes, it's *the* new place, my dear,' said Betsey, her huge blue eyes dancing. 'Much more exciting than Knightsbridge – and of course Mayfair is just all hotels now. Kensington is full of young people. Now tell me, Ned, any wedding bells on your horizon yet?'

'Oh, no,' said Ned quickly. 'Far too busy at the moment. Plenty of time when I'm settled in my career. Anyway, like you, I'd hate to steal Princess Elizabeth's limelight . . .'

'Of course,' said Wendelien, laughing. 'Very unselfish of you. The only thing I can't understand is why she's chosen November. Such a dreary month.'

'I know, but the whole idea, I have on the best authority, is to cheer the country up, and I do believe it will.'

'We're told she's having to produce coupons for her dress, just the same as everyone else,' said Betsey.

'Oh, darling, really, you can't believe that nonsense. With the dress being made by Norman Hartnell! And something like two and a half thousand guests! I don't think so.'

'Well, I do actually, and I think it's all lovely,' said Betsey. 'And it's been such a wonderful long romance. Imagine, she first fell in love with him when she was thirteen. And I thought what Sir Winston said about it being a flash of colour on the hard road we have to travel or something romantic like that – exactly right. You see, every single person in the country will come round in the end. It'll be a wonderful day.'

She was right. Certainly, the juxtaposition of a currency crisis, a cabinet reshuffle and the scheduling of an emergency Budget did not bode well for the occasion; nor a formal protest by a group of Labour MPs to the Chief Whip about the extravagance. But love – or at least romance – carried the day, and into every echelon of society.

Indeed, the night before the wedding Tom came home to find Laura poring over the *Daily Mirror*, which carried a map of the procession's route thoughtfully printed for its readers, and the news that people were already staking out places in the Mall.

'Laura, really,' said Tom. 'I'm surprised at you.'

'I'm a bit surprised at myself,' said Laura, 'but I do like Princess Elizabeth –'

'You can't like her – you don't know her.'

'You know what I mean. She's so sensible, somehow, did her bit in the war, joined the ATS . . .'

'Laura, what has got into you? That was a work of fiction. More or less.'

'No, it wasn't. There were lots of pictures of her doing work with vehicles. And she was in uniform. I mean, Princess Margaret, she's different. Always at nightclubs and things –'

'Laura! I think being pregnant must be affecting your brain. I would never have believed you could even read such rubbish, never mind believe it.'

'Well, it probably is,' said Laura placidly, 'but even your Mr Bevan seems to approve of it.'

The point was, it seemed, that a young and handsome prince and a beautiful and radiant princess proved in the end irresistible; there was a need for a fairy story, and that grey November day provided it with delightful aplomb and, as it proved, perfect timing.

# Chapter 13

## 1948

It was quite – no, it was extremely – no, so far it had been unbearably painful. Or was she just a coward, making a fuss about nothing? In which case, how was she to cope with childbirth itself? The doctor – not the empathetic young woman she had imagined would be caring for her, at this mecca for care of women by women, but a tough, hard-faced, middle-aged creature with rough, probing fingers – was approaching her again, followed by what seemed like a crowd of young women.

'Gather round,' she said, 'and listen carefully. This woman, aged twenty-eight, has a history of three spontaneous abortions. Consequently, we make a diagnosis of cervical incompetence.' Well, that made her feel a real failure, Laura thought and how she hated that word 'abortion', her mind cringing from it as her body cringed from the assault it was about to receive. She knew it was the medical term for a miscarriage, but it was so ugly, sounded so harsh. 'Therefore she would seem a good candidate for cervical cerclage.'

'Miss Curtis, would you care to define for us precisely what that is?'

Miss Curtis, who was more the sort of doctor Laura had imagined she would find here, young and sympathetic, and who looked terrified, cleared her throat and said, 'A stitch, Miss Moran.'

'A stitch.' Miss Moran looked at her witheringly. 'And where would we be placing this stitch, I wonder? In her arm? Her cheek?'

'No, Miss Moran. In her cervix.'

'And how would we describe this stitch? In medical terms? Miss Kennedy?'

'A suture, Miss Moran.'

'Ah. Well, that didn't take so long. Congratulations. I hope none of you are hoping to qualify too terribly soon. Yes, we shall be placing a suture in Mrs Knelston's cervix, and this will give her a better chance – I do not say a certain one – of carrying to term. I shall of course perform the procedure myself, but one of you may examine her before and afterwards in order to note the placing. Now, Miss Curtis, would you tell us the date of the first cervical cerclage?'

'I – think – that is, 19– no, 1890.'

'Incorrect. Anyone else?'

A girl who looked a good option to replace Miss Moran in a dozen years or so said, '1902.'

'Correct, Miss Burne. And the success rate is fair. You do realise that, I hope, Mrs Knelston? That this is not a guarantee of successful delivery, six months or so hence?'

'Yes,' said Laura. 'It was explained to me on my first visit.'

'And tell me, Miss Scott, when do we, or rather the midwife or obstetrician, remove the suture?'

'At the onset of labour?' said Miss Scott, her voice hopeful rather than confident.

'Correct. It is crucial therefore that the midwife is aware of its presence. Otherwise there could be unfortunate consequences, such as tearing of the cervix. Why unfortunate, Miss Kennedy?'

'I – I – well, it would make future conception less likely.'

'Correct. Or even impossible. Now – get her prepared, please. I shall be ready in ten minutes. '

If there had only been one word of kindness from Miss Moran, Laura thought. One hint that her permission might be sought, for what seemed to be a multiple assault by the students on her already tender person, what followed might have seemed less dreadful. She was moved to an operating theatre, told to climb onto a table, swabbed down, shaved, her legs thrust into stirrups, and a brilliant light shone up her vagina. When Miss Moran arrived, only Miss Curtis had the consideration to whisper, 'I don't think it should be too bad.'

But it was much too bad. The double internal examination, first by Miss Moran and then Miss Kennedy, and then the barked instructions from Miss Moran to keep completely still as she advanced on her with needle and suture thread. She managed to keep still, but she did cry out – twice. Almost worse than the rest was when she was finally released from pain, Miss Moran instructed not just Miss Kennedy, but also one of the other girls to examine her.

On her release from the stirrups, she managed to say thank you. Then, with a sudden infusion of her normal spirit, she said, 'I would just like to say something. When I read of this procedure, Miss Moran, I gathered there would be some kind of anaesthesia available. It would have been easier to bear when I was confronted by the reality had I known this was not the case.'

'Anaesthesia!' said Miss Moran. 'This is a free hospital, Mrs Knelston, not some expensive nursing home. If you found that painful, then I would suggest you need to confront the reality of childbirth before it is too late.'

She pulled off her surgical gloves, nodded at the girls.

'Take her back to the recovery room,' she said. 'You may stay for half an hour, Mrs Knelston, and then you may leave. Providing you are not experiencing any pain, of course. Do make sure you rest for the next few days – don't go racing back to your domestic chores at home, or you could regret it.'

'Miss Moran,' said Laura, 'I am experiencing considerable pain already, but that is entirely due to your ministrations. And what I shall be racing back to, as you put it, are not domestic chores, but my position as head of a primary school. I shall tell any girls who show an interest in studying medicine that a little kindness might not go amiss during painful procedures.'

The girls surrounding her drew back a foot or two, as if to disassociate themselves from such heresy, until Miss Moran had gone. Then they followed her: all except Miss Curtis, who whispered, 'Well done. She's a brilliant surgeon and obstetrician, but I wish she would be a little kinder. I certainly intend to be – if I ever qualify, which is a bit unlikely, I'm afraid. Can you walk?'

'I think so,' said Laura, wincing as she eased herself off the surgical table. 'And thank you so much for your consideration.'

She felt dizzy suddenly and sank down again. 'I'll get you a wheelchair,' said Miss Curtis. 'And then some tea. Just wait a moment.'

She sat with Laura while she drank the tea. 'You look better already, Mrs Knelston,' she said.

'I feel it,' said Laura, 'And thank you again. I'm Laura, by the way.'

'Jillie. Jillie Curtis. I don't know if I'll ever make a surgeon.'

'Well, I hope you do,' said Laura, grinning. 'I hope you're chief surgeon here and you can sack Miss Moran for unkindness, or even brutality.'

'I'm afraid that's a bit unlikely. She really is top of her tree. Where are you going to have your baby?'

'Hilchester General,' said Laura. 'Little town near Winchester.'

'I hope it goes well.' Jillie Curtis looked thoughtful for a moment, then said, 'You should really go somewhere that's a centre of excellence, you know. With your history. I'm just wondering –'

'Yes?'

'My uncle is one of the chief obstetricians at St Thomas'. I wonder if we could arrange for you to have your baby there – he's a complete sweetie.'

'But why on earth should they take me? What right would I have?'

'Oh, Laura,' said Jillie Curtis, smiling her sweet, gentle smile, and shaking her head in mock reproof. 'Medicine's exactly like everything else – it's not what you know, it's who you know. Look, I can't make any promises, but I'll ask him and write to you. Give me your address. Quick, I can hear them coming back.'

A week later, a letter arrived for Laura from Jillie. It said she was afraid it might be rather difficult for her uncle to find room for Laura in his ward, but if she was really worried, he would of course do his best. *It's all to do with the new National Health Service,* she wrote. *There's so much more pressure on beds. Let me know, Laura, and if you are really worried I know my uncle will find a bed for you somehow.*

Tom read the letter and looked at Laura, his face incredulous.

'I can't quite believe this, Laura.'

'What?'

'That you should be considering having your baby in some hospital where, should you go there, it would mean pulling strings, jumping the queue, in a way I couldn't possibly condone. Surely you can see that would be totally against the principles of the National Health Service? I couldn't possibly allow it.'

'Oh, is that so?' said Laura. 'You wouldn't allow it? And what right do you have, Tom Knelston, to allow or not allow me to have my baby at one of the best hospitals in England?'

'I'm its father,' he said. 'And that gives me the right.'

'It does no such thing. And you,' she added, 'should just listen to yourself. You get more and more like your own father every day.'

'Laura, it's just not right.'

'If it's right for our baby, it's right,' said Laura firmly. 'And I will be the judge of that. You may have an extensive knowledge of the law, Tom, but you have none of obstetrics, as far as I know. Now, I have work to do.'

But even as she shut herself in the bedroom and threw a couple of Tom's books at the wall, she knew he was right. She should not be taking the place of some woman who had a right to it; on the other hand, if it did give her a better chance of delivering a healthy baby, she felt she should take it. She finally decided to see what the ante-natal clinic had to say, how familiar they were with the process of cerclage. If she felt they were competent she would stay with them. But she would not be told whether or not to do so by her husband.

Diana looked at Wendelien across Victor Stiebel's salon, with a kind of desperation in her eyes.

'Oh, Wendelien, this is all so wonderful,' she said and burst into tears.

'Darling, darling Diana, why are you crying then?'

'You know as well as I do.'

She had come down to London to purchase an outfit for her brother Michael's wedding: a blessed break from the flat dullness of her life in Yorkshire.

'Of course I do. Well, I did tell you not to go up there.'

'It was hardly sound advice,' said Diana fretfully.

'If you'd followed it, you'd be much happier now.'

'Maybe. Only I wouldn't have Jamie; he almost makes it all worthwhile.'

'Only almost?'

'Well, no, completely. I couldn't imagine life without him. And Johnathan – well, he is so sweet and he loves me very much. So I'm lucky, aren't I?'

'No,' said Wendelien, 'you're not. Well, only a bit. Other people have babies and husbands and enjoy their lives as well. And don't have wicked witches to contend with. Is she really no better?'

'Worse. Hates me. Won't let me help, won't let me do anything. Johnathan just can't see the problem. Says I'm making a marvellous job of it all. You know, I'm President of the WI now and—'

'Goodness,' said Wendelien.

'Oh, shut up. And I'm on the committee of the Royal South Yorkshire show.'

'Who's in charge?'

'Guess. And Johnathan's Deputy Lord Lieutenant of the county now, and there's a lot of stuff to do with that. I could become a school governor, if I wanted. Last week, he asked me if I thought I'd like to learn about sheep. You know. Four-legged, woolly things. '

'What is there to learn about them?'

'Oh, all the different breeds, and so on. He's thinking of introducing a new breed and he suggested I might like to investigate that, take responsibility for it even.'

'Diana,' said Wendelien firmly, 'you cannot spend the rest of your life introducing sheep to one another.'

Diana giggled, then suddenly burst into tears. 'Don't mock me. It's all I've got.'

'I know, and it's not enough.'

'And now he's talking about a little brother or sister for Jamie. If he says once more how jolly that would be I'll scream.'

'Right,' said Wendelien. 'That does it. We have to act fast. Before you get preggers again.'

'It's not terribly likely,' said Diana. 'He's always so tired.'

'Well, that's something. Now stop crying, and I'll think of something. He will be coming up for the wedding, I presume?'

'Yes, of course. Mummy and Daddy have asked the wicked witch and Sir Hilary obviously, but I don't think they'll come. He is more and more lost to us, completely batty really, so she couldn't bring him and I don't see how she could leave him.'

'Oh, I do hope she does come,' said Wendelien. 'I'll have a few words to say to her.'

'Wendelien, don't even joke about it.'

'I'm not. Now come on, are we settled on the blue? What about the hat? Shall we get it here, or look further afield? You know who dresses here quite a lot, don't you? Moira Shearer – you know, the divine red-headed ballerina. God, she's beautiful. Have you seen *The Red Shoes*, her film?'

'No, of course I haven't,' said Diana irritably. 'The only thing I've seen for months is the local dramatic society's performance of *Private Lives*. It was frightful.'

'Sorry. Anyway, Victor was saying something about *Vogue* being here the other day, choosing dresses for her.'

'Oh, dear, don't tell me any more. You are so lucky, Wendelien, you've just no idea.'

'Well, it beats introducing sheep,' said Wendelien. 'That's for sure.'


Laura looked so lovely, Tom thought; with her ripe, full belly, her skin more peach-like, her curls shinier. She was seven months pregnant now, justifying the torture she had endured at the Elizabeth Garrett Anderson Hospital, although it had left emotional scars. She had decided, after some exhaustive questioning, to remain at Hilchester General, but she took her time telling Tom. He had a long way to go yet, she feared, before understanding the place of the modern husband.

It had been a lovely summer, and since temporarily leaving St Joesph's, she had spent as much time as she could sitting in the sunshine either in the local park, or in her sister's garden, where she went more than once to stay for a few days.

She was serious about going back to teaching; though she had promised to see how she felt when Miss or Master Knelston arrived. Tom was very keen for her to devote herself entirely to the baby, and then to several more besides. Asked by Laura how he thought he would support this new, large family, and indeed where he would house them, he said that Mr Pemberton had already promised him a substantial raise, and had hinted at a loan that would enable them to put down a deposit on a little cottage on the outskirts of Hilchester.

'I didn't like to ask quite how much,' he said to Laura, 'but he seemed to be talking about a hundred pounds. Which would be about a quarter of the price. The rest we should be able to get a mortgage on. Imagine us, Laura, owning a house.'

Laura said briskly that she had no difficulty in doing any such thing, and that Tom's loyalty to Mr Pemberton came close to feudal at times, but when she told her mother the amount being discussed, Edith told her she didn't know how lucky she was.

'I'm not saying it's not right, and of course Tom has been very loyal to Mr Pemberton, but it's not usual. So if you've got half the sense I hope you have, you'll tell him how grateful you are. Nothing demeaning about showing good manners, Laura.'

Mr Pemberton seemed very excited about the imminent baby. Having no grandchildren of his own to look forward to, it had given him quite a new lease of life. Mrs Pemberton had succumbed entirely to her depression and was in a nursing home. Living alone, surrounded by ghosts, he took great comfort from the youthful energies and patent happiness of the young Knelstons. He did have to admit finding Laura's visits, or rather her burgeoning physical presence, rather embarrassing, and had a little trouble finding somewhere to fix his eyes when she was in the room, other than on her. Tom had asked rather anxiously if he would mind her visiting, since she would very much like to thank him for his great kindness to them both, and once he had adjusted to her shape and size, he found himself looking forward impatiently to each visit – especially as she invariably brought a large cake she had baked herself.

Laura had returned from one of her visits to Mr Pemberton, and was slightly wearily climbing the stairs to the flat, when the door burst open and Tom, looking as if he might explode himself, appeared through it.

'Now what?' said Laura, smiling at him. 'Don't tell me – Aneurin Bevan has heard about the baby and wants to be its godfather.'

'Almost,' said Tom. 'Almost as good as that. Laura – I've been asked to be one of the two delegates from the branch of the HLP at the party conference in Blackpool this September.'

'Oh, my goodness,' said Laura, pushing past him, and lowering herself carefully onto the sofa. 'That really is exciting, Tom. Let me see the letter.'

'Here,' he said, handing it over with great care as if it was fashioned from fine china and might break. 'Here, look, can you believe that?'

'I can, yes,' she said, having read it, and smiling up at him, thinking that one of the reasons she loved him so very much was his inability to perceive his own value. 'I think it's wonderful just the same, completely wonderful, just like you are, Tom Knelston. Oh, I'm so proud of you. If only I could come too.'

'Well, maybe you can,' said Tom. 'I'll – I'll ask.' It was a measure of the enormity of his achievement that he would even consider such a thing. 'I'll talk to Mr Roberts tomorrow. See what he says. You never know.'

'No, you never do. Mind you, the size I'm getting, I'll need two seats rather than one . . .'

The next day brought more exciting news still; Mr Roberts, the chairman of the Hilchester branch of the Labour Party, said that there was to be a debate on the subject of the plight of the ex-servicemen. 'I'm going to put you forward to speak on the subject. Just at one of the fringe meetings, naturally, not the main conference. We're very proud of you, Tom,' said Mr Roberts, suddenly rather pink in the face. 'You've done very well. If only your father was here to see all this.'

'If only,' said Tom.

There was a silence; then Tom said, 'Er, Mr Roberts, I was wondering if – that is – whether – if – I mean –'

'Come along, Tom, spit it out.'

'Well, whether Laura could come. To the conference.'

He was so sure Mr Roberts would say no, that when the reply came, he said, 'I didn't think it would be possible.'

'And you thought wrong. She can come. She's a member of the party, after all. Of course, she'll only be able to be there as an observer, and won't be able to speak. Although –' he cleared his throat, looked at Tom rather awkwardly – 'I would have thought, in her condition, she must get rather tired. Of course, it's your decision but with most of the delegates being male . . . Well, you will I'm sure consider your decision very carefully as to whether she will feel comfortable there.'

'Indeed,' said Tom. 'Thank you for your thoughtfulness. She does get tired, yes, but if I am to speak, she will want to be there and to hear me. And I will want her to be there.'

'Yes, I understand,' said Mr Roberts. 'I just wouldn't want you to be distracted, by worrying about her, you know.'

'I won't be,' said Tom. 'She won't let me be. She is a very committed member of the party. Thank you so much, Mr Roberts. For everything. I won't let you down. Will Mrs Roberts be attending?'

'No,' said Mr Roberts, and a very quiet sigh escaped him. 'She will not. I fear she has never shown the interest in politics Laura does. She feels they are not for her. Mind you, with the five children, she has quite enough to occupy her. But I regret it just the same.'

Yes, I expect you do, Tom thought, remembering the attitude of the men towards the female members at his very first meeting, when Laura had confronted them over the washing-up. Possibly Mrs Roberts would be a devoted party member now without that attitude. Well, he had been lucky. And now he could go home and tell Laura the news. She would be so pleased.

\* \* \*

They struck lucky with their B&B. Anne Higgins, whose house was only a fifteen-minute walk away from Blackpool Sands, supplied not only a very pretty double room right next door to the bathroom, but a large and comfortable double bed. 'Looks like I knew you were coming,' she said, smiling at Laura's stomach, protruding from her carefully buttoned navy woollen coat. The coat had been the subject of a brief but quite fierce argument between Tom and Laura; she had wanted a red one, but Tom, mindful of Mr Roberts's clear concerns about Laura's condition and people's possible attitude towards it, had urged her to buy the navy. She had told him she knew perfectly well why he preferred it, and anyway, red would be a more suitable colour given that they were not attending a Tory conference. Then, suddenly and uncharacteristically, she gave in. He was not to know that for perhaps the first and only time in her life, she had decided to put her wifely duties before her most deeply felt attitudes.

The days of the conference passed in a complete blur. They travelled up by train, together with Mr Roberts, who gave them a lift in his taxi to Mrs Higgins's guest house.

Having settled in and with a couple of hours' daylight to spare, they made for the seafront, and walked along the huge, sweeping beach, gazing up awestruck at the famous Blackpool Tower. 'You know,' Tom said, reaching for Laura's hand and smiling happily, 'I really love it here.'

Laura too liked the heady bracing air, replacing the gentle southern breezes of Hampshire, the apparently limitless landscape, the grey sea reaching out to infinity. It was cold and she liked that too; her head felt very clear, her energies increased.

'Maybe one day, you might be an MP for some northern constituency, and we could come to live up there with the children. I like Mrs Higgins too, I like her bluntness. I've heard this about northern folk, how they call a spade a spade, that sort of thing.'

'Yes, well, what we can definitely do,' said Tom, 'next summer, we could all come, bring the baby up for a holiday, let him – her – ride on the donkeys, show her how to dig sandcastles. It'd be so lovely.'

'It would,' said Laura, reaching up to kiss him. 'Although not many babies nine months old can ride a donkey. I know she's going to be a genius, but . . .'

Next morning – after Mrs Higgins's magnificent breakfast of bacon, eggs, black pudding, mushrooms and fried bread, followed by hot toast and marmalade and as much tea as they could drink – they walked down to the ballroom and enrolled; then they attended their first session, followed by another and another and yet another. It was a heavy schedule; they had not expected to be so fully occupied. Some of the speakers were inspiring, some brilliant, some frankly dull.

There were a great many drinks parties and dinners as well, to most of which they were not invited, hosted by legendary names and bodies: the BBC, the great unions, the newspapers. The most impossible party to get into, unless you were a truly great name, Mr Roberts had told them on the train as they travelled up, clearly eager to show off his knowledge, was the *Daily Mirror* bash.

'Hugh Cudlipp – you'll have heard of him, brilliant chap, been editing the paper since he was twenty-six. He's Welsh, so you'll approve, Tom. Commercial traveller's son, bit like your Aneurin. They're friends, of course. Keep an eye open for him. He's not very tall, crinkly fair hair, always in a rush, never stops talking. Or drinking,' he added, slightly disapprovingly.

A great deal of drinking went on. After every major speech, which meant after every session, people gathered to pass opinions and drink. Tom saw Bevan several times, beaming benignly, a glass of beer in his hand; and he did catch sight of the great Cudlipp, recognisable from his photographs, pushing his way impatiently through the crowds. They were all there, the great names, Attlee, Herbert Morrison, Ernest Bevin, Stafford Cripps, Denis Healey and of course, making Laura's entire week, the glamorous redhead, Barbara Castle. Tom felt he had strayed into some new, magical kingdom, where anything was possible.

Bevan's speech was inevitably the highlight for Tom; he stood on the platform, his wonderful voice turning his vision of free healthcare for all into poetry, a kind of anthem, utterly at ease, yet filled with his extraordinary energy, his unique style; it was said it was almost unreportable, his ability to mix – as Michael Foot famously put it years later – fire and ice.

And, of course, Tom spoke. At a small hall, outside the main conference area; the meeting was sponsored by the Lest We Forget Association founded to support the ex-servicemen. Tom was an active and loyal member of the Hilchester branch. He was so nervous beforehand, he was completely unable to eat all day; but as always, as soon as he began, his passion for the subject and his concern for the cause absolutely overtook him and filled his head and his heart and his voice. There was more than one quite seasoned delegate at the meeting who felt that a part of the future stood before him. He spoke, most touchingly, of an event he had attended at Stoke Mandeville Hospital where many paralysed patients were cared for and helped as far as was possible in rehabilitation. 'I went to an archery competition in the grounds, and every entrant was in a wheelchair. It was wonderful to see the spirit of competition and excitement experienced by men who a year or so ago must have felt their lives were quite over.'

When the meeting ended, he and Laura went out into the dusk and walked for over an hour along the sands, silent at first; Laura had been taken unawares by the pride she had felt in Tom that evening, and perhaps something more than pride. Looking at him on the platform, with his considerable height, and a little weight put on, she saw how physically impressive he was, even with his limp, and extraordinarily good-looking, pushing back his wild auburn hair, his green eyes blazing from his expressive face. He wasn't merely Tom to her any more, not merely the husband she loved so much. He was something else, something special: promise, integrity, the future.

They went back to Mrs Higgins's guest house and climbed the stairs to their room, where they lay in the big bed in silence, holding hands, contemplating, in their different ways, the new future they felt they had discovered and indeed begun.

# Chapter 14

## 1948

'Excuse me – Miss Curtis?'

'Yes. Yes, that's me. Can I help you?'

Jillie smiled at him, such a nice young man, tall, good-looking, with amazing green eyes, although he was very pale and almost gaunt-looking.

'I hope so. Yes. I'm Tom. Tom Knelston. I wrote to you, asked if I could see you and you said to come today.'

'Oh, of course. Yes, do please forgive me. I've been on duty nearly all night, I'd forgotten – only temporarily – you were coming. Shall we go and have a cup of tea somewhere? There's a good café down the road.'

'Yes. That might be nice. Thank you.'

His voice was attractive, she thought: deep, almost musical, but again, very weary-sounding. Well, if his wife had just had her baby, he would be weary.

It had been such a nice letter, very brief, simply saying his wife had been seen at the hospital in the spring, for 'a cervical stitch' and had told him how kind she'd been, and he'd be very grateful if she could find the time to see him. He had a few questions she might be able to answer. Jillie hoped she'd be able to help. Six more months in the company of Miss Moran had left her uncertain of her own name.

They set off down Grafton Way; it was very cold. Struggling for small talk, Jillie remarked fatuously, she felt, upon how seasonal it was.

'Perhaps we'll have a white Christmas,' she said. 'Although we had one last year, of course, and that should have cured us all of wanting another for a long time. Did you get snowed up, Mr Knelston?'

Tom said he did, yes, although not till after Christmas. He didn't expand upon the subject.

'Right,' said Jillie, pausing in front of a rather cheerful-looking café, its door hung with paper chains. 'I quite often come here, it's very nice. In fact, I'm meeting an old school friend here later for lunch; we're going to the pictures this afternoon.'

'That sounds nice,' he said, and she realised that between everything she said and his answer there was a pause, as if he was digesting with great difficulty what she had said and how he should reply.

She pushed open the door, leading the way into the warm, steamy room. 'Is that table all right?'

'Yes, fine. Shall I take your coat?'

'Oh, thank you.' She unwound her long scarf, handed that to him too. 'There's a coat stand over there, by the door.'

She waited till he sat down, then said, 'Do you want anything to eat? They do lovely iced buns here.'

'No, no,' he said, 'just tea for me.'

'Right, well, I think I'll have one – I'm hungry. And Alice won't be here for ages.'

'Alice?'

'Yes. She's the friend I'm meeting. We were at school together. She's a nurse at St Thomas'. You'd probably have met her if your wife had been able to have her baby in London. She was so interested in Laura's story.'

'Yes, I see,' he said.

'Such a pity about that. Anyway, what can I help you with? Or rather, what do you think I might be able to help you with?'

'It's difficult,' he said. 'Very difficult. But I read something and – well, I just thought it worth asking.'

'Right. Well – fire away.'

He looked down into his tea, stirred it rather helplessly. 'It's – difficult,' he said, again, after a long pause.

'Let me ask you some questions, then. That might help. I presume it's to do with your wife. And the baby?'

Another very long pause; then, 'Yes,' he said. 'Yes, it is.'

'How – how are they? Was it all right, did they look after them well at the hospital?'

'No,' he said. 'I wouldn't say well, not well at all, no.'

'Oh, I'm sorry. But she's all right now, I hope? They both are? Was it a girl or a boy?'

'A girl,' he said. 'A lovely little girl.'

'How nice.'

'Yes.'

'And – your wife? Laura, wasn't it?'

'Yes, Laura, that's right.'

'Is she recovering well? The baby must be about – let me see – a month old now, sleeping a bit better, I hope. Not giving you too many bad nights?'

'She – she – no, not really.'

'Good. Well, you're lucky, then. Lots of babies go on waking up for months . . .'

There was a very long silence; then he said – and the words came out in such a rush that she thought she must have misheard, in fact she did say, 'I'm sorry, I didn't quite follow . . .'

'I said,' he repeated, his voice louder now, as well as slower, 'there is no baby. She died. And Laura died too.'

For the rest of her life, even when she was a distinguished obstetrician of great experience and had confronted many tragedies, that moment remained with Jillie as a measure of the most unimaginable and dreadful sorrow. She sat, helpless and silent, staring at Tom Knelston across the table while around them people chatted and smiled, quite oblivious to his tragedy. As he looked away from her, and down into his tea, she realised that something had fallen into it, followed by another, and that those things were tears; and then he looked up, and she saw there were more, uncontainable, and that he was mortified by them, dreading that others in the café would notice them and worse, be curious about them. A man shedding tears in public. That, for that one short moment, was the greatest of his concerns, and she acted with an absolutely correct and compassionate instinct and passed him one of the paper napkins so that he might wipe them away and sat rummaging through her handbag looking for nothing, nothing at all, until she heard him clear his throat and say, 'Sorry.'

'It's all right,' she said carefully. 'You mustn't worry about it. Let's just wait a bit, shall we, and then maybe get some more tea, and if you want to, you can tell me more about it.'

'Yes,' he said. 'Yes, thank you – that sounds a good idea.'

And they sat, very quietly, until he said, 'I'm all right now. I'd like to tell you some more, I think, please. And ask you some questions as I said in my letter.'

'I'll do my best to answer them, Tom. But I should warn you, I'm not very far advanced in my training – it may be beyond my area of expertise.'

It had been a case of placenta previa. 'That's when the placenta lies across the opening of the uterus into the birth canal, effectively blocking the baby's exit,' he said.

'Yes,' Jillie said, 'yes, I know.'

Laura had had an appointment with the midwife, just three weeks before the baby was due. The midwife had pronounced the heartbeat strong, but said the baby's head was still not engaged in the birth canal. Laura had asked if this was something she should worry about, and the midwife said no, not at all, she had known cases where the baby's head didn't engage until labour had begun. 'I might have suspected a breech, but I can feel baby's bottom, quite high, all in the right place. No, I'm sure it's just that he or she is in no hurry to join us just yet, and very sensible too, in this freezing weather. I hope we're not going to have another winter like last year. Now I'll just take some measurements, check on baby's size – and next time you come, we'll talk to doctor about removing that stitch.'

So Laura had gone home, quite happy, assured that her baby was just right, and they had had supper and she had said she was very tired and might go to bed early if Tom didn't mind. And when he had gone into the bedroom, she had been fast asleep, smiling, still with the light on, a copy of the recently published *The Diary of a Young*

*Girl* by Anne Frank lying open on her huge stomach. Tom had removed it gently, got into his pyjamas, kissed her tenderly and whispered that he loved her. She hadn't replied, but had smiled and sighed sleepily and sunk deeper into sleep. It was, for the rest of his life, a comfort that those were his last words to her and that she had clearly heard them.

He had woken to her screaming; it was just light and he had struggled awake, sat up, switched the light on and seen why. The room was a bloodbath. Not just the bed, but the floor, and even some of the walls; the blood kept coming and coming, unstaunchable – towels, spare sheets soaking in moments.

He had rushed downstairs and out to the phone box, called an ambulance; and then raced back to the room and the horror.

She seemed to be in no pain, just terrified, but already losing consciousness; the baby was born in the ambulance, their little girl, perfect, beautiful, but dead. Laura died within ten minutes of arriving at the hospital.

They had been very kind, he said, and it was still something he was clearly grateful for. They took them off immediately, out of sight, Laura still on the stretcher, the baby carried by a nurse, and had refused to let him follow; but when he said, after sitting shocked and still in the emergency area, please, please, could he not hold the baby, a nurse had said it wasn't usual. Why, in the name of God, was it not usual? Jillie wondered, struggling to maintain calm as the story was told. What could be more usual than that a parent would wish to hold a dead or dying baby and why should they not? Then, apparently, another nurse appeared and told him to follow her, and led him into a little room and said, 'They're just giving her a little wash, then we'll bring her in,' which they did. He had sat looking at her, at his daughter, so perfect and white and still, and tried to believe that it had really happened, that she would not suddenly draw a breath and cry, and he held her very close, trying to warm her for she was already growing cold, and telling her she was beautiful and he loved her.

And then they came for her and took her away and he didn't argue, he didn't have the strength, and they asked him if he would like to see Laura and he said yes. They led him to her, on a high bed, under a white sheet and again, she looked so perfect, so normal somehow, and he had taken her hand and kept turning it in his and kissing it over and over again, and then he had stood up and bent over her and kissed her face, the face he loved so much, the rosy dimpled face that was neither rosy nor dimpled any more but white and sweetly serene, and he sat and told her he loved her, that he would always love her, her and the baby, the baby they had agreed they would call Hope. That was what she carried with her – hope for their family and its future – and of course he would see they were never parted, but be together for the rest of time, lying in the little churchyard at West Hilton where Laura would be surrounded by people who loved her and would have loved Hope. Then a doctor came and said he must ask Tom to leave now, and he did so without arguing or without even questioning why, and when he went back to find his little daughter, his little Hope, she had been moved from the cubicle where they had sat together, and she was nowhere to be found for quite a long time, and he had hunted, increasingly desperate for her until the first nurse, the kind one, who had arranged for Tom to see her and hold her, had said she had been taken to the morgue but she wasn't sure what would happen to her next.

'What do you mean?' Tom had said. 'She's my daughter. I want her to be with her mother and I want them to be buried together.'

And Tom suddenly became angry and walked out into the casualty area, shouting for a doctor. They kept telling him to be calm and to wait and he said he had been very calm and he couldn't wait, in case they were taken away, Laura and Hope, and began rushing through all the doors into all the rooms and cubicles, and finally a doctor did appear and said would he please be quiet, and Tom said how could he be quiet, would the doctor be quiet if his wife and baby had both just died and he had no idea where they were? The doctor suddenly stopped and stood very still and said, 'I'm sorry, Mr Knelston. So sorry, come with me.' He had led Tom into what was obviously his own room and explained that post-mortems would have to be done, it was essential, so that they could try to discover what had caused the tragedy in the first place. 'Post-mortems?' Tom had said, staring at him. 'You mean you're going to . . . to . . .' but he couldn't even finish the sentence it was so horrible. The doctor said he could withhold his permission if he so wished, but it could be helpful to other women and other babies; and it was too much finally for Tom to confront or bear and he said no, no post-mortems. He wanted Laura and Hope kept as they were, quite perfect, and that as soon as he possibly could, he would arrange for them to be taken away to where he wanted them to be.

And that is where they now lay, Jillie discerned, after listening carefully and quietly for as long as seemed necessary; in the little churchyard at West Hilton, the village where Tom had been born and grew up and where he and Laura had been married.

'And I hope,' she said gently, 'that is in some way a comfort?'

'Yes,' he said. 'Yes, of course it is. A very little way.'

She looked at his life, the bleak, solitary life of a young widower, loveless, childless, and she felt in that moment that she knew where her heart must lie, for she could feel it aching for him.

'But,' she said gently, after a long silence, 'you said you wanted to ask me something?'

'Yes,' he said. 'Yes, if you don't mind?'

And she thought how minding what he asked her would be the least, the very least of it. The very least she could do for him was answer, however difficult. And it *was* difficult, sitting in that cosy steamy café surrounded by smiling, happy people looking forward to Christmas.

'Please ask. And I will try to answer.'

'All right. Well, the first question is, could having the stitch – you know, the cervical stitch –'

'Yes.'

'Could that have caused it? Or made it more likely even?'

And filled with a relief that was palpable, that she moreover could pass on to him, she was able to say no, there was absolutely no way that the cervical stitch could have caused the condition that had so dreadfully ended the lives of Laura and her little daughter. She could see it was what he most wanted, indeed needed to hear, for he took a deep, almost life-giving breath and half smiled at her.

'They did say it couldn't have but I didn't quite believe them, I had to know.'

'Of course.'

'Because I did read that it could be caused by, well, by previous surgery.'

'Well, real surgery, a Caesarean section perhaps, could cause scarring and that in turn might affect the endometrium – that is the lining of the womb. But not a cervical stitch, no. Most emphatically not.'

He nodded and was silent for a bit, draining his already cold cup of tea.

'And the other question?'

'Oh. Well, that's harder for you to answer, I'm sure. But – well, I have to know as much as can. I feel I owe it to Laura.'

'Of course.'

'So, the thing is, what I can't help wondering. If she had had really good care, such as she might have had at St Thomas', where you so kindly tried to get her a place, might they have detected it? And prevented it?'

His expression was now so agonised, so full of fear at her possible answer, that Jillie found herself quite unable to speak; she sat staring at him, was trying to shape a careful, truthful, yet kindly response, when the door of the café opened and someone was suddenly at their table and the someone said, 'Jillie, hello, am I early? So sorry, shall I—'

And Jillie looked up and saw it was Alice standing there – and she was at once filled with relief and anxiety. Relief that she had a respite before answering this question, and anxiety that poor Tom Knelston, who had already confronted one strange woman under the most extraordinary, painful circumstances, must now confront another. She jumped up, hugged Alice and said to Tom, 'Would you excuse me one moment?' and pushed Alice towards the door.

'Jillie! What is this? What's going on?' said Alice, half laughing, half indignant.

'Alice, I'm so sorry to do this to you, and you're not really early, but could you possibly go away for maybe quarter of an hour and then come back? I'll explain when we're having lunch, but I can't ask this poor chap to endure meeting you.'

'Am I really so hideous?' said Alice, smiling, her blue eyes dancing. 'Jillie, is this a new boyfriend? You could have told me. Yes, all right, all right, I'm going, but I will be back in fifteen minutes flat. I'm cold and wet and hungry, so you'd better be finished by then – and I don't want to play gooseberry this afternoon, if that's what you're thinking.'

'OK. But – oh, goodness, quick question, don't ask why. Do you think placenta previa could be diagnosed while the baby was still in utero?'

'Gosh, you don't ask for much, do you? I've only been doing my midders for two months, but – um – well, maybe, head not engaged at term?'

'Oh, God,' said Jillie. 'I was afraid you might say that. I thought so too. Oh, Alice, what am I going to do?'

'I can't answer that question, I'm afraid, because I have no idea what this is all about. I'm going to go and walk round the block, and then I'll be back and—'

'Yes, all right, all right. Fine. Now go away.'

Tom was already standing up and winding his scarf round his neck when Alice returned. Jillie introduced them; but he was so exhausted by the trauma of the morning, of reliving the events of the past month, that he could scarcely see Alice Miller, but he did absorb the fact that she was blonde and not very tall and smiled very politely at him, which was nice of her considering she'd been sent back out into the foul weather for his convenience. Her voice as she said, 'How do you do, Mr Knelston,' was very light and clear and rather posh, like her friend Jillie's, and clearly the school they'd been at together was not one Laura would have taught at.

Jillie walked with him to the door and shook his hand and said he mustn't hesitate to contact her again if he wanted to. She gave him a telephone number which she said was her home; and he told her, truthfully, she had been more helpful than she could possibly know and went out into the sleet which was now lashing London, feeling calmed and even, briefly, comforted. For Jillie Curtis had told him that while it was just possible that Laura's condition might have been diagnosed had she been in the maternity ward at St Thomas', it would have been extremely unlikely, and the only certain symptom was the onset of bleeding which of course had come too late for anyone to have saved her, however great their skill.

'Which is true,' said Jillie staunchly, as Alice looked at her. 'That is the only certain symptom . . .'

'And the head not engaged?'

'That's not certain. She was three weeks from term. She hadn't even had the stitch removed. Don't look at me like that.'

'You lied,' said Alice. 'And I'm not looking at you like anything and I would have said the same thing, but it wasn't completely true, was it? Did he mention anything the midwife might have said about that?'

'Well . . .'

'Jillie!'

'Well, he said she'd said the head wasn't fully engaged, but sometimes it wasn't, right until the woman went into labour.'

'Which is true. But—'

'But nothing. It is true. Then she just said that the next time Laura came to the clinic, they'd probably take the stitch out.'

'Well, that's all right then. Obviously not even an issue. But—'

'Don't,' said Jillie, putting her hand over Alice's mouth. 'Don't say it again, please. I didn't lie. If it was anything, it was a sin of omission. So can we please not talk about it any more? Oh, God, Alice, what a morning.'

'Yes. Poor, poor man. What a terrible, dreadful, awful thing.'

'Oh, Alice, I tell you something. I'm never going to forget this day as long as I live.'

'Actually, I don't think I will either,' said Alice. 'Such a sad, sad story. He was awfully handsome,' she added, sipping thoughtfully at her tea. 'Did you notice?'

# Chapter 15

## 1949

Finally. After all those years, starting at Oxford before the war, his training interrupted by it, Ned was an honorary at St Peter's, with his own rooms in Welbeck Street; not without some nepotism, of course, and Ned was first to admit it, both regretful and thankful for it. The night he had actually signed the lease on the rooms, and celebrated it with some rather good champagne in the company of Michael Southcott, he had thought that this was his reward for putting up with his father for every moment of his thirty-two and a half years. It was no more than he deserved.

He had also signed a second lease, on a small house in Chelsea; he was tired of living at home under Sir James's hyper-critical nose, and as his father said, it would come in handy when he got married.

'Time you got on with that now,' Sir James had said more than once. He was learning to crush the panic, to smile and say yes of course, but surely he had enough challenges for a year or two now, building up his practice, gaining experience. 'That's all well and good,' Sir James had said, 'but all the best girls will be taken the rate you're going. You mark my words, you could be sorry.'

Ned said he would do his best.

His house was a pretty little Victorian cottage, just off the King's Road, with two bedrooms and a tiny back garden. He moved in with no furniture, apart from a rather fine bed from Heal's which had been his mother's. His father was delighted to see the back of it. It was rather large for the room, but he had always loved the bed, used to lie on it with his mother when he was a small boy, while she read him stories and sang nursery rhymes to him. After she ran away with the artist, his father had threatened to burn it for firewood, but it had remained in the big house in Knightsbridge, a source of happy memories for Ned throughout his childhood. When he came home from prep school for the holidays, wretched, hardly able to believe now the unimaginably happy time when his mother had lived in the house, he would creep in and lie on the bed, summoning her back by sheer force of memory – her perfume, her smile, her lilting voice.

He was forbidden to go in there by his father; but one night, creeping from his room along the corridor to hers, gently pushing open the door, he saw his father standing with his back to him, looking down at the bed. It was the first time he realised that his mother's departure from their lives had hurt his father as much as it had hurt him.

He had seen very little of his mother over the years; just the occasional letter or even surprise visit to school, always with a time limit, a train to catch, someone to meet, perhaps once or twice a year; usually Christmas presents, always birthday presents, but by post. That she did not try to see him more hurt him horribly. It wasn't until he was much older that he had understood that she was kept from him by law until his eighteenth birthday, when she had returned to his life, sought him out at his rooms at Oxford, bearing ridiculously extravagant gifts, all brought from Paris – a long silk scarf from Hermès, an exquisite leather attaché case from Galeries Lafayette, and an amazing panama hat with a wide floppy brim which she had found in the flea market one Sunday morning and having found it, she said, could only visualise Ned's face beneath it.

'Now come along,' she said. 'Time we became friends again, you and I.'

And half unwillingly, half intrigued, he had let her take him to lunch at the Randolph, very aware of the interest she caused, so chic and so beautiful still, with her cloud of dark hair and great brown eyes, so like his.

It took a while, but eventually she began to make inroads on his hostility and his hurt, explaining that Sir James had put upon her all manner of legal restraints, and threatened her and her lover with physical violence should she even try to see Ned. Many years later, she told him, her artist lover, insanely jealous of the beautiful little boy she wept over nightly and begged to be allowed to see, had threatened to leave her.

'And are you happy, my darling?' she said. 'Are you in love, is there some beautiful girl I should know about?'

He said there was not, but that he was very happy. She stared at him intently for a moment or two, then said, 'Or some other sort of beauty, perhaps? You can tell me. Of all people I will understand.'

He had blushed furiously, said he didn't know what she meant. 'Darling, of course you do.'

'Mother—'

'It's all right. I won't breathe a word, of course.'

'Well, you won't,' he said, suddenly angry at this entirely unwarranted invasion into his most private life. 'Because there is nothing to breathe a word about. Please, can we stop this at once? Or I shall have to leave and that would be a pity.'

'It would. But if *ever* you do need to talk to me about anything, anything at all, then please remember my view of life is not quite the same as most of the people you are surrounded by. All right? Oh, you look so handsome in that scarf,' she added, winding it round his neck. 'Now, tell me, what sort of a doctor do you want to be? A surgeon, like your father?'

And he had explained that he might want to be a paediatrician. 'That's a doctor who looks after children.' And she had said how wonderful, and then, said that she and the artist – 'Michel as he is known in Paris, although of course he is as English as you or I, and really it's Michael' – were thinking of coming back 'quite soon' to England to live.

'This awful war business, so worrying, it's spoiling everything for everybody. Anyway, we're not prepared to risk our lives, and we think we'll go and live in Cornwall; there are lots of artists and artists' colonies there, and Michael will be very happy. He's too old to be called up, of course.'

'And will you be very happy?' Ned asked and she looked at him and said probably not, but she had little choice really. 'I can hardly leave him, I don't have any money. Anyway, we rub along together very well . . .'

That had been the last he had seen of her for many years. Impatient and even bitter at the new desertion, for he had hoped to see more of her after the birthday conversation as he thought of it (although it had contained subject matter that had frightened him considerably). Then one evening, there was a ring at his new Chelsea doorbell and there she stood – a little older, a little grey in her wild dark hair, her clothes neither fashionable nor unfashionable, but the usual riot of flowing layered multicoloured fabrics, her arms outstretched, and impossible to turn away. She had got the address, she explained, from the housekeeper at his father's home. 'Dear Mrs Ellis, she was always very fond of me . . .'

He asked her in, stiffly at first, but it didn't last – it couldn't against her enthusiasm, her exclamations of delight at the pretty house. 'And my bed! Oh, how lovely to see it again, Ned, and to know that you liked it so much. I would never allow your father into it,' she added, absent-mindedly pulling the counterpane straight. 'It was mine, my refuge, my queendom.'

It was his turn – after more than a dozen years as he pointed out – to take her to dinner; they went nowhere smart or famous but to one of the small restaurants on the King's Road that were becoming fashionable, and she told him that Michael had died. 'Quite suddenly, of a heart attack.'

'I'm sorry,' he said and she smiled her conspiratorial, enchanting smile and said, 'I don't think I am. He was just as much a bully in his way as your father. I only went off with him because he was an escape, and I only stayed with him because I had no alternative. He's left me quite a lot of money – they sold well, those chocolate-boxy pictures of his – so I shall be all right. I shan't come back to London. We have a pretty house in Cornwall, near Fowey, very nice, lots of friends, and I shall stay there.'

'Right,' said Ned, with a rather unfilial stab of relief, for the thought of Persephone becoming a part of his daily life was alarming. 'But what will you do?'

'Oh, darling, I have a little business of my own – I make cushions. You have no idea how much people want cushions; in fact, they want mine so much I have had to find people to help me make them. I enjoy it very much. Now, talking of being alone, how about you? Any girlfriends? Fiancées? Wives?'

'No.'

'Ned, you're in your thirties . . .'

'I know,' he said, 'but I simply haven't had time. I've done nothing but work ever since I came back from the war.'

'Ned, darling, there is always time for love.'

'Not for me there hasn't been.'

'And still nothing else, no one else?'

'No,' said Ned, angry suddenly. 'Mother, please. I don't want to have to leave you here, but—'

'All right, darling. I'm sorry. So, these poor sick children you look after – what are they suffering from?'

'Oh, so many things,' said Ned, feeling himself calmer as he talked. 'In the hospital we get the acute cases – convulsions, appendicitis, diphtheria, tuberculosis, and of course this dreadful thing, leukaemia, which is cancer of the blood. I have been doing some work on that, and I've discovered that in some cases, simply a fresh blood transfusion will bring them into a remission.'

But she was looking round the restaurant, smiling at people at other tables; and he gave up, resigned, wondering why he had thought for even a moment that she would really be interested in anything he had to say.

'Tell me,' she said. 'Was there a wild mutiny with the doctors when this new arrangement, the National Health Service, began?'

'There wasn't,' he said, adding, 'I'm surprised you even know about it.'

'Well, of course I do. I was once a doctor's wife, after all – it interested me. All the stories in the papers, this man Bevan, wildly attractive I thought, telling the doctors what to do, they can't have liked it.'

'Well, in the end they – we – didn't mind. Now, shall I walk you back to your hotel?'

'No need,' she said, but he did and then wandered home slowly, reflecting on her visit, on all her visits, so rare, so irritating and yet for all that, so special.

The launch of the National Health Service really had been something of an anticlimax: after all the headlines and the speeches and the BMA voting against it, it had been launched that summer and in the hospitals, at any rate, on that day, 5 July, you would have been hard-pressed to know anything important had happened at all. Doctors and nurses arrived, looked after their patients as they had always done, performed operations, ran clinics, delivered babies, and at the end of their day left again.

Ned couldn't remember anyone saying, 'Oh, my God, the Health Service has started'; nobody said we won't be doing it like that any more; nobody even said thank God for the Health Service. It just happened.

It affected the honoraries, like his father and him, hardly at all. In fact, privately, away from the headlines, where many of them thundered about not allowing the government to tell them what to do, they were arguably happier and certainly better off.

They had always given their services free to the hospitals, sometimes paid an honorarium, hence their title of honoraries – sometimes not, making their money from their private practices. Now they were paid by the NHS as well, per session – eleven in each week maximum – and beyond that could do as many or as few as they wished. It suited them very nicely. Even Ned's father could find little to complain about. The much-vaunted spectre of government busybodies standing in operating theatres and by patients' beds, telling the doctors what to do, had disappeared like so much hot air.

Now, Ned thought, he had everything he had ever wanted: work he loved and was absorbed by, a pleasant lifestyle, a good income. But he made a decision that night, as he walked home through the long summer evening, shaken by the conversation with his mother. It was, as his father and his friends, his colleagues and his superiors, all kept telling him, time he got married.

If Ludo Manners could raise a large and happy family, then maybe so could he; but it was a terrifying prospect. Could he do that – live a lie, pretend to everyone, even to himself – make such a marriage work? But the alternative, carrying on as he was . . . suspicions would arise, the occasional lapse was fraught with huge danger, and as a life, it was a terribly lonely one.

He sank into his big easy chair when he got home, poured himself what must have been a triple brandy, and tried to concentrate on his dilemma. As always his mind absolutely refused to focus on it.

'Well, wasn't that lovely?' Diana collapsed onto the sofa in her parents' drawing room, kicked off her high heels and took the glass of champagne her father had passed her. 'Thank you, Daddy. Funny how it can revive you, when you've already had too much.'

'It was a perfect day,' said Caroline. 'Darling Betsey! Daughters-in-law can be such hell, and here are we, sent this angel. Her parents are so nice too. Lovely house. I do like Berkshire – if I ever had to choose another county, that would be it.'

'God forbid,' said Sir Gerald, irritable with a growing hangover, picking an argument as he was inclined to do on such occasions, 'that we should even think about living somewhere else.'

'Oh, darling, I know. And I'm not. I just said I liked it.'

'Betsey's dress was wonderful, wasn't it?' said Diana, oddly exasperated by the comparison of two counties she would have killed to live in, banished as she was to the wretched wilds of Yorkshire.

'And darling, may I say again, yours is quite lovely,' said Caroline. 'You looked beautiful. Didn't she, Johnathan?' she added, as he came into the room. He looked distracted.

'Sorry?'

'I said Diana looked – looks – beautiful in that dress?'

'Oh, yes. Well, she always does. Now – darling – I don't know if you heard the phone just then?'

'No,' said Diana, a sense of alarm creeping over her. 'I didn't.'

'Well, it was Mother. She, well, I'm sorry, but I think I'm going to have to leave first thing tomorrow.'

'Oh, Johnathan, no!' Diana looked at him, unable to disguise her horror. 'I thought we were going to stay a few days.'

146

'We were. And of course you may, if you like. But Father's taken a turn for the worse. Mother fears a stroke – only a small one, but she's terribly worried.'

I bet she is, thought Diana, terribly worried that her darling son is away from her, possibly even having a nice time, with his wife and son, a few days' break he had certainly earned,

'Oh, Johnathan,' said Caroline, flashing a warning look at Diana. 'I'm so, so sorry. Of course you must get back. We can put you on an early train, and you and Jamie too, of course, Diana . . .'

'I – but I have a few arrangements for next week,' said Diana helplessly, seeing it all disappearing, her trips to London, lunching with friends, going to a matinee with Wendelien, leaving Jamie behind with his grandmother and his nanny, treats in prospect that had sustained her sanity for the past month or more. 'I . . .'

'Well, Diana, they hardly matter, surely?' said Caroline. 'Not if Vanessa needs you all back at Guildford Park.'

'Oh, she doesn't need all of us,' said Johnathan hastily. 'She did specifically say she didn't want to spoil Diana's plans.'

'Well, that's exceedingly generous of her,' said Caroline. 'Isn't it, Diana?'

'Exceedingly,' said Diana.

Next morning, Johnathan safely on the train to London and thence to Yorkshire, Diana most willingly accompanied her parents to church. As they drove away, they passed a tall, gaunt figure walking down the hill towards the churchyard.

'Oh, look,' said Diana, 'it's Tom Knelston, isn't it? He looks dreadful.'

'Oh, my goodness,' said Caroline. 'Diana, I completely forgot to tell you, how awful of me. Poor, poor man, the most dreadful thing, absolute tragedy.'

'What?' said Diana, craning her neck to look back at Tom, who she could now see was carrying a huge armful of wild flowers,

'His wife and baby both died.'

'Died? Both of them? How terrible. I wish I'd known, I'd have written . . .'

'I'm sure you would. I've been so distracted, this year, with the wedding and everything. I am sorry. Yes, it was just before last Christmas.'

'Last Christmas! Oh, Mummy, that's appalling, you should have told me! Why, how, whatever happened?'

'Some freak gynaecological thing, his mother told me. Everything seemed fine, she was three weeks away from having the baby, and . . .'

They had reached the Manor House by the time Caroline had relayed the tragedy; Diana jumped out of the car. 'I'm going back. I must speak to him, he must have thought none of us cared. Honestly, Mummy, I just can't believe you didn't tell me.'

'Well, darling, I'm sorry,' said Caroline, slightly irritably now. 'It's not as if he's a friend or anything. I didn't think you'd be so upset—'

'It doesn't matter that I'm upset. It's him, for God's sake. Anyway, I'm off to find him. Don't wait lunch if I'm not back. And tell Nanny to make sure Jamie has his cod liver oil. I think it got forgotten yesterday in all the excitement. Oh, here, take my hat, would you?'

'If I didn't know it was impossible,' said Caroline to her husband, looking after Diana as she strode down the drive, 'I'd say she felt something more for that boy than sympathy.'

'Oh, don't be so ridiculous,' said Sir Gerald. 'She hardly knows him. And he's the postman's son, for God's sake.'

Tom was just getting up from where he had been sitting by Laura and Hope's grave when he heard Diana's voice. He tried to visit them most Sundays; being so near to her was comforting. He would sit actually on the grave, his hand resting on the headstone, the lovely headstone, so simple, no angels or flowers or crosses, just the words that he had spent so many hours and so much heartache getting exactly to his satisfaction. *Laura Knelston*, it said, *beloved of Tom Knelston. And Hope, their daughter, beloved of them both, and with Laura for ever.*

People had queried the wording, had said endlessly, surely he meant to say 'beloved wife of Tom Knelston' but he said, no, the fact that she had been his wife was of no real importance, what mattered was that she had been his beloved; had filled his life with happiness, with tenderness, with joy. It was important that people should know about Hope too, that she, although no one had known her, except him for the briefest while, was a part of him, and of Laura, and even while taking her mother away from him, she was important; she had made them a family, however briefly and sadly. For a while, she had been so very much alive; she had lain in their bed at night, a small important presence, albeit unborn, moving, kicking, making them laugh, a promise of their future, of the family they would shortly be. He would never forget, ever, he knew, the hour he had spent with her, holding her, looking at her small, peaceful face, her perfect, beautiful self; he would never know more of her than that, but he did have it, the memory of that presence, that beauty, and it was a great deal more than nothing, lying beneath the earth in her mother's arms.

He would talk to Laura, telling her everything he had been doing, how much he missed her, who he had seen, what they had said, that without her he was only half himself. He tried, tried so hard, to live on as she would have wished. He could imagine her impatient disdain if he spent all his days grieving, spreading sorrow: 'For goodness' sake,' she would say, 'is this all you can manage for me? I'm really not very impressed, Tom.'

What he tried to manage for her was something quite different, requiring a courage he could not have summoned without her, without having lived with her and loved her and known her: the courage to smile, to talk to people, to care about all that they had shared together, the ideas, the ideals, the plans, the future, to show that she had not lived in vain. That was her legacy, through him; and he refused to squander it through grief.

He told her if he had enjoyed something, if someone had made him laugh, would give her the most minute details of political meetings, anything ridiculous, or pompous, of any new members, especially ones he thought she would like. He told her about days in the office, about how hard Betty tried to cheer him up, about how continuingly upset Mr Pemberton was.

'Sometimes I quite dread it,' he had said, only that morning. 'He is so sympathetic, but I could do with a bit less of hearing about how lonely I must be, and how sad.'

Mr Pemberton had even taken to suggesting they went to the pub together for a drink after work on Fridays. 'I can't refuse, of course, but we sit there, not talking much, and always, when he thinks it's time to go, he says, "Well, Tom, what would we do without each other these days."'

He had had some special news for her that day; that he was about to be admitted as a solicitor, fully qualified, an incredible achievement, the result of so much work, so much determination. It hurt to tell her, thinking how proud she would be, how joyful, how full of admiration; but at the same time, knowing those things gave him a kind of pleasure. And at the same time, pain; and even as he thought he must be getting back, leave her for now, as he kissed his fingers and ran them over her name, the letters were blurred with tears. He stood up, then, forcing a smile. 'Sorry,' he said. 'Sorry, Laura. Sorry.'

And then he heard his name called; and a few yards away from him he saw Diana standing there.

'Oh,' he said. 'Oh, hello.' And stood, not sure what to do or say further; but in a moment of extraordinary and unexpected gentleness, she stepped forward and reached up and kissed his cheek and said, 'I'm so sorry, Tom. So very sorry. I didn't know, or I would have come to find you before.'

He was astonished by it; by the gentleness, and even more by her courage in coming to him. So many people avoided him, pretended they hadn't seen him; he had even known them cross the street as he approached rather than confront his grief. It was a mystery to him, this behaviour. What could they fear should they approach him and say how sorry they were? That he would break down, or even turn away from them himself? Was his pain really of so little importance to them, less than their own embarrassment, that they were not prepared to risk it, to risk some kindness, some concern?

But he had grown used to it; and had anyone asked him how Diana Southcott might behave, he would have expected her to be the worst of them, of the avoiders. Proffer him the cold shoulder rather than the sweet kiss, the gentle words, the obvious sorrow on his behalf.

She drew back, then said, 'I'm sorry, you probably want to be alone. Or with Laura. Is that her grave?'

He nodded.

'May I – may I see?'

'Of course,' he said, and she stood there quietly, reading and rereading the words, and then turned to him, and said, 'How lovely, and how lovely that they are together.'

'Yes,' he said. 'Yes, well, I wanted that. It was important.'

'So important. Oh, Tom. How unhappy you must be.'

'Well – I am,' he said, and then, 'but I try not to be. She wouldn't have wanted that.'

'You're very brave. I never met her, I wish I had. She must have been a very special person.'

'She was.'

There was a silence. Then she said, clearly feeling there was nothing more that she could usefully say, 'Well, I must be getting back. But I'm so glad I found you today. And so very sorry I didn't manage it before.'

'Oh, no,' he said. 'It's lovely that you came today. Thank you.' And then astonishing himself, 'May I walk you back to the house?'

'Of course. I'd like that.'

And they talked on the way of a few important and a few unimportant things; she was clearly afraid to talk about Jamie, but he asked about him. 'I met him when he was very young, remember?'

'Yes, of course I do. Well, he's a real boy now – and his lovely blonde baby hair is now quite, quite dark.'

'And – do you like it any better, up there in Yorkshire?' he asked and she stared at him and laughed and said, 'I'd forgotten I'd told you that. No, I still hate it.'

'Why?'

'Oh – so many things. It's cold, it's bleak, even in the summer it's bleak. The people are odd. I don't have any friends, not that I would call friends. I miss London, I miss my family. Goodness me, I must stop. It's not all bad.'

'Isn't it?' he said and his green eyes boring into hers were genuinely interested.

'Mostly,' she said, 'I'm afraid it is, but you are not to tell anyone I said so. Ever.'

'Of course. And your husband, does he like it up there?'

'Oh, he loves it. Absolutely loves it. But then he comes from there – it's different if you do. It's another country.'

'Of course. I sometimes think,' he added, amazed that he should confide in her, 'that I would do well to move away, to live somewhere quite different.'

'Really? To do what?'

'Well, I have become very interested in politics. It's the only thing I can imagine taking – or partly taking – Laura's place in my life. Giving me something to care about again.'

'I can understand that,' she said. 'You mean you'd like to be an MP?'

'Yes. Ultimately. Meanwhile to work for the party in some way. The Labour Party,' he added, with a smile.

'Yes, well, I didn't see you as a true blue Tory,' she said, smiling back. 'It would be wonderful for you, I can see that. And Laura would have liked it,' she added, astonishing him with her perception.

'Indeed. And of course, it would be better than another woman,' he said and she actually laughed and he laughed too. They had arrived at the Manor House. 'It's been lovely talking to you, Tom. I'm so glad I was here today. I'd ask you in,' she said, after a pause, 'but you wouldn't like it, would you?'

'Not really,' he said. 'And nor would they. Although I'd like to meet your husband.'

'He's gone back to Yorkshire, his father's not well. We were only here for Michael's wedding – my brother, you know . . .'

'Yes, of course I know. I like your brother. He was always very friendly to me at village cricket matches. I suppose he's an important doctor now?'

'Very important. A surgeon. Oh, now there's Mummy watching us out of the window, wondering what on earth's going on. I'd better go in. Take care of yourself, Tom. Goodbye.' And she reached up and kissed him again on the cheek and then turned and walked up the drive towards the house.

\* \* \*

'Diana,' said her mother as she walked in the door. 'Diana, you really can't stand about in broad daylight kissing people like Tom Knelston.'

'Oh, really, can I not?' said Diana, and there was real anger in her eyes as she looked at her mother. 'You wouldn't have minded if it was one of Michael's friends, would you? Ian Bellinger, for instance, or Ned Welles. I'd like to know the difference. Only of course I do.'

'Diana—'

'Now, have I missed lunch? Shall I go and eat it in the kitchen, with Cook, or up in the nursery with Jamie? That would be better, wouldn't it, more acceptable.'

'We haven't had lunch,' said Caroline. 'You can eat it in the dining room with us. Nanny has taken Jamie for a walk.'

'She seems to have taken leave of her senses,' Caroline said later to Sir Gerald, watching Diana playing with Jamie in the garden. 'I do hope her situation in Yorkshire isn't making her so unhappy she'll do something silly.'

'Of course it won't,' said Sir Gerald. 'That pretty head is screwed on quite firmly. She knows what she's got up there, even if she doesn't like it very much. Sherry, darling? Or rather another sherry. We seem to have been drinking it for hours, waiting for her.'

'Do you know I think I might?' said Caroline.

# Chapter 16

## 1950

The conference was dreadful. He had missed the previous year's, unable to face it, but Laura haunted this one still, a shining-eyed, excited ghost, her baby sticking out through her navy coat, filled with the wonder that they were actually there. At least it wasn't in Blackpool this time. Every day hurt more than the day before.

And yet he knew he must go. It was what he most cared about now, the party and his politics, and the new future he wanted. As always his hero, Aneurin 'Nye' Bevan, did not fail him. For Bevan, it was a good conference. He had had a bad two years; first there was the infamous speech when he had proclaimed the Conservatives to be 'lower than vermin' and unleashed a row of gargantuan proportions, causing himself and his party immeasurable harm. Then another row over a demand for an extra £52 million for the National Health Service, and the consequent accusations of improvidence. He still managed to emerge as the author of a new, glorious socialism for the years ahead.

Listening to his speech, Tom felt his heart lift; that alone would have justified his decision to come. But he was rewarded for it personally too, for his courage. It led him into his new future, in a way he could never have expected.

'Tom Knelston, isn't it?' A booming voice spoke out of the din, as he waited to go into a session. Looking round, he saw the huge figure of Donald Herbert bearing down on him. Donald Herbert was one of the big names around the party, a power behind the throne. He ran a hugely successful delivery business: dozens of lorries and vans bearing his name wove their way round the country every day. His employment of hundreds of drivers and his reputation as a generous and infinitely fair boss made him both popular and influential within the TGWU. He had stood for a couple of seats, but failed, rather more spectacularly than his large ego could endure. Now he contented himself with having a large circle of political friends – many of them hugely influential and rich, like Lord Stansgate and Lord Longford and, perhaps even more importantly, prominent journalists – giving large dinners for political friends and acquaintances, drinking in the bars at the House of Commons and eating in its restaurants, and generally having access to many of the heavyweights in the party. He was a favourite with the press, being a colourful character, and was known to have dined with Cudlipp several times.

This afternoon, he was certainly living up to his sartorial reputation, the suit a brown and beige houndstooth check, and the bow tie a brilliant yellow. Tom stood up, stammering his greeting.

'I came to your meeting when you spoke last year, no, it was the year before that. Bloody good, I thought. Meant to congratulate you at the time, but had a drinking engagement. How's that pretty wife of yours? In the family way, I seem to recall.'

'I'm afraid she died,' said Tom who had learned that raw, painful statements were infinitely preferable to stumbling euphemisms, in terms of getting such moments over.

'Oh, my God, how awful.' Herbert spoke with the unmistakable accent of the public-school boy; Tom was always amazed to meet the few who had crossed the playground (as he had heard it expressed), to become socialists and prominent ones at that. 'I'm so sorry. Christ, how ghastly. I feel dreadful now. Look, let me buy you a drink. I wanted to make contact with you anyway. This session's going to be pretty dull, you know, won't hurt either of us to miss it. Let's go and find a bar.'

Tom, shocked that anyone should choose to miss a session, but flattered beyond anything that Donald Herbert should want to speak to him, nodded and followed him obediently to the nearest bar.

'What's your poison then, young Tom?'

Tom longed to ask for a whisky but was fearful that he might have to buy Herbert a drink in return. 'A pint of bitter would be very nice, sir.'

'Might join you in that. No need for the sir stuff. As I said, I thought your speech was bloody good. You have a flair for it. Can't be learned, that sort of thing. What did you do in the war?'

'I was out in the desert with the sappers,' said Tom. 'With Monty.'

'Were you, by Jove. So was my brother. Said it was pretty bloody tough!'

'It was. Wouldn't have missed it, though. And you?'

'Air force. One of the lucky few who didn't get shot down. What's your job out on Civvy Street?'

'I'm a solicitor.' He was still mildly amazed he could say that.

'Interesting. So is my brother. You two seem to have quite a lot in common. He's a bit older than you, of course. He's got a practice in Islington. You?'

'Oh, I work for a firm in Hilchester,' said Tom. 'Near Southampton,' he added. 'I've been very lucky. The senior partner's helped me enormously. I'd never have made it without him.'

'Oh, you probably would. You should be a barrister, with a gift for speaking like yours.'

'I don't think so,' said Tom, smiling at him. 'I've got the opposite of a private income for a start.'

'What's your background then?'

'My dad was a village postman,' said Tom. 'I went to the grammar school.'

'Did you? And now you're a solicitor. Bloody well done. And what a good example for the rank and file. Marvellous story for the press. I must ponder on that one. Want another one of those?'

'Oh – oh, let me,' said Tom.

'Don't be so bloody silly. I might switch to Scotch. Fancy one?'

And Tom found himself looking at a double.

'Right. So do you have political ambitions, Tom?'

'Oh, I most certainly do. It's all I want now.'

'Is it indeed? Well, with your background, or rather what it says about you, and your gift for speaking, not impossible. But you won't get far sitting in a country solicitor's office in a cosy town near the south coast. You want to meet a few relevant people. Christ, I must go. It's been good to meet you, Tom. I'm sorry about your wife. And remember what I said, get up nearer the action.'

As if it was that easy, Tom thought, looking after Donald Herbert's huge figure as he lumbered out of the bar. He was sure he'd never hear from him again.

He was wrong.

This was when he missed Laura so much. When she wasn't there to tell things to. Or advise him. Or be pleased for him. Or all three.

'I've had this letter,' he'd have said, still staring at it in disbelief. 'From a solicitor in London, Donald Herbert's brother. He's asked me to go and see him, says he could have a job for me.'

And of course she'd have said go. But then what would she have said?

'He's offered me a job, in his practice in Islington,' he'd have said. 'He does a lot of work for the Labour Party. Pro bono. Really a lot of it.'

'Well, you must take it of course,' she'd have said. 'It sounds a wonderful opportunity to me.'

'But how can I leave Mr Pemberton? It would break his heart.'

'Tom,' she'd have said. 'You either break Mr Pemberton's heart and get nearer the future you want, or you stay with him and keep him happy, and forget all about everything else.'

Alice was in love. Inevitably with a doctor. A house surgeon, to be precise, newly qualified, idealistic, fiercely ambitious. He worked tirelessly round the clock, with not a single free weekend, stumbling sleepily from one of the small rooms allocated to him and his colleagues in the hospital whenever required, to perform an incredible range of operations. His name was Philip Jordan, and he was tall and very skinny, with rather untidy brown hair and very bony wrists. The other nurses teased her about her claims that he was good-looking. She supposed, if she was honest with herself 'pleasant' would have been more accurate. He had blue eyes and a wide, if slightly lopsided, smile, and as she said to Jillie when she was describing him, anyone who looked good in scrubs was hardly ugly. He was, as he stressed to her on their first date, 'a pretty junior member of the firm' which consisted of the consultant surgeon, the assistant surgeon, the registrar and him.

'But my God, am I learning a lot, and fast! During the past four months, I've done twenty-six appendectomies, nine varicose vein operations, three haemorrhoidectomies and an umbilical hernia repair. Oh, and two above-the-knee amputations.'

As chat-up lines went, it wasn't exactly polished but Alice sat entranced.

She had enjoyed midwifery throughout her time at St Thomas', and one of her proudest moments was when, after assisting at a difficult birth, she was accorded the honour of having the baby named after her.

'But I didn't do much,' she said, settling the mother finally back into bed, handing her the baby to nurse.

'Yes, you did,' the girl said, smiling wearily at her. 'You made me feel I might just survive.'

Above all, Alice loved the drama of the operating theatre. She was entirely unfazed by the gore, or the surgeons barking out orders, the more temperamental ones literally hurling instruments across the room if they were not what they'd asked for. The surgeons were the most arrogant and the most revered among the honoraries, holding as they did literally life or death in their hands. But Alice also never failed to marvel that even they had to defer to Sister on their ward rounds.

Alice and Philip became a couple of sorts. They enjoyed the same things: going to the cinema, walking across Hampstead Heath, listening to traditional jazz on the gramophone, and dancing to it occasionally at Humphrey Lyttelton's club at 100 Oxford Street. Such outings were rare; mostly they were confined to snatched hours in the hospital, long conversations over meals in the canteen, much of it about his work – rarely hers – and rather intense occasional snogging sessions in the junior doctors' rooms. Alice didn't mind. She was completely in love and very, very happy.

She was in her third year now, and a qualification as a state registered nurse was in sight; but she had decided to do a fourth and get her Nightingale badge, prized and recognised everywhere in the world.

Alice loved nursing as much as she had instinctively known she would. She loved its order, its sense of purpose; she saw it as charting a course across difficult terrain, taking intense pleasure as her patients recovered, while slowly learning to remain philosophical when they did not. The first few deaths had upset her, of course, but the probationers were well prepared for them; although the death of a baby or a child shook her dreadfully. The very first one, a baby, born dead with the cord round its neck, was completely incredible as well as shocking, so great was Alice's faith in her profession and its powers. She fled to the sluice and stood leaning on the sink, sobbing and shaking, not merely at the death but the mother's grief. It was Sister who found her, and was oddly gentle with her, explaining that acceptance of their limitations to prevent such things was important, and should only serve to reinforce a pride in what they could do. Alice took that philosophy with her for the rest of her working life. The comradeship of the other nurses was also a huge help; people who had gone through it too, experienced the pain, the grief. She learned from Philip that the banter, as he called it, the cheerful comradeship of the other doctors, the acceptance of death as a fact of life, was essential.

She was frustrated, of course, by what could not be done. There was no known treatment for so many things, the worst it seemed to her being heart disease and of course, childhood leukaemia and the worst excesses of polio. They were at the most famous and respected hospital in the country, or so they had been told, and knew that no one, and no other hospital, could do more. That gave her confidence too.

As a less serious by-product they knew of course that they were, as Nightingales, the most socially superior. Indeed, the junior doctors and students had a saying: 'Barts for tarts, Guy's for flirts, Thomas' for young ladies.' It might not have been relevant to their nursing skills, but it was something to enjoy. Besides, behind her wide blue eyes, her apparent unremitting sweetness, there was a steeliness to Alice; her seniors recognised it, and appreciated that it was very much part of her armoury in becoming not just a good nurse but an excellent one.

So, successful and happy in her work as she was, she was also, at the age of nearly twenty-two, still a virgin. Hardly a unique state of affairs; the spectre of pregnancy hovered over every unmarried liaison. She had never been remotely tempted to risk such a horror: had never loved or even fancied anyone enough. She had had boy-friends all her life, from the tennis club days onwards. It wasn't just her prettiness; she was sparkly and fun, and possessed of great energy. She had been very fond of some of the boys, had wished herself, and even at times fancied herself, in love. And she enjoyed what limited sexual experience she had had. But the fact remained that in her world, girls remained virgins until they were at the very least engaged, and for most of them, married.

Philip Jordan, however, had plans to change all that.

Wendelien Bellinger had a new friend, Blanche Ellis Brown, a fash-ion editor on *Style* magazine, a fashion glossy recently launched which its backers hoped would in the fullness of time rival *Vogue*. Blanche had been poached from *Vogue*, and was a rising star in the magazine firmament. Sharply chic herself and ferociously ambi-tious, she also had an eye for the new look in fashion and fashion photography, which she transferred with considerable style to her pages.

And there was very much a new look; largely due to the fact that a different breed of camera, small and portable such as those made by Rolleiflex and Leica, were replacing the cumbersome variety, which had confined fashion shots to the studios. Suddenly models were being photographed on beaches and boats, on the streets and at the wheels of cars. The great and inventive photographers, most notably the Americans Richard Avedon, Toni Frissell and Irving Penn, were creating the most exciting images.

Blanche was loving her new job, and the circulation of *Style* was climbing slowly but steadily northwards.

'But what I need now, above all,' she said to Wendelien as they lunched at the Connaught one day, 'are some new faces. There just aren't enough models. Good ones, that is. Many of them will only work for *Vogue* anyway – ridiculously loyal.'

'Can't you just offer them more money?' said Wendelien, who had a severely practical streak.

'Doesn't work. It's the cachet of *Vogue*, you see. Where one goes they all follow. They're like a flock of beautiful sheep: Fiona Campbell-Walter, Suzy Parker, Anne Gunning and Barbara Goalen. It's so hard to tempt them away. The Fords have just been over – Eileen Ford's agency is number one in America – and they've done a tie-up with Lucie Clayton here. I'm hoping that will bring a few new ones in.' She giggled. 'The Fords actually stayed here for a couple of days, and were asked to leave, as all the models heard they were here and were bombarding the switchboard. Didn't quite go with the Connaught image. You know it's the only hotel in London that takes guests on personal recommendations only. Anyway, they were asked to leave. So –' She suddenly sat back and looked intently at Wendelien across the table.

'Whatever are you doing?' said Wendelien, laughing.

'Just wondering if you'd do – you do wear clothes awfully well – but sorry, darling, no offence, but you've not got quite the bones.'

'Thanks.'

'But if you have any beautiful friends, ideally of an aristocratic persuasion, steer them in my direction, would you?'

'Funny you should say that,' said Wendelien.


'Welcome home, darling,' Wendelien said to Diana over the lunchtime menu at the Ritz a week later. 'You look marvellous. How did you escape this time?'

'It's Mummy's birthday. She's having a little party at the weekend. Not big enough to warrant Johnathan coming down, but I made it an excuse. I really don't think he minds much if I'm there or not, he's so busy.'

'How is life generally up there? Any better?'

'Worse,' said Diana flatly. 'My only comfort is Jamie, who is adorable. I thought he was the beginning of a new marriage for us both but I'm afraid the farm is more important to Johnathan even than Jamie. I've brought him and Nanny down with me – Mummy loves to spend time with him. She complains endlessly about him being her only grandchild, but of course Betsey's pregnant now, so she'll have a bit more to do.'

'But you're not preggers?' asked Wendelien, her voice carefully casual.

'No, not yet. Thank goodness. How about you?'

'Oh, well, Ian is getting quite keen and actually I wouldn't mind one myself now – all one's chums are at it – so watch this space.'

She patted her flat stomach gently.

'You're so lucky,' wailed Diana. 'You all have each other – it's so lonely having a baby up in Yorkshire.'

'You must have found one friend, surely?'

'Not really. They all hate me. No matter how hard I try with the wretched WI and everything.'

'Well,' said Wendelien, 'I've got a little idea for you. A little idea that might make your life seem a bit brighter. How long are you here for?'

'About four days.'

'That should be long enough.'

'For what?'

Wendelien told her.

'Wendelien, I couldn't. Even if they thought I was good enough, and had the bones –'

'Which you do.'

'How could I, when I live all the way up there? They're not going to bring their cameras and clothes up to Yorkshire, are they?'

'But that's the whole point, it's not a full-time job. No one's going to ask you to come and live down here permanently. It'd just be an occasional break for you.'

Diana looked wistfully into her cocktail. 'Well, it sounds wonderful. I don't want you to think I'm not thrilled and flattered. I am. But Johnathan wouldn't like it.'

'It wouldn't be very often. And the wicked witch would love it, give her something else to hate you for.'

'Now that is true!' said Diana, laughing. 'Oh, Wendelien. How – how amazing it would be.'

'So, will you at least meet my friend Blanche?'

'I'd love to. That'll solve everything straight away, as she'll just say I haven't got any bones. How is it going to work, are you going to march me into her office?'

'By a happy chance, she's going into Hardy Amies this afternoon, and I thought you'd like to have a look at the suits.'

'Wendelien, I'm really not in the couture league any more,' said Diana. 'My allowance from Johnathan is quite modest.'

'Diana,' said Wendelien patiently. 'Blanche doesn't need to know that. We'll go to Amies and look at the suits.'

'But . . .'

'But nothing. Stop fussing and order your lunch. Only don't eat too much, your stomach might stick out.'

'No, all right,' said Diana humbly.

And thus it was that much later that afternoon, Diana found herself in the studio of one Kirill (christened Cyril) Bell, being posed and unposed, and given what seemed to her ridiculously extravagant positions to strike, and then told to act naturally – as if such a thing were possible – having what they called test shots done, which Kirill promised to Blanche by first thing next day.

And first thing next day, Blanche rang Diana and said her pictures were 'absolutely divine. I'm amazed, the camera really likes you, so rare,' and she had exactly the look she wanted for a feature on tweed suits for the October issue.

Diana said she was very flattered and pleased, but she'd have to talk it over with her husband, as she lived in Yorkshire, and had a small child. It would all mean quite careful planning, and when was Blanche thinking of for the session?

The next day, Blanche said, and she'd need Diana to come up that afternoon to try on some of the clothes. 'Maybe get your hair cut and styled. It's a bit long.'

'Tomorrow!' said Diana. 'I thought you said the October issue.'

'It takes three months to get an issue together,' Blanche said patiently. 'Here we are, mid-July, bit late already. It's not a problem, is it?'

Diana's sense of yearning for this wonderful new world was tempered by panic. 'I really do need to talk to my husband. He might not like the idea.'

Blanche's voice grew slightly impatient. 'I hope he does – we've wasted a lot of time and effort otherwise. When can you get back to me? Shall I make an appointment for your hair this afternoon anyway? Oh, and we can't do the pictures in town obviously – the photographer wants some woods, and the art director's found what will pass for some on Hampstead Heath. It's a very early start. We can meet here, about seven. What's your shoe size? I'll get you those. Normally models bring a selection of their own, but obviously you can't do that at this sort of notice.'

'I'm staying with my parents in Hampshire,' said Diana, rather helplessly. 'So I don't think—'

'Well, perhaps you could stay with Wendelien,' said Blanche, her impatience clearly increasing by the moment. 'Look, I've got to go. Can you sort all this out and let me have an answer by twelve? I need to know if I can rely on you or not. There is a lot hanging on this feature.'

Getting hold of Johnathan was clearly an impossibility. In the summer he was out on the farm until darkness. So it was her mother she had to win round. Diana put the phone down and went to find her.

Caroline was rather excited by the whole thing. Diana carefully presented it as a one-off, and said she would of course ask Johnathan the minute she could get hold of him.

'I should think he'd be rather proud. It's not as if you're going to be away longer than you said or anything. My goodness, how thrilling. And Jamie will be fine here with us. So yes, of course you must go and get your hair done! Ring this woman back, and don't worry about anything.'

It was only when Diana heard her mother boasting on the phone to one of her friends when she went home to collect Jamie, that she realised that, for rather suspect reasons, her mother could become a great ally in this great new adventure she seemed to have tumbled into.

# Chapter 17

## 1950

*Biggles*? *Just William*? *The Boy's Own Annual*? Whatever did boys of nine like to read? If anything. And what about boys of six? Here she was, thinking Foyles would solve all her present problems. This was her last chance to shop before Christmas.

Jillie sighed, heard a similarly heavy one to her left and realised that a man was studying the girls' line-up equally distractedly. She gave him a sympathetic smile and then realised he was rather familiar.

'Oh! Hello! It's Mr Knelston – Tom – isn't it? What a nice surprise. You look as desperate as I am.'

'Oh, yes, hello,' he said and as she advanced towards him holding out her hand, he promptly dropped an armful of books on the floor.

She bent down, retrieved a couple and then said, 'I'm Jillie – Jillie Curtis, from . . .' She faltered, afraid she had stumbled into territory too painful for Tom to contemplate. 'From the Elizabeth Garrett Anderson – we met last year.'

She waited for him to turn and walk away, but he did neither; he smiled his wide, oddly generous smile and said, 'Yes, of course, I remember you. How are you, Miss Curtis? Thank you,' he added, taking the books from her.

'Jillie, please. I'm very well, thank you. Although I'd feel better if I knew what little boys liked to read. Do you know? Age nine and six. *Just William*, would they like that?'

She realised she was gabbling, just to fill the awkwardness, but he smiled again and said, 'Oh definitely. And perhaps that boys' album –'

'What about *Biggles*?'

'Bit grown up. And for the six-year-old, well, how about *Thomas the Tank Engine*?'

'Oh, lovely! Of course. I'd never have thought of that, thank you.'

'Pleasure. Maybe you could help me. With two girls, aged eight and nine.'

It must be so hard for him, Jillie thought.

'Oh, at that age I loved *What Katy Did*. And *Anne of Green Gables*. And *A Little Princess*. They're all ideal.'

'Look, they're all here, in the same section. Thank you very much. Well, that's me settled. Are you done?'

'I am. Now, I warn you, they have the most complicated system for actually buying a book here, but there's no help for it.'

'I'll follow your lead then,' he said. After they had stood in at least two more separate queues, they emerged into the Tottenham Court Road and, after a rather long hesitation, Tom said, 'If you've got time, can I buy you a cup of tea, to say thank you?' They went off to the rather grand Lyons Corner House on the corner of Oxford Street.

'So what are you doing up here?' Jillie asked after they had ordered tea and toasted teacakes. 'It's a long way from Southampton?'

'I've moved up to London. I'm working for a solicitor in Islington and we do lots of legal aid work. Do you know about legal aid? People who can't afford solicitors can get financial help from the government. It's very different from my last job.'

'In what way?'

'Well, that was all about farm and small estate sales, lot of probate work, conveyancing of course, all very –' He hesitated. 'Respectable? Yes,' Tom said and grinned. 'It was dreadful leaving my boss, of course. He's been so good to me, saw me as a sort of second son. But I knew Laura would have told me to move on and start again. So I moved to Herbert & Herbert. Sometimes the clients are anything but polite, but then they're desperate, being evicted from their homes without reason, domestic violence even. It's – well, it's a lot more interesting and much more – lively. I do enjoy it.'

'Good. I'm so pleased.'

'And then I also do quite a bit of work for the Labour Party.'

'Legal work?'

'No. Dogsbody work. Pounding pavements. Delivering leaflets. Putting stuff in envelopes. Speaking at meetings, sometimes. We're gearing up for the next election.'

'Oh, yes,' said Jillie. 'My parents have been talking about it quite a lot. They're great socialists. Or think they are.'

'Really?' he said, not knowing quite how to react. 'Anyway, Islington North is pretty solid Labour. I think we'll get in again.' He stopped talking, took a bite out of his teacake, then looked at her awkwardly. 'Sorry, probably the last thing you want to talk about.'

'No, actually my cousin, who's a political journalist, was talking about it the other night when he came to supper.'

'What paper is he on?'

'The *Daily News*.'

Tom was momentarily stunned into silence by this piece of information; the *Daily News* was a paper of huge importance.

'Which party does he think is going to get in?' he asked.

'The Tories. Sorry, Tom. So where do you live – have you got a house or what?'

'I've got a flat. In Islington, just off the Angel. Part of a house, very small. Property's much more expensive than it is in Hampshire. I live alone. So – what about you? Are you an important doctor now?'

'Absolutely not. Long way to go, about two more years till I take my finals. I'll probably fail,' she added. 'I'm pretty hopeless. But I have to keep trying.'

'I'm sure you won't fail. So where do you live?'

'Oh, with my parents. Who live rather conveniently in Highbury. I told you, my parents are socialists.' She grinned at him. 'Not that you'd recognise them as such. So are most of their friends. To be quite honest, it makes me cross. They live in huge houses. Give lots of dinner parties. Employ domestic staff, make endless excuses for sending their children to expensive schools, say they'd be much happier if they were at local schools, but the education just isn't as good and why should their children and their chances in life be sacrificed because of their principles? Anyway, I must go. I have to buy lots of cheese and olives and stuff like that. My parents are having a party on Saturday. They said I could invite a few friends of my own, so I said I'd get some of the food.' She looked at him. 'You – you wouldn't like to come, would you? You'd be very welcome.'

'It's very kind of you, but I don't really like parties. Laura loved them,' he added. 'She made me go to them with her. But I hated them, even then.'

'Well – if you change your mind . . . Anyway, I expect you're busy, Saturday before Christmas.'

'Not really. Although the local Labour Party are having a sort of party that night. I shall have to go to that.'

'Why? I mean, why do you have to?'

'Because,' he said, very seriously, 'it would look bad if I didn't. You have to do these things if you want to make your way in politics. It's what I've got now. Instead of Laura. It's not enough, of course. But it helps.'

'Well, that's good,' said Jillie, thinking that if anyone ever considered taking Laura's place in Tom Knelston's life she would have a very hard time of it. 'Look, if you change your mind about the party – here's the address.' She scribbled it down on one of the paper napkins.

Walking back to his flat, Tom thought about Jillie.

He realised she was the first girl he had noticed as a girl, since – well, since. He decided she was attractive, with her gleaming straight brown hair, her rather dark green eyes, and her curvy smiley mouth with one tiny dimple tucked underneath it. Large dimples reminded him too much of Laura's, but this small one was all right. She was tall, and very slim, again suitably different from Laura, and he liked her voice, which was slightly husky and low-pitched.

Alice lay on the small bumpy bed, curled into a ball of misery, pulling the blanket over her head, and started to cry. That Philip, who she loved so much and had thought loved her, could do this awful thing, deliver this cruel ultimatum. Oh, she had heard of men doing it before, of course, but if anyone had told her Philip would . . . !

'Alice,' he'd said. 'I am very fond of you and I love being with you. But you're saying you won't have sex with me unless I tell you I want to marry you. Is that what you're saying?'

She had nodded, terrified at what he might say next.

'Well,' he said, turning away from her, onto his back, 'we might have a bit of a problem. Why, for God's sake? I thought you said you loved me?'

If only she hadn't; if only she hadn't let it slip out as she stopped kissing him just for a moment, loving not just him, but the way he kissed her, pushing her into so many sensations, new, overwhelming, enjoying the feel of his hands on her, longing for more, knowing she mustn't. It had made it all so much worse.

'I do,' she said. 'I do love you.'

'Well then, why not?'

'Because – because it's wrong. Having sex before you're married is wrong. It ought to be – well, special.'

'Alice, if we have sex it will be very special indeed.'

'That's not what I mean. I mean, it would cheapen it. It wouldn't be important enough. I'm a virgin, Philip, you know I am. I'm scared.'

'Oh, Christ.' He sat up, looked down at her. 'You're scared of getting pregnant. Is that it? Because I swear you won't. I've got some rubber johnnies, of course I have. You don't have to worry, Alice. I'll take care of you, I won't let that happen. So if that's all it is – come on, Alice, trust me –' He lay back down again, started playing with her breasts. Somehow she pushed his hand away.

'Philip, no. I'm sorry. I can't. That's not all I'm scared about. I'm scared that it doesn't mean as much to you, and I don't think it does. I thought – I thought you loved me.'

'I'm very fond of you, Alice. I've gone out with you longer than I've ever gone out with anyone before. What more do you want? You're not suggesting I should ask you to marry me, are you? Alice, really!' He sounded almost amused. 'Even if I thought I might want to marry you, how could I know? How could you know, for that matter? Look, we're only doing something very natural. It's not wrong. It's no more wrong than the rest of what we've been doing this afternoon.'

She was silent. He sighed and sat up again.

'You're absurdly young for your age, you know that? You're a child. I hadn't realised. Well, I'm sorry, Alice, but there is no way I'm going to lie to you and say I want to marry you just to get into your knickers. At least I'm honest. You'll have to find someone else, someone more high-minded, to share all your ridiculous hang-ups. So – very sadly, Alice, I think we should go our separate ways. I'm on duty in an hour anyway. I'll go and get a meal and you should get back to the nurses' home and – well, have a good look at yourself. The world's changing, Alice. It's not the same as when your mother was a girl.'

He leaned over and kissed her, then stood up, started pulling on his clothes. She lay, watching him, somehow managing not to cry.

The party was quite dreadful. If Tom hadn't experienced many similar ones over the years, he would have been shocked. The hall had been decorated with balloons and paper chains and a rather sparse Christmas tree, listing dangerously to the left. There were a few bottles of red wine, some beer, and a lot of almost empty plastic cups. Everyone was very drunk. Tom had several times already been dragged onto the dance floor by a series of girls, each more drunk than the last, and tried to follow their increasingly random steps.

He had arrived late, at eight o'clock, and was already, at nine, wondering how soon he could escape. He stood now, a refugee from the dance floor, nursing a plastic glass of warm bitter, smiling at everyone he knew, agreeing it was a very good party, and occasionally sharing in the relief of some more serious conversation about how the Labour Party would be fine and they'd get in again: no one was going to let the Tories undo all the good that had been done in the last five years.

Finally, at nine thirty, he decided he would slip away and was just making for the door when a young man barred his way, held out his hand and said, 'Jim Dunne, *Islington Gazette*. Can I talk to you? One of the men here said I should ask you for an interview.'

'I'm surprised you value his opinion,' said Tom with a grin. 'I'm not very important.'

'He seemed to think you would be. Would that be your wish for yourself, in the New Year?'

'I – I suppose so. Yes. It's such a wonderful party. Look at the fine politicians we have. So how can we fail? The Welfare State, education, and of course the National Health Service, all looking after people from the cradle to the grave. Of course I want to be part of it. And to have a voice in it.'

'Do you think people need looking after? Can't they look after themselves?'

'I think a lot of them need help,' said Tom, choosing his words with care. 'There are still too many inequalities, too much shameless exploitation of working people.'

'What do you do, Tom?'

'I'm a solicitor. I work for a firm that does a lot of legal aid work, giving representation to people who could never normally afford it. And I do a twice-weekly session at the Citizens' Advice Bureau.'

'So what would your next step be? Would you hope to be selected as a candidate? Who would you model yourself on?'

'Oh – Nye Bevan, of course. He's done the most incredible things for this country and its people. He's not just a visionary, he makes the visions come true.'

'Right.' Jim Dunne put his notebook away. 'Thank you. You've been very helpful, Tom. Keep me posted on your progress.'


'Alice, do stop crying,' said Jillie, her patience just slightly tested as the hour for her guests' arrival drew nearer and Alice continued to demand her full attention.

'I know it's awful for you, but I really must get on a bit now. I haven't started on the mince pies and I need to ring my cousin Dan –'

'I thought it was Josh who was coming.'

'He is, Dan's another cousin. He's making the punch and I have to ask him to get some more rum. Then there's all the cheese to put out and . . .'

'Oh, I'm sorry,' said Alice, blowing her nose. 'Really sorry. Look, I'll do the mince pies, it'll take my mind off it all a bit. Just as long as you do think I did the right thing –'

'I really do,' said Jillie, moving towards the larder door before Alice could collapse in a heap on her again. 'Now look, here's the pastry, the mincemeat's in those jars. I got it at Selfridges, so it should be all right, and I've already got the oven at the right temperature. I'll start chopping the fruit for the punch – oh, there's the door now, that'll be Dan, so too late to get any more rum.'

Alice only planned to stay at the party for a short time – Jillie wouldn't let her duck out altogether, saying it would do her good. She had never felt less festive and she looked awful, she thought, as she studied her ravaged face. She had a quick bath in Jillie's bathroom, and pin-curled her hair, put on the dress she'd bought specially for the party. It was a waste not to wear that, a navy taffeta that made her eyes look bluer still. By the time she'd put on some foundation and some mascara and some coral lipstick, which she also dabbed on her cheeks, she had to admit she didn't look too bad.

She ran down the stairs and bumped into Dan, who was carrying the huge silver punch bowl into the dining room. He gave an appreciative wolf whistle.

'You look lovely, Alice,' he said and suddenly life didn't seem quite so bad.

Tom felt less depressed after his encounter with the journalist. He always enjoyed talking about the party and what it had done for the country. He felt that not enough people recognised it. And it was very nice to hear that other members – all right, only local ones – thought he had a future within it. Maybe he did. Maybe he should be more pushy.

He looked at his watch. Only just ten. If he went home now, he'd never be able to go to sleep. In fact, he felt rather alert and psyched up as Betty Foxton from Pemberton's used to say. Dear Betty, he missed her and her mothering, which had increased after Laura died. He had no one to mother him now, or even care about him; it formed a huge part of his loneliness.

The people downstairs in his house were having a party. They'd asked him, but they really weren't the sort of people he'd want to party with. The man was an estate agent – who Tom regarded with almost as much suspicion as he did the landlords they worked for – and his wife was a secretary to some civil servant who were all, in

Tom's view, in spite of their supposed neutrality, Tories. They all went to public school for a start. It was either home or walking the streets, a dismal choice. And then he remembered Jillie Curtis, and her invitation to her party. Could he go? All those posh people, but maybe – you never knew – he might meet an influential champagne socialist.

He stood still, trying to decide, and then a bus came along that said *Highbury Road* and that seemed like fate giving him a nudge. Taking a deep breath, he got on it.

Josh Curtis, Jillie's other cousin, was on the same bus. Unlike Tom, he was keenly looking forward to getting to the party. It wasn't just that it would be fun, and he liked his aunt and uncle very much, and Jillie too, but it would be absolutely packed with the sort of important and influential people he could use as future contacts.

The *Daily News*, the paper he worked for, was a middle-market broadsheet, edited by Harry Campbell who had been raised and trained on some of the finest newspapers in Fleet Street; and the *Daily News*, very much Harry's creation, was hugely admired. His proprietor, the eccentric Scottish millionaire Jarvis McIntyre, who had bought it as an ailing weekly just after the war, was determined to produce a first-class daily and had given him his head; and Harry had hired an extraordinarily talented team. A picture editor, who had poached half a dozen of the best photographers in Fleet Street and then displayed superbly the rich haul of pictures they supplied him with every day; a news editor with an incredible talent for giving every major story some unexpected twist; a fashion editor who saw her job as something of a daily war in itself, to be waged against every other fashion editor in the business; and a bank of writers, some staff, some freelance, whose words were not only devoured by the paper's readers, but also quoted and re-quoted in every weekly periodical, and most news programmes on the BBC.

It was, in its politics, slightly right of centre. Its political editor, Clive Bedford, was renowned for his extraordinary ability to express a complex argument in, at the most, two comparatively brief sentences; and its sports writers were the envy of even the tabloids. Most important of all, Harry Campbell had that most precious of editorial skills: he knew what his readers were thinking almost before they did. He understood their dreams and aspirations, recognised their fears.

At a time when circulations were measured in millions, the *Daily News* was running out in front with the best of them, behind the *Daily Mirror* and the invincible *Express* of Lord Beaverbrook, but giving the other popular mid-field papers, the *Mail*, the *News Chronicle*, the *Manchester Guardian* and the *Sketch*, a very good run for their money.

Josh knew he was lucky to be on the Bedford team. He was extremely ambitious, he wrote well, and had a talent for ferreting out a story that makes an excellent journalist out of a good one. After a year of working for the paper, he was only just beginning to relax and not expect to be fired every day.

Alice was just deciding she could slip away. The party was at full throttle, everyone was quite drunk, and although she'd had not too bad a time, and even felt almost cheerful for a bit, it was wearing off now and she really wanted to creep under the bedclothes in her room at the nurses' home, do a bit more crying and go to sleep. The violent emotion had left her terribly tired. Also, she had just drunk at least three glasses of champagne and they had had a very strong effect.

She looked at her watch. Nearly eleven. She excused herself from the rather earnest spotty chap she'd been talking to and went upstairs to find her things. There was a bus in ten minutes from the end of the road, she'd catch it easily if she left now.

She was just crossing the hall when Jillie appeared.

'Oh, Alice, you can't leave now. That handsome boy who's been mooning after you all night was just asking where you'd gone.'

'Jillie, I don't want to talk to any boys, however handsome. Sorry. It's been lovely and thank you, but I'll miss my bus.'

'All right. Oh, but look, he's waving at you, you might at least say goodbye.'

Tom stood outside number five Channing Road, and decided there was no way he could go in. It was a huge detached four-storeyed house, with wide steps running up to the front door. Through the unshuttered windows of the hall he could see small groups of people chatting and laughing. He would have to confront them before he got into the party itself. There was no way Jillie was going to answer the door. He'd just go back – it had taken up some time at least. At that moment a car pulled up and four people got out of it, a boy and three girls; they looked at him. 'You coming in?' said one of the girls. 'Good, we're not the only latecomers.' And she virtually pushed him up the steps and rang the bell, so that he was at the front when the door opened.

And by some miracle it was Jillie who stood there; she smiled at him and said, 'Tom, how lovely that you're here, come in, come in, and you lot too, of course, better late than never. Alice, look who's here – it's Tom Knelston. You remember him, don't you? Now you can't leave for a bit. Get Tom a drink and introduce him to a few people.'

'I'm sure you don't remember me,' said Tom helplessly, but Alice smiled, the pretty smile that he did remember, and said, 'Yes, of course I do. How lovely to see you. Come on in, give me your coat.'

'You look as if you're leaving,' said Tom. 'And I—'

'Well, I was, but I've just missed the bus, and there isn't another for an hour. What would you like to drink? There's beer and a bit of rum punch left and lots of rather cold red wine. The bar's in here – follow me.'

And she took off her coat and set down the attaché case she was carrying, and led Tom through the huge hall, with its wide sweeping staircase and wood-panelled walls, into what was clearly a dining room, equally huge, with shelves of books and dark red floor-length velvet curtains at the windows. A long table, set with a white cloth covered with wine stains but no bottles of wine, a great many bottles of beer, and an enormous silver bowl with a ladle which was actually empty apart from a few rather sorry-looking bits of fruit.

'Oh dear,' said Alice. 'Looks like it's beer.'

'I'm fine,' said Tom. 'I've been drinking beer already anyway.'

'Gosh, you've been to another party, have you? How smart.'

'Not very,' said Tom. 'It was given by the local Labour Party.'

'Goodness,' said Alice. 'You must tell Jillie's parents. They'll be frightfully impressed, they're great Labour voters.'

'Yes, Jillie did tell me that.'

'We'll go and find them in a minute. Now there's food in the kitchen and I do know there's lots of that left. Are you hungry?'

Tom suddenly realised he was. He followed her and found himself in some kind of new, exotic country with hundreds of people, it seemed, some very familiar, others more vaguely so. He spotted at least two cabinet members, one from each party, several lesser MPs who he remembered from the conferences, a couple who had starred in a series of musical comedies on the screen and another actor he had seen in a rather mediocre thriller. He also recognised one famous actor he had actually seen at the Old Vic and a distinguished novelist he recognised from the cover of his books. All of them talking, laughing, drinking, drawing one another aside from time to time, to reveal – he imagined – some confidence or other, kissing or embracing one another every so often for no apparent reason, pulling one another from group to group. Almost all of them good-looking, the women beautifully and, in many cases, imaginatively dressed. There was a lot of red to be seen, and a great many bosoms, much pairing of low necklines and dazzling jewellery, and high-piled hair, or frequently on the younger members of the cast – for it was, he decided, exactly like watching a play – long untamed Pre-Raphaelite curls. The men were colourful as he had never seen men before, in velvet jackets and flamboyant ties, many of them of the bow variety, waving cigars and what were clearly glasses of brandy about, all smiling benignly at him as he passed.

Everything was as different as it could possibly be from the party he had just left.

Tom was oddly easy to talk to, Alice discovered. They sat on the stairs and he ate an incredibly large number of sausages and an equally incredible number of mince pies; he obviously didn't feed himself properly, she thought, her tender heart lurching. He talked about his new life in London without Laura. He loved his new job, he said, and felt he was doing something really useful. Then he suddenly stopped. 'Sorry. This isn't party talk, is it?'

'I don't like party talk,' said Alice, only slightly untruthfully.

'No, it wasn't very polite of me. You're nursing, aren't you? How's that going?'

'Oh, pretty well. I do absolutely love it.'

'Do you know all these people?' said Tom, looking round, and she could tell they were exactly the sort of people he rather disapproved of, while reluctantly admiring them at the same time.

'Oh, just a few of them. They're all right, really – I know what you're thinking.'

'I'm sorry, I wasn't thinking anything, not in that way.'

'Yes, you were,' said Alice, giggling; then the scene with Philip came vividly back and quite suddenly, exhausted and overwrought, she burst into tears.

'Oh, no, don't, don't – what is it, what did I say?' said Tom.

A long silence, then: 'Well – well, I broke up with someone just today,' Alice said. 'Someone I was very fond of.'

'I'm sorry. Very sorry. I don't suppose you want to tell me why?' Tom asked, praying silently that she wouldn't.

Then just in time, because she really was in danger of telling him all about it, which really wouldn't have been a good idea, the front door opened and four more people came in, a couple of whom she knew, and one of them, dressed in a red velvet smoking jacket, looked at Tom and said, 'Good heavens. It's young Tom Knelston, isn't it? Hello, Tom, what on earth are you doing in this fleshpot?'

And Tom jumped up, scarlet in the face, and held out his hand and said, 'Good evening, Mr Herbert.'

And he was introduced to the other three as a promising young politician. 'Works for my brother, for his sins. Enjoying life are you, Tom? Come along into somewhere quieter and tell me all about it. Jillie, there you are, my darling. Happy Christmas to you. Tell me, is young Josh here? I'd like Tom to meet him, think they'd have rather a lot to say to one another.'

And Alice, seeing that this was the end of any kind of intimacy with Tom for the rest of the evening, and that another hour had passed, slipped away to catch her bus, wondering if she would ever see him again and thinking that it didn't matter either way, because she was never going to get over Philip.

# Chapter 18

## 1951

'Alice, hello. Happy New Year.'

'Thank you. And to you.'

'Did you – did you have a nice time?'

'Not particularly.'

'Oh. I'm sorry. So you didn't hear from – from –'

'I didn't hear from anybody,' said Alice. 'Now I really must go. I'm about to go on duty for a twelve-hour shift on casualty and I can't be late.'

'Of course. Alice, I'm sorry.'

'Nothing to be sorry about. See you soon. Bye.'

'Bye,' said Jillie. 'Sorry.'

'And stop saying sorry.'

'Sorry.'

Jillie felt bad. Alice had been hoping, she knew, to hear from Tom Knelston. They had got on so well, or so Alice had thought. 'Even though he did disappear to talk politics with that Herbert man and your cousin Josh, so I left.'

'And did he say he'd like to see you again?'

'Not exactly,' said Alice.

'Well, when he couldn't find you, when he came back after all the political stuff, he asked me for your phone number.'

'Oh, gosh. My goodness. Well – well, maybe then . . .' Alice's voice rose with excitement. 'Well, I'll let you know.'

But there had been no phone call. Christmas came and went and now the New Year and Alice thought it really didn't look very hopeful.

Jillie had had a rather exciting evening, which made her feel guiltier still. She had been invited to a dinner party by her aunt and uncle – only, as they told her rather unflatteringly, because they were a female guest short.

They did this quite often – her uncle was a famous St Thomas' obstetrician. He knew, since she was both pretty and charming, that she would make a most pleasing addition to their parties. The person she was to replace, she discovered, was a distinguished art historian, and against all odds, the evening had turned out to be a great deal better than she had expected. A very great deal better.

It had started rather unpromisingly. Before dinner there were twenty people in the drawing room drinking champagne, nineteen of them horribly successful. She was introduced to what seemed to be about a dozen hugely prominent doctors and surgeons, three barristers, two politicians, an architect who appeared to be redesigning the whole of London and his wife who was running some extremely high-profile charity, while raising five children. Jillie stood smiling and shaking their hands, then standing in complete silence, drinking her champagne rather too fast. Then, in the dining room, she found herself next to one of the most handsome men she had ever seen: even allowing for the flattering effect of his dinner jacket.

'Hello.' He was smiling at her and holding out his hand to shake hers. 'We didn't meet out there, which is good, I think. Nothing worse than finding you're sitting next to someone you've been talking to for half an hour already. I'm Ned Welles,' he added. 'And you are?'

Looking back over the evening from the safety of her bed, she just couldn't stop smiling. He had been so lovely to her, had seemed to be really interested in her and what she did and who she worked for. 'Ah, Miss Moran, how is the old dragoness?' Then he wanted to know about her ambitions for herself. 'Nobody ever fails who trains under Moran, she won't allow it. Besides, I can tell you're clever, so why on earth should you fail?' Then later (having returned to her after a decent interval talking to one of the barristers), 'Goodness, that was challenging. Now tell me, do you have a boyfriend? What does he do?' He appeared rather pleased when she said she hadn't.

He had even, before the evening ended, returned to her from the library where most of the men had gathered, and said, 'I'm being a party pooper, but I have a difficult day tomorrow. Jillie, it's been lovely talking to you, and I'd very much like to see you again. Could I have your telephone number?'

It was Laura, of course: that was the thing. He really would have liked to see Alice again, just to take her to the pictures, or for a meal at a Lyons Corner House, nothing too serious. Tom found her sweet and thoughtful; she was also extremely pretty and seemed perfectly happy to hear about his political ideas and ideals, while implying that while she did agree with them she had a few of her own. He had fully intended to ring her within the next few days. Somehow, every time he plucked up his courage, he would see Laura's face – concentrating on her work, or on something she had just said; hear her voice expressing her approval, or even disapproval, of it, see her brown eyes fixed on him; or looking up from something she was reading and wanted to discuss with him – and he would put the piece of paper back in the drawer again. Laura was still too close, her presence too vivid. He would feel disloyal, he knew, as if he was being unfaithful to her; and besides, he knew she wouldn't really approve of Alice.

'Spoilt,' she would say. 'Very nice but privileged.'

He just knew that Laura would be shocked that he was going out with such a person. Or not even going out with, just spending time with.

'Getting ideas above your station, Tom Knelston,' she would say. 'I'm surprised at you. You'll be joining the Tories next.'

So the weeks went by and he didn't ring Alice, and then it was too many weeks. She'd have forgotten all about him, and no doubt found a new boyfriend and besides, he was very busy. Once the 1950 election had been safely won (albeit with a greatly reduced majority), Donald Herbert had been pushing him up the political ladder. He insisted on funding a dinner jacket for him, telling Tom he could pay him back when he was in the cabinet. Then Herbert made sure he heard many of the more important debates in the House, introduced him to many of the more junior MPs and took him to meet the PR people at Transport House. He also introduced him to the Marquis of Granby pub nearby, a major haunt of the press. He managed to persuade Josh Curtis to quote Tom in a couple of articles, as a representative of the new breed of young, politically minded young men.

His conversation at the Labour Christmas party with the local journalist had turned into a full-scale interview complete with photograph in the *Islington News* and had caught the attention of several people in the party. He found himself being wheeled on at more and more meetings and press conferences; the crowning glory was being quoted very briefly in the *Daily Mirror* as a 'young man with a burning desire to go places, preferably in the footsteps of his idol, Aneurin Bevan'.

The article also mentioned a new Tory candidate, a young woman called Margaret Roberts, dismissing her roundly, claiming contemptuously she was one hundred per cent out of the 'Tory top drawer mould, an Oxford graduate', while failing to mention that her father ran a grocer's shop and she had won a scholarship to grammar school. Tom felt mildly interested in her and resolved to follow her progress.

When a safe Tory seat became vacant, in the heart of middle England, Donald Herbert insisted he at least had a stab at becoming the Labour candidate and he spent a miserable three weeks addressing either contemptuous local meetings or the half-amused selection committee who cut him off mid-presentation and told him he was wasting his time. When the day for selection came, he trailed home last of all the candidates, wishing he had never agreed to so ritualistic a humiliation.

None of which mattered in the least, Donald Herbert said, over a consoling beer at the pub.

'It's just to give you a feel for it, no more. Think of it as practising scales or something. Ever learn the piano?'

Tom said, no, never, 'but my late wife used that analogy occasionally'. A sudden vivid picture of Laura at the piano at various school functions, her brown eyes, brilliant with a mixture of anxiety and pleasure, darting endlessly from her music to the performers and back. It hurt; he cleared his throat.

Donald Herbert looked at him thoughtfully, then stood up and said he had to be getting home. 'I haven't been home for days; my wife's pretty long suffering but she has her breaking point. Night, Tom.'

'Goodnight, Mr Herbert,' said Tom, and watched him walking out of the pub, envying him that he had a wife to get back to rather than a painfully empty sitting room, a half-made bed, an unused stove, and a silence that was almost a noise.

Loneliness had become the heart of his life; weekends were the worst, when he sat reading, listening to the wireless, trying to force himself to concentrate on the political news, making a contribution to a pamphlet or newsletter, or going out for walks in Highbury Fields and watching families, and struggling not to think of Hope, no longer a baby but a small child, a two-year-old ghost, tottering across the grass, laughing, picking flowers, falling over, being lifted up and comforted. There were couples talking, joking, holding hands, but he walked alone, an outcast from it all, isolated from togetherness, from sharing, wondering, albeit absurdly, if they were all looking at him, pitying his alone-ness, pondering at the reason for it. He longed, even more absurdly, to go up to them and to disabuse them of their sympathy and puzzlement. To say yes, I am alone, but once I was together, together with the woman I loved beyond anything, and our unborn child. Finally, unable to bear it any longer, he would go home, and lie on the bed, staring at the ceiling and raging at the cruelty of whatever malign force had condemned him to this awful, endless pain . . .

He would weep sometimes. He had an old sweater of Laura's that he kept lovingly folded in a drawer and when he felt especially bad he would get it out, and hold it as once he had held her, gently at first, then frantically, clutching it to him, burying his head in it, crushing it, tears drenching it. Catharsis achieved, he would very gently shake it out and hang it over the foot of the bedstead to dry, and lie staring at it and wondering for a while whatever was to become of him. Then he would take a deep breath and stand up, pull on his coat, and go out to buy a Sunday newspaper or perhaps a copy of the *New*

*Statesman* and lie on the bed reading. Gradually the pain would fade as his mind became reabsorbed in the present and the other things he managed against all odds to care about, and he could lay Laura once again to rest.

'Darling, this is rather thrilling. You didn't tell me about this.'

'What?' said Diana casually, although she had been waiting all morning for someone to spot the picture in the *Sunday News* fashion pages, of her and a handful of other models, most of them much more famous than she was. The picture had been taken by John French, one of the greatest fashion photographers of the day, working with the fashion editor, Camilla Jessop.

He had dressed them all in black and white, each by a different designer, and photographed them on a staircase specially built in French's studio. The caption was *The Faces of the Fifties*, and the picture went right across the entire page. Diana had been very lucky to be chosen – it was a huge accolade after such a short time of work, half of which had not even appeared.

Her first session with Blanche had been the most wonderful and extraordinary experience. Wonderful in that it had been such fun, such heady glorious fun. Diana insisted she could do her own make-up, but she could see very swiftly it was completely beyond her, as Blanche's assistant Lorelei produced a box of theatrical-looking make-up, with a dozen lipsticks and shaders and at least six brushes. 'Don't worry, I'll quite enjoy it and it's not very difficult, you'll pick it up in no time. And I can see René's done a super cut on your hair so we won't need to do much with that.'

And sitting in the studio dressing room, draped in a large cape and listening to a lot of extremely scurrilous gossip, a discussion as to whether this photographer and that designer (both fairies) were having an affair, how pathetic various other fashion editors' pages had been recently and how when Lady Mary Someone had come into the studio to be photographed in her wedding dress, she'd spent the whole time flirting with the photographer and Lorelei had heard them arrange to meet at the Connaught later that evening. Then they all piled into an enormous six-seater Riley, its huge boot filled with clothes, more of which were piled on top of her and Lorelei, and drove up to Hampstead Heath where Blanche and Kirill were waiting impatiently, parked near the Ponds.

'What have you been doing, for heaven's sake? Diana, let's have a look at you, yes, that hair's definitely an improvement. Lorelei, too much lipstick, but otherwise not bad. OK, now I want to do the Worth suit first, so if you could just get into that.'

The dressing room was the car; it wasn't easy, certainly not the skirt and blouse, and although there was a blind in the rear window, there was nothing in the others, and there were several moments when she was just sitting in the car in her slip, and various passers-by were waving and whistling, but she managed to not mind that simply by imagining the wicked witch was watching, and enjoying her outrage. When she got out of the car, and had tried on about six pairs of shoes and had three or four different hats plonked on her head, and Lorelei had put on some more mascara and wiped off some of the lipstick, replacing it with colourless gloss, she was sent off to stand by the pond.

'Don't look at the camera,' Blanche said. 'I want you to stare just beyond it, as if you'd seen someone you knew.' She suddenly found she knew exactly what to do and changed her expression from pleased recognition to cool dislike and then suddenly a sexy stare straight into the camera, which seemed right in spite of Blanche's instructions. Kirill said, 'Good, good, now can we try a move, no, darling not forward, just a change of body position, no, you're not a schoolgirl in a prayer meeting, it's sex we want, just thrust a hip forward, that's better, now raise that hand just a bit. Lorelei, have we got any pearls? Come on, quick, quick, we really haven't got all day. Now, Diana, touch the pearls as if you're checking they're still there and look at me.' And somehow, after a few false starts, as he directed her, he started saying, 'Yes, that's right, that's good.' She learned fast, moving just a few inches at a time, putting her weight on a different foot, her shoulders turned this way and then that, or even standing straight placing her feet slightly apart. It was heady stuff, like being able to sing in tune, or ride a bicycle for the first time, and Diana could see that Blanche had stopped frowning quite so much.

It was the longest day Diana could ever remember; they were shooting until after seven, dodging the clouds, then waiting until the light was gentler.

She wore six outfits, all tweeds, some with hats, some not, had her hair combed and tweaked and re-combed until her head was sore, her earrings pulled on and off until her ears were quite raw, her make-up changed over and over again, once taken right off because it was just too heavy. Once she had to change behind a bush, into a long tweed evening gown – she was past caring by then, would have stripped right off if she'd been asked. Her head ached, her feet throbbed, she was hungry, only allowed half a sandwich in case it made her stomach stick out, and terribly thirsty, because she didn't dare drink much in case she wanted to pee. In fact, she did have to go once, behind a tree and did rather mind that, and couldn't under-stand why nobody else wanted to, and then realised none of them had had babies. At the end of it, throbbing all over with exhaustion, she thought she had never enjoyed a day more in the whole of her life.

'Well,' said Blanche, smiling at her as she collapsed, shaking with weariness, into the back of the Riley. 'I must say, Diana, that really wasn't bad. For a first time. I think we've got some pretty good stuff there. Well done.'

'I enjoyed it,' said Diana truthfully. 'Oh, God, look at the time, I had no idea. My mother will be worried to death, she's been looking after my little boy all day.' Then realising she hadn't given Jamie more than a moment's thought since early that morning, added, her voice stricken, 'God, I hope he's all right.'

He was of course: perfectly all right, fast asleep, and her mother was far from reproachful; and Nanny, a very down-to-earth Yorkshire girl, clearly felt it had all been rather exciting and wanted to know all about it when Diana went up to kiss Jamie goodnight.

She walked down to the drawing room where Caroline was wait-ing with a bottle of champagne.

She'd even been paid two guineas an hour. She thought now, as she sat in the drawing room, wolfing down supper from a tray, regaling her mother with the details of her day, that if today had gone well and she was asked to do some more work, she would be able to spend more time in London, and not only need fashionable clothes but be able to afford them for herself. But maybe that was too much to hope for. It didn't even occur to her to ring Johnathan.

Blanche phoned in the morning and said the pictures were good and that Kirill was thrilled. She would certainly like to use Diana again if the right opportunity came up.

'You look far more stylish than I dared hope,' she said. 'When I showed Miss Banham, the editor, she was really rather pleased. She said you looked a little tubby in some of them, but I'm sure you can deal with that before next time, and we can choose the shots carefully. Kirill has a marvellous printer whose forte is retouching. Kirill says he can shave your stomach outline quite easily.'

'So you'll definitely be using some of them then?' Diana was unabashed by this insult, thinking she would go onto a complete starvation diet immediately if that was going to ensure her a future in this wonderful new world.

'Well, of course we'll be using them. We're not going to waste a day's shooting and all that expense. Now do give your phone number in Yorkshire to my secretary, won't you, so I can contact you easily when I need to. I don't suppose you have an agent yet – perhaps you should get one. Give Lucie Clayton a call, they might take you on.'

Diana didn't even bother telling Johnathan about her day, or possible new future. But a moment of pure joy came, even greater than when the October edition of *Style* thumped through the letter box and there she was – or was it her, that aristocratic, fine-boned creature, looking as if she owned Hampstead Heath as she posed and smiled and scowled and strode across it?

Her mother-in-law appeared at her front door a week or two later and said she'd heard from a friend that there was someone who looked rather like her in a copy of *Style* magazine. 'Not that I'd read it, obviously.' Is it possible that they were one and the same?

Diana, smiling at her sweetly, said yes, they were indeed. Vanessa asked what Johnathan had felt about it. Diana said she hadn't told him. Vanessa said that as his wife, Diana should have asked his permission. He might have felt unhappy or uncomfortable about it.

'Vanessa,' said Diana, smiling at her, 'there's only one picture where I'm not actually wearing gloves. I cannot imagine it making Johnathan uncomfortable. Would you like to see them for yourself? Just to be reassured?'

She was clearly rather shaken by the five pages of the magazine and had the grace to say that Diana did look quite smart, then said she had really come for the minutes of the AGM of the WI which were needed urgently for the local paper. She made it sound as if the front page of *The Times* was at stake.

A week later Diana received a call from Blanche asking her to come for some Christmas party fashion. 'Can you be here for Thursday? Kirill has expressly asked for you. Several girls, of course, not just a solo turn.'

Diana knew that nothing, not even Johnathan's expressly forbidding it, would keep her from such happiness. Two days later she, Nanny and Jamie were on the London train from York, to stay with her mother. Far from forbidding it, Johnathan seemed rather relieved she wasn't going to be sitting at home on her own while he embarked on a series of talks he was giving to sundry farmers' unions across the country.

The December issue of *Style* carried three double-page spreads of girls in the most outrageous party clothes Blanche and Lorelei had been able to find, including one of Diana wearing a simple black silk sheath by Jacques Fath which Blanche had accessorised with a sort of bridal veil also in black. Diana had thrown it back in a pose of extraordinary abandon, and was half laughing in an indisputably and extremely sexy way. Every other girl in the shot faded into the background; it was always said later that it was the photograph that had really launched Diana's career.

# Chapter 19

## 1951

It was a magnificent speech. Roaring through the Commons in that unmistakable voice, at once so strong and yet so musical, rising and falling like the valleys and hills that had shaped him and his principles and his every belief. The valleys and hills indeed were at the heart of the speech: for this was a small stone, he said, 'falling down towards a valley that would become an avalanche'.

The items in question were quite modest; spectacles and dentures would entail a small charge. 'But,' Bevan thundered, as his audience sat silent. 'Prescriptions? Hospital charges?'

'And he finished,' Tom said to Alice, who was working extremely hard on maintaining her expression of intent excitement, 'by saying there was only one hope for mankind and that is democratic socialism. And that there is only one party in Great Britain which can do it – and that is the Labour Party. And it was terrible – not only the Tories, but the Labour Party seemed to be against him in the House. They're even saying now he's destroyed the Labour Party's chances in the election. How could that be, when he is so true to them, and their principles?'

'Tom,' said Alice gently. 'Tom, eat your food. It's getting cold and it's a bit of a shame, seeing as I spent two hours cooking it.'

'Sorry,' said Tom. 'I'm sorry, Alice, and it is very nice, of course. Very nice. Thank you.'

'So what do you think will happen to him next?'

'What, now he's resigned? I don't know. He's still looking after housing, of course. But we may not win the election anyway, and . . .'

Alice tried to suppress a sigh. When Tom was in full flood like this, nothing stopped or even slowed him. She wondered what Laura had done on these occasions. She wondered increasingly about Laura these days, while not wishing to in the least. Indeed, she had done ever since that first rather amazing day two months ago now, in the middle of February, when there had been a message on the notice-board at the nurses' home to say Tom Knelston had rung her and could she call him back.

Her first instinct was not to. To ask for her number on New Year's Eve and to put it to use over six weeks later was hardly morale boost-ing. Then she suddenly noticed what the date was. She looked at the note saying there were some flowers for Sarah Jane Harding to col-lect from the kitchen, and thought about the fact that she would be very much alone in the sitting room, and decided that, if only for the one evening, she should swallow her pride and call Tom Knelston back.

She tried to imagine what might have propelled him finally into action. All right, it was Valentine's Day, but he seemed the opposite of romantic in that sense. She decided she should ring Tom back, however much she would like to play it cool.

He answered straight away, which she found rather encouraging; he was obviously waiting for her to ring. 'Tom Knelston, hello?'

He did have a very nice voice; it was deep and contained only the slightest burr of Hampshire accent – she liked that burr.

'Hello, Tom. It's Alice here. Alice Miller,' she added, rather unnecessarily.

'Hello, Alice. How are you? Thank you for ringing.'

'That's all right.'

There was a long silence. Alice began to panic. What could she say? The silence grew. She felt herself feeling rather dry in the mouth. This was ridiculous. He'd rung her.

'I'm sorry,' he said finally. 'So sorry, Alice, for not ringing before. It was very rude of me. It's a long time since New Year's Day.'

'Well,' she said, aware how fatuous she was sounding, 'not that long.'

'It is. Six weeks. Six weeks and three days, actually.'

Alice giggled. She couldn't help it.

'Well, never mind. I wasn't counting,' she added untruthfully. 'Anyway, you didn't say you were going to ring.'

'Didn't I? I meant to. Well, I told Jillie I would. When I asked her for your number.'

'And,' she said, smiling into the phone, 'and how was I supposed to know that?'

'Well, of course you weren't. Anyway, I did mean to. It's really nice of you to ring me back now. I'm not very good at this sort of thing. I – I just wondered if you'd like to go out one night.'

'I'd love to, Tom. Thank you.'

'To the pictures, perhaps? Have you seen *Harvey*?'

'No, I haven't.'

Nor did she want to.

'We'll go on Saturday. We could go to one of the Corner Houses for a bite first, if you like. Maybe the one in Piccadilly? At six?'

'Sounds fine.'

'Good.' There was a bit of a silence, and then he said, 'Goodnight, Alice. And thank you.'

She put the phone down, smiling at it rather foolishly.

She might have been just a little less joyful had she known that what had actually prompted Tom to finally make the phone call was almost – no, entirely – due to Jillie Curtis.

Two evenings earlier, not having seen Jillie since her party, Tom was trudging towards the bus stop through an icy rain, after a particularly frustrating and depressing session at his Citizens' Advice Bureau surgery in the main Islington library. He'd had them all that evening, all the desperates as he thought of them, each one saddening and enraging him more than the last. People sacked without any real cause, people evicted from flats or rooms which, however unsuitable, provided some kind of home, people with ruthless landlords putting up already extortionate rents, people desperate to get a

191

council house. These people brought Tom closer to disillusion with the government than anything else. They had achieved a lot, but not enough. There were just too many in need. And the housing programme was a particular failure.

That night the world seemed filled with depressed, unfortunate, helpless people; and he was failing them all. He knew he ought to be going to Transport House and checking over some press release to check their legality. But somehow he couldn't. Maybe he should forget politics, maybe he should concentrate on his career as a lawyer. It could be a more positive, more fulfilling thing to do and he could make some money, feed his self-esteem. Then, as if on cue, supporting the heresy, temptation arrived.

'Tom! Hello! How lovely to see you. I always forget you belong up here now in the frozen north. Isn't it freezing?' It was Jillie, looking pretty and warm in a red coat with a hood, rosy, happy.

He smiled back at her, said, 'Hello. Nice to see you.'

'Where have you been and what have you been doing? Something noble and useful I expect —'

'Not very,' said Tom. 'Failing a lot of people at my Citizens' Advice surgery.'

There was a slightly awkward silence and then to his astonishment Tom heard himself asking her if she had had supper and if not, would she care to join him.

'I'm afraid I have,' she said apologetically, adding, 'with Alice, actually. We went to the pictures, saw such a silly lovely old film called *The Red Shoes* all about a ballerina who married a conductor and threw herself under a train because she couldn't choose between him and the ballet.'

'It sounds — very good,' said Tom politely.

'Well, it was fun. And then we had a quick supper at the Corner House. I don't think I could eat another now, fun as it would be.' She hesitated, then said, 'Look, there's nowhere open now anyway, and you obviously need food after advising all those citizens. Why don't you come back to my house? My parents are probably out and there's always soup in the fridge, I'll warm that up for you. Go on, Tom, it would be lovely for me. Otherwise I'll have to do what I should be doing, and revising the construction of the pelvis. About as much fun as the citizens, I should think.'

And Tom heard himself climbing into Jillie's little red Morris Minor. 'This is the love of my life,' said Jillie as she switched on the engine. He felt no sense of injustice on behalf of all the people who didn't have cars and had to stand at bus stops, getting cold and wet, just huge gratitude and pleasure; emotions repeated as they climbed the steps to the great front door of number five Channing Road, and walked into its beguiling warmth and charm.

'Right,' said Jillie, 'to the kitchen. Oh, here's some nice fresh bread, and some cheese, and a pot of Cook's special raisin chutney. How about a beer? Daddy always has some in the cellar.'

Tom sat, drinking the soup and eating the bread and cheese, and enjoying the beer, feeling any sense of guilt melt away. And enjoying the company of Jillie, who was drinking from a huge cup of tea and eating ginger biscuits, chatting and smiling. Then, suddenly, he heard himself say, 'How – how is Alice?'

'She's fine,' said Jillie. 'Working very hard. She's decided she wants to be a theatre nurse. She likes the drama of surgery, the sense that you're getting something done. My –' She hesitated, blushed, then said, 'I have a friend who's a surgeon, he says the same thing. So much of medicine is slow. Treating with drugs, with rest, with good nursing. Surgery, you have a chance to put things right, straight away. Of course sometimes it goes wrong, but when it goes right, then you're God, you've given the person their life back.'

'I see. This friend, this surgeon, is he very successful?'

'He will be. He's only just become a consultant. An honorary, as they used to be called.'

'And – what sort of surgery does he do?'

'Paediatrics. Working with children. He doesn't just operate, of course, there's a lot of the other sort of work too. Putting crooked limbs and knock knees into plaster casts, all sorts of minor children's ailments, tonsils, appendicitis, that sort of thing. Then he's very interested in –' She stopped. 'Sorry. You don't want to hear all this.'

'It's interesting. Have you known him long, this surgeon?'

'No, I met him on New Year's Eve. But we, well, we see a lot of each other. He's very nice.'

'So – so is he your boyfriend?'

'Just about. A very new one, though. How about another beer?'

'That would be – very kind. Oh, this is so nice. To be talking to you while I eat. Instead of all by myself, I mean.'

'Oh, Tom,' said Jillie, looking quite shocked. 'That sounds like a dreadful way to be living. So alone.'

'It is. But – it's the way things have worked for me. Laura died, and the baby died, so of course I'm alone.'

'Yes, of course you are. Tom, I'm so sorry.'

She fetched the beer, sat looking at him, clearly not knowing what to say.

'It's all right,' he said, smiling at her. 'I'm quite used to it.'

'I know but . . .'

Then, and he would never have managed it had he not felt so totally relaxed, and been halfway through the second beer, and wanting, besides, this warm sociable evening to go on and on, and because suddenly he really wanted to know . . .

'Has – has Alice got a boyfriend?'

'No, Tom,' said Jillie, her expression carefully blank. 'No, she hasn't.'

'I see. I just wondered. I mean, we did get on very well at your party. I'd really like to see her again. If you don't think she'd mind me getting in touch after all this time.'

'I think she'd be delighted.'

'Do you? You see, I really did mean to ring her. I should have done. Only – well, it's hard to explain. I still feel so – I belong to Laura, you see.'

'Of course you do. And I suppose you feel disloyal. Even thinking of going out with someone else, getting involved with them possibly?'

'Yes. Yes, I do. I loved her so much.'

'But—'

'Please don't,' he said. 'Don't say she wouldn't want me to be lonely, she'd be happy for me to be with someone else. Everyone says that, it's not the point.'

'I wasn't going to,' said Jillie. 'I was going to say I should imagine you want to stay on your own, however lonely you are, because it's how you keep her alive.'

'Yes, that's exactly right,' he said, astonished at her perception. 'Exactly. I can keep her – well, not alive, but alive in my memory, everything about her. I can't have her blurred.'

'Oh, Tom,' said Jillie and there were tears in her eyes now. 'I am so, so sorry. It was cruel, what happened to you, so unbelievably cruel. But – forgive me – you have to think of yourself too. You're clever and you've done so well, and you're ambitious and you could be really successful, I think, and I love the way you're a real socialist. But I think being so miserable and alone all the time – and this has nothing to do with Alice, you certainly don't have to ring her – but being so lonely is holding you back. Making you not believe in yourself, and making you negative. What would you think about that?'

'I – I'm not sure,' said Tom.

'And all right, of course you don't want to be disloyal to Laura, but I do know one thing – and don't forget I met Laura – I thought she was one of the bravest, most positive people I ever met, and I just know she wouldn't want you to be wasting your life. She'd want you to do justice to yourself.'

Tom sat in silence for some time; it wasn't an awkward silence, it was rather the reverse, it was easy and comfortable and rather happy. He let Jillie's words work their way into his head. 'Jillie, thank you for that. Of course you're right. She'd – well, she'd be furious with me.'

'I don't know about furious,' said Jillie, 'but maybe rather sad.'

Two days later, still with nothing accomplished, Tom realised, as he walked into the newsagent to buy his *Daily Mirror*, that it was Valentine's Day. What happened next became, as they say, history.

# Chapter 20

## 1951

'Have you had many lovers before me?' The question posed, very gently, startled her a little; they were sitting on a bench in Kew Gardens, where they had been walking on the new, fresh grass, surrounded by the shrubs and trees all coming into life again, in the annual lovely miracle known as spring. It was Sunday and he had asked her to walk there with him.

Since Jillie would have loved anything in Ned's company, even a tour of the local sewage works, she rapturously agreed, and he had picked her up in his dark green MG convertible; whenever they had to stop for some traffic lights he would put his hand over hers, or raise it to his lips, and look at her with that smile of his, and everything in her seemed to lurch, not just her heart but her stomach, and her head and her thoughts. She looked at him rather anxiously now, wondering why he should have suddenly asked her, and what he would like her answer to be.

Jillie's romantic life had been fairly uneventful; she had only had a very few boyfriends, and no really serious ones, although she did not quite share Alice's view on the retention of virginity, nor the importance of it in a young woman's life. Growing up in the home that she had, such opinions would have been almost impossible to hold. Her parents moved in liberal circles, their friends being writers, artists, the more intellectual breed of politicians (mainly left wing) and musicians. Her father had a great predilection for traditional jazz and was indeed most knowledgeable about it. Ned's prowess on jazz piano had delighted him.

The people Jillie had grown up with were, therefore, for the most part free thinking, unconventional and possessed of a rather easy moral code. Jillie's mother had told her, when holding a general and unusually frank (for the times) discussion on such things, that it might be ideal to go to the altar a virgin – although she wasn't even sure of that, since sexual compatibility was one of the most important factors in a marriage – but the really important thing was not to have to rush to it pregnant. She then sent Jillie to her own gynaecologist who instructed her in the complexities of birth control, and particularly the usage of the Dutch cap, so that when and if Jillie should fall in love, she could make her own mind up as to exactly how far physically she should let matters develop. But except for one relationship, she had never felt a desire to take things further than the pleasant petting which she found only mildly exciting.

Ned Welles was like no one she had ever gone out with – older for a start, and an ideal companion. Charming, good-looking, urbane, amusing – she relaxed into their relationship easily and happily, flattered by his patent interest in and devotion to her. Ned took her all over London; to the smartest restaurants of the day – Le Caprice, Le Gavroche, Prunier's – and to nightclubs and bars – especially the American Bar at the Connaught.

He took her to Covent Garden and the Old Vic, as well as the West End theatres and the Hollywood musicals they shared a passion for. They had seen the film version of *On the Town* three times and the stage version of *South Pacific* twice.

It was as if he was trying to dazzle her, and indeed she was at first, but then as the months went by, she became first bemused and then puzzled. For Ned had made no sexual move on her apart from kissing her – with varying degrees of enthusiasm. He had never touched her breasts, let alone her legs. There was none of the constant stroking and touching and hopeful journeying into areas shielded by bras and stockings and knickers and girdles. Occasionally he would tangle his hands in her long brown hair and bury his face in it, while murmuring things she could hardly hear, apart from frequent repetitions of such words as 'darling' and 'sweetheart', but that was as far as he would go; and then he would draw back and gaze into her eyes with his burning dark ones and tell her how lovely she was, and – that precious once or twice – that he loved her. She didn't mind the lack of sexual activity, but it puzzled her, especially for a man of his age who must, surely, she thought, be more sexually experienced than she.

Ned smiled, clearly reading her thoughts, or at least the tenor of them, and took her hand and said, 'Darling Jillie, don't look so worried. I just – well, I just want to know. It's important to me.'

'Of course it is. Well, lots of flirtations and that sort of thing and one –' she hesitated, but felt she had to tell him – 'one important one.'

'Important in which way?'

'I just adored him,' she said, for prevarication seemed pointless. 'He was my first great love.'

'And – what happened?'

'It all went wrong,' she said, hoping that her expression was as blank as her voice. 'Just horribly wrong.'

He simply nodded, and to her huge relief and pleased surprise did not ask how or why; just said, 'Poor darling.'

'Oh, I'm over it now. It would never have worked, anyway, he was about a hundred times cleverer than me.'

'Jillie, you do love to do yourself down. It's silly. When you are clearly so clever.'

'I know,' she said, half surprised at the observation. 'I suppose it's coming from such a brilliant family with so many brilliant friends. I mean, if your parents had had, within their immediate circle, a dozen professors of literature, several Oxford scholars, two Royal Academicians, and of course—'

'Those are your mother's associates, the Academicians?'

'Yes. And I mean, look at her!'

'Yes, all right,' said Ned, laughing.

'And then frequently round the dinner table, we have prize-winning novelists, several leading politicians and – well, what have I done, scraped through my second MB? Come on, Ned, admit it. Not even an also ran. Now even my cousin Josh has won some Press Association award for the most promising political writer of the year. Of course I do myself down. I'm the family dunce. Thank God I'm an only child. It's the one great blessing bestowed upon me.'

He smiled, leaned forward and kissed her.

'Then may I say, I find the family dunce clever as well as beautiful, and charming. Thank you for answering my question so honestly,' he added, and he looked around, and seeing no one too terribly near them, took her in his arms, and kissed her quite thoroughly. 'Jillie Curtis, I adore you. And I admire your mind as well as the rest of you; I find it interesting and contemplative – a rare thing especially in someone as young as you – and original. Now – shall we go and have our tea?'

And so they made their way towards Richmond and the Maids of Honour Restaurant, and it was charming, rebuilt since the war when it had been bombed, with great attention to its past so that it still had a thirties air to it and with wonderfully old-fashioned waitresses and exquisite china.

'Now,' he said, as she admired, as she was clearly supposed to do, the cake, 'I have an invitation for you. To another tea.'

'With?'

'My mother.'

'Your – mother?'

'Yes. Don't look so frightened. She really doesn't deserve that at all.'

'I'm – I'm not. Just – well. A bit surprised.' And swiftly restored to happiness, because why else could he wish her to meet his mother if he did not regard her as fairly important in his life?

'Well, she doesn't come to London often. She lives in Cornwall, as you know. But she is coming up for a couple of days next week – although not to stay with me for we should murder one another in a very few hours – and she wants to meet you. I've told her a bit about you, and she wants to know more.'

'Oh. Well, that sounds lovely. I'd like that very much.'

She knew little about the legendary Persephone, merely that she had run away from Ned's father when Ned was just a little boy, and that he had, with what she guessed was fairly extreme understatement, 'missed her rather'.

'Good. Well, I thought the Ritz would be nice. Next Saturday. Or are you working?'

She shook her head.

'No, I'm not. But my parents want me at home that evening for some important politician – only because as usual they're short of a female guest. I wish I could invite you too.'

'I wish it too. But I understand these things, and anyway, I should be available to St Peter's. I will have done a difficult operation the day before.'

'Which is?'

'You're so sweet, the way you're interested in what I do.'

'I'm not sweet,' she said almost irritably. 'It's my world too, you so often seem to forget.'

'I'm sorry,' he said, clearly distressed by this. 'Very sorry. Of course it is. I'm operating on quite a young child, just three, with what is apparently a recurring appendicitis. The symptoms fit, but I feel uneasy about it. You know how one has these hunches? One of the things I love about medicine is its resemblance to a jigsaw puzzle.'

Now he was flattering her, treating her with a knowledge and experience she entirely lacked.

'So three thirty, shall we say? In the Palm Court.'

Jillie had heard Persephone was very beautiful. It was true. Shining, dark, thick, thick hair, wound into a rather old-fashioned chignon, though she was fashionless and ageless with huge dark eyes just like her son's, soft, powdery skin, an astonishingly smooth brow, and a curvy, perfect mouth. She wore a dress in purest sky blue, with a skirt that hung almost to her ankles, and a slightly darker blue jacket and the highest of high heels. She was sitting with Ned at a table in the Palm Court and she stood up and held her arms out to Jillie, as if welcoming her, which Jillie rather hoped she was. When she drew her close to her she smelt wonderful. Jillie was told it was the lovely thirties scent of Arpège.

She patted the seat beside her, and told Jillie that her hat was the most adorable thing she'd ever seen, and then asked her endless questions, clearly prompted by the intense curiosity that was her trademark, about her friends, her family and her career. Jillie, charmed beyond all measure, quite forgot her determination to disapprove of Persephone at least a little for making Ned so unhappy as a small boy, and forgot also to ask him about the operation the day before; she fell beneath Persephone's spell as Ned watched and listened, smiling benignly and ushering in extra tea, cakes and champagne.

When Jillie had left, after a shower of Arpège-scented kisses and hugs, Persephone looked at Ned and said, 'Well, darling, I can see why you're thinking of marrying *her*.' And then added, summoning more champagne, 'But I really don't think you should. It would be awfully wrong.'

# Chapter 21

## 1951

'Mummy and Daddy have asked you to Sunday lunch. Could you possibly bear that? They really want to meet you. I know it's not the sort of thing you'd most like, but –'

Mummy and Daddy. Sunday lunch. How that summed it all up. All Tom's anxieties, all his misgivings. And how he resented them, because really Alice was so lovely, and he was so happy with her. Loneliness banished, despair gone, wounds healed; he felt whole once more. He had told Laura, of course, had gone to see her, begged her forgiveness, asked for her blessing. He had felt, as he knelt by the grave – what? Nothing. He had waited a long time, for some sense of peace, of rightness. It didn't come and he had left, anxious, almost afraid. How could he do this? he wondered, as he sat on the train back to London. How could he turn his back on what they had had, their perfect, perfect life and love?

For what he felt for Alice was not the same. She irritated him sometimes, she argued with him over his ideals, told him he should move into the real world. She fussed too much over her appearance, as Laura never had. She had always made the most of herself and had disliked her too-short legs, her slightly heavy breasts, her unruly hair, but she could do nothing about them as she would say. To Tom she had been beautiful anyway. Alice, not sure of Tom's admiration, was always fretting about her hair, her lovely fair curly hair: it was too long, it was too short, it looked silly up, untidy down. Then she would worry about her weight when she was already so slim, turning away things like cake and chocolates. 'It's so daft,' he would say. 'You're perfect, eat all the chocolates you want,' and she would laugh and say that if she did, then he would see the difference in no time. She had a certain fondness for the kind of books Laura would have scorned – romantic novels, historical rubbish by someone called Georgette Heyer – and he would often find her reading the women's pages in the *Daily Mirror*, when he had brought a particularly brilliant political article to her notice. In spite of all this he was so extremely, wonderfully fond of her. He didn't quite dare let the word 'love' out, for that surely would have been a final betrayal.

It was hardly a whirlwind romance, Alice reflected. It was some months now that they had been going out. They were both so busy, Tom with his politics – one election the year before, which his party, as she thought of the Labour Party, had won by a hair's breadth, and another coming up in October. She, with her nursing, and its strict schedules and endless studying to be done most evenings.

Tom worked so hard for the party – she wished she cared about it, as Laura clearly had. It was so important to him, it really did govern his life. Her concerns were more personal and romantic (until of course it came to her nursing which she cared very passionately about). She feared she was far too frivolous altogether for Tom, and spent much of their time together making a huge effort to appear more serious.

'I just feel so inadequate,' Alice wailed to Jillie, 'trying to match up to her, to the wonderful Laura. I absolutely hate her – isn't that awful? I just feel she's there all the time, cleverer than me, more beautiful, a better cook, a more worthy person altogether.'

'Alice, she wasn't. Not more worthy, not cleverer, certainly not more beautiful – I don't know about her cooking, of course. Listen, don't try to be her, because you can't. Be you – you can see he loves you.'

'He's never said so. Never.'

'Well – I'm sure he will. You're happy when you're together, aren't you?'

'Terribly happy. He's so – so – sweet. So kind. So tender hearted. He says the dearest things to me. Like I've made him happy again when he never thought he would be. Like he keeps thinking about me, just being glad I'm there. Like he can't believe how lucky it was he met me.'

'Doesn't sound as though he's not sure about you to me. Alice, stop fretting. Just enjoy it. Do you love him?'

'Oh, Jillie, I do absolutely love him, although of course he is quite – odd. I've never known anyone remotely like him before, he's so serious and so intense, but I hate not being with him. He's even distracting me from my work, makes it seem almost unimportant. I got ticked off by Sister yesterday, nothing's ever done that, nothing and nobody, not even Philip.'

'Good heavens,' said Jillie, laughing, 'that does sound serious. And talking of Philip, has Tom – I mean, do you –'

'No,' said Alice firmly, blushing. 'Of course we've talked about it, and he absolutely understands how I feel and he says he would never force me to do anything I wasn't happy with, but actually – well –' She looked at Jillie slightly shamefaced. 'Actually, I can imagine doing it with him. I love him that much. All the things that I always believed, like it's wrong if you're not married, or at least totally committed, I can feel myself changing my mind about. I mean, if he'd asked me to marry him I definitely would. Go to bed with him, I mean. I tell you what, I jolly well want to,' she added, blushing again.

'Well, you know what I think about it anyway.'

'Yes, yes, I do. And I never thought I'd come to agree with you. So – while we're on the subject –' She looked very directly at Jillie. 'Are you? With Ned?'

'No,' said Jillie, and it was her turn to blush. 'I'm not. I wish I was. But he's never even asked me, and I can't work out why. I mean, maybe he just doesn't fancy me.'

'Oh, don't be silly. He's crazy about you, anyone can see.'

'Well, I don't know that he is,' said Jillie. 'We seem to have totally hit the buffers. Sometimes I think he just sees me as a friend. It's been going on an awfully long time, but then like you, we're both fearsomely busy.' She sighed. 'Anyway, we're not talking about me, we're talking about you. I just think that, somehow, you've got to put Laura behind you. Not forget about her – you can't – but stop comparing yourself with her. She's been dead for what –?'

'Three years,' said Alice. 'And I'm sure Tom knows how many days. But actually, in his head, I think only about a week. Honestly, if she was alive and she'd left him, I could cope. But you can't fight a perfect memory. And sometimes, I just know he's thinking about her. Even when we've been kissing, or he's lying on the bed holding me, he suddenly goes away, not really, but in his head, I can feel it, and I know he's thinking about her.'

'Well, Alice, I think you have to confront it.'

'What do you mean?'

'I think you have to talk to him about it. Tell him how you feel. Then it's in the open, you can discuss it and if he obviously does – did – still feel more for her than he does for you, you'll know where you are. Otherwise she is never, ever going to go away.'

'It's lovely to see you. You're looking marvellous. Love the hair.'

'Do you? I thought it might be a tad too short, but René does usually know best. You look pretty good yourself, Wendelien. Considering. How's it going?'

'The pregnancy? Better. It was ghastly at first, now the worst thing is feeling tired all the time.'

'I should be getting some beauty sleep myself,' said Diana. 'Not that I'm short of it. Being pregnant sounds a bit like life in Yorkshire, supper and then early to bed. While Johnathan stays up, working,' she added with a sigh. 'Not that if he came to bed it would be exactly exciting.'

'Oh, Diana. I'm sorry.'

'Oh, it's all right. It's just boring boring boring. I should go mad without my second life. Here's the barman. Let me treat you. Are you allowed cocktails?'

'Just a little one. I'll have a Buck's Fizz. The orange juice part will be good for me. And – it isn't difficult, getting away?'

'Not in the least. He just looks at me in that weirdly vague way and says, "Fine, darling, whatever you want." He did say that when Jamie starts school next year he won't be able to come with me, but that's all right, he doesn't have to, and although Mummy will miss him, it'll be easier in lots of ways.'

'And who is this session for?' asked Wendelien.

'Oh – *Vogue*,' said Diana carelessly, as if such a thing was utterly commonplace, 'with John French. I'm thrilled, he makes one looks so marvellous, not a wrinkle or a droop to be seen – it's all in his lighting, you see, it bleaches everything out. No one can work out quite how he does it, it's a sort of magic. And he's extraordinary to work with. He's queer, of course, but so gentlemanly and he just loves women. The more ladylike the better.'

'He must like you then,' said Wendelien.

'He does seem to. He says I have the bones. But I'm afraid I'm absolutely not his first choice. He works most of the time with people like Fiona Campbell-Walter and Barbara Goalen. You can't take a bad picture of either of them. You can of me, I assure you. But he directs so brilliantly: terribly painstaking, spends hours just getting a foot or a hand or the angle of the head exactly, exactly so. Never touches the camera himself.'

'What do you mean?'

'Well, he gets everything set up, lights and angles and everything, and spends hours working out the composition and the poses with one of his little boy assistants – standing in for the model, I mean. They look so sweet in their black jeans and T-shirts, posing as if they were in ball gowns, and then finally you get called in and he tells you where he wants you to stand and how, and then after about another half-hour fiddling, he summons one of the assistants, stands back, folds his arms, and says, "Now!" very peremptorily. The assistant presses the button or the Rolleiflex lead or whatever. He'll do that a few times, and then you have to move a fraction, or he tells the fashion editor to tweak the dress an inch, and then, when it's all exactly as he likes, he does it again. Fascinating. Tiring, though,' she added.

'And what sort of clothes tomorrow?'

'Evening. Hartnell and Hardy Amies. I've been told to bring lots of costume jewellery; I haven't got that much, but as it's *Vogue* they usually supply quite a lot themselves. And evening shoes. Last time I got ticked off for only having two pairs of gloves. I must do a bit of a stock-up this time. Will you come with me? Or are you too tired? I'm staying on an extra day. Just for fun, really, and to do a bit of shopping. Mummy will love it and Johnathan just won't notice.'

'Are you sure about that?' asked Wendelien. 'It seems strange to me.'

'Wendelien, honestly, I'm sure. He has absolutely no interest in what I do in London, and what's more he doesn't care. He wouldn't even mind if I had a lover, I swear. God, I wish I did,' she added, and Wendelien was quite shocked by the seriousness of her expression, the ache in her voice.

'Well, I can't quite believe that he really doesn't care,' Wendelien said. 'And he must see the pictures in the magazines. It does sound a bit – odd.'

'He *is* odd,' said Diana dismissively.

God, it had been a mistake. A dreadful, shocking, obscene mistake: Johnathan felt so angry with himself. How had he made it? How had he been blind enough, deaf enough even? Everything she said now drove him to distraction. How could he not have seen it was witchcraft, that she had worked some spell, confusing him with her beauty, her charm? Why had he lacked the sheer common sense to see that she was using him to get what she wanted: the fashionable life in London, the chic house, the smart friends?

How had he thought she could possibly want what he wanted, care about what he cared about? He supposed she had tried at first; and he could see it was hard for her, the brutal weather, the harsh, forbidding landscape as it must have seemed to her – and yet so lovely when you got to know it, with its crags and waterfalls and great stretches of moorland with its ever-changing colours and vast, amazing skies.

It was so painfully obvious that she was never going to fit in. All the women he knew up here in Yorkshire had done their best, asked her to join things and to help with things and had in the early days asked them for meals. She had given a few and they had felt bound to reciprocate. She had so clearly not enjoyed their dinners, sitting looking bored while the talk ranged from farming to county shows and county politics. Of course, it wasn't as charming as London gossip. But it all mattered to him, and he would have hoped she would make an effort on that account. His mother wasn't easy, he could see that, but she had tried very hard at first to be welcoming and she had so much to cope with. Not once had Diana gone over to sit with his father or take him out for a drive, amuse him just for a few hours. That, more than anything, hurt and angered him.

As for sex, Johnathan literally couldn't remember when they had last made love, and he was miserably aware that even there she found him a disappointment. He should have ended the whole thing immediately after the war, when he had known, could see as they sat there in that bloody restaurant in the Savoy how much she would hate it and how hopeless it would be. He could have done it there and then, cleanly, easily. He could have made her a generous settlement and they could both have begun again, for there had been no children. There he always stopped, thinking of Jamie, his beloved Jamie with the floppy dark hair and the wide brown eyes and the hero worship and the assumption that he was the source of every possible wisdom. Little Jamie, stomping round the farm after him, afraid of nothing, not the hugest shire horse, the most massive bull, the largest herd of cows – as long as Johnathan was with him, holding his small hand in his big one. He was his constant companion, sitting beside him on the tractor, following the plough with him, stomping through the muddiest field, watching, his eyes huge with wonder as the lambs were born.

He had bought him a pony for his fourth birthday, a sweetly sturdy Yorkshire Fell pony, darkest grey, the colour of the Yorkshire crags, with the black shaggy mane and long tail that were the breed's trademark, steady as a rock but fast, or would be one day when it was asked of him. He loved to ride with Jamie when he had time, which was rarely; but Diana had usurped him there, for she had plenty of it to fill, and he never disliked her more than when watching her riding out of the yard, Jamie on the leading rein, heading for the moors, looking back and chatting and smiling at him.

He didn't know what to do. He would have loved to have got rid of her but he couldn't divorce her now. He had no grounds and besides, that could mean losing Jamie, or certainly risk losing him. The only way he could be sure of getting custody, or fairly sure, was if she could be convicted of adultery. That seemed, given her present mode of behaviour, a real possibility; but getting proof would entail sordid procedures like having her followed by a private detective, and the resulting court case would be squalid beyond belief. Maybe that didn't matter; his mother would be delighted to be rid of Diana, she hated to be so much as in the same room as her, and it really would have no effect on their position in Yorkshire and the circle they moved in. And most people would be sympathetic, kind even; nobody liked Diana and although no one ever mentioned it, her increasingly frequent absences hardly spoke of a successful marriage.

But then he thought again – how would it affect Jamie? If nothing else, Diana was a good mother, surprisingly patient, loving and fun, endlessly inventive with games and treats, reading to him by the hour, playing the tedious make-believe games he loved. Did he really have the right to deprive Jamie of that?

All these things and more Johnathan pondered as he rode the tractor one long, lovely spring afternoon, when Yorkshire agreed to soften just a little and yield some blossom in the hedgerow here and an occasional cluster of daffodils in some hidden hollow there: and when he knew he would get home to an empty house after Diana had set off again to London.

Unbidden, the thought of Catherine came into his head.

# Chapter 22

## 1951

Sunday lunch with Alice's family had been all right; a bit painful, genteel even, with sherry beforehand and a small glass of red wine with the excellent lamb, and apple pie to follow with many references to some Mrs P who'd made it; he'd liked Mrs Miller, she was smiling and welcoming and rather engagingly nervous, spilling her husband's sherry as she passed it to him, and rushing round with a tea towel mopping it up, when it would have been better to leave it; Mr Miller he was less sure of, he seemed a bit of a tyrant.

There was no domestic help in the dining room, but clattering from the kitchen indicated the presence of some kind of minion; Tom offered to help with the clearing away but Mrs Miller looked very shocked and told him to go and join her husband Alec in the drawing room – this was the only reference to Christian names, and it was clear that they would remain Mr and Mrs Miller for the foreseeable future.

He had feared there would be veiled references to their relationship, and worse, its future, but none came. Later Alice told him she had been on tenterhooks throughout for the same reason. There was never any knowing what her father might say or do.

They left before tea; Alice could see that Tom was sated with gentility and perfectly mown lawns – twice referred to admiringly by Mrs Miller in terms that made it very plain this was Mr Miller's pride and joy. Mr Miller pumped his hand and said it had been very good to meet him and Mrs Miller smiled up at him and told him he would be welcome any time.

'Alice tells me you're going to the Festival of Britain together,' she said. 'Do let me know what you think of it – we're hoping to go, aren't we, Alec?'

This was clearly as much news to Alec as it was to Tom. On the train he said to Alice, 'You don't really want to go to that thing, do you?'

'Of course I do, I'd love to. Please, Tom, I think it'll be really good.'

'OK,' he said, 'as long as you listen to my speech this evening. It's to the local TGWU. Donald Herbert says it's going to be very well attended, and Jillie's cousin, Josh Curtis, is coming. I'm a bit unsure about parts of it. Well, most of it, to be honest.'

This was a new honour for Alice; she flushed crimson with delight and said she'd love to and spent the next hour feverishly wondering if Laura had simply sat admiringly and listened on such occasions, or made a lot of helpful and/or critical suggestions.

It was when he knocked his wine over that Jillie realised that Ned was in a truly distraught state, totally unlike his usual self-assured, easy self. He'd been edgy all evening, criticising the route the taxi driver had chosen, complaining about the table they'd been given at the restaurant, failing to tell her how lovely she looked. That was quite a relief – it got a bit repetitious and tedious at times. Twice he left the table to make a phone call. She assumed he must be worried about a patient, but when she asked him, he said no, everything was fine. He also rushed their dessert order, demanding the bill immediately afterwards. When she asked him mildly what was the hurry, he said he'd reserved a table at Claridge's and he didn't want to be late.

Jillie said it seemed rather a shame to rush a nice dinner just to go and drink some more somewhere else, and he almost snapped at her, saying he'd planned the evening rather carefully at her two favourite places, and the idea was to please her, not him. She drank her coffee in silence; but then suddenly in the taxi, he leaned over her and kissed her and said he was sorry, he was being a brute, and maybe they should just go to his house if that would be better, and she said better for what and he said she'd find out soon.

So the taxi was redirected to Markham Street, and the minute they arrived, he rushed into the kitchen and she heard a clinking of glasses and the fridge being opened, then a pause while he was clearly cancelling the table at Claridge's, and then he reappeared in the tiny drawing room, bearing a tray with two glasses and a bottle of champagne. He put it down on the low table next to her and she couldn't help noticing it was Veuve Clicquot Vintage, pretty special even by Ned's standards. She leaned back and looked at him as he reached for the bottle and said, 'Ned, what is going on, have you got something to tell me?'

He put the bottle down again, and looked at her very steadily and said, 'No, ask you,' and then he actually went down on one knee and said, 'Jillie, will you marry me?'

Her first thought was that he could never have done that in the champagne bar at Claridge's so it was as well they weren't there; and her second was of how absolutely adorable he looked kneeling there, literally at her feet; and her third was of total astonishment followed by, she was almost surprised to discover, complete and absolute joy. 'Oh, Ned,' she said. 'Of course I will. Of COURSE. Thank you.'

'Really?' he said, in tones of such disbelief and pleasure she actually laughed.

'Well, of course. I can't think of anything more wonderful. I really can't!' And then he sat down beside her and kissed her for a long time, really rather passionately, and she responded, loving it, longing for more, and thinking that if ever an occasion was auspicious this one was, with his bedroom upstairs and the moment so perfect; but the invitation, or even the suggestion, didn't come, although he began to caress her breasts and her stomach, and to tell her how much he loved her, and since that was clearly what he wanted, then she wasn't going to spoil the perfection of the moment.

'I am so, so glad,' he said suddenly, breaking off, pushing a strand of her hair back, smiling into her eyes. 'I was so afraid you'd say no.'

'Ned, why? When you know how terribly, terribly fond of you I am?'

'Yes, but it's not been very long – January to now, less than six months – you might not have been sure.'

'Well, I am. Perfectly sure. I long to be Mrs Welles, more than anything else in the world, and I'm going to be such a good one, such a perfect wife.'

'All you have to do is love me,' he said. 'That's all I ask.'

'Then you don't have anything to worry about,' she said, and then, suddenly, almost hopeful, 'Would you like me to give up work?'

'Now why should I like that?' he said, smiling at her. 'I love that you know the world I work in and care about. And I'll be incredibly proud of you when you qualify as a surgeon. Unless you want to, of course.'

'I'm not – sure,' she said. 'I'll think about it. I mean I've got a long way to go still. But then it would be awful to waste it. Maybe when – when we have children?'

'Goodness,' he said. 'You are thinking ahead.'

'Getting married is about thinking ahead, surely?'

'Yes, I suppose so. But really, it is your decision –'

'Think of the hours, though. When I'm a houseman. And I'd have to live in sometimes.'

'Well – yes. That might be hard. Oh, why are we spoiling this wonderful occasion worrying about something so relatively unimportant?'

'It would only be important if you cared about it. About the implications.'

'Yes, but I don't. Now let me give you some of this very special champagne and let us drink to Mr and Mrs Welles.'

'Mr and Mrs Welles,' said Jillie, raising her glass to him and then setting it down again. 'Now can we do some more kissing, please?'

# Chapter 23

## 1951

'How's it going then? You enjoying it?' Donald Herbert raised his glass to Josh.

'Yes, I really am. It's bloody tough, of course. And Bedford is a bastard – constantly spiking my stuff, saying it's not original, not sharp enough, not political enough.'

'Well, that's his job. He wouldn't be political editor of one of the country's most successful newspapers if he was a kind and cosy chappie. How do you get on with Harry Campbell?'

'Hardly ever see him. But I admire him beyond anything. People are always saying he's a bit like Cudlipp, has the same charisma, same passion. He's certainly got the Cudlipp philosophy, that a newspaper should have a mission.'

'And what's the mission of the *News*?'

'To support the ordinary man,' said Josh. 'The invisible one without a voice, who can't make his grievances felt. He's still having a hard time, that man – and his wife and family – six years after the war's ended.'

Josh Curtis and Donald Herbert were having what had become a regular chat in El Vino's bar in Fleet Street, opposite the Law Courts, where journalists famously drank and gossiped, often all afternoon.

'Do you know,' said Josh, warming up now, 'only a third of households in this country have a proper bathroom, and one in twenty don't even have running water? It's a bit of an indictment of you lot, don't you think?'

'I do,' said Donald Herbert. 'But the answer's not easy. There just isn't room for everybody. The old East End houses, for instance, are built incredibly densely. There's just not the room to build decent homes. Either people have to be moved out of London, which they don't want, or some of these high-rise places have to go up.'

'Yes, and there's resistance to them, of course. Old biddy called Dame Evelyn Sharp, she represents the Ministry of Housing, says people will be upset by the sight of them. I bet she doesn't have to wash in a tin bath by the fire.'

'Well, that sounds like a great story to me,' said Herbert, 'so why don't you write it. Give it a strong political angle; get some interviews with these people . . .'

'Don't you think I wanted to? But when I mentioned it to Clive, he liked it so much he made me do all the research, then wrote it himself. Campbell loved it. See what I mean?'

'Well, yes. Bloody annoying. But that's newspaper life, young Josh. It's not a tea party. You'll have to pitch a story to Campbell yourself, maybe one day when Bedford's away. Want another one of those?'

He nodded in the direction of Josh's glass.

His glass filled for the third time, Josh looked at Donald Herbert anxiously. 'But I don't want you to think I'm not enjoying it and I do know how lucky I am to be there at all, and I know I have you partly to thank for it –'

'Well, only partly. Your cuttings from the *Western Morning News* were pretty impressive. All I did was make sure Bedford read them, and gave you a chance. I'll see what I can do, try and find you a story from the inside track. We're going to lose this next election, that's for sure. So there'll be plenty of material in that. Meanwhile, just keep your head down and do what Bedford tells you. Even if you don't want to do it. Only way to learn.'

'I know. Actually, I've got one to do tomorrow. About the Festival of Britain. More of a feature really, nothing political, and personally I think the place is a bit depressing, but apparently Campbell's keen on covering it and told Bedford to get on with it.'

'Right, well, good luck with that. Look, I must go. I have a company to run, keep forgetting about it . . .'

He hadn't forgotten about it, of course; he never did for an instant, Josh thought, looking after his large figure as he made his way out to the Strand. He was currently regarded as a possible, if not probable, elevation to the House of Lords at the end of the present parliament and Josh knew he was lucky to have him as a mentor; he also really liked him. He had met him at the Curtis household, at one of their evening soirées.

Thinking of them reminded him of the news about Jillie's engagement. There was to be a party shortly to celebrate; and he had been invited. He was very fond of Jillie, hoped the Welles fellow was worthy of her. He must contact her and congratulate her. He wondered if she'd give up her medical studies; shame if she did. There were precious few married women working; most men demanded – and got – one hundred per cent attention to themselves. Well, if he was ever lucky enough to find a wife, he'd let her do whatever she liked. The women's editor on the *News*, Philippa Parry, was a great champion of women's rights and commissioned many stories supporting this view. She always got a huge postbag from frustrated housewives after one of these. 'But then the poor things just go back to their washing,' she said to Josh one day, as they waited for the evening conference. 'It's such a slow battle. I thought the war would have done it, but they've all just slipped backwards into the kitchen. Or rather been driven there.'

She liked Josh; she found him amusing and liberal minded, not to mention rather attractive. She wished he could get more stories into the paper, but that was a slow battle too; it had taken years of fashion reporting of the most basic kind before she had finally gained any kind of authority. And that was entirely due to Harry Campbell, who had worked with her years earlier, and when a slot came up on the *News*, he called her in.

'I want a lot more than reports on frocks and the height of heels,' he said. 'I want the women's pages to be like the rest of the paper: a strong statement of what we stand for. Which means giving women a voice, so they can express their concerns and ambitions. Delivering that is all you have to do.'

Twenty-four hours later, Josh was stationed by the entrance of the Exhibition on the newly glamorised South Bank. With him were John Booth, photographer; Joanna Biggs, fashion reporter; and Donald Herbert, who had been lunching at the Savoy with Harry Campbell and found himself suddenly dispatched in the middle of a superb fillet of beef to 'keep an eye on this shoot at the Festival. Nobody senior there and I'm not entirely happy about it. Your protégé's going, young Tom Knelston, and he'll be glad to see you.' As indeed Tom was.

Tom was interested in the Festival of Britain only in as far as it was known to be the brainchild of Attlee and another of his bids to cheer the nation up. He was fascinated by such public-relations enterprises. So far it had been a success, and this being a blessedly sunny warm day, it was already busy. They were all clutching copies of the *South Bank Exhibition Guide* with its jaunty logo incorporating Britannia, and a row of red, white and blue flags, designed at considerable cost. The two most famous segments of the exhibition (timed to coincide with the centenary of Prince Albert's Great Exhibition) were the Dome of Discovery which contained a series of exhibitions on such worthy subjects as the Land, the Earth and the Sea, and the Skylon, a slender steel needle-like construction almost 300 feet high. And the new Royal Festival Hall, acoustically perfect, it was said, and already booked to host the world's finest musicians for months and even years ahead.

Gerald Barry, the festival's director, had described the whole thing as a 'tonic for the nation', and while it perhaps lacked the sparkle normally associated with tonic, being for the most part grey and constructed in concrete, the nation, or such of it as spoke to Josh Curtis, seemed of a mind to agree with him. After two hours things became repetitive; there were, as Donald Herbert remarked, only so many ways for people to admire it, and was there nothing more exciting for Joanna to write about than the British uniform for outings of overcoat, hat, gloves, umbrella and nicely polished shoes?

Then Donald Herbert had the idea, which not only transformed the feature and the photographs, but propelled Joanna's byline into sixteen-point, and tipped Tom Knelston's comparatively ordered life into potential disarray for years to come.

'What we should do,' he said, 'is head down to Battersea, to the Pleasure Gardens. Bet we'll get a jollier crowd there.'

He was right: the Festival Pleasure Gardens, opened by Princess Margaret, were filled with people in much more holiday mood. A glorified funfair, it had attracted much controversy, felt to be not in keeping with the more serious purpose of the festival. There was particular criticism of the fact that it was open on Sundays. However, the public were determined to enjoy it, and indeed it much more closely resembled the tonic described by Gerald Barry than its more earnest neighbour up river. Its centrepiece was the big wheel and the queue to ride upon it extremely long. The inhabitants of the queue that day were young and, greatly to Joanna Biggs's relief, more interestingly dressed, many of the young in jeans and that new phenomenon, the overgrown sweatshirt known as a 'sloppy joe', munching contentedly on toffee apples and candyfloss as they waited. Girls giggled and boys postured for John Booth's camera, flashing tirelessly into the evening light; Joanna became increasingly inventive, pulling boys' hats off and plonking them onto their girlfriends' heads, and Donald Herbert, feeling his work done, was emboldened to pull out the whisky flask he kept permanently in his pocket and take increasingly frequent sips of it. They were all beginning to feel they had done their job when there was a sudden cry of 'Tom! Tom Knelston, hello!' and they all turned round to see a beautiful girl, tall, dark, aristocratic, wearing what only Donald Herbert could say for sure was mink, and extremely high-heeled shoes, waving at them from the hot dog stall.

The wave was followed by some imperious beckoning; obediently, they trooped towards her, Herbert looking at Tom with an entirely new expression on his face, veering between awe and irritation, and as they reached the stall another woman, also be-minked and high-heeled, came towards them holding out a gracious hand.

'Do come over. How marvellous, just as we were giving up. My name is Blanche Ellis Brown from *Style* magazine.' It really was too good to be true, Donald thought. 'We've been shooting all afternoon. The other girl's gone, but we wanted one last shot of Diana here, on the big wheel, or possibly the carousel, and needed a good-looking man to be beside her. Precious few of those here, I can tell you, but – well, you wouldn't mind, would you?' She addressed her remark to Tom, although Donald Herbert, Josh Curtis and even John Booth were all beaming hopefully at her. It wasn't until she said, 'Diana tells me you are old friends,' that they were forced to realise it was Tom she was actually addressing.

Tom could only smile sheepishly and submit to having his raincoat removed by Joanna, who was beside herself with excitement. A study of his cheap suit saw the jacket of that removed as well, his tie loosened, his top shirt button undone and he was set beside Diana on a carousel horse smiling uncertainly into Booth's camera. The proprietor of the carousel, who knew a publicity opportunity when he saw one, stopped and started it as often as required. Diana, a seasoned practitioner of the photo shoot, took command, and the final shot had Diana and Tom on the same horse, Diana side-saddle, her face turned to Tom and both of them laughing.

'I can't thank you enough,' said Blanche, as they finally scrambled off. 'Yes, please do use the pictures, as long as you credit *Style*. Thank you so much, Mr Knelston – you should get someone to sign you up, you're a natural. Diana, what are you going to do now, darling? I have to get back to the office, get those coats locked up for the night, and that diamond bracelet and earrings, if you don't mind.'

'Pity, I was going to try and make off with them,' said Diana. 'Where's the car? All my stuff's in it. Look, Tom and the rest of you, why don't we go for a drink, we're so near the Savoy.'

'Marvellous idea,' said Donald Herbert. 'I was having lunch there several hours ago, before the editor sent me off here. I can pick up where I left off. Halfway through a bottle of rather nice claret, I seem to remember.'

'And you are?' said Diana, studying him with interest.

Thus it was that twenty minutes later, Tom found himself in the cocktail bar at the Savoy. He had a vague, uneasy feeling that he should have been somewhere else, doing something much more worthy, but he really couldn't remember what. Since all that mattered was that Alice was on duty, he should just try to enjoy it. Which he was. Very much. As he sat there, watching Diana, waving for the waiter, ordering champagne, taking in the surroundings, which were scarcely familiar in themselves, but which induced a sensation he could recognise from being in Jillie's house – and even, he reflected with some surprise, being in the Southcott house with its glorious warmth that freezing day surrounded by books – he settled back in his chair, took the champagne from the tray the waiter was offering him and surrendered to – what? A sort of rich pleasure, a sense that this was quality in its purest sense, and that while this was not where he belonged, he had reached it and not without some difficulty, and having the ability to recognise that, he had every right to enjoy it.

So he sat there in the bar, smiling at Diana who was unmistakably happy to be there with him. Delighted to be able – just for once – to be in command of the situation, sipping at champagne and feeling neither overawed nor uncomfortable but easy and able to enjoy the whole, surprising experience in a totally unsurprised way.

The picture of him and Diana in the *Daily News* the following morning, taking up a large part of the third page, aroused a variety of emotions in a variety of people. It was the main feature story in the paper that day: the rest of the page and the one opposite showed a number of smaller photographs, including one of Donald Herbert eating candyfloss. Diana was described by Josh in his caption as *top model Diana Southcott* (she had agreed with Johnathan at the beginning that she would be known by her maiden name) and he as *rising star of the Labour Party, Tom Knelston* (Tom had agreed to this wild overstatement after his third glass of champagne, urged on by Donald Herbert and Diana). Harry Campbell, the editor of the *Daily News*, was delighted as he was able to show Jarvis McIntyre, his ultimate boss, that he had done what he asked and made a splash of the festival; Donald Herbert was gratified at doing what he had been looking for an opportunity to do for a long time and bring Tom to the public's attention; Blanche Ellis Brown was thrilled at the pre-publicity for one of her fashion pages, and her new top model discovery; Diana Southcott was extremely pleased with herself, not only for getting some personal publicity but for finding a reason to claim Tom Knelston as more than just a childhood acquaintance; Tom Knelston was deeply embarrassed and anxious about Alice's reaction, and to a lesser degree that of the local Labour MP and indeed the party chairman. His apprehension about Alice's reaction was correct; she was so angry on reading the article, brought to her notice by several of her colleagues, that she had to go into the sluice and throw several bowls of water at the wall, before rehearsing word for word what she would have to say to Tom when she saw him that evening; words delivered with such vitriol in the hallway of the nurses' home where he was waiting for her with a rather weary-looking bunch of daffodils that he felt them like physical blows, her nurse's cap hurled onto the floor and the daffodils with them.

'I thought you didn't want to go to that "thing", as you called it. So what changed? Some fancy posh bird in a fur coat? I wonder how your beloved party would view that? I thought you were a socialist, Tom Knelston. All over, is it, now you're hobnobbing with top models? How did you meet her anyway? Just happened to bump into her? As you wandered through the park? All by yourself. Or were you with your loud, vulgar friend Donald Herbert? I never could see the attraction of that man, Tom. He's just – gross. Well, you're very welcome to the whole disgusting lot of them. I just wonder what Laura might have had to say about it? You could at least have warned me, but I don't suppose you care enough about me to even consider that. Well, never mind. I never want to see you again, Tom Knelston, as long as I live. So you can just get out of here and go and find Miss Southcott. Only if she's got any sense, she won't waste her time on someone like you. Do you think she'll sit for hours listening to your boring speeches, or your ambitions for the National Health Service? I very much doubt it. I don't suppose she's been near a public hospital in her entire life. Now just get out of here, and –' she was crying now, the tears somehow increasing the force of her rage – 'don't touch me, just don't, stop it, Tom, stop it, I hate you, or I would if I didn't despise you. What are you—'

For Tom, standing there, initially meek and apologetic, had slowly, in the face of this onslaught, become overwhelmed with a quite different emotion, one of intense and quite shocking desire for her. He had never seen this Alice before: passionate, raw, careless of what she was saying. The sweet, submissive girl had, as he watched and listened to her, become a woman, strong, brave, honest, fighting for what she had and what mattered to her. He raised his voice above hers and said, 'Alice, stop it. Stop it now, at once. You're being stupid. And I—'

'Oh really? Stupid? No one's ever complained about it before.'

'Well, perhaps they should have done. Perhaps you'd have grown up a bit. Instead of going around thinking you're perfect, doing so well at that expensive school, and at your nursing, and your parents . . .'

That did it; she went for him, physically, lunged at him, slapped his face, pummelled his chest, screaming that she hated him. Suddenly he caught her wrists and held her off and – what was he doing now? Smiling, for heaven's sake, smiling and then half laughing. She lashed out with the only weapons she had left, her feet, and kicked him in the shins.

'Don't laugh at me!' she said. 'Laura might have been perfect, but I tell you what, Tom Knelston, you most certainly aren't. You're arrogant and quite often boring and rude and—'

'Laura always said my mother should have put me over her knee more often. Said she spoilt me. You seem to be in agreement with her over that at least.' He rubbed his ankle, grimacing. 'That quite hurt, you know.'

Alice stood back, breathing heavily. 'Good, I meant it to. And yes, I think Laura was right.'

They stood there, the pair of them, six inches apart now, their eyes fixed on one another. Then suddenly, Tom reached for Alice's hand, and with his other hand very gently stroked her cheek. 'I was just wondering if you might consider marrying me? Arrogant, boring and rude as I am?'

'Marry you?'

'Yes. Marry me.'

'Oh,' said Alice. 'Oh, my goodness. Oh, gosh. Crikey. Crumbs.'

'Is that a posh way of saying yes?'

'Look, I just want to get one thing out of the way. This obsession with class that you have is so tedious. I can't help being born into whatever class it was. Nor can you. So can we just stop talking about it, for ever?'

'For ever is a very long time. But for a bit yes, of course. And having got that out of the way, what is your answer?'

'What do you think it is, you rude arrogant, boring, incredibly lovely man?'

'I don't know. You'll have to tell me.'

'It's yes, of course. Yes, yes, yes!'

Alice looked at him. He was smiling. She realised that he had become someone different. Someone more confident, less confused. Which was exactly how he felt, although he couldn't have told anyone why.

'Now,' he said, and she took the hand he held out to her. 'We're going to get a taxi – yes, not wait for a bus, the way most people have to do, because we aren't most people; we're privileged, thank God – and get the hell over to Islington, and if you don't come then you really never will see me again.'


An hour later they were in Tom's mercifully recently changed bed; Alice had been duly deflowered and while not entirely enjoying it, could see the huge potential of it at least and she had agreed, in a rather quavery voice, that they should marry in the fairly near future.

'Very near if I'm pregnant,' she added, with a hiccup. 'But Tom, are you sure about all this? It's a bit sudden. You're not going to change your mind, are you?'

'No. I'm not going to change my mind. And it's not really sudden. I'm a bit thick, that's all. I couldn't see how much I loved you.'

'I still don't quite understand.'

'You don't need to.'

And with that Alice had to be, if not content, at least fully persuaded, and was very happy to be so.

# Chapter 24

## 1951

Tom's enthusiasm for the June wedding, so yearned after by both Alice and her mother – a mere two months after the announcement of the engagement – was something of a surprise as well as a relief to both of them. Alice quite simply couldn't wait to become Mrs Knelston and to commence her role by wafting down the aisle on her father's arm in a dress and veil as much like those featured in the pages of wedding magazines as possible. June was *the* month to be married, everybody knew that; warm, sunny, with gardens at their rose-filled, lush-lawned best. It was also perfect for honeymoons, ideally in a seaside location. Mrs Miller did have a slight anxiety that it might look just a little too hasty, as if Alice might have something to hide beneath the bouquet, but a rather embarrassing conversation reassured her on that score. Although when the wedding date actually had to be set for the middle of July, the church being so fully booked through June, it came as something of a relief.

Tom's enthusiasm, which he would not have admitted to Alice even under torture, was due to two facts: he knew that the election looming in the autumn would consume a great deal more of his time than a wedding and was also impressed by the frequent assertions of Donald Herbert that a pretty young wife would do his political progress no harm. The sooner his journey to the altar and then the honeymoon was completed, the better it would suit him. The only problem was that he seemed unable to choose a best man; he knew his brothers would be horrified by the idea, far too shy to stand up and make the requisite speech. Alice had suggested one of his workmates, but he said he didn't care enough about any of them to award them the honour. Which was all very well, but time was passing and plans generally made. He told her not to fuss, it really didn't matter that much surely; he suggested Donald Herbert which frightened her to death, until she found he was teasing her. 'Well, if we can't find anyone else, he'll have to do it,' said Tom. He was taking a perverse pleasure in the whole affair, it being the only way he could fall short of total submission to her plans.

This did not mean he was not in love with Alice; he was, deeply so. The more he got to know her, the real her, rather than the one she had been so carefully presenting to him, the more he loved her. She was very much her own person and now she had shaken off the spectre of Laura as rival, the more she pleased him. She didn't have Laura's intellect, but she was loyal, caring, and tender hearted almost to the point of absurdity. Her tendency to accept people at face value he found particularly refreshing, embedded as he was in the cynicism of the politician class. She had a charm and eagerness to socialise that Donald Herbert was not the only person to appreciate. She also thought Tom was the cleverest, most gifted person she had ever met.

Having been something of a recluse since Laura died, and not possessed of a social circle before he met Alice, Tom found the constant invitations that came their way, both formal and informal, almost bewildering. Alice had more friends than anyone he had ever known and an extraordinary tolerance of people's shortcomings. He found himself constantly in the company of a great many people he would never previously have exchanged the time of day with; it wasn't easy, but he did it for Alice because he loved her. He really did love her.

Alice was so happy she found it difficult to believe. She woke up in the morning glowing with it and fell asleep at night suffused with it. Her wildest dreams of Tom had had him telling her he loved her and that some day maybe, they might have a future together. That he should be marrying her in a very few weeks seemed close to impossible. It was as if Tom had stepped over some barrier that night of 'The Row', as she thought of it. He wasn't very romantic, that was for sure. 'You know I love you,' he said slightly irritably when she hinted that the odd compliment might have been nice, when she was wearing some new dress or had changed her hair. 'I don't see what more you want.' She hastened to tell him that indeed she didn't, she was just being foolish, and he would agree that she was. She still had a considerable rival in the form of the Labour Party, but she could accept that; his beliefs and ambitions were as much part of him as his auburn hair and his glorious smile.

And sex – well, sex was so wonderful. She couldn't believe she had lived through twenty-three years – or at least through a grown-up life – without discovering how wonderful it was. She found herself looking forward to an evening in bed with him as passionately as she would once have looked forward to being taken to the theatre or out to dinner. The month she was on night duty, deprived of this glorious new pleasure, was almost unbearable. She became irritable and altogether miserable. When she told Tom he flushed with pleasure and said nothing could have pleased him more.

'Well, don't you miss it?' she said plaintively, in their snatched meetings over early supper or breakfast, and he said he did, of course, but he had grown accustomed to such deprivation in the long years on his own.

They had decided she would continue working until she was pregnant and when the first baby was unarguably on its way, they would look for a little house with a garden just slightly further out of central London, in Ealing perhaps, or Highgate, neither frighteningly expensive. He was so easy about the wedding; she would have expected him to be awkward, questioning all sorts of aspects, but he simply agreed to everything. Guest lists, venue, food, champagne, even what he was to wear. The thought occasionally rose unbidden to him of what on earth Laura would have made of it, but he banished it. She would either have mocked him or despised him, probably both. She was in another country now, remembered with great love, but he had left her there, safe, together with Hope.

❖ ❖ ❖

Alice's parents had slightly mixed feelings about Tom as a husband for their beloved only daughter. They thought he was charming, and might well have considerable prospects, but these were of a rather vague variety. They did concede that being the wife of an MP could be very prestigious, but he wasn't one yet and might never be. Anyway, he wouldn't be a Conservative MP but a socialist one.

They were a little nervous about Tom's family, and their attendance at the wedding; how would they fit in with their own friends? They were probably unsophisticated. It was very fortunate, they agreed, that neither of Tom's brothers was to be his best man, but like Alice they were finding the absence of any other suggestion increasingly irritating. Finally Mrs Miller decided she could hardly leave meeting the Knelston clan until the wedding day and suggested that as many of them as were able, but certainly Tom's mother, should come for the day one Sunday. She wasn't quite sure how they would all get there, and was slightly surprised to discover that all the families, and even the unmarried daughter, had cars, and that Arthur, Tom's next brother down, was rather well off, being a successful builder. He would bring Mrs Knelston and two or three other cars would come too.

Alice was delighted with this plan; she had still not met Tom's mother. Now, suddenly, she would meet the lot of them, and had already decided she would like them very much.

Finally, one evening in bed, she discovered the reason for Tom's reluctance; his mother, who was only in her mid-fifties, was what he described as 'confused'. Dementia from an early age ran through the female line of the family and poor Mary had fallen victim to it.

'I just can't think why you didn't tell me,' she said crossly. 'What did you think I might do? Forbid her to come to the wedding, refuse to have anything to do with her?'

Tom, looking at once wretched and embarrassed, said he supposed he'd thought she might find the whole thing hard to cope with.

'Do you really think so little of me?' said Alice. 'I'm very sad for you all, of course, but that's about it.'

'I'm sorry. Yes, it was wrong of me. But she certainly won't be able to come to the wedding, Alice. It would be impossible. She's quite likely to rush up to the altar and kiss me when we're taking our vows.'

'It seems such a shame,' said Alice. 'Surely one of your sisters could take care of her, take her out if she thought she was about to do something – odd.'

'It all happens rather suddenly,' said Tom. 'Hard to predict. And once she's on her way, there's no stopping her. I don't want you worried about her in the middle of your wedding.'

'*Our* wedding,' said Alice briskly.

'Sorry. Our wedding. But it's – well, it is your big day, isn't it? That's all I mean.'

'I would hope it was yours too,' said Alice. Then, 'Look,' she said into the silence. 'Bring her, Tom, please. To the reception at least. And I still think if one of your sisters sat at the very back with her . . .'

'No,' said Tom. 'Not in the church. But yes, the reception.'

'Good. I'd better give my mother due warning though.'

'Oh, Alice . . .' He leaned across the bed, reached for her hand and kissed it. 'In case you don't know, I do love you.'

'Just as well,' she said, 'since there's only about six weeks to go for you to change your mind.'

She left him feeling happier, but in the taxi started worrying whether he would have kept such a thing from Laura. She felt quite sure he would not.

'Damn you,' she said aloud, to the brave tragic ghost who seemed destined to be her life's companion. And then again, 'DAMN YOU.'

Jillie's wedding was not to be in June; nor in July. Ned said he wanted them to enjoy their engagement. It was such a happy time, there was so much to do, a house to find – the cottage was far too small for two of them – his private practice was growing, and absorbing more and more of his time, and besides a big wedding, such as Jillie would surely want, was a large enterprise, and required a great deal of organisation.

Jillie, who would have married him in a registry office, with witnesses pulled off the street, the sooner to become Mrs Welles, agreed to all this with a dutiful cheerfulness. He was right; the cottage was tiny and her parents did want a big wedding, and he was terribly busy with his work.

'But I just think,' she said to Alice one night, managing to interrupt the urgent flurry of consideration over whether the bridesmaids should have white ribbons or blue on their pale lemon taffeta dresses, 'I just think if he really loved me as much as he says he would at least have some kind of notional date in mind. I mean, don't you think it's a little bit odd?'

'I – suppose so,' said Alice, torn between total agreement with this and not wishing to upset Jillie further. 'But you mustn't forget he's quite a bit older than you and he's got a very complicated life to sort out –'

'What's that got to do with it? He's the same age as Tom and Tom's been married before.'

'He has indeed,' said Alice with a sigh. Jillie ignored it. 'Then there's the – the sex thing. I just don't understand it.'

'Still nothing?'

'Nothing. Sometimes I feel like a sort of – sort of much-loved sister.'

'Golly,' said Alice, contemplating the joy of her bed life as she called it, the swooping, sweeping pleasure, the consuming, greedy invasion of her senses the moment Tom touched her, just the sheer joy of experiencing it and of knowing she was giving the joy back to him. It was so much part of love, surely. How could Ned not be sharing this with Jillie, or at least wanting to share it? Something was wrong, terribly wrong; but she couldn't begin to imagine what it could be.

Ned had chosen Ludo as his best man – of course. Ludo, who had known from the very beginning. Ludo, whose example he had followed. Ludo, who had encouraged him with his own happy marriage, his large, growing family. Ludo, who had assured him he was doing the right thing, that he would be happy, as would Jillie, as would their children. Ludo, who had made a wonderful speech at the engagement party, that gathering of the great and the good in the house in Highbury. Ned had been so proud that night, so proud and so happy, so sure of himself, so certain of his love for Jillie, of hers for him.

And so welcomed into the family: his future father-in-law, in the most wonderful erudite speech, told how proud they were to have him joining them, how happy for Jillie; but it had been that night the fear had begun, that he would fail Jillie, not only privately, but publicly and dreadfully. He lay awake, quite literally into the dawn, haunted and afraid, and since then the fear had resisted denial.

His mother had come to the party, as well as his father; probably the first time they had met since across the divorce courts, and of course they did not meet then, not really. His father had made a stiff little speech, and Persephone had just wafted about, in a cloud of cream silk and lace, looking rather naughtily bride-like, stunning people and charming them with her beauty. She had taken a great shine to Tom, had told him that, apart from her son, he was the most handsome man in the room, and Alice could see he was absurdly taken by her in return. Well, he clearly liked a bit of class in his women. That Southcott woman who had been riding the carousel with him; there was no denying the rapport between them as they sat there, laughing at one another, his arm round her waist. While making his excuses and protestations, he had revealed more than he realised, talking of her kindness and genuine sorrow at Laura's grave, their childhood years interwoven by village life, their first proper meeting as he stood in the ditch, and how every word of it, remembered so vividly, told not so much of her attitude to him, as his to her.

Yes, yes, he said impatiently, as he and Alice lay in bed that night – for she had returned perhaps unwisely to the subject – of course Diana was beautiful; she was a top model, for heaven's sake. That didn't alter the fact that she was a perfect specimen of her breed, spoilt, snobbish, vain; and then rather spoilt the effect by adding – unwisely – that he had been surprised by how gentle and natural a mother she clearly was.

'Tom,' said Alice suddenly. 'What did you think of Ned?'

'I liked what I saw of him. Which wasn't much, was it? But he was very nice to me. Jillie had done her bit, told him about the politics thing, and he asked me about that. And he's all the right things for Jillie, isn't he?'

'What do you mean?'

'Well – charming, successful, good-looking –'

'I don't know why you should think those are the sorts of things that would matter to Jillie,' said Alice, slightly irritably. 'She's not a shallow person.'

'I didn't say she was. Quite the reverse. But she's grown up in that sort of set-up, hasn't she? She'll expect to be kept in the manner to which she's been accustomed, as they say.'

'I think that's a horrible thing to say,' said Alice.

'Oh, don't be ridiculous. It's true.'

'All right. But what sort of a person do you think he is? Do you think he really loves Jillie?'

'Oh, Alice, don't be absurd – how can I tell? He seemed to be very fond of her, but then they were getting engaged, weren't they? He was hardly going to be anything else.'

'So he didn't seem – odd in any way?'

'What sort of odd?'

'Oh, I don't know.'

'Alice, he seemed exactly like most people from his class to me. Maybe a bit less self-confident. But then, that wouldn't be surprising, given his childhood, that father and that mother.'

'No, I suppose not,' said Alice, giving up. 'Jillie wants us to have dinner together one night, the four of us. Would you like that?'

'You know I'd hate it,' said Tom. 'But for you, yes, I suppose so. After the wedding. I tell you one thing I didn't like –'

'Yes?' said Alice, wondering if it was going to be deeply significant.

'That shirt he was wearing.'

'What was wrong with it?'

'Hideous colour. Almost yellow. I mean, nice suit and then ruin it. How could he do that?'

Tom noticed clothes, both men's and women's. Alice had been surprised by this at first, wondering why when it was apparently out of character. He had submitted, without protest, to being kitted out in morning dress, and had then taken her on an expedition to buy his going-away suit, and astonished her by choosing cream linen, an open-weave white cotton shirt which he insisted would be worn open necked and – most astonishing of all – a panama hat with a distinctly wider brim than the conventions of the time would allow.

'I shall have to look to my laurels,' she said, laughing as he modelled it all for her later. 'You'll outclass me completely. None of the going-away pictures on our piano.'

'It would be nice to have a piano,' said Tom suddenly, arranging his linen suit carefully on a hanger, 'and not just for putting pictures on. If we bought that house in Ealing, the one with the room with French windows, it would go very nicely. You could maybe teach me and the children to play. I'd like our house to have lots of music in it.'

'Like the Bevan household?' said Alice, her eyes sparkling at him. She was teasing him, but he took it seriously and said yes, music was so important, it reached out to everyone, whatever their circumstances and education. 'If I was education minister,' he added, 'I'd make music the first lesson of every day in every school.'

'Would you like to be education minister? Don't tell me you're going off health?'

'No, of course not,' he said, sounding shocked. 'That will always be the most important thing to me. It's at the heart of every civilised society.'

'And yet your Mr Bevan has resigned.'

'He had to. He couldn't tolerate the watering down of his ideals.'

'Well, there's a job ready and waiting for you,' said Alice, giving him a kiss. 'And no, I'm not teasing you and you know I'll do everything in my power to help make it happen.'

She had no idea what she was promising.

# Chapter 25

## 1951

Every time Diana thought about Ned and Jillie's engagement party – or looked at the handsome, elaborate invitation, designed by some arty member of the Highgate elite, no plain gilt-edged stiffy for the Curtis clan – she felt sick. It wasn't that she still fancied Ned, but she still, in some distorted way, blamed him for her agreeing to marry Johnathan. She had never forgotten that night at the Savoy, and his rather public rejection of her and how she had fled to Johnathan to save face; she knew it was absurd, but she couldn't quite face the prospect of seeing him become so splendidly and publicly engaged, when it was so precisely what she had wanted for herself. In the end a gloriously simple solution occurred to her: 'Can we make some excuse?' she said to Johnathan. 'I just can't face it.'

Johnathan said he was very surprised, and that surely all her old friends would be there. 'Doesn't matter to me, of course, I'd love not to go, so yes, make whatever excuse you like.'

Which she did, saying that things were very busy on the farm, and it would be very difficult for Johnathan to get away.

She was busy trying to be a good wife, for a while anyway, so time spent quietly together in Yorkshire was what she thought of as good-will in the bank. She was waiting for a suitable moment to tell Johnathan that not only had she been booked for a three-day session, shooting evening gowns and furs for the all-important September issue of *Style*, the biggest issue in the year, where advertisers spent more money than all the others put together, but she'd been asked to go to Paris in January to shoot the collections. Every time she thought about that, her skin crawled with excitement. She had never 'done' Paris, and although she knew it was desperately hard work and you had to work through the night quite often, and you got to see almost nothing of Paris apart from its photographic studios, it still gave you a cachet, a standing as a model that nothing else could do. If you'd never done Paris, you just weren't quite the thing; and Diana wanted to be quite the thing more than anything. She thought, all other things being equal, he would agree. The only thing was that Johnathan was becoming increasingly insistent on their having another child.

Jamie, he said, was alone too much, needed a little brother or sister. Diana didn't point out that it would be about three years before the little brother or sister became any kind of a companion for Jamie, by which time he would have gone away to prep school anyway. She wasn't exactly a good wife, so the least she could do was give him another baby. But if she was pregnant, she wouldn't be going to Paris. Using contraceptives was out of the question – he would know; she would just have to hope.

And Johnathan did seem very determined. He came home earlier, spent more time with her when he was there and actually managed to persuade his mother to let Diana take over some of the farm paperwork, so that she was more involved – which she had always wanted, and argued (to herself at any rate) that their marriage would have been far happier for it. As Sir Hilary was worse, and very frail and in need of more care, Vanessa was actually quite grateful. There was no help for it, Diana thought, she'd just have to do what Johnathan wanted. She had sufficient sense of fairness to see that. The sex as always was dull – but more frequent.

At first she was lucky; her next period duly arrived and Johnathan, grateful that she was patently trying to do what he wanted, agreed, a little sadly, that she should go down to London for the three-day shoot for the September issue.

She had the most marvellous time. She was recognised now as

being, if not one of the top models, then very high in the second division. Of course she wasn't Barbara Goalen, whose elegant dark beauty was rather similar to her own, and who dominated the field, along with the other greats, Anne Gunning (fortunate, Diana often thought, that she had chosen to work under her unmarried name) and Fiona Campbell-Walter; but she had a reputation for incredibly hard work, and also for her skill at doing her own hair and make-up imaginatively. Moreover, she would help other, less talented, and newer girls do theirs. John French had once actually called her the Monet of the make-up box; she was incredibly proud of the title.

He wasn't shooting the September issue, of course; he was booked exclusively for *Vogue*. But there was a new photographer on the scene, American, whose photographs had the look of Irving Penn; one interview with him in the *Sunday Times* said he had the gift of sprinkling his pictures with glamour dust. He and Diana had developed a rapport and he booked her whenever he could. As always in such partnerships, a kind of alchemy worked between them; their sessions were charmed. No photographer could draw out Diana's glamour, her gift of making it sex-charged, as Freddie Bateman could. And he was young and attractive, with thick blonde hair and a preppy glamour of his own: and most assuredly not queer. Diana fancied him wildly, and he her. Nothing had happened yet, but it was said in the business it was inevitable.

The pictures they produced were extraordinary. He didn't go for anything excessive – no wild exteriors and settings like the young Norman Parkinson – and his style was quite formal in the beginning at any rate, his posing careful, his lighting in the John French mould, bleaching out imperfections, enhancing bone structure; but with Diana there was a rawness, almost an insolence, that he brought in as well. She stared directly into his lens, hungry, sex-charged, and yet untouchably beautiful. When Freddie Bateman arrived with the contacts he knew perfectly well what treasure he was delivering; he stood, arms folded, smirking with excitement, while Blanche Ellis Brown, examining them, was to be heard shouting with excitement.

'Darling,' said the editor, putting her head round the door, 'no orgasms in the office, please!' But called over to the table, given a magnifying glass, she was as excited as Blanche and said there were at least three covers there, and she had no idea which to choose. The art director was called in; usually very cool, he became quite noisy and voluble himself, and suggested they used two pictures on one cover – that, in itself, would cause a huge stir.

Blanche was so excited she called Wendelien Bellinger to see if Diana was still in London and if she'd like to come over and see the pictures. Diana, who wasn't going back to Yorkshire till the morning, said a whole herd of wild horses wouldn't keep her away and abandoned Wendelien and her new baby with a certain guilty relief. When she arrived there was something of a party going on; Blanche had produced a bottle of champagne, and both Freddie and Cedric, the art director were there; they all raised their glasses to Diana and, struggling to appear cool, she took her glass and smiled at Freddie with a look of complicit satisfaction. He returned the look rather seriously and kissed Diana on the cheek. 'She's one hell of a broad,' he remarked to the room in general.

Diana rather liked being called a broad; it had unladylike, raunchy connotations. It wouldn't have gone down well at all in Yorkshire society, she reflected.

'Thank you,' was all she said; but when the champagne was all gone, and Freddie suggested they went on and shared another bottle at the Connaught, where he was staying, she said she couldn't think of anything she'd love more.

'You sound so ridiculously English,' said Freddie, laughing, and Diana said what else should she sound like, and he said he had no idea but the way she looked in the photographs, a Brooklyn growl would be quite appropriate.

'I don't think I'm sure what a Brooklyn growl sounds like.'

'Come along,' he said, holding out his hand to her. 'Let me give you a lesson. And maybe we'll have Martinis, rather than more champagne. It'll help get you into character.'

Blanche and the other two exchanged glances and expressed huge regret that they were unable to join them; but when they had gone

Blanche said anxiously that maybe one of them should have gone 'to act as chaperone – she is a married woman after all'.

'Blanche, darling,' said Cedric, 'you just saw before you the beginnings of a great affair. Do you really want to see it stillborn?'

'Well, yes, I do,' said Blanche. 'I feel highly responsible.'

'Oh, don't be so silly. Diana Southcott is a very sophisticated, hardheaded young woman. Perfectly capable of saying no all by herself. Or choosing not to.'

'Well, exactly,' said Blanche.

# Chapter 26

## 1951

The wedding somehow got into the papers. Well, one paper. The *Daily News*. Quite a prominent item, quarter of a page complete with picture, there it sat on page 4, captioned, *Tom Knelston, marked out as a young man to watch in the political scene, was married on Saturday to Alice Miller, a nurse at St Thomas' Hospital.*

Everyone had been surprised by the choice of Josh as best man, even Tom himself. But time had been pressing on him, and a decision had had to be made, and suddenly he thought that Josh would be as good as anyone; he liked him a lot, he had met him the night he had properly met Alice, and he was a cousin of Jillie's.

His brothers thought he was selling out to what they thought of as the opposite side. The Sunday lunch had been a fairly dismal failure, despite Alice's superhuman efforts to make it work. The brothers were uncomfortable and silent, and their wives likewise. Tom's sisters made a big effort and really liked Alice, thought her efforts to greet Mary and make her feel at home and welcome were touching and genuine, and were fascinated by her life as a nurse.

It was actually Donald Herbert who suggested Josh as best man. Tom was having a drink with him one night, voicing his concerns about who he might choose. The real subject under discussion was the forthcoming election, which Donald was cheerfully certain would be won by the Tories and an apparently revived Winston Churchill, but Tom's forthcoming nuptials were clearly rather in the forefront of his mind and the vacant position of best man in particular.

'He's good fun, you get on well, you certainly share political views, you both love Real Ale. Why don't you think about it? Or I could do it,' he added.

Tom had an uneasy feeling Donald was not entirely joking.

Alice didn't really mind. She liked Josh and thought he was fun, and had forgiven him for the Battersea funfair debacle. 'I think it's a lovely idea,' she said to Tom.

And really, how much did it matter? She had had a wonderful wedding day, the sun shining, Tom looking amazing in his morning dress, and telling her he loved her at least ten times, both in his speech and quietly, in odd, unexpected moments of privacy; then again when they finally arrived at their honeymoon destination, a pretty, secluded cottage they had rented for a week, on the south Devon coast near Kingsbridge. She had half hoped for a fancy hotel, but Tom had said it was asking too much of him and his principles to stay in some lackey-filled establishment. 'I would just feel too uncomfortable, Alice, I'm sorry.' The Millers, who were giving them the honeymoon as a wedding present, were probably more disappointed than Alice was, but they clung tenaciously to the bridal suite for the weekend at the Salcombe Bay hotel, saying it was too late to cancel. It was rather wonderful, filled with huge vases of flowers and a bottle of champagne on ice waiting for them, with its huge bed, and balcony overlooking the estuary. Tom submitted to this with a good grace and, extremely clearly, enjoyed his four-course dinner and the dancing afterwards, in the hotel ballroom; he fell asleep very suddenly as soon as they got into bed, which was a bit of a disappointment to Alice, but she went out onto the balcony and looked at the moon shining on the water, and although it was hardly a substitute for sex, she felt extraordinarily happy and blessed. It was only when she got back into bed that the anxiety came to her unbidden as to whether he slept through his wedding night to Laura: and then she couldn't sleep for hours.

❋ ❋ ❋

The cottage was lovely, though, and seemed to act on Tom like an aphrodisiac; they spent most of the week, it seemed to Alice, in the big bed in the small, whitewashed bedroom, the windows open to the lovely sea-washed air.

# Chapter 27

## 1951

She couldn't be pregnant, could she? Not so easily, so swiftly, so terrifyingly soon?

What was she going to do? How was she going to cope with it? Who could she tell? She felt totally trapped, her mind and emotions twisting and turning this way and that, the terror as responsible for the sickness as her hormones and the tiny, life-engulfing creature growing inside her.

Alice was also pregnant: joyfully, radiantly, nervously pregnant. She was also surprised at the speed of their accomplishment. It would probably have been wiser to wait a little longer, to complete the purchase of the small house they had chosen in Acton. But Tom was so keen to start their family, and she had deliberately left her Dutch cap behind for their honeymoon. She'd hated it from the beginning, it was the opposite of romantic. She'd just assumed she should go back to it once they were home again. Which indeed she did. And when Alice, too busy to notice, passed the date of one period and when, two weeks later, she threw up horribly when she woke, she blamed the chicken she had eaten the night before. Then, finding nothing to blame the second morning, she looked a little nervously at her diary as she sat on the bus (still feeling fairly queasy) on her way to St Thomas' and realised that, yes, the dates at least fitted perfectly.

She told Tom that night and he was overwhelmed with a beaming, almost exultant pleasure; entirely untinged – as she had feared it might be – by anxiety, or even, far worse, by thoughts and memories of Laura and Hope.

'Now look,' said Alice, after absorbing this joy and finding it increased her own a hundredfold, 'we can do a test. This frog thing, you know –'

The frog thing, the Aschheim–Zondek test whereby her urine would be injected into a frog and two weeks later, if indeed she was pregnant, it would start laying eggs, was revolutionising anxiously pregnant women's lives, reducing the two-month or so wait for certainty to as many weeks.

'What you must do is tell Sister immediately – you need to establish your leaving date.' Alice, who was dreading this, knew what must be done. 'And Alice, I do want you to look after yourself, very carefully. I don't want you working and getting overtired, which you know you do.'

'All right,' said Alice, recognising the first signs of anxiety in him, the legacy of the three miscarriages for poor Laura. 'I promise.'

And the third morning of horrid noises in the loo left them both in no doubt; there was a small new Knelston on its way.

Diana felt very much in need of the frog's services. Too afraid to go to her GP or even the local hospital, she went to an expensive private clinic in York where the smooth, rather smug gynaecologist there rang her two weeks later to confirm her pregnancy. Johnathan still had no idea; he was usually out long before she woke, and conveniently, she was usually sick mid-morning, rather than first thing.

Because she had to talk to someone, she went to London for two days, on the pretext that her mother was unwell, and stayed with Wendelien; unwise for many reasons, not least that Archie, Wendelien's baby, was at an enchanting age. Diana loved babies anyway; she had enjoyed Jamie's babyhood hugely, once the birth was over. Wendelien, of course, counselled termination: 'It's the only thing, darling, you can have it done really well in a nursing home. Only one night there, and then you can go home again, feeling fine, all over.'

'Yes, but it might not be Freddie's. In fact, it's quite unlikely – it's probably Johnathan's. He's been very ardent, desperate for another baby.'

'Diana,' said Wendelien, 'you really can't know that.'

'I know I can't know. But—'

'And what does Freddie look like?'

'He's – oh, well, he's blonde and—'

'Diana,' said Wendelien severely. 'Johnathan is dark. You are dark, Jamie is dark. Eyes?'

'Freddie's? Green.'

'Yours – dark. Johnathan's dark.'

'Yes, all right,' said Diana irritably. 'I get the message.'

'And – time in your cycle?'

'Oh, right in the middle. But then, I practically seduced Johnathan the night I got home, I felt so guilty and bad. So—'

'I still think you can't risk it. How on earth are you going to explain a green-eyed blonde to Johnathan? Well, look, I can help with places. It's not a problem. So go away and think about it. But please, darling, be sensible. There can always be other babies.'

'I know,' said Diana. 'But Wendelien, I just don't know if I could do that. Just get rid of it. As if it was a bit of rubbish. It's so brutal.'

'And telling Johnathan you're having another man's baby isn't?'

All the way back to Yorkshire, Diana sat motionless, staring out of the window. Of course Wendelien was right; a termination was the only safe, sensible thing to do. Johnathan would never know, would never have to cope with the pain of what she had done. Her marriage would be safe – he would quite likely divorce her if she told him. They could start again, immediately; probably in two months she'd be safely pregnant again. By him.

It wasn't as if she was in love with Freddie Bateman, nor he with her. He was gloriously, wonderfully sexy and exciting and it was so flattering that he fancied her. They'd had a heavenly time, but God, how could she have been so stupid.

But she knew. It had just been too much for her; irresistibly too much. Years of boredom in Yorkshire, a dull husband she wasn't in love with, who made the sex act about as thrilling as a bowl of unseasoned porridge. To be suddenly with someone who made her feel alive and hungry in every tiny unexplored corner of her body, someone funny and appreciative, someone who lived the dream of the new world she had just found herself in, this glorious world, all glamour and style and wit and charm, someone moreover with whom she could bring something to that world, who raised her beauty and her own sexiness to new, dizzy heights, who made people exclaim over her and adore her, and desire her. How could she have said no to him, as he plied her with cocktails and racy gossip and then flattery and dirty talk, and finally, first suggestions, then pleas, then increasingly open insistence that she go up to his room and thus his bed? Where, for the first time in her life, she discovered what sex could be for her, how she could climb and reach, and fly and soar, how she could laugh as she rode the pleasure, and cry as she came, how all her thoughts and emotions, her past and her present, could fuse into this one amazing thing. How at last she knew what she could do and be.

For Freddie, it had been nothing like that. Another lover, another conquest, no doubt all of them beautiful – some more than she – some more sensuous, some more experienced, some undoubtedly younger. They had made a little magic, no doubt of that, rather as they did when they worked together, for what did he do then than make love to her with his camera, and she, responding through his lens, drove him on? But that had been the end of it until the next assignment, the next assignation; he would recoil at what she had to tell him, if she did, and so of course she would not.

But she shrank from the sensible thing, the wise thing. She found herself in a whirlwind of distress whenever she thought about it, about tearing this tiny precious growing thing from its safe haven, abandoning it, and to what? What became of these small live creatures – were they just disposed of, flushed down the clinic lavatory, thrown into its sluice? The thought was impossible to bear. Whatever else she did, she could not do that, and long before the train reached York station, she had made that decision at least. For all the others she had, at the very least, time.

\* \* \*

244

'Oh, Alice, how lovely. How very, very lovely. I'm so happy for you.'

'I'm pretty happy for myself.'

'And – when?'

'April. A spring baby.'

'Is Tom all right?'

'Yes, he's very happy. I know what you mean – I thought it might make him sad or anxious, but no, he's just delighted. With himself as well as me.'

Jillie laughed. 'Men!'

'I know. My sentiments exactly. Now I want to ask you something.'

'Yes.'

'I want you to be the godmother. Will you?'

'Oh, Alice, I'd love that. Thank you. Of course I will.'

'Good. The only one, as I'm determined it will be a boy. Actually, even if it's a girl, I still don't want you having to share her. Tom won't care if we have two godparents or twenty, he's a total non-believer, as you know – only has things like christenings and weddings to keep me and my parents happy.'

'It's odd, that.'

'I know what you mean. When he goes to see Laura at the little churchyard, I wonder where he thinks she is, if anywhere. I mean, he does still go, quite often –'

'Do you mind?'

'Sort of. But – I shouldn't. I've never asked him about it. Although he hardly ever talks about her, except to say things about her political beliefs, or her teaching methods, I don't think he'd refuse to answer if I asked him.'

'He never suggests you go with him?'

'Never,' said Alice.

'Or that you'd like to?'

'No. I'm not sure that I want to, but – I do wish he'd ask. It really does make me feel very – very shut out. And of course I worry about her, all the time.'

'In what way?'

'Well, whether I'm doing well enough. Living up to her. Whether she made a fuss about being sick, or whether she complained about

245

being tired all the time. It's awfully difficult, competing with some-body perfect.'

'Alice,' said Jillie firmly, 'you'll drive yourself mad. You said yourself that Tom said she wasn't perfect, and you just have to accept that. He loves you, he's told you so many times.'

'I know,' said Alice. 'Most of the time I do manage. But I still feel he's shutting me out. And this is worse. More difficult. We're living through what took her away from him.'

'Yes, but you said he's beside himself with happiness. You have to accept that, or you'll spoil the whole thing for yourself and him. I can see how hard it is, but you just have to. Now look, I wasn't going to tell you, steal your thunder, but I'm going to distract you. I've got some news.'

'Oh, Jillie, what? What what what?'

'We've sort of got a date. And it's really good, because you'll be over the baby, and I want you, of course, to be matron of honour.'

Alice squealed with pleasure, hurled herself into Jillie's arms.

'Jillie, Jillie. That is so lovely. When?'

'July next year. I just finally put my foot down. I said June or nothing and he said not June, and I was all ready to throw the ring at him, but then he said he was delivering his paper in June, you know the one on premature babies, but how would July be? So . . .'

'So that's wonderful,' said Alice. 'And I'd adore to be your matron of honour.' And then added, looking panic-stricken. 'What on earth does a matron of honour wear?'


Every milestone made him more terrified, more amazed at what he had done. Getting properly involved with her. Realising how much he loved her. Telling her he loved her. Getting engaged to her. Celebrating it with that ridiculously excessive party. And now agreeing to a date. Why had he done this, why? Why hadn't he listened to himself? He knew, of course: it was safety, the fading of the likelihood of discovery; respectability, a seal on his successful life.

He had resisted talking to Ludo for a long time; it formalised the folly, let the daylight in. But finally, after a particularly demon-filled night, he sought him out, unloaded his fears, sought counsel. And

Ludo had been wonderfully supportive, had held out for him, tanta-lisingly, the example of his own happy, fruitful marriage.

'Honestly, Ned, marrying Cecily was the best thing I ever did. She's such a sweetheart, and without blowing my own trumpet, I think I can say I've made her very happy. I adore the children – you can't beat a family, for sheer, bloody contentment.'

'No,' said Ned. 'I'm sure. But – did you want – I mean, did you . . .'

'Of course,' said Ludo. 'Well, I loved her. I wanted to be married to her. I wanted to be married. So much.'

'Yes, but –'

'But if you really want to know, I was also in a bit of a pickle. I'd got a bit over-involved with a rotter. There was talk. He began to threaten me and I was extremely scared. I'd have lost my job, my friends, well, most of them. Nobody who hasn't lived through that fear can possibly begin to imagine the total horror of it.'

Ned, very soberly, said, 'It's all-consuming. It invades you. Fear not just of disgrace but the loss of everything you've got.'

'Some people say they're going to make a stand, and look what hap-pens to them. End of a normal life. Unless they're artists or actors. They seem to be all right. They have each other, they're not sweating, alone, afraid to do anything in case it gives them away. There's a sort of respectability all of its own. If you're rich and famous like Cecil Beaton, fine. Society loves them, says what fun they are. Quite a cachet to have at cocktail parties and so on. But I'm a stockbroker, Ned. What would have happened to me? Clients all vanished. Off every hostess's list. Probably have had to go and live abroad. My father would have insisted on that. Anyway, I chose Cecily. And it's been marvellous. As it will be for you. Courage, old chap. You're not mixed up with anyone dangerous, are you?'

'No, no,' said Ned. 'I just – sometimes – still go to one of the clubs, you know. Practically throw up before and after, for fear someone sees me. Or knows me.'

'Well, as long as it's only the clubs. Not those pubs. They're danger-ous places.'

'I know. But I need to feel I'm with my own kind. Just occasionally.'

'Well, that'll have to stop,' said Ludo. 'After you're married.'

'Of course. I know that.' And then after a long, agonised silence: 'So did you ever – ever have any of those treatments?'

'Yes. Yes, I did. Ghastly. You know how they work? They show you pictures of beautiful boys and then they give you an emetic first orally, then by injection. You're not just sick, you feel ill, horrible, for hours, days. They do it again and again. Then, at bedtime, they give you an injection of testosterone and show you slides of attractive women. Again and again. They claim great success – ten out of twenty-five was one figure being bandied about. I honestly wouldn't recommend it – it didn't work for me. It was a loathsome experience, guaranteed to put you off sex for life. With anyone or thing.'

'But you – you and Cecily –'

'Look,' said Ludo. 'I love Cecily. I truly do. She is the centre of my life, she holds me together. I couldn't live without her. I don't find making love to her very difficult. She's very attractive and I've always liked pretty women. The damnable thing about all this, the most damnable of all, is that what we are, different – it makes us criminals. Christ, when I think of other criminals who are considered on a par – murderers, paedophiles, men who beat up women – they're probably thought preferable to us. At least they're "normal", in quotes. It's too frightful.'

Just talking about it with Ludo, in this normal civilised way, as if they were talking about the weather, made him feel infinitely better.

'I mean, look at your situation, a doctor! Working with children, for Christ's sake. You'd be done for in days if it became known. No one would trust you with their children. You'd almost certainly lose your consultancy; your hospital would sack you. Your life as a doctor would be over. You could even end up in jail. It's so wrong. So desperately wrong.'

'Those are all the things I'm afraid of,' said Ned. 'But hurting Jillie, most of all.'

'Look,' said Ludo. 'You love Jillie, don't you?'

'I adore her,' said Ned. 'That's why I'm so fearful for her, as much as me. How hurt she'd be, how used she'd feel. It seems wrong to expose her to that risk.'

'I felt the same. It was a gamble. But it paid off, it was all right.'

'Does she –? Well, does she know?'

'If she does, it's never been acknowledged. I think she knows *something*. But she doesn't *know*. She's very . . . innocent, led a very sheltered life.'

'Which Jillie hasn't,' said Ned. 'She's about to become a doctor, her family are rich, bohemian Londoners. I don't quite understand why one of them hasn't suspected it at least.'

'Well, they're obviously broad-minded. They like you, clearly they love Jillie, and they trust her to know what she wants. Which is you. Lucky man. She's gorgeous.'

'I know she is, I know,' said Ned almost fretfully. 'And she'll be a marvellous obstetrician.'

'What a team!' said Ludo, laughing. 'Oh, go on, old chap. Stop agonising, marry the girl. Be happy with her. Have lots of sprogs. Powerful things, children. They bind you together as nothing else can. Now, I want to be your best man. I promise not to lose the ring, or leave you naked and drunk, padlocked to a tree, as Billy Francis did to poor old Dudley Buchanan. G and T?'

'Of course you must be my best man,' said Ned, taking the drink gratefully.

But already the loathsome, duplicitous thoughts had begun. If there was ever talk about him, might not Ludo's closeness to him, and the gossip around Ludo, begin again, feed people's suspicions further? God, what a hideous world he was about to enter, with his bid for 'normality'. Worse, in many ways, than the one where he lived now.

It was the heat, of course. Exceptional for September. She was just terribly hot, she was not going to faint. And the noise. The peculiar mixture of sounds that define agricultural shows: the band, the instructions barked endlessly through the loudspeakers, cattle noise vying with horse noise. But she was fine. This was important, the first time she had been asked to actually participate in anything at the show; Johnathan was so proud of her, she couldn't let him down.

She had taken huge care with her appearance, and knew she was dressed exactly right: nothing showy, just a cream linen suit with the newly popular half hat in red; red shoes with modestly low, almost chunky heels; and red clutch bag. Every inch a Lady with a capital L.

An hour later, as the last contestant went clear, she felt exhausted, and actually now rather sick, and asked if she could possibly have a chair. The afternoon stretched endlessly before her; maybe once she'd presented the cups, she would be able to leave.

The president's wife, Marjorie Harper, was walking towards her now, followed by some minions bearing a table and a large number of silver cups. God, so many: did she have to present them all? She really did feel rather odd. Hang on, Diana, hang on. Deep breaths.

Johnathan still didn't know. She had somehow kept it from him, she wasn't sure why – buying time, she supposed, while she decided what to do. It was no clearer now what that was than the first day she had suspected the whole dreadful nightmare.

The president's wife was speaking now, about her she realised: 'Mrs Gunning, whose husband Johnathan has played such a crucial part in the development of the show, will now present the cups to the winners of the Under Thirteens, the Under Fourteens and the Under Twelves. Mrs Gunning . . .'

There was clapping but it was rather odd clapping, coming in waves, the sound receding and advancing; Diana stood up, smiled at Mrs Harper, picked up the first cup, which seemed inordinately heavy, and began to speak. Then the ground began to sway and lurch beneath her feet and with infinite grace, she crumpled, sank onto the ground, somehow managing to hang onto the cup as people helped lay her out straight, proffered folded jackets as pillows, and a loud-speaker asked for St John's to come over to the collecting ring. Then suddenly Johnathan was there, looking down at her with such infinite and kind concern, and he knelt beside her, and she said, 'So sorry, Johnathan, so sorry, but I'm pregnant.' Then she was on the stretcher, being borne away from the field and the shame and the remorse of the whole dreadful disaster, and into the St John's tent.

Only it wasn't a disaster, for as she sat cautiously up, sipping some rather lukewarm sweet tea, Johnathan appeared, with a beacon-like smile, and even as she stammered out an apology he said, 'Darling, don't keep apologising, it's marvellous news. Pity you didn't tell me before, but nobody really minds at all. Now finish that tea, and I'll take you home in about ten minutes.'

At home, he was tender and solicitous, touched by her explanation that she had been waiting for the three months 'safety ground' and for the doctor to give her absolute assurance, lest it prove to be a false alarm. She didn't want to disappoint him.

'It's marvellous,' he said again. 'Absolutely bloody marvellous. Maybe this time, we'll have a girl. Not that I mind which, of course,' he added hastily.

Yes, a little girl with blonde curls and green eyes, Diana thought, wincing at this rather clear vision; but then she forced it out of her head again. She would just have to find some blonde relative in her family whose genes had suddenly surfaced. Meanwhile, she must take the happiness on offer and make the very most of it. This new little person would have to work hard, to console her from what she would be missing: no modelling for a year at least, no trips to London, no Paris. As the strain of the day added to her general distress, she started to cry. She excused herself, saying she was overemotional – it was her hormones, and if Johnathan didn't mind she was going to have a little rest; then she went up to her bedroom and wept for hours.

# Chapter 28

## 1951

It really was rather awful being pregnant. Once the first rapture was over, Alice continued to be sick every day, and to feel exhausted and bone weary all the time. She felt ashamed and inadequate, having been assured by Tom from day one that she was about to feel better and more energetic than she ever had in her entire life – clearly Laura had bloomed like some prize rose bush – and managed somehow, by the time he came home, to appear smiling and healthy, to pretend she was enjoying the meal she had cooked, although it made her feel desperately sick, and to show great interest and enthusiasm for any news he had.

The election was called for October, partly as a result of the King's poor health. He had had a lung removed and was an extremely sick man; he was about to embark on a trip to the Commonwealth, and he feared for the effect on the country of an election in his absence, and wanted matters settled before he left.

The Conservatives, with their slogan of 'Britain Strong and Free', and many new fresh faces, were able to present youth and promise.

Tom worked very hard during those few months, assisting the local MP any way he could, not merely with the promised envelope stuffing and poster deliveries, but preparing halls for meetings, sweeping floors, setting out chairs, and more than once manning the great tea urns, so integral a part of parish and political life. He did a great deal on election day of that process known as 'knocking up' – knocking on doors as it drew towards evening and trying to ensure the people behind had voted. He attended the count, but as morning broke, the Conservatives had won by a majority of seventeen. The Old Bulldog was still in power.

'I'm sorry but I do want to have this baby in Welbeck Street, under Sir Harold's care.' Diana looked at Johnathan across the supper table. 'I know that didn't quite work out last time, but I still feel I was incredibly lucky then and Sir Harold makes me feel safe.'

She had expected Johnathan to protest, but he was so happy these days about the baby that he simply smiled at her and said, 'Of course. I completely understand. And this time, hopefully, I'll be able to be there. Not actually at your side, of course, but very near at hand –'

'Oh, Johnathan, you're so sweet,' said Diana, 'and thank you. But there really isn't any need.'

The image of herself holding the newly born blonde green-eyed baby, desperately claiming a blonde green-eyed great-great-grandmother while Johnathan's joy turned to suspicion, swam into her head.

'Darling, this new little one is more important than anything on the farm. Now make the arrangements as soon as possible. Have you told your mother yet? I presume you'll be staying with her?'

'Yes, of course, and she's thrilled. I will be staying with her.' The very thought of being with her family, near London and her friends, made her feel quite dizzy with happiness. 'Johnathan, you're an angel. And thank you.'

'Nothing to thank me for, I just want you to feel as safe and happy as you can. Now I'd quite like an early night, if you don't mind.'

'Of course. I think I'll listen to the wireless for a bit. There's a marvellous serialisation of one of Angela Thirkell's novels, being read by Dulcie Gray.'

He came over and gave her a kiss on her forehead and went out. Their marriage had taken a turn for the better altogether lately; well, that was worth a great deal, she thought. Please please, dear God, I know I don't deserve it, but let this baby have dark hair, eyes immaterial. I can handle that. She knew He must be extremely busy, but she felt sure God would give her wishes in the matter prime consideration. She touched every piece of wood within reach in case He didn't, and then chided herself for being ridiculous.

'Tom? Donald Herbert. Look, I want to talk through a few things with you. I might even have some news. You free this evening?'

'I could be.'

'Right. Savoy at six OK with you?'

'Well, if it's all right with Robert, my leaving the office early yet again?'

'Don't you worry about Robert. The American Bar.'

Tom put the phone down, feeling discomfited. He never failed to be shocked by Herbert's choice of dining and watering holes. Still, it would be interesting to watch capitalism at its most bloated. He wondered idly if he was dressed smartly enough for the Savoy and then thought if they turned him away it would be a strong message that he had been invited to the wrong place.

They didn't turn him away and Donald, wearing a dinner jacket, was seated at a small round table, being hovered over by a waiter. He waved at Tom as he came down the steps into the bar.

'Hello. I was just debating getting a bottle of bubbly, but we'll never get through it in time. I'm taking Christine to the theatre. That being so, what's your poison?'

Tom was deeply tempted, but didn't quite dare, to say a pint of bitter. 'Gin and tonic, please.'

'Good man. Make that two,' Donald said to the waiter. 'Doubles. And some of your excellent brazils and those salted almonds, if you'd be so kind.'

The waiter half bowed – God, this was disgusting, Tom thought – and backed away from them. Tom studied the clientele: men in dark suits, some in dinner jackets like Herbert, the women in full-skirted dresses, a couple of them in what were very much evening coats, again mostly made of taffeta with large collars that were almost an extension of the elaborate necklaces they wore.

'I do like women in cocktail dresses,' said Herbert, looking at a blonde dressed in black, with a very low neckline and modestly tight three-quarter sleeves. 'I always think they show them at their best. Still get the legs to look at, and the tits as well.'

The blonde recognised his admiration from across the room and acknowledged it with a slightly cool half smile; she had the most lovely mouth, Tom thought, full and curvy, enhanced with some brilliant red lipstick. While he was looking at her, the drinks arrived, small bottles of tonic water to add to what looked to him like half tumblers of gin, and he took one sip of his and suddenly it happened: the feeling which he was beginning to recognise, an easing into it all and that he did, after all, like being here; it felt comfortable, it suited some small, greedy part of him. He took one of the almonds, savouring its sweet saltiness against the richness of the gin and tonic, and relaxed and said to Herbert, as if it were an idle question, the answer to which he might act upon and go himself, 'So what are you going to see?'

'*The King and I*, musical, at Drury Lane. I'm not mad about the things myself, but Christine loves them – have to keep her sweet somehow, she doesn't have a lot of fun, poor woman. Now look, I want you to think about standing for some hopelessly Tory seat –'

'What would be the point of that?' said Tom, almost alarmed.

'Practice, dear boy, practice.'

And then, as he listened, tried to see the sense in what sounded like a most fruitless enterprise, Tom looked up and saw Diana Southcott (as he would always think of her) coming down the steps into the bar. She was wearing a cocktail dress in dark green taffeta, her dark hair swept up, her long legs flattered by some very dark stockings and extremely high heels, and she looked so lovely that Tom felt a lurch somewhere he supposed to be his heart. Which was nowhere near his actual heart, he thought. Slightly lower, somewhere more carnal, more invasive: and he called out to her, as she had to him at the Pleasure Gardens, called out her name, and with no idea of her married surname, simply 'Diana' had to suffice. He hoped she wouldn't mind.

She clearly did not; she walked towards them smiling, apparently delighted. Tom stood up to greet her, holding out his hand, but she ignored it, offered her cheek to kiss, and as he complied he felt the warmth of her, smelt her perfume, rich and musky.

'Well, hello,' said Donald, the emphasis on the second syllable, standing up and holding out his hand. 'It's the lady of the round-abouts. Donald Herbert, sure you won't remember me.'

She shook his hand and said, 'Of course I do.'

'Join us for a drink, won't you? Or is some lucky fellow already here waiting for you?'

'Not a fellow, a girl,' Diana said. 'In any case, I'm early. So yes, thank you, that would be delightful. A dry sherry, please.' Much summoning of the waiter ensued, and further bowing and grovelling; she sat down on the chair opposite Tom, and picked an almond out of the dish.

'My favourite,' she said. 'How clever of you to know,' and she smiled at Donald, before biting on it and closing her eyes in mock rapture.

'Oh, I have many powers,' said Herbert, picking up on her mood. 'An ability to prophesy being only one of them.'

'Well, that must be very useful in your profession,' said Diana. 'So, tell me, were you dreadfully disappointed about the election?'

'Oh, not for an instant. Churchill was on the warpath. But we put up a pretty good fight.'

'And did Tom help you?'

'Immeasurably,' said Herbert. 'I had hoped his hour might have come.'

'What does that mean?'

'Well, that he would have had much more chance of making his way in politics. In fact, even as things are, I'm looking for likely by-elections. So he can stand as an opposition candidate.'

'I don't understand,' said Diana. 'I thought you'd lost the election.'

'We have. But whatever party's in, there has to be an opposition. With representatives for every seat.'

'Tom!' said Diana. 'You're going to be an MP! How terribly exciting.'

'I'm afraid that's extremely unlikely for many years. But if it happened, yes, it would be exciting,' Tom said.

'Don't talk yourself down,' said Diana. 'I'll vote for you.'

'Well, that's very kind, but I'm afraid it doesn't work quite like that.'

'Look,' said Donald Herbert. 'I'm afraid I shall have to go. I'm taking my wife for supper before we see *The King and I* this evening –'

'Oh, how terribly clever of you to get tickets,' said Diana, as if he had managed to unlock the Enigma code. 'I hear it's booked solid months ahead.'

'Oh, we have ways.'

'And is that part of the English political system?'

'You could say that. Anyway, Tom, do you want another of those before I settle up?'

'No, thank you,' said Tom, realising he was feeling distinctly light headed. 'No, that was very good, Donald. Thank you.'

'My pleasure. As has been meeting you again,' he said to Diana, raising her hand to his lips and kissing it.

Old bugger's flirting with her, thought Tom, not sure whether to be amused or annoyed and wondering if he would ever be able to behave the same way. Women seemed to like it. And what are you doing, thinking about what women like, Tom Knelston? You, with a pregnant wife at home, a pregnant wife that you love very much.

And then . . . rather to his shame, he did nothing to hurry his departure.

'So Tom, what are you doing here, in this bastion of privilege?' Diana's dark eyes looked at him in a kind of challenge.

'Not my idea,' said Tom. 'Donald summoned me. He's in charge of my rather futile attempt to become an MP. So I have to dance to his tune.'

'Well, it seems like a pretty nice tune to me,' said Diana. 'Seriously, Tom, whatever you're trying to do, I wish you the very best of luck with it. Tell me about you? I know you're married, I read it in the *Daily News*.'

'What on earth are you doing reading the *Daily News*?' said Tom, genuinely surprised.

'I try to read all the papers. It's such a good way of really keeping in touch with everybody and everything. Especially up there, where people are so narrow-minded. I love the *Daily Mirror*. The way it doesn't give two hoots about what important people think, and its campaigns. You know, getting a better deal for old people. Anyway, you're married – very pretty, your wife, I thought. Lovely wedding dress. Now – here's to you. Good luck.'

'Thank you,' said Tom. 'I'm going to need it.'

'We all need luck,' said Diana soberly.

She had pulled a small, enamelled cigarette case out of her bag, and a tortoiseshell lighter. Her hands, as she lit her cigarette, were shaking slightly.

Tom wondered if he should ask her what she meant, and decided it wouldn't be wise. Instead he said, 'Are you down in London to do some modelling?'

'No,' she said briefly, and looking at Tom in silence for a moment as if making some kind of decision. Then she said, 'No, I'm not modelling at the moment. I was seeing my gynaecologist.'

Tom felt nonplussed. Clearly no gentleman could possibly ask a lady why she was seeing her gynaecologist; but then why tell him at all, if she didn't want the conversation to halt altogether?

'The thing is,' she said, solving his dilemma, 'I think it's time I had another baby. For Jamie, as much as anyone.'

This was safer. 'How is Jamie?' he said.

'He's very well, growing up too fast. He'll be away at school before I know it and I shall miss him terribly. He's my best friend up there, you could say.'

Tom knew better than to suggest that Jamie need not go away to school, and therefore not be terribly missed. Boarding school was one of this strange tribe's rituals, to be followed at all costs.

'So, do you like it any better up there now?' he asked, this being the nearest he could get to the matter.

Diana looked at him and smiled. 'You're so sweet, Tom. Remembering all my moaning. No, I suppose you could say I've got used to it. Where do you live?'

'In Acton,' said Tom. 'And Alice – my wife – is pregnant.'

'Really? How lovely.'

'I don't think she thinks so. She feels dreadful.'

'Poor her,' said Diana. 'Do you feel dreadfully worried all the time?'

'Not dreadfully,' said Tom. 'But worried, yes.'

'Because of what happened to Laura?'

'Yes.'

He sat, looking at her, and thinking one of the main reasons he liked her was that she met things head on. And after a moment fuelled by the gin, he said so. 'Most people dance round the subject of Laura's pregnancy. Thank you for mentioning it. It's like the way you came to find me at her grave that day. I've never forgotten that, how you just said what you felt. It was, well, it was so welcome. And surprising.'

'Why? Oh, because you think I'm a toffee-nosed brat without any proper feelings. I hope your view is changing a bit now. I like to think of *you* as a friend, I must say. Tom, will you be my friend?'

'I would love to be, Diana,' he said, rushing, half knowingly, headlong into danger.

'Well, that's just so nice,' she said and leaned forward again to kiss his cheek. I—' and then she stopped suddenly and pulled back, an expression of intense pain on her face. Then it cleared.

'Oh,' she said, relaxing, 'that hurt.'

'What was it?' he said anxiously.

'Bit of indigestion. I get it a lot. Look, there's Wendelien. I'll introduce you. You won't like her.'

'Then maybe I should just go.'

'No, no. But don't stay. Anyway, you must get back to your lovely Alice.'

'Yes, I must,' he said, thinking he actually didn't want to get back to the weary, sickly Alice he hardly recognised as much as he should.

'Here we are, Wendelien,' Diana called to her. She jumped up and embraced her, then said, 'Wendelien Bellinger, Tom Knelston.'

Wendelien, also extremely pretty he thought, held out her hand.

'He's not staying,' said Diana firmly. 'He's been keeping me company while we waited for you. Tom, darling, thank you for your company.'

She kissed him yet again; he knew he should be wincing at the 'darling' but in fact he loved it. It was a moment to savour, all part of this spellbound forbidden territory.

'My pleasure,' he said. 'It really was. Goodbye. And goodbye, Mrs Bellinger.'

And with great reluctance he moved away from them and the temple of grovel and privilege that he liked so much, and knew he shouldn't, and walked back to the foyer of the Savoy, and out into the cool evening where he tried to return to normal while he waited in a very unprivileged bus queue.

'Wow, he's a looker,' said Wendelien. 'Seemed rather sweet too. Diana, you're not –?'

'Of course I'm not,' said Diana irritably. 'He's just a – ow. God –'

'Darling, whatever is it?'

'Awful twinge. Had another one just now. That's better. Indigestion, I'm sure. I – oh, dear. I must just pop to the ladies. Order yourself a drink and I'll have another sherry, please. Dry. See you in a tick.'

'Diana, you look awful. Shall I come with you?'

'Darling, don't fuss. I'm fine. Honestly. Just get me a drink, and some salted almonds. Too delicious.'

'It was a girl.' Her voice was thick with tears. 'A girl. Why did it have to happen, why couldn't they have stopped it? Useless, useless doctors. I can't bear it, I absolutely can't bear it. It's so, so unfair.' And she started crying in earnest.

# Chapter 29

## 1952

Alice was now six months pregnant, no longer sick, but far from blooming. She was extremely tired, and the initial kicking of the baby, so exciting the first few times, became an exhausting and near-painful event that continued throughout every night, and kept her awake.

'This has to be a boy,' she said to Tom. 'A star footballer. He'll be playing for England.'

Tom, while pleased to hear of his son's putative future on the football pitches of England, was more excited on his own account. He had been summoned by the national agent to Transport House and was told he was being put forward for the shortlist of Labour candidates for Middleston, a leafy suburb on the outskirts of Birmingham. Although the Tories would hold on to the seat, having increased their majority in the election, the agent had told Tom he had a good chance of being selected as candidate.

'They want someone young and your profile is much higher than it was with the party; the other two are no more likely than you to be adopted, in fact, rather less. One unmarried – as for the other, I've unearthed that he was once a Young Tory and we can spread the dirt quite nicely. It'll be bloody hard work if you get selected, lot of pavement pounding and speeches to half-empty halls, but the campaign manager is a bloody good bloke and he thinks you've as good a chance as any. So – what do you say? It'll mean being away from home a lot, and a lot of flag raising by your wife of course, but . . .'

Tom didn't hesitate. 'She'll be game, and of course I'll give it a go. When can I go up there, get started?'

'The minute poor old Barton announces he's standing down.' Tom was worried that Robert Herbert would resent his absences, but he seemed rather impressed.

'So is that a yes?'

Excited and disproportionately hopeful, he went home to tell Alice.

It had never occurred to him for a moment that he might ask her how she felt. Alice found it necessary to point this out, whereupon he reminded her of her promise at their wedding to put his ambitions in the Labour Party before anything, and she fled to their bedroom in tears.

'Oh, for Christ's sake,' said Tom, following her in, looking down at her with something close to dislike as she lay on the bed. 'Don't you realise this is a real chance of my actually achieving what I've dreamed of for the whole of my life?'

'And if you get adopted,' she said. 'Will we have to move up there? Leave this lovely house? Will I have to have the baby in a strange hospital, with no friends around me? Which of course I will, but don't you think you should have at least asked me how I felt about it?'

'Curiously, I assumed you'd feel about it the way I do,' said Tom. 'As my wife, sharing my ambitions, my feelings, everything I want for both of us, all of us, as a family. Clearly I was wrong. Love – and marriage, indeed – don't seem to mean the same things to you as they do to me. I think I'll go out for a while. I'm not enjoying your company very much at the moment.'

'Tom – Tom, I didn't – I mean I do, Tom, please don't go, please.'

'I don't see any reason to stay, quite frankly,' and he was gone, the door slammed behind him.

Alice stopped crying at once, stunned at what she had done. Failing him totally, breaking her promises, whingeing and whining like the pathetic women she so despised. When – no, don't think about Laura, don't, Alice, it won't help: but of course she did, imagining Laura's great eyes shining, voice tremulous with excitement, asking what she could do, now, at once, saying how wonderful it was.

Tom came in after a couple of hours, clearly drunk, and looked at her with something close to dislike.

'I'm sorry, Tom,' Alice said immediately. 'So very sorry. Of course I'll do everything I can. It was just a bit of a shock.'

'Clearly,' he said. 'I'm rather sad it should have come as a shock; it seems I should be more careful in future. I certainly don't want to force you to do anything against your will.'

'It's not against my will, it really isn't. I want to help you, I want you to succeed. I do, Tom, I do. You've got to believe me. Please, Tom, please.'

'Well, I'll do my best,' he said. 'And in answer to your rather self-absorbed questions, we wouldn't have to move to Middleston. If I was actually elected, I would be working at the House. We'd merely have to go there at weekends, if that was acceptable to you.'

'Tom –'

'But since that is highly unlikely, there would be no question of it. So you wouldn't have to have your baby away from everyone you know, as you put it.'

'I wouldn't mind, Tom. It would be worth it, of course it would. How can I make you believe me?'

'Well, there is one thing,' he said, 'since you ask – you can have the baby at Acton Hospital. Forget all that nonsense about having it at St Thomas'. It's not our local hospital, and you having it there reeks of privilege. You know how unhappy I am about it.'

'Of course I will. I'm sorry,' said Alice, bidding a silent and sad farewell to being somewhere she knew every inch of and where she had delivered babies herself and would have been under the aegis of Jillie's uncle. 'I didn't know you felt so unhappy about it.'

'I think you did,' he said, 'but we will leave it at that. Now, I have some reading to do. You look tired. Why don't you go to bed, have an early night?'

'Yes, yes, I will. Good idea,' said Alice.

But she was still awake when he came to bed, hours later. She pretended to be asleep. Some part of her, along with the shame at her behaviour, was in shock. It was the first time she had ever seen Tom's ruthless side, and indeed, his potential for cruelty. She found it disturbing, and worse, rather frightening.

In the event, Tom didn't even get selected; he sat through an interview by the committee during which they treated him so derisively he almost walked out. The national agent broke the news, followed by a call from Donald Herbert shortly afterwards.

'Just put it down to experience, which is crucial in this game. You didn't do too badly in your interview.'

'Really? It felt as though they couldn't wait to get me out of the room.'

'No place for paranoia in this game,' said Donald. 'Anyway, I thought I'd take you and Alice out to dinner, by way of consolation.'

Tom often doubted if Donald had a heart. He felt slightly ashamed and rang Alice to tell her.

'I didn't get selected. But we're going out to dinner. Donald's taking us, consolation prize. It'll be somewhere pretty grand, so wear something really nice.'

'Don't be silly, Tom. I haven't got anything really nice. Just a couple of smocks, remember? One of which you said reminded you of what your mother wore when she was doing the housework.'

'I would never say anything like that.'

'Well, you did. Anyway, it doesn't matter.'

'Well, go out and buy something. We can't afford it, but the occasion merits a bit of an overdraft.'

'All right, and thank you. But Tom, wouldn't it be better if you went alone?'

'No, Alice, it wouldn't be better. This is a joint enterprise, and Donald wants to treat us both.'

There was a hint of the ruthless Tom she had seen for the first time so recently. The last thing she felt like doing was going out into hot crowded shops and pushing her vast self into a series of hideous garments that wouldn't fit her, but she knew she had no option.

'All right, Tom, I'll do that,' she said. 'And please thank Donald for including me.'

This was a mistake. 'Alice,' said Tom, 'do I have to say it again?

This is something we're doing together. Of course you should be there tonight.'

'Tom? Tom Knelston? Is that you?'

He knew that voice. Cut-glass posh, slightly husky. But it wasn't quite itself. Not as self-assured, or as strong.

'Diana, what is it? You sound upset.'

'You recognised my voice. I'm flattered.'

'Of course I did. Is something the matter?'

'You could say so. Tom, Friend Tom – you haven't forgotten, have you, you promised to be my friend?'

'Of course I haven't forgotten.' But he hadn't thought it meant anything, just an idle flirtatious request.

'Good. I really need to talk to you. Can you meet me this evening?'

'Well –'

He had promised Alice to be home very much on time. He owed her a lot – they'd had a successful dinner with Donald Herbert – and she wanted his help decorating the nursery.

'Tom, please. It's really important.'

'Well – all right. But I can't be long. Where were you thinking of?'

'I'm staying at Wendelien's house, but she's away. Could you come there?'

'Well – well, yes, all right.' It was probably safer than some public place. 'Where is it?'

'They've moved to a little mews off Baker Street. Padster Mews, number nine. Just whenever you can get away.'

'Six? Six thirty?'

'Marvellous. Thank you, Tom. I'll have a gin and tonic at the ready.'

'You'd better not,' he said. 'I'm going to have to invent a very lengthy client meeting for Alice. At which there would be no place for gin and tonic.'

He didn't reach Padster Mews until almost seven. The buses were few and slow; and then it was hard to find. It was very pretty of course, and number nine had clearly been built across two sets of stables.

'Can I get you anything? A beer, coffee . . . ?'

'Cup of tea would be nice. A large one.'

'You shall have it. Oh, Tom, I'm so glad to see you. Let me just get your tea and I'll start.'

She was back quickly, bearing two rather small mugs of tea. 'These are the biggest I could find.'

'Thank you. Now – come on. You have all your friend's attention.'

'All right. I might cry a bit.'

'That's OK. I'm used to women's tears.' He looked at her. 'Well, you're not pregnant. As you were planning. Didn't it work out?'

'I – well, I wasn't actually planning it. That was a lie. I *was* pregnant. Just over three months. But – well, I lost it.' Her voice shook. 'It was so sad, I really, really wanted that baby. Anyway, Johnathan came down, and he was dreadfully upset too; he couldn't have been sweeter. And when we got back to Yorkshire, even the wicked witch was kind to me. But it didn't help. I got more and more depressed, couldn't sleep, cried all the time, and Johnathan kept saying there could always be another baby, stupid things like that.'

It didn't sound that stupid to Tom, but he didn't say so.

'Then, out of the blue, Blanche called – you met her at the funfair that day, the fashion editor of *Style*. Anyway, she said how sorry she was to hear about the baby, but she still hadn't got anyone for Paris – for the collections, you know –'

Tom nodded wisely.

'And it was like the sun suddenly coming out, and I just knew, absolutely knew, that was the thing to do. Go to Paris, work hard and then come back and maybe then I'd feel brave enough to have another baby. Anyway, I went to talk to Johnathan, and said how I felt so much better, just thinking about it, and I hoped it would be all right – I'd only be away for a week. And he went very quiet, and said he'd think about it and the next day he came into the morning room and accused me of having an abortion.'

'What!' Tom was shocked. Literally, physically shocked. He had wondered about Johnathan, of course, how he could be so tolerant as to let his wife come to London for days at a time, to be photographed and feted, leaving her husband and little boy to fend for themselves – although of course there was always the omnipresent staff, Nanny and the housekeeper; it was different if you were rich.

But – clearly it wasn't. The long-suffering, patient, generous-hearted Johnathan was like any other man, hurt, angry and jealous.

'Yes. He said it was very odd I had chosen to go to London then, when it was just within the time limit for an abortion; that it was my way out of it, and my excuse to go on going to London and "racket about with your friends" as he put it. I was so shocked and hurt, I didn't know what to do or say, I just went to my room and stayed there.

'There were three awful days when he wouldn't even speak to me. Finally I said to him at breakfast that if he wasn't going to speak to me, and he thought that badly of me, I might as well say yes to Paris.

'Whereupon he said if I did go he would divorce me, he had plenty of grounds. I don't know that he has. Oh, Tom, it's so dreadful. I'd never see Jamie again. I don't know where to turn. Or what to do. But the worst thing, and you've got to believe me, is that I would never, ever have an abortion. I just wouldn't, I couldn't.'

She started to cry. Tom put first one arm round her shoulders and then rather nervously the other, and held her while she sobbed, saying nothing, occasionally stroking her hair and once or twice kissing the top of her head; and she clung to him as if she was in actual physical danger, as if he was some kind of rock, a refuge against the storm that raged about her.

Finally she released herself with a huge shuddering sigh, and tried to smile, her face swollen from crying and oddly distorted. 'What shall I do, Tom? I just don't know what to do. Oh, look, please have a drink, I need one so terribly and I can't drink alone, it's such an awful thing to do.'

What an extraordinary creature she was, Tom thought, talking as if drinking alone was as heinous a crime as – well, having an abortion. He released her carefully, set her back from him on the sofa and smiled.

'I think in this particular instance, it would be all right. You have a gin and tonic and I'll just have tonic. I daren't arrive home late and drunk.'

'Is your wife such a tyrant?' she said, getting up and going over to what he presumed was that mysterious thing, a drinks trolley.

'No, she's an angel,' said Tom. 'She's incredibly supportive in many ways and I don't deserve her.'

'Well, I hope she deserves you, Friend Tom. Now what should I do? Please tell me.'

'I honestly don't know,' said Tom, sipping his tonic. 'But people do say horrible things when they're hurt and upset. I'm sure he was very unhappy about the baby too.'

'Yes, well, you of all people should know that,' said Diana soberly.

'I do,' said Tom quietly, drinking the tonic water rather fast. 'Anyway, what should I do?'

'Well, don't give up on Johnathan yet,' said Tom. 'I know it was a terrible thing to say, but unhappiness makes us cruel. I've said some pretty harsh things to Alice from time to time. I'd put quite a lot of money, if I had any, on his coming round and apologising. If he doesn't, if it goes on, then obviously you have to think again.'

'I should never have married him,' said Diana sadly. 'It was very wrong of me.'

Tom looked at her sharply. 'Why do you say that?'

'Because I didn't love him,' said Diana. 'All right then, I'll try to do what you say. And should I go to Paris, do you think? It really would cheer me up.'

'Absolutely not,' said Tom, sounding as stern as he could. 'You'd wipe out any goodwill at a stroke.'

She sighed, then managed a watery smile.

'All right. I'll do my best. But I can't promise anything. You've no idea what it's like living with someone who hates you. Or at best dislikes and mistrusts you. That hurts. Oh, Tom, dear Friend Tom, I know you've got to go, but thank you so much for coming and listening to me, and advising me. Just talking to you has made me feel better. I just hope I can do the same for you one day. Contrary to what you might think, I'm very good at keeping secrets. Go on, home to Alice the angel and I'll hope to see you very soon.'

She was very tall, hardly had to reach up to kiss him, but she did, a long, gentle kiss on the lips. It was confusing, that kiss, albeit not in the least carnal. Tom said good luck, and half stumbled out of the front door and down into the perfectly groomed Padster Mews, where he stood for a while, taking deep breaths and steadying himself.

She was danger, was Diana Southcott. He was more aware of it with every meeting. He started to run, hoping for three things. That Alice wouldn't be too cross with him; that he had no lingering whiff of Diana's heady, heavy perfume about him; and that she would not go to Paris.

# Chapter 30

## 1952

Paris was wonderful. Diana hadn't enjoyed herself so much since her coming-out year. Of course it wasn't all parties and fun; it was hard work. But she loved it.

Going to Paris to be photographed in haute-couture clothes sounded as if you wafted about from designer to designer, drinking a lot of champagne and eating wonderful Parisian food. But you saw very little of Paris, merely moved from studio to studio in a series of taxis, and as everyone was working and needed to stay fully alert, it was unwise to drink much. There was certainly no eating of Parisian food, except a few morsels here and there, lest a pound might creep onto one's slender frame. And slender it had to be. There was only one example of each garment, and that was the one worn by models at the shows; if you didn't fit into it – and they were all about the same size – you were useless and sent home. Diana only ate the equivalent of about three meals in the entire week she was there.

The real work took place at night, and very often until dawn. During the day, the fashion editors were at the shows, seated on tiny uncomfortable gilt chairs in appalling heat. They would arrive at whatever studio had been arranged, already exhausted. Photographs and even sketches were forbidden at the shows; there was a strict embargo of several weeks before anything visual could leave the showrooms. All that was permitted was descriptive copy, and perhaps a drawing of a hat or some gloves, as shown on the programme.

This was the law laid down by the Chambre Syndicale, the all-powerful body that controlled the fashion business in Paris, lest the wholesalers, the stark enemy of couture, should rush out cheap copies and have them on the streets in days at a fraction of the cost. It was not for this that six months' intense, expensive work had been done, by some of the most dedicated and brilliant designers, pattern and toile makers, dressmakers, shoemakers. And jewellers, for many of the evening and cocktail dresses were exquisitely embroidered with dazzling coloured and crystal jewellery. At the end of a show there would be a stampede by the editors to 'reserve' one or more dresses from the *directrice* that they could photograph; often to be told – unless they were near the front of the queue – that it was booked continuously for days. And so through the night, studios all over Paris were alive. Much of it was spent waiting, for taxis trundling across Paris, bearing a garment being photographed by another magazine, and the more popular the garment, the longer the wait for its release. Bargaining went on, as one fashion editor telephoned another in their respective studios: 'I believe you've got Cardin 23 – if you send it over I'll send you Balmain 48, which I know you're waiting for.'

It was strictly forbidden to take a dress out of the building to photograph it, but some photographs where there were accessible roof spaces were taken in the lovely, early Parisian dawn. Diana found herself at five o'clock one morning climbing a fire escape ladder up to a studio roof, wearing a Balenciaga evening gown, its hem held up with Sellotape until she reached the top in safety; the result was glorious but the risk horrendous. As Blanche said cheerfully when they were safely back in the studio, drinking the black coffee that had become their staple diet, 'I don't know which would have been worse, Diana, if the dress had been damaged or you.'

There were a few parties; but for the most part attended by the fashion editors, not the models. Sometimes if you'd been working particularly hard or being creative you'd be taken along, or if you had an 'in' with the editor, but on the whole they were by invitation only. Diana managed to wangle her way into the party given by Sam White, the wonderfully charming American who ran the Paris press agency for the *Evening Standard*. She was told she was lucky because it was legendary and indeed it was: more like the traditional view of Paris week, held at the Ritz, with limitless champagne and dozens of famous faces.

Diana worked with some of the greatest names in fashion photography, including her beloved John French, and returned to England exhausted, happy and having learned a great deal. She felt she had been to some enchanted place, a wonderland to which she could return many times, should she so wish. It all rather depended on what she – and Johnathan – decided to do.

'Jillie –'

It was only six in the morning, but Tom knew she wouldn't mind being woken.

'Yes. Tom, is something the matter with Alice . . .'

'There is nothing the matter with Alice. She is very well and so is our son.'

'Your son! But it's almost three weeks until B Day!'

'I know. But he started making his presence felt around seven last night. And was born half an hour ago.'

'Oh, Tom, how lovely. What's he called, and how much did he weigh, and when can I go and see them both?'

'Not till visiting time,' said Tom. 'Six o'clock this evening. He's called Christopher but to be known as Kit. No reason except we like it. He's the jolliest little chap, six pounds twelve ounces, and Alice was just amazing, so brave, made no fuss at all. I was allowed in to see them about ten minutes after he was born, and the midwife said she wished all the mothers were like Alice. She was sitting up, all rosy and pleased with herself when I went in, and so happy, I've never seen her so happy. I can't quite believe it's over and he's safely here. I know I kept saying I wasn't worried, but of course I was.'

'Of course,' said Jillie. 'Oh, I can't wait to meet him.'

Alice sat in bed, cuddling Kit, and thought how lucky she was.

She had hoped so much for a boy so that there could be no question of competing with Hope's memory, and here he was, born so quickly and comparatively easily.

Motherhood became her as much as pregnancy had not. She felt strong and well and amazed everybody by getting out of bed in the afternoon and walking to the bathroom. Her milk flowed, and while the other mothers struggled to get their babies latched onto the breast, she felt Kit clamp his small greedy mouth round her nipples and suck until he was replete. After which he slept, for up to four hours at a time. She was much envied for this, especially the night feeds when, summoned to the nursery where all the babies slept, she was only out of bed for about twenty minutes, after which they both went back to sleep.

Alice begged to be allowed to go home early but they refused: 'You need the week here,' the ward sister said, 'to rest and get your strength back. I know you've got a very easy baby, but when you're home as well as looking after him, you'll have to do the laundry – and there'll be an awful lot – clean the house and look after your husband. They don't like playing second fiddle to their babies, you know, whatever they may say. Also getting home unsettles baby, he'll be difficult for a few days which will make things harder for you.'

But if Kit felt unsettled, he kept it to himself; he appeared to like his nursery, and the mobile strung across his cot entertained him mightily. He continued to sleep a great deal. Alice put him out in the garden in his pram whenever she could, under the apple tree, where he seemed to take equal pleasure watching the leaves move about in the sunlight; it was a beautiful spring, and almost every day he lay there all morning sleeping or gazing contentedly round him. He smiled for the first time when Alice lifted him out of his pram for his two p.m. feed. 'I know it's half an hour early,' she said to him, 'but if you don't tell anyone, I won't. Then we can get to the park early, sit by the pond.'

And his answer, as he gazed up at her, was some wobbly working of his face as he struggled to get it under control, a little awkward at first, but then settling into the undoubted wonder of his first smile. Alice was so excited, she wanted to ring Tom and tell him. Since she was not allowed to ring him in the office, she rang his mother instead.

* * *

'I do hope we haven't made a terrible mistake,' said Jillie, looking anxiously at her husband to be. 'Or rather,' she added, 'that I haven't made one.'

'My darling girl, why ever should you think that?' said Ned. A student of body language would have noticed a slight but distinct change in his.

'Ned! Don't be silly!' Jillie threw down her pen. They were making one of the countless lists that litter every path to every wedding service and celebration.

Geraldine Curtis had set the number of people invited. 'Perfectly straightforward,' she said. 'Fifty for Ned, fifty for you, Jillie, fifty for our friends, fifty for Persephone and James's. Strictly speaking the marquee only holds one hundred and fifty, but please God the sun will shine, and people can spill out into the garden.'

'I mean, it's perfectly obvious,' Jillie said now, glaring at Ned. 'It's Ascot week. I just hadn't realised.'

'Realised what?' said Ned patiently.

'Oh, Ned, don't be stupid. Lots of people will be going, it's Ladies' Day. Why didn't any of you think of it?'

'It was arranged rather a long time ago,' said Ned. 'We checked our own diaries, family birthdays, all that stuff.'

'None of those things can possibly compare with Ladies' Day at Ascot. We'll just have to change the date.'

'Jillie,' said her mother rather firmly, 'we have very few friends who go to Royal Ascot. Now if it was a first night at the Old Vic or Stratford, or even Covent Garden, it might be more serious, but I did check all those.'

'Well,' said Jillie irritably, 'I'm simply not convinced.'

'I think perhaps I should be going,' said Ned. 'I've done my list. If you think we should change the date, then let's discuss it at another time.'

'Of course we can't change the date now,' said Jillie. 'Don't be so ridiculous.'

If only, Ned thought, as he pulled the MG out of the drive, if only his worries were just guest lists and dates. He went home and played Scott Joplin 'Rags' for almost an hour, to try and calm down.

* * *

Jillie spent quite a lot of time during this period with Persephone, who she increasingly liked. She was such fun, enjoyed everything, and was full of admiration for Jillie's future career. She also didn't seem to have the blind devotion to her son so many women did. She clearly adored him, but she was very aware of his faults, and laughed about them with Jillie – his obsessive tidiness for one. 'It's the navy training.'

'Well, I'm rather obsessively untidy, so goodness knows what will happen,' said Jillie, laughing.

Persephone asked her if they had found a house yet; Jillie sighed and said they hadn't. 'We'll just have to slum it in Ned's cottage in Chelsea, but it really is tiny. I'd have settled for half a dozen of the houses we've seen, but not one was right for Ned. I don't know quite why.'

Persephone thought she knew but was unable to say so. The wedding was fantasy, which Ned had always been good at, while a house, making a home, was real life, and he simply could not confront it.


Diana and Johnathan had reached an uneasy truce while they tried to decide precisely what to do. Hostilities had reached crisis point; each feeling the other had committed the ultimate in cruelty. Johnathan with his accusation of Diana having an abortion, Diana with her wilful departure for Paris in January.

Long term they didn't know what to do. Divorce would affect Jamie's life horribly, and Johnathan had no real grounds. Diana did, that of mental cruelty, but it would be extremely hard to prove and the case would be sordid. And so they went along, polite in company and with Jamie, silent when not; sleeping in separate rooms, eating when possible at different times – waiting for some helpful nudge from fate to show them the way.

# Chapter 31

## 1952

'Oh, Tom, not this weekend.'

'Yes, Alice, this weekend. It's essential.'

'Well, why didn't you tell me before?'

'I didn't know before.' Tom had been asked to present the prizes at Acton grammar school on Saturday evening. 'Some bigwig from Oxford was coming but he's pulled out at the last minute, and they've asked me to do it instead. Of course I must go, and of course you must be there with me. It's a marvellous opportunity to be seen and the local press will be there. We won't be late, so you can leave Kit with your mother.'

'She might be busy – you can't just assume she'll come up here.'

'She's never busy,' said Tom. 'Anyway, what's so special about this weekend?'

'Jillie's having all her bridesmaids to supper on Saturday. It's only a week till the wedding.'

'Golly,' said Tom, 'good thing it's not this weekend. We'd have to miss it.'

Alice would have liked to think he was joking; but she knew he wasn't.


'Ludo, I need to see you. Can you have dinner tonight?' His voice sounded shaky even to himself.

'Not tonight, old boy, sorry. Tomorrow?'

276

'Tomorrow's fine. Thanks, Ludo. Look, do you mind if we eat here? I've made a steak-and-kidney pie by way of a diversion. Is that all right?'

'Of course. Do I take it you have something rather personal to discuss? Got plenty of whisky, have you?'

'Plenty,' said Ned. 'Although not nearly as much as I did a week ago, I'm afraid.'

'Sounds bad.'

Tom was brilliant at the prize-giving. Sitting behind him on the platform, Alice thought she had never been prouder of him. The opening to his speech almost made her cry.

Having thanked the mayor and the headmaster for inviting him, he said, 'You should all – and I mean *all* of you, not just the prize-winners today – be extremely proud of yourselves. This is a wonderful school, but I won't say you're lucky to be here. Because you're not.' The headmaster gave him a startled, none-too-friendly look. 'You're not here because your fathers pay a large sum of money every term so that you can attend. Although the education you're receiving is every bit as good, if not better, as you would be receiving at a private school. No, you're here entirely through your own efforts, through hard work and determination, every single one of you, and coming here is a prize in itself. So well done. Your families should be proud of you, and you should be proud of yourselves.

'I went to a grammar school myself, in a small town in Hampshire. I lived in a very small village where my father was the postman. From there, I went on to work for a solicitor, as a clerk, and now I am a qualified London solicitor. And I am proud, very proud. Particularly of the system that got me there. Undreamed-of opportunities are available through the grammar schools for every child in the land. Make the most of yours. Which I'm sure you are doing.

'And now to the business of the evening . . .'

The local paper called his speech inspirational, and carried a photograph of Tom, captioned, *Labour figure tells grammar-school boys to be proud of themselves.*

It was almost better than being at Jillie's wedding supper, Alice thought, reading it.

Ludo sat looking at Ned, appalled. Things were even worse than he'd thought. Ned had recently gone against Ludo's advice for treatment under the auspices of professional psychiatrists from a large London hospital, the purpose of which was to 'administer and evaluate treatment for homosexuality', said Ned.

'There were things we had to do which I can't tell even you, they were so appalling. Well you've been through it, you know. Christ, it was dreadful. But I did it. I felt I had to, for Jillie, because I so sincerely love her. I've done absolutely the wrong thing in asking her to marry me, and for letting things reach this stage.'

'When was this?'

'Couple of months ago.'

'Any help?'

'No. Absolutely none.'

'Ned –' Ludo hesitated. 'Ned, you shouldn't have let it get to this point. I know that's not what you want to hear, but –'

'You're right, but I have to face things now, call a halt. Jesus. Two hundred guests, eight bridesmaids, huge party in the garden afterwards, the great and the good all there, including my mother. Who's been fantastic. She guessed, of course, but coming from the circles she lives in, she understands and accepts and is absolutely supportive, but she's angry with me for letting it get to this stage. But every time I decided to talk to Jillie, I would think of the awful consequences for me and my courage would fail.'

'You poor blighter,' said Ludo.

'But now I have to. However ghastly it is for her as well as me, it's better than marrying her under false pretences, to save my face. I'll tell her the truth and urge her to tell it too. I'm not having her humiliated more than she has to be.'

'I'm not sure the truth is what she'll want to tell,' said Ludo, 'but we'll see.'

'There was a case in the papers last week,' said Ned. 'Some poor chap got caught soliciting. Wasn't really, he just approached someone who was sitting on a park bench, struck up a conversation with him. But the police were onto this man, watching him, they'd had a tip-off and – well, that did it. They were both arrested, charged with gross indecency. Gross indecency, Ludo, for making a friend. They weren't even holding hands, for God's sake. The police just loathe us, they'll do anything to catch us, send decoys into public lavatories – it's dreadful. So wrong. So desperately wrong.'

His whisky glass was empty. Ludo poured him another.

'Thanks. Anyway, I just needed to see you. Tell you what I was going to do, and I'd – I'd like to be able to talk to you afterwards, if you're around.'

'Yes, of course. I'm in the flat all week. Look, I can see now how lucky I am I suppose. I'm what's now known as "bisexual". I daresay you've heard of James Lees-Milne, the art historian –'

'Yes, yes, of course.'

'He's bisexual; fell in love with Tom Mitford at Eton, and then years later with his sister Diana. Anyway, when I went to bed with a girl, I was all right. Although I much preferred the boys, certainly when I was young. But the dangers – well, the first time we talked, when I told you –'

'That was brave,' said Ned. 'I'll never forget that, Ludo, how much it helped me.'

'We were pretty drunk, as I recall,' said Ludo.

'Well, it made me feel a lot less crazy,' said Ned. 'And I hoped you felt you could trust me.'

'I did. And I do still. But you must get it over, Ned. Go and see Jillie tomorrow, no later, for her sake.'


'Ned's coming round this evening,' said Jillie to her mother over lunch. 'Says he wants to talk to me, can't think what about. Now look, I know it's a bit late in the day but I'm thinking of changing my hair.'

'What, for your wedding?' said Geraldine, her voice rising in horror. 'Darling, it's much too late, the poor hairdresser will have a fit.'

'Well, it's better than walking down the aisle in front of all those people, knowing I could be looking better,' said Jillie.

'I think you look lovely as it is. And so did all the girls on Saturday.

You know, when they wanted to see the dress and you did your hair with the tiara.'

'I know, but they hadn't seen the new way. Alice would have understood,' she added. 'So sad she couldn't come. She really is the most devotedly supportive wife. I'm afraid I shan't be nearly as good – I've got terribly behind with my studies as it is.'

'Well, you know my views on that,' said Geraldine. 'I don't really approve of that sort of devotion. Women, even wives, have a right to their own lives.'

'I know and I think Alice feels like that deep down. But she's buried it, she's so haunted by Laura's ghost.'

'Yes, it must be very difficult, living up to a paragon.'

'I bet she wasn't really a paragon. I bet she had loads of faults. But in Alice's mind she was, so she just can't help trying to be one too. Anyway, back to my hair . . .'

'Jillie, please don't. These last-minute things are so hard on everyone.'

Ned arrived at six on the dot. He was very pale, and Jillie realised for the first time that he had lost a lot of weight. I should have noticed, she thought. It's because I've been so wrapped up in myself.

'Hello,' she said, giving him a kiss. 'Come in. This is a bit of a treat. How are you?'

'Oh – fine.'

'You look as if you're not eating enough. I mean, brides are meant to lose weight but I don't think bridegrooms are. Stay for supper when you've finished talking about whatever it is. We'll probably be eating in the garden, it'll be lovely. Shall I tell Mrs Hemmings to find a bit of extra everything?'

'Er, no. Let's talk first at least,' said Ned. 'Where shall we go where we can be sure of being left alone?'

'Gosh, it's serious. Well, why don't we go to my bedroom? Whatever can it be? I'm hugely intrigued. Come on.'

Her bedroom was large, more of a sitting room where she worked and studied, with a desk, a chaise longue and a couple of easy chairs, as well as her bed. It was a beautiful evening, and the windows were wide open, the curtains blowing in and out of the room with the breeze. She paused in the doorway, looking at it thoughtfully.

'I love this room,' she said. 'I shall quite miss it. Oh, what a thing to say to you. Sorry, Ned.'

'That's – all right.'

'Well, shall we sit down? Where would be appropriate? The chaise longue, perhaps.'

She crossed to it, patted the space beside her. 'Ned, darling, you're as white as a sheet. Would you like a drink? I'll go and get you a whisky.'

'No, no, don't,' he said, and he didn't even sit down, just stood in front of her, clearly waiting to speak.

'All right,' she said. 'Go ahead. Have I done something awful? I'm terribly sorry if I have. I know I've been a bit of a bitch lately, I—'

'You haven't,' said Ned, 'but I have.'

'Well, I promise not to be cross.'

'You can be as cross as you like,' said Ned. 'Jillie, look at me. I want you to listen very carefully to what I have to say.'

He took a deep breath and told her that he couldn't marry her. And then he told her why.

# Chapter 32

## 1952

'It's disgusting.' Tom's voice was full of hostility. 'Disgraceful. I cannot understand how anyone can behave like that.'

Since he was reading the paper, Alice thought that whatever it was, the Conservative party must be doing it. She was right.

'We started all these reforms,' said Tom. 'Now they're claiming it was entirely due to them. God, I hope Gaitskell goes for him in Question Time. Just listen to this: "In every way the nation is better off under this new Conservative government. Its health –" health! I suppose they brought in the National Health Service – "education, nutrition – rationing is almost over – identity cards are gone, and wartime regulations almost at an end. Wages have trebled." Oh, I can't go on. We did every one of those things, or were well on the way with them . . .'

'It is dreadful,' said Alice carefully, 'I agree. But it's the way of the world in politics, isn't it?'

'I suppose so. But I'm going to write to this paper – your friend Josh Curtis wouldn't print this rubbish in the *Daily News*. I think I'll ring him in the morning, or maybe now –'

'Well, I'm going to take Kit to the park,' said Alice. 'You'll have some peace and quiet to think about your letter.'

She picked Kit out of his playpen and hurried away, before Tom could decide she should ring Josh, or want to discuss some other plan altogether.

It was a lovely October day; golden and warm. She tucked Kit into his pram, and pushed it out through the front door and down the street. Kit struggled to sit up, his latest accomplishment. He smiled at her, showing one white half-emerged tooth. He was a lovely golden brown colour himself, having spent much of the summer outside. He really was a remarkable baby. His temperament remained level and cheerful, even when he was clearly in some discomfort from his teeth. Alice, who refused to take any credit for his behaviour, was much envied for it. She insisted he had simply been born happy, but both her mother, and Tom's married sisters who they saw occasionally, thought otherwise. 'It's because you're so calm, darling,' her mother said. 'You enjoy it all. They pick up on that sort of thing.'

Whatever the truth, Alice was grateful. And particularly over the past three months, when Jillie, as her best friend, had needed so much companionship and comfort and she had had to leave him to play by himself as Jillie wept and talked and begged to be with her. More than once she had had to spend the night at number five, with Kit; Geraldine Curtis, grateful to have someone to share the burden of her distraught, humiliated, heartbroken daughter, had Jillie's old cot brought out of the attic and fitted it with new covers, bought toys for him, stocked up with Cow & Gate and often gave him his bottle if Alice seemed stressed as she prepared it and said Jillie was crying and she wanted to get back to her.

She would never forget the wail of grief that came down the telephone from Jillie that dreadful evening: 'Alice, something dreadful's happened, you've got to come, got to. Get a taxi, I'll pay. Is Tom in?'

'Yes, of course. He'll look after Kit. I'll be over as soon as I possibly can. Is your mother there?'

'Yes, but it's you I need really. Oh, Alice –' and then came the wail, like some animal in pain. Which of course, Alice thought afterwards, she was. A wounded animal.

Geraldine, white and drawn, let her in.

'I'll let her tell you what's happened, Alice. It is dreadful. I – she's coming, Jillie,' she called, as Jillie appeared at the top of the stairs, swollen eyed, shivering with shock and pain.

'I just don't know how he could do it to me,' she said to Alice, who sat frozen with horror listening to the dreadful news. 'He says he loves me. How can he love me, Alice? He's humiliated me, hurt me, deceived me for all this time.'

As the dreadful evening wore on, as Jillie tried to make sense of the situation, and her parents to decide what best to tell people, Alice cried quite a lot herself. This was cruelty beyond anything she could imagine. She could offer no comfort, beyond her company and her sympathy. She held Jillie in her arms while she sobbed and said how could she have been so stupid, so trusting?

'Not so stupid,' Alice said gently. 'You were worried about the – the bed thing from the beginning, weren't you?'

'Yes, of course.' That appeared to steady her momentarily. 'I suppose I'd tucked it away somewhere, decided not to think about it. Oh, Alice, what are we going to tell people? What are we going to say?'

Downstairs, Peter and Geraldine Curtis were trying to solve that very dilemma.

'It's not for us to tell people the real reason,' Geraldine said.

'No, of course not. That has to come from him. It'll be the end of his career – he could even be arrested.'

'Although I'd quite like to see him behind bars, in solitary confinement for the rest of his life,' said Geraldine. 'But not for that reason, of course. Just as a punishment for what he's done to Jillie.'

She and Peter, intensely liberal minded, were appalled at the way homosexuals were treated by the laws, had joined one of the many campaigns to change them. It would be unthinkable to give the real reason for the cancellation of the wedding; but what one could they give?

Jillie had said she didn't want the real reason known. 'Not to save his skin,' she added. 'Just because it makes me look so stupid and naive.'

Geraldine went upstairs to Jillie, knocked on the door of her room. She was quiet now, lying on her bed, staring in front of her. Alice sat beside her looking helpless.

'Alice – Jillie – I'm so sorry to press this, but we do have to get an announcement out, both in the form of personal letters to our friends, and in the press, tomorrow morning if possible. Certainly to our friends.'

'I've got one suggestion,' said Alice. 'Couldn't you just say that Jillie and Ned have decided, by mutual agreement, not to get married? Then it doesn't sound as if Jillie is in any way a victim.'

'I think that, or something like it, could well be the answer,' said Geraldine slowly. 'It will give rise to gossip, of course, but anything will. Jillie, what do you think?'

'I think that would be all right. I keep telling you, say what you like.'

'I'll go and talk to Peter,' said Geraldine. 'Put the suggestion to him.'

Peter said he thought it was the best suggestion by far: 'But we'll have to tell Ned. Personally, I'd like to horsewhip him, but if he doesn't know he may concoct some quite different explanation of his own. I'll ring him.'

Ned answered at once.

'Ned,' said Peter, 'I haven't rung with recriminations – there's nothing I can say that could possibly express my anger and disgust at what you've done to my daughter. I simply want your approval to this suggestion of the announcement we'd like to put out.'

'I'll approve anything. You can tell the truth if you like,' said Ned wearily.

'I wouldn't dream of such a thing. No, this is the form of words –' Ned agreed instantly.

'Good. I'd only like to add that if I hear you are telling people anything else, I shall take you to court and sue you for breach of promise. Or rather Jillie will. And then it possibly would all come out. I'm not threatening you or blackmailing you, I've no interest whatsoever in your future. My only concern is for Jillie and her reputation and emotional well-being. Do I have your word?'

'You do.'

'Good.' Peter put the phone down. And then sat thinking how much he liked Ned and had been looking forward to having him as a son-in-law. God, this was a damnable business.

✻ ✻ ✻

The announcement was made, the presents sent back, and after the inevitable tidal wave of gossip and shock, everyone got on with their lives and forgot about it. Except, of course, the main players in the drama, who continued to grieve and to withdraw from human contact as best they could. Geraldine's friends tried to wheedle another explanation out of her; she told them firmly there was none, and if they raised the subject again, their friendship would be at an end. Mercifully, there was no conjecture in the press as to any other reason, although reporters haunted number five for a few days, trying to find one.

Nobody in the world, outside the immediate closed circle, knew the real reason – apart from Ludo Manners, and of course Ned's mother who had been fearing that something of the sort might happen for many months. She too kept silent. There was a fairly distressing scene when she telephoned Jillie and asked if she might come and see her; Jillie told her that she would rather be fed to the lions than have Persephone in the house.

'I cannot think you have anything to say to me that I would wish to hear. Please leave me alone in future.'

Persephone travelled from Cornwall to see Ned the day after the announcement was made.

'Well,' she said, looking around at the disarrayed house, littered with whisky bottles, and at his white face, his eyes red rimmed with exhaustion and grief. 'At least you had the courage to do it in the end. For which I have to admire you. But oh, Ned, why, why did you ask her to be your wife?'

'Because I was afraid,' said Ned, his anger at the laws that had driven him to it dispersed briefly to Persephone. 'Afraid of being found out, branded, of imprisonment, although I believe one can opt for what's known as chemical castration, given a fairly liberal judge. It has a very unfortunate effect on the brain, and indeed the whole of one's body, as a side effect. I'd be afraid of losing the position in my profession I have worked so hard for, and indeed of losing most of my social circle. And I genuinely love Jillie so very much I thought it would be all right. I longed to spend the rest of my life with her, to have children. But it was not to be.'

'Well, they've let you off very lightly,' said Persephone, 'with that announcement. They'd have been within their rights to tell the truth.'

'I know that. I told them if they did I would not deny it. But they are an intensely liberal family. One evening at dinner I remember Peter raging at the iniquity of the laws against homosexuality. They had some QC present, who of course disagreed with him; I remained as silent as I could, but I said I agreed with Peter. He asked me if I had any homosexual friends, and of course I said I didn't. Which I don't.'

'Not even Ludo Manners?' said Persephone.

Ned looked at her in wonder. God, her antennae were effective.

'No,' he said firmly. 'For God's sake, Mother, he has four children, been married to Cecily for fifteen years.'

'I know,' said Persephone. 'And wasn't that precisely what you were planning?'

He was silent; then said quite savagely, 'If you ever utter one word of suspicion about Ludo I swear I shall kill you.'

'Darling, don't be so ridiculous. Now, I'm going to clear this place up and then we are going out to dinner. I've booked a table at the Caprice.'

'Mother, I can't go to the Caprice. I can't go anywhere. I'm an outcast.'

'Well, you can't stay here for the rest of your life. Otherwise, all the sacrifices you've forced on poor Jillie will be in vain. You are becoming a well-known paediatrician – don't squander that as well. Go and have a bath, shave, put on a decent suit and drive me to the restaurant.'

It was probably the most difficult and the bravest thing Ned had ever done, apart from telling Jillie he couldn't marry her; but Persephone was right, he had to do it sometime. Most people there that evening who knew him nodded a little coolly, but then ignored him, clearly afraid of some involvement. Persephone met a couple of friends there, who joined them for coffee and brandy, and even made Ned laugh. He went back to work at St Peter's and opened his rooms in Welbeck Street the following Monday.

❖ ❖ ❖

Jillie went to see Miss Moran and asked her for a further month's leave; Miss Moran said her attendance levels had been so execrable she was of a mind to ask her to leave altogether. 'There are many, many girls who would give all they had to be in your position here. You have abused it disgracefully. However, you don't look well, I have to admit. Take one month from now. You will return then and work as you certainly haven't worked this summer.'

'Miss Moran, thank you. I can promise you, I am about to become one of your best pupils.'

'I really don't think that is remotely possible,' said Miss Moran. She paused, clearly in thought, then turned and said, 'I was sorry to hear about your marriage. But really, I'm sure you'll come to see in time one is much better on one's own. Men are such a brake on one's life.'

And then she was gone.

For the first time in weeks, Jillie laughed.

# Chapter 33

## 1953–4

'I simply don't understand it,' said Tom. 'It really is quite beyond me. 'I'm with John Osborne –'

'Who's John Osborne?'

'This brilliant new playwright,' said Tom slightly irritably. 'Surely you know he wrote *Look Back in Anger.* He calls the Royal Family a fatuous industry. My view exactly.'

'Well, you'd better not let any of your Labour voters hear you say that. They'd lynch you.'

It was true. Coronation fever gripped the nation and royal fervour was at its peak. It had begun with the death of George VI. The lovely young Queen Elizabeth, mother of two small children, and her absurdly handsome husband became the darlings of the press. The New Elizabethan Age was written about every day. The date was set for the coronation, 2 June. A national holiday was declared; every town had street parties and carnivals planned.

An argument raged about televising the event. A fairly new phenomenon, television had been pronounced by the Archbishop of Canterbury as 'potentially one of the great dangers of the world'. The Duke of Norfolk, who was masterminding the whole thing, was also opposed to it, believing it would rob the ceremony of its mystique. The press wanted it; it was a little-known fact that the Queen, young, shy and already nervous at the prospect of what would be a huge ordeal, did not. But in the end, the cameras were in the Abbey, and the reverently respectful voice of Richard Dimbleby provided the commentary.

The country drowned in a red, white and blue sea of flags and bunting. People came to the capital in their thousands to celebrate, and on the morning of 2 June, when it was announced that the Union Jack had been set on the very top of Mount Everest, it was as if some benign force was guiding the day, ensuring its place in history. Anybody who was anybody had a balcony, or at least a window to watch the procession from; tickets were sold for the stands in the Mall, changing hands on the black market for as much as £50, while seats on balconies that lined the route cost as much as £3,500.

People dressed up in their very best clothes simply to watch it on television; those who were not among the privileged few who owned a set were invited into their friends' and neighbours' homes. The hit song of the day, crooned by one Mr Donald Peers, was entitled 'In a Golden Coach'.

But as if begrudging the people total euphoria, it rained. Hard. On the many thousands who had come to camp out, all along the route, and indeed on the long, long procession of foreign kings and queens, dukes and duchesses, princes and princesses. The star of the procession, apart from the Queen, radiantly beautiful, was undoubtedly Queen Salote of Tonga, who insisted on having the roof of her carriage open and sat waving, smiling determinedly, and getting extremely wet.

The coronation also brought into the public eye one of the great royal romances of all time: that of Princess Margaret and Group Captain Peter Townsend, equerry to the King and, after his death, to the new Queen. Townsend, who had been a fighter pilot in the war, was extraordinarily handsome, exceptionally charming – and divorced. Margaret, less troubled by the rigours of her royal duties than her sister, more beautiful, more glamorous, and certainly more spoilt, could see no reason why she and the group captain should not marry; and the press saw a new royal drama to fill their pages, sending the curtain up on the unarguably intimate evidence of the way the Princess picked a bit of fluff from the group captain's uniform, stroking the lapel as she did so. A new fever, more thrilling than any since the abdication of King Edward VIII, seized people's imagination. The *Daily Mirror* ran a poll by way of a voting form on its front page as to whether Margaret should be allowed to marry her great love; there were seventy thousand replies and only just over two thousand said she should not. Other papers took a more serious and respectful approach, debating the matter carefully. The *Daily News* adopted a middle road, giving a male columnist a whole page to come down against the marriage, and on the opposite page, the women's editor rhapsodised in her inimitable way on its golden possibilities.

The palace, and indeed the church and the government, were in a flat spin. A temporary solution was found; Townsend was sent to Brussels, the Regency Act was changed, and Margaret was given the two years until her twenty-fifth birthday to make up her mind.

Tom's first words, when Alice told him she was pregnant again, were, 'I hope that doesn't mean you won't be able to come to the conference in October.'

'Tom!'

'Well, it's important, I –' And then he realised he had overstepped the mark as her eyes filled with the easy, hormone-induced tears.

'I'm sorry, Alice. I'm a brute. I sound like a nineteen thirties husband.'

'Yes, you do. A very bad example of one, I'd say.'

'I'm truly sorry. It's wonderful news. But I thought –'

'That I was being careful. Well, I am, usually. But if I could just say "caravan" to you –'

'It would stir up some pretty good memories,' said Tom, grinning reluctantly.

They had rented a caravan in August, and driven it to Hampshire, settling in a caravan park not far from Sandbanks, the glorious stretch of golden beach opposite the Isle of Wight. They were lucky with the weather, seven days of sunshine; Kit was ecstatic, displaying his building skills as he patted his bucket prior to tipping out what Alice decided must have been a hundred sand pies. They also got him a rubber ring and he bobbed about in the warm water, laughing, his fists beating up waves, his feet thrashing up and down, propelling him along.

They were so happy, sated with sunshine, and the sun acted on them like an aphrodisiac; after supper the first night, Tom put his arm round her, and kissed her shoulder.

'You taste of salt,' he said.

'So do you.'

'How about a new experience?'

'What's that?'

'Shall we call it carasex?'

'We could. Kit's very fast asleep. Now look, I'll just get my –'

That was when she discovered she had failed to pack her Dutch cap.

Saying no was unthinkable – she was drenched with desire. She cast a quick review of her cycle, decided she was at a point when conception was almost impossible, or so Jillie had told her, long ago, and went back to Tom.

It was glorious, a tangle of entirely new sensations, it seemed, created by the sun and the wind and the freedom from everyday anxieties, for Tom as much as for her.

'Crikey,' he said, when finally she came with a huge wild cry, 'they'll hear you on the Isle of Wight.'

'And what's wrong with that?'

'Nothing. Except they'll be jealous. Oh, Alice. I love you.'

'And I love you. And I'm so happy.'

It happened, twice more that week, Alice continuing to put her faith in Jillie's doctrine.

Jillie, it turned out, was wrong.

She had arranged for her mother to look after Kit so that she could go to the conference; and had been looking forward to it. Now it loomed over her, a horrible ordeal. She just couldn't face it. As for Mrs Higgins's breakfasts: the very thought made her heave.

In the event, Mrs Higgins, in whom she had confided about the pregnancy, said she knew exactly how Alice felt. 'Morning sickness, poor wee girl, worst thing in the world, and you having to be all bright and chirpy and impress people. I'll do you some nice toast, lass, and anything else you fancy, just let me know. For some reason it were brown sauce with me, I could eat anything so long as it had brown sauce on it, but I can see that doesn't appeal.'

In fact, Alice did really fancy something, and that was smoked haddock; Mrs Higgins said she'd cook it for her every morning.

'Oh, Mrs Higgins, you are so kind. And – you don't have any Marmite, I suppose?'

'I do, my lovely, I do. On your toast?'

And so, every morning Alice ate dry toast and Marmite-flavoured smoked haddock, and it got her through the day.

By the last morning, Tom still hadn't been asked to speak; he was bitterly disappointed. Then suddenly someone dropped out of a debate on education and Tom was asked to take his place.

The Labour government had an inbuilt resistance to grammar schools; the new comprehensive ideal, of one school for all with no punishing examination at eleven and offering every kind of education, from the academic to the technical, seemed to them far fairer. There were a very few trial schools, but it was far too early to judge the system on its results.

The debate was a hot one; Tom could see the dangers of selection at eleven, it was potentially life-wrecking, but having benefited himself so enormously from the grammar system, and being a shining example of its virtues, he spoke passionately in its defence. He had made himself felt more strongly than any of his mentors or supporters had dared hope and on the train home the next evening, reading about himself as one of the stars of the previous day in Josh's column in the *Daily News*, and featuring in a rather smaller way in a couple of reports in the nationals, Tom leaned across the compartment to Alice and said, 'Thank you for coming and making such an effort for me. I know it wasn't easy for you, feeling as lousy as you do, but it really did pay off in spades. I'm very lucky to have you.'

Alice was so surprised, she nearly fell out of her seat.

Jillie had returned to the Elizabeth Garrett Anderson, and the rather doubtful mercies of Miss Moran. She was working very hard, mostly to ease her new, loveless, single existence, and doing better than she ever had before. She found the practical work slowly less scary and, under Miss Moran's fierce gaze, could now make an incision and even move into the organs beneath it without trembling with terror.

Her hurt and her humiliation were still intense; she remained withdrawn and for several months spent all her spare time in her room, or at Alice's house. Her personal life felt very dead; she was numb to positive emotion, had been made a fool of, she felt. She was, she reflected one night as she got ready for bed, although not for sleep (that was a luxury only awarded her by the sleeping pills she removed from the pharmacy when nobody was looking), a spinster which was bad enough, and a virgin which was worse. She scarcely recognised herself from the radiant creature of the spring and summer. Although she was too level-headed to consider taking the whole bottle of pills, she often felt her life was pointless and not worth continuing. It was not a good state of mind.

Tom was making his name as a speaker, was asked to speak at appropriate local functions and debates, either linked in some way to health or education, in which he was also becoming something of an expert. Then he was summoned in the middle of January to Transport House, to a meeting with the national agent, who informed him that there was a by-election coming up. 'Terence Bright, the present member for Purbridge, has just been diagnosed with Parkinson's, poor chap,' he added piously. 'Now this is a marginal, and your main rival, given this is a Tory-held seat, is an old codger, James Harvey, classic Tory, ticks every bloody box and I wouldn't think you'd have a chance if it wasn't for a new industrial estate being developed in the area, bringing in lots of Labour voters, so you could just make it. We'd like you to go for selection at least; there are a couple of other contenders, but you made a pretty big mark at the conference with that speech of yours. What do you think?'

Tom managed to stammer out that he thought it sounded very good indeed.

'Good man. Get down there as soon as you can, get to know the place and its people. The agent down there is very good, very experienced. Date's not set yet, but you've got about a month. Go and see the PR people on your way out, but meanwhile –' and he launched into a string of procedures.

Tom walked out of the building two hours later as if on air. Alice was less enthusiastic, sick and weary as she was, but took her cue from Laura and said it was wonderful. Laura haunted her increasingly now that the honeymoon period of their marriage was so well in the past, and particularly now, when she was sick and weary from her pregnancy. Whenever Tom was cross, or even thoughtless, she never reacted simply and honestly. She thought of Laura, what she would have done or said, and tried to do the same.

Consequently, she became increasingly confused and anxious; on bad days she felt she hardly knew what she thought about anything any more, was lost in a spiral of self-doubt and insecurity. She also became obsessed with the fact that he had never taken her to Laura's grave. Laura lay there, in the churchyard in his village, a precious, private part of his life that Alice was to be eternally kept from. It was as if he had a mistress, but one she could not possibly fight and certainly not confront.

Some situations were easier than others to deal with: and this was one of them. Laura would have been as excited and determined as Tom, so Alice's path was clearly marked. Next day she found Purbridge on the map; and was so excited, she broke the rule and rang Tom in his office.

'Sorry,' she said, 'but you'll just have to win this seat. And I'm sure you will.'

'Why this sudden enthusiasm?'

'Tom, do you realise what's quite wonderfully near it? Sandbanks! If that's not an omen, I really don't know what could be. Our lovely Sandbanks, where this little one started her life. Clearly she has to go on living there, doesn't she? I think she's a girl, by the way.'

Tom, masking the irritation with her that he increasingly felt, agreed it could be seen as an omen. Anything that was going to make her put more effort into his cause could only be a good thing.

❖ ❖ ❖

The other two prospective candidates were, in theory, promisingly less suitable, one extremely left wing, the other unmarried. 'People like a family man,' said the national agent.

Poor Terence Bright turned out to have a heart condition as well as Parkinson's; his doctor said he should resign immediately, or he wouldn't answer for the consequences.

Alice was spared much of the practical work of a supportive spouse; even Tom could see that with one very small child and a fairly advanced pregnancy, she couldn't possibly be expected to constantly travel hundreds of miles to appear on platforms beside him. However, one terrifying ordeal was obligatory: her interview by the selection panel. This took place at Labour Party headquarters in Purbridge; a large, ugly Victorian building, apparently devoid of any form of heating. Alice was shown into a very large room, with crumbing lino on the floor and grimy windows; a vast table was the only furniture. Three people sat at the table, a rather stout woman and two men, one of them, Richard Darrett, the chairman of the selection committee; he stood up as she entered and indicated an upright chair set several feet away from the table. She could never remember being in so unwelcoming an environment and wondered if the Conservative set-up was any better.

She presumed she was intended to sit down, and did so, rather nervously, tugging her skirt down over her knees and hoping the very modest make-up she was wearing wouldn't be considered tarty. They nodded approvingly on hearing that she had a small child, and would shortly have another and that, apart from caring for the family, her only occupation was supporting her husband in his political ambitions.

'Now, there is one thing that worries me,' said the woman. 'It appears you attended a private school.' She made this sound rather as if Alice had spent time in prison.

But Alice was ready for this one. 'Yes, but only because of the war. It was a boarding school in the depths of the country. My parents lived on the outskirts of London, and they naturally wanted me to be safe. But I believe passionately in the grammar-school system.'

They all nodded approvingly; there were four grammar schools in the Purbridge area, two for boys, two for girls. She knew she was on safe ground; she had taken great care with her research.

'And – would you be able to support your husband by joining him in the constituency at weekends? There will be a lot to do. Not just his surgery.'

'You mean the school visits, the amateur theatricals, the concerts, organising help in various ways for people who need it? Supporting local charities? Yes, of course. I shall enjoy all that very much.'

On and on it went. When Alice joined Tom and the constituency agent, Colin Davidson, in the dreariest pub she had ever been in, she was close to exhaustion.

'I'm afraid I was hopeless,' she said. 'I'm sorry, Tom, I did my best.'

Three days later the selection of the new Labour candidate for Purbridge would be made and the result announced; Tom had gone down for the occasion, desperately nervous, none too hopeful. Alice wanted to go, but he told her it would be such a depressing occasion and there was no point her being there.

'You can be waiting at home for me with a consoling supper and some nice cold beer. I still can't get over having a refrigerator.'

'Nor can I,' said Alice. 'But Tom, are you really so sure you haven't been selected?'

'Absolutely. I don't know why I ever agreed to go for it,' he added gloomily. 'Must have been mad.'

Next day she was strapping Kit into the pram when the phone rang. It was Tom.

'Mrs Knelston?'

'Yes. Tom, you know it's me, what's the matter?'

'You are addressing the prospective Labour MP for Purbridge. I can't quite believe it myself. I'm over the moon, I can tell you. And a lot of it is thanks to you. So very well done and thank you, Alice. I've got to go now, give an interview to the local rag. God, it's exciting. We'll go out and celebrate tomorrow when I get back.'

Alice couldn't think of anything she'd like less; she was so tired she could hardly hold her knife and fork at supper at home, but she managed to express delight. They couldn't afford to go out to dinner so it probably wouldn't happen. But she was wrong. Donald Herbert took them out to dinner again, to the Boulestin on the edge of Covent Garden.

'It's a charming place, thought it would be slightly less masculine than Rules which I had considered, and this is your treat as much as Tom's. You did wonderfully well, Alice.'

They both smiled at her and raised their glasses; she smiled back, and thought how nice it was to be considered of value in her own right for once. One day, maybe, just maybe, she would go back to work . . .

But first there was the election to get through.

Ned's practice had grown slowly over the past two or three years. Paediatricians were a comparatively new breed and it was taking time for the public to accept them. His National Health practice at St Luke's, where he recently moved, was very busy, however; and seemed to have a purpose that the private practice lacked, insofar as he saw desperately ill children. They were often malnourished – through ignorance and laziness, rather than poverty as they would have been before the war – existing on diets of chips, sweets, and canned vegetables and fruit, and the new much-admired convenience foods like meat pies that were largely pastry, sold in tins. He began to make a name for himself in child nutrition, explaining to mothers that fresh food and plenty of milk provided the vitamins that built bones, encouraged growth, and improved their dental health as well.

Like Jillie's, Ned's social life was almost non-existent, due to fear rather than lack of opportunity. He was exceedingly nervous at first that the truth would come out; but so far nothing more than the vaguest suspicions were expressed. He was desperately lonely, and missed Jillie dreadfully. His mother had become his only companion; together they went to restaurants, theatres and the cinema.

One night in the interval of Robert Anderson's *Tea and Sympathy*, waiting for Persephone to return to the bar from the ladies, he heard someone call his name, and turning, saw Diana Gunning waving at him above the crowd. For the first time in his life he was actually pleased to see her. The same applied to her; she had been genuinely saddened at the news of his cancelled wedding and in her new persona as famous top model, admired and feted wherever she went, she felt none of the old animosity.

'Ned, darling, how lovely. How are you?'

'I'm very well, Diana, thank you. I see you – or rather your photograph – everywhere. Do you enjoy your new life?'

'So much. I'm just back from New York, spending a few days in London before I go home to Yorkshire. Ned, I was so sorry to hear about your cancelled wedding. I never met Jillie, but everyone says she's adorable. All very sad. And it must have been ghastly doing it at the last minute like that, terrible decision. Jolly good for you both, though; far better than marrying the wrong person.'

'Thank you, Diana,' said Ned, realising with some surprise that she was the first person not just to actually confront the issue, but to do so in a calm and sensible way. 'It *was* ghastly. The most difficult decision I – we,' he added after an imperceptible pause, 'have ever made.'

'I should think it was. Oh – hello,' she said to Persephone who had returned. 'I'm Diana Gunning. Old friend of Ned's. Well, I hope we're friends,' she added with a conspiratorial smile at Ned.

'Of course we are.'

'I'm Persephone. Persephone Welles. Ned's mother.'

'How lovely to meet you,' said Diana. 'Oh, dear, there's the bell. I'd better go and find my friends again. The Bellingers – you know them, don't you, Ned?'

'A little. Well, it was wonderful to see you, Diana. Thank you for coming over.'

'Beautiful creature,' said Persephone, when she had gone.

Lying in bed that night at the Bellingers', Diana thought about Ned. He was still so sublimely handsome, and charming in that gentle, soft way. And quite old for a bachelor.

Almost middle-aged. She wondered what could have driven him to cancel the wedding at – what – four days' notice. Must have been something very serious. And to be at the theatre with his mother. With whom he was obviously very close. A shaft of light suddenly shot through Diana's brain. Gentle. Soft. Bachelor into middle age. Cancelling his wedding at the very last minute – she had not missed the pause between the 'I' and the 'we'. And – at the theatre with his mother.

'Of course,' she said aloud. 'Of course. He's a fairy. My God. Poor Ned. Poor, poor, lovely Ned.'

She had spent so much time with homosexuals over the past few years, her instincts were very sure. Everything suddenly made perfect sense.

# Chapter 34

## 1953–4

It was the most excruciating tension Tom had ever experienced. He knew, whatever happened, he would never forget it. The huge rather bleak room, oddly quiet, only a murmur of sound, people pacing its boundaries, sometimes alone, sometimes with a companion, heads close together, engaged in important conversation. The platform, on which he would be standing when he learned his fate. The rows of long tables at which people sat, tipping the contents out onto the area in front of them, tidying them into a neat stack and then counting, endlessly. It was a crucial by-election, and Tom's profile was high: the TV cameras were there, the first time an election had known this experience.

This was the culmination of all the weeks of walking the streets, knocking on doors, receiving sometimes a welcome, sometimes abuse, reciting the mantra until he hadn't the faintest idea what the words meant, handing over, if he was lucky, posters saying *Vote for Knelston for a fairer Britain.*

Tom was popular in the town among Labour supporters; he had worked so hard, made huge sacrifices, spent long weekends without Alice as he made speeches, judged competitions, awarded prizes, attended party meetings, drank horrible watery warm beer in disagreeable pubs, ate disgusting food at endless dinners, courted town councillors, and wondered occasionally why he had ever wanted to be an MP.

Tonight, Alice was with him – Kit left with her mother – a fake smile fixed on her face, chatting up the councillors, flirting with the men she knew, Colin Davidson particularly, Tom's agent who had worked every bit as hard as Tom; all of them pretending to be calm, assuring each other that they had done all they could. Which they had.

The numbers made no sense at first; he couldn't take them in. William Forbes, Liberal, five thousand, two hundred and ninety-two; Tom Knelston, Labour, seventeen thousand, four hundred and twenty-seven – that sounded like a lot – James Harvey, Conservative, seventeen thousand, nine hundred.

Then there was a great roar of applause, and clapping and cheering, and – well, that was it, it seemed, James Harvey had won, beaten him by about five hundred votes. He had failed, he wasn't an MP, not the Labour member for Purbridge. All that work, all that shoe leather, all those evenings, all for this – failure.

He felt, pathetically, like crying; but he smiled as James Harvey pumped his hand, smiled at Alice as she kissed him and slipped her hand into his, smiled through James Harvey's acceptance speech; and then stepped forward to the microphone and started to speak himself, aware of the cameras, both flashbulbs and TV. Half angry, half despairing, but fired up suddenly to speak the truth as he saw it about the Labour Party and its beliefs.

Afterwards and for many years, people said it was the best speech he ever made. He thanked the people of Purbridge who had always treated him with courtesy and made him welcome. He thanked those who had worked so hard for him. He said he was naturally sorry that he would be unable to speak for Purbridge in the Commons, because he had so much to say; he spoke of the philosophy of the party, that the weak should have a voice, have rights.

He spoke passionately of the National Health Service, one of the party's proudest achievements. 'We are all shocked by apartheid,' he said. 'But that was exactly what we had here, before Bevan launched the National Health Service. Good healthcare for the fortunate few with money; little or none for the unfortunate many.' He spoke of Labour's heart, of its passion to see justice done, of its determination to educate every child in the land, its promise that every family should be in decent, rather than adequate, housing. He looked extraordinary, standing there, eyes blazing, his hair wild as he pushed his hands through it every now and again. His speech was entirely unprepared; it took him by surprise, never mind his entourage. They and all those Labour voters, watching or listening at home, shook their heads in disappointment that they had not got this extraordinary young man as their representative, and more than a few hundred Tories had the same thought. When at last he became aware that his time was up, he stopped abruptly, and said, 'Let me say, I will never, as long as I have breath in my body, abandon the party I love and all it has done for this country and indeed for you.'

The next day it could have been assumed that Labour had won the by-election. Tom got far more coverage than the winning candidate. His potential, his talent for oratory, combined with his looks, his charm and his credentials – humble beginnings, grammar-school education, young family, pretty young wife – meant the press pounced upon him like some huge bird of prey, picking him up, flying off with him, up towards the sun.

Substantial quotes from Tom's speech, referring to his passion for the National Health Service and his hero, Aneurin Bevan, appeared in the *Daily Mirror* and the *Herald*. The *Mirror* showed a picture of him at the count with Alice.

Tom, stunned by the reaction, sat at his desk at Herbert & Herbert as everyone in the office came to congratulate him.

'But I lost,' he kept saying. 'I didn't win.'

Donald Herbert arrived, almost as excited as if Tom had won. 'You *have* won, Tom,' he kept saying. 'You, Tom Knelston, political force, the future is yours – nobody can take it from you.'

Tom gave in and decided to bask in his own glory; he seemed, entirely by accident, to have gained a foothold into history. He was summoned to Transport House, feted there, promised a win in the next election. Alice, interviewed in the *Daily Sketch* in a feature that filled half a page, spoke of her faith in Tom and the Labour ideal.

* * *

Once the excitement, the euphoria, had gone, once he was back where he had been, an ambitious nobody with no constituency, Tom was as close to depression as he had ever been. This was not the wild grief he had experienced after Laura died; it was a dull heavy misery. Whatever people said, however much he was feted, and his speech quoted, he was a failure, and it hit him very hard. He went endlessly over 'if only's in his mind. If only he'd knocked on five more doors each day, if only he'd made a better speech at that librarians' dinner – he'd been tired and a bit lacklustre, he knew – if only he'd supported the young mothers trying to open a crèche a bit more enthusiastically, if only he'd written a better speech for the Rotary Club, if only he'd done all those things, then he might have got five hundred more votes.

Useless for Alice to tell him he was wonderful and it was only a very short year to the general election and another chance to win, or for Donald Herbert to promise he'd see him into a safe Labour seat; useless for Robert Herbert, who promised him a junior partnership in a year's time, to tell him. He felt he had let not only himself down but also the Labour Party. He was a failure; and he couldn't cope with it. As a miserable Alice said to Jillie, he had never known failure. All his life, apart from losing Laura – which was a dreadful thing but the blame for which could not possibly be set at his door – things had gone well for him, at school, at Pemberton & Marchant, during the war, and then at Herbert & Herbert. From his first tentative dip into the world of politics, he had succeeded.

Jillie said that was true, but failure was a necessary ingredient to life's mix and everyone should know something of it. 'Look at me, I'm finding out about it too.' Tom would get over it and be a better person and a better politician for it. Alice hoped she was right, and later decided she had been wrong.

The small Miss Knelston, for whom neither Alice nor Tom had yet thought of a name, duly arrived three weeks early, just as her brother had, in the middle of the following April. She was almost as equable as her older brother – her birth as easy, and even swifter – and she lay, looking out at the world through eyes as wide and blue as his, clearly well satisfied with what she saw.

It was one of Tom's sisters, who gave her her name.

'I once had a doll who looked a lot like her,' she said. 'Big blue eyes and little round mouth. She was called Lucy.'

'Lucy!' said Alice. 'That's lovely. If Tom likes it, then Lucy she shall be.'

Tom liked it very much, but Kit's version was Loopy; Alice rather feared that might stick.


'Cheer up, Gunning. You look as if you'd lost a shilling and found sixpence.'

'I haven't found anything at all, actually,' said Jamie.

'What's up, old chap?'

'Oh, doesn't matter.'

'Course it does. We're meant to be blood brothers, remember. Come on, spill the beans.'

'Oh, all right,' said Jamie. 'But you are not to tell anybody, Richards – this is top secret.'

'Blood brothers don't tell on each other,' said the small Richards. 'We mingled our blood, didn't we?' And indeed they had, pricking their fingers and letting the drops of blood fall on a saucer and then mingling them carefully.

So behind the squash courts, which was the accepted place for confidence sharing, Jamie told Richards the appalling news.

'I got a letter from my mother this morning. She and my father are getting divorced.'

'Oh, crikey,' said Richards. 'That is a bit rough. Funny way to do it, in a letter.'

'They're coming to see me on Sunday. Both of them. My mother said this would give me a chance to get used to the idea, before we all talked.'

'Oh, I see. How rotten. Sorry. But you know Northfield's parents are divorced. He says it's really excellent. They both want him to like them best, so they give him amazing presents – his father gives him the top-class Meccano set, then his mother a full set of *Biggles* books and so on. Not all bad, you see.'

Jamie contemplated this for a moment, then said, 'I'd rather have two parents than a Meccano set.'

305

'Well, of course,' said Richards. 'I'm just pointing out it's not all bad.'

Diana was in her version of behind the squash courts: a pub called the Salisbury in Charing Cross Road, waiting for the equivalent of her blood brother, one Tom Knelston. She wasn't quite sure if she was waiting in vain. He had been quite cross when she called him, saying he was working on a difficult case and had to have the documentation finished by the last post.

'Well, I'm sorry, but I need to talk to you, Friend Tom. Very badly. Couldn't we meet after work?'

'No, Diana, we couldn't. I've got a wife and two small children at home, and I need to be there, helping Alice. She has a lot to do. She has to share me with the Labour Party as it is.'

'Couldn't you pretend I was an official of the Labour Party?'

Tom tried and failed not to laugh. The concept of Diana Southcott, with her fame and beauty and her expensive clothes, taking on the persona of the Labour Party was so absurd it was funny.

'There, you see, I've made you laugh. It'll cheer you up meeting me at the Savoy. It can't be *that* much fun at home with two tinies grizzling and filling their nappies.'

'Kit and Lucy don't grizzle,' said Tom firmly and loyally.

'What lovely names. Now come on, even if they don't grizzle, I'm sure they fill their nappies.'

'Well, they do but Diana, even if I did meet you, it couldn't be at the Savoy. Someone might see me. It's hardly a suitable venue for a prospective Labour MP.'

'All right. Wherever you like. I know, there's a lovely pub in Charing Cross Road called the Salisbury. It's full of fairies. They love it there. Which reminds me, I want to ask you something. Will you meet me there? I really do need you, dear Friend Tom.'

Twin visions swam before Tom's eyes. One was of him removing a well-filled nappy before putting its owner into the bath and dealing with it, and then, bath-time done, washing the nappies, putting them through the mangle and hanging them outside; these were his regular evening activities as soon as he got home. The other was sitting in the Salisbury, the lovely pub in Charing Cross Road, all brass railings and etched glass, with a beautiful woman who was desperate to talk to him.

'No,' he said firmly. 'I really can't.'

Alice had had a bad day; Lucy did grizzle occasionally when things were not entirely to her liking. Kit found it hilarious to imitate her. The noise had been going on all afternoon, and her head ached. She looked at her watch: Tom would be home soon and then she'd feel better. Although she did have something to tell him which certainly wouldn't make him feel better. The one time Tom had suggested sex (that was yet another misery for her, his appearing to have completely gone off the whole thing) she had been so relieved, so hungry for it, she had decided not to go through the spell-breaking procedure of fetching and inserting her Dutch cap. Now, two weeks later, her period was a day overdue. Only a day – but her cycle ran like a clock. The thought of nine months of vomiting and exhaustion with two small children to care for at the same time, was too awful to contemplate.

'I'll have a gin and tonic, darling, please.'

'OK. Now Diana, before we start, I have to leave by six thirty. I promised Alice I'd be home by seven and even that'll be cutting it fine.'

'I'll be quick,' she said. And watched him fondly as he went over to the bar, his tall figure and dark red hair cutting a swathe through the crowd.

God, Tom was good-looking. And so sweet. Alice was a lucky girl. He returned with her gin and tonic and what looked like a tomato juice.

'Cheers,' she said, 'and thank you so much for coming. Is that a Bloody Mary?'

'No,' said Tom. 'A tomato juice. I'm not arriving home drunk as well as late. Now, what's the matter?'

She took a large sip of her drink and hesitated, looking into the glass. Then she said, 'Johnathan wants a divorce. He wrote me a curt little note saying he wants to instigate proceedings. Gave me the name of his solicitors, to make it all easier and quicker.'

'I'm so sorry. But . . . has he got grounds?' She looked down into her drink; then up at him. He couldn't quite analyse the expression on her face. It was – complex. Hurt, irritation, amusement and – what? Humiliation?

'He's providing them,' she said, and smiled, a brisk bright smile. 'It's him who wants the divorce. So, aren't I lucky?'

'He's providing them? But –'

'No buts, darling. Apparently he has some woman up there. Mainstay – or one of them – of the local community. Name of Catherine. Very nice and admirable, but not exactly a looker. I can't imagine what he sees in her.'

Tom could imagine it all too well. Kindness. Loyalty. Appreciation. Love, even. He didn't say all that, of course. 'Diana, not all women can be beautiful fashion plates.'

'No, of course not. I'm being bitchy. Obviously she gives him everything I don't. And we couldn't go on as we are. He deserves a proper decent wife. Apparently she's marvellous with Jamie and he "adores her", according to Johnathan. Now that does hurt.'

'It must.' He tried to imagine the pain of another man in Kit's little life, another man who played with him and hugged him and made him laugh. It was awful.

'Anyway, I deserve it all, of course I do. And it's so lucky for me he's got Catherine, not least because he might have delved into my life, looking for grounds. Well, he'd have found them, of course.' Her dark eyes were brilliant with tears. 'Darling, get me another drink, would you? A double this time.'

Something akin to jealousy was going through Tom. A nasty pernicious little worm that was boring its way into somewhere at the heart of him, and that completely, illogically hurt.

He went to the bar again, and got himself another tomato juice, went back.

'I had an affair,' she said. 'With a photographer. Freddie Bateman. He's awfully famous, have you heard of him?'

'Rather strangely, not,' said Tom, grinning suddenly and thinking how totally Diana must trust him to be giving him all these details. It made the worm feel less insidious.

'He's American. Awfully good-looking and a complete bastard, of course. Oh, dear . . .' Her eyes brimmed with tears. 'Sorry, Tom, sorry. It's so nice to be able to talk about it.'

'Well, I'm glad I can do something to help, and I'm sorry. But – forgive me for asking – why are you so upset about Johnathan wanting a divorce? You don't seem to care about him in the least, you've got a life of your own, and you don't move in the kind of circles that are going to ostracise you.'

'It's just that I feel very rejected. I mean, I did love Johnathan in the beginning. He certainly loved me.'

'And – this Bateman fellow?'

'It's the thought of losing Jamie that really breaks my heart. I know I'm a pretty terrible person, but I am a good mother. I love him so much, and the thought of only seeing him – well, how often would I see him, do you think? I mean, he wouldn't be taken away from me altogether, would he?'

'Most unlikely,' said Tom. 'It's not my bag, but I do know that much. Given that Johnathan's admitting adultery himself. You're Jamie's mother, his natural mother. You'll almost certainly get custody. It's only that –'

'What?'

'Well, you can't offer the kind of home a little boy like Jamie is used to. In the country, riding, which you say he loves – I presume you're moving down here?'

'I can get a flat. A nice flat. And he doesn't just care about ponies, he loves going to the pictures, and the theatre – well, pantomime, anyway. I could even take him to Battersea funfair,' she said, with a sudden smile. 'Perhaps you could come too.'

'I don't think so,' said Tom hastily. 'What about your job? You're always out and about and abroad.'

'Oh, I can book myself out when Jamie's with me. That's not a problem. No, it's just my rights to have him at all that I worry about.'

'You have plenty of rights,' said Tom gently.

'Would you be my lawyer? Represent me. I know you'd be awfully good. Start work on the case until I can find someone of my own?'

'No, Diana. I can't do that. In the first place I don't know anything about divorce law, and in the second – well – no. I'm sorry.'

'So am I,' she said, and her dark brown eyes seemed to probe into his. 'Very sorry.'

'But I can recommend someone very good, either up in Yorkshire or down here in London. Someone who you'll like, and who will make out a good case for you.'

'Thank you. Down here, I'd think, wouldn't you? Now, let me get you another drink to say thank you. Same again?'

'Yes, please,' said Tom and then looked at his watch and called after her, 'Diana! No. I've got to go.'

But she didn't hear him, or pretended not to. She came back in a remarkably short time, and said, 'There you are. Only I asked them to put a drop of vodka in it so you can see how much nicer it is. It's called a Bloody Mary.'

'Oh, Diana, no. I can't drink that, Alice will smell it and –'

'No, she won't,' said Diana. 'Vodka is undetectable on the breath. You'll be fine. Now taste it. Isn't it good?'

Tom had to admit it was good, and that suddenly he felt good too, and – more than that – entitled to it. He'd had a hard day as well as Alice, after all, and he had to go down to Purbridge first thing in the morning. An hour's escape from it all didn't seem such a lot to ask. He'd just tell Alice the meeting had gone on a bit.

'It's lovely,' he said. 'I've never tasted vodka before. Thank you, Diana.'

'My pleasure.' She smiled at him, then leaned over and kissed him on the cheek. 'Dear Friend Tom. What would I do without you?'

'A great deal, it seems,' he said, and tried not to think about what it would be like to kiss her properly. 'Now. You said you wanted to ask me something else. What was it?'

'Oh, yes. Yes, so I did. Now don't try and fob me off by saying you don't know, because you must do, and remember, I'm not one of your terrible people who think they should be flogged, I love them, some of them are my best friends. And I shall know the answer anyway, just by looking at you. Is Ned Welles queer? Is that what the whole cancelled wedding thing was about?'

# Chapter 35

## 1954

'I just don't know how you can be so cruel. It's not my fault. If it's anyone's it's yours. Although how we can be talking about it in terms of such a negative emotion, I don't know.'

'Is that so? Alice, we have two babies already; the house stinks of nappies, you're exhausted and are about to become more so. We have no time together, no chance to talk about anything except how many so-called clever things Kit has done and whether Lucy is gaining weight. And then you expect me to give three cheers because all of the above is about to increase by one hundred per cent. Well, I can't. I'll support you to the best of my ability—'

'That's very good of you.'

'—but you're rubbing salt into the wound by demanding I should be pleased about it.'

'You – you bastard!' Alice experienced a wave of such hatred, such resentment of Tom, she felt physically faint. 'How dare you talk to me like that? Anyone listening would think I'd gone out and got pregnant by my lover. I can tell you, right this minute, I wish I had a lover to get pregnant with.'

'Oh, don't be so ridiculous.'

'I'm not being ridiculous. Tom, this is your baby. You might not remember the night of its conception. You came home late, drunk, and practically forced me to have sex with you –'

'I have never forced you to have sex with me. That's a filthy thing to say.'

Alice promptly felt violently remorseful. 'I'm sorry. I shouldn't have said that. I love our sex life. It's gorgeous. I'm sorry, Tom –'

He said nothing, just nodded rather remotely; but she knew he had accepted the apology.

'What I meant was, Lucy was only a few months old, I was still sore and exhausted and it was the last thing I wanted, but I thought I owed it to you.' This wasn't quite true, but she wanted to hurt him.

'Oh, spare me. Of course some of the blame is down to you. Why couldn't you have got your bloody contraception sorted?'

'I – I don't know,' said Alice, suddenly miserably guilty. The fact was she hated the whole awful business of the cap, messy, fiddly, and at that stage it hurt just putting it in. But Tom was right; that was her responsibility. He trusted her. On the other hand, she had been trying to please him, to cheer him up as he struggled to do his bit as a father. And he was very good, he did help. She felt very contrite suddenly.

'I'm – I'm sorry, Tom,' she said. 'You're right. I should have used it. It won't happen again.'

'Too bloody right it won't,' he said, killing the contrition at a stroke. Down the corridor Lucy began to wail; he looked at Alice with cold dislike and said, 'I'm going to the pub. It's quiet down there by comparison.'

Alice sat feeding Lucy and crying at the same time, her tears falling on the small, downy head.

Diana was staying at Claridge's, while she looked for a flat.

She'd decided the Bellingers had done enough for her, and although Wendelien had once been such fun, motherhood had claimed her and she talked endlessly about the children, even asked Diana if she would ask one of the photographers she worked with to take some pictures of them. Diana tried to imagine John French's reaction to such a request and shuddered.

She had been working for him for two days, modelling knitwear. Knitting had shaken off its rather dowdy wartime image, and been reborn as something luxurious and highly fashionable. The 'chunky knit' had been invented, with its big bold shape and thick wool. *Vogue*'s instruction was to 'buy two sizes larger than usual, and fill in a V-neck with scarves, or rows of pearls'. French didn't entirely approve of them, although he did admit they were rather fun. He was happier with the other new trend, of tight polo necks tucked into skirt or trousers, although he said they could look 'just slightly tarty', adding carefully to Diana, 'But never on you, darling.'

She could have gone back to Yorkshire that afternoon, but Jamie was away at school and the atmosphere in the house was poisonous. It was all very depressing. The divorce process was under way. She had taken Tom's advice on a solicitor and was relieved and privately surprised by his choice, half fearing some left-wing personage of rather modest social standing. Hugh Harding was the reverse: public school, middle-aged, extremely courteous, with a Lincoln's Inn practice and huge experience; he assured her, in response to her anxious questioning about Jamie, that Tom was quite right and it would be extremely unlikely that she would not get custody of Jamie, not least because Johnathan was admitting adultery.

'So I will write to this firm in York, saying your husband has admitted adultery, and that you want a divorce. I will issue a petition for you in the London Divorce Registry, which is situated in Somerset House in the Strand. Not the jolliest place, I might say, or that section of it – corridors full of weeping women and their solicitors.'

'I won't be doing any weeping,' said Diana firmly. 'And I have an income of my own.'

'Indeed, I can see that. You have a London address?'

'I'm looking for a house to buy in Kensington.'

'Excellent. After that there will be a lot of other tedious correspondence about the child, property, money, settlements and so on. Now, may I assume that you can offer the child a good home, and that you will be available to take care of him in the holidays? You say he is at prep school. In the case of any brief absences, there will be a nanny?'

'Yes, of course. I imagine you are referring to my modelling career. I assure you I accept bookings at my own discretion. I would never be away if Jamie was staying with me. Oh, and my parents live on the Surrey–Hampshire borders. He is very fond of them and we can go there together to stay, and ride in the holidays and so on.'

'That all sounds very satisfactory. Of course, your husband will be entirely responsible for financially supporting the child – school fees, the nanny and so on. Your personal settlement would be a matter for negotiation.'

'I really don't want any money from Johnathan,' said Diana firmly.

'Mrs Gunning, that would be an extremely unwise path to go down. Let your husband make his offer, and we will consider it. So – is everything clear? Am I to assume I should go ahead?'

She told him he was to assume that and left rather quickly, taking a cab to the Savoy – conveniently close to Lincoln's Inn – where she ordered a large gin and tonic, and sat in a dark corner of the bar, determined not to cry. She was surprised to find how difficult it was. A deep sadness seized her. Things had gone horribly wrong, but there had been happiness, once. She had walked down the aisle with genuinely good intentions, had been deeply fond of Johnathan, if not actually in love with him. It was – well, it was horrible, all of it; and a future, less glossy, more lonely, lay stretching ahead of her. She wondered if she could ring Tom Knelston. She hadn't seen him for weeks, and she could thank him for the solicitor. It would be a good excuse. She could cite her need for a friend.

Friendship, she thought, as she looked up his number; it was scarcely a description of her feelings for him. She had, she acknowledged to herself, a serious crush on Tom Knelston. She fancied him to death, and the extreme unlikelihood of a happy outcome for her made it all the more intense. He was so bloody good-looking for a start, with those extraordinary green eyes and dark, dark auburn hair, so exceptionally tall and well built, even given his war-wounded leg – and he had a surprising flair for choosing the clothes that suited him, though he could afford so few. It gave him style, and marked him out as an individualist.

But it was also that he was so sexy – and scarcely aware of it, which increased it a hundredfold. When Tom Knelston's eyes bored into hers it was not to flirt, it was with a genuinely intense interest. When those eyes wandered over her, explored her cleavage, studied her legs, it was a fearlessly honest appreciation of what she possessed. When – or, far more likely, if – he made a move, advanced physically upon her, it would not be with diffidence, not a request; it would be a sure, steady confidence that she would want him as much as he wanted her.

She was put through quite quickly, always a good sign; and when she had made her request for 'a chat with a friend', he agreed almost at once.

'Alice is –' He stopped suddenly, and she wondered what on earth he had been going to say. But instead he said, 'Terribly busy with the children, and then tonight she's got Jillie Curtis coming round – I'll be glad to be out of the house.'

Diana wasn't sure this was a flattering reason for wanting to see her, but she didn't dwell on it; he was coming, that was what mattered. He even agreed to meet her at Claridge's; she took that as an encouraging sign. Recklessness often preceded a decision to take things further.

She took a cab back, ordered a half-bottle of champagne from room service, and drank it while lying in the bath. She was fairly drunk, she realised as she got dressed; she hadn't eaten all day, and the champagne's effect on her empty stomach was fairly immediate.

Two hours later, wearing one of the ubiquitous cocktail dresses, in bright red taffeta, tight waisted with an almost excessively low neckline, her hair swept up in a chignon, a cloud of Carven's Ma Griffe perfume surrounding her, she walked into the cocktail bar where Tom was waiting for her.

He stood up, slightly dazed by her beauty, her sexiness, thinking how dangerous it was to be meeting her today of all days when he and Alice, poor, weary, white-faced Alice, were still facing one another across a chasm of reproach and resentment. But the thought of being with Diana was compelling. Her phone call and his acceptance of her invitation had opened the gates, albeit briefly, to some kind of nirvana, a paradise of style and chic, where no babies cried, no nappies needed his attention, where he was smiled at, kissed, welcomed. She almost certainly wouldn't be able to understand his misery, or help him out of it. It was simply that she was so far removed, with her beauty and her glamour, and the absurd combination of naivety and sophistication that gave her her charm; it was such a relief from his own world. That, with its combination of professional failure and domestic struggle, seemed to hold nothing for him. An hour of her company promised relief, however temporary. It was a crazy, dangerous adventure, he feared, the whole thing, but one that, having been considered, was irresistible.

'I wanted to thank you for Hugh Harding, but it's you who seem depressed,' Diana said, looking at him thoughtfully over the gin and tonic she had requested. Tom was downing rather fast a Bloody Mary, to which he had been quietly addicted ever since she had introduced him to it in the Salisbury. Since the only person he knew who could fund such a habit was Donald Herbert, he had only had half a dozen since. Herbert had been intrigued by this new addition to what he called Tom's upmarket repertoire and enquired how it had come about. Tom refused to tell him, said rather vaguely that he had just come across it. Herbert gave him a sharp look and said, 'I see Diana Southcott's hand in this. Am I right?' Then he looked at him very seriously. 'Don't let her get her long red talons into you, Tom, whatever you do. She's lovely and very sexy, and quite clearly after you, for which I envy you.'

'I'm sure she's not,' said Tom rather feebly, trying to crush the streak of pleasure he felt at the concept.

'Of course she is. But at the stage you're at in this game, you can't afford a scandal. Later on, when you're established, you can risk a bit, but now people will never forgive you. Your public, such as they are, are in love with you and Alice and your family, filled with youth and innocence; hold on to that, Tom, it's very precious and not to be thrown away.'

Tom felt violently irritated. 'There is no question of Diana getting her talons into me, as you put it,' he said. 'And anyway, I think I can be trusted to make such judgements myself.'

He sounded pompous and he knew it.

Herbert looked at him, his eyes unreadable; then he said, in a voice Tom had not heard before, a voice at once amused and sharp, 'Don't be too sure of that, Tom. You have a long road to travel yet, most of it unfamiliar to you, and if you are tired of my company, then let me assure you I can find other pilgrims on the same journey and leave you in peace. But think carefully before you decide on that. You're in treacherous company, Tom, surrounded by potential enemies. You need to be with people you trust; trust is the most important thing in this business.'

Tom felt immediately panicked. He owed everything to Donald Herbert – he would have got nowhere at all without his help, nor much further without it now. 'I'm sorry, Donald,' he said quickly. 'I'm behaving like a brat.'

'Your absolute prerogative,' said Donald. 'I'm just advising you not to fly too near to the sun. Now drink your fancy drink and let's discuss the possible dates of the next general election.'

This conversation came back to Tom sharply now, as the waiter approached with the drinks on a tray; he looked round the bar, thinking he had been foolish to come at the snap of Diana's imperious fingers.

'Darling,' Diana said, pulling out her cigarette holder and filling it with one of the turquoise Balkan Sobranie 'cocktail cigarettes' that were her latest discovery, 'are you depressed?'

Tom, thinking not for the first time how extraordinarily perceptive she was for one so self-obsessed, found himself going against all Donald Herbert's advice, and said he was, just a little. Then she moved slightly nearer to him, engulfing him in Ma Griffe and suggesting very gently that she would be happy to hear why if that might be helpful. 'That's what our friends thing is all about, isn't it?' And Tom went against quite a lot more of the advice, and told her far, far more than he sensibly should have done.

# Chapter 36

## 1954

Jillie had passed her finals. Not particularly well, but at least passed. It seemed scarcely credible after everything she had been through: all those years of being mocked and belittled by Miss Moran, the endless lonely hours of studying, the terror of the vivas. But she had done it and that lovely summer evening, the dappled sunlight falling onto the pavement, she walked home smiling foolishly. Then fiercely, she longed to have someone to tell, other than her parents and Alice, someone who would rejoice with her, someone like, well, yes, someone like Ned. She thought then that if she did ring him and tell him, even as things were, or rather were not between them, he would rejoice, genuinely and with a full heart. But she knew it would be wrong beyond anything, that however much they had loved one another – and it had been love – the line had been drawn and could never be crossed again. She would be tearing open wounds that were beginning finally to heal.

She still missed him, she was lonely for him; and even as her parents raised their champagne glasses to her in congratulation, Alice's excited squeals still in her ears, she thought how far she still was from finding anyone who could begin to replace Ned in her life and in her heart, and felt very sad.

The divorce had gone through. Diana and a stony-faced Johnathan had sat in one of the corridors in Somerset House and were duly ushered, together with both their solicitors, into an extraordinarily gloomy room with a T-shaped table, where the Registrar listened to the solicitors outlining the financial arrangements that had been agreed, he then rather wearily pronounced himself satisfied with what had been agreed, made an order giving Diana custody of Jamie, and granted a decree nisi. It was all extraordinarily painless, and extraordinarily depressing – so much so that Johnathan accepted Diana's offer of tea at the Savoy (champagne version for her, standard for him) and they sat together, sunk into one of the deep sofas, desperate to find some positive aspect to the whole thing. Which of course, long term, there was, and for both of them; but that afternoon went down in their joint memories as one of the most negative of their entire lives.

The waitress who served them clearly decided they must have had a bereavement and spoke to them in hushed tones; Diana cheered up a little as the champagne went down, remarked upon the fact with something approaching a giggle. Johnathan didn't manage the merest smile; and reflecting on the whole thing later that evening, Diana could see why.

For what indeed was a divorce, but just the death of a marriage?

'Darling, you're looking a bit peaky,' Persephone said to Ned. 'When did you last go for a walk, in the fresh air?'

'I don't have time to go for walks.'

'Well, I'm glad you're so busy, but it doesn't suit you.' Persephone looked critically at Ned across his tiny drawing room. She had come to London on one of her periodic visits; to do some shopping, meet old friends, see her son. Who did indeed look less than his best: pale, hollow eyed and very thin.

'Well, let me at least take you to dinner, feed you up a bit. Where would you like to go?'

'Oh, I'm a bit – depressed. You'd be better off dining with one of your friends.'

'I don't want to see any of my friends. I want to see you. Anyway, you are my friend, I hope. How about Aurora's? It's so pretty there and nice and quiet this evening, I should think.'

Ned forced some gratitude into his voice. He didn't want to go, but said, 'Yes, why not? That would be lovely. Thank you.'

* * *

319

Ned went upstairs to change. Aurora's suited his mother. One of the prettiest restaurants in London, in the heart of Kensington, with its ravishing conservatory, wonderful flowers everywhere and waiters who were genuinely courteous and helpful, it exuded charm. As she did. He was lucky to have her; he wondered why she irritated him so much and why he didn't make more use of her, as the confidante and friend he needed so badly. Apart from Ludo, he was oddly friendless: terrified of being too close, of revealing too much, of just feeling at ease. That was an odd thing to fear, he thought, struggling with his cufflinks; something few people could know.

Aurora's proved ideal; not full but far from empty, lots of pretty women and good-looking, well turned-out men, none of whom they knew.

'Right, darling. Shall we start with champagne?'

'Oh, I think so. But my treat, please.'

'No, sweetie, this is most definitely on me. I had a little windfall this week, some shares came up trumps. And—'

'Mother, you should put little windfalls away, not turn them into champagne and expensive dinners.'

'And how boring that would be? Now I must tell you, I've got a new beau.'

'Really?'

'Yes, he's complete heaven, quite naughty, had three wives and goodness knows how many mistresses, awfully good-looking, and really quite sophisticated.'

'In Cornwall?' said Ned, astonished.

'In Cornwall. The last wife had a house there, and she left him for once, not the other way around. She's frightfully rich, got a flat in Paris and another house in London somewhere, so she told him he could keep the Cornish pile.'

'Good God,' said Ned. 'Some chaps have all the luck. What's he called, this paragon? Or rather non-paragon.'

'George Tilbury.'

'And is it a nice house?'

'Quite nice. Thirties, big pile of a thing, on the cliffs at a place called Polzeath. He likes it, as you would, wouldn't you? He can play lord of the manor and drink cocktails on the verandah, that sort of thing.'

'And you really like him?'

'Well, not *specially*, if that's what you mean. But he's fun and he has a rather splendid old car, an Allard, and he takes me out and about. I make him laugh, he says.'

'Well, he's lucky to have you,' said Ned. 'I hope he appreciates you.'

'Oh, darling, he does. Lots of lovely presents and things. He's very keen. But I'm keeping him hanging on.'

'So, you're not actually – living with him?'

'You mean as in sleeping with him? Heavens, no. He'd like me to, but I wouldn't dream of it. Not yet anyway. I value my independence far too much. Ned –' She caught him off guard. 'What's really the matter?'

'Oh,' he said, giving in to her finally. 'I'm just not – not happy.'

'Well, darling, I can see that. But why?'

'I'm lonely,' he said simply, his eyes meeting hers with absolute frankness. 'So lonely. I miss Jillie so much. I really loved her, you know; she was my best friend, my confidante. She was so interested in my work, in what I planned to do, we talked about everything under the sun, politics, religion, where we wanted to travel – just everything. Except – well, you know.'

'Yes. She's a lovely girl. I liked her so much. It must be dreadful for you.'

'It is rather. I keep thinking I'll find another friend. Like her. But of course I won't, how can I? No one has time to spend with a miserable old bugger – sorry.' He laughed for the first time. 'A miserable old bloke like me.'

'What about another miserable old bloke like – well, you? Is there no one?'

'Who I trust? No. I wouldn't even try and find someone, I wouldn't dare. Oh, it's not so bad, in absolute terms, I realise that of course. I'm successful, getting rich, I'm busy all day, more and more in the National Health system – actually, it seems more worthwhile.'

'Ned! You're not turning into a pinko.'

'I might. Now that really would shock you, wouldn't it?' He laughed.

'About the only thing that would, I daresay. But then I come home, and – nothing. No one. I go to concerts, stuff like that, but always on my own. And musicals, you know how Jillie and I loved them? I can't bear to go to any now. It just hurts thinking how much we'd have enjoyed whatever it is. I get asked to dinner parties sometimes – not often these days, because I'm frankly not very good company.'

'Oh, darling. I'm so sorry. I wish I could help.'

'You can't. No one can. Don't worry, you're not going to wake up one morning and read about some doctor who's slit his wrists or anything. I'm not that desperate. It's probably only a phase, I'll get through it.'

'It's more like a life sentence, if you ask me,' said Persephone. 'Oh, it's all so unfair, so wrong.'

'I know. It *is* wrong. Not us, them. But the world isn't going to change just because I'm a bit lonely, I'm afraid. There is talk of relaxing the law, some MP is keen. Fine chance of anything happening. Oh, my God, look who's just come in. There, see, in the black dress and the mink.'

'Good Lord. How lovely she does look? Who are those people she's with?'

'The Bellingers, Wendelien and Ian – she's an absolute poppet. Oh, Diana's seen us. Do you mind? We'll have to chat a bit.'

'Of course I don't mind. I liked her very much when we met her at the theatre. But why doesn't she ever have a husband with her?'

'They're getting divorced, apparently. He's fed up with being on his own in Yorkshire and he's got some new lady he wants to marry. He's even providing the grounds.'

'It seems to me,' said Persephone briskly, 'you do get about occasionally, darling. That's quite a bit of gossip you've just passed on to me. That didn't come from nowhere.'

'Oh, I know,' said Ned, and then added, 'She wanted to marry me once. When we were all very young. Diana, hello, and Wendelien and Ian, lovely to see you.'

'Pity she didn't,' said Persephone lightly, with one of her sweetly malicious smiles, and then stood up and offered her cheek to Diana to kiss.

# Chapter 37

## 1954

'Guess who's asked for you for a fur shoot?' Blanche's grey eyes were dancing as she looked at Diana.

'I don't know. Norman Parkinson?'

This was more wishful than realistic thinking; she had still not cracked 'the Parks ceiling', as she thought of it. He used only the very, very best girls: his wife Wenda, Fiona Campbell-Walter, Anne Gunning. He had also worked a lot with Barbara Goalen, who Diana probably most closely resembled, but she was not amongst his top favourites. She was one step removed in his estimation, she knew, from Barbara – just slightly less ladylike, less sophisticated – and indeed the sexiness of her glamour was what made her special in her own way, and sought after by the more imaginative younger breed of photographers. 'Not Parks. Your old beau, Freddie Bateman. Next week and a peach of a job. He wants to take you to Austria or somewhere like that, maybe St Moritz, for four or five days. God, you'll have fun.'

'But there won't be any snow yet, surely?' said Diana.

'I suppose you're right. I hadn't thought of that. Well, he seems to think if you go high enough. He's calling you tonight, from the States, around eight our time, so you will be in, won't you?'

Diana would. She had a hot date playing Cluedo with Jamie, his latest passion. He was spending the last week of his holidays with her.

She had done her very best to entertain him, and they had indeed had fun; they had been to the Tower of London and to Madame Tussauds – he had specially loved the Chamber of Horrors – had watched the Changing of the Guard, and the Household Cavalry riding down the Mall, and had spent two days with Diana's parents, where they had done a lot of riding.

'Diana, hi.' Freddie Bateman's expensive East Coast voice cut across the Atlantic. 'We're to work together again, I hope.'

'Hope so, Freddie. Nice of you to ask for me.'

'Darling, it wasn't nice at all. I love working with you, it's fun and we make great pictures. Now then, Blanche rang me and said – and I must admit I hadn't thought of it – there won't be any snow yet on the slopes, too early. So that was a great idea. Any others? I'm determined to do this job.'

'Well – I did have one idea. Sounds a bit wild, but what about a giant fridge? Jamie, I saw that. Put Colonel Mustard back immediately.'

'Who's Jamie? Should I be jealous?'

'Desperately. He is my favourite male in the entire world. He's seven, my son.'

'If he's a Cluedo player, count me in. I am probably the best Cluedo player in the universe.'

'Really? You're such a modest soul, Freddie.'

'I know. It's part of my great charm. Now perhaps you could explain about this fridge?'

Diana put Jamie back on the school train with rather less regret than she had experienced before – it was hard work entertaining a small boy in London – and then went to meet Freddie at the Connaught. She had ordered a coffee and was in the lounge, carefully settling herself in front of one of the vast urns of flowers, when Ned Welles walked in.

'Good Lord,' he said.

'Hello, Ned. I am truly not trailing you all over London.'

'It would be very dull for you if you did,' he said, smiling. 'I go from home to hospital and back again –'

'This isn't a hospital.'

'Oh, isn't it? Damn! I thought it was.' He smiled at her, that slightly careful, heartbreaking smile that had ensnared her so long ago. 'I'm meeting a chap who's working on the treatment of leukaemia in children.'

Diana could actually have very happily listened to this for some time, but Freddie Bateman appeared, kissed her rather ostentatiously on the mouth and said, 'Good morning, beautiful lady.'

'Good morning, Freddie.' Irritated by his display of possessiveness, she drew back and looked at him coolly. 'Ned, this is Freddie Bateman, photographer. Freddie, Ned Welles, distinguished paediatrician.'

'Morning,' said Freddie dismissively. 'Darling, I thought we need to get out pronto and down to Smithfield, and the butchers.'

'Freddie, *I* was waiting for you, not the other way round, and I've ordered coffee. I intend to drink it. Sorry. We'll be fine. Could you bring another cup?' she said to the waiter. 'And Ned, what about you?'

'No, no, thank you. I'm fascinated as to why you're going to visit butchers at Smithfield. You must tell me another time. My mother has threatened to invite you to dinner with us before she returns to Cornwall; perhaps then? Should there be any awkward pauses in the conversation, which seems a little unlikely.'

'How very, very sweet of her. Tell her I'd love to come, whenever it is. My evenings are suddenly emptied of games of Monopoly and Cluedo, and even gin rummy.'

'Ah, Jamie's gone back to school?'

'He has. I'm exhausted.' She stood up and kissed Ned's cheek. 'Bye for now, Ned. Lovely to see you.'


'Boyfriend?' asked Freddie, slightly irritably, as the taxi made its way down Mount Street.

'Not any more. Once, maybe.'

'Well, maybe you could concentrate on me for a while.'

Interesting. He was jealous. And even with the highly charged sexual atmosphere he lived in, and his exposure to homosexuality on an almost daily basis, his sensitive antennae had clearly not even twitched. She would have liked to tell Ned, reassure him; he lived on a knife edge of fear, but it was hardly a subject she could broach over dinner, even with Persephone. She really liked Persephone; she was fun and different, and infinitely charming. And so beautiful.

'Right. Well, here we are.' The cab had arrived at Smithfield Market. She tapped on the glass division. 'This'll do, thank you.'

'Wow, this is gorgeous! I didn't expect this. All that wonderful ironwork, and it's so big, all those arcades. Love it. You clever girl.'

Freddie stood beaming, surveying the great colonnades of Smithfield Market, Victorian commercial architecture at its finest: the glass domes, the finials on the roofs, the clock towers at either end.

'It's like a church. This sure beats the meatpacking district in New York.'

'I expect it does. Actually, just over there is the oldest church in London, St Bartholomew the Great; I'll show it to you later. My godmother was married there. Right now we have to find a lovely friendly butcher.'

The butchers all proved lovely and friendly – to Diana at least. The arcades, divided into stalls, housed shops, and behind them, they were told, were the vast refrigerators that stored the meat. But the vast refrigerator rooms were plain, no arches or domes or painted ironwork – just rows of slaughtered animals. 'It's all a bit brutal. And they don't even look cold,' said Diana. 'Shame. Nice idea though.'

'We can fix that,' said Freddie. 'Dry ice, we can bring it in, it'll send up clouds of the stuff. We could use a couple of these guys in their overalls as props; it's all only background, we'll use some exterior too if it kills me, and you'll make the pictures. Nothing brutal about you.'

Freddie threw the contacts onto Blanche's desk four days later. 'They're sensational,' he said modestly.

They were. Diana stood there, wrapped in sable and ermine and dark brown mink, and one particularly glorious full-length white fox, the clouds of dry ice rising round her, the porters going about their business apparently unconcerned, the carcases hanging just slightly out of focus behind her, and thus not distressing to the more tender-hearted readers of *Style*. She had worn a much paler than usual make-up, with huge smudged brown eyes, her lovely mouth a brilliant red, her hair drawn tightly back, so as not to distract in any way from the fur.

'My God,' said Blanche, 'these will make the papers, I wouldn't wonder. You two are an amazing team. I love them. What would you like to do next? Swimwear in a reservoir?'

'That's a good idea,' said Freddie.

'It's a terrible idea,' said Diana. 'Swimwear somewhere very, very warm. Otherwise count me out.'

She was interested to discover that Freddie no longer seemed particularly attractive. Maybe because of the dreadful business of the miscarriage, maybe because she knew him better, but for whatever reason, she had no desire to go to bed with him. He was mildly indignant about it the first night, having given her a wonderful dinner at the Connaught, but by the second had found some other gorgeous creature to lure into his room.

It was odd, Diana thought, because when they were working, and through the lens, she could almost see the raw attraction between them; but the lights off, the cameras packed away, they were just easy, professional friends. And they were a great team, they sparked ideas off one another, Freddie inspired her; her body seemed to come alive with ideas and energy and even risks for him. Only Norman Parkinson could persuade models to do the unspeakably dangerous things that she did.

Freddie watched her incredulously over the next few weeks, as she climbed a tree in Richmond Park to reach a mistletoe clump, so that he had to use his latest toy, a telephoto lens, to properly display the drama; as she rode a bicycle down Piccadilly without holding the handlebars; or sat in the open doorway of a helicopter as it took off, her long legs dangling.

When these came out, in the *Daily Mail* as well as *Style*, not only her mother but also Johnathan made disapproving phone calls.

'You are still a mother,' were his terse words, 'even though you seem to give less and less time and thought to it. Jamie told me he was really frightened when he saw the pictures, wanted to ring you and make sure you were still alive and hadn't fallen out.'

Jamie did indeed say this to his father; to his classmates, he boasted shamelessly about the fame and beauty and courage of his mother, adding that he couldn't wait to try it himself.

Diana and Freddie didn't quite realise it, but they, along with a very few other photographers and models – including of course Parkinson and his coterie – were in the vanguard of an entirely new, free-thinking approach to fashion photography. The clothes were still comparatively formal and glamorous, but the pictures took hold of them and gave them a shake. Freddie and Diana were seen as entirely original, to be relied upon to produce pages that were startling, and filled with humour as well as glamour. *Vogue* tried to put them under contract, but they refused; *Style* had provided their first showcase, and with the great Ernestine Carter of the *Sunday Times* booking them for a story about the new ease in fashion, as displayed by the genius of Coco Chanel, they felt altogether rather pleased with themselves and the way their careers were turning out.

'Get you out to the States next,' said Freddie, as he said goodbye to her after a month-long spell in London. 'I'd like to see you in *Glamour* magazine. You familiar with that?'

'Not very. It's Condé Nast, isn't it?'

'Yup. Used to be called *Glamour of Hollywood*. Now it's very much us, tag line "For the girl with the job". So a bit forward looking. It would suit you. And us. I'll go and see them, let you know.'

'Yes, sounds fun. Well, as long as you don't start working on it with some American girl.'

'Darling, I really only like working with you these days,' said Freddie. 'We seem to have struck a gold seam.'

'Not a mine?'

'Not quite. Seams are more exciting, they have to be really worked for. Bye, darling.'

'Bye, Freddie. I'll miss you.'

London seemed rather empty and her life with it.

She wondered how she might fill it up a bit, and, as always on such occasions, her thoughts turned to Tom.

# Chapter 38

## 1954

'Diana? This is Persephone Welles. Hello, my dear. Apologies for not being in touch before, but I had to dash back to Cornwall. No, nothing serious, of course, just some stupid man being more so than usual. Anyway, I'm back now and staying with Ned, and we would love you to dine with us either tonight or on Thursday. Any good? Oh, splendid. And shall we say Aurora's? You obviously like it there, as do I. Seven thirty then? See you then. Goodbye, Diana.'

But when Diana arrived at Aurora's, Persephone was alone.

'Hello! How lovely you look. I feel like an old frump.'

'Persephone, don't be ridiculous. How could anyone be less of an old frump than you? You've got such style, so original, I just follow the fashion.'

Indeed, Persephone did look amazingly stylish, in a dark red crushed velvet dress, thirties style, with a handkerchief hem, and a long shrugged-on dark navy cardigan jacket, soft and loose, skimming over her tall slender body, and rows and rows of different sizes of fake pearls.

'Well, you see, for so long I had no money, and I cared so desperately about clothes, so I just learned. I hoarded everything, never got rid of something because it was out of fashion. I bought cheap clothes if the colours were good, I learned to sew and made a lot, even bought some clothes at jumble sales. My only extravagance was shoes. I will *not* wear old shoes. When I couldn't afford proper ones,

I bought tennis shoes, and dyed them. Anyway, Ned *is* coming, but not yet – some emergency at the hospital. It's his NHS one, not his private work – he'll often take other doctors' evening shifts because he doesn't have a family to get back to. Anyway, I'm not entirely sorry because I want to talk to you about him. I think you can help. He told me you wanted to marry him when you were young.'

'I did. But it was impossible. I was so, so spoilt, no one with any sense at all would have looked at me, and I married on the rebound. It was a terrible mistake.'

'Not quite the rebound, I imagine. You weren't engaged?'

'No, no, of course not, but – I'd decided.' She laughed. 'And of course –'

'Of course. Now we both know, don't we, about Ned. No need to spell it out.'

'No need,' said Diana, accepting the glass of champagne the waiter had brought and raising it to Persephone.

'It all makes me so sad,' said Persephone, raising hers back. 'Condemned to a half-life, just because of some stupid attitudes. Anyway, we can live in hope. There seems to be a little at the moment. Although poor John Gielgud, booed and hissed when he came on stage – did you hear about that? The courage of the man, walking onto a London stage when he'd just been convicted of – what's it called?'

'Importuning?' said Diana helpfully.

'Yes, exactly. How can people who call themselves civilised behave like that? And his own profession, not much better – a minority tried to get him expelled from Equity, so that he wouldn't have been able to act at all.'

'Do you know him?' asked Diana curiously.

'I met him once or twice. The man I left Ned's father for was a distinguished painter, he did a lot of theatricals. He didn't paint Gielgud, but one went to parties, of course, met people.'

'What a life you've had,' said Diana, smiling at her.

'Anyway, back to Ned . . . the thing is, he's desperately lonely. He's terrified of being – challenged. Especially since breaking the engagement to that lovely Jillie. Do you know her?'

'No, I don't. And if you want me to take him out, show him a good time, I'm afraid it wouldn't work. He'd be suspicious *and* wary, would refuse any invitations, I'm afraid.'

'Really? How disappointing. But I do have one idea. There's to be a big ball, in early December, fundraising for the hospital, St Luke's Chelsea, and he's agreed to take me. He more or less has to go, but I shall tell him this evening that you're joining us – I'm sure there's some man you can bring. One of those photographers, perhaps, or are they all queer too?'

'Some of them,' said Diana, laughing, 'but not all. Anyway, I wouldn't bring one of them.'

'No, Ned might think you were matchmaking, which would be quite dreadful.'

'I can find someone of a most unremarkable make-up. And I could also ask Wendelien Bellinger and her husband: they'd love to come.'

'You are a splendid girl!' cried Persephone, and she got up and flung her arms round Diana, kissing her rapturously and almost knocking the champagne from her hand.

Ned arrived, clearly exhausted. 'Sorry, no dinner jacket, Mother, but I thought better to come and disgrace you like this than be another half-hour late.'

'Darling, it's fine. Have a glass of champagne quickly and tell us what you've been doing.'

'I don't think that'd be at all a good idea,' said Ned. 'It would put you off your dinner. Just let's call it emergency surgery. Anyway –' He took the glass gratefully. 'Hello, Diana, so nice to see you.'

'Just seeing her – or rather looking at her – is extremely nice,' said Persephone. 'More than nice, she looks amazing. You should hire yourself out just to be gazed at, Diana, only I suppose that's exactly what you *do* do.'

'Sort of,' said Diana, smiling at Ned. He smiled back warmly, clearly happy to be with her, and more important still, at ease.

'Only don't go hanging out of any more helicopters, Diana,' he said. 'It was the most frightening thing I've ever seen.'

'Not you too!' said Diana. 'My mother and my ex-husband are both nagging at me about it, and telling me to be more careful. It was just – fun. And such a good photograph, you must admit.'

'Quite possibly. But no photograph would be worth risking your life for, surely.'

His expression as he looked at her was genuinely anxious. She leaned forward and kissed him on the cheek.

'It's all right. I won't do it again. I promise.'

'Good,' he said, smiling.

In spite of everything she knew and understood and had learned of him that evening, it was really rather lovely to have him so concerned about her.


Dinner was fun – in a charmingly random way. Persephone talked about her youth in the thirties and the wilder aspects of the war: 'Marvellous evenings at the dear old Dorch, goodness it was fun, champagne cocktails, things like grouse which one might have thought were extinct, salmon –'

'It sounds quite disgraceful to me,' said Ned, but his eyes smiled into his mother's.

He had always had the ability to combine rather engagingly a strong moral code of his own – certainly when it came to more minor transgressions – with an easy acceptance of the lack of one in others.

'Well, of course it was,' said Persephone, 'but we enjoyed it.'

'And that makes it perfectly all right, I suppose?'

'Not perfectly, but better. I mean, no point drinking champagne and thinking what a nasty taste it had, now would there be?'

'I suppose not.'

'Oh, Ned, of course not!' said Diana impatiently. 'I mean, suppose I stole some jewellery and then looked hideous in it. What a shame that would be.'

'I can't think you'd ever look hideous in anything.'

'Well, thank you, but you're dodging the moral issue.'

'Nothing moral about that issue,' said Ned, grinning.

'Oh, OK. You win. So,' she said, 'how is the practice doing?'

'Well – the private one is slow, but paediatrics is a new field, more like orthopaedics in a way, knock knees and so on. Lot of tonsils, of course. God, there can't be many tonsils left in London. However, the NHS practice is going extremely well, orthopods glad to get some help – and then, more to the point, it's led me to what I have decided is my real cause in life. Something I care passionately about, where I can really make a difference, I think.'

His face was very serious.

'Darling! So solemn! Whatever is it about?' said Persephone.

'It's about the human side of medicine. Nobody seems to be aware how wrong it is, what's going on at the moment – actually bad medicine, in my view. And I'm determined to change it.'

# Chapter 39

## 1954

'You should be ashamed of yourself! I promised Jean I wouldn't say anything to you but I have to do something about it.'

'Look, Mr Miller – Alec – I'm sorry, but I don't know what you're talking about?' said Tom on the other end of the phone.

'Well, you should. Do you remember your wedding day? You've broken those promises. To love, cherish and honour her. She wouldn't look – and behave – the way she does if any of that applied. I've never seen a woman look less cherished.'

Tom finally understood what was being said to him. And why. He opened his mouth to reply, but Mr Miller was talking again. 'Well, I'm not having it. She's staying here until she's recovered a little. She's very against it, said she was going home, but as she was leaving this afternoon, putting Lucy into the car in her carrycot, she just – passed out. Have you seen the size of her? I can't believe you have, or you'd have done something about it. She's a wraith. She's not eating, says she can't, and yet she's feeding that baby – words fail me. Her mother's worried sick about her. Look, I won't mince words – she's pregnant again, isn't she? It's disgraceful in my opinion. You should be leaving her alone – that's what any decent man would do, give her some peace.'

Tom put the phone down. He couldn't reply without being intensely rude. He was angry, angry beyond anything at Alice, for running to her parents, complaining about him, whining behind his back. It was absolutely disgusting. Where was loyalty, where was love in this? She was even clearly implying that the new baby had been conceived against her will, practically turning him into a rapist. What could he do, how could he live with this level of disloyalty? It was not to be borne.

He was just rather half-heartedly tidying the kitchen that evening, thinking at least he'd have an unbroken night, when the front door opened and Alice stood in the kitchen doorway, holding a sleeping Lucy in her arms.

'Can you bring Kit in, please? I can't manage them both.'

'You should have brought your father with you to help,' he said, his voice raw with rage. But he strode out into the street, reappeared with Kit and carried him upstairs. When he passed Alice on the landing he didn't even look at her.

Coming down again, he found her slumped on a chair in the kitchen.

'Apparently, I'm starving you. That's what your father implied. I could make you a sandwich, would that help? I'm afraid a three-course dinner, which he clearly thought was your due, is beyond me.'

'Tom?'

He bustled about, rather ostentatiously cutting bread, grating cheese, boiling the kettle for tea. He didn't speak.

'Tom, I'm so sorry my father rang you and said all those things. It was terribly wrong of him. I didn't even know he'd rung until Mummy told me, after I – I –'

'Fainted? Very dramatic. And what did Mummy think you should do about it all? Sue me for divorce? Leave me? Do tell me, please.'

'Tom! I didn't go there to complain, truly I didn't. I just thought a day with them would be nice. Restful. Mummy's very – helpful.'

'And I'm not, is that right? Well, Mummy doesn't have to pay the bills as well, does she? Doesn't have to go to work, just potters about, saying what can I do now, darling, apart from keeping your nasty brutish husband away.'

'Tom! You know I'd never, ever say anything about that sort of thing.'

'I don't think I do know, actually. Otherwise how did your father have such a clear picture of my behaviour? Which is not that of any decent man, apparently. I should be leaving you in peace. Dear God, Alice, if you wanted that why not say so?'

'Tom, I hadn't told them about the baby. It never seemed the right time. And you know how seldom we – I – see them. It came as a shock.'

'A shocking shock. Poor Mummy and Daddy. No wonder they want to take you in, give you shelter.'

'I was going to ring you later, ask you if you'd mind if I stayed the night. Just the one. Then when I heard what Da— my father had done, I was so upset I just left.'

'Really?'

'Yes, really.'

'And what about this poor wraith-like creature I am supposed to have created – how did they know about her? About how I never give you any food, watch you starve.'

'Tom, don't be so ridiculous. Of course I am very thin, everybody says so, but I don't feel like eating much of the time, I'm still being sick. When this little one is born, I'll be better straight away, you know I will.'

'Yes, and you can be sure there won't be any more. You'll find yourself living with a very decent man.'

'Oh, Tom, *please.*'

'Well – it's disgraceful, peddling that sort of rubbish about.'

'I wasn't peddling any sort of rubbish. I – I love our sex life, you know I do –'

'I could be forgiven for not knowing recently, but I'll let it pass. Does Daddy know that?'

'No, of course not,' said Alice wearily. 'As if I'd say anything like that to him. I suppose it was just a conclusion he jumped to – that generation, you know, they see it all differently.'

'And you made no attempt to put him right?'

She sighed, sipped at her tea. 'How could I?'

'Very easily, I'd have thought. I'm disgusted at you, Alice, absolutely disgusted.'

'Yes, I've got that message,' said Alice wearily. 'Look, I am very tired, it's been a very long day.'

'Not my fault.'

'I didn't say it was. But I'd like to go to bed – we're not getting anywhere.'

'As you wish.'

She got up, threw the uneaten sandwich in the bin.

'Hey,' said Tom. 'That's a terrible thing to do, throwing away perfectly good food. The children would have eaten that.'

'Strangely enough, the children don't really like very stale sandwiches,' said Alice and then with a sudden return of her old spirit, 'Perhaps you'd like to take it out and offer it to some poor deserving person on the street.'

'Oh, don't be so ridiculous,' said Tom irritably. 'I only said it was terrible to throw food away. You do it a lot.'

'Well, if you can suggest what I do with it, I will.'

Tom glared at her. 'I don't know. It's not my department. You could make stuff into soup or something. I would have thought,' he added just a little too quickly. Alice felt the familiar flood of jealousy and for once converted it into words. 'Oh, I see. Is that what Laura did, make leftovers into delicious soup? Difficult with a cheese sandwich, I'd have thought, but I'm sure she'd have managed.'

'Oh, Alice, for Christ's sake, grow up.'

Lucy started crying. Alice fled upstairs, crying too.

In bed, still hoping to make amends, she reached out tentatively for Tom; he ignored her. She tried again. He turned over. It was a very clear message. Well, she'd given it out herself enough times, she supposed. Suddenly she was aware of how undesirable she must be, with her droopy breasts and flabby body. She started to cry. She couldn't help it. Tom turned over sharply.

'For heaven's sake,' he said. 'You've done that to me often enough.'

'I bet you never refused Laura,' said Alice. It came out in a rush, stupidly vitriolic. She hadn't meant to say it.

'For Christ's sake,' said Tom. 'Alice, you've got to get over this absurd obsession with Laura. It's extremely tedious.'

Anger shot through her. 'Well, I'm sorry about that. It's a hard act to follow, you know, the perfect wife.'

'You are being bloody ridiculous. I've listened to quite enough garbage for one day. I'm going out. I'll come back when you've pulled yourself together.'

'You can't go out now. Where are you going?'

He didn't reply.

Tom had no idea himself where he was going; he walked all the way to Shepherd's Bush, where he found a lorry drivers' café. He bought a cup of tea and a bacon sandwich and sat down in the window, staring gloomily out at the green. He felt very depressed.

Life seemed reduced to screaming babies, shouting toddlers, a house that seemed to permanently carry the whiff of dirty nappies, and a wife who did nothing but criticise him. And then go running to her parents, complaining about his brutish behaviour. Which was so unfair. He did what he could, an awful lot more than his father, or even his contemporaries; but she seldom said thank you, seemed to regard it as his duty. She turned him down in bed, and had this bitter jealousy both of the Labour Party and of his first wife. Who had frequently turned him down in bed, he remembered, telling him she was too tired – and almost smiled at the memory. The difference was that she had said it cheerfully, confidently. But it would do no good to tell Alice that. Her jealousy of Laura was impossible to deal with; there seemed no solution. Except to leave Alice, and that was unthinkable; he loved her far too much.

He felt something close to tears at the backs of his eyes, and put his hand in his pocket to pull out his handkerchief.

An envelope came with it, addressed to him by hand at Herbert & Herbert. It had come days ago and he'd stuffed it in his pocket, vowing to tear it to shreds and put it in a litter bin on the way home. Only he hadn't. Of course. He read it now.

*Diana Southcott has moved*
*to 17 Berkeley Court, Lower Sloane Square, SW3. Tel SLO 1274*

He had rather liked the 'Southcott'. It sent out a clear message that she was no longer a Gunning.

Underneath she had written by hand, *If you ever need a friend* . . .

Of course it was unthinkable. Of course he wouldn't ring her. And certainly not now. It was half past ten.

Diana met him at the door of her flat, wearing cropped jeans, a huge yellow sweater, very little make-up and a cloud of Dior perfume. Half an hour earlier, when he had rung, saying, 'I think I need a friend,' she had been dressed in a black cocktail dress and very high-heeled shoes. She had given the metamorphosis a great deal of thought.

'Come in, Friend Tom,' she said. 'Drink?'

'No, thank you. Some coffee would be nice.'

She made a pot of it, and set it on the coffee table in front of them.

He looked round. The large drawing room was filled with furniture that exactly echoed the style in her parents' house; the only difference being that all the pictures were stylised coloured prints of birds, their names written underneath in cursive writing, and the fireplace, clearly never to hold a fire, had a huge urn of flowers in it.

'I'm looking for a house for me and Jamie. I think I've found one, in Kensington, but it all takes such an age. It's lovely, bit more room than here, perfect for when I've got him. Which isn't that much, even though I got custody as you said I would. I mean, he's away at school and then he has half each school holiday with Johnathan.'

'Doesn't sound much, certainly.'

'Well – he seems happy enough. He should be, we're both spoiling him rotten. And it means I can concentrate on my career . . . So – why do you need a friend tonight, Tom?'

He realised he would have to tell her, having arrived so dramatically, but it sounded rather petty when he did.

She disagreed. 'It does sound rather awful. What a ghastly chap. Ticking you off for claiming your conjugal rights, so to speak. God, I'd have been furious.'

Tom said he had been. 'I don't really think Alice went running to her parents, complaining. It would be very out of character. So I feel bad now for shouting at her about it. Leading to the worst row we've ever had. It was – bad of me.'

'Not at all. Maybe she didn't do that, but you'd had this awful pasting from her old man. You should stop trying to be perfect, Tom, none of us can be. I should know,' she added, and smiled at him. He looked away; there was an invitation in that smile that he couldn't quite ignore. 'Tom, do have a drink. You'll feel better. Just a tiny glass of red, maybe, or a very small whisky?'

'Oh, all right,' he said. 'Very small whisky. Very small.'

It wasn't small, of course; and once it had hit him, he found himself telling her more and more, the fact that family life was pretty much hell, and that Alice seemed completely indifferent to his political success.

'I need someone to really support me, come to meetings and dinners, that sort of thing. And she – well, she can't. Not at the moment.'

'Because?'

'Because she's so exhausted. And tied to the children.'

'You could get a nanny,' said Diana.

'Don't be silly, Diana. Would-be Labour MPs, especially the disciples of people like Bevan, don't have nannies.'

'I bet they do. Well, can't help, I'm afraid. I suppose I could come to the dinners and stuff with you.' She grinned. 'Only joking. Oh, Tom, I'm so sorry.'

'Well, it's not the end of the world.'

'No, but I can see it hurts.' She got up from the sofa. 'Another whisky?'

'No, thank you. I'll have to be going soon.'

'Why? No rush as far as I'm concerned.'

'No, but I don't suppose she's asleep. Probably getting worried. I was angry when I left, and there were a lot of slammed doors. Not very husbandly behaviour.'

She sat down on the sofa again, rather closer to him than before.

'It doesn't sound to me as if she's being very wifely. Don't suppose there's much sex either, in spite of what her dad says.'

'Well – you know,' said Tom, reaching for his empty glass.

'Yes, I do know. Actually, I'm quite with her there, I have to say. After a baby everything hurts and you're exhausted and –'

'Yes. I know all that, of course. Which is why it's so bad of me.'

'To want it? Of course not. It's entirely natural. You're too hard on

341

yourself, Friend Tom.' She leaned forward and kissed him: just on the cheek. 'Well, if it's any comfort, I am hugely proud to know you and of what you've done. I really am. It's taken a long time, and a lot of work. It's a bit like modelling, in a way. It looks so easy, just standing in front of a pillar or something, wearing a nice dress. Nobody knows about the boredom of a lot of it, doing the same thing over and over and over again, or of smiling until your face twitches, or longing to pee and not being allowed to move for hours. That's very like an election, I should have thought.'

'A bit,' said Tom, smiling at the absurdity of the comparison.

'Anyway, I mustn't keep you. I can see you're feeling remorseful. With absolutely no reason, I'd say. But please come again. I'd love to see you any time. Come and let me give you a hug . . .'

She stood up, held out her hand to pull him up.

'Dear Tom. I hate to see you so unhappy. Ooh – gosh, nearly fell over.' And she collapsed back onto the sofa, laughing.

That did it. She knew it would.

His arms were round her, his mouth on hers; she remembered thinking that if the sex was anything like the kissing, it would be astonishing.

It was absolutely astonishing. She could never remember feeling such excitement, such aching desire, such desperation to be touched, stroked, explored, entered. She was taken through new boundaries that night, scaled new heights, rose and fell from those heights in a glorious cycle, reaching, reaching for the pinnacle, and when she was finally there, triumphant, shouting with the pleasure of it. She was slowly, slowly sinking into peace when she smiled at Tom, and said, 'What a good friend you are, dear Tom.'

And Tom, stricken, terrified at what he had done, said, 'Diana, I must go. I really must.'

It was hardly a romantic finale but she didn't mind. She had finally accomplished her mission, that of seducing Tom Knelston, and it had been glorious, and gloriously requited, she knew. He would be back. She was sure he would be back.

And Tom, while vowing as he sat in the cab that he would never go back, knew it was more than probable; and even if he didn't, a boundary had been crossed, and he had stepped into another country – a dangerous country from which there could be no return, no matter how much he wished it and however hard he struggled to find a way.

# Chapter 40

## 1955

'Jillie? It's Josh.'

Jillie promptly felt irritated. Josh was most unlikely to be inviting her out in the accepted sense, could only have two other reasons for ringing her. One, an obligatory attempt to cheer her up; two, a desire to pick her brains over some article he was writing. She wasn't sure which of the two options was less attractive and decided it was the cheering-up one.

It turned out to be a curious combination of both.

'Hello, Josh,' she said cautiously. 'What can I do for you?'

'Well,' he said. 'I wondered if you'd like an evening out. Next week.'

'Josh, darling,' said Jillie, 'it's very sweet of you but the answer is absolutely not, thank you all the same. I much prefer my own company just at the moment.'

'No, no,' said Josh. 'I have no intention of trying to cheer you up or anything ghastly. No, friend of mine from Oxford, haven't seen him for years, name of Julius Noble –'

'What a wonderful name.'

'I suppose it is. Anyway, I bumped into him the other day, as you do, and I want to ask you a favour. On Julius's behalf.'

'I hope it's not too onerous. I'm so tired I can't concentrate on anything. I'm doing a locum at St Mary's, Paddington while I try and find a job, never worked so hard in my life. Tell me what it is before I say I will.'

'I don't think it will be onerous. It might take an hour or so.'

'An hour will be all right. Not so sure about the "so". Anyway, what is it?'

'Julius has a fiancée. Nice girl. She was with him. She's a writer. And she wants to talk to you about being a surgeon.'

'A writer! Goodness, how grand. I feel quite nervous already.'

'Don't be silly, half the famous writers in England have been to your house. It's she who should be nervous. Actually, her books are quite silly. Love stories, you know.'

'Is she famous? What's her name?'

'Eleanor, but everyone calls her Nell. Eleanor Henderson. She's not famous, she's only had a couple of books published. She wants to know how scary your first operation is, what an operating theatre looks like, who's in charge. Oh, and what it's like being a woman surgeon – she's very interested in that. I'd be awfully grateful.'

'All right,' she said. 'I can't do it next week, because I'm doing nights, but the following week I can. Why don't you all come here? Mummy won't mind and actually, I think they're away then.'

'Well, that's very kind,' said Josh. 'Give me a date and I know they'll fit in with you.'

She had put the phone down when she realised she hadn't asked what Julius did. Or what he was like. Why had she agreed to this? When she really didn't have time and she hated meeting new people? Oh, well: too late now. It was only one evening, after all.

Loud screams filled the corridors; Ned, who had been on his way home, dropped his briefcase and ran towards the children's ward. He found a complete lack of concern among the nursing staff: two probationers were giggling, Staff Nurse Lambert was writing a report.

He glared at her. 'What on earth is going on in here?'

'No need for alarm, Mr Welles. Just Joanna Brigstock, making a fuss.'

'She must be screaming about something. She's had a tonsillectomy, it leaves them in a lot of pain the first few days.'

'She'd had a bad dream. That's all. Nurse Wallace is with her now, trying to settle her. She'll have all the other children awake if we're not careful.'

'I'll go and see her.'

'Mr Welles, she's far better left with Nurse—'

Ned walked through the ward, the children asleep for the most part. Joanna Brigstock was weeping silently now, tears rolling down her flushed little face. A nurse stood looking down at her rather helplessly. Ned smiled at her. 'Don't worry, nurse, I'll take over.'

'But Staff told me to settle her. I don't think she'd like you doing it.'

'You can stop worrying about her too,' said Ned. 'I'll take the blame for anything either she or Sister don't like. I'm quite brave.' He grinned at her. 'Off you go. Now,' he said, sitting down on the bed, smiling at the small Joanna. 'Crying's not allowed in my ward. What's the matter? Can I help?'

She shook her head and turned away from him, stifling the sobs.

'Joanna,' said Ned, 'it's bad for your poor throat to cry. It needs you to be asleep, resting it.'

Silence.

'Is it very sore?'

She nodded, still not looking at him.

'How about a little tiny bit of ice cream? Do you think that might help?'

Ice cream was on the menu for all tonsillectomy patients; so was jelly. She turned her head on the pillow, nodded, half smiled.

'I'll be back.'

He made his way to the kitchen, took a small tub of ice cream from the big fridge, found a spoon and was just leaving when the night sister appeared.

'Is there anything I can do for you, Mr Welles?'

'No, no, Sister, thank you. Everything seems in excellent order.'

'I see.' She looked rather pointedly at the tub of ice cream. Ned smiled at her.

'Joanna Brigstock's obviously in pain. I thought a bit of ice cream might help.'

'Mr Welles, this is hardly the time for a child to be given such food.

We don't want her vomiting. And if the other children wake up, they'll all want it.'

'I don't think either of those things will happen. If they do, I promise I'll deal with it. And I think a little ice cream combined with a bit of attention would help Joanna.'

'Very well.' She sighed heavily, clearly envisaging disasters on an apocalyptic scale. 'If you insist. Give it to me.' She held out her hand. 'I'll get one of the probationers to feed her.'

'No, no, I'll give it to her. Something's troubling her. I'd like to talk to her.'

'Very well,' said Sister again, her face etched with disapproval. A consultant, feeding a child! It was most unsuitable. But Mr Welles was renowned for his slightly odd behaviour. There was much gossip about him in the nurses' room, she knew, particularly about his film-star looks, and the fact that he was not yet married.

One theory was that he had had his heart broken in his youth and never loved anyone else; another that a much adored fiancée had died.

'Or maybe,' one girl had said, 'he's – you know, one of *those*.'

'He couldn't be. He's a consultant. That's impossible.'

'Oh, I don't know. I've heard the most ordinary, normal people are that way,' said someone else. 'They just keep it covered up.'

'Hardly normal.'

'Well, you know what I mean. Mind you, I think—'

'We are not interested in what you think, Nurse Brown.' It was Sister's voice, cutting through the chatter. She had clearly heard every word. 'I would like the subject changed and not raised again. And since you clearly have too much time on your hands, you can do the napkin round.'

'Right,' said Ned now, to the small Joanna, putting the ice cream tub into her hot little hands. 'Tell me what the matter is. And what's this?' He pointed to the bundle of blanket she was clutching.

'I'm pretending it's Teddy. They took him away.'

'Who took him away?'

'The nurses,' she said, her voice shaky. 'They said I might get blood on him. And I need him. I haven't got Mummy or Daddy – Teddy was instead. Sort of.'

'Well, in a minute I'll go and find him for you and make sure it doesn't happen again. Now, how is that throat feeling?'

'Much better.'

Ned left the hospital with a heavy heart. The encounter with Joanna Brigstock and its implications had upset him. Every day he became more distressed by the grief caused to the children. He felt that children needed their parents more than ever when they were ill. As for depriving them of their teddies – that was appalling. Night Sister had handed over Joanna's most reluctantly.

Something close to a lovers' meeting had taken place between Joanna and Teddy, who was sweet faced, blind in one eye, hugged almost bald. She had clutched him to her, covering him with kisses, and then had laid down, cuddling him under the bedclothes, and was asleep in five minutes. It was, Ned supposed, a victory for his views, but it would take many such to see them taken seriously.

Nevertheless, each day saw him more determined to make that happen: no matter what cost to him.

# Chapter 41

The morning of the dinner with Josh and his friends was supremely beautiful, the sun breaking slowly and gently through the early drifting mist, soaking up the heavy dew; the tops of the trees ghostly pale; the shrubs below still a young, fresh green. Jillie, leaning out of her bedroom window, smiled at it, and blew it a kiss, a rather fanciful trick of her mother's when confronted by any particularly glorious view, and hoped it would be a good omen for the evening.

Her parents were indeed away; she had told Mrs Hemmings to poach a small salmon, and to serve it with baby new potatoes from the vegetable garden, or rather the useful garden as her father always called it, and summer pudding for dessert. She could never do wine, so when he arrived, considerately early, Josh was dispatched to her father's cellar to choose. He came up fifteen minutes later, looking rather dazed. 'That is a real treasure trove he's got down there. Anyway, I've found a really nice white burgundy, and a Sauternes to go with the summer pudding. I've put them in the fridge. Lucky people, getting all this.'

'Well, let's have a cocktail in the morning room, shall we, before they arrive. Something really easy like Bellinis,' she said, reminded painfully only when Josh arrived with the jug of peach juice and the bottle of champagne that Bellinis were the drink she and Ned had always had on special occasions. No longer the wild grief, just – joylessness in everything.

Too late now, though; she took her Bellini, smiled at Josh and drank it with reckless speed. It would help: it had to.

She was just slightly tipsy when the car scrunched on the gravel; just enough to be a tiny bit dizzy, and – she could feel it – flushed. She stayed in the morning room, while Josh let them in. Nell came in first – pretty, brown-haired, with a dimpled smile – holding out her hand, saying how kind of Jillie this was; and then Julius appeared from behind her.

She told herself it was the Bellini, on top of her exhaustion, that did it – the sweet shock of something, a slight unsteadiness as the ground seemed to shift in some odd way, a sense of recognition of something, rather than someone, something promising, something warm, something confusing. She took his proffered hand, put her own into it, rather than shook it, then said, 'You are so welcome,' in response to his echo of Nell's gratitude, and meant it. Never was any moment, any fragment of time, more welcome.

He was tall and slim, with brown eyes and rather wild dark hair; his natural expression was serious, but when he smiled it was like a child's, a sudden brilliant expression of delight. He wore very nice clothes, which she liked – Ned had always looked marvellous, but conventionally so. Julius was more avant-garde – dressed in a very nice suit, the jacket a little longer, more waisted, than would have been considered the norm. His shirt was white silk, his blue tie almost cravat wide, tied in the loose 'Windsor knot', and his shoes brogues in style, but in very soft, light brown leather. Had Diana Southcott been present, she could have explained that his was the perfect personal interpretation of the Edwardian look that was so fashionable for men, expressed at its extreme by the Teddy Boys with their greased quiffed hair, their over-tight trousers, their narrow leather ties; Jillie only liked the fact that he looked unusually stylish, and had clearly given some consideration to how he dressed for the occasion. She wished promptly that she had gone to more trouble herself than the blue fine wool shirtwaister she had dragged irritably from her wardrobe.

Nell's dress, which she had not taken in before, was, she noticed also rather irritably, quite special: a shirtwaister too, to be sure, but in green and white spotted silk, with long, very full sleeves, gathered on the shoulders and then caught in at the wrist.

Then she wondered why she cared so much what any of them was wearing. She offered them Bellinis, smiling graciously at their admiration of the house, and again at her hospitality, and said, 'I don't know how much help I can be to you, Nell, but I'll try.'

Nell said, 'The thing is, I do take my research terribly seriously, and hate getting things wrong.'

'Quite right,' said Jillie. 'Well, I'll try not to let you down.'

'Thank you.'

And then, feeling she had done enough for her for a moment or two, turned to Julius and said, 'And Julius, what do you do?'

'I'm an antiques dealer.'

'How perfectly lovely. What fun.'

'Yes, it is. Some of the time, anyway.'

'And – do you specialise in any particular period?'

'Yes, deco mostly. It's coming back in, fortunately for me, especially the ceramics, and of course the bronze pieces, the borzois—'

'He is terribly knowledgeable about it,' said Nell, just a little automatically. 'And he can tell repro from real just with the briefest glance.'

'Darling, not really,' said Julius. 'I often make mistakes, actually,' he said, turning back to Jillie, laughing at himself. 'Terrible one the other day, paid over twenty guineas for something worth ten shillings.'

'But that's jolly rare,' said Nell. 'Usually you're a genius at it.'

'No more than you are at your writing,' said Julius, smiling at her.

How sweet they were, Jillie thought. Totally in love. Lucky, lucky them.

'Well, you must tell us more about it later. My mother loves deco, especially Clarice Cliff, in fact she's got a complete tea set –'

'My God,' said Julius. 'Really? Not – not in the crocus design?'

'Not sure. We can go and look later, it's in a cabinet in the morning room.'

'I'd love that.'

351

'You would, wouldn't you?' said Nell. 'Gosh, we didn't expect this, both of us so lucky.'

'I hope you'll go on thinking so,' said Jillie. 'Tell me, Nell, who is your publisher?'

'Well,' she said, rather reluctantly, 'at the moment I'm between publishers.' She blushed, and then giggled rather self-consciously. 'Which actually means I haven't got one – quite. But I have got a very good agent.'

'That's more than half the battle,' said Josh. The evening was working out rather better than he had expected. So far anyway. He hadn't seen Jillie so animated for a very long time.

'She'll find you someone soon,' said Julius. 'You're so good.'

'Well, let's go in to dinner, and you can tell me about it, the plot and so on,' Jillie said, thinking that this mutual adoration society could quite quickly get boring.

'Wonderful,' said Nell. 'Can I help, Josh?' He was gathering glasses together, overloading the tray rather dangerously. They disappeared towards the kitchen.

Jillie stood up and smiled at Julius. She felt odd, being alone with him. As if it was dangerous. How stupid. But he clearly felt it too; the easy relaxation had gone, and he was obviously thinking rather wildly of something to say. Finally, he managed to remark on the beauty of their garden.

'And so big.'

'Yes, we're very lucky. Or rather they are, I really shouldn't be here at all, bit old to be living at home but I've only just passed my finals. Now I have to find some hospital that will have me. I'm doing a locum at the moment.'

'You can't stay where you've trained?'

'No, sadly not. They only keep about one student each year, and she has to be outstanding. I'm not. And Miss Moran, the big white chief surgeon, has taken against me, unfortunately. I'm not very good and I irritate her.'

There was a silence. Then Julius said, 'I can't imagine anyone being irritated by you.' He spoke very seriously, presenting the opinion not as a meaningless compliment, but something he needed to say.

'Well,' said Jillie, 'I am a bit nervous and clumsy, and those are two things surgeons absolutely cannot be. And – well, I missed a lot last year, about six weeks altogether.'

'Were you ill?'

'Sort of – let's go in, shall we?'

'Sorry,' he said, looking stricken, sensing a forbidden territory. 'I'm so sorry, I didn't mean to cross-question you –'

'No, no, it's fine. Honestly. You weren't,' she said, flustered on his behalf. 'Come on, hope you're hungry . . .'

They were finally gone; she felt exhausted. Nell's questions had been predictable, easy to answer – yes, it was a man's world, surgery, you had to prove yourself twice as good as they were; no, the worst hostility tended to come not from the other doctors, you just had to flirt with them. Jillie didn't exactly like her – she was quite outstandingly self-confident – but her questions were well thought through, and she seemed genuinely eager to learn.

Jillie did ask them when they planned to get married and Nell said, 'Oh, next spring soonest – so much to arrange, isn't there, darling? We've actually only just got engaged.'

Jillie offered her congratulations, then asked Julius if he would like to see the Clarice Cliff tea service in its cabinet and he stood there, gazing at it, his face very solemn, and then turned to her with his brilliant smile, and said, 'Thank you so much. It's – well, it's wonderful. Wonderful things.'

He sounded rather like Harold Carter, confronted by the tomb of Tutankhamun for the first time, as reverent and as astonished.

'It's been the most wonderful evening,' he said, his brown eyes very serious on hers. 'I've loved it. You've been wonderful to Nell –'

'Not at all. And congratulations again on your engagement.'

And may you never know, she thought, the tears back behind her eyes, the misery of it not ending as you think it will.

Lying in bed, wide awake, she felt disturbed, confused even. Julius had done odd things to her; made her feel – goodness, what had he made her feel? Aware, she realised finally, for the first time for many months, aware of herself, as if she mattered, indeed as if anything at all mattered. For so long, she had plodded dutifully along: working, because it was the only thing to do, while not caring too much what the outcome was; being pleasant to people, while feeling no interest in them whatsoever, while avoiding them indeed whenever she could; holding herself back, locking her emotions away as things not to be trusted, not released. Julius, with his intense enthusiasms, his untidy charm, had broken into her passivity, had made her want to know more of him, more of what he thought and enjoyed and disliked and desired. She felt for him, in the purest sense, felt herself involved by the charm, the enthusiasm, the way he dressed, the way he talked, the way he was.

But he was not hers to be explored, to be sought out, investigated: he belonged to Nell. He was forbidden, dangerous territory and disturb her as he might, she had no option but to turn her back on him and walk away.

# Chapter 42

Jillie didn't actually ever intend to go in, of course. That was intensely out of character. It was a pretty little gem of a shop in the King's Road, the big window filled with deco wonders. Jillie noticed it before she saw the sign over the door that said *Noble Antiques*. She was looking for a birthday present for her mother, and felt she might have found it in a beautiful marble and bronze clock, a full-breasted winged lady stretched out above the face, and would have gone straight in had she not seen the sign. Whereupon she was seized with ridiculous shyness, that Julius might think she was pursuing him – though why should she, him being practically married. But she had not been able to quite forget her reaction to him as he took her hand, a month ago at least now, the warmth, the increased intensity of colours and sounds . . .

Inside it was literally a treasure trove, of cabinets that were lovely in themselves, some mirrored, filled with china and pottery, of clocks ranged along several shelves, of statues, chairs, tables, dressing tables, of sets of hairbrushes and combs and hand-held looking glasses, of pretty limpid lamps with great fringed shades. She stood there, smiling, Julius quite forgotten, thinking this would solve the birthday problem not just today but for many years to come. There were footsteps and Nell stood in front of her, looking – well, clearly not suspicious, for how could she be, but not entirely welcoming.

'Oh, hello,' she said, and her light, pretty voice seemed to have developed a new edge. 'How nice to see you. I was so grateful for your help, my agent said that chapter was the best in my draft – and

I'm sorry, you just missed Julius, he's gone dashing off to see some woman in Surrey.'

'It's not Julius at all,' said Jillie. 'I'm looking for a present for my mother and I noticed the clock in the window, the marble one, the lady with wings –'

'Oh, yes, I liked that. I was hoping Julius would give it to me, but –'

'Oh, well, in that case,' said Jillie, 'forget it. He's probably intending to give it to you. There's plenty of other lovely stuff here. What about that dressing table, how much is that?'

'I haven't the faintest idea,' said Nell, 'but I can find out for you, everything's listed in this book. Let's see, dressing table, well, sixty pounds, but hasn't she got a dressing table?' And Jillie said yes, yes, of course she had, but she would love to have this instead – and it was extremely charming, a semicircle of bright polished oak, with three circular mirrors, one large and central, the other two on either side of the curve. How displeased her mother would be, presented with such a dressing table, for she was fond of the one she owned which had been her grandmother's, but that displeasure could hardly meas-ure up to Nell's, still clearly hostile. 'So, yes, I might take that, or rather buy it. Do you deliver?'

'Of course,' said Nell. 'Goodness, what a lovely present, lucky her. Well, look, I'll tell Julius you were here.'

'But only because of the shop,' said Jillie firmly and then thought she must sound at least half mad, for why else should she be in the shop, if it was not to pursue Julius, which of course she was not.

'You can write a cheque and he'll arrange the delivery. When is the birthday, by the way?'

'Next month,' said Jillie. She really could not afford sixty pounds, especially for something she didn't want, nor her mother either. 'So if you could have it delivered at the weekend, that'd be wonderful, because they're away –'

'Oh, I'm afraid I can't possibly say,' said Nell. 'Deliveries are noth-ing to do with me, I'm only sitting in as a favour, but I'll leave a note for Delia, the girl who usually does it.'

'Oh. Yes, well, thank you, Nell, that's really kind, gosh, I must fly. Give my – my regards to Julius, won't you?'

'Yes, of course. So glad we could help you. And thank you again for your help to me.'

Then she ushered Jillie to the door of the shop, rather firmly, as if fearing she might stay any longer. And Jillie walked away down the King's Road towards Sloane Square, feeling foolish, cheated and depressed.

Tom was trying to make up his mind quite how he was going to deal with Diana. He could never see her again, of course – but he had to tell her and didn't quite know how. A phone call seemed rather casual, a letter could be ignored. So maybe he did have to go and see her. But when? And where? A visit would be dangerous: he didn't trust himself to resist her. The sex had been extraordinary, beyond anything he had ever known. He kept reliving it in his mind and at times at unsuitable moments.

He wished with all his heart he hadn't had sex with her. He liked being her friend, he liked her, he liked being with her, she was funny and fun, and he loved just looking at her. Tom appreciated style; and he didn't get much of it at the moment. Caring for small children left precious little energy for adding a bold necklace or tying a scarf in a particular way to make a dress stand out. Of course he didn't blame Alice, but he missed it. The friendship with Diana had supplied it in spades. Now he'd spoilt all that, broken the spell, changed the friendship into something dangerous and forbidden that had to be ended.

Diana had decided that she really didn't like him at all. She had been charmed by him at first, glad he had been seated next to her as he was charming and attentive, and very good-looking.

They were at the St Luke's Hospital ball, and had a really very nice table: Ned, of course, looking divinely handsome; Persephone and her boyfriend George Tilbury, a nice old buffer, handsome and with very nice manners; Wendelien and Ian Bellinger; Ludo and Cecily Manners; and one of the sisters from the hospital – there was a representative on every table – who was more beautiful and more charming than any sister had a right to be, called Anna Fitzwarren. The young man she had decided didn't like, Ned's registrar Philip

Harrington, was another representative of the hospital. His father, Sir Digby Harrington, was on the board of governors of the hospital, and a distinguished surgeon himself.

Diana had taken enormous trouble over her appearance – partly because she liked the stir she caused, partly because she wanted Ned to admire her. She had borrowed a dress from Hardy Amies – one of the perks of her trade – it was red silk, with a great swooping skirt spilling from a tiny waist, and a particularly daring bodice, skin tight but parting just above the cleavage line, thus empasising her lovely breasts, and lest they might be missed, further embellished with gold and silver embroidery.

She had arrived on Ned's arm, swathed in a great white fox stole, her hair swept up in a chignon, her make-up bold: heavy black eye-liner and brilliant red lipstick. She was at least six inches taller than any other woman in the room, partly because of a pair of four-inch heels endowed by Rayne. So lovely did she look, there was no one, male or female, in the room who did not stop whatever they were doing to stare at her. As she bent to kiss Persephone, who was already at the table, the staring focused on her breasts which threatened – or was it promised? – to spill out of their embroidered casing.

'My darling, how beautiful you look,' Persephone cried. 'Ned, doesn't she look just too, too amazing?'

And Ned, playing up to Diana's game for once, said, 'Truly amazing, yes.' He looked her quite openly up and down before kissing her hand and settling her in her seat.

Philip Harrington had arrived rather rudely late, Diana thought. In her book, if you were to attend so glittering an affair, you made sure to get away hours before necessary. Then she chided herself as she shook out her napkin and smiled graciously at him. Perhaps registrars did not possess such powers over their lives. But she noticed that Sister Anna Fitzwarren had clearly made note of the late arrival and her eyebrows rose on her aristocratic forehead just for a moment. Good, thought Diana. He would suffer for it in the days to come.

But after that Philip made a great effort to be agreeable and charming, signalling to the waiter more than once that her glass was in need of refilling, or her napkin needed retrieving, having slithered yet again off the great expanse of her skirt.

It was quite far into the evening that he said it; dancing had begun and Diana was much in demand, first with Ned, to establish her position as guest of honour on his table, then Persephone's beau, who had a rather showy style that amused her. And then of course Ian Bellinger and Ludo Manners; she was just sitting down, breathless and laughing, when Philip Harrington joined her.

'I was going to ask you if you would do me the honour of dancing with me,' he said, 'but I can see you would rather sit this one out.'

'I would indeed, and thank you for that piece of perception. What a wonderful occasion this is, isn't it? Are you enjoying it?'

'Oh, very much,' he said.

'And how long have you worked at St Luke's?'

'Oh, I got my job, as it's called, a position at a hospital—'

'Yes, I do know,' said Diana coolly. 'My brother is a consultant at the London and of course I've known Ned all my life, so I'm familiar with medical terminology.'

'Well, I got my job here just about six months ago.'

'And – you like it?'

'Oh, very much. Paediatrics is quite a new field, but one I'm very interested in, and some of Mr Welles's work is quite pioneering. So I'm very fortunate and appreciate it.'

'Good. And your father works here, I believe.'

'Yes, he's over there,' said Philip Harrington, indicating a stout, red-faced man dancing a rather inexpert foxtrot with a woman who would clearly have wished to be partnering almost anyone else in the room. 'Would you like to meet him? I'm sure he'd be delighted to be introduced.'

'Yes,' said Diana bravely, thinking only of Ned and that this entire evening was, as far as she was concerned, in his best interests and to further his career and also to develop their friendship just a little. 'Yes, I would very much. Thank you.'

Sir Digby proved exactly as she might have expected: pompous, overbearing and none too bright. Until her brother had qualified she had assumed doctors must all be brilliant people, but he had assured her they were not. 'Everyone hero-worships them because they have the power of life and death in their hands, but honestly, it's not a difficult subject, medicine, it's all facts. You need a good memory and a facility to apply what you know to the case in hand.'

'Well, I must be getting back to my table,' she said as soon as she possibly could. 'Mr Welles's mother is on her own.'

'Ah, is that who she is?' said Sir Digby. 'Pretty woman; I believe there was some scandal, long ago of course. Welles seems very devoted to her. Not many men would bring their mother to such an event, but then she does seem most delightful.' And then, 'Welles has never married, has he?' said Harrington, with a suddenness that shocked her.

'No, not yet. He was about to, about a year back, but it was broken off. In fact, I planned to marry him myself when I was very young. We were childhood sweethearts.' May God forgive me, she thought, or rather Ned . . .

'Did you, by Jove. So what changed your mind?'

'Oh – common sense, I would say, on his part. I was only nineteen. But so much in love.'

'And – is your husband here tonight? I see you are married.' He nodded at the wedding ring and huge diamond on her left hand.

'No, sadly, we're divorced.'

'Oh – pity. Now look, I see that Mrs Welles is dancing again and this is one of my favourites.' The band had struck up with the old Astaire song 'The Way You Look Tonight'. 'Don't suppose you'd do me the honour, would you?'

'Of course,' she said, summoning her warmest smile. Put up with it, Diana, stay friends with this one, it's important.

She survived – just – then made her excuses and allowed him to lead her back to the table, where Philip Harrington was sitting alone. He stood up, pulled back a chair for her.

'Hello. Hello, Father. Having a good time?'

'Delightful, quite delightful. Goodnight for now at least, Mrs –?'

'Gunning,' said Diana. 'Goodnight and thank you for the dance.'

'My pleasure entirely. My regards to Welles. Tell him we're very pleased with his work here, especially the new stuff.'

'Shall we dance?' said Philip Harrington.

'That would be lovely,' said Diana.

'My father isn't the best dancer,' said Philip, steering her into a rather expert waltz. 'How are your shoes?'

'Oh – fine,' she said, laughing politely.

There was silence for a turn or two; then he said, 'So – have you known Mr Welles a long time?'

God, both of them.

'Yes, a very long time. And when I was a debutante we went out together,' she added.

'Oh, really? And was he as handsome then as he is now?'

'He certainly was. Half the girls in my year were after him.'

'Lucky fellow.'

'Yes. And he's a very nice person too. Goodness, that dance was over quickly. Now, if you would just take me back to the table, I can see Mr Welles is on his own. Thank you so much, Dr Harrington, you do – let me put it politely – treat a girl's shoes with more respect than your father does.'

He laughed. 'That is putting it very politely. Now, here we are. I return your partner to you, Mr Welles. I feel honoured to have danced with her.'

And he went off.

Seeing they were alone, Diana said, 'Ned, afterwards – I think we should talk. Just briefly. Can we go back to your house? Don't look like that. I'm not going to try and seduce you, I've learned my lesson there!'

'Don't be silly,' he said, laughing. 'Yes, yes, of course. My mother and her dashing gentleman friend are staying at the Dorchester. Should I be worried at what you want to talk about?'

'I don't think so.'

They were actually joined in Ned's small house not only by the Bellingers, but Ludo and Cecily. Cecily was tired – hardly surprising, Diana thought, with four children to care for, nannies and apparently limitless money notwithstanding. They had decided to stay in town rather than make the long drive home. Ned invited them in to use his phone to find somewhere to stay; it required a few calls, but the Berkeley offered to open its doors to them; they then all six settled into that greatest of social joys, the post-mortem.

'Great evening,' said Ludo. 'Thanks for inviting us, Diana. Ghastly chap, that Digby Harrington. What a boss, Ned. Do you know, he was at my prep school? I suddenly remembered the name. Everyone was terrified of him. He had an appalling reputation as a bully. Tormented the small ones, heads down the lavatory, you know the sort of thing.'

'I'm afraid I do. Well, I don't suppose he's changed. Mind you, he's not as bad as Sir Neil Lawson, he's the real head honcho, absolute brute.'

'Oh, Ludo,' said Cecily, 'how can you even think of sending the boys away? I wish you wouldn't.'

'Oh, they'll be all right,' said Ludo easily. 'It's different these days, anyway, nobody gets away with that sort of thing any more.' He looked at his watch. 'Time we were going, I'm afraid. Anyone want a lift? We're headed Knightsbridge way, as you know.'

'No, we've got our car,' said Ian. 'Thanks all the same.'

'Diana?'

'No, I've still got too much lovely champagne left – if Ned doesn't mind me staying to drink it.'

She hated doing it, but felt it too important not to warn him about Sir Digby and his insistent probing.

He grew very pale, drank an enormous Scotch very fast.

'A spy,' he said. 'Oh, God.'

'I simply don't understand it,' she said. 'Why they're so bothered. I'd have thought they'd both got better things to do. But there's no need to panic, Ned. Just – be careful. They're a nasty pair. You heard what Ludo said about Sir Digby. No reason to suppose his son's any different. But everyone else there, and I met loads of them tonight, clearly loves you. And what do they have to go on? Never did anyone lead such a blameless life. I don't know how you can stand it.'

She spoke lightly, but he said, 'I have to. You can see why now.'

'Indeed.'

'More champagne?'

'No, thank you, I've had far too much already. I really must go, if you'd call me a taxi.'

'Of course. I haven't asked about you. Is everything all right in your world? Do you have anyone yourself at the moment?'

'Oh – no. Not really,' she said, her mind swooping back to the evening at her flat, and Tom Knelston kneeling above her on her sofa, kissing her frantically. 'No. Not with any future in it, anyway.'

'Well, I'm sure there will be. Someone, I mean. Meanwhile, it's so very good to have you as a friend, Diana. I wish we'd become so long ago. I have so few.'

'Me too.' The very word 'friend' produced a vivid image of Tom. 'Now listen, I understand you like the theatre. Maybe we could go together sometimes. At best it would be fun, and at worst –'

'It could allay suspicion,' he said and laughed and kissed her, very gently, on the mouth. 'I'd like that very much. Only not – not –'

'Not musicals,' she said. 'Because of Jillie, I know. But you like the ballet?'

'I love it.'

'Me too. And all this new theatre stuff? Osborne, Wesker –'

'Very much.'

'Opera?'

'Naah.'

'You know, we really are made for one another,' she said, laughing.

# Chapter 43

'Darling, do leave me alone.'

'What?'

'I said, please leave me alone.'

'I am leaving you alone.'

'No. You're hovering. You know I can't concentrate when you're hovering.'

'I'm sorry, I call this sitting and reading.'

'Well, I call it hovering. And I've got to get this synopsis done by tomorrow, for this woman who might take me on as her editor.'

'Sorry. Shall I go into another room?'

'No, I'll still know you're there. Can't you go out and look for things?'

'Oh – yes. Yes, all right.'

He really didn't like the way she talked about looking for things. It belittled what he did dreadfully, the painstaking following up of trails, the hunts through catalogues. Everyone thought he was the dominant one in the relationship, and everyone thought wrong. Nell was very much in charge; she had a temper and he was actually rather frightened of her when it was aroused. She also had a gift for making him see things from her point of view, so that suddenly he felt bad for being there and having nothing to do but read when she was so busy. But it was Sunday, the only day he had to himself, when the little shop in the King's Road was closed. It was very nice once a week to just relax and read the papers, and try not to think about any of it. But this particular Sunday that was clearly not to be; Nell had her synopsis to write, and that was what mattered. He dropped a kiss on the top of her head, said he'd see her later, and went out to his car.

Julius Noble the third, as he was known in his rather dynastic family, was a gentle soul, just thirty and extremely clever. He had been an Eton scholar, and left Oxford with a double first in Greats and very little idea what he might do next. His father, Julius the second, had died of tuberculosis when Julius was only seventeen, leaving a vast fortune, inherited initially from his father, made from the manufacture of arms in the First World War, but later converted, with considerable entrepreneurial skill, to the manufacture of engineering tools, in particular for the burgeoning post-war housing industry. Julius entered Oxford therefore a millionaire many times over; he was saved from exploitation there by the simple fact that he had no idea of it. His uncle, terrified of the money being wasted, had set up a complex series of trusts, which allowed Julius a modest income; any requests for more had to be put first to him and thence to one of a range of trustees. He was allowed his first capital sum, a modest five hundred thousand pounds, at the age of twenty-one, his first million at twenty-five, and two more at thirty. A considerable sum was still held by the trustees and would be released on his marriage with further instalments upon the birth of each child.

The least avaricious of people, he had bought an extremely pretty but modest Victorian stucco-faced house in St John's Wood, which he had enjoyed furnishing so much that it had led to his present career in antiques. He owned a rather large and splendid pre-war Bentley (he did like cars) and a small but well-powered Morris for zipping about town. But he had shown no interest in the things his uncle had so feared; horse racing left him unmoved, gambling bored, and all three of his serious girlfriends had been well-brought-up, well-behaved young women, who he liked to take to nice restaurants and buy pretty things for – jewellery, silk scarves and for Nell, a rather spectacular diamond ring. Nell was, of course, aware of his wealth, but she came from an old banking family and looked for no more than being kept in the considerably comfortable manner to which she was accustomed.

Julius's only real extravagance was his wardrobe; he loved clothes and regarded them, in their most expensive and stylish form, as a necessity; most of the top floor of his house was given over to them. Racks of suits, rails of shirts, piles of sweaters, stacks of shoes, all handmade, not to mention belts, scarves and hats, filled what would have made a very adequate flat. He would sometimes wander among it all, reminding himself what was there, making notes of what he might buy or how he might add to them.

Today, even this held no charm for him; especially as Nell was inclined to mock his collection, saying it was really not very manly. She did dress quite interestingly herself, and lived in a little house in Kensington; not far, Julius realised, as he drove home, from where Jillie Curtis had entertained them so graciously a few weeks ago. He had been rather fascinated by Jillie; she wasn't exactly beautiful, but she had wonderful bones, he had thought, and he liked her voice, which was light and rather musical. There was a slight sadness about her which intrigued him and had stayed with him. He had felt too the emotion that had come between them, indefinable, unexpected. But Nell was of a jealous disposition, and since he had been with her, he had never allowed himself even to seem interested in another woman, even to admire a film star or actress. He loved Nell; she was clever and amusing and passionate and, while not beautiful, very pretty. Most of the time she was just about sufficiently interested in and impressed by his work; for the rest, he told himself, nobody was perfect.

He must ask Josh if Jillie had found a permanent job yet; the least they could do, in return for her help, was congratulate her if she had. Once home, he rang Josh, and when he heard that she was working in Hackney, wrote her a short note in his florid handwriting, congratulating her, and saying how much he hoped they could all meet again soon. But whether Nell was there or not, he wanted to see Jillie again, of that he was sure.

Alice knew at once something had happened. Tom sounded different, charged somehow. He came into the house and called to her, his voice compelling. It was early, the children had not yet had their tea, and the place was in chaos. He ignored it and walked into the living room, making a pathway through half-built bridges, knocked-down castles, overturned trains, and sank into the large, lumpy easy chair that was so surprisingly comfortable.

'Hello,' he said and smiled at her.

It was a long time since he had come home and seemed pleased to be there. In the forced cheerfulness, the uneasy peace that they had lived in for months now, he had simply walked into the house, hung up his coat, kissed her briefly and gone straight into his domestic tasks, with neither enthusiasm nor complaint.

'Hello,' said Alice. 'Sorry about the mess. You're early, I didn't—'

'Oh, never mind the mess,' he said. 'Yes, I am early. I've had the most extraordinary afternoon.'

'Really? What?'

'I was in the House,' Tom said. 'I'd been sorry to miss yesterday when there was the launch of the debate, between the parties. On the question of the nuclear deterrent. You know that's Bevan's great cause now, or rather what we do about it.'

'Yes, of course,' said Alice, thinking of the thousands of things Tom had told her about the nuclear debate in the preceding months and how little proper notice she had taken of the most burning issue of the age.

'Yesterday, Churchill spoke, and I would have loved to have heard him. He can't make many more speeches and much as I loathe his politics, we both know what he did for the country in the war and how revering him is somehow in our bones.

'Apparently though, the speech was not particularly good; and today was the official opposition debate. And Bevan spoke, and Alice, he was magnificent. I wrote down several phrases, but listen to this: "Neither the scientists nor the military men have an answer to the problems of the world. It is now time for a little more wisdom." Alice, he was so wonderful.

'But the real point is that Churchill then struggled to the dispatch box and spoke again. He is so old, and so small – I swear he's shrunk – but his voice – oh, Alice, not so strong, but still as wonderful. He revealed that he had wanted to call a meeting with Eisenhower and Malenkov, the new Russian in power, but that – and this is the first anyone had known of it – he suffered a stroke. Then he apologised to Bevan for what he called the "exceptional intervention into his speech", bowed to all sides of the House and sat down again. It was so marvellous, Alice, to be there, and you know, people are saying probably the last time he would speak in a major debate in the House. I saw history this afternoon, and it was wonderful.'

'It must have been,' said Alice, and for the first time in months she felt she had Tom back, the Tom she had fallen in love with, the passionate enthusiast, the irrepressibly ambitious man.

'It's so dreary, so much of politics, so many boring events and tedious meetings, so hard to hang on to what it's all about, and then something like that happens and you remember: the power of it all, and the ability to change people's lives and indeed the world. Now –' and he seemed to remember properly where he was – 'I expect you'd like a cup of tea. I would. I'll make it. And I will do the nappies and the story, but then, I'm afraid, I have to go and meet Donald. He thinks not only was it a momentous occasion, but there's bound to be an election pretty soon. I'm sorry, Alice.'

'That's perfectly all right,' said Alice, as graciously as she could. Which under the circumstances, was really very gracious indeed.

It had been an extremely difficult, if not unhappy, few months, since the dreadful day of her father's phone call. Gradually, uneasily, Alice and Tom had worked their way back into some semblance of a working relationship; his hostility underlying it, her remorse and resentment, in equal measures, half helping, half hindering the process.

She struggled to be cheerful, more efficient, not so much for Tom's sake but for their marriage. Which clearly had to continue somehow. When she had had this baby – and early April was not an age away – she would feel well and strong again, and she even made an effort to be at least a little more active in bed, but except for very rare occasions, like Christmas, he seemed totally disinterested. At the moment the very thought of sex made her feel sick – but a new emotion had entered her, one that crept into her head and her heart and that try as she would, she could not quite dispel. It was fear: fear that he had found someone else, someone free and young and sexy, who had time and energy for him, who could give him what she was failing so miserably to provide. She tried, tried so hard to crush the fears, and for the most part she succeeded, but sometimes, when she was alone, or worse, in the early mornings as she sat feeding Lucy, it would enter the silent house and her heart, the awful fear, and she would wonder what she could do about it, and then face the fact that there was nothing at all, and that confronting him with some nameless creature would make him as angry as when she railed against Laura. And so she struggled on, and struggle it was.

Tom was out a lot, often at the weekends. She hated the weekends in many ways. All her friends were with their husbands, and she couldn't go to her parents any more, the rift between them was far too wide. If her father had apologised to Tom, then bridges might have been built. Jillie was available at the weekends sometimes, and loved to come and see her and the children, although she was also being rather odd, Alice thought. She seemed to have something on her mind and was very erratic in her moods, flying quite high one day, and quietly subdued the next. She had a new job that she loved, obstetric registrar at quite a small hospital in Hackney, working for a woman who was just as brilliant as Miss Moran but a great deal more compassionate, and Alice envied her that more than anything, having a place and a purpose in the outside world. More and more she resolved that when the children were old enough she would go back to work, whether Tom agreed to it or not. Raising a family was not enough on its own to be the only purpose for living.

Meanwhile, she had no option but to see it that way. She had more than once dragged her vast bulk – and it did seem particularly vast this time – to Purbridge if there was some dinner or ceremony to which wives were invited. But she had an uneasy feeling that Tom found her size and condition almost embarrassing, and the complexity of the arrangements for the children, now that she could no longer ask her mother, tedious. In the end, he announced he was grateful for her efforts to be supportive, but perhaps they should now be put on hold until after the baby was born.

Tom was meanwhile in a different kind of limbo – or was it more like hell? Of raging guilt, a realisation of the puny power of his own will, joined by a kind of self-justification that something had to make his life worth living; that he was doing all he could for Alice, and that his visits to Diana Southcott represented almost the only pleasures in his life.

For he had not been able to give her up, of course. Those forays into a wild, joyful, multicoloured country, from one that was otherwise strictly monochrome, were absolutely irresistible as were the evenings that contained them; the beautifully furnished, orderly house, into which he was welcomed with delight, where he was plied with delicious food – prepared by Diana's housekeeper, whose other function, for which he thanked her silently every time, was to wash up in the morning. It was shocking, disgraceful, inexcusable, he knew that, and God only knew what risks he ran. He trembled sometimes to think of what Donald Herbert would have had to say to him, had he known.

Every time he left his beautiful mistress in her equally beautiful surroundings he vowed this would be the last time. And like all adulterers, he found himself drawn back again and again for just one more time, one last glorious gratification. He was bewitched not just by her but by all that she gave him, and life without her now, in all its drabness, had become quite simply unthinkable.

'Well, young Tom,' Donald Herbert said as they sat in the Savoy bar, and raised their glasses to what seemed a now inevitable election. 'Cometh the hour cometh the man. I hope you're ready for this.'

'Of course I am,' said Tom.

'Good. Because if you think you've been nursing your constituents before this, you're about to discover what that really means. Every hour God sends, you have to be there, once the gun has been fired. Of course you know the form, you've done it already at the

by-election, but this time you're going to win, I'm absolutely confident. I hope you feel the same way.'

'I think so,' said Tom. Confidence was not quite flowing in his
veins.

'Well, you must tell yourself you do. If you don't believe in yourself,
nobody else will. Now then: the word is May, with a small minority
mooting July.'

'Will Attlee lead the party?'

'Unfortunately, yes. I would rather Gaitskell. No Tom, not Nye,
he'd be a disastrous leader, charismatic as he is. Everyone knows the
party is riven at the moment and Attlee at least spells unity. They
have Eden, attractive figure, well known enough by now; perhaps a
bit too much of a Tory stereotype – but that could play into our hands.'

'You think we have a chance?'

'Not really. Not the party. But you do, and that's the main thing.
That constituency of yours is going to see a big swing. There are many
more working-class voters than there were, Tom, it's all yours for the
taking. When's that baby due?' asked Herbert, suddenly.

'Early April.'

'Hmm. So Alice won't be much use to you until the end of April
earliest, then?'

'Not out on the stumps, no, 'fraid not.'

'But maybe a few crucial appearances towards the end. All constituents love a wife, and if she's got a baby, she's double value. And a
new baby – well, beyond price.'

'I'll talk to her,' said Tom, 'but it really will have to be a very few.
She won't be very strong.'

'If she can get out on just the last few days, knock on a few doors
with you, be there at the count . . .'

'Oh, I'm sure she can do that,' said Tom. 'She really wants to help.'

'Of course. Bad timing, the whole thing, but it can't be helped.
Well, look, I must get home, promised Christine I wouldn't be late.'

He stood up, pulled on his coat and held out his hand to shake
Tom's.

'You're off home now, are you?'

'Yes,' said Tom, slightly surprised by the question. 'Of course.'

'OK. Best wishes to Alice. One last thing,' said Herbert suddenly, taking him completely off his guard. 'This is no time for scandal, Tom. One hint of it and you'd be done for.'

'Of – course.'

'Yes. Just thought I'd mention it. Word gets round horribly fast, as you must know. It's not worth it, Tom, not at the moment at any rate. Night, then . . .'

And he was gone. Tom sat down abruptly on his chair again; his heart was racing, he felt he might be sick. Christ. Donald obviously knew – something. And if Donald knew – Jesus. Well, he'd have to finish it now. The new incentive would get him through.

Diana would not be pleased, though. To put it mildly.

# Chapter 44

'What's this?'

'What's what?'

'This sold note on the little dressing table.'

'Well, I hate to state the obvious, but it's a sold note.'

'And you didn't think to tell me about it?'

'Sorry, Julius, I forgot.'

It wasn't worth getting cross with her; she would just get crosser back.

'Who did you sell it to?'

'To Jillie Curtis.'

'Jillie Curtis? Was she here?'

'Yes. She was. She just walked in, one morning when you'd gone out, and wanted to buy something for her mother's birthday.'

'But – she must be waiting for it. You should have told me.'

'I forgot. Sorry.'

Julius went into the tiny office and dialled Jillie's number. Since it was midday and she was mid-operating list, the only answer he received was from the housekeeper. Having met Mrs Hemmings and hugely enjoyed her cooking, Julius was able to leave a friendly and fairly coherent message for Jillie. He then returned to cataloguing a series of prints he had bought that morning, while wondering, in his fantasy-prone way, if it was possible for a human being to actually explode with anticipation.

She finally called him back that evening at home at seven. She sounded wary.

'Hello, Julius?'

'Yes. Hello, Jillie. How are you?'

'I'm very well. A bit tired. And you?'

'Very well. Not a bit tired. Or is that annoying?'

'No. No, of course not.'

'I sometimes think it's really annoying if one is exhausted and nobody else is. Well, anyway, Jillie, I am so sorry not to have got back to you about the dressing table that you bought. And of course that I wasn't there, that I missed you.'

'It doesn't matter at all,' she said. 'Honestly. It was only two or three days ago.'

'Well, it's very nice of you to be so forgiving. When would you like me to deliver the dressing table?'

'It would have to be a weekend and preferably this one, as my mother's away and so no danger of her seeing her present.'

'Well, I'll bring it up on Sunday. Sunday morning, if that's all right?'

'Wonderful. You do your own deliveries, do you? Because a driver could—'

'Even if I had a driver, which I don't,' he said, 'I wouldn't dream of sending him to your house. I want to see you.'

Her. He wanted to see her. Oh, stop it, Jillie, where do you think this is going to get you?

'And your mother's bedroom, of course. It'll be fun.'

'Well – fine. Marvellous. Come for coffee. And of course,' she added, in infinitely careful tones, 'bring Nell.'

'Can't do that. Sunday is her great working day. I'm not allowed near her on Sundays, really.'

'Well,' said Jillie and suddenly she didn't feel tired any more, she felt rather wonderful, as if she had just woken from a very long, very refreshing sleep. 'Well, in that case you and I will have coffee. But – we may have to hide the dressing table for a bit.'

'We'll put it wherever you wish,' said Julius. 'About eleven, then?'

'About eleven.'

By a quarter to eleven on Sunday morning, Jillie had changed four times – dress: too dressy; skirt and blouse: too dull; jeans: too casual;

capri pants, oversized white shirt, red sweater slung round her shoulders: just right. She had laid coffee in the morning room and was positioned – pretending to read the *Observer* – in a window seat on the landing, that being prime position to see anyone coming into the drive.

By a quarter to eleven, Julius was sitting four roads away, in his vintage Austin van, the dressing table carefully stowed in the back, knowing he shouldn't be early, reading the *Sunday Times* and checking his watch every alternate minute. At five to eleven, he decided it was all right to be slightly early, and drove carefully into the drive of number five. Pausing to look up at the house, he saw a blurry figure at an upstairs window and moments later, the front door was opened by someone who could have been Audrey Hepburn, had she not been more beautiful.

He felt quite odd, contemplating her; after days and hours of remembering her, thinking about her, anticipating her. He jumped down from the van and said, 'Hello,' and she said, 'Hello, Julius, this is so kind of you.' Adding, 'What a glorious van.'

Julius patted its pale blue bonnet and said, 'Well, I think so. She's not exactly practical, always breaking down, but she suits her cargo so well, I couldn't bear to turn up with something like – well, your dressing table – in a 1950s Ford.'

'Well, no. Although I can see it might be better from a business point of view,' said Jillie. 'Look, why don't we go and have coffee before you unload? Would you like some orange juice or something? Mrs Hemmings does a big jugful on Sunday mornings.'

Julius said he couldn't think of anything more wonderful than some of Mrs Hemmings's orange juice, and while he waited in the morning room for her to return with it, admiring the extraordinarily pretty rug on the polished floor and the small Staffordshire pieces in a cabinet by the fireplace, he reflected on what a perfect environment Jillie had grown up in and wondered where the sadness came from and how on earth he would find out. Because, having seen her again, heard her voice again, watched her move again, he wanted to know every single, small and large thing about her.

\* \* \*

'Now,' he said when he had eaten a large number of biscuits, drunk two glasses of the orange juice and two cups of coffee, and they had discussed the relative headlines in the *Observer* and the *Sunday Times*, 'I think we should go and unload the dressing table.'

'Will you be able to manage on your own?' said Jillie anxiously. 'No gardener around, it being Sunday, although I'm very strong.' He assured her the dressing table was not heavy, not very big, and in no way a problem.

'Then I must move my car out of the garage, and we can put the table in its place, covered up, and maybe a couple of tyres or something in front of it.'

He watched as she emerged at the wheel of her pretty little dark green Austin.

'That is *lovely*,' he said, as she got out of it.

'Well, thank you. I love old cars, so does Daddy. He has a most beautiful pre-war Mercedes – go and have a look if you like.' He went in, and gazed almost awestruck at the pale blue creation, with its lovely low lines, swooping running board, and huge array of lamps.

'It's glorious,' he said. 'Does he drive it?'

'Oh yes, every week – not Sundays, because he can't bear Sunday drivers, but one day in the week if he has time he takes it for a run down to the coast. I used to go with him, when I was little, and then in the holidays, but now of course I can't.'

And Julius said, while knowing he should not, 'I have a special car, a 1930s Bentley, that likes a run, and I don't mind Sunday drivers, so if that would make up for the loss of your Mercedes rides, I'd love to take you sometimes.'

And Jillie, also knowing she should not, said carefully that that would be lovely some time, and then rather rushed him into getting the dressing table out of the van and into the garage, lifting the dust sheet he had placed over it to admire it politely.

'She's going to love it,' she said untruthfully.


'Josh. Sit down. I want to discuss something with you.'

Harry Campbell's face was unreadable as he looked at Josh across his vast desk.

Josh looked back, wishing his could be the same. It was a bit of a gift as a journalist, as in poker: and actually the qualities that made a good poker player – courage, appearing to know more than you did, keeping steely calm under pressure and of course the blank face – were all enormously helpful in pursuit of a difficult story.

'Right,' Josh said.

'It's homosexuality. And the attitude of the law. I think we should run a piece about it, possibly make it a cause. We need one, haven't had a good one for a bit. I like us to be unpredictable, and I think our readers – amongst whom of course there must be many such – are educated enough to take it. Well, some of them.'

'Ri–ight.' Presumably he meant in favour, Josh thought, but there was no real telling with him.

'What's your view on it, eh? Let's get that established first.'

'I think it's appalling,' said Josh simply. 'Really shocking.'

He hoped this wasn't going to lead back to Ned and Jillie's wedding. Campbell had been very good about it at the time, not pressed him in any direction, but if he had a bee in his editor's hat, there was no telling.

'Well, do you think the readers would cope with it?'

'I – think it would be pretty brave,' said Josh honestly. 'I mean, we do lean to the right. Some of them could agree, but an awful lot wouldn't. We could lose some of them. If we made it a cause, that is.'

'Well, let 'em go,' said Campbell easily. 'Plenty more where they came from.'

Josh knew that was far from what he really thought; he counted every additional thousand readers as treasure beyond price. He also knew it meant Campbell was serious about it.

'Anyway, Josh – do some research first. I'm not wild about quite a lot of it, mind you. Cottaging – you know, meeting in public lavatories – for instance, makes me heave. I just don't like injustice and persecution. Or blackmail, which is where it so often leads. Find a few people you can talk to, then get back to me, all right?'

'All right,' said Josh. 'And thanks.'

Harry laughed. 'You may not be thanking me in a week or so. This is not an easy one.'

\* \* \*

It wasn't. By the end of ten days, he had a lot of rather dull factual stuff, which would form the bare bones of the piece, but now he wanted gossip – gossip and froth from a completely fresh perspective. And it was proving hard to find.

It was Jillie who had the idea: he had taken her out to dinner at the Trocadero, to thank her for her help with Julius Noble and his fiancée, and found himself, after three Martinis and some excellent lobster thermidor, telling her about the article.

'It's brave of the *Daily News*, or rather Harry Campbell, and I think he's going to make it a cause for the paper.'

'Oh, really?' said Jillie. Her face was carefully blank and Josh knew why; he had always suspected the reason behind the cancelled engagement, although it had never been confirmed by anyone, in or out of the family, and he hoped she didn't think he was trying to draw her on the subject.

'Yes. And I think it would be a wonderful thing if he does. The whole thing is so filthily unfair, and as Campbell says, it's turned into a witch hunt. I hate the labels too: "gross indecency". Look what happened to Turing. The police had him marked down, and somehow after reporting a break-in, he was charged with it, arrested, and forced to undergo what they called hormone therapy. No wonder he topped himself.'

'I didn't know that,' she said.

'Oh, I've unearthed a lot of similar stories. They've all been turned into criminals.'

'Where is this leading, Josh?'

'Oh – nothing you can help with. But I'm a bit stuck at the moment for what I'd call gossipy stuff, bit more light hearted, even scurrilous if you like, don't know where to find that. Your lobster all right?'

'Lovely, thank you. You should ask someone in the theatrical profession – they seem to get away with it. Noël Coward wears it like a banner.'

'Well, he's hardly likely to answer my calls, is he?'

'What about an interior designer? Or a photographer?'

'The photographers on the *Daily News* are hugely homophobic, most of them.'

'Here's an idea, then. That model, Diana something, the one you had photographed on the big wheel at Battersea with Tom Knelston. God, Alice was so angry – anyway, I bet she'd be a good source. And she owes you a favour. You could say you gave her her big break, put her on the front page of your paper –'

'Hardly. But she's a good idea. Thank you, Jillie. Now – pudding?'

'I couldn't. But it's been a lovely evening, exactly what I needed, thank you.'

She arrived at Scott's looking amazing, in a mink coat and Cossack hat to match. She ordered a gin fizz, one of the specialities of the house, and sat sipping at it, waiting for the questions to come. After about ten minutes, her dark eyes brilliant with amusement, she said, 'Josh, you'll have to ask me soon, whatever it is, or I'll have to go. I've got a photographic session in half an hour. The photographer will not be amused if I'm late, nor the client. So come on, what is it?'

And shocked into directness, Josh asked her whether she had any queer friends or acquaintances amongst her fashion connections who would talk to him openly about their lives in London today. 'What I'm looking for is gossipy stuff.'

She looked at him thoughtfully. 'I should think so. They'd have to trust you, though. Could they?'

'Of course. Absolute anonymity.'

'I mean, I couldn't be more in sympathy with what your paper's doing, I have to say. The whole thing makes me sick with rage. Poor people, turned into criminals for just – well, just being themselves. Give me a few days, and I'll see what I can do. Now I must dash. Lovely drink, thank you. And if you want a safe place to talk, you can use my house. Nice neutral territory and they'll be more relaxed. I'll do some ironing or something in the kitchen.'

'That's very kind of you,' said Josh, trying and failing to imagine Diana ironing.

'Well, darling, I could say you gave me my big break.'

He laughed.

'What's so funny?'

'That's what Jillie – my cousin – said. I thought she was mad.'

'Jillie who? Do I know her?'

'Jillie Curtis.'

'Is she your cousin?'

'Yes, she is.'

'Good Lord,' said Diana.

Tom was being much nicer suddenly. Alice couldn't quite believe the difference. The angry, resentful man she had been living with for months had been replaced by someone cheerful, helpful and best of all affectionate – although he didn't seem to want sex, which was a relief. With her eight-month stomach between them, it would have been pretty difficult anyway. She really was very big. Delilah, the large midwife who had been assigned to her at Acton General, and who she loved, had assured her it was not the twins Alice so desperately feared, simply her third pregnancy in as many years, and her stomach muscles had more or less given up the struggle.

Tom's only thought these days, apart from his chances in winning his seat, was how he could end the relationship with Diana. It was a nightmare; he woke to it, worked with it, talked to his constituents with it and went to sleep with it. Twice, he had arrived at her house, resolved to tell her, and twice he hadn't got half a sentence out before she was at him, her lovely mouth on his, her perfume surrounding him, her desire driving his – and twice he had left again, desperately remorseful. The election had not yet been called – but he knew it couldn't be long and he had to be free of her by then.

He was also distracted over the political shenanigans of his idol, Nye Bevan. The Health Service long set aside, Bevan had a new obsession, his involvement with the Campaign for Nuclear Disarmament. He was tearing the party apart, defying his own leader, as well as the bulk of its members, to such an extent that he was, in that pre-election spring, expelled.

Tom, naturally peace loving, had gone twice to some of the great

CND rallies and stood with his like-minded colleagues, feeling a profound sense of pride and commitment to be part of them.

The whole thing had inspired some of Bevan's greatest speeches in the House aimed directly against many of the most powerful members of his party, which included his leader. Tom managed to get into a few of the speeches and sat entranced, listening to what was to him music, watching the famous gestures, the arm waving, the sweeping hand movements.

Donald Herbert, half amused, half anxious, begged Tom to keep his opinions to himself. 'Most of the party is against him,' he said, 'and much of the country. You cannot afford to be a rebel, Tom, not at this stage; you must give people what they want.'

Which did not include an adulterous MP, Tom thought; and rang Diana from his office next morning, to tell her he needed to see her urgently.

The Knightsbridge evening with Josh had been fixed for the session in Diana's smart little house; 'I've got a photographer's assistant for you,' she said on the phone to Josh. 'Feisty little sod, quite prepared to spill the beans, and if that doesn't work, a young actor. Who, actually, you can see anyway, another evening, if you like.'

'What's his name?'

'We agreed it was safer for him if you didn't know it.'

'But I would never, ever use it.'

'I know that and you know that but he doesn't. You're to call him Nick.'

'Right. So – which evening?'

'Thursday,' said Diana.

'I'm going to be very late this evening,' Tom said. 'I'm so sorry, Alice. I'm whizzing down to Purbridge for a meeting.'

'It's all right, I understand, you know I do. But don't expect me to be awake and all agog to hear about it, because I'll be well into the Land of Nod.'

'I'm pleased to hear it,' said Tom, giving her a kiss. The Judas kiss, he thought, shame reaching deep into him.

❊ ❊ ❊

'Nick' did indeed excel on the gossip: meeting places Josh was amazed by, clubs that looked like ordinary houses, a coffee bar, the Mousehole in Swallow Street, the Spanish Bar in the depths of Fortnum & Mason.

'You should visit it, Josh, it's wonderful, all embossed leather. And the Grenadier Pub, behind Hyde Park Corner, it's near Knightsbridge Barracks, of course, which is an absolute hotbed. The police are dreadful, of course, they set up honey traps in pubs and so on; and then fix their prey. I had one friend who was living with someone very quietly, and he had some drunken maniac driving through his front garden. He called the police, but before that they had to make up the spare-room bed; they knew they'd be checking for such things. Your trade behaves pretty badly, I might add. If you are going to do something for us, it's none too soon.'

He picked up the vodka Martini Diana had made him.

'Another one?' she asked Nick. She had begun by stationing herself in the kitchen, but could find nothing to do, so had ended up joining them.

Josh, feeling his task almost done, accepted too. She made them, but as she poured them into fresh cold glasses, said, 'Now look, you two, I want you out of here at eight thirty at the latest. I've got someone coming to see me at nine, and I don't want my drawing room awash with dirty cups and glasses, all right?'

She was beginning to regret agreeing to see Tom the same evening as Josh; but he had sounded very stressed.

'The worst thing, in a way,' Nick said, 'is the waves of panic after a high-profile case – like the Montagu one. I have friends who destroyed suitcases full of letters and photographs, most of them harmless, for fear of discovery, and made bonfires of keepsakes. It's dreadful, the terror. Lots of the rich just move abroad; Robin Maugham, for instance, sails his yacht permanently. Some move to places like Tangiers and Rome. But if you're an ordinary man, trying to earn a living, you just have to get on with it and live with the fear.'

Diana thought of Ned; living with the fear, all his life. A half-life, really. It was almost unendurable.

'Of course, I'm lucky,' Nick was saying. 'I live in a tolerant bit of society, but if you don't, then . . .'

'Sorry, chaps,' said Diana, 'this has to come to an end.'

It was only eight thirty but Diana wanted to have a bath before Tom's arrival.

'Nick, thank you so much,' said Josh. 'And you, Diana. Would you like me to help you clear up?'

'No, thank you,' said Diana quickly. 'I'd rather do it myself.' She was a bit on edge, Josh noticed: maybe her visitor was a new boyfriend. Whatever the reason, they owed it to her to leave her in peace.

Nick left first, kissed Diana, and said, 'See you next week, lovely lady.'

'Oh,' she said. 'Yes, I'd forgotten. That lovely pleats idea. On location, aren't we? Hope so.'

'We are. Off to Winkworth Arboretum. Leaving at dawn. Well, seven. Don't be late.'

'I'm never late,' said Diana indignantly, and it was true, she was not. Punctuality was as essential a quality in a model as height, slenderness and good hair. Many was the lovely young thing struck off her agency's books for keeping an important photographer waiting.

Tom had misjudged the time of his journey; he arrived in Buckley Mews at eight fifteen. He was foot-weary, and his head ached. Surely to God she would let him in now. Well, all right, maybe not quite now: he'd wait for a bit then ring her doorbell.

God, he was tired, tired and terrified. Feeling wretched; apart from anything else, he knew how much he was going to miss her in his life, not just the sex, but the fun, the glamour, the danger. It was all such a far cry from the little house in Acton. He needed to sit down. There had been some seats in the square that led to the mews and he went back and sank gratefully onto one, put his head between his knees for a moment, then sat raking his fingers through his hair in an effort to tidy it, pulled out a handkerchief and wiped his sweaty forehead. He thought how dreadful he must look, and then, hopefully, that she would find him so distasteful she would just let him go.

He looked at his watch again: twenty-five to nine. Just five more minutes and he'd only be quarter of an hour early.

* * *

'Diana, thank you again,' said Josh. 'Marvellous stuff, and he's given me another lead as well. I'm so grateful to you. Martini wasn't bad either.'

'Good. I enjoyed it too. Now look, I really am going to push you out. I hope we'll meet again. I think it's fantastic what your paper's going to do.'

'Night, Diana, thanks again.'

'Night, Josh. My pleasure.'

He walked slowly down the mews; the houses were all brightly lit, with outside lights. It looked like a film set.

She really had been in a hell of a rush: almost flustered. Probably one of her many lovers was coming. Not that he knew how many lovers she had; but he couldn't imagine anyone as gorgeous and fun as she was leading a nun-like existence.

He kept remembering things Nick had said that he hadn't written down, and paused to make notes. It was so easy to forget tiny details and they were what brought a piece alive. He had interviewed a minor Tory cabinet minister once for the paper, exceedingly dull he had been too, except that whenever Josh asked him a question he didn't want to answer, he cleared his throat loudly. It clearly gave him time to think, but it also gave Josh clues about what the areas were. Harry Campbell had actually praised the piece. Josh couldn't remember him doing that since. Finally satisfied, he put his notebook back in his pocket and walked briskly towards the square.

A man was sitting on a seat next to a lamp post. He was clearly waiting for someone, kept looking at his watch. There was something familiar about him . . . He was signalling to taxis as the man stood up, turned round into the full flood of the lamplight: he was very tall, with – wait a minute – dark red hair. It was Tom Knelston. What on earth was he doing here? A taxi with its 'for hire' lights on came towards him; Josh put down his arm, shook his head at the driver.

Tom was walking now quite slowly towards the mews. He took one last look at his watch and then speeded up, as if he had made some decision or other. Josh followed him, cautiously slow, afraid Tom would see him, fearing now, dreading what his destination might be. Surely not, please, dear God, not Diana's house. Not Tom, the perfect family man, married to his cousin's best friend. Must be someone from the Labour Party, they were half of them filthy rich, lived in places like this.

But Josh stood stock-still now that Tom had arrived at his destination, terrified that he'd see him. And indeed Tom did turn round, furtively, checking the mews. Josh ducked behind a car that stood outside one of the houses. And then Tom raised his hand and rang Diana's doorbell and – Christ, there she was, dressed in a silky dressing gown, bare-footed, her cloud of hair loose around her shoulders, signalling to Tom to come in quickly, raising her face for a brief kiss.

And then she closed the door, leaving Josh with questions he would have given anything not to be asking, answers that he desperately shied away from even as he found them.

# Chapter 45

It was talked about everywhere for those first few days, in drawing rooms and pubs, bedrooms and clubs, and even the bars and dining rooms of the House of Commons. In tones that moved from delighted to shocked and every variation between; it formed debates, inspired gossip, and at best, gave rise to much sober thought.

The piece was not run under Josh's byline, but as a leader in the paper. 'It'll have more authority that way,' Harry Campbell said. 'The paper's view, rather than that of one single person – but good work, Josh. I'll rework it myself, I'll enjoy it. Haven't written a leader for months.' Josh sighed, but he had been half-expecting this.

Headed 'Living with the Fear', the article called for an urgent review of the laws regarding homosexuality, *in order that men of all sexual persuasions may live quietly at home, with a chosen partner. That is all we would ask of those that create and then vote upon the laws of this country. We do not condone the excesses, the more unsavoury aspects, of the homosexual lifestyle; but the vast majority of these men do not indulge in any such practices. These are law-abiding, worthy citizens, who live out frequently lonely lives in the shadow of blackmail and the constant fear of arrest. We have in this country what amounts to a witch hunt, an echo of McCarthyism. It is not an attractive sight. There are encouraging signs: MPs on both sides of the House are of the same opinion, and indeed a change in the law is, we are told, under consideration, at least by the Home Secretary.*

It took some courage for Harry Campbell to give the final go-ahead to the article, that time which another great editor was later to call the lonely hour. He knew the uproar it would create, that at worst the proprietors of the *Daily News* would call for his resignation. He had to persuade them of the rightness of his decision to run the piece, and that had been difficult enough, but he knew that if public and official opinion went against the paper, they would demand his head on a plate without a second thought. But he took the risk: and he was right. On balance, it seemed to be agreed amongst his readers that the paper's view was a not unreasonable one. There was the inevitable soar in circulation figures on the day of publication and the few following, as letters poured in, many from that most famous scribe 'Disgusted of Tunbridge Wells', but many too from supporters in the establishment professions: solicitors, teachers, even the Church, mainly anonymous, but a few signed.

A few weeks later, there were signs of a small but steady climb in circulation, as the readership welcomed the paper's thoughtful, liberal attitudes.

'Yes, of course I read it,' said Ned to Diana; she had requested his company for dinner the week after the article came out. 'I thought it was very good.'

'Do you think it'll help?'

'Maybe, a bit. Any easing of public opinion is welcome.'

'Is that all?'

'Oh, Diana, I don't know. Look, I'd rather not talk about it here, if you don't mind.'

'Here' was the Caprice, her choice. Ned didn't really like it very much; the food was good, but the pink tablecloths always made him feel faintly bilious.

He looked at her closely. 'You didn't have anything to do with it, did you?'

'Me? How could I have? How's it all going at St Luke's? Are you happy there?'

'Yes, of course. I'm fighting a bit of a battle at the moment. Well, quite a big battle. It could turn out to be a war.'

'Goodness. Who with?'

'Sir Digby. Your friend from the ball.'

'Oh, him. Nasty piece of work. What on earth are you fighting him about? I'm not sure that's a good idea, Ned.'

'You sound like my mother – she really took against him.'

'Did she?' said Diana, her voice over-casual.

'Yes, said he was a pompous old fart and she wouldn't trust him further than she could spit.'

'I'm with her there. I really wouldn't get on the wrong side of him, Ned. Anyway, what are you fighting with him about?'

'My new crusade. Allowing mothers into hospital with their children.'

'Oh, yes. It's such a good crusade. Well done you; I suppose he's totally opposed?'

'Yes, of course. He positively enjoys seeing these wards full of listless, miserable children. And what makes it worse, if one of the mothers does come in, if there's a crisis of some sort, they become terribly upset when she has to go again, crying, screaming even. And then all the nurses – who've been ingrained in this ghastly doctrine – say there, you see, he or she was much better when the mother wasn't coming in. Much more settled. How I've come to hate that word. When I do my rounds at night, sometimes, at least a quarter of the children are crying, most of them silently. It's heartbreaking.'

'So what do you do?'

'Oh, I try to comfort them, find their teddies and so on. I'd read stories if Sister would allow it, but of course, she thinks I'm being ridiculous. Sorry, am I being boring?'

'No, of course not,' said Diana. 'It's fascinating. But you couldn't have mothers with every child, surely? Just hanging round, getting in the way? It would be chaos.'

'Of course it wouldn't. They could help with mealtimes, washing, all the things the nurses are too busy for. And settling the children for the night. I absolutely know it would be better for everyone. Most of all, the children would be far easier to look after medically, if they were relaxed and happy.'

'And is Sir Digby actively against you?'

'That's an understatement. We had a meeting about it the other day, and he said I was making a mountain out of a very small mole-hill, that children were in here to be made well, not mollycoddled.'

'It's a pity your father isn't still alive, he could help.'

'My father? I don't think so, Diana. You're talking about the man who sent me off to school at seven.'

'Oh – hello.'

It was Julius.

He had phoned Jillie the Friday after Dressing Table Sunday as she thought of it and said, 'Well, your car or mine?'

'Sorry?' she said, stupid with surprise.

'I thought we'd agreed on a spin on the heath – or even a bit further today?'

'Oh – yes.'

'Are you not free?' he said and his tone was so disappointed she almost laughed for joy.

'Yes, yes, I'm free. Oh, do bring your car, much less complicated. I can't wait to see it.' And then, her voice politely hopeful, 'Will Nell be with you?'

'No,' he said. 'As I told you, she likes to keep Sundays for herself. She'll be really glad to know I'm busy, and in no danger of turning up on her doorstep.'

'But does she know in what way you're going to be busy?'

'No,' he said. 'But I will tell her, of course. You know, Jillie, I'm my own man, as I read somewhere the other day.'

She could hear the smile in his voice, and that made her able to suddenly see it; he had a rather particular smile that she had noticed that first evening, which started as a look of extra seriousness and then slowly, almost cautiously, became the wide, delighted grin. Dear God, she was smitten with this man.

That first Sunday had been fine; he'd turned up in his truly glorious 1935 Bentley Saloon, dark green, with swooping running board, huge chrome fog lights and a cluster of smaller ones above the front bumper.

'Oh, my goodness,' said Jillie. 'What a lovely thing. I feel I should be better dressed to deserve it! Look at me, poor Cinderella, I shall go and change.'

'Quite unnecessary,' said Julius gallantly, for he was dressed with storm coat, leather helmet and high boots over his cream trousers. 'You look wonderful.' Adding, 'You always do,' which made her feel as if Cinderella had arrived at the ball. Nevertheless she fetched her own greatcoat, and wound a scarf round her head, leaving the ends trailing down her back. 'Careful,' warned Julius. 'We don't want any Isadora-style accidents today.'

'I will be. But it's not a convertible, is it? Or should I say she? A great ship of a car like this one should surely be a female. Now my parents are out, or my mother would have thanked you for the dressing table.'

'Nothing to do with me. What did she make of it?'

'Oh, she loved it,' said Jillie, 'but it was too small.'

This was quite untrue; her mother hadn't even seen the small dressing table shrouded in its dust sheet in the garage, next to the Mercedes. If she had, she would think Jillie had taken leave of her senses. Which, Jillie thought, half sadly, half amused, was exactly what she had done. She had looked at Julius and shaken his hand, and sense had just gone in one breath, leaving her senseless, stupid with – what? Not love, of course, she had learned her lesson on that one, on love at first sight. That was what she had felt for Ned, love had flown into the room and settled on her and him; and how foolish, when one knew nothing of a person – absolutely nothing of the most important things. She knew nothing of Julius either, and so clearly this was quite, quite different; she just thought he was very – interesting. And attractive. And had dark eyes like Ned's and a sense of style like Ned and that was all it was about really, they were a type, her type. It had been a lovely drive; out onto the heath, towards Highgate, and they had a drink in a pub there, and thus on, further than they had realised for lunch at another pub, so engaged were they with one another, talking and laughing and enjoying the day. It wasn't until it suddenly seemed to be growing dark that Julius said, 'Oh, my goodness, I shall have to switch the lights on, and then I think we should be going back. And we haven't had any lunch. I meant to buy us a splendid feast. I'm so sorry, you must be starving. Next week I'll get Mrs W to make us a picnic, she's awfully good at them.'

'Who is Mrs W?'

'My housekeeper.'

'Ah.'

Clearly, she thought, a man of means: owning a car like this as a plaything was not usual in young men, and there wasn't a great deal of money to be had from antiques, surely.

The next Sunday it was her turn, and she turned the Austin southwards, down to Richmond and the park; where they found the Pen Ponds, twin lakes housing an amazing assortment of birds and he leapt out of the car and said, 'Right, here we are,' and took out the picnic hamper he'd stowed in the boot. Such wonders it contained, almost Dickensian in its bounty, half a ham, a chicken pie, cold pickles, a freshly baked loaf (only just cool), some wonderful cheddar cheese and then for dessert, a peach tart.

'My goodness, we could feed the five thousand with this,' Jillie said.

'I know, Mrs W takes the feeding of me very seriously. Now look, the sun is shining. We could carry the basket right down to the lake, and eat there, I see a seat. Would you risk the cold?'

'I would risk anything,' she almost said, but managed to say just 'it' instead, adding that it would give them an appetite, and they sat in the sunshine, tossing fine scraps at the swans and ducks, and then they went for a stroll and then again, before they knew it, it was growing dusk and they had to drive home. He stayed for supper and met her parents, who were clearly absolutely charmed by him, and when he had gone her mother said, 'Darling, what a delightful young man.'

Jillie knew what she meant, which was 'what a suitable young man'. She explained that actually Julius was engaged to somebody who was writing a book on Sundays and was just a friend, no more, whereupon her mother said, 'Ah. I see. But – darling, don't get hurt again . . .'

'Mummy,' said Jillie, 'there's no question of my getting hurt. He's just a friend, I told you.'

'Who clearly admires you very much,' said Mrs Curtis briskly.

It was on the fourth Sunday that it happened. They had been in the Bentley, taking it for its own outing to Richmond, when Julius, having parked, suddenly said, 'Look, the Sunday after next there's a vintage car rally in the wilds of the Surrey-Hampshire border. Bit like the Old Crocks Run. I've got the Bentley's name down, so to speak – would you like to come with me? I've asked Nell, but she's too busy. I'd love to have some company – would you do me the great kindness of coming with me?'

'Oh!' said Jillie, and it was as if someone had handed her a priceless gift (which in a way they had). 'Oh, Julius, I'd love to.'

'I'll pick you up. It starts quite early – seven in Richmond.'

'Shall I dress up? Mummy's still got the outfit she used to wear for the Old Crocks – I could borrow that. Hat and all.'

'Wonderful.'

Was she mad? She was mad. Quite, quite, and very immorally mad.

She went up to her room and sat down at her dressing table, staring into the mirror: wondering if her wickedness showed on her face. It didn't seem to. Her face didn't seem to have gained any evil lines or twists; extraordinary that it should not have, but then the whole thing was extraordinary, this half-formed, half-acknowledged, totally impossible thing. What was Julius, newly engaged, thinking about? He could submit so cheerfully to banishment from his fiancée every Sunday and not only submit to it, but condone it? And what was she doing, acquiescing to it, allowing herself to enjoy it? When the one thing she knew, knew with certainty, was that she would not be instrumental in breaking up an engagement.

# Chapter 46

Tom looked at Donald Herbert and tried to analyse what he felt. None of it nice: a bit sick, shocked, scared, and yes, disillusioned. That was almost the worst. Actually, he felt most of these things most of the time these days; his life, once so hopeful, so happy, so under control, had become a quagmire, where nothing was as he had thought, nothing as it had seemed.

He had believed so fervently in the beginning, in the early days, in the power of politics to right wrongs, rectify injustices, level inequalities; its practitioners, like-minded, idealistic people, using that power wisely and well. Gradually, he had come to see it was not like that at all, that the very people able to achieve the most for others wanted to achieve things also for themselves and were the best placed to do so: and that power did indeed tend to corrupt, and absolute power corrupted absolutely.

For the gist of what Donald had said was that the prospects of the party winning any new seats in the election, even one as promising as Purbridge, were remote, and that Tom stood almost no chance of getting in.

'The party want you there on the back benches, and the National Agents told me they're proposing to drop you into a dead cert. Trimworth South, up near Leeds, Labour majority last time twenty-two thousand. Chap there desperate to retire and you'd stroll in, your profile being what it is now, and some other young hopeful can take over Purbridge.'

'But—'

'Tom, don't turn this down. You need to get in, or it's God knows how many more years in the wilderness. It means a bit of extra work of course, by-election almost straight away, new people to impress, but we've still got six weeks, it'll be a doddle. No offence, old chap, but they'd vote Labour if the candidate was a donkey.'

'Thanks.'

'Now don't get aerated, Tom. Just take the chance and be grateful. You'll regret it if you don't.'

Tom looked at him; thinking of all the friends he had made in Purbridge – his agent, all the local Labour councillors. All right, not exactly friends perhaps, but warm acquaintances, most of them. He thought how welcoming the people had always been, how he had come to know the head of the boys' grammar school quite well, how he'd promised the staff of the secondary modern that he would work tirelessly to get it improved so that a place there would be an opportunity, not a mark of failure. And Alice, hoping to move there, spend the summers on the golden beach at Sandbanks, how she too had made a few friends, even in the short time she had spent there, including the matron of the local hospital. They trusted him, these people, trusted him to improve things for them, take up their causes, be on their side. Now they were to have some stranger dumped upon them, who they might like less, and find less hard working.

'I'll have to think about it,' he said to Herbert.

'You're allowed twenty-four hours. If you decide against this proposal, you're a bigger fool than I ever expected. You finished with Diana Southcott yet?'

This came out so suddenly, so shockingly, that it was impossible to do anything but answer.

'Yes,' he said. 'And no.'

'What's that supposed to mean, for Christ's sake?'

He had to tell him; he'd find out soon enough. 'She – she said if I stayed away from her, she'd come and see Alice, tell her all about it. And that she'd go to the press.'

'Christ Almighty. That's all we need just now. You're a bloody idiot. You should have listened to me the first time I warned you about her.'

'I know,' he said. 'I'm sorry.'

'So what are you going to do?'

'I don't know. I thought the only thing was to keep seeing her. She – she said once a fortnight would do.'

Donald Herbert laughed loudly.

'She really has got you by the short and curlies, hasn't she? Some woman, that one. Brains *and* beauty. You must have some pretty special qualities, Tom, I'll give you that. Not much use in this situation, though. You'd better agree to my other proposal, or I really will give up on you.'

He walked out of the bar. Tom watched him, feeling, as he did most of the time these days, extremely sick.


It was Sunday again; they seemed to come round with gratifying speed, too fast really, Jillie thought, given their absolutely finite lifespan. They had taken the Morris out in the Sussex direction, along the Hog's Back; had a sandwich at a pub, chatting about the rally the following week as they got into the Morris again.

'What I loved best about the Old Crocks Day when I was a little girl,' said Jillie, switching on her engine, 'were all the people on the way watching by the road, waving and cheering. I used to pretend I was the Queen. Oh, I really am *so* excited!'

She looked at him and smiled, and he smiled his slow, careful smile back; and then, quite without warning, he said, 'You are so very sweet, Jillie, I do love being with you,' and he leaned forward and kissed her. On the mouth. And it started safely and innocently, and then it became dangerous, hugely so. She felt herself responding, fought against it, couldn't, just couldn't, kissed him on and on, hungry, greedy, unable to believe what was happening to her, to both of them. It was like an electric shock, her whole being was jolted by it; and then he drew back and said, 'Oh, dear.'

No more was said by either of them, but she put her foot down and drove home as fast as she could, parked outside the house without even turning the engine off; and waited for him to get out. But he put his hand out onto hers and said, 'That was my fault – incredibly stupid of me. I do hope you'll forgive me.'

She said, her voice cool as she could manage, 'I think it was both our faults, and I actually don't think there's anything to forgive. Goodbye, Julius. I hope you enjoy next Sunday.'

'Thank you,' he said, and there was clearly no question of his arguing about it, for which at least she was grateful.

She went indoors, and ran up to her room, and shut the door and cried. The pain was awful, dreadful, but even in the midst of it, she knew it was not as bad as it might have been, had they progressed further. There was no harm done, Nell had no idea, nobody knew. Really, she was lucky, it had just been fun, lovely charming fun, like Julius himself indeed, and now it was over.

What was the matter with her, she thought, starting on a new hanky, that she couldn't find an ordinary, nice, unattached, attractive man who was attracted to her, a man who was free to love and to love her; did she have an unhappiness wish, as some people had a death wish? Whatever the reason, it was over; she must not, could not even consider, seeing Julius again. He was barred from her: as he should have been from the beginning, and for that she told herself, in a fresh wave of misery, drenching the clean handkerchief, she had only herself to blame.

She managed to arrange to be on duty the next Sunday, and was lucky to find herself extremely busy: three C-sections, a breech birth, and a hysterical midwife who had missed a clear case of pre-eclampsia, which Jillie spotted just in time. When she got home that night, weeping with exhaustion rather than sadness, her mother, having comforted her with the unbeatable combination of nursery food (fish pie) and a couple of glasses of rather grown-up wine, said, 'Oh, your friend Julius Noble telephoned you. He asked if you could ring him back. At home.'

She nodded and said all she wanted to do was have a bath and she would ring him next day; which, exerting enormous self-control, she did.

'Hello.'

'Hello, Jillie.'

'How was yesterday?'

396

'I didn't go.'

'Oh, I'm sorry.'

'Yes, me too. Look, Jillie – Jillie, I wonder – could you regard what happened as a bit of foolishness? We're such good friends, and we do enjoy our Sundays – and it's not as if we've fallen in love or anything. And I thought – well, I would so like us to stay friends. Go for the odd drive. It seems silly to throw all that pleasure away.'

Either he was extremely stupid, Jillie thought, or he was a fantasist. Or he really couldn't face life without her. Whatever the reason, she knew what she must do.

'I mean – it won't happen again,' he said. 'The – the foolishness, I mean. So what do you think?'

'I think,' she said, trying to keep her voice calm, 'that's not a good idea. I really do. I've enjoyed our Sundays too, but – no, Julius. Goodbye.'

And she put the phone down. It had been quite horribly tempting. A reprieve at least from pain and loneliness and disappointment: but only a reprieve.

For a little while, she felt a glow of virtue and calm from knowing she had done the right thing. It didn't last for very long.


'Mr Welles! Glad I caught you. Wonder if you could spare me a minute of your very valuable time.'

It was the chairman of the board of governors of St Luke's, Sir Neil Lawson, a gentle-voiced tyrant and professor of cardiology; it was said that he was the only living being who could make Matron feel nervous. Ned was certainly no exception.

'Yes, of course, Sir Neil. Now?'

'No time like the present. My office, five minutes?'

'I'll be there.'

Sir Neil's office was large, overlooking the gardens of the hospital; every inch of wall space was taken up by framed certificates, telling of triumphs in examinations, honorary degrees of universities, international awards, and photographs of himself at what were clearly important ceremonies, or shaking hands with distinguished people from the Duke of Edinburgh downwards.

He was a tall, thin man with a shock of white hair and steely grey eyes, and wore, no matter what the season, a black worsted three-piece suit with a white shirt and a bow tie in a rather bilious green with white spots.

Ned knocked on the door, and on the imperious command of 'Come' went in. He knew at once he was for it; Sir Neil had his back to him, studying the gardens, and did not turn round for a full minute. When he did so, he greeted Ned with a charming smile.

'Mr Welles, do please sit down.'

Ned sat on the chair on the other side of the desk, and waited.

It didn't take long to begin.

'Mr Welles, I understand you are doing the most splendid work in paediatrics; particularly in the area of premature infants and their incompetent lungs. We are fortunate to have you with us.'

Ned waited. This in no way accounted for the general aura of displeasure, conveyed by Sir Neil's icy stare that had immediately followed the charming smile. He was right.

'However,' said Sir Neil, 'I have received some – complaints would be too strong a word – criticism, about one aspect of your wards and your running of them.'

'Really?' said Ned.

'Yes. I speak of what appears to be almost a fixation about the children in those wards and their mothers. You will know, I imagine, to what I refer?'

'Yes, indeed,' said Ned. 'And if it appears a fixation, then that only reflects the depth of my concern.'

'Which is?'

'That the children are not just unhappy, but disturbed by the disappearance of their mothers for several days and at worst, weeks, at a time.'

'Yet they respond to your treatment or surgery, they recover, they are reunited with their mothers and they go home healed.'

'Apparently healed,' said Ned. 'Physically, yes, but I have come to believe, talking to the mothers when they bring their children for post-operative checks, that the trauma to the children of the separation is considerable. They have nightmares, they are anxious, clinging, they cry easily.'

'Oh, please. All children cry.'

'Not to the extent some of these children do.'

'Could it be that they are the more difficult, over-sensitive children, hospitalised or not?'

'It could,' said Ned. 'But I do not believe so. When I do my night rounds, I invariably find several of the children weeping silently, in a state of what I can only describe as despair. I try to comfort them, to reassure them, but—'

'Yes, and it is this that various sisters have complained about.'

'Complained? They haven't done so to me.'

'Well, that would be difficult for them, wouldn't it? Your being their consultant. But I understand that other children wake, there is a general air of confusion, disarray, in the wards – and this isn't a good thing in a hospital. Calm and quiet is what we look for in all our wards, Mr Welles. But particularly in the paediatric ones. Calm and quiet heal as much as good medicine and good nursing do.'

'Forgive me, Sir Neil, but I would put it to you that the calm and quiet we require of these children is frequently the calm and quiet of despair, not order.'

'And I would put it to you, Mr Welles, that in the opinion of myself and several of my colleagues you are wrong, that you disrupt and disturb the children in your reforming zeal.'

Ned was silent; then Sir Neil said, 'I hear that you have some idea that if the mothers stayed with the children all day, then the children would be happier.'

'Yes, and recover faster, sleep better –'

'And do you not think the mild chaos you are causing at night would be hugely multiplied by day, wards full of ignorant mothers, getting in the way of the nurses?'

'With respect, Sir Neil, I think the mothers could be a great help with washing, feeding, playing with their children, reading to them –'

'Mr Welles,' said Sir Neil, his voice heavy with distaste, 'we are trying to run a hospital here, not some kind of children's party. Now can we have no more of this, please.'

'So you won't even consider my ideas?' said Ned. This was a mistake.

'No, I won't. And I don't want to hear them mentioned to anyone. Next thing we know, the mothers will be demanding access to their children whenever they fancy and I will not have it. Is that quite clear?'

'Yes,' said Ned, careful with his words as always. 'Quite clear. Thank you.'

'Josh? Tom Knelston.'

Josh felt a rush of panic. He had tried very hard to forget the image of Tom on Diana's doorstep, being greeted by what could only be described as an inviting kiss – and failed.

He had been shocked: profoundly, morally shocked. He was aware that this was scarcely a suitable emotion for a journalist to experience. But while Tom and he might not have been the close friends people assumed, given that he had been best man at his wedding, they were friends; and until then he had liked him as a man, and admired him as a politician in waiting. Far closer, though, was the other link: that his cousin Jillie was Alice Knelston's best friend. Jillie adored Tom, she thought he was wonderful.

'Yes?' he said now, hearing his own voice cooler than usual.

'This a bad time? If so, maybe we could meet. I need your advice – and it might even be a story for you.'

It couldn't be, could it? Josh wondered. He couldn't actually be calling him to talk to him about his infidelity. He decided he needed time to think and said, 'Yes. Bit busy right now. Could we talk tomorrow after work? I presume it's not desperately urgent.'

It could be, he supposed; Alice might have found out about Diana, delivered an ultimatum, and demanded an answer by tomorrow. Well, if that was the case, tough.

'No, no, not terribly, tomorrow evening will do. I'll warn Alice. She gets pretty sick of me being out every other night.'

I expect she does, Josh thought; poor, sweet, weary Alice. The last person to deserve such treatment. 'We can make it quite early,' he said, more from a wish to save Alice than anything else. 'I have to be back for a conference at six, could have a quick drink somewhere near here at five.'

'Cheshire Cheese?'

'Fine. See you then. Please give my love to Alice,' Josh added. The poor girl needed all the support and affection available to her.

'I will. She's pretty fed up, little bugger's really huge now. Thanks, Josh.'

Bastard, thought Josh. Absolute two-faced bastard.

Tom had been speaking the truth about Diana. He had told her that he didn't want to see her any more, it had been wonderful while it had lasted, that he would miss her of course, but that Alice was growing suspicious; she was about to have a baby and he owed it to her to try to be a good husband and father.

'Besides, once this one is born, I'll be even more needed at home. I won't be able to spend hours out of the house every other night.'

'Darling! Would that it were every other night.'

He was silent.

'Well,' she said. 'This is a bit of a bombshell. I'm sorry, Tom. Friend Tom. Can we still be friends?'

'No,' he said. 'No, I don't think that's a good idea. It wouldn't work.'

'Why not?'

'Because if I was with you I'd have to go to bed with you.'

'Well, I suppose that's something. To soothe my ruffled ego.' Silence. Then, 'And – I must admit, my feelings too. There must be something wrong with me. First my husband, now my lover, both want to get rid of me.'

'There's nothing wrong with you, Diana. You're a very beautiful, very clever woman.'

'Not clever or beautiful enough, it seems. Well, Tom, thank you for being honest with me. I appreciate it. And it has been fun. Such fun, indeed, I think we should have just one last glimpse of it, before you go.'

'Diana, no!'

'But why not? What harm can it do? You're here, you've made your getaway for the evening. You'll be out for an extra hour or so; what's that, set against this blameless future you envisage?'

'Diana, I'm sorry but no. It's over. It would be – well, a travesty, to – to –'

'What? Oh, Tom, come on. For old times' sake. No? All right. Just kiss me goodbye. Please. Dear Friend Tom –'

And at that he was lost. The goodbye kiss went on and on, Diana collapsing under him, laughing, just as she had that first night, wanting him as she had that first night – she became irresistible again.

'Well,' she said, sprawled naked on the sofa, watching him dressing, unable to meet her eyes, his face a study in guilt and remorse. 'You know what, Tom? I don't fancy life without that occasionally.'

'Diana, I said—'

'Oh, I know what you said. It made me very sad. So *au revoir*, then, I think, dear Friend Tom,' she said. 'Not goodbye.'

'Diana—'

'No, I really don't want to lose you now. I decided that about – what? – twenty minutes ago. Just as I – well, you know what I mean. Anyway, I want you to continue your visits. I need them, you know. I spend many, many evenings alone here. You have your Alice – who do I have? Occasionally Jamie, sometimes a few friends, but most often just me. So I need you, Friend Tom, I really do, and I don't want to do without you. So please continue to come and call—'

He interrupted her. 'Diana, that's impossible, I told you, very sadly for me at any rate, it's—'

'If you don't come,' she said, her voice quite different suddenly, 'if you insist on saying it's over, then I'm afraid I shall have to visit Alice and explain where you've really been all those evenings. I'd love to meet the children, I do really like children, as you know, and I'm also quite curious to meet Alice.'

Tom sat down abruptly on a small gilt chair that stood next to the drawing-room door; it creaked ominously. Rather like his life, he thought. His legs had become shaky and jelly-like, an unpleasant accompaniment to the nausea rising in him.

Diana was pulling on the silk robe she had been wearing for his arrival; he looked at her and she smiled brightly, as if she had just offered him a cup of coffee.

'Or – or should I say, I could go to the press. That would never do so near the election, would it? When you'll need all the good write-ups you can get. So, what with one thing and another, Friend Tom, I think you'd be much better preserving the status quo, don't you? Shall we say two weeks from now? For your next visit? Now, will you excuse me, darling, I've got to change – I'm having dinner with a girlfriend.'

She walked over to him, kissed him briefly on the lips, and then disappeared up the stairs. Tom somehow dragged himself onto his feet, let himself out of the house, and stumbled down the mews.

# Chapter 47

Diana actually had no intention whatever of going either to Alice or the press. She simply wanted to make Tom sweat a bit. She had been hurt by his rejection, more than she would have expected. She loved him in a way; felt she had loved him for years. Their relationship had always been oddly close, from the first time she had properly talked to him, in her parents' house when he had fallen in the snow, right until she had finally achieved what felt like a lifelong ambition and got him into bed.

Although – she was sure no one would believe her – she did value him above all as a friend; someone to talk to about her life and its problems, to laugh with, to have a drink with. He fascinated her, with his rise from poor village boy, his unshakeable socialist principles, his determination to improve people's lives, his devotion to what he seemed to regard as an almost sacred cause, that of the National Health Service.

But then she had also, from that very first exchange between them when he was standing half-naked in a ditch, fancied him sexually; he was so extraordinarily good-looking, with his dark red-gold hair and green eyes and his countryman's physique, tall and very strong. There was the element of sadness about him now too: the loss of the wife he had adored, the baby he would have adored, was the stuff almost of Greek tragedy. He was also extremely sexy and her hours in bed with him were an ongoing surprise and delight. Now it was to end, and rather like her early passion for Ned, her main emotion was humiliation.

She was clearly, she thought, drinking glass after glass of wine that night, smoking cigarette after cigarette, doomed to unhappiness in her love life. Where for her was the calm, happy marriage her best friend Wendelien enjoyed with her Ian; or the sparky, sexy partnership of her brother Michael and his Betsey; even the peaceful affection of her own parents, about to celebrate their fortieth wedding anniversary? What was the matter with her, that she chose so disastrously wrongly for herself: first Ned, then Johnathan, sundry lovers who took their pleasure from her and then departed again – most notably Freddie Bateman? And now, Tom Knelston, so firmly married, although she was fairly sure Alice was no real replacement in his heart for Laura. Why couldn't she find someone who was suitable, for God's sake, sexy, sophisticated, available – a nice divorcé would do – and loving? It was the loving she seemed to fail with every time.

She had worked out a little cat-and-mouse game she was going to play with Tom. If he turned up within the two weeks she had specified she would give him a kiss, pat him on the head – notionally – and send him on his way. If he didn't, she would make a phone call or two to his office, perhaps send a note: and see what happened next.

In April, she had a wonderful trip planned, shooting two features with Freddie Bateman in the States; one, seriously glamorous, in New York, and then the second one, which she was much more excited about, on the wild windswept beaches of Massachusetts, places which had become so famous it made her spine tingle just to think about them – Martha's Vineyard, Nantucket and Cape Cod, home to the famous Kennedy clan.

She and Freddie were now growing famous for their ingenuity; the fur shots at Smithfield had been really groundbreaking, and Blanche Ellis Brown, in particular, who had first put them to work together (and never failed to claim credit for doing so), had come to rely on them to find a story where she could not. So it was with the New York shoot; she had invited them to lunch in her office that very day, shown them a few of the clothes, and said of course she did have one idea, but how about them? It was Freddie who came up with the 'Day in the Life of New York'. Twenty-four pictures shot on the hour, round the clock. It was a well-known fact that New York never slept. 'We'd have everything from one of those crazy downtown diners, with Diana chatting up some truck drivers, to dancing at some fantastic nightclub. That way we'd get in every iconic New York landmark, and a huge range of clothes. What do you think?'

Diana clapped, leaned towards him and kissed his cheek. She rather enjoyed encouraging the fiction that they were still lovers.

'Brilliant!' said Blanche. 'Absolutely brilliant.'

'So – what was your idea?' Freddie asked her.

'Oh – not even worth discussing,' she said quickly.

'I knew she didn't have one,' said Freddie to Diana later. They were drinking cocktails in the American Bar at the Connaught, where he was inevitably staying.

'You are naughty.'

'I know. I enjoy it. Now, we must make sure they book us into the Carlyle in New York. Terribly smart, darling, *the* place right now. Wonderful jazz in the café; we could maybe use it for one of the shots, it's all marvellously deco . . .'

'I can't wait,' said Diana. It sounded exactly what she needed just now. And suddenly, Freddie looked rather attractive again.

She was just sipping thoughtfully at her third Martini (and finding him more attractive still) when Donald Herbert's flamboyant figure loomed over her.

'Miss Southcott. How lovely to see you. How are you?'

'Now you know you should call me Diana,' she said, reaching up and offering him her hand. 'I'm very well, thank you. This is Freddie Bateman, a friend from the States. He's a very famous and wonderful photographer. Freddie, Donald Herbert, well-known politician.'

'Hardly a politician,' said Herbert. 'I just paddle about in the shallows.'

'That makes it sound so cosy,' said Diana. 'I'd ask you to join us but we're about to leave.'

'I wouldn't think of intruding on you,' said Herbert, 'and in any case, I'm meeting someone myself.'

'Not our mutual friend?'

'No, no. But speaking of our mutual friend, Diana, I believe you and he had some unfinished business the other evening.'

'It might not be,' said Diana coolly. 'Unfinished, I mean.'

'I do hope it can be,' said Donald Herbert. 'It would be most unfortunate if his career was to come into difficulties now. I'm sure you wouldn't want that either.'

'I'm afraid I have no interest whatsoever in his career,' said Diana. 'Whether it was in difficulties or not.'

'I see. Well – just thought I'd mention it. This could be his big moment.'

'How exciting for him. Well, Freddie and I have work to do. Please excuse us, Mr Herbert.'

'What was all that about?' said Freddie curiously. 'Not your usual type at all, darling.'

'What a ghastly thought. If he was my usual type, I mean. And you really don't want to know what it was about: a pathetic little tale. Come on, Freddie, drink up, and I'll take you out to dinner. How about the Berkeley?'

She suddenly felt very annoyed with Tom. Running to his boss, or whatever Herbert was, blubbing about her threats, and obviously begging him to help: it was pretty pathetic, really. Clearly, she came a very poor second to his career; and that was not something she was used to. If Herbert thought a word from him could obtain her silence and her sympathy, he had another think coming. There might yet be some fun to be had from the situation.

# Chapter 48

'They said in your office that you were just popping out for half an hour. And they promised to give you the message.'

'What message?'

'Oh, nothing important,' said Jillie, her voice curdled with sarcasm. She was standing on Tom's doorstep. 'Just that Alice had gone into labour.'

'Oh, my God,' said Tom. 'Where?'

'She's in hospital. And she's had the baby. It was terribly quick, touch and go she might have had it here. It's a boy,' she added. 'If you're interested.'

'Of course I'm interested, for God's sake,' said Tom, hardly taking in the good news, so heavy were her reproaches, so great his guilt. 'Oh, God, this is awful. Jillie, I'm so sorry.'

'Apologise to her, not me. Luckily I had the day off and came whizzing over. She was really frightened, Tom.'

'Why didn't she call an ambulance?'

'Small matter of the other children. She could hardly take them with her.'

'Yes, well, her mother should have been here,' said Tom. 'She was coming for the week.'

'Maybe, but the baby wasn't to know that. It decided to come early. Determined little creatures, babies. And the next-door neighbours both out, and most of her friends round here not on the telephone. Tom, you must have realised it could happen any minute. You should have kept properly in touch. Where were you, for God's sake? It's hours since we first phoned your office.'

'Oh, it was political stuff,' said Tom. 'Not always easy to get away. Look, Jillie, can I come in?' For in her rage she was still occupying the whole of the doorway. 'I'd like to phone the hospital.'

'Yes, I expect you would,' said Jillie, turning and walking into the house, Tom behind her.

'And go and see her. If it's allowed this late. If I can, would you – that is, can you –'

'Look after the children? Yes, of course. For Alice's sake, rather than yours. God, Tom, I just cannot get over your behaviour. It honestly makes me wonder if you weren't engaged on something rather more personal than political business.'

'I don't know what you mean,' said Tom. He turned away from her to the telephone.

'I think you do know what I mean,' said Jillie, but he could tell it was a wild bluff, just from her expression.

'Well, you're –' he started and with a merciful intervention from fate he got through to the hospital, and then to the ward.

'Ah, Mr Knelston. Well, your little one's going to spend his life in a hurry and no mistake. All's well though, a big boy, eight and a half pounds. He spent the first hour telling us he didn't like it here, cried non-stop, but he's quiet now.'

'And – how is my wife?'

'She's well. Very well under the circumstances. Glad it's over . . .'

'Could I – could I come and see her?'

'You most certainly may *not*,' said the nurse. 'Visiting hours end at seven, as you should know.'

'Yes, but if I'd been in the hospital when she had the baby, I'd still be there now,' said Tom, in a desperate attempt to call logic into play.

'Ah, but you weren't,' said the nurse. 'Mrs Knelston was hoping until the very last minute for a message, but . . .' Her silence was a reproach, stronger than any words.

'Well, could I speak to her? On the phone?'

'Now how do you think I'm going to manage that? Cut the phone free of its wires or something? So you'll just have to wait until tomorrow. Afternoon visiting, three to four.'

'Oh, yes, I see,' said Tom miserably. 'It seems a bit hard.'

'Yes, well, it was quite hard for Mrs Knelston to go through labour not knowing where you were.'

'It seems a terribly long time for me to wait.'

'I daresay you'll get over it,' said the nurse. 'But I can give her a message from you, if you like.'

'Oh – yes, that would be very kind. Could you give her my love and say how sorry I am?'

'I will. And that you'll be in tomorrow at three?'

'Yes, please.'

Tom put the phone down and turned to Jillie.

'No chance of visiting her, as you probably gathered. Or even speaking to her.'

She was looking almost sympathetic.

'That's hospitals for you. I should know.'

Tom thought briefly and treacherously of what a private hospital would offer: a private room, a phone, probably husbands allowed to visit any time. Well, if he got in next time he'd argue for the right of any husband to be with his wife, any time, including while she was in labour, the early stages anyway.

He sat down; Jillie poured him a cup of tea.

'If I had my way,' she said, her hostility apparently forgotten in the face of his obvious distress, 'husbands could be with their wives in labour. If they wanted to be, of course. And for the first twenty-four hours after the birth, he could visit any time at all.'

'I was just thinking that very thing,' said Tom, sipping gratefully at the tea.

'Perhaps you should talk to Josh about it.'

'Josh? He's a political writer, surely,' said Tom, a vivid re-enaction of his discussion with Josh two hours earlier sweeping into view. 'He wouldn't be interested in maternity wards.'

'He might. His paper's always looking for good causes. And if you were an MP, it would become quite political. Worth a try.'

'It's certainly an idea,' said Tom. 'Although that's looking less and less likely, I'm afraid.'

'What, you becoming an MP? I thought it was more or less a dead cert.'

'Not any more.'

'Why not? What's happened?'

'Oh – complicated. You don't want to hear about it now.'

'I might. I've got nothing else to do this evening.'

But at that moment Lucy woke up from a bad dream, screaming, and just as she was settled Kit woke up and was not to be silenced except by the promise of a story; Jillie, having helped with Lucy, had no stomach for reading and left.

It was going to be great fun having a third child to add to what increasingly resembled a mob, Tom thought; none of them would ever get any sleep at all.

Alice had been, as always, transformed by the actual birth of her baby. Tom arrived next afternoon, to find her not even in bed, but sitting in the chair next to it, rosy, smiling, a silent, sleeping infant in her arms.

'Hello,' she said to Tom and raised her face to be kissed.

'Hello, Alice. How are you?'

'I'm absolutely fine, thank you.'

'I am so sorry about yesterday.'

'What, your going AWOL? Oh, it's all right. Really. I mean, it was a bit alarming at one stage, but Jillie kept me calm, and called the ambulance and honestly, by the time I got here, everything was happening so fast, I forgot about you. Well, you know . . .'

'Jillie hauled me very thoroughly over the coals. She was furious and so she should have been.'

'Well, maybe. But today – who cares? I just assumed it was political stuff.'

She did not mention – and indeed they were half forgotten, lost in her new happiness – her increasing doubts about Tom's fidelity, as every attempt to find him was frustrated, every plea for a return phone call fruitless, and how even the pain of childbirth faded in comparison with the savage rage consuming her. But Jillie had sent a message to say that Josh had confirmed that he and Tom had been together for hours in The Cheshire Cheese, discussing election matters, and that then Tom had said he simply must get home.

'Alice, you're a saint.'

'Not really,' she said and smiled at him again. 'Make the most of it, it won't last. Best not let my father hear about it, though. Anyway, this is your new son. Quite a whopper.'

Tom looked at the baby: sleeping determinedly as only newborn babies can, a mass of dark hair on his small head, the tiny snub-nosed face utterly peaceful. Once he opened his eyes, deep dark blue, and then closed them again and drifted off once more.

'He's very sweet,' said Tom, smiling. 'Can I?'

'Yes, course. Here –' She passed the baby over, and Tom sat cradling him, struck as always by the extraordinary yet ordinary miracle that saw a moment of lovemaking become a tiny being just nine months later, a being that would grow, that would first smile at him, and then laugh, and then learn to do amazing things, like walking and talking, and have tantrums, and demand stories and join his brother and sister as the centre of his parents' world.

'He's very sweet,' he said again, finding (as always) his voice oddly choked, his eyes filled with tears.

'Isn't he? It's amazing. And it's true what they say, they do bring their own love with them; I was changing Lucy's nappy yesterday and she was giggling, you know how she does, and I thought to myself how I could never love anyone as much as I loved her and Kit, and then this little one arrived and I looked at him, as they put him in my arms, and I just felt this great wash of love. Tom, can we call him Charlie?'

'Any particular reason?'

'Only the same as usual – I really like it, and it seems to suit him.'

'Charlie it is,' said Tom, thinking the last thing he could do after his appalling behaviour was deny Alice her choice of name. 'He's a fine chap and you're a clever girl, and I don't deserve you.'

'Probably not,' said Alice, reaching up to kiss him.

'Now, I need to talk to you about something very important.'

'So soon?' she said. 'Can't I have just one day of thinking about nothing but my baby and you do the same, like everyone else in the ward?'

'Sorry, but no, you can't,' said Tom, and outlined his dilemma. Did he stay as the constituency's candidate for Purbridge, and probably not get in, or did he go to a new one and almost certainly get in? It would affect her greatly, and he wanted her to be absolutely behind him.

'Well,' said Alice with only the briefest hesitation, 'it seems very straightforward to me. Of course you should stay with Purbridge. You've worked so hard and made so much progress there, so many friends and acquaintances, it just seems such a slap in the face for them if you say, "Sorry, chaps, I'm off somewhere else now, so I can be sure of getting in." Anyway, miracles do happen – you might get in there. And besides, we're going to move there, aren't we? To lovely Sandbanks, without which we wouldn't have Lucy. Oh, dear. Now I'm crying. Sorry, hormones I suppose.'

Tom pulled a distinctly grubby handkerchief out of his pocket and tenderly wiped her face.

'I feel exactly the same. I'm so glad you agree. But Donald says I'd be a fool to turn this new constituency down.'

'If you ask me,' said Alice briskly, 'Donald can be a bit of a fool himself at times. Why are you smiling at me?'

'Because I've got the old Alice back. The Alice I love.'

'Where is this other place? Heart of industrial Birmingham, did you say?' At which point Charlie suddenly started to cry very loudly.

'There you are,' said Alice. 'Charlie doesn't like the sound of it either. Best stay with Purbridge, Tom. Or we'll all be sorry . . .'

Donald was furious; even more so than Tom expected.

'You won't get any gratitude from the people of Purbridge, if that's what you're thinking. You're an idiot, Tom, and I hope you realise it.'

'I don't think so,' said Tom. 'Politics are about principles, it seems to me. I've always felt that and I always will.'

'Oh, really? Pity you didn't stick to them when it came to personal matters. Hanging round Diana Southcott as if she was a bitch on heat. I saw her the other night, by the way. She said she had no interest in your career when I said it would be ruined if she caused a scandal. More or less said she was going to carry out her threat.'

Tom's stomach felt as if it had dropped several yards through the floor. 'God, Donald, the last way to get Diana on our side is to go crawling to her. She totally despises that sort of thing.'

'I didn't go crawling to her. Just presented a straight picture. Tom, I've been around a lot longer than you have. I know a woman on the make when I see one. She'll be wanting something soon, to keep her quiet, you mark my words. And it won't be your over-active dick.'

Tom sat looking at him very steadily for about thirty seconds. Then he stood, picked up his coat and hat, and walked out of the pub without saying another word.

But he felt badly shaken and had to walk for at least half an hour to calm himself down, before going home.

Home was not quite what he had hoped it would be once Alice was back to her old self. Charlie Knelston, once woken from his new-baby trance, proved an awkward, irritable, restless child, with a digestion that troubled not only him but everyone else in the household. Wails of pain filled the house from as early as three a.m. to as late as midnight; the only things that pacified him were his mother's breasts, and Alice sometimes felt she had no life, no calling other than proffering the poor weary things, once so pretty and purveyors of such pleasure, into Charlie's greedy, frantic little mouth.

The only other thing that rendered him silent, especially at night, was being pushed round the streets in his pram. Alice was so tired she had no idea what day it was, what meal she was cooking, or even what time. She feared she had become a bad mother to the other children, having very little time for them, and snapping at them endlessly because she was so tired. Once or twice she slapped Kit, who was being extremely naughty, taking advantage of the general chaos; once Tom was witness to this; he was shocked and said so.

'I cannot believe you did that. You know we agreed we would never hit our children. It's a brutal thing to do, taking advantage of our superior size and power over them. You mustn't ever do it again.'

'I know that was wrong of me,' she said, 'and I'm sorry. But I'm so tired! Kit is being extremely naughty and just you try being endlessly patient all day, every day. You might even do a bit of slapping yourself. I wish you were at home more, Tom, it would be such a help.'

Remorse struck Tom. 'Alice, I'm truly sorry, I can't. You know I'm fighting an election. Every minute counts. I'll make it up to you when it's over, I swear to you.'

He desperately hoped these were not empty words. As well as worrying about the election, he was on constant tenterhooks, afraid that Diana would suddenly make her threats reality. He never turned the corner of the road without a stab of terror that her car would be there, outside the house: and if it was not, never opened the front door without fearing a furious Alice recounting how Diana had visited her that day. If Diana's revenge was to make him suffer, she was certainly succeeding.

He had told Josh what his decision was about Purbridge: Josh was impressed, while clearly sharing Donald's view that, short term, it was not going to do him any good. He said that nearer the time he would put an item into the diary section of the paper which should help Tom, establishing him as a person of principle and loyalty. Not that anybody knew when the time would be: Eden hadn't even called the election yet, although Churchill had officially resigned. It all added to his general tension.

Of the other half of their conversation he made no mention.

It was now three weeks since he had told Diana he couldn't see her any longer – and despite her threats he missed her: not just the quiet, civilised evenings in the pretty house, or even the brilliant sparky sex, but Diana herself. He tried very hard to analyse his feelings for her. Clearly he wasn't in love with her – he loved Alice, however much his behaviour might belie it and he certainly didn't allow himself any foolish fantasies about being with Diana all the time. But she made him laugh and seemed genuinely interested in his political career, while disagreeing violently with the shade of his politics. She was truly that rare thing, a good friend: the sex had been a sort of side dish, dipped into to better savour the main ingredients – although clearly it would be difficult explaining that to Alice, let alone the press.

There was nothing he could do, plainly; except perhaps hope – and of course pray. But as he doubted the existence of the Almighty – he couldn't help feeling that even if He did exist, He was unlikely to help him conceal several acts of adultery from his wife – he did nothing.

# Chapter 49

Blanche's voice down the phone was odd. A touch of bravado, a bit of faltering, an unmistakable choke as she finished bringing the shocking news.

She had been fired. Along with the editor. The editor! When did they get fired? And the art director, the whole creative team, in fact.

'But – who's fired you?'

'Mr Big –' her name for the American proprietor, a sweet, benevolent man, who had inherited the whole *Style* stable from his own father – 'Mr Big has died.'

'Oh, no!'

'Yes, and the dreaded Master Big has taken over.' Master Big was the son and heir, obnoxiously brash, entirely lacking in his father's courtesy and charm. 'With ideas about relaunching, new editors – including, guess what, his girlfriend – new titles. He's decided he doesn't like English *Style*, he wants a whole new look and relaunch.' Her voice broke.

'Oh, Blanche, I'm so shocked.' Diana had a lump in her throat herself. *Style* had made her, and Blanche was truly talented, a visionary when it came to fashion. She had had countless offers from other magazines and even a couple of newspapers, but she always turned them down, loyal to *Style* which she said was her natural habitat.

'Anyway,' she said now, her voice and emotions clearly under control. 'I'm afraid it's from today –'

'What? Can they do that?'

'Well, yes, they're paying me for my notice period. Some Yank broad is on the plane even as we speak, taking up residence from Monday morning, and I've been told to cancel any features from June onwards. Which, since we put your shoot back two weeks, more's the terrible pity, means goodbye to your American dream.'

'Shit,' said Diana. 'Have you told Freddie?'

'I was rather hoping you would. I can't take many more of these phone calls, and there are a few sessions booked even sooner than yours. So, if you wouldn't mind terribly, I'd be so grateful . . .'

'Of course,' said Diana. 'And Blanche, let's meet next week for a drink.'

'Lovely. Call me in a few days when I'm a bit less frantic. Lot to do, not least clearing my desk.'

Blanche's desk was famous for its clutter, every inch of surface taken up with sheets of photographers' contacts, pages ripped from other magazines, scribbled reminder notes to herself, invitations and letters waiting to be answered. Diana could never believe the order Blanche could pull from this chaos. 'Well,' she said feebly now, 'if there's anything I can do –'

'Sweet of you, darling, but I don't think so; see you next week.'

Freddie was outraged: 'Poor darling Blanche. Look, I'll be over next week, I'm shooting something for *Flair*, and I've been summoned to *Vogue* as well. I'll see what I can do. You'll be around, I presume?'

'Yes, where else might I be?' said Diana. She suddenly felt very depressed.

She had been looking forward to this trip so much; it was the only really exciting thing on her horizon at the moment. The only thing altogether, she realised. Her social diary was not as full as she would have liked, she had no other bookings for any other magazines; her birthday was coming up and she supposed she could give a party, but it was her thirty-fifth, and would rather remind people, especially in the fashion business, that she was no longer young. OK. So Barbara Goalen was apparently immortal, and so was Fiona Campell-Walter, but they were goddesses, and she belonged to a more mortal band.

Once forty she'd be done for, apart from the odd booking if she was lucky for 'Mrs Exeter', the elegant, sophisticated *Vogue* creation, Exeter being a synonym for 'older'.

She suddenly thought about Jamie; maybe she could see him for half-term week. He was increasingly good company, and they had had a very good time in London seeing shows and films and were working their way through the sights. He was getting very tall and at the age of eight could easily be taken for ten. He was still a charming child, but there was no denying he was very spoilt; he only had to mention that he wanted something to his father than it arrived: he had a bigger horse, one of the new transistor radios, an electric gramophone, and Johnathan had set up a complete train layout for him all round one of the attic rooms.

'You want to be a little bit careful, darling,' Caroline said to Diana when she told her mother she thought they might look out for a new pony for Jamie for the autumn hunting season. 'He's well aware that you and Johnathan will do anything for him, just to keep him on your side, and he's beginning to use that. It won't really do any harm to say no to him once in a while.'

'Maybe not, but I'm not going to risk it,' said Diana coolly. 'I think I know my own child well enough to make judgements about how I bring him up.'

Caroline wasn't quite brave enough to say that having Jamie a maximum of twelve weeks a year was hardly bringing him up.

Diana telephoned Johnathan.

'Hello,' she said.

'Oh, hello.' His voice was very cold.

'How are you?'

'Pretty well, thanks.'

'And your parents?'

'Mother's fine. Father needs round-the-clock care now.'

'I'm sorry.'

He was silent.

'Well, I'll be brief. I wondered if I could have Jamie to stay for half term, rather than him coming up to you. There's a new production of

*Over the Rainbow*, which I wanted him to see, and some lovely children's concerts at the Festival Hall.'

'I'm afraid that's out of the question.'

'Why?'

'Catherine and I are getting married that week.'

'Goodness. Well – congratulations.'

'Thank you. I'm surprised you haven't seen the announcement or Jamie didn't mention it.'

'No, he said nothing. Obviously he didn't think it was very important,' she added, her voice edged with malice.

'I doubt it. He's very excited about it and playing a big part in the ceremony.'

'How nice. Well, it's been a long time coming, we've been divorced for quite some time.'

'Yes, indeed. But Catherine's mother's been very ill, and we wanted to wait until that was resolved. Fortunately she's much better. And now we want to be married as soon as possible, as Catherine desperately wants to have children.'

'How delightful. Well, congratulations, Johnathan. I hope it all goes very well.'

'Thank you. And I'm sorry I can't oblige over Jamie.'

'Oh, it doesn't matter.'

But it did.

She went for a walk, made for the Bayswater Road, and down to Selfridges. She didn't quite have the heart for buying clothes, but she needed some cosmetics, and she could have lunch there. That should cheer her up. She bought a copy of the *Daily Mail* to read over lunch and then, having purchased rather more Coty powder, Elizabeth Arden lipsticks and Revlon eyeliner than she would get through in a year, settled down to a chicken salad, and opened the paper.

It was predictably full of election news; Mr Eden was putting into his busy schedule three live television broadcasts, where members of the press would question him. It was, the *Daily Mail* informed her, the first election to be fought on television. She studied the picture of Eden; he was an extraordinarily good-looking man. He left poor

Attlee looking like an elderly hobgoblin. She wondered idly if Josh would be one of the press; then decided he was clearly too junior. But his boss, Clive Bedford, might. She would watch the programme, see what he was like. It was a good paper, the *Daily News*; she liked it. It treated you as if you were intelligent. The leader they had run about homosexuals had been very good; Josh said they were considering turning it into a campaign now. That reminded her of Ned; he was a good dinner companion, she would phone him and see if he was free tonight. That would be fun. Better than an election broadcast.

There was a paper boy outside Selfridges; on an impulse, to see if Josh had any stories in it, she bought a copy of the *Daily News* and caught a taxi home to Knightsbridge.

Ned's secretary at his private rooms said she wasn't expecting him back that day as he was operating. She would leave a message for him to ring Diana back. 'But he's got a very long list, Miss Southcott, I doubt if he'll be able to ring you before eight.'

Diana sighed. This wasn't her day. She made herself a cup of coffee, and leafed through the *Daily News*; more of the election. She was about to close it when an item intruded on her consciousness.

*LABOUR CANDIDATE RESISTS PRESSURE TO SWITCH CONSTITUENCIES, page 5.*

Very slowly, very carefully, as if it was some priceless silk blouse she was dealing with, Diana opened the paper at page 5. There, occupying almost a quarter of the page, was the story, byline Josh Curtis.

*Labour Party hopeful, Tom Knelston, considered by many insiders to have a bright future in politics, has shown that all too rare quality in the business, loyalty. Offered what is known as a safe seat to contest in the imminent election, he has refused, in order to remain with Purbridge, a Tory-held seat, where he was selected as Labour candidate some time ago.*

*'I feel I belong in Purbridge,' he said. 'I have made many good friends there with whom I share values and enjoy working. And we will continue to work together for the better, fairer future that only Labour can bring this country.'*

*Mr Knelston is well known for his admiration of Aneurin Bevan and is passionate about the National Health Service and its ideals. He is very much a family man, and his wife Alice recently gave birth to their third child.*

There was a photograph of the family man and his wife and children sitting on a sofa. Diana, feeling oddly calm, studied it closely. Alice was pretty, she noticed, with blonde – albeit extremely badly cut – curly hair, and a wide smile; she was cradling the baby, while the two older children sat between their parents, their father's arm around them. It was a charming photograph.

Slowly, the calm left Diana, to be replaced by a twisting fury of rage and jealousy. Loyal, was he? A family man? She had a very clear vision suddenly of Tom, standing naked in front of her in her bedroom, grinning joyfully post-sex, holding the bottle of champagne she had just sent him to fetch from the kitchen. Very loyal. She wondered what the paper would make of that side of his story – his many friends in his constituency might well feel differently about his values – and, as she sat there, a conviction began to grow in her that they really did deserve to know.

Ned had indeed had a long list; had it not been so long, had he not been so tired, things might all have been very different. He would have simply walked home, had a large whisky and fallen asleep in his chair to the strains of *La Bohème*, the eight-record version of which Persephone had just given him.

However, he was very tired; his judgement was thus slightly impaired and his temper short. As he removed his scrubs and dressed, he realised that he could hear loud crying coming from the direction of the children's ward, urgent, desperate, terrified crying. Disturbed, Ned hurried to the entrance of the ward, where he found a young child, the source of the screaming, clinging to his mother; a hapless nurse, clearly responsible for him, was trying to calm him, while Sister endeavoured to prise him away.

'What on earth is going on here?' he said, more sharply than he would normally have done. 'You'll have the whole ward awake at this rate.' Indeed, several small people were already sitting up in bed, clearly fascinated by the ruckus.

Sister turned to Ned and said impatiently, 'It's nothing serious, Mr Welles. Billy's in pain, and he keeps being sick, he's been sent up from casualty, and he won't let his mother go and she more or less refuses to go. He'll settle in a while if we all leave him alone.'

'Of course you can't leave him alone,' said Ned, the word 'settle' unsettling him almost to violence. 'Poor little chap. He's obviously frightened out of his wits. God Almighty, I would be. What's he been brought in for?'

'Acute appendicitis. Appendectomy first thing in the morning. Mr Sharp's seen him and said to have him ready first on the list.'

Graham Sharp was perfectly competent, in Ned's view, although at the age of forty had probably reached the peak of his career.

'He doesn't consider it necessary to do it tonight?'

'No, Mr Welles, he does not,' said Sister firmly. 'Now, Billy, you're much too big a boy for that silly crying. Say goodbye to your mother and come with me, and we'll get you into bed.'

Billy peered into the darkened ward with its long row of beds, and screamed even louder. Sister recommenced her prising, yet more children sat up in bed, and Billy's mother said, fresh tears flowing, 'I don't know what to do.'

Ned lost his temper. 'Sister, can we stop this nonsense at once. Would you please allow Billy's mother to get him into bed and stay with him until he's asleep, or certainly calmer. And you,' he said, turning to the nurse. 'You get all those other children tucked up again. I'm sorry, Mrs – sorry, I don't know your name –'

'Johns,' said the mother, wiping her eyes on the back of her hand. 'I'm ever so sorry, sir, he doesn't usually behave like this, but –'

'But he's in a very frightening situation. Of course. Now, Billy –' and he squatted down in front of the little boy and took one of his hands – 'you do have to stay here, I'm afraid – we have to make your poor tummy better – but Mummy will be with you for as long as you want her to be. Which is his bed, Sister?'

Sister, beyond speech, pointed at an empty bed at the end of the ward; Ned led Billy and his mother to it, pulled the curtains round them and said in little more than a whisper, 'Do you have any pyjamas with you?'

Billy shook his head.

'We didn't know he'd be staying,' said Mrs Johns. 'I'm very sorry.'

'Of course you didn't. We have some he can borrow, I'm sure. What about a teddy or something?'

'Well, there's his dumdum as he calls it,' said Mrs Johns, producing a distinctly grubby muslin nappy from her bag, 'but the nurse said he couldn't bring it, said it's dirty.'

'Well, it won't do him any harm tonight,' said Ned, taking it. 'Tomorrow we'll have to get it washed, I'm afraid, but that's no problem. Now I'm going to find you some pyjamas, young man. You wait here with your mummy.'

He walked out to the nurses' desk, where three goggled-eyed nurses were clustered, whispering and giggling, and asked one of them to find Billy some pyjamas and take them to him. 'And let him keep that grubby bit of cloth until he goes down for surgery in the morning. Mrs Johns is going to stay with him until he goes to sleep. Is that quite clear?'

'Yes, Mr Welles,' they said in chorus.

Ned nodded and went into Sister's office. She was white with rage.

'Mr Welles, I cannot have this sort of thing in my ward. The disruption is dreadful. What's more, you have totally undermined my authority and I shall make a formal complaint in the morning.'

'That is absolutely your prerogative,' said Ned. 'I'm sorry if you feel undermined, but I would like to point out that it is not your ward, it's the children's. The disruption has entirely ceased, if you notice, and Billy himself is quiet and as happy as can be expected for a child who has undergone such a significant trauma as he has today and who indeed is undoubtedly still in pain. Goodnight, Sister. I shall be in my room for another half-hour, should there be any further problems.'

Sister was silent; Ned, who had longed only to get home in the shortest possible time, walked to his room and sat down wearily at his desk. Where he found, finally, among other messages tucked under his blotter, the one from Diana; he decided to ignore it until the morning.

# Chapter 50

'Hello? Is that the *Dispatch*? Would you put me through to the diary editor? Sorry, I don't have his name. Oh, yes, please, that would be most helpful. Let me just write that down. Leo, is that right? Leo Bennett? Could you transfer me, please? Yes, to him personally. Thank you.'

Diana had woken up feeling almost excited at her plan. Oh, this was going to be fun. Tom's last day as upright family man and principled politician. Diana thought of him, safely in his family-man bubble, canvassing on doorsteps, addressing meetings, people smiling at him approvingly – and how efficiently and swiftly that bubble was going to be burst. Sorry, dear Friend Tom. Nothing can save you now.

It would be nice to talk to Diana, Ned thought, about his troubles at the hospital. She was, in spite of certain absurdities, possessed of a large degree of common sense and her reactions to his dilemma would almost certainly be helpful. She was the only person he could have this particular conversation with. His mother was back in Cornwall, and besides, was rather lacking in common sense. He would ring Diana, apologise for not getting back to her sooner, and invite her to dinner that night.

Her phone was engaged. Well, he'd go to the canteen, get a sandwich, then try her again.

'Hello? Is that Leo Bennett? Oh, I see. Well, when will he be out of conference? No, I really do want to speak to him myself. Yes, if you could ask him to ring me, that would be very kind. My number is SLOANE six two four. Sorry? Oh, my name is Southcott. Diana Southcott. Thank you so much.'

Back in his room, Ned rang Diana's number again. It was still engaged. God, women talked a lot. He'd try her once more and then it would have to wait. By which time she'd almost certainly be fixed for the evening. Well, there was always tomorrow . . .

Diana had decided on the *Dispatch* (rather than the *Daily News*) after some consideration. It was, apart from being high Tory, widely acknowledged to have the best diary in Fleet Street, and certainly the best diarist. Good-looking, charming and witty, Leo Bennett inveigled himself into the lives of not only his subjects, but also their underlings, and managed to extract their stories with an almost chilling ease. His rivals regarded his success with irritation and resentment, but the reason was simple. People liked him; indeed it was hard not to. Moreover, within the constraints of his calling, and his frequent statement of the old Fleet Street adage that a good journalist would sell his own grandmother for a story, he was a nice man. He was kind, considerate and particularly fond of children; he had famously remonstrated, and ultimately come to blows, with a father in a children's playground who had been hitting his small son about the head. He was also a brilliant mimic, and could assume any accent on demand; his default mode was fairly classless BBC, spiced up with a slight northern twang, but for professional purposes it was Old Etonian which had certainly not been acquired at Eton. He had spent a couple of years at a minor public school whence he was expelled for climbing up the fire escape of the local girls' school where he would meet and exchange fairly chaste embraces with one of the prefects.

His father was an extremely rich industrialist from Manchester, now resident in the Surrey Hills, who had been determined his two sons and his daughter should grow up Gentlemen and a Lady; the daughter, Teresa, had obliged by doing very well at her convent school, and then proceeding to a finishing school in Paris, where she learned to speak French, cook, arrange flowers and get in and out of a car keeping her knees neatly together. Marcus, the younger son, had been a model student at his prep school and was about to go to Charterhouse, from where he was most unlikely to be expelled.

Michael Bennett had refused to spend a penny more on Leo's education and sent him at fifteen to the local secondary modern, where he made a host of friends. One of them, Ronald Tims, became a very successful burglar and introduced him to all sorts of useful skills, most notably lock-picking, and to his sister Janette, who worked at the local Boots store and relieved Leo of his virginity. Leo still bought Ronald dinner twice a year, partly because he liked him and partly because of his wide range of talents and intimate knowledge of many of the large houses in London – and its families.

At sixteen, feeling that school could teach him little more, Leo told his father he wanted to be a journalist; one of Michael Bennett's friends, met at Masonic dinners, was Mark Drummond, the proprietor of the *Dispatch*, and he hosted a lunch for the three of them. Drummond, quietly impressed, arranged for Leo to start work immediately in the post room.

Post rooms were famously the launch pads for many a successful career, providing daily contact with the great and good of a company and the chance to impress them; Leo was hard-working, cheerful and efficient and, after a year, Drummond made it known that he should be promoted, either to the showbiz pages or the diary. The diary editor, a shrewd Fleet Street veteran, looked at Leo's background and track record and claimed him instantly, and there he typed copy, read proofs, ran errands and fed scandalous stories to the diary reporters which often proved to have sufficient substance to warrant publication.

After a year, he was promoted to reporter himself and by the age of thirty was deputy editor; five years later he became diary editor, his handsome face smiling from the sides of buses and posters for the *Dispatch* as well as above his page every day.

He was hurrying out of morning conference, late for lunch at the Connaught with a Rank starlet, secretly engaged (or so she said) to a young peer of the realm, when he met Stuart his assistant hovering in the corridor.

'Some woman says she has a really important story for you. She's waiting for you to ring soon, otherwise she's going to the *Mail* . . .'

'Original. What's her name?'

'Diana Southcott. I looked her up, she's a model. Up there in the top ten, it seems. And very well connected – mostly with the fashion riff-raff, but divorced from the son of a baronet.'

'Perhaps I should ring her before I go. Janey,' he said to his secretary, 'could you get Diana Southcott on the phone for me? Stuart has the number. Straight away . . . oh, and tell the Connaught to have some champagne on ice for Miss Brown – such an original pseudonym – when she arrives.'

'I will. She just rang, though, to say she's arriving early, and can't be there for more than an hour . . .'

'Oh, fuck. Well, I'll call Miss Southcott when I get back. Ring her and keep her sweet, would you?'


'Diana? It's Freddie. Listen, I've been to *American Fashion* and they've bought the New York feature idea, want us to do it. I know, isn't that thrilling?'

'Truly thrilling,' said Diana, her voice genuinely awed. *American Fashion* was a post-war, brilliantly packaged, glossy, high-fashion magazine, but quirkier than *Vogue* or *Bazaar*, with a social section which covered all the smartest parties, first nights and benefits, guaranteeing a sizeable sale to all those featured, as well as their friends and relations, before it even began on its fashion circulation. 'You're a genius, Freddie . . .'

'I know it. Only problem, timing. Do you have your case packed?'

'Well, my model bag, obviously, because it always is.'

'Excellent. It's all you'll need. Apart from a few clean pairs of knickers.'

'Oh, don't be silly –'

'I'm not. They only want the one feature this time round, and they're in a hell of a rush for it – we got lucky and coincided with four blank pages to fill, some feature rejected by the editor, so it'll be a

428

flying visit, literally. Our plane leaves tomorrow afternoon. I'll meet you at the Cromwell Road Terminal at three, OK? They're flying us first class but they're booking us in for three nights – at the Pierre!'

'The Pierre! Oh, my God, this is so exciting. You know I've never been to New York . . .'

'I do know, my poor little country bumpkin. OK, I'll leave you to pack while you ponder on my amazing cleverness.'

'Yes, all right,' said Diana. 'God, do you think I'll have to hang over the rail at the Empire State?'

She put down the phone, reached for the message pad and started to make a packing list. The Pierre! One of the top hotels in Manhattan, seated magnificently on Fifth Avenue, overlooking Central Park. Soaring high above New York, its top floors home to many of the city's broadcasting giants, home from home to the likes of Elizabeth Taylor and indeed most of Hollywood royalty – it required a lot more from her than the few pairs of knickers Freddie had suggested.

'Diana? It's Ned. I'm so sorry to have been such an age getting back to you, I didn't get your message yesterday. Long list and then trouble with Sister, and now I've been summoned by the big white chief. What? Oh, later today. I'd like to tell you about it. And you've been on the phone for ever. What do you girls talk about, for heaven's sake?'

'I wasn't talking to a girl. I was trying to talk to a man. A particular man, yes. And talking to lots of others in the process.'

'Sounds mysterious. Would you like to have dinner with me tonight? Then you could tell me about that as well. Unless you'd rather not! Well, I thought we might go to the Savoy. It would have to be late, though, say nine, that all right for you? Good. See you there.'

'Hello. Yes, this is she. Oh, Mr Bennett. How kind of you to make time to call me. This is a very – personal – story. You can't manage a drink, I suppose? No. No, sweet of you but I can't make dinner either. How about lunch tomorrow? Where? Oh, that's very nice of you. I think I'd like to go to the Berkeley, if you're really letting me choose.

I have to be at the air terminal at three. I'm working in New York for a few days. It's a political story. Well, about politicians. One politician to be precise. I don't want to give you a name. I will tomorrow, though. Good afternoon, Mr Bennett. So sweet of you to call.'

Pity, in a way, that it had to wait another day. But then it was a day nearer the election. Which meant it would probably damage him that bit more.

# Chapter 51

'Mr Welles! Yes, do come in.'

The tone wasn't just icy, it was deep frozen.

'Thank you,' said Ned. He smiled warmly at Sir Neil, hoping to effect even the mildest thaw. It was not successful. He sat down in spite of not being invited to do so, which was clearly a mistake.

'I thought we had seen an end to this nonsense,' Sir Neil said.

'Nonsense, Sir Neil?'

'Yes, bloody nonsense, mothers being allowed on the wards. I hear there was an appalling scene on Bates. Screaming, children out of their beds, discourtesy to Sister.'

'There was indeed, until I said the mother might stay with her child and – *settle* him. After that, everybody settled.'

Ned used the word deliberately, it being bandied about so much on the paediatric wards. 'I admit I was rather short with Sister Bates. But I was trying to improve the situation and she wasn't cooperating. I did apologise to her in the morning.'

'What she described was hardly shortness, Mr Welles. It was considerable rudeness.'

'Well – I'm sorry.'

'This can't go on. I will not have the hospital disrupted in this way. The staff don't know how to cope with it, the mothers who are not allowed on the ward resent the fact that others appear to be –'

'Both those things could be immediately rectified,' said Ned, 'if we could just establish the fact that mothers are permitted to be with their children.'

431

'No!' It was a roar. 'No, no, no.' He had turned an interesting shade of near-purple. Ned wondered idly if he would be up for manslaughter if a fatal heart attack ensued. It didn't.

'While you are working here, Mr Welles, you will abide by the rules of this hospital. Good surgeon you may be – outstanding, I hear from some sources – but no one is irreplaceable. The board of governors and I are agreed that if you do not abide by the hospital rules you will be asked to leave.'

There was a long silence; finally, Ned stood up and walked to the door. His hand was on the doorknob when Sir Neil spoke again; his tone lower, full of menace.

'Mr Welles?'

'Yes?'

'I think I should tell you there are rumours about certain aspects of your – what shall I call it – private life that I dislike intensely. I would like to think that they are, like most rumours, unfounded, but I would like your solemn assurance that this is absolutely the case.'

'I'm afraid I don't know what you mean,' said Ned. He felt now that he was lost, no longer bravely standing up for the rights of the mothers and children in his care, but flailing helplessly in a rip tide of terror.

'I think you do, Mr Welles. I refer to the kind of disgusting conduct that belongs in the sewer; that no normal, decent man would even consider. I don't intend to spell it out further. Now, I would like that assurance within the next few days, or your future might look a little different.'

Another day, safely got through. Tom wondered if he was going to have to spend the rest of his life like this, terrified of the story getting out. Surely, in time, she'd find another victim, start playing with him, poor bugger: only of course, if he was entirely honest with himself, she was hardly the only one to blame. He had not exactly been dragged kicking and screaming into her bed.

He paused in his present task, preparing a speech for a rallying meeting in Purbridge the next day, not that it required much preparation; he could have recited all his speeches without a pause, so frequently did he deliver them.

He was seeing Donald Herbert tonight; Donald had not exactly forgiven him for his refusal to do the right thing, as he saw it, but he seemed to have decided to help Tom anyway.

Their meeting was to be at Donald's house in South Kensington, a huge pile just off the Old Brompton Road. The unfortunate Christine had been responsible for the decor. It was rather dull, like Christine herself: a great deal of beige carpeting, chintz curtains and covers, not a proper picture in sight, the walls and surfaces of the reproduction furniture adorned with countless framed photographs of the Herbert family, with one vast painting of the entire clan – fifteen of them, three generations – hanging over the fake fireplace in the drawing room. This evening they were to spend in what Donald called the snug, the home of the television, shelves of political books (he didn't seem to read anything else) and a very flashy radiogram. Donald had invited Tom round to watch the very first TV debate, chaired by Anthony Eden, with four other senior politicians, including 'Rab' Butler and Iain Macleod, all questioned by members of the press, one of whom was the legendary Hugh Cudlipp. The questions were spontaneous and had not required approval. Tom wished only that the Labour Party, with Nye Bevan and Gaitskell among them, had envisaged something similar; but then he thought that Attlee would have had to chair it, and changed his mind. Eden was suave, good-looking and relaxed. Attlee, while unarguably clever, probably more so than his counterpart, had the charisma of a bowl of cold porridge.

Donald had invited Alice too and Tom had begged her to come, but she said that short of bringing Charlie with her it was impossible. He disliked all strangers, and reduced the few available babysitters to tears, and the one occasion Alice had tried giving him a bottle, acting on a suggestion from the district nurse, had been a resounding failure. She had offered Charlie a few ounces of Cow & Gate; he took a tentative suck while she held her breath. His face screwed up in disgust, and he clamped his mouth firmly shut and turned his small head away from her. Alice wearily put the bottle down and unbuttoned her dress. Charlie clamped his mouth round her nipple, with a look that very clearly said, 'Don't you try that again'. He didn't even gaze up at her adoringly while she fed him, as the others had. It seemed a very long time since anyone had gazed at her adoringly. Certainly not Tom.

He agreed that taking Charlie was not an option, and set off alone. Christine, who clearly liked him, greeted him with a large vodka tonic.

'I've got some sausage rolls here,' she said, putting a dish of about fifty down on the coffee table. 'And some of my fruit cake to follow. You look as if you need feeding up.'

Tom accepted the drink and ate his way manfully through about five sausage rolls before giving up. 'I'm sorry – more in a while, maybe.'

'How about a piece of cake then?' Christine said. 'Or I've got some shortbread.'

'Christine, he's had enough,' said Donald, his voice tinged with exasperation. 'Why don't you go and tidy up the kitchen while Tom and I talk business. I'll call you when the debate begins.'

'You don't need to,' said Christine, rather heavily. 'I can tell the time. And the debate's at eight thirty.'

Tom thought briefly and sharply of how Laura might have reacted to similar instruction some ten years earlier and Alice too, for that matter, and wondered why Christine put up with it. He supposed it was because they were different generations.

'Well,' Donald said, 'someone did a small poll in Purbridge last week – it's not impossible you'll win. They really do seem to love you down there, so unless you get some particularly bad publicity over the next couple of weeks, you're in with a fighting chance.'

'Good,' said Tom, taking a very large slug of the vodka tonic; and then, 'I'm doing an interview with the local paper tomorrow, before the meeting, so that should do some good.'

'Yes, indeed. What we really need is more of what young Curtis did for you. I'll have a word tomorrow.'

'Oh, please don't,' said Tom.

'Why not?'

'Well – you know journalists hate any suggestion that they might write what they're told.'

'I do. I also know half of them haven't got a thought in their heads and are quite grateful for a story.'

'But I don't see what else he could say, or rather write,' said Tom. 'He's written about me, Alice, the children, and far more than anyone ever wants to hear about my devotion to Bevan and the NHS.'

'Yes, well, we might pursue that one. Maybe you could tour Alice's old hospital. I'll see what the PR people come up with. Meanwhile, no sound from your upmarket mistress, I presume? She was definitely bluffing, don't you think?'

'Oh, definitely,' said Tom.


'So I'm having lunch with Leo Bennett, he's the diary editor of the *Dispatch*,' said Diana. 'I'll give him the sort of story journalists dream about.'

'Yes, I see,' said Wendelien. She had been summoned to the Ritz by Diana because she had something on her mind and needed a sounding board.

'Is that all you have to say? I mean, it'll do for Tom.'

'And his family,' said Wendelien quietly.

'Well, family men shouldn't put it about. That's not my fault.'

'Oh, really? He just rang you up one day, did he? No prompting or anything like that?'

'Wendelien, what's the matter with you? Aren't you on my side?'

'Yes – but I'm not sure in this case that means encouraging you to do this.'

'But why not? Apart from the mealy-mouthed little wife?'

'You don't know she's mealy mouthed. From that interview in the *Daily News* she sounded quite feisty.'

'Oh, Wendelien, please! She's a pathetic little mouse, and anyway, Tom will be able to fob her off with some travesty of an explanation.'

'Diana, what has got into you?' Wendelien sounded quite exasperated. 'What wife was ever easily fobbed off with stories of her husband's infidelity?'

'Well, all right,' said Diana, looking slightly less sure of herself. 'But I don't think you quite realise what this has been like for me, Wendelien. Just dumped. And him assuming I'd never tell on him. Then reading all that rubbish about him being a family man and his devotion to them all. Honestly, I nearly threw up, it was so repulsive. You might ask why he didn't think of me and my feelings when he gave that interview.'

'Yes, I can see it was dreadful for you,' said Wendelien. 'Don't think I don't sympathise. But have you thought about the harm to you as well?'

'What do you mean? I'm not going to tell him I was the woman in question, for God's sake.'

'Diana, don't be absurd. They'll know, of course they will. Even if you deny it, they'll work it out, it won't be difficult. Think of Jamie –'

'Jamie!'

'Yes. Think how he'll feel seeing his mother all over the front pages of the newspapers, branded as some kind of upper-class tart.'

'It's for the diary, not the front page. And they won't know it's me, whatever you say. I'll say it's a friend.'

'Oh, really? Diana, I'm amazed at you. How can you of all people be so naive about the press? Look, Tom's a hot story, especially since he appears to be being given the full publicity treatment by the party. They're not going to leave it at that.'

Diana looked at her, and for a moment Wendelien could see she was faltering. There was a long silence; then she said, 'Well, I can't stop you, obviously. But –'

'No, you can't. Anyway, I've fixed to see Leo Bennett tomorrow, so – nothing I can do, I'm afraid.'

'Diana, don't be ridiculous. You can cancel the lunch, say you haven't got a story after all.'

'Of course I can't. It would be really – really unprofessional.'

Wendelien stood up. 'I must go,' she said. Her expression as she looked at Diana was not friendly. 'What are you doing now?'

'Having dinner with Ned. His idea, not mine. We're great friends these days.'

'How ironic,' said Wendelien. 'Better not tell him what you're going to do.'

'He'd understand.'

'I don't think he would. He's an extremely moral person. He'd hate the idea of your wrecking Tom's marriage.'

'Oh, do shut up about wrecking his marriage. If it was a good one, he wouldn't have had an affair in the first place.'

Wendelien was silent. Then her face softened and she leaned down and gave Diana a kiss.

'I'm sorry to have been such a bore,' she said. 'It's only because I care about you so much.'

'I'm used to it from you,' said Diana. 'Being boring, I mean. Ever since you became a mother.'

Wendelien stood up again, looked at her with a mixture of dislike and hurt. 'I'm sorry about that,' she said. 'You'd better not waste good champagne on me in future.'

'Don't worry, I won't. Bye, Wendelien. Enjoy your evening with your husband and family. It must be nice to be so perfect.'

Wendelien was less hurt by this than she might have been; it meant her words had struck home, and Diana was rattled. And when she was rattled, she went flailing about, inflicting as much hurt as she could. By breakfast tomorrow at the latest, Wendelien knew she would have phoned to apologise.

'Good evening.' Anthony Eden's handsome face, his well-modulated, upper-class voice and his easy charm emerged from the television set. God, he was an asset to that party, Tom thought. He fitted it like an expensive glove. If only the Labour Party had someone like that. Bevan, of course, would have been the perfect fit, but he was at loggerheads with almost the entire party.

'Now this evening we are going to have the first of three television debates.' Eden smiled at them all, going on to explain that the editors of several national newspapers were to ask him questions, the content of which he had no idea.

He sat flanked by his ministers, who smiled slightly less assuredly at the camera. Rab Butler looked distinctly uncomfortable, Iain Macleod possibly more so.

'He's got health,' said Donald. 'Not making too bad a fist of it.'

Tom studied the editors. The only one who really interested him was Hugh Cudlipp: God, he was amazing. The charisma crackled out of him.

'Good evening,' he said to Eden, as his turn came. 'Hugh Cudlipp, *Daily Mirror.*' Humour suddenly appeared on his face. 'As you know, we are not among your chief flatterers.'

Eden smiled in agreement.

'But I have always had the greatest regard for your integrity.' More smiles.

'There are two sorts of Toryism,' Cudlipp went on. 'That of a small majority and that of a big majority. The Toryism of the small majority is what I would call a more humanitarian Toryism. The Toryism of a big majority, on the other hand, sees a neglected housing policy, broken-down slums and massive unemployment. If you are elected with a large majority on May the twenty-fifth what kind of Toryism will we see?'

'Clever bugger,' said Donald. 'Straight for the jugular and so well phrased, you have to work out that he's actually being very insulting about the Tory record.'

Diana was more disconcerted by Wendelien's reaction than she liked to admit, even to herself. What had started out as almost a jape, was turning into something much more serious and almost dangerous. Wendelien was quite right, Leo Bennett and his team would undoubtedly work out that she was the wicked adulteress in Tom Knelston's story; it made it much more glamorous and exciting, and they would go to town on it. And while that could make her sound glamorous and exciting also, it could backfire badly and hurt Jamie. She really didn't want that.

And there wouldn't be a single person in London who didn't know about it. It might damage her professionally, although she doubted it. But socially? Her large and rather eclectic circle of friends would probably, for the most part, be amused by it, although some would definitely be not. She could live with that. To Tom she gave little consideration, either to his career or his family; he had used her and hurt her badly and he deserved everything he might get. Dressing for dinner with Ned, she felt irritable and almost depressed; as if she was being deprived of some huge treat.

She decided to sleep on it and see where her instinct led her in the morning; for Wendelien was quite right, she could easily cancel her lunch with Leo Bennett.


'Darling Ned, I'm so sorry I'm late. I – well, I got held up.'

'Nothing serious, I hope.'

'No! Goodness, no. It's actually rather exciting – I'm flying to New York tomorrow. With Freddie Bateman, my photographer friend.'

'Is he the one who has you hanging out of helicopters? Don't you go jumping off the Statue of Liberty.'

''Fraid I've got to,' said Diana. 'It's part of the brief.'

'Diana!' He looked genuinely anxious, so much so she was touched. Then he grinned. 'Very funny.'

'Yes, I thought so.' She sparkled at him over her champagne. 'I'm jolly excited, anyway.'

'I bet you are. Now, I heard just today from Ludo that Johnathan is getting married again. True or false?'

'Quite true.'

'Anyone you know?'

'Well, I've met her. Terribly dull. And a goody-goody. It makes me wonder what Johnathan was doing with me.'

'He loved you, I expect.'

'Do you think so? He pretty well hates me now. And probably with good reason. Oh, it was so wrong, what I did. Marrying him when I – well, when I knew I didn't love him. I married the pre-war lifestyle, the London house, the social scene; being dragged off to Yorkshire just finished everything.'

'Well, it must have been a terrible culture shock. I'm not sure I could cope with it either. I'm not a country mouse any more than you are. Anyway, let's order quickly, and then we can talk. I need your advice.'

'Mine? Ned, I am really not the sort of person you should take advice from. Unless it was about whether you should shorten your skirt or cut your hair.'

'I think I could decide both those things for myself. No, I want to talk to you about something even more important than that.'

She laughed, picked up the glass of champagne the waiter had poured her and said, 'Well, here we are, having supper at the Savoy, where you broke my heart all those years ago.'

'Not quite broken. Minor fracture, perhaps.'

'Ned! At the very least, a major one.'

'Oh, all right. Anyway, I thought we should lay that ghost. We've never been here alone together since.'

'No, of course we haven't. Oh, Ned. How I adored you. You were so handsome – well, you still are, of course – and so charming, and so special.'

'And you were so beautiful – and you still are – and so charming and so special. You could have said we were made for each other. Except for the one little thing.'

'Yes, the one little thing. You didn't love me.'

Diana looked at him. There was something different about him, and she couldn't quite work out what. He seemed less terminally anxious, more relaxed. It was lovely to see.

'Do you know,' she said, 'I don't think I've ever been in love. Except with you, and that doesn't count.'

'Oh, darling, that's so sad. Not even that photographer chap?'

'Who, Freddie? No, absolutely not. But no, I've never gone weak at the knees, or felt anyone was too good to be true. Anyway –' she laughed, a light, manufactured laugh – 'I suppose I have a little time yet . . .'

'Of course you do. There's probably someone walking along the Strand right now, thinking, "I'll just pop into the Savoy for a night-cap" – and there he'll be, and there will go your knees.'

'I doubt it.' She sighed. 'It's not very good for morale. I keep wondering what's wrong with me, what a bad person I must be.'

'Diana,' said Ned, 'you are not a bad person. You are so far from that. You're actually a very good person.'

'Oh, Ned. If only.'

'No, you are. All right, you might not be accepted into a convent . . .'

'God, I hope not.'

'But you were a very good wife to Johnathan –'

'I was a terrible wife to Johnathan.'

'No, you weren't, you went up to Yorkshire to live, for God's sake . . .'

'But then I kept running away. To show off in front of the cameras.'

'Yes, but you're so good at it, and you always went back to Yorkshire. And you've told me how hard you tried to make it all work and you're a wonderful mother, anyone can see that. And Johnathan blaming you for that miscarriage, that was so outrageous, and yet you never hit back – and you're such a good friend, so loyal and always there when I, at any rate, need you, and I'm sure for everyone else too . . .'

'Oh, Ned, stop it,' said Diana, laughing. 'This is all very flattering, but it's a bit rose-tinted. I was really mean this afternoon to Wendelien.'

'Well, I'm sure she'll get over it. But properly mean, in a way that would really hurt someone – I know you would never do anything like that. You're just not capable of it . . .'

There was no doubt he meant it, his smile as he finished his testimony to her non-existent virtue very sweet. She suddenly felt extremely uncomfortable.

'Tell me what you want advice about,' she said. 'What's your problem?'

'Well. The big white chiefs at the hospital don't like me. They've demanded my allowing mothers into the wards stops, or rather I stop trying to insist on it. Sisters are on their side too. And I can't, Diana, or rather I won't. It's wrong, it's brutal, it's like being back at prep school, only at least we were fit and well and understood what we were doing there.'

'Well, that's easy. Of course you must fight on.'

'Easier said than done. The chairman of the board of governors of the hospital, charmer called Sir Neil Lawson, really does hold the whip hand – he can make my life impossible, get rid of me altogether if he wants to. In fact, he threatened to, if I didn't drop my campaign.'

'Bastard.'

'Indeed. And there's more. He said he'd heard rumours about what he called my private life.'

'What? That's that pig of a Digby Harrington.'

'And without my assurance that they're unfounded, as he put it, he will make quite sure everyone in the hospital knows. Diana, it's awful. I don't know what to do.'

'Oh, Ned, what a mess.'

'I absolutely don't know what to do. I can't turn a deaf ear to those children crying, just do my job and go home. And anyway, what about the other threat? I can't lie outright, I simply can't.'

'Of course you can't. But – oh, Ned, I wish I could help. I'll try, of course, but –' She felt suddenly deeply sad, felt tears welling, brushed them away.

'Oh, God,' he said. 'I'm so sorry, Diana. I'm afraid I've given you a rather dismal evening . . . would you like to dance?'

'Not dismal at all,' said Diana. 'But I'd love to dance. Just once. Then I must go, I've got a busy day tomorrow. Even before I get on the plane.'

'What are you doing in the States? Tell me, divert me. Being photographed stark naked, galloping along a beach at dawn, standing up on a horse?'

'No, but it would make a great picture. I'll suggest it to Freddie. Thanks, Ned. Maybe you could find a new career as a fashion editor? Oh, listen, come on, it's a foxtrot, my favourite.'

They both danced rather well; people watched them from their tables, smiling, and several of the other dancers stopped to admire them. As they passed a neighbouring table on their way back to their own, a man, unmistakably American, beckoned to them.

'That was great,' he said to Ned. 'I don't know which of you dances better, you or your wife.'

'Oh, she does,' said Ned, smiling.

As they sat down again, Diana looked at him, her eyes dancing.

'There you are,' she said. 'There's your solution. You can marry me, that'll scotch the rumours. Then we can buy a great big house, and who will know what goes on behind the doors?'

Ned laughed. 'Brilliant. It would almost be worth doing, just to see people's reactions.'

'What do you mean, almost? Am I really such an appalling prospect?'

'You're a wonderful prospect. Brains and beauty. And I'll tell you what people's reaction would be, they'd say we should have done it years ago.'

'Well, there you are. And probably we should. Now look, I really must go.'

'Oh, yes, you've got this busy day tomorrow. So if it's not riding a horse starkers along a beach, what is it?'

'Oh – it's sort of admin,' said Diana. 'Terribly complicated. You really don't want to hear about it.'

Which of course, she thought, as she kissed him briefly before climbing into her taxi, he wouldn't.

# Chapter 52

'I've persuaded Campbell to let me come and cover it,' said Josh. 'It's quite a story. Support visit from a minister. And what a minister, for God's sake.'

Tom had that morning been telephoned in his office by a very VIP cabinet minister to say he would be coming to Purbridge that week. 'To join you on the stumps for the day,' he said. 'Might help a bit, you never know. Seeing as it's too close to call. Attlee's idea. OK with you?'

'Yes,' said Tom. 'I mean, yes, of course. It would be terrific, thank you very much indeed.'

'Right, right. Well, we'll meet you at the local HQ? That is, couple of my staff and me. Shall we say eight a.m.? I'm relying on you to get a good programme together and the earlier we start the more we can cram in. Till Friday, then.'

'Friday,' said Tom to himself in awed tones, and the minute the line cleared, he rang Josh. Clearly impressed, he told him he'd ring back, and did within thirty minutes, with the news that he would be there as well. 'Quite a coup, Tom. The powers that be obviously consider you a very important marginal.'

'Yes, well, we are. It's terribly close, according to the polls. Only thing is, what on earth do we – I – say to someone like that? I'll be totally out of my depth.'

'Oh, rubbish. You won't have to say anything to him anyway, he'll be far too busy even to speak to you. They're all the same, Tom, they make these grand gestures of supporting you, when all they want to

444

do is support themselves, play to the gallery, get people hanging on their every word. It's just an ego trip, really. He'll arrive in a cloud of glory, shake your hand and then he'll be off, telling everyone how marvellous he is. Not in so many words, of course, but – anyway, I presume your agent will have some programme worked out for him?'

'Yes, of course,' said Tom. 'We've got two car-manufacturing plants, the high street and the working men's club.'

'Sounds good. And it'll boost your column inches by loads. You'll see.'

'Hope so. Apparently, some constituency or other, also too close to call, is literally measuring the columns, by the inch, to see who's winning the publicity battle each day.'

'Well, this'll put you up into the yards, I reckon. Anyway, it's marvellous,' said Josh. 'You should get Alice to come. She's such good copy.'

'I'm trying. It'll mean her bringing Charlie, that's the only thing. Her mother can take the other two, but he's such a nightmare. Screams all the time.'

'Won't matter,' said Josh. 'He's a baby. The minister might even kiss him.'

'He'd be a brave man,' said Tom, laughing.

'They'll do anything for a photo. Even at that level. No, tell Alice to come, tell her I'll be there, I'll look after her.'

Tom looked at the phone slightly doubtfully as he put it down. Josh knew about Diana and he was very fond of Alice. He didn't think Josh would deliberately tell her, but he could easily give something away, with a thoughtless word, a careless joke even. Christ, he was in a mess. A filthy, foul mess. And it was all his own fault.

He telephoned Alice and asked her if she'd come to Purbridge in two days' time. 'We have a minister coming. It would be wonderful if you could. You can bring Charlie.'

'Really?'

'Yes. It's desperately important this, Alice. Everyone says you should be there.'

'Everyone meaning Donald, I suppose.'

'No. Everyone. Including Josh.'

'Josh!'

'Yes. He said it was terribly important you came. He's covering it, said to tell you he'd look after you.'

'I don't need looking after,' said Alice irritably.

'I know. But Charlie might.'

'Josh has offered to look after Charlie?'

'Yes – if he has to.'

Diana was late arriving at the Berkeley. It was not entirely intentional; indeed, she was renowned in her social circle for arriving slightly too early for her hostess's comfort. But she had spent too long packing, partly because she kept stopping to rehearse what she was going to say to Leo Bennett, and then had trouble getting a taxi. So that by the time she arrived at the restaurant, it was one fifteen rather than the agreed one o'clock and her hair was uncombed, her nose unpowdered. The maître d' bowed and said the gentleman had only just arrived himself, which was at once soothing and irritating since clearly he would have been late if she had not. The combination of those emotions, combined with the further complications of still not being quite sure what she was going to say, made her mildly cross, and when she was cross her dark eyes became even more brilliant, her lovely mouth a little fuller. Leo Bennett, therefore, found himself almost shocked by her beauty. And she, for her part, taking the hand held out to her, was aware of only one thing: not (as she absorbed later) his dark blonde hair, nor his almost navy blue eyes, nor his height (considerable), nor his suit (grey, perfectly cut), but only that her knees, which had, until that moment, been their normal strong selves, had become strangely weak.

'Miss Southcott,' he said, bowing very slightly over her hand, then waiting while she removed her coat and gloves, retaining her hat, and settled herself onto her chair before smiling at him graciously across the table.

'I'm so sorry I'm late,' she said. 'I'm flying out to New York this afternoon, as I think I told you, and my packing got the better of me.'

'How very smart,' he said. 'To be flying to New York. Do you know it well?'

'Not at all,' she said. 'In fact, it's my first visit. So I'm very excited.'

'I expect you are. Where are you staying?'

'The Pierre.'

'Ah, New York's finest. You will suit one another,' he added, his extraordinary eyes smiling very deeply into hers. 'Now, would you like a glass of champagne while we order, or are you a cocktail girl?'

'Both, please,' she said. 'That is, a Buck's Fizz, if I may.'

'Of course. Now, just so you know, they are called Mimosas in New York.'

'Oh – thank you. Useful information, as I intend to be drinking quite a lot of them. But I think I should warn you, you might not want me to order anything, because I've decided I don't have a story for you after all. I did consider just cancelling on the telephone, but I decided that would be cowardly and ill-mannered and I do try very hard to be neither.'

Leo Bennett turned to the waiter, who had been listening to this with some interest, and said, 'One Buck's Fizz, please, and one vodka Martini,' then turned back to her and said, 'I'm sure you are never either cowardly or ill-mannered and I am also sure that we shall enjoy our lunch very much whether you give me a story, or recite nursery rhymes –'

'Not sure about nursery rhymes,' she said, 'but I am rather good at Winnie-the-Pooh –'

'I too. Maybe we could do a duet; you can be Kanga and I will be the bear of very little brain –'

'Very well. Although I like Tigger –'

'But he's a boy –'

'He is indeed. I like playing boys. Being tall, I always had to be the boy when we did ballroom dancing at school, and whenever I took part in the pantomime in the village hall, I was principal boy.'

She smiled at him; now that she was sitting down, her legs seemed restored to their normal strength. He was extraordinarily good-looking though, and charming, and fun; bit of a treat for lunch.

While he, for his part, though fairly annoyed, was in no way inclined to tell her so. There was always another story and there was always an alternative route to it, having been given the faintest trail. Had she been plain, or dull, or badly dressed, he would have felt more than fairly annoyed, but it was a long time since he had met someone who was not only beautiful, but charming and intelligent, and she seemed, therefore, to be of more value than her story. Which might, in any case, be of no value at all he reflected (although given her intelligence and obvious sophistication, that seemed unlikely).

'Well – that's very nice of you. But you must let me pay for my own lunch; I'm clearly not earning it.'

'Miss Southcott –'

'Diana, please.'

'Diana. I am gentleman enough to find the very thought of a lady buying her own lunch – while sitting at my table, that is – extremely disquieting.'

'Well, that's very nice of you. Thank you.'

'I'm sure it will be my pleasure. Now, what would you like to eat?'

Diana really had had no clear idea as she rushed into the restaurant late what she was going to do about her Tom story, but as she followed the maître d' to the table, she had discovered she knew with absolute clarity. It had nothing to do with her fondness for Tom (considerable), or her concern for his career (negligible), or her sympathy for Alice (debatable); it was all about Ned.

Diana was used to people admiring her looks, her sense of style, her breezy courage, her willingness to work until she was beyond exhaustion, but she was quite unused to them admiring her character. Most people indeed did not admire it at all, she knew; and especially in Yorkshire, where they felt quite the reverse, her self-esteem had plummeted to painfully low levels. But having Ned, good, kind, morally upright Ned, who she genuinely loved and admired so much, tell her he knew she would never do anything bad, never try to hurt anyone, had had a profound effect on her; she had lain awake for a long time, smiling into the darkness, savouring that moment, that pronouncement, and hoping, rather hopelessly, that it was true.

The morning had found her less principled. Tom's behaviour still

hurt, his sending Donald Herbert – or so it had seemed – to inter-
vene for him still stung, and his public claims to be a family man
enraged her. She had been influenced by Wendelien's attitude, her
concerns for Jamie, and to a lesser extent her own reputation; but
revenge would be sweet and within her grasp, and it was a vision hard
to relinquish.

Just the same, she had decided against seizing it, in the moments
as she crossed the restaurant. People always recognised her in such
situations, smiled at her, pointed her out to their friends; admired her
for her looks, her style, her fame. If she did give Leo Bennett Tom's
story, she would be recognised still more; but for less charming reasons. Wendelien was quite right; she would be the adulteress, the
woman willing to break up a family and a young wife's heart; and,
indeed the destroyer of her lover's brilliantly promising career. And
she would, in many ways, be seen as the greater sinner; people always
took the man's side, found excuses for him, cast stones at the
adulteress.

She didn't want that, she wanted to continue to be admired, smiled
upon, regarded as Ned regarded her; all these things and more, she
realised, in those moments on her way to the table. And then her
knees went weak: and everything in the world was changed.


'So,' said Leo Bennett, 'what shall we talk about? As you have no
story for me.'

'I – can't imagine,' she said, smiling first down into her drink, and
then rather boldly directly at him.

'How about you? As in you and your life?'

'Not terribly interesting.'

'I'm sure it is.'

'Not really. How about yours?'

'Fairly interesting, although I say it myself. But I can't spend the
next hour and a half talking about myself; how about we swap fact for
fact?'

'All right,' she said. 'But I insist you go first.'

'No, ladies first. I'll start you off. Are you married?'

'Not any more. I'm divorced.'

'Because . . .'

'Oh, the usual sort of thing,' she said, unwilling to reveal the huge and genuine hurt she had sustained over Johnathan's divorcing her.

'Ah. But I am sure your husband was gentlemanly about it and did the right thing, lady in the Brighton hotel and so on . . .'

'Of – of course,' she said. 'Now that's enough of that; are *you* married?'

'Like you, not any longer, but three times, I'm afraid. Children?'

'Yes. One son. Aged eight. Love him to pieces. You?'

'No, to my great regret. I have lots of godchildren, though. And I take my godfatherly duties very seriously, believe it or not. I like children.'

'Why?'

'I like their honesty, the way they either like you or they don't; I like the way the plainest child is attractive, given your attention; I like their clear view of things, the original things they say.'

'You really do like them, don't you?' she said, rather charmed by this. 'Most people give such stupid, false reasons.'

'I know. I agree. Your turn. Tell me, what do you like doing? When you're not working?'

'Oh – goodness. I don't have any interesting intellectual hobbies, don't even like the theatre that much. I like horses and I love riding –'

'Do you have a horse? Do you hunt?'

'Yes, to both. My horse, a sweet mare, is a hunter, bit long in the tooth now to take out, doesn't like big gates and things –'

'Do you?'

'Not any more, to be truthful. '

'Then she sounds ideal. I like horses too, though I don't hunt.'

'So what else do you like doing?'

'I'm not sure it's not your turn. But I like good food and wine, pretty ladies – oh, and I love my work.'

'So do I,' she said with a fervour which surprised him. 'Absolutely love it. Don't know what I'd do without it.'

'Nor I mine . . .'

And so it went on. Until suddenly, Leo Bennett looked at his watch – gold, Patek Philippe, and said, 'You know, I could sit here happily for the rest of the day, but if you are going to make your plane, I think you should leave in the next five minutes –'

'Oh, God,' she said, looking at her own watch, telling her inexorably that it was quarter to three. 'You're right, I must go –' She stood up, held out her hand and then dropped it again, bent and kissed him on the cheek and said, 'Thank you so, so much for the most wonderful lunch and for being so nice about it all, and I do hope you find something else to put in your column tomorrow,' and ran out of the restaurant.

Sitting in the taxi, she felt mildly remorseful; she had wasted hours of his time, pushed up his expenses by at least five, possibly six pounds – lunches at the Berkeley didn't come cheap, especially when champagne and a bottle of white burgundy were on the bill – and his only words had been to thank her for her company and tell her to enjoy New York.

In between fretting at the traffic on the Cromwell Road, she thought about him. He was not just absurdly good-looking and beautifully dressed, but also sexy and funny and fun. She felt slightly silly, he had affected her so much. Of course, it was extremely unlikely she would ever hear from him again. Which was a pity . . .

'Here we are, madam –' the taxi had swung into the entrance to the air terminal – 'told you we'd make it easy. Let's just get that case of yours out and find a porter –'

'Diana, where the fuck have you been?' It was Freddie, looking wild eyed. 'We've only got five minutes to check in and find our bus. Come on, for God's sake – I'll get the cab, you go in, I've done everything, we won't be able to sit together probably now, I tried to get them to hold a seat, but they refused. It really is too bad of you –'

Diana made her way into the terminal; she always forgot how easily Freddie panicked and, as a result of it, lost his temper – it was his most disagreeable characteristic. Now if only Leo Bennett was going to New York, that really would be fun.

Leo Bennett walked into his office, whistling under his breath. His secretary, Janey, looked at him expectantly.

'Good lunch?'

'Very good.'

'Good story?'

'No story.'

'Oh.'

Janey waited for further instructions; usually an unproductive lunch was followed by an irritable instruction to her to trawl through the cuttings library at the very least. It didn't come.

Instead, a thoughtful pause, then, 'Could you dig out all the stuff on the countess and the ballet dancer, darling? Quick as you can.'

'Sure, but I thought you said it wasn't worth a row of beans.'

'Well, I'll just have to find a magic one amongst them. Like Jack's, you know?'

'Er – yes.' She stared at him; he was in a funny mood. Very funny.

# Chapter 53

Oh, God, it couldn't be. But it was. Him. Unmistakably, horribly him. Now what did she do? He was carrying two glasses of wine across the bar; if she was quick, bolted for the ladies, she might just—'Darling. Look where you're going. I think I'd better get our drinks.' It was her mother; she had taken her to see *The Diary of Anne Frank* as a treat: 'You look so badly in need of cheering up, darling,' she had said, waving the tickets over the breakfast table. Hardly cheering-up fodder, Jillie had thought, having read the book, but it was kind of her mother and she was trying very hard to enjoy it. Now almost impossible, having discovered Julius and, she presumed, Nell was in the audience.

He had rung her every day for a while, saying, 'I think we should talk,' or, 'I'm missing you terribly.' At first she said, 'I don't see the point,' but as he persisted, she had moved on to simply putting the phone down on him; finally the message seemed to have got through.

She felt terrible still; any virtuous glow that such strength of will might have rewarded her with, entirely eluded her, her only comfort being that she would probably never have to see him again.

Now the worst had happened: had materialised before her eyes, and under the worst possible circumstances. Had she only been with some handsome, attentive man, at least her pride would have been saved; but she was with her mother. Who went to the theatre with their mother, for God's sake? Lonely, friendless, certainly boyfriend-less people, that was who – and almost worse, she was wearing the same shapeless dress she had worn all week, having come straight from the hospital. Julius looked as marvellous as always in a black velvet suit and pale blue shirt, and no doubt, if Nell was there, she would be looking equally marvellous.

He had seen her and waved one of the glasses at her – looking, she had to admit, and how nice that was – totally delighted.

'Jillie!' he said, reaching her finally. 'How very nice, how are you?'

'I'm – very well,' she said primly, longing more than anything to hug him, kiss him possibly, tell him how wonderful it was to see him. 'Is – er – is Nell here?'

'Yes,' he said. 'Yes, she's in the ladies.' No hiding place there, then. 'Jillie,' he said then. 'Jillie, I wanted to –' but there was her mother, smiling, and worse, there was Nell saying, 'Jillie, how lovely –' and Julius was offering to get them all another drink.

Then the five-minute bell went, which meant release and relief. Only then Julius said, 'Look, have you eaten? We're going to Simpson's for supper afterwards, would you like to join us?'

'How very kind, and yes, why not?' said Geraldine. 'Jillie, wouldn't that be fun?'

And Jillie was still trying to find an excuse, any excuse at all, when the final bell went and Julius and Nell disappeared, and Jillie looked at her mother and said, 'Mummy, I can't go to Simpson's dressed like this. I simply can't, and anyway, I'm awfully tired, you know I am.'

'Well, it's too late now,' said her mother firmly. 'It will seem appallingly rude to change the arrangement.' Whereupon Jillie burst into tears, in the mercifully almost-empty bar and said, 'You should have asked me, not just accepted for us both. I can't go, I just can't.'

'Oh, darling!' said her mother. 'All right, I'll get a note to them. Do you want to leave now?' and Jillie, struggling to contain not just her tears but her grief, said, 'If you don't terribly mind, I'm so sorry . . .'

'I don't mind. The whole idea was to cheer you up – it's backfired horribly, and I can see why. Let's go and find a taxi and get you home.'

She said no more until they were safely at number five; there, making hot chocolate for them both, she said only, 'You should have told me, Jillie,' embraced her daughter and sent her up to bed.

Jillie lay awake for much of the night, alternately weeping and thinking that whichever of the good fairies had attended her christening had done her a great disservice in bestowing upon her such high principles, and reflecting also that, if things had been the other way round, Nell Henderson would probably have hesitated for no more than a moment before setting to work procuring Julius for herself.

'The beef all right?' Julius asked now.

'What? Oh – yes, lovely, thank you.'

'Good. My kidneys are superb.'

And they then returned to their respective thoughts: Nell of Seth Gilbert, her rather attractive editor; Julius of Jillie Curtis in terms distinctly unsuitable for a couple who were planning their wedding to one another . . .

The day with the cabinet minister had gone extremely well. He had been far more proactive than Josh had predicted, eager to meet the constituents, to ask them of their voting intentions, absorbing any hostile reaction with calm good humour. He suggested to Tom that he offered to drive supporters to the polling stations – 'Never fails to please 'em, swung many a don't-know round' – smiled obligingly at the press, and even – as Josh had predicted – kissed several babies, including Charlie, who didn't scream in protest.

He also took rather a fancy to Alice, who was looking inevitably tired, but very pretty in a white blouse and red skirt and jacket. He sat next to her at the lunch at the working men's club, and insisted on asking for second helpings for her of the chicken on the menu, claiming she needed feeding up.

He was clearly impressed by the number of people who knew both her and Tom, who made reference to things they had attended, the supermarket openings, the prize-givings, the concerts.

'Bloody boring, most of them. You deserve to win,' he said, pumping Tom by the hand at the end of the day. 'You've obviously worked extremely hard down here, and even if you don't win, I can tell you I'm not the only one to have you marked as part of the party's future. I like the way you've hung your cap on the NHS and Nye Bevan too. It's a way of standing out. If only he'd follow your example, rather than getting into a lather over the wretched bomb.'

Tom was so overwhelmed by the concept of Nye Bevan following his example that he went completely white; watching him, Alice really thought he was about to faint.

She discovered as they drove home, Charlie now giving up all pretence of being the good baby he had been impersonating all day, and screaming the entire way, that she had enjoyed her day out. 'I'll do this again,' she said to Tom, 'providing Mummy can have the other two. And if you really think it helps.'

Tom said there was no think about it, it did help enormously; and the household went to bed that night in a rare state of peace and harmony, Alice deciding that from tomorrow, screams or no screams, Charlie was going on the bottle.

Tom's last thought was that he had, with a dollop of good luck and a degree of cunning, navigated some fairly stormy waters. His constituents seemed pleased with him, and wherever possible he told them that he had been offered an alternative, but had turned it down out of loyalty to them. Alice actually wanted to move to Purbridge, or rather Sandbanks, and Diana seemed to have decided not to do her worst – whatever that might be.

# Chapter 54

'You know, of course, the top floors of the Pierre are modelled on the Royal Chapel at Versailles?'

'I – didn't actually,' said Diana, 'but that is completely fascinating.'

'And did you know that the gala opening dinner was prepared by Escoffier himself?'

'No! How incredible,' said Freddie.

'Yes. And of course he was guest chef here in the early years.' The voice of the public-relations officer charged with the task of showing Diana and Freddie round the hotel was growing chilly.

'I had imagined you would be more au fait with the facts.'

'We only heard yesterday – while we were still in England – we were to shoot part of this feature here,' said Diana. 'The whole thing has been a huge rush, as you can imagine.'

The PR officer, whose unlikely name was Metro, looked slightly mollified. 'Of course. Well, you must decide for yourselves where you will be doing the photographs – but I would imagine the ballroom would suit you best.'

'Marvellous idea, and thank you for the suggestion, but of course we are very much in the hands of the fashion editor,' said Freddie, who had already decided that Diana tumbling temptingly out of a silk negligee, and leaning over one of the Pierre's floral-painted basins, doing her make-up in the magnifying mirror above it, would be the Pierre's contribution. It had transpired that they were staying there free as a quid pro quo for using it in one of the shots:

always a tricky situation, with both sides determined to get their pound of flesh.

'Oh, really?' The tones became chillier still. 'We were very much given the impression that we would have carte blanche – more or less – on the feature.'

'Well, perhaps a touch of crème, I fear – there will have to be a little give and take,' said Freddie, and then seeing that this piece of verbal whizzery was wasted on Metro, added hastily, 'But do please show us the ballroom, so we can start to plan our pictures.'

Mollified, Metro led them to the vast acreage of the ballroom, with its twenty-three-foot-high ceiling, a fairy-tale forest of chandeliers and windows that would not have disgraced a cathedral.

'Marvellous,' cried Diana, taking her cue from Freddie. 'Just perfect. But – as Freddie says, we mustn't get carried away.'

'And now, darling, we must go,' said Freddie to Diana. 'We're going to be late for dinner. Thank you so much, Metro, for your time and all the fascinating information.'

'My pleasure entirely,' said Metro. 'Now, I'm having a complete information pack sent to your rooms; anything else, you have only to call. May I ask where you are dining?'

'Oh – with friends,' said Freddie carefully. 'At the Oyster Bar at Grand Central.'

An hour later, happily settled in the tiled vaults, wrapped in a plastic bib and halfway through her dozen Maine oysters, Diana had only to argue with Freddie over which precious hour of their day the place should occupy.

'One vital advantage this has,' said Freddie, 'is it could be noon or midnight. The light never alters.'

'We can't waste noon light,' said Diana.

'Of course not. I think small hours. Oh, no – shit – it closes at midnight. OK, then, how about rush hour?'

'Rush hour'd be good.'

'Only thing is, light's nice enough then for Central Park.'

'You did say dawn for that.'

'Yeah, I did. OK, we'll pencil in six p.m. Then seven for the yellow cab. Good thing we haven't literally got to do it in twenty-four.'

'Why?'

'My darling girl, where do you think you're going to change?'

Diana looked around her and shrugged. 'Here? Not much different from behind a bush on Hampstead Heath. That was my first day ever modelling. I was so excited I'd have stood naked in Piccadilly Circus. I feel a bit like that now,' she added with a grin.

'That's why you're such a great model,' said Freddie, kissing her on the cheek. 'You've never got tired of it. Now come on, we should get back to the Pierre. We're meeting Ottilie there at nine.'

Ottilie, a terrifying Valkyrie-style six-foot blonde, with a face like an iceberg and hair like hemp, plus her retinue, were waiting for them in the foyer, with a mountain of clothes.

'Hi,' she said, her expression daring a smile to come near it. 'Let's go up to your room, Diana, and we can unload these and plan the shoot.'

She stalked towards the lift; Diana and Freddie followed meekly.

'It's all right,' he hissed in her ear. 'It's the American way. They feel they have to frighten everybody.'

'Oh. She's succeeded.'

But once talking about shots and clothes and locations, a remarkable change came over Ottilie. She didn't exactly smile but her face eased into an approximation of one; she knew a good idea when she saw it, liked a lot of theirs, threw in several of her own; and she was swift to seize opportunities and use them: so when a yellow cab broke down in the middle of Third Avenue, steam pouring from its bonnet like a volcano, she told Diana (also dressed in yellow) to get behind it and start pushing. Or hiring a helicopter – 'I'll argue with Miss Dickens about the cost' – so they could fly past the Chrysler building in all its lace-like loveliness, with Diana's profile etched against it.

They went up to a jazz club in Harlem, where she slipped the trumpeter ten dollars to let Diana blow it for two dizzy minutes; and agreed they should take the Staten Island ferry at two in the morning, and then had Diana, wearing a huge-skirted white ball gown, standing recklessly on the boat rail, with only the make-up lady hanging onto her dress for security, waving to the Statue of Liberty as they went past.

The entire shoot took three days, not two, and at the end Ottilie hugged them both and said they had been 'quite good'.

Next day, their last, they got a call from Miss Dickens's secretary; could they come down to the offices right away.

'This is it,' said Freddie. 'She hates them.'

He always said that; it was the only time he ever displayed any lack of confidence.

*American Fashion* was based just off Times Square. It was rather unglamorous, very different from *Vogue* or *Style*, too many people crammed into too few offices. Even Miss Dickens shared her office with not only her secretary but also the beauty editor. She was unlike any fashion editor or editor Diana had ever seen, being tiny and rather timid looking, with mousey brown hair, half-moon spectacles, and clothes that looked at least five years out of date.

'She says she's too busy to go shopping or get her hair done,' Freddie said. 'She makes a thing of it; she can look fabulous, I'm told.'

The room was filled with now-familiar people: Ottilie, the beauty editor, the accessories editor, Miss Dickens's assistant. The desk was entirely covered with sheets of contacts. Miss Dickens was looking at them with a magnifying glass, occasionally pushing one towards Ottilie, and saying something in a low voice; she totally ignored Diana and Freddie as they came in. The silence was a long one; Diana was just beginning to think Freddie for once was right and she did hate the pictures when she put down the magnifying glass, looked at them over her half-moon glasses and smiled, a delighted child-like smile.

'I *adore* them,' she said. 'Absolutely adore them. What a team you are. These are way, way beyond anything even Ottilie has produced before and I can tell you, that is something. This one with the taxi – and the trumpet – oh, and you practically falling off the Empire State, Diana – they're just fantastic. I am *thrilled*. I'm giving them four spreads, not two. We can't really afford it, but they'll pull in a lot of advertising. Well done. Both of you. Now look, are you free tonight, because I want to dine with you.'

'Miss Dickens, you're having dinner with the Elizabeth Arden people tonight,' said her assistant.

'And Miss Arden herself might be there,' said the beauty editor. She looked as if she was about to burst into tears.

'Oh, I can't help that,' said Miss Dickens. 'Tell them I died or something.' But Diana, who had learned a great deal about advertisers and their importance, said, 'Miss Dickens, we can meet you after dinner. Can't we, Freddie?'

Freddie, who was planning to meet an old girlfriend for dinner and hoped to persuade her back to the Pierre for the rest of the night, hesitated, clearly dismayed, and then said yes, of course they could, asking hopefully if that mightn't be a little late for Miss Dickens; she drew herself up to her full five feet and said she wasn't senile yet and she'd meet them in the King Cole Bar at the St Regis at eleven.

They arrived early, as Freddie said Diana ought to have time to enjoy the famous Maxfield Parrish mural of Old King Cole, which she did, but was marginally more enchanted by the doorman's brass booth at the entrance. They sat drinking what Diana remembered from her lunch with Leo Bennett to call Mimosas. She had hardly had time to think about him since, but found herself reflecting on him now with some pleasure and whether she might try and find some excuse to see him again when she got home.

Miss Dickens arrived late: she had clearly not considered the Elizabeth Arden people worth dressing up for and wore the same high-necked ankle-length tea dress as she had for her meeting with Diana and Freddie. She ordered some tea for herself, and sat back in a chair that was far too big for her, her tiny feet not even reaching the floor, and looked at them both intently.

'Right,' she said. 'I want to discuss something with you. I know we've only done one session, but it's quite enough to convince me. As you know, I'm new at *American Fashion* and I'm still building my reputation and my team. I'd like to offer you a contract. The two of you working together, usually one feature a month, but you must be prepared to do two, to be shot generally over here. That's because of the clothes, of course, no use featuring English clothes that the readers can't get. But under exceptional circumstances, like a royal wedding – we do so love the royals – then it would be shot in England. Or you can go somewhere quite different, of course, providing the clothes were American: the Bahamas, or Ireland – wherever your inspired fancies took you. But this would have to be your base. What do you say?'

Persephone read Ned's letter, and then read it again and then again, smiling more and more as she did so. This was beyond her wildest hopes for him; she found it hard to believe it could finally have happened.

*I have found someone I love,* he had written, *and I wanted you to be the first person to know. Someone I am happy with, at peace with, someone who makes me laugh and talk and think. I'm not ready yet to tell you who, because we don't want to go even slightly public with it yet; he has family considerations, and needs to think about it all carefully. I know you will find this extremely difficult (!) but it will do you no good to try and tease it out of me. I just wanted you to know. But it seems so wonderful, and I feel different, stronger, braver. God knows what we are to do about it – we can't actually live together, of course – but the time we do spend together is so precious, so special, and such fun and I hope together we can work something out.*

It was a sad little document in its way, Persephone thought – two adults finding love for one another, and unable to acknowledge it except to a very few people – but it was lovely to know Ned was so happy. She felt very happy herself, and was touched that he trusted her enough to tell her.

Alice woke up in the night from a horrible dream in which she was screaming and screaming – and then realised it was real, and it wasn't her screaming, it was Kit. She rushed into his room and found him clutching his stomach, his legs drawn up in what was clearly agonising pain; as she took him onto her knee, shouting for Tom, Kit vomited all over her.

'Tom! Tom! Ring Dr Redmond, would you? Now, quickly. There's something terribly wrong.'

* * *

By the time Dr Redmond arrived, Kit was much calmer, the pain clearly easing, but pale and listless.

Alice liked Dr Redmond. He was the ideal, trust-inspiring family doctor, middle-aged, patient, kindly faced.

'Right, young fellow-my-lad, let's have a look at you. Put him on the bed, would you?'

He felt Kit's tummy for a long time. Then he said, 'His abdomen is still quite soft which is a good sign. I'd say it was a grumbling appendix. His symptoms are classic. Let's see how he goes in the next few days. Keep him quiet, plenty of fluids. If it happens again, of course let me know. They used to rush them into surgery at the first symptom, now we leave it for a few days, see if it settles. All right? I'll be getting back to bed, I think. I'd advise you to do the same.'

'Right,' said Tom. 'Thank you so much for coming out at this terrible hour.'

'Oh, it's all part of the job.'

Dr Redmond followed Tom out of the room. Alice could hear him uttering calming clichés before the front door closed.

'Nice chap,' said Tom, coming back into the room. 'Very good of him to come at this time of night.'

'I suppose,' said Alice. 'It's no more than he should do, though – this is your wonderful National Health Service we're dealing with. I still don't feel very happy, Tom. What if it's something more than appendicitis? It just feels – wrong to me.'

'Alice, he's a very experienced doctor. And with respect, he knows a lot more than you do. Come on. Back to bed. You're probably going to have a difficult day tomorrow.'

No change there then, thought Alice wearily.

# Chapter 55

He was all right. No, that was unfair. He was more than all right, he was very nice. Interesting. Mildly amusing. Quite good-looking in a quiet sort of way. Light brown hair, grey eyes, tall, fairly – if conventionally – well dressed, but then she'd had enough of flamboyant dressers, they seemed to trail trouble in their wake. He was a medic too, a surgeon at St Thomas'. She'd met him through her uncle, who'd invited her to a lecture on developments in anaesthesia. At the drinks reception afterwards they'd been chatting and her uncle had spotted them together and suggested they came to supper with him. Jillie looked at him suspiciously.

'Your aunt's agreed to join me; I'd already invited Patrick.'

'Oh, no, Uncle William, I can't. I've got work to do.'

'Come on, Jillie, all you ever do is work. You know what they say, all work and no play –'

'Makes Jill a dull girl,' said Jillie, smiling at him. 'Yes, all right, I give in.'

She did indeed feel very dull; Julius had lit her up, made her feel sparkly and special. Since then, the lights had all gone out. She didn't have great hopes of Patrick in that direction, but at least it wouldn't be yet another evening reading in her room.

They went to a small restaurant in the Strand; the chat was easy and interesting. It emerged that Patrick Brownlow was a gastroenterologist and had been working in Edinburgh, had only just come to London. At the end of the evening he asked her if he could have her phone number and she (only a little unwillingly) gave it to him. Since then, they had seen a couple of films and eaten a few meals together, always at small, unpretentious restaurants. It was all oddly soothing after the excesses of Sundays with Julius. She wasn't in love with him, but she did like him, and felt happier than she had for some time.

And then one night, after seeing a play, they decided to go to a small, slightly smarter restaurant called Angelo's in Albemarle Street. They walked into the restaurant rather briskly as it was pouring with rain, with Patrick's arm round Jillie's shoulders (where it had never been before) in order more easily to share his umbrella, and almost collided with Nell Henderson and Julius Noble who were leaving.

Jillie managed a smile, the introductions and an expression of delight when Nell announced that her book was to be published. 'And it's all thanks to you – everyone loves the surgeon bit best.'

After some graceful protestations, Jillie handed her wet coat to the maître d' and, with a sweet smile at Nell, said goodbye.

To Julius she spoke not a word.

Julius was not, anyway, in a chatty mood because Nell wanted to postpone the wedding date.

'The thing is, darling, that's precisely when they want to publish my book – not a good idea. The clash, I mean.'

Julius's suggestion that the publication might be postponed rather than their wedding got a very poor reception. 'Darling, you can't possibly realise how lucky I am to be getting published by these people at all; I can't start arguing with them about dates. Please don't be difficult, Julius, it's so easy to change our date.'

Julius said mildly that he wasn't being difficult, merely a little disappointed, and it was a good thing they hadn't sent out the invitations yet; they then spent most of the rest of the meal in silence.

Finding the next morning that, along with feeling like a discarded handkerchief, he was experiencing something close to relief – and wondering, not for the first time in recent weeks, if their marriage was actually such a good idea – Julius thought he would ring Jillie and beg her yet again for a meeting. But after a little more careful thought

465

over his breakfast, he decided against it; she had clearly found someone else and it was equally clearly at least a little serious.

Nobody who was present forgot the night that Mr Edward Welles and Sir Neil Lawson faced one another literally over the bed of a child in Mr Welles's ward, and did battle over her.

It began with the crying; the crying of a sick, frightened child for her mother. Sister looked at the ward clock, saw that it was after nine, and breathed a sigh of relief that Mr Welles had had a very long list; he had pulled off his surgical gloves and operating mask a full hour earlier, said he was exhausted and looking forward to getting home. With luck, they could settle the child themselves. Sister was growing very weary of the problems caused by Mr Welles's interference. Not just the interference in itself, but the unpleasantness of having to report it to Sir Neil (these were his strict instructions now), of recording every detail of what happened, and at times being called into Sir Neil's office, along with Mr Welles, and having to act as witness – and in such a way as to make it very plain that Mr Welles and his methods caused disruption and distress to the other patients, the nurses on duty and indeed to herself.

The problem was that several of the nurses, the younger ones anyway, agreed with Mr Welles. The children did settle more quietly and happily if their mothers were allowed to remain with them until they went down to theatre, and certainly, if they were very poorly afterwards; Sister couldn't work out at first how these women managed to find out how their children were post-operative, and, if the news was not good, to arrive at the entrance to the ward. But the answer was simple: if it was a difficult case and the child was high on his list, he would tell the mother to wait in the waiting room. Sir Neil's wrath when he heard this reputedly brought him close to heart failure.

They couldn't go on like this, or rather she couldn't, and in fact Sir Neil had promised her he was gathering cases and then intended to hold a meeting with the entire medical board of the hospital and get Mr Welles dealt with once and for all; but it seemed like a long time coming. She had resolved that she would put in a formal complaint herself if the next episode was not dealt with to her satisfaction.

But Mr Welles was still in the hospital, had been worried about one of the day's cases, and, wanting to make a final visit before he went home, walked straight over to the little girl's bed (without seeking permission from Sister) and attempted to comfort her. He was not entirely successful; the child's tears turned into near-hysteria as a result of his sympathy, at which several other children, also operated on that day, began to cry as well.

Ned was demanding to know why he had not been told of Susan's distress when Sir Neil Lawson, who was also most unusually still in the hospital, stalked into the ward, white lipped with fury, demanding silence; and, literally shouting across Susan's bed, to an audience of frightened children, tremulous nurses and a deeply satisfied Sister, demanded that Mr Welles should leave her to the care of the nurses, and go immediately to his office.

Ned, driven to his own fury, refused, 'until I have first examined and then calmed this child to my satisfaction'. They faced one another across the bed, shouting, each refusing the other the respect and indeed courtesy that was their due. It was appalling, as Ned afterwards admitted to everyone, for morale, for the children, for the nurses. The children were upset and anxious for days.

He had no right, he knew, to set himself single-handedly against the philosophy and discipline of an undoubtedly great hospital; he had ruthlessly used his position there to turn comfort into confrontation, order into anarchy. He had behaved in a way that he had no right to do; and he resolved that he should approach his campaign in future quite differently,

Sir Neil kept him waiting for over half an hour. When he arrived, still clearly fuming, he called Ned in and didn't even tell him to sit down.

'That was shocking, appalling behaviour. I cannot tell you how distressed I was.'

'You don't need to,' said Ned quietly, 'and I shall have letters of apology to Sister and to the nurses involved delivered in the morning. And to you, of course, Sir Neil.'

'I'm afraid I require rather more than that. I want your absolute assurance – and most certainly in writing – that you are dropping this absurd campaign of yours, as of now, and that we will hear no more about it.'

'I'm afraid I can't give you that,' said Ned. 'It is too important to me. And, I still believe, to the children themselves. But I shall approach it differently – there will be no more confrontation in the wards, I assure you.'

'Then I shall have to ask for your resignation. This is a large and important hospital and I cannot risk its running being disturbed by what I can only term crackpot theories. And I would remind you also of the other matter of which we spoke, Mr Welles.'

A long silence; then Ned said, 'Very well. If that is how you feel, then you will have my resignation in writing in the morning. Meanwhile, I apologise for my behaviour, and for the undoubted distress I have caused.'

Whereupon he left Sir Neil and the hospital calmly; but he arrived home with a sense of foreboding, aware that he had not only lost his job, but also made an enemy of one of the most significant members of his profession.


Two days later Kit had another attack. As he walked into the kitchen, he suddenly lay down on the floor, his legs drawn up, screaming, in between sobbing and saying, 'Tummy, tummy.' And then he vomited. It was an absolute replay of the last time.

Alice laid him tenderly on the sofa, ran to the phone and dialled the surgery number: could Dr Redmond come and see Kit immediately. Dr Redmond was out on his rounds, and wouldn't be back for at least two hours. She could come to the surgery if she liked, and then she'd be sure of seeing him, otherwise he wouldn't be making any more house calls until at least five.

'And you can't contact him?'

'No, of course not. I only do it in the most acute emergencies. Of course, you could take your child to casualty.'

Alice looked in at Kit; he was quieter. Maybe . . . but it was only a pause, and then the screaming began again. God, this was a nightmare.

'I'll bring him to the surgery,' she said. 'Thank you.'

Kit's screams were now joined by Charlie's. Alice visualised sitting in the surgery for up to an hour, with three children, two of whom were screaming, one possibly vomiting; she wasn't sure if she would be able to bear it. She rang Tom, without any hope at all: he was on his way to Purbridge. She did have a couple of friends in the road, but they had three children apiece; she could hardly wish Charlie on them.

And then she thought of Mrs Hartley, her next-door neighbour who had more than once offered to help Alice. 'My grandchildren are all teenagers – how I miss them. I'd love to have one of yours if you were stuck one day.'

She was, surely, stuck now?

She knocked tentatively on Mrs Hartley's door, and explained her predicament. Could she possibly have Charlie? 'We won't be more than an hour, two at the most.' Mrs Hartley beamed at her.

'You be as long as you like,' she said. 'I'd love to have the baby. I've offered to help and I meant it.'

'Oh – thank you,' said Alice. 'Thank you so much. I'll get his bottle and his carrycot.' She hoped she sounded like the mother of a child who enjoyed his bottle and lay gurgling in his carrycot for hours on end.

She returned in minutes with Charlie in the carrycot, the bottle tucked at his feet; Mrs Hartley reached for him eagerly, as if Alice was giving her some long-yearned-after present.

'You go on, lovey, you don't want to lose your place. I'm sure the doctor will be able to sort Kit out; he does look bad, though. Come on, then, Charlie, we're going to have a lovely afternoon together.'

Alice, feeling rather like an executioner, thanked her and left, put the other two children in the back seat of the car, Kit swathed in towels against further vomiting, and drove to the surgery.

'Yes, well, you were right to bring him back,' said Dr Redmond. 'But I stand by my original diagnosis. He's quite quiet again now, and his abdomen is quite soft – it follows the pattern of appendicitis exactly. Very distressing for both of you, but not serious.'

'Yes, but –'

'Yes?'

He sounded slightly less patient.

'If it's not, what might it be?'

'Well, hard to say. But I'm confident it is.'

'And – how long would you leave it? Before operating, I mean? Supposing he got peritonitis as a result, then—'

'Mrs Knelston, I do assure you Kit is a long way from developing peritonitis,' said Dr Redmond, his expression carefully patient.

'How can we be sure of that?' Irritation was making Alice brave.

'Well –' He hesitated, then said, 'I can arrange for him to see a consultant, if you like. How would that be?'

'Well – mightn't it take weeks?'

'Good heavens, no. You've been reading the newspapers, they love running down our National Health Service. Maybe a couple of weeks, no more.'

'But Dr Redmond, this has happened twice in three days. Surely—?'

'Look, Mrs Knelston, I can't do better than that. Bring Kit in if he has another of these attacks, of course, but I'd put money on it all settling down within a week. Now, if you'll excuse me . . .'

They were clearly dismissed.

And now, thought Alice, I've got to face Mrs Hartley. Who will probably never speak to me again.

Mrs Hartley was beaming as she opened the door. A blissful silence lay behind her in her house.

'What a little angel,' she said. 'Oh, we've had such a lovely time. He took his bottle beautifully and then just lay on the floor, playing with some old rattles I found, and I sang to him, poor child, but it made him laugh. Anyway, he's asleep now, in his carrycot. I'll just get it unless you'd like a quick cuppa –'

Alice could think of nothing she'd like more than a quick cuppa, but she had visions of Charlie waking up, taking one look at her and starting to scream, and after thanking Mrs Hartley profusely, she took the carrycot and went home.

'You little monster,' she hissed at Charlie, as she set him down on the floor.

Tom arrived home exhausted and in no mood to start fretting over the health of Kit, who was fast asleep.

'Hell of a day,' he said. 'Doorstepping, non-stop. Several people told me to bugger off, several more to mind my own effing business. Oh, politics is fun. Well, only ten days to go. Whatever happens it can't be worse than this.'

'Tom, I'm sorry you've had such a bad day,' said Alice carefully, 'but I'm really worried about Kit. Supposing it isn't appendicitis, supposing it's—'

'Supposing it's what? Look, he's fine, Alice, sleeping like a – a baby. Obviously, whatever it is can't be serious. And Dr Redmond is getting an appointment with a consultant. What more do you want?'

'I – I want to be convinced,' said Alice. 'And I'm not. He's in such pain when it happens. We had children in Thomas' with appendicitis and it can be horribly painful, of course, but it wasn't really like that – and if it is his appendix it could rupture and then—'

'Alice,' said Tom, 'you're being a typical nurse, thinking you know more than the doctor. Look, I'm sorry, but Kit seems fine to me, and I need to get some sleep. I think I might stay in Purbridge tomorrow and the next few nights. The journey is a killer. Now, you are still on for polling day, aren't you?'

'If Kit's all right.'

'Oh, Christ,' said Tom and stalked out of the room; Alice heard him going upstairs.

'Bastard,' she said, too quietly for him to hear but it still made her feel better. Was the election really more important than his child's health?

It seemed it was.

'Diana Southcott?'

She knew that voice. Posh with an edge, she would have labelled it. Like its owner. She had been wondering if she might hear it again of its own accord, or whether she might have to use subterfuge. But no subterfuge required. Good start. Very good start. She'd only been back twenty-four hours.

'Yes. It's me.'

'Leo Bennett.'

'Oh – hello,' she said. She didn't want him getting all pleased with himself, thinking she'd recognised his voice straight away. Even if she had.

'How was New York?'

'It was amazing.'

'Good. Did you like the Pierre?'

'Loved it.'

'Do any shopping?'

'Didn't have time.'

'God. They really were making you work.'

'Of course,' said Diana, slightly primly.

'I rang,' he said, after a moment's pause, 'just on the off chance you might have changed your mind.'

'About the story? No, absolutely not. Sorry, Leo.'

'That's OK. I thought that's what you'd say. But you know . . . never give up.'

'I'm sure you never do,' she said.

'Occasionally. How would you feel about lunching again anyway? Without having to worry about what you were or weren't telling me?'

'I'd feel quite happy,' she said, smiling down the phone. 'But not yet, I'm working all day the next few days.'

'You really do work hard, don't you?' he said. 'In that case, why don't we make it dinner instead? If that could be sooner . . .'

They arranged to meet two nights later. Diana wondered how her knees would react to seeing him again. Maybe it would only happen on the first meeting.

# Chapter 56

Oh, no. Please, please, no. Not again. He'd been so well the last thirty-six hours . . . now he was lying on the kitchen floor, thrashing about with pain, screaming, 'Tummy . . . tummy . . . tummy . . .'

It was six thirty in the morning. Tom had just left, not that he would have been any help, Alice thought, racking her brain for someone who might be not Dr Redmond. Oh, of course, of course, she should have asked her before.

'Jillie? It's me, Alice. Look – I know it's a lot to ask but could you – could you possibly come over? There's something the matter with Kit. Recurrent abdominal pain. Three times now, each episode more severe. He's screaming with pain, legs drawn up, vomiting . . . temperature a hundred and two –'

'Sounds like appendicitis.'

'I know, so the doctor has said, twice now. But I think it's something else. I *know* it's something else. No idea what. Jillie, please come.'

'I'm on duty this morning, Alice. Operating. I was just leaving.'

'Jillie, please. I'm really scared. I don't know what do to.'

A moment's silence; then Jillie said, 'Let me give them a ring. I'll see what I can do.'

She rang back in five minutes. Five very long minutes.

'It's OK, I'm on my way.'

Alice met her at the door, gave her a hug. 'Thank you so much for coming. I'm so scared. He's really unwell. Come through, he's in the sitting room. Oh, God, Jillie, what on earth is that?'

There was an explosion as something extremely unpleasant, red in colour, came shooting out of Kit's pyjama trousers.

'I don't know, not really. But can I have a look at your bottom, Kit, darling?' said Jillie. 'I'll try not to hurt, I promise.'

Jillie spent a little while examining him, then said, 'I can feel something – in his rectum. He needs to see someone urgently. What's your GP like?'

'Hopeless. He just keeps saying it's appendicitis.'

'Well, you're right, it's more than that. Kit needs to see a specialist quickly.'

'The GP finally agreed to that yesterday. He's writing to someone.'

'Writing! It's a lot more urgent than that, I'm afraid.'

'But where – I mean, who?' She looked at Jillie with panic in her eyes.

'I think you should take him to see Ned,' said Jillie quietly. 'He's one of the best paediatricians in London and he'd see him this morning, I know.'

'You really think he needs to be seen that urgently?'

'Yes, I do.'

'I'll call him then. Do you have the number for his rooms?'

'Yes. Here –'

Alice rang the number. It rang for quite a long time. She looked at her watch.

'It's only nine. Would he be there?'

'He should be. If not then I – well, I do have his home number.'

'Of course. God, Jillie, this is good of you. I – oh, good morning. Is that Mr Welles's secretary?'

'Yes. Can I help you?' The voice didn't promise great helpfulness.

'I – wondered if I could speak to Mr Welles? I'm a prospective patient. Or rather my child is.'

'I'm afraid not. Mr Welles doesn't speak directly to patients without a referral. So – I'm afraid . . .'

'Could you hold on a minute?' Alice put her hand over the phone and looked at Jillie. 'He doesn't speak to patients without a referral.'

Jillie hesitated, then said, 'Give the phone to me. Jennifer, this is

Jillie Curtis. Yes. I'm very well, thank you. Look, I need to talk to Mr Welles. I've got a very sick child I want him to see. It's desperately urgent. What? Oh – yes. Yes, I'll hold on.'

She had become very pale. Alice tried to imagine what she must be feeling, how painful this must be. She reached for Jillie's hand and held it; Jillie smiled at her, rather wanly.

'Oh – Ned, hello. Yes, I'm very well, thank you. And you? Good. Ned, I'm with Alice Knelston. Her little boy, Kit, is very unwell. Stomach pains, vomiting, fever. No, I don't think so. But he's producing what we were told to call a redcurrant stool. Does that mean anything to you? Yes, I thought it would. Look, can you see him this morning? I think it's really urgent. Yes, of course, I'll tell her. Thank you, Ned. Thank you so much. Bye.'

She turned to Alice.

'The red poo is very significant. I thought it was, but I didn't feel confident enough to say so. We're to get Kit up there just as soon as you can. We can take my car. Fine to bring Lucy. I can look after her, but I'm not sure about Charlie –'

'It's OK,' said Alice. 'The lady next door, the love of Charlie's life, will have him. I'll just go and make a bottle and take him in there.'

Mrs Hartley was delighted. 'A whole morning with my little sweetheart. How lovely! Come to Nana, darlin'.'

Charlie gurgled delightedly at the sight of her. He never gurgled . . .

'Oh, Mrs Knelston –' Mrs Hartley looked stricken suddenly. 'I hope you don't mind me calling myself Nana. My own are all grown up, and it's so lovely to be one again.'

Jillie said she was delighted to think of Mrs Hartley as Charlie's nana, and handed him and the bottle over. 'I'll bring in the carrycot and some nappies in a minute. Thank you so much. I hope we're not too long.'

'You be as long as you need. Poor little Kit, what a shame. We'll have fun, won't we, Charlie? How would you like to go to the park, eh?'

Charlie gurgled again.

✳ ✳ ✳

'There's one thing I must do before we go,' said Alice. 'Tell Tom. I'll ring him straight away. Are you OK with Kit?'

'We're fine. Only be quick. We don't want to be late for Ned.'

'Promise I won't . . . Tom, it's me. Look, Jillie's here. She's very worried about Kit, says he needs to be seen by a specialist right away. She's very kindly arranged for him to see Ned, this morning. Straight away. Ned Welles. Yes. Yes, Tom, that Ned Welles. Now, actually. We're just leaving. I just thought I'd better let you know. What? Yes, of course I know he's a private doctor. What? No, of course I'm not going to cancel the appointment. Why should I? Tom, this is your son you're talking about. Who is very, very ill. And possibly needs surgery right away. I beg your pardon? No, Tom, I won't listen to you; I can't believe you actually said that. No. Yes, of course I realise what I'm doing. Do you realise what *you're* doing? Putting your principles before your son's life. I can't believe it. No. No, I will not go and see Dr Redmond again. Apart from anything else, he's got no particular knowledge of paediatrics, whereas Ned is a paediatric surgeon. Look, I've got to go. Ned is fitting us in between patients. Jillie's driving us up. No. No, I'm sorry, Tom, I'm not going to wait for you to come home. If you really want to see me you can come to Ned's rooms. I can't listen to any more of this – it shocks me, it really does.'

And then, as she put Lucy's shoes on, shaking with rage and shock at Tom's reaction, came the dreadful, ugly thought. Would Laura have done this? Gone against one of the most sacred tenets of Tom's life? Defied his most deeply held belief? Would she? Or would she have done what he wished, battled on with the NHS, seen that Kit got the same swift treatment from them; whereas she, getting it through contacts and privilege, was doing what Tom most hated and despised. And as she stood there, suspended by indecision and her fear of not being a good wife, as good a wife as Laura had been, Jillie, her voice urgent now, called her to hurry, and Kit started crying again with pain and fright.

Tom put the phone down. He was literally shaking with rage. Alice, his wife, taking his son to see a private consultant in Welbeck Street. He thought for a moment he was going to be sick. How could she betray him like this? She knew how passionately, how deeply he cared about the National Health Service, how he hated privilege, and the rights it bought to do things like seeing top consultants immediately, getting special care, jumping queues. It was so wrong, such appalling injustice: and she was putting her name – *his* name – to it. With a general election only a week away, when his loyalty to the National Health Service, his hatred of privilege, were under such scrutiny. He had been so proud of his speech, comparing the system of private doctors and hospitals, where only the rich could go, with apartheid. Now it could come back to haunt him.

It only needed one person to have seen Kit at Ned Welles's rooms, or to have heard he had been there, and – well, he could see the headlines.

'*Knelston the Bevanite sends sick son to Welbeck Street*' ... '*Bevan betrayed by his disciple*' ... '*What price principle now, Mr Knelston?*' God, it was awful. Terrible. He would be ruined. How could Alice have done this to him? Of course Kit mattered desperately, but he didn't seem that ill, he'd been larking about in between attacks, apparently perfectly well. And the GP was sending him to an NHS consultant. It surely couldn't take that long, they could press to have it hurried along ... and there was always the emergency department.

Kit lay quietly on the examination table in Ned Welles's consulting room, displaying the listlessness that always followed the attacks, and allowed Ned to examine him without complaint.

When he had finished, Ned said, 'Good boy, you were very brave. Now – come and sit on Mummy's knee again.' Within minutes he became drowsy, held in Alice's arms like a baby, exhausted by the events of the morning.

'Right,' said Ned. 'Well, the good news is that I know what's wrong – well, I'm as certain as one can ever be – and that it can be fixed surgically. The bad news is that it's been allowed to develop – in no way your fault, Alice, or even your GP's. It's very rare – and he's pretty ill.'

'So – what is it?' asked Alice.

'It's something called intussusception. Did you ever come across it at Thomas'?'

'No. I'd have suspected it if I had.'

'Of course you would. It's pretty rare. And very unusual in any child much over two. Basically, the gut folds into itself, bit like one of those folding telescopes. Then, because it's anchored by blood vessels, it can't go any further and it causes an obstruction. And then it will swell, and if not treated, the bowel can necrose, leading to peritonitis. Kit's high temperature leads me to suspect there's a danger of that. Peritonitis, that is.'

'But why the spells of being perfectly all right?'

'In the early stages, it can un-telescope, so to speak, and all is well until it does it again. But each time, it tends to take longer. And finally we reach the stage Kit is at, where it is well and truly blocked. Surgery can cure it, but we don't have much time. Now, I can fit him into my private list this afternoon, if you would like me to.'

'How dangerous is the operation?'

'If the bowel has not necrosed, not particularly. It's difficult, of course, all surgery on small children is, but I'm confident about it. The main danger now is delay.'

'Then – then we mustn't delay,' she said, her voice sounding shaky even to her. 'Oh Ned, Ned, it is so good of you to do this.'

'Well,' he said. 'I think you've been pretty good to me. All of you. I am more grateful for your discretion than I can ever tell.'

She knew, of course, what he was referring to. She merely smiled at him and said, 'Please, please, do go ahead. Where do you operate?'

'St Mary's Chelsea. Small private hospital, but I have an excellent team. You may as well go straight there. I'll alert them, and get Kit's case first on the list. And I'll ask Jennifer to sort out a room for you – that's if you want to stay.'

'Of course I do.' There was a knock on the door; the icy Jennifer, now warm and friendly, put her head round it.

'Mrs Knelston, your husband is here. He—'

'How very timely,' said Ned. 'Ask him to come in, Jennifer, if you would. I'll explain the situation to him.'

'I might take Lucy out for a bit,' said Jillie hastily.

'No, said Alice, 'please stay.'

Tom was ushered in, his eyes brilliant with what Alice knew was anger.

'Good morning, Tom,' said Ned.

'Good morning,' said Tom. 'Look, it's very kind of you to see Kit but I'll take him and Alice home now. And Lucy. You appear to be sheltering my entire family.'

'Tom, you will *not* take us home,' said Alice, shocked into a new level of determination by his arrogance and near-rudeness, Laura fading, temporarily at least, into the background. 'Of course we can't go home; we have to take Kit to St Mary's Chelsea where Ned is going to operate on him this afternoon.'

'No, I'm afraid he's not.'

'And I'm afraid he is. Ned, please tell Tom what you just told me.'

Tom listened in silence; then he said, 'I'm grateful, Ned, of course, but that is only your opinion. I don't want Kit put through surgery until we are quite sure your diagnosis is the correct one. Also, for obvious reasons, I want him treated on the NHS.'

'The NHS is a wonderful organisation,' said Ned, his voice very calm. 'I work for it, and I believe in it as much as you do. But it would be highly unlikely that Kit could have this surgery done under its aegis in time. Had he been diagnosed earlier, it might be different. You could go to casualty, of course, but even then, hours would be lost. He is dangerously ill, Tom. Time is of the essence.'

'Again, that is only your opinion,' said Tom. 'Look, I'm very grateful for your help. But I cannot allow this operation to go ahead this after-noon and certainly not at that particular hospital. I'm sorry.'

'Tom, how can you talk like that?' cried Alice. 'Kit could die. You're putting your absurd principles against your son's life.'

'My principles are not absurd.'

'They are under these circumstances,' said Alice. 'Anyway, it doesn't matter if they are or not, because neither I nor Kit are coming home with you. Ned, we'll see you this afternoon.'

Ned looked at her, his dark eyes anguished.

'You must resolve this between you, of course,' he said, 'but I beg you to do so quickly. I cannot stress enough the danger Kit is in. And there is one other very important thing. If you decide on what I am convinced is the right action, I need one of you to give me your written consent. That's the law, as I'm sure you will know, Tom. I –' He stopped.

'I'm afraid I'm not prepared to do that,' said Tom.

'Tom!' Alice was shouting now. 'That is a truly wicked decision. You're putting your political career before your son's life.' She stopped, looked down at the sleeping Kit, and said abruptly, 'You think people will find out, don't you, and that will destroy you politically. That's what this is about. You're so desperate for success and power and all that ridiculous, horrible stuff, you're prepared to risk Kit's death. Tom, you can't do that. Please, please, tell me you can't.'

Tom was silent; then he said, 'No, Alice, I won't agree to what you want – so wrongly, in my opinion. It's got nothing to do with my having success and power. I find that infinitely insulting. It's to do with what I believe in. It's about justice, nothing more or less. Justice for the individual. And I care passionately about that. Don't you understand?'

'No, I don't. Especially not when it is our son's life at stake. But it doesn't matter, because I'll sign the form.'

'No,' said Tom, and his expression as he looked at her was of open dislike. 'No, Alice, I absolutely forbid that. And I feel quite sure, as Kit's father, my wishes would outweigh yours in a court of law.'

Panic struck at Alice, panic and something else even more powerful: shock that Tom could display such paternalistic arrogance – the arrogance he had deplored, as he had often told her, in his father.

And then, something extraordinary happened. She felt Laura move onto her side. She would not have stood for that: for being told what and what not to do by her husband. It would have been abhorrent to her, against all her feminist principles. She might not have followed the course Alice had chosen, but she would have put Kit first, in whatever way she thought best. Alice knew that. And she would have fought Tom, if she believed she should. Alice suddenly, and with great clarity, had no doubt about it, and in that moment Laura changed: from being rival and enemy to ally and friend. So engrossed was she in this revelation, that Alice hardly realised Ned was speaking again.

'I'm afraid you are wrong there, Tom,' he said. 'The law, as it stands, gives preference to whichever parent is in favour of any surgery, be it the father or the mother.'

Alice looked at Tom, and said, 'Right. That's settled then. Ned, give me the form or whatever and I'll sign it.'

'Alice, please,' said Tom, and there was desperation in his voice now. 'Please try to see it my way.'

'I see it very clearly your way. And I don't like what I see. You want to stop Kit from having the best possible care in the least possible time, and there's only one reason as far as I'm concerned. You don't want to betray your own principles, not just because you do hold them so passionately, and I accept that, of course. But also because you're afraid of being seen to be betraying them, caught out if you like, and endangering your political career.'

'That is untrue and unjust.'

'Oh, really? Well, I'll try to believe that. But in just a couple of hours Kit could be receiving the best surgery available. Why should you deny him that?'

'I don't accept it will necessarily be the best. It's available, yes, wonderfully available, but why the best? The finest surgeons in the land work for the NHS –'

'Could I just remind you,' said Ned, mild still, but with an underlying threat in his voice, 'that those surgeons include me? For many, many hours a week. At a very fine teaching hospital. Whose theatres and support staff just happen *not* to be available to me this afternoon. And who, should I turn up there now, with a request to use their facilities for Kit, would almost certainly turn me away.'

Tom was silent for a moment, then he said to Alice, 'If you go ahead with this, totally against my wishes, then clearly there's nothing I can do to stop you. I would hope you would see how unhappy that makes me, and that it would trouble you. Please, Alice, please, for my sake consider that at least. And could I remind you that – that –' He paused, clearly struggling with a mass of painful emotions. 'When Laura died, and I asked you if it still would have happened, if her care would have been what some would call better, had she been under Jillie's uncle at St Thomas', you and she both assured me she would not. Surely that must mean something to you.'

They faced one another across the room, gladiators in a life-and-death struggle: Jillie watched them, half fascinated, half fearful. And then Alice spoke, her eyes brilliant, her voice low with rage and fear, but quite strong.

'Tom, we lied,' she said.


'I think,' Jillie had said, after Alice had made her poisonous confession, 'I think I'll wait outside.'

'I'll come with you,' said Ned. 'In any case, I have other patients to see. Please tell Jennifer when you have come to a decision, Alice – and can I just remind you that time is passing and Kit is in danger. Whatever you decide.'

'But I thought – I thought you said you could save him?' Alice's voice was thick with fear.

'Alice, Jillie was right, there are no certainties in medicine. You know that, of course you do. He is a very sick little boy and it's a difficult operation. Of course I can't guarantee anything although I do feel confident. But I do repeat, time is of the essence. You must make your minds up very soon, if he is to have the best possible chance.'

'My mind is made up, obviously,' said Alice, giving Tom a look of such implacable hatred that Jillie winced. 'And since that is sufficient for Ned to go ahead, there is no need for any delay.'

'And the form?'

'I'll sign the form,' said Tom, very quietly.

# Chapter 57

The operation was delicate, and took longer than anyone had expected. To Alice, waiting in the parents' room, and to Tom, banished to the general reception area two floors below, the afternoon seemed endless and terrifying.

Once Tom ventured upstairs: 'I was afraid I would miss Ned if I was down there, when he had finished, you know.'

'I'll see you are informed, of course,' said Alice.

'Alice – Alice, please will you let me just try and explain—'

'You couldn't,' she said.

'But—'

'Tom, please, just go away. I shall never forgive you as long as I live. I think the best thing you can do is go back to Purbridge. You've got *really* important things to do there.'

He left; she went back to her chair and sat hugging a cushion. How had she let this happen? How could she have put Kit's life in danger, accepting what the GP said, not taking him somewhere she trusted immediately? Was she mad? Or just feeble? She thought of Kit as she had last seen him, dressed in his tiny hospital gown, lying like a doll on the trolley as they wheeled him down to theatre. He had been so brave, hadn't cried or made a fuss, just lain there, his fair hair neatly combed back; only his blue eyes, wide with apprehension, to hint at what he must be going through.

As they stood in the lift, a little hand came from under the blanket groping for his mother's; Alice took it, kissed it, tears blinding her.

Silence; then a sudden wail: 'Teddy. Want teddy.'

'Darling, I can't—'

'Teddeee.' The small face crumpled, the chest heaved with the beginning of a sob: losing Teddy was breaking Kit, as the pain and the fear had not.

'Kit —'

'It's all right, Mrs Knelston,' said the nurse who was accompanying them to theatre. 'You can go and get his teddy. We'll wait. Mr Welles likes the children to have anything they want at this stage, to feel as comfortable and happy as possible.'

What an amazing man he was, Alice thought, running upstairs and searching frantically for Teddy, finding him finally under the cot where Kit would sleep. No wonder Jillie had loved him so much.

Reunited with Teddy, Kit smiled a seraphic smile.

'Teddy brave,' he announced.

'Teddy is very brave.'

'Stay now, Mummy.'

'I will.'

And stay she did, holding Kit's hand up to the moment when he lost consciousness, lying limp and still, even Teddy no longer required.

And Alice, terrified beyond anything, went to the parents' room and sat there, willing Kit to be strong, strong enough for his small body to withstand all that was required of it.

She looked out of the window, thinking about Kit, the astonishment and wonder of her first sight of him, his first smile, his first laugh – a slightly hoarse, deep chuckle, nothing like his light dancing voice – his first steps – tottering determinedly across the sitting room from one chair to the next, a long and perilous journey for his sturdy little legs. Kit lying sweetly and peacefully asleep in his pram in the garden, under the apple tree. He always smiled in his sleep; as if to show that his dreams, like his life, were sweet and happy. Please God, it would continue and safely, that short, precious, happy little life. That short, fragile little life.

\* \* \*

A clearly exhausted Ned came smiling into the room two hours later, assuring her that all was well. 'The bowel hadn't necrosed. He's still unconscious and quite poorly, but absolutely not in danger. Although – another twelve hours even, and it could have been a very different story.'

'Can I see him?' said Alice, tears of relief streaming down her face.

'Not yet. But when he comes round he'll need you to be with him. In this hospital, mothers are welcome to stay with their children round the clock.'

'That's amazing,' said Alice. 'Thank you.'

'Now I must get back to theatre. I've several more operations to do yet, one almost as difficult as that one. Kit will be in his room in an hour or so.'

'Oh, Ned,' said Alice, 'how can I ever thank you?'

'Well –' Ned hesitated, then said, 'There might be something Tom could do. When he's an MP, that is. I haven't got time to discuss it now, but another day perhaps. Where is Tom?'

'Oh – downstairs in reception, I think,' said Alice coolly, as if that was a perfectly normal place to wait while your child was having life-threatening surgery.

'But he is still here?'

'I imagine so.'

'Alice –' said Ned gently and then stopped, clearly thinking better of what he was about to say. 'I'll go and find him, tell him the good news.'

'Oh, no, you're far too busy . . . I'll—'

'No, I'd like to see him. I'm never too busy to speak to parents,' said Ned. She hoped he wasn't sending her a coded message that he didn't believe she would tell Tom. He couldn't think she was that wicked.

'Look,' said Tom, after they had seen Kit through a painful and nauseous awakening and he was in a more normal sleep, 'why don't I go home. Relieve poor Mrs Hartley of Charlie. Then you can stay here.'

'Well, if you have the time that would be extremely kind,' said

Alice. She spoke as if he was a fairly distant acquaintance. 'Thank you.'

'Alice! They're my children, for God's sake.'

She didn't answer.


'Tom?' Donald Herbert's voice was at its most hectoring. 'What the hell do you think you're doing at home, with only days to go to polling day?'

'I'm sorry, Donald, but I can't be anywhere else. Kit has just had life-threatening surgery and—'

'Yes, yes. Where's Alice, can't she hold the fort?'

'Not at the moment,' said Tom firmly. 'She's at the hospital with Kit.'

'Well, she can't be there all the time?'

'I'm afraid she is.'

'How extraordinary. Well, if you don't get back to Purbridge sharpish, you won't have a cat in hell's chance of getting in.'

'Just hearing you talk like that makes me wonder if I want to,' said Tom and put the phone down.

It rang again immediately. 'What was that for?'

'Oh, things you didn't say. That you hoped Kit was going to be all right, what was wrong with him, that sort of thing.'

There was a silence; then Donald said, clearly reluctantly, 'I'm sorry. How is he?'

'As well as can be expected,' said Tom. 'He's going to live if that's what you mean. But he might not have done.'

'What hospital is he in? I'll send him a – a toy or something. And some flowers for Alice, she must be getting pretty fed up.'

'Honestly,' said Tom, not answering the question, 'please don't bother. It wouldn't be worth it. I'll go back to Purbridge next Tuesday, Donald, best I can do.'

'Tuesday! For Christ's sake, that'll only give you forty-eight hours.'

'Sorry. I can't leave till then.'


Donald put the phone down, swore briefly; and then realised that this was possibly a situation they could make capital of: in the form of publicity, a sympathy vote. No one could resist a sick child, and if it was done skilfully, stressing how Tom was putting his child before his career, he'd come out of it looking like a hero. They might even do a picture of Tom with Kit in his hospital bed. Now that was a really good idea. He'd get in touch with his agent immediately and suggest it. Silly bugger should have thought of it anyway. It was possible the PR boys at Transport House would be interested too. Especially after Tom's triumphant day with the cabinet minister.

If only, if only, Tom thought, he had someone to talk to. He felt weak, almost faint, physically as well as mentally, shocked at the drama of the day, the dreadfulness of Kit's illness, at Alice's casting aside his feelings and views as things of no import. Perhaps, he thought, perhaps if she had asked him, if they could have discussed it, properly and carefully, he might have agreed, albeit with huge misgivings, that she should take Kit to Ned. Of course, there had been no time for that, and he tried to think how frightened, how desperate she had been, but there had been nothing, not a glance in that direction, just a blind, careless lack of respect for his deeply held, lifelong beliefs, about justice, equality and the strong's responsibility to care for the weak. They came, those beliefs, as close to a religion as anything he knew; they provided the standard he tried to live by, albeit rather unsuccessfully of late, the justification for much of what he did. It made him look very differently at Alice, at their relationship, at what he had assumed was her love for him.

But what was even worse was her revelation about Laura. He forgave her and Jillie the lie they had told him, designed as it was to save him pain – and what would have been the point of the truth? It had comforted him, that lie, helped him through the grief and the loneliness: there had been nothing, he was able to tell himself, that anyone could have done to save her. Not he, not the doctors, not the nurses and the midwives who had checked her and smiled and told her all was well every week at the hospital and sent her on her brave, confident way. Now it seemed something could have been done. Then, just as today, he had put his principles first, holding fast to his faith, and Kit might have died, as Laura and Hope had died, and all to be laid at his door.

It had been a dreadful cruelty that he had had to learn of it, and in the way that he had. He could tell from the expression on Jillie's face that she was shocked. He had, to be sure, raised the matter in the first place today, and Alice could – perhaps would – have defended it on the grounds of strengthening her case. But she would not have let him have his way, would not have watched quietly as he took Kit to another doctor, to another hospital. She would have died herself before she had allowed that to happen. And so, there had been no need for that truth, that cruel, savage truth that left him helpless with pain and remorse, as if he had only lost them, his lovely wife and daughter, that very day. Grateful as he was for Kit's life, long after he had put Charlie and Lucy to bed, he sat staring into the past, both near and distant, and weeping as if he could never stop.

# Chapter 58

Diana picked up the phone.

'Ned, darling, hello, can I come and see you?'

'Well, it's not the best night. I'm completely exhausted, had a dreadful day yesterday –'

'What was so dreadful about it?'

'Oh – two very complex operations. Anyway, I've promised myself an early night, leaving on the dot. I'm not operating, just ward rounds and admin. Then home and collapse.'

'Oh, Ned, please. I've missed you. And I want to ask your advice about something. Something important.'

He hesitated, then, 'All right, but just one drink, then you'll have to go.'

'What time do you finish?'

'Five.'

'Fine, I'll come at six. I've got you a present anyway, from New York.'

'How lovely. Yes, all right, six; and then you must leave at seven. I'm sorry.'

'Goodness, don't overwhelm with me with your hospitality.'

Diana was driving up the King's Road, had turned into Oakley Street, then realised she was very near the hospital. She could pick him up, give him a lift. He never took his car to either of the hospitals, he liked to walk, but if he was that tired . . .

*\*\**

It was quarter to five when she walked in; she didn't announce herself. She sat down, deliberately screening herself behind a pillar, lit a cigarette, and picked up a magazine from the table. Five o'clock came, quarter past . . . so much for Ned's idea of leaving on the dot.

A lift came down; two men and a girl got out. One of the men was Ned, but he didn't see her, screened as she was by the pillar; and anyway, he wasn't alone. The girl was with him and they were engrossed in conversation; she couldn't hear what they were saying but she could see the girl quite clearly. And recognised her. From her photograph. Recognised her pretty, heart-shaped face, her blonde hair – less curly, a bit unkempt in fact – recognised her long, slender legs. She realised she had studied that photograph rather thoroughly, after all . . . Tom's perfect wife, as described in the article at any rate.

It was odd, looking at someone and knowing you'd been in bed with her husband. Been given considerable pleasure by her husband. About whom you knew all sorts of intimate things. Very odd.

Alice had now seen her. But she had no idea, of course, who she was looking at. That was even odder, Diana thought: like being invisible. Alice looked very tired: tired and upset. But why on earth was she here? It was hardly Knelston territory: completely the reverse, indeed. Tom would die rather than set foot over such a threshold.

Suddenly, Diana couldn't bear it any longer; there would be no use asking Ned what Alice was doing there, he was incredibly discreet about his patients. She walked forward, smiling, and said, 'Ned, darling, hello.'

She was quite safe, he had no idea about her and Tom; there would be no denouement. He looked surprised to see her, and obviously more than a little annoyed at her interrupting his conversation with Alice.

'Diana, what on earth are you doing here?'

'I came to pick you up, give you a lift home. I was just passing, and I thought as I was coming for a drink anyway, we could move the whole thing forward.' She smiled at Alice, held out her hand. 'How do you do? I'm Diana Southcott.'

'How do you do?' said Alice. She smiled at Diana, but it was clearly an effort. She had a pretty voice, Diana noticed, a voice that told of an expensive education: a cut above Tom socially, then. Interesting.

'And are you – one of Ned's lucky patients? Oh, no, how silly of me, it would have to be your child, or children . . .'

'I – no – that is –'

'Diana, I'm sorry,' said Ned, and now he was looking seriously annoyed. 'But you'll have to excuse us. It was kind of you to think of giving me a lift, but I'm mid-conversation with Mrs Knelston, as you see, and I'm not quite ready to leave. I still have a couple of patients to see. In fact, I think I shall have to postpone our drink.'

'Perfectly fine,' said Diana airily. 'I'll ring you in a few days. Good-bye, Mrs Knelston, so nice to meet you. I hope whoever the patient is recovers soon. Bye, Ned.'

'Sorry about that, Alice,' said Ned. 'That must have seemed very rude. I'm afraid she has a hide like a rhinoceros, as they say. She's a famous model.'

'Really? She is very beautiful. She seemed to know you rather well.'

'Oh, we were young together,' said Ned. 'Went to lots of dances, things like that. Now then, as I was saying, Kit is doing beautifully. Don't worry about the inflammation round the wound. It's a natural reaction. I'll call in again tomorrow, of course. Has Tom been in?'

'No,' said Alice flatly, her face expressionless, 'he hasn't. He couldn't risk being seen.'

'Alice,' said Ned gently, 'try not to be too hard on him. He's had an awful shock too.'

'Really? Ned, he was all ready to sacrifice Kit on the altar of his beastly politics.'

'I don't think it was quite like that.'

'Of course it was. And I can never forgive him.'

'Never is a long time. And don't forget he had to sustain the news about Laura too.'

'I know. That was bad of me.' She sighed. 'Far better he never knew. But it was sort of – relevant. Anyway, I'd better get back to Kit.'

* * *

Diana sat on her sofa, smoking, drumming her long red fingernails on the telephone table and waiting for what seemed like an eternity for the phone to be answered. If she ran a hospital she'd see callers got a better service than this. Suppose she was an emergency, suppose –

'St Mary's Private Hospital.'

'Oh – hello. I wonder if you can help me. I want to send a present to one of the children there. Can I just address it to the room?'

'Yes, of course. We'll send it straight up.'

'Right. Then I wonder if you could tell me his room number. His name is –' God, she realised she had no idea which of the children it was. 'The name is Knelston.'

'I'm afraid we don't give out any information about our patients.' The voice was soothing but firm.

'I see. But I have got the right hospital at least? You do have a child called Knelston there?'

'As I said –' less soothing now – 'we don't give any information. I'm sorry. Might I suggest you check with the child's parents?'

'Yes, of course.' She didn't want anyone reporting strange phone calls to Alice. 'Thank you so much.'

Well, she'd only been double-checking. It was quite clear the child was there. But – in a private hospital? Why?

The press office at Transport House weren't terribly interested in Tom Knelston when Donald rang them next morning, or about whether or not his child was in hospital. With only a few days to go to the election, they had better things to write about.

'Might be different if he was actually an MP. But he's not. Not a big enough name.'

Lucy had just fallen downstairs from the landing where she was rather pathetically looking for Kit, and was screaming while Tom held a cold handkerchief to the rapidly swelling bump on her head when the phone rang.

'Yes?'

'Tom? It's Donald. Look, we like the idea of a picture of you and Kit in the hospital for the local press. Thought it would help. They're going through hell up there without you. Can't Alice's mother take over?'

'No,' said Tom shortly, 'she can't.'

'But Tom, it's your entire political future at stake.'

'Can't help it.'

'Right, well, tell me what hospital the child is in, get down there soon as you can, and I'll organise a photographer. Then we can do a heart-rending interview.'

A flood of bile rose in Tom's throat; he realised he was shaking. He set Lucy down, told her to go and play with her dolls.

'I most definitely don't want to do that either,' he said. His voice sounded odd, even to himself.

'Why the hell not?'

'Kit nearly died. He's still very sick. I'm not having him used as an accessory to some PR campaign.'

'Don't be ridiculous, Tom – what harm will it do? He hasn't got to do anything.'

'Yes, he has. He's got to be photographed. Stranger in the room with a camera. Flashbulbs going off. He's much too ill for such nonsense.'

A long silence; then, reluctantly, 'All right, Tom. Have it your own way. But let's have a picture of you going into the hospital, carrying a big teddy or something. You can give the interview, or quote rather, there and then. How would that be?'

'Donald, you don't seem to understand. I'm at home because I'm looking after the other two and because I need to be available to be with Alice, in case something suddenly goes wrong.'

'Why should it go wrong? He's had the surgery, hasn't he?'

'Yes, and as I keep saying, it was quite major and it was only yesterday. Now please, can we stop this nonsense and let me get on with what I'm trying to do, which is take care of the other two children. I'll go back to Purbridge on Tuesday, as I promised.'

'Well, give me the name of the hospital at least, so I can—'

But Tom had put the phone down.

Donald was not deterred. He decided to ring a few of the news desks himself, see if he could get them interested.

* * *

Tom's phone rang again, five minutes later. It was his agent.

'Look, Tom, sorry to hear about your boy. But he's OK, I understand.'

'Well, he's more or less out of danger now, but he's pretty rotten still.'

'I can't tell you how difficult it is for us, coping with this, last weekend before polling day. Can you at least give me a statement I can put out to the local press? It would be such a help.'

Tom thought. 'Yes, all right, I can do that.'

'OK then. Soon as you can. Ring the office, give it to them. I'm doing my best out on the stumps without you. And if there's any chance, Tom, you can get down here sooner –'

'Yes, all right. But it's unlikely.'

Tom returned, distracted by a lurking sense of dread, to the already miserable task of looking after Lucy who was now very quiet.

He soon discovered why; she had climbed onto the kitchen table and was eating her way through a jar of honey, dipping her fat little fingers into it and licking them, like a small contented cat.

Ned had woken with an unexpectedly light heart. His future was looking very interesting, he decided. He would be very sorry to leave St Luke's, but he had his private practice still and although that was hardly going to occupy him full-time there were plenty of other hospitals – less prestigious, perhaps, but maybe that could be for the best; they were perhaps likely to be less set in their ways, to welcome new ideas.

He had told Jillie of his resignation and the reason, as they'd talked that day; she said she had been horrified herself by the misery and fear she had seen inflicted on children in the name of order and efficiency.

'I'll tell Uncle William, if you don't mind. I'm sure he'd be interested too.'

'Thank you.'

It was a nice morning, very nice actually, the sun had definitely got its hat on, as his nanny used to say. And then there was the wonderful new addition to his life. He smiled foolishly into the shaving mirror as he lathered on Mr Taylor of Jermyn Street's luxury shaving cream: one of the few rituals he had copied from his father. He wasn't used to such happiness; it was a delightful sensation.

A quick ward round and then he was free.

Diana was at René's salon in South Audley Street having her hair done. Tonight she was having dinner with Leo Bennett, and she wanted to look her very best. She had bought a black taffeta and lace dress and she was planning to wear that, with some extremely high heels and her grandmother's ropes of pearls, so much more beautiful than the modern ones, creamy and so flattering to the skin tone.

She had managed to book with René himself, despite it being Saturday; he was proud of her as a client, and there were several pictures of her hanging in the salon, framed pages from various magazines, mostly *Style*, and one of the two of them together that had been in *Tatler*. Of his most famous client, the Queen, there were, of course, no pictures at all. René was famed for his discretion.

Diana was looking forward to the evening; at worst it would be huge fun, like Leo himself, and at best – well, she just had a feeling about him. There was the knee test, of course, that would be interesting.

And then, this afternoon, she was going to make her phone call to Tom.

'Josh?'

'Yes.'

'It's Clive. Look, I know you're not working officially, but I am, and we do have an election on Thursday and . . . do I need to go on?'

'No,' said Josh resignedly.

'Good. I've just had a phone call from someone at Transport House PR. About Tom Knelston.'

Josh was silent. He felt instantly apprehensive; anything to do with Tom Knelston inevitably meant trouble,

'It might make a diary piece. Apparently, he's deserted his post in Purbridge; one of his children is in hospital having had dangerous surgery – but he's all right now – and instead of pounding the pavements down there, Tom's at home minding the kids and being the perfect dad. It wouldn't be terribly interesting if it wasn't that Purbridge's such a close call and it's political suicide what he's doing. Give him a ring, there's a good chap, try and find out what's going on, where the child is, that sort of thing. Cheers, Josh.'

'Tom? Tom, it's Josh. How are you? I hear one of the children is ill.'

'Yes – Kit,' said Tom shortly. 'How did you know? Jillie, I suppose?'

'No. From Clive actually, Clive Bedford, my boss. It came from the PR department at Transport House, apparently.'

'Oh, God.'

'Yes. Well, anyway, Clive thinks it could make a diary item.'

'What, a sick child?'

'No, you idiot, you not being down in Purbridge where every vote counts. Is Kit very bad?'

'He was yesterday,' said Tom bleakly. 'He could have died.'

'Christ. No wonder you're at home. How is he today?'

'Better, thank you. Out of danger, more or less. But Alice is with him and I want to be on hand, and anyway, there's the other children.'

'Yes, of course. So – what was it? Did it mean surgery?'

'God, yes.'

'And –?'

'Well, it was successful and today he's better,' said Tom.

'OK – and what was it?'

'Something very rare.'

'God, Tom, don't go overboard with information, will you? Look, you can just tell me to get off the phone and stop bothering you if you like, but they're going to go on pestering you if you don't say something. Especially if I report failure. They'll start to think there really is something to write about.'

'Well, there isn't. Oh, all right. Kit had something called intussusception, an obstruction of the bowel. He was operated on, and now hopefully he's recovering.'

'Right. And you're staying at home because . . . ?'

'For God's sake, Josh, because the other children have to be looked after. Because I want to be near Kit just in case he has a relapse. Because I want to support Alice. Is that so extraordinary?'

'Knowing you, a bit extraordinary. You're fighting for your political life, Tom. Every hand you shake this weekend, every door you knock on, every word exchanged in every street, could make a difference, get you another vote. You must know that. You've waited and worked for this all your life. I can see why you wanted to be near Kit yesterday and today, but if he's recovering, why not at least give some interviews? Maybe at the hospital? Which hospital is he in, by the way? Why couldn't Alice give an interview?'

'She'd think it was a totally inappropriate thing to ask,' said Tom, ignoring the question about the hospital. 'She was terrified yesterday, we both were. Our child could have died. What's an election, compared to that?'

'Nothing, of course,' said Josh. 'And I'm playing devil's advocate to a degree. But I can't see why you don't give an interview. It would buy you lots of sympathy, and probably votes; people would understand why you weren't there, instead of thinking you just couldn't be bothered. Look, I'll write it and you can vet it. God knows, you should be able to trust me by now. It'll go in the paper tomorrow – thousands of your supporters will read it.'

'I – can't,' said Tom. 'You don't understand.'

'No, I don't,' said Josh. 'Well, don't blame me if you get the whole bloody pack on your tail. Because you probably will, you know.'

'Why should I?'

'Because you're being so bloody mysterious. People will think you've got something to hide, if you go on refusing to talk about it to anyone. I mean, I'll do my best but a bald statement about your son being ill in a London hospital – which one is it, by the way, Great Ormond Street?'

'I wish to God it was,' said Tom. It came out, unbidden; he would have given anything to take it back.

Josh didn't miss the intensity in his voice.

'OK, so where then? Where is he?'

'Oh – he's – Josh, look, just – just fuck off, will you? Leave me alone.'

Josh suddenly felt violently angry with him. Angry and hurt. To be addressed in those terms by Tom, who he had done so much for over the years, been his best man purely because Tom couldn't think of anyone else, written what had felt like endless articles to further his career, kept quiet about his affair with Diana – and now he seemed to be implying that he would splash any information he could elicit across the front page of his paper in twelve-point. In which case, he deserved precisely that.

'Tom,' he said, 'I really don't appreciate being treated like this. I've done a lot for you – including, I might say, not mentioning to anyone that I saw you arriving at Diana Southcott's house the night I was there doing an interview. I'm beginning to regret that discretion.'

He put the phone down; it rang again almost immediately. But it wasn't Tom, as he had expected, it was Clive Bedford.

'Well? Got anything yet?'

'Not yet,' he said, and then added, 'But give me a bit more time.'

By lunchtime, every National Health hospital, large and small, in the Greater London area had confirmed that they had no child called Kit Knelston in any of their wards. It was very odd. And then he thought of the agony in Tom's voice when he had asked him about Great Ormond Street.

In a moment of absolute clarity, he knew. Kit was in a private hospital: that would explain everything. And almost certainly, he thought, the one where Ned Welles worked. Josh hesitated a moment or two and then rang Tom.

Tom sounded panicky to put it mildly. 'Josh,' he said.

'Yes?'

'I – well, I can explain about – about Diana.'

'Really? I can't think how.'

'Well – not explain. But make it look better.'

'I don't see how it could. Fucking about with her, when Alice was at home, trusting you, needing you. She's just had a baby, for Christ's sake. You really are a bastard, Tom Knelston.'

'I know. Why – why didn't you say anything before?'

'Because I couldn't bear to, to be honest. I couldn't think of anything to say to you. I'm very fond of Alice, and she's struggling to cope. The only reason I didn't spill the beans is because I didn't want her to know about it. It would have been a terrible thing to do to her. So I hope, for rather nobler reasons than yours, that she never needs to. But some other journalist might get on to it. You're pretty high profile in a minor way at the moment, you know. Anyway, perhaps you'd like to tell me how it's better than it looks. I'm fascinated.'

'It's over,' said Tom. 'I went there that evening to finish it. I haven't seen her since.'

'Well, that's extremely good of you. And are you so sure she won't say anything?'

'No, I'm not. But she hasn't so far. I can only hope that continues.'

'I wouldn't put money on it. She won't like being dumped. Why did you finish it anyway? I wonder. Were you just taking the moral high ground? It couldn't have had anything to do with an election coming up, I suppose? Adultery – not a vote winner.'

Tom was silent.

'You've turned out a pretty poor example of a human being, Tom Knelston,' said Josh. 'I used to quite like you, admire you even. Not any more. Bye then.'

He put the phone down. He had meant what he said: he wouldn't go public on Tom's adultery, for Alice's sake. But the hospital he had chosen for the treatment of his child, if it was a private one, that would also be quite damaging . . .

Ricky Barnes, a young mustard-keen trainee reporter on the *Daily Sketch*, having been given nothing to do so far that day, decided to find a story for himself. He flipped through various notes lying on the desk, and saw one scribbled from the PR department at Transport House. It was almost indecipherable but the subject matter was one Tom Knelston. *Would-be MP, sick son, interview?*

Ricky's ambition was to be a political editor one day; here perhaps was a chance to get some insight, however ephemerally, into what seemed to him the incredibly intriguing world of politics. He called Transport House, said he was investigating the story about Tom Knelston: could they tell him any more? They could: Knelston was Labour candidate in an extremely crucial marginal constituency. On this, the last Saturday before polling day, he was not out there, making speeches and knocking on doors, but at home looking after two of his children, while a third, the eldest, was in hospital. Transport House had phoned the *Sketch*, among other papers, and suggested an interview but didn't know which hospital the child was in.

*Not worth it, no interest to readers*, had been scrawled over the note in the news editor's red pencil, but in the absence of anything to do, Ricky took himself down to the cuttings library and looked up Tom Knelston. He sounded interesting: had risen from humble beginnings, had a real chance of being elected, and was a great Bevanite and a passionate believer in the National Health Service.

Ricky decided the news editor just might be wrong; Knelston would very possibly have something to say about his personal experience of the NHS. He pulled out a pack of Woodbines – all he could afford; one day it would be cigars like the legendary Hugh Cudlipp – settled down at his desk and began on the gargantuan task of finding where Kit Knelston was. He discovered, like Josh, that no National Health hospital in the entire London area had a patient called Kit Knelston in its children's wards. Which, if you thought about it, was quite interesting. Either Master Knelston was home, which meant Mr Knelston was lying about his reason for not being in his constituency – or he was in a private hospital. Another hour elapsed; the private hospitals were less forthcoming about their patients but he persevered.

Annabel Smyth had only been working at St Mary's for a week, most of the time in accounts. This was her first day on the reception desk, and she was only doing that as a favour for Miss Roberts who had wanted to leave early to go to the cinema.

'It's not difficult,' Miss Roberts said. 'Mostly people wanting to speak to their relatives. If they ask for any of the doctors, put them through to Matron.'

A man who didn't sound too much like most of the callers rang halfway through the lunch hour. He sounded very young and his voice was distinctly cockney, Annabel thought, but then she thought he might be calling from a florist or something; and he was extremely polite and apologised for troubling her, so she confirmed that yes, Kit Knelston was in the hospital and in room one hundred and five.

Tom had been briefly asleep on the sofa when the phone rang. Lucy was having her after-lunch nap; it had turned into a deep, deep sleep and he was buggered, he thought, if he was going to wake her. He had tried to talk to Alice, but apart from telling him in her new cool voice that Kit was doing fine, she refused to say anything.

He had tried to ring Josh several times to apologise, but he wasn't answering his phone. Well, Josh wouldn't betray him, even if he did find out where Kit was. He was far too loyal. This must be him now; he'd offer him copious apologies, and—'Hello, Tom. It's me. Your friend Diana.'

His voice was gratifyingly shocked; the silence before he answered more telling still.

'For God's sake,' he said finally. 'What do you want?'

'Nothing much. Just a chat. I miss our chats, Tom.'

Further silence.

Then, 'I met your wife yesterday,' she said. 'I thought she was lovely; very pretty. We had a nice chat.'

'But – but where? I don't – understand.'

'Oh, at the hospital. Where your son is. How is he today? Or is it the little girl?'

'No, it's – it's Kit. He's – he's doing all right. Yes, thank you.'

'Very nice hospital, I thought. How did you come to choose it?'

'I – I didn't.'

'Really? Oh, I know. Through Jillie Curtis, who of course is Alice's best friend? And knows Ned Welles? Well, you went to the right man, he's supposed to be brilliant. I know him very well, had a huge crush on him, actually wanted to marry him.'

Tom felt sick.

'You mustn't say anything to anyone about Kit being there. In that hospital.'

'Well, I'll try not to. It is quite intriguing, though.'

'Diana, I cannot tell you how important it is that it doesn't get out. It would be the end of me politically.'

'I can see that. Well, yes, I'll try and keep it to myself.'

'Diana – please!'

This was fun. This was high-quality revenge.

'Tom, I told you, I'll try not to talk about it. I can't think who'd be terribly interested. Although I have got a new boyfriend –' she reached out, touched wood; she didn't usually tempt fate in that way – 'who edits the diary pages of the *Dispatch*. He might be interested . . .'

'Oh, God. Diana, you can't. And – you didn't say anything to Alice? About, well, about us?'

God, he was a self-centred bastard. His marriage clearly came well behind his career in his concerns.

'Well, a bit. Just mentioned that we'd had an affair, nothing else.'

'What? Jesus Christ. And how did she – I mean –'

He sounded close to tears; she laughed aloud. 'Tom, of course I didn't. I'm not that sort of girl.'

'You said you – you might. That night. The last time I saw you,' he said, his voice almost unrecognisable in his relief.

'That was only to tease you. I did think of telling the press at one point. Reading all that rubbish about what a wonderful family man you are. Pretty tacky, it seemed at the time. But – I didn't. Bit of a temptation, though. Anyway, what I've rung about today really was to enquire after Kit's health, poor little boy.'

'He's – he's better, thank you.'

'I'm so pleased. And then I did think I'd ask you about your choice of hospital. Private! What happened to practising what you preach, Tom?'

'Stop it!' he said, and now she could hear not anger, but genuine dreadful pain in his voice. 'Just stop it. It wasn't like that, I – I –' And then she heard something extraordinary, his sobs, loud, racked sobs, and then his voice, breaking with pain, said, 'If you only knew what I've done, what I did. God, Diana –'

Diana knew real grief when she was confronted by it. And she had been very fond of Tom, still was, she supposed, and was distressed by his patent despair.

'Tom,' she said quietly, all the banter gone from her voice. 'Friend

Tom, what is it? It can't just be about Kit. Or even your career. Do you want to talk about it? I'm here all afternoon, got nothing to do. I can just sit and listen. You never know, it might help. Has in the past. Or I could come over and see you?'

'Diana, don't be ridiculous. You can't come here. That really would be madness.'

An hour later, a taxi drew up.

# Chapter 59

'Tom? It's Alice. Yes, Kit's fine. I'm afraid I just had a phone call from a journalist. Yes. No, not the *Daily News*, the *Sketch*. God knows. Well, he came through to the room, and asked me if I was Mrs Knelston. I asked who was calling and he told me. His name was Ricky something. He wanted to speak to you. What? Well, of course I didn't. I said you were out at the moment. Then he asked me how long you'd be and I put the phone down. No, he hasn't rung again, but I'm afraid he will. If he does, what do you want me to do?'

Well, it had happened now, and there was nothing to be done about it. Or was there? Should he talk to this journalist, try to have a reasonable conversation with him, put his case – Kit dangerously ill, rare condition, knew surgeon personally – or what? Refuse to speak to him? Deny it? Could hardly do that, the man had already spoken to Alice.

Once he could have asked Josh for help but Josh was quite possibly writing his own article, denouncing him as a hypocrite. He deserved that, Tom thought. How had it happened, how had he turned into this prime shit? Who had repeatedly slept with a woman who was not his wife. God, it would serve him right if Josh put that into his article too – this shit who told lies easily and thoughtlessly, who was foul tempered with his family, totally unappreciative of his wife. What, in the name of heaven, would Laura think of him now?

'Well, let's see if you can get hold of the bloke,' said Bob March, news editor of the *Sketch*. 'Not that much to go on if you can't. And he's of no great interest to anybody except his constituents. You make him sound as if he was Nye Bevan himself.'

'But he wants to be,' said Ricky. 'That's the whole point. He came into politics because of Bevan. He hero-worships him, never stops quoting him – he's a bloody hypocrite.'

'Yeah, I know, but they all are. As I say, if you can't get a quote from him, it's not really worth a row of beans. Full marks for initiative, though, young Barnes. Well done.'

Ricky didn't want full marks, he wanted to write his story. He lit yet another Woody and dialled St Mary's number again. This time they didn't put him through. He tried the Labour Party headquarters in Purbridge and asked if Tom Knelston was there, and got very short shrift. And Tom Knelston's home number was perpetually engaged. There really was sweet FA he could do.

Unless he went to his home – it was only in Acton – and doorstepped him. It would be better than nothing.

'Josh? Josh, it's Tom. Look, I'm very sorry about earlier. I shouldn't have spoken to you like that.'

'No,' said Josh, 'you shouldn't. What do you want?'

'Your advice,' said Tom. 'The *Sketch* are on to me.'

'Could be worse. Could be the *Express*. Right-wing righteous indignation is a terrible thing.'

'But what should I do? What's the best way to deal with it?'

'What do you mean by "on to" you exactly?'

Tom told him.

'Give him a quote, otherwise he'll just make it up. Don't blame it on Alice, just say you were desperately worried, Kit was clearly extremely ill, you weren't getting anywhere with your GP or you couldn't get hold of him, and you knew someone at St Mary's who could see you at once. It doesn't sound too clever, whatever you say, smacks of hypocrisy, which it is – I know, I know – but it'll give him something to write. Refuse to say any more, tell him you've got to get off to see Kit, or bath the children, anything really. Tell Alice not to speak to any of the press, obviously. I'll write something similar if you like –'

'Josh. I can't expect you to do that.'

'To be honest, Tom, it's purely self-interest. If Clive sees this story in the *Sketch* and I've come up with nothing he'll think I'm useless. Does Ned know about this, by the way?'

'No. Not as far as I know.'

'He won't be pleased. He hates any sort of publicity and this isn't the best sort. Inevitably his name will come into it. You'd better tell him, before you do anything else.'

'Oh, Christ,' said Tom. 'This gets worse and worse.'

Alice was reading to Kit; he was just growing drowsy. His temperature had gone up in the afternoon, over a hundred and one; the nurse in charge of him had called the house doctor, and the house doctor, who had never seen a case of intussusception before, and didn't know exactly what he was dealing with, was a little alarmed and called Ned as he had been instructed.

Ned had come at once; he was clearly in a bad mood, not entirely due to the news that the press were, as Alice put it, 'about'.

'I suppose it was inevitable,' he said. 'Well, as long as they don't start trying to get into the premises. Last time something like this happened, a reporter pretended to be delivering some drugs or something, and got into a patient's room, complete with tape recorder. They really are an appalling lot. Josh being a notable exception, of course. I sometimes wonder what he's doing in that business.'

Alice looked alarmed. 'I hope no one will get in here.'

'Of course they won't,' said Ned irritably. 'Our security is much better now. Anyway, Kit's fine. Possibly a minor infection, nothing serious – we might give him a dose of penicillin. It is the end of the day, temperatures often go up. Well, you should know that.'

'Yes, of course,' said Alice meekly, 'it was just that the house doctor thought –'

'Yes, yes, I realise that. Well, I hope you have a reasonable night with him. I'll look in again in the morning.'

'There's no need –'

'Well, you don't know that, do you?' said Ned, his voice distinctly edgy. 'Hopefully not, but let's make that judgement tomorrow. Good-night, Alice.'

'Goodnight, Ned. Thank you.'

She smiled rather nervously at him as he left; she hadn't seen him anything but composed and charming before.

Tom had undressed Lucy and was about to put her in the bath when there was a ring at the door; maybe it was Mrs Hartley, returning Charlie. He wrapped Lucy in a towel, carried her down-stairs, and opened the door. A young – very young – man stood there, holdall at his feet. Tom thought at first he was a door-to-door salesman,

'Good evening, Mr Knelston. Ricky Barnes, *Sketch*.'

He rummaged in the holdall and pulled out a notebook.

Some kind of void opened up in Tom's guts. He felt violently sick. He actually thought he was going to shit himself, or throw up. This, on top of a very emotional hour with Diana, was unbearable. Thank God she had gone at least. The visits could have coincided. He leaned against the door post, took a deep breath and said, 'I have nothing to say to you, I'm sorry.'

'Not even about your little boy? Who's been very ill, I understand. How is he, Mr Knelston?'

'He's – a bit better. Thank you.'

'I'm glad. But – still in hospital?'

'Yes. Of course. He had major surgery yesterday.'

'Ah, yes. At St Mary's Hospital Chelsea, I believe.'

'I don't propose to discuss that with you,' said Tom.

'I see. St Mary's is a private hospital, is it not?'

'I said I wouldn't discuss it.'

'Interesting choice, given that you are a member of the Labour Party, and a great fan of the National Health Service, wouldn't you say? And the general election only a few days away. I'm just wonder-ing how your constituents would feel about that.'

And then Tom made his fatal mistake.

'It's nothing to do with my constituents,' he said. And thought,

Shit. Shit. That was not a good thing to say. Ricky Barnes clearly thought so too.

'Really? I wonder if they'd agree with you. I don't suppose many of them could afford a private hospital. What was it that made you decide to do that, to take your little boy there? I've read a speech of yours in which you refer to private medicine as a form of apartheid.'

Tom remembered Josh's words and decided he couldn't make matters any worse. Perhaps Ricky Barnes had a softer side.

'We were – desperate. My son was extremely ill. Time was of the essence. We – we knew the surgeon at St Mary's –'

'Ah. That would be Mr Edward Welles. Right at the top of his tree, I believe. How fortunate that you knew him.'

'Look,' said Tom. 'I've had enough of this. Just go, please.' He shifted Lucy onto his other arm, tried to close the door. But Ricky Barnes's foot was jammed in it. So they really did do that, reporters, Tom thought inconsequentially. Then he said, 'Please remove your foot.'

'I will. Just going –'

He dug into the holdall, produced a camera and fitted a flashbulb on it, all in one incredibly quick movement, and the flash went off.

'Thank you. This must be your little girl, Lucy, isn't it?'

'Get out,' shouted Tom. 'Just go away. Leave us alone.'

It couldn't have been worse.

Mrs Hartley was just walking down her own path with a sleeping Charlie in his carrycot when the flash went off. She was startled, but continued on her way. This was proving a very eventful afternoon. What with that obviously very smart woman arriving in a taxi, wearing such high heels Mrs Hartley couldn't imagine being able to walk in them, and then Mr Knelston arriving, white as a sheet, with Lucy, asking if she would mind taking the child for an hour or so, and then returning to pick her up, looking as if he had been crying – she'd been afraid it had been bad news about Kit, but he assured her it wasn't – well, it was very different from most Saturdays in Acton.

A young man was walking towards her; he smiled.

'Good evening. Ricky Barnes, *Sketch*. You're a neighbour of Mr Knelston's, I presume.'

'Looks like it,' said Mrs Hartley. She didn't know much about the press, except that it was not to be trusted. 'Let me past, please. I've got a baby here, who could be catching his death thanks to you.'

Ricky Barnes remained where he was.

'I just wondered how well you know the Knelstons. Are they good neighbours?'

'Very good indeed. Now –'

'I understand their little boy is in hospital?'

'He might be.'

'Oh, so you don't know about it?'

'I don't know anything that's any business of yours,' said Mrs Hartley firmly.

'Is that another of their children?' He indicated the sleeping Charlie in his carrycot.

'It is. I've been looking after him. Now if you don't get out of my way I shall call the police.'

How she was going to do this without a telephone she wasn't sure, but Ricky Barnes wasn't to know that.

'So you didn't know that the little boy was in a private hospital?'

'Look,' said Mrs Hartley, 'Mr and Mrs Knelston are the best parents you could hope to meet. Wherever they've decided to take Kit for help, you can be sure it's the very best place and with the best intentions. And that's all I have to say.'

'Right. Fine. Thank you, Mrs Hartley. You've been most helpful. Goodnight.'

Hoping she hadn't been helpful in a way the Knelstons would not have wished, Mrs Hartley proceeded down the path and opened their door.

Tom, watching from an upstairs window, thanked the Deity that he had insisted Mrs Hartley had a key, in case she needed something for Charlie if he wasn't there. If he'd had to open the door, Barnes would have been in again.

'Mr Knelston? Here's Charlie. I've just seen some reporter who was on your path.'

'Thank you,' said Tom, taking the carrycot, 'and I'm sorry if he bothered you. What did he say?'

'He wanted to know all kinds of things, but mostly which hospital Kit was in. Or rather if I knew it was private. I told him it was none of his business.'

'Good. Thank you.' So far, so good. He'd been afraid she'd have been flattered into talking too much.

'You're welcome. And I told them wherever you'd taken Kit to it would have been the best place, and with the very best intentions.'

That wasn't quite so good; but better than it might have been.

'Well, thank you, Mrs Hartley. You did well, getting rid of him.'

'I told him I'd call the police if he didn't go away.'

'Now why didn't I think of that? And thank you for having Charlie all day, of course.'

'Oh, we've had a lovely time. I'll have him again tomorrow, then you can take Lucy to see Kit. Or I'll have her here, whatever's best for you.'

'Thank you, Mrs Hartley, Er – just as a matter of interest, what do you feel about my taking Kit to a private hospital? Does it seem wrong to you?'

'Mr Knelston,' said Mrs Hartley, 'if Kit was very ill, which he was, I wouldn't blame *anyone* for going private. Not if it was urgent. We wouldn't have the choice, mind, and casualty at Acton General isn't too bad for waiting. But if it was life or death, and I could see someone quicker, I would. I should think any parent would say the same.'

'I do hope you're right,' said Tom. 'Goodnight, Mrs Hartley. Thank you again.'

He still felt dreadful, sick and shocked. He rang Josh again in desperation, told him what had happened. Josh was clearly horrified.

'I'm afraid that's it. If he got a photo . . . what were you doing?'

'Carrying Lucy wrapped up in a bath towel.'

'That's good. And what did you say exactly?'

Tom told him to the best of his recollection.

'There was one – one particularly unfortunate thing –'

'Which was?'

'I said it was nothing to do with my constituents.'

'Jesus,' said Josh.

He warned Tom that it might be followed up by other papers. 'And you could get more doorstepping, a whole mob might descend. If that happens, don't go out unless you absolutely have to. Say "no comment" to any questions, and take the phone off the hook.'

'I can't,' said Tom. 'Alice might need to ring me about Kit.'

'OK. Well, you ring her every hour or so. Was Ned mentioned?'

'I'm afraid so.'

'Oh, God. By name?'

'Yes.'

'But not by you?'

'Er – no. He just asked if Ned had done the operation. I said it was none of his business.'

'Right. Well, I've written my piece, let's hope it helps.'

'Thank you, Josh, I don't deserve it.'

'No, you don't,' said Josh coldly.


He rang Alice, told her what had happened. For the first time she sounded less hostile. How long would that last?

'Oh, God, Tom, how awful. I'm – I'm sorry. But – how did they find out?'

'You know the press. It's their stock-in-trade, finding out.'

'Well, I hope they don't turn up here.'

'Me too. Er – anyone outside now?'

'Don't know. Can't see the street from here. I'll go down the corridor.'

She was longer than he would have expected; when she came back she said, 'There is a man lurking outside. And I went down to reception, asked if anyone had tried to come in, or asked for me. She said they hadn't, so I told her if they did to send them away. Oh, Tom. I'm scared.'

'Don't be. No one will get in there. But I do think it could all get quite – difficult. Anyway, it's happened, can't turn the clock back.'

She was silent.

'Josh is writing an article about it too,' said Tom.

'What! How could he?'

'Alice, he's doing it for the best. If they all know, better a helpful article from him, defusing the situation. Which he's promised.' He sounded exhausted, drained of emotion. The nightmare evening had continued, confronting Donald, and a torrent of abuse down the phone.

'Now, if you do have to go out in the morning, ignore anyone who tries to question you. And I'm afraid there could be quite a gang of them. But it would be better if you didn't go out at all.'

'I won't.'

Another silence.

'Alice?' said Tom. 'We need to talk.'

'Yes. Yes, I agree. Not tonight, though.'

'Of course not. But – soon. Maybe after the election.'

'Oh,' she said, and there was infinite bitterness in her voice, 'the election. Yes, of course.'

'Alice –'

'Tom, we said not tonight.'

'No, all right. Well, I'd better go. I'll ring you later, just to check all's well there. Don't ring me. The children are fine, both asleep. Goodnight, Alice.'

'Goodnight, Tom.'

The chill between them could be felt even down the phone lines.


Diana lay in the bath with a glass of champagne, struggling to recover from the emotional exhaustion of her hour with Tom. She had never thought to feel anything close to sympathy for him again, but looking at him, hunched over on the sofa, his head buried in his arms, hearing the deep sobs racking him, she did feel it, and it was with genuine tenderness that she said, 'Oh, Tom, my darling Tom, I am so, so sorry,' and moved to sit beside him, her arms round him, drawing him close to her, her own tears mingling with his.

It had been the Laura part of the story that moved her; if Alice had flouted his wishes and taken Kit to a private hospital, that was fair game – and she felt something close to admiration for her, for refusing to be browbeaten by Tom's politics and putting Kit's needs first. But to tell him that she had lied to him about Laura's death, that perhaps it had been needless, that without his obstinacy in refusing the better hospital, the greater skills, Laura and Hope could have been alive today, that was cruelty of the most savage kind. Wilful, dreadful cruelty, such as she would not have suspected the sweet-faced, gentle Alice capable of. It was the same kind of destructive cruelty, born of grief, targeted with savage accuracy, that had driven Johnathan to accuse her of aborting their baby; and she knew, from her own unhealed wounds, how truly dreadful the pain could be.

He clung to her, sobbing, and they sat there for a long time; then he sat back and looked at her, took her hand and said, 'I loved her so much, Diana. I would have died for her, willingly, and instead of that I killed her. If I had said yes to Jillie's offer, Laura would be alive today. Laura and Hope, and—'

'Tom, you don't know that.'

'I do,' he said. 'I do know it. There were signs that would have saved her, signs that were missed – I've looked it up since – that would have told them, alerted them, things that could, should have been done. She would have been safe those last dreadful days, and I left her in danger.'

'You can't be sure that the other hospital would have picked up on those signs, Tom, they—'

'I do know.' He was shouting now, angry with her and the platitudes she was offering, and she could see why.

'I'm sorry,' she said quietly, 'and yes, I expect they would. And Tom, my heart breaks for you, it really does. But—'

'I never really loved Alice,' he said, interrupting her. 'I can see that now. She was sweet and kind – or so I thought – and she loved me and it was the end of my loneliness, but what I felt for her was nothing, set against my love for Laura. I should never have married her, it was wrong . . .'

'Maybe. But you did. And Tom, you must put Laura behind you, leave her in peace.'

'I will, I will try.'

'You must.'

'You're very wise, Diana. You know, I often think I love you more than I love—'

'Don't say it.' She put two fingers on his mouth. 'You don't love me.

Well, only as I love you, as a very special, extremely sexy friend.' She paused, then said with a glimmer of a smile, 'Fine pair we'd make. Selfish, stubborn, devious – goodness, just be grateful you've been spared that, Friend Tom.'

He managed a ghost of a grin then, blew his nose, and wiped his eyes.

'You're right. Of course.'

'And think of the children we'd have had. Appalling. Whereas I'm sure yours are as nice as mine. Thanks to our spouses.'

'Not sure about Charlie,' he said. 'The devil's somewhere in his ancestry. Oh, Diana, how am I ever going to forgive Alice? Or trust her? Trust is such a big part of love.'

'It is indeed,' she said, 'and you won't forgive her, any more than I've forgiven Johnathan about – well, you know, the baby. But she has things to forgive too, don't forget. Pretty bad ones. Like – well, you and me. She may not know about me – yet. But she still might find out. And then her trust in you will be gone.'

'Well – yes, it would. And Josh knows, he saw me arriving at your house that night he was there too.'

'Really? Well, he won't tell. Much too nice. Sweet boy,' she added rather absently.

'No, but he's a journalist. Dangerous.'

'Alice could find out any number of ways. The point is, you've done each other great wrongs. As had Johnathan and I. It helps, Friend Tom, in the recovery process, admitting that sort of quid pro quo.'

'Oh, Diana. You've made me feel better. I know I'm not allowed to say it, but I do love you. There. I won't do it again. Last time.'

'Good,' she said briskly.

'Look – I think you'd better go now. Mrs Hartley next door will be bringing Charlie back, and I promised her I'd collect Lucy soon.'

'And I have a hot date with a gossip columnist. How he'd love to get his hands on this story. But he won't. Don't worry.' She stood up, and then bent to kiss him.

'Goodbye, darling Tom. Be brave.'

'I don't have any choice.'

'No. You don't, I'm afraid.'

# Chapter 60

'I think,' said Leo Bennett, 'we should go on to dance somewhere. You know what they say about dancing?'

'What do they say about dancing?' said Diana, meeting his eyes. What was it about looking into eyes that was so sexy? How did it convey you to some molten place deep within you, a place that moved and stirred and hungered? How did that happen?

'They say it's a vertical expression of horizontal desire.'

'Oh, really?'

She would have been quite happy in that moment to have moved straight to horizontal, but she didn't want him thinking she was a tart. She was sure his life was littered with women who had thrown themselves at him, and she had no intention of joining them. If any throwing of anyone was to be done, then it was to be him at her.

'Oh, yes,' he said. 'Where would you like to go? How do you like the Café?'

'De Paris? Love it.'

'OK. You never know, it might be one of Princess Margaret's nights.'

'Well, that would be exciting. I've never seen her.'

'She's very beautiful. She was there the other night, made an amazing entrance in a white fur coat. Spoilt, though.'

'Well, she's a princess. She would be. She should have been allowed to marry Townsend. I would have done it anyway, whatever those old fogeys said.'

'Do I detect a romantic here, beneath the cool exterior?'

She was rather pleased about the cool. It was what she aimed to project, but rather feared she didn't always come over that way.

'I'm quite romantic. Sometimes.'

'I see.'

'What about you?'

'Oh, I'm very romantic. That's why I've had three wives. Keep falling in love.'

'You don't have to marry them, though,' she said, intrigued.

'I know,' he said and sighed. 'I just get – carried away. I'm quite a helpless chap really.'

'You don't seem in the least helpless to me,' said Diana briskly. 'Come on, let's go dancing.'

'Apparently, we should have come last week,' he said, as they settled themselves at a table gratifyingly near the band. 'Noël Coward was doing the cabaret.'

'Oh, my God. How marvellous! I wish you hadn't told me.'

'Well, I'm here,' he said, looking mildly put out.

'I know. Sorry. But he is one of my all-time idols.'

'Champagne?'

'Please. The thing about champagne is it takes you back to where you started. Makes you feel the evening's just beginning.'

He laughed. 'I think I know what you mean.' A Sinatra sound-alike was crooning 'Moonlight in Vermont'. 'Come on. I want to express my horizontal desire.'

He danced very well. So important, Diana thought: such a barometer of sexiness. Johnathan had been a terrible dancer, she should have taken heed of that fact. Although she'd known, of course, all along; no use pretending it had been a surprise.

She looked around as they sat down again; you so often saw famous faces here. She couldn't see any.

'Who are you looking for?' he asked, amused

'Oh, just someone famous. I like seeing them off duty, so to speak.

It amuses me. Specially if they're in a bad mood. I once saw Grace Kelly here.'

'In a bad mood? I don't believe it.'

'No, just clearly bored. Goodness, she's beautiful. She was with her beau, that French actor, Jean-Pierre something.'

'Aumont.'

'Yes, that's right. I suppose you know hundreds of famous people?'

'Met them, let's say. Very few of them would say they knew me. Anyway, there's no one here for you tonight, I'm afraid. Oh – yes. Billy Wallace. Over there, look.'

Diana looked; Billy Wallace, one of the so-called Margaret set, officially acknowledged – by the press at any rate – as one of her suitors, was escorting a girl off the dance floor.

'He gives new meaning to the term "chinless", doesn't he?' said Diana with a giggle. 'She can't like him for his looks.'

'No. But he has huge charm and he's very, very nice. I've met him several times, over the years.'

'What a glamorous life you do lead, to be sure, Mr Bennett.'

'Yours can't be exactly dull.'

'No, it's not. Actually, maybe you can advise me.'

She told him about the New York offer.

'Darling, it sounds a terrible idea to me. Don't go.'

She liked the 'darling', although it probably meant nothing.

'Why not?'

'For a start, it's probably the loneliest place in the world. Anyway, what about your little boy?'

'I'd work around his holidays. They don't need me there full-time.'

'Diana, you know as well as I do, that won't work. There'll be a crucial fashion shoot you've got to go to California for, exactly coinciding with his half term.'

She looked at him with interest. 'You sound as if you speak from experience.'

'Our esteemed fashion editor has children. I hear her constantly wailing about such dilemmas, in spite of what seems to be a fleet of nannies. And what do you think your ex-husband would have to say about your upping sticks and going to the States?'

She shrugged. 'He'd just see it as a way of seeing more of Jamie.'

'And you wouldn't mind that?'

'Well, of course. But I just want to do this. And it wouldn't be for long, I'll be too old to model soon.'

'Well, I think you'd find it hard for all sorts of reasons. Anyway, having just found you, I don't like the idea of your moving to the other side of the Atlantic.'

She liked that. As much as the 'darling'.

She smiled at him, leaned across the small table and gave him a kiss.

'Let's see. Now if you'll excuse me, I must go to the ladies.'


She was sitting on the loo, holding her skirt round it with great difficulty, when she heard the door open.

'Well, I see our Leo hasn't wasted any time. How long since he finished with Celia?'

'Oh, not long – two weeks? Maybe three. She's still sobbing, poor creature. He really is a prime bastard. Just dropping her like that, without a word of warning.'

'Well, to be fair, a warning would be as bad. Either a man's madly in love with you as he professes to be, or he isn't. But he'd more or less said he was going to propose. What a bastard.'

'Especially when he's still married to Baba, technically speaking. Mind you, she's very beautiful this one.'

'Yes. She looks familiar, don't know why.'


Diana sat frozen on her porcelain throne. She couldn't go out now – could she? But it would be a long wait if she didn't. While first one and then the other used the second lavatory, did their make-up, debating Leo and his sexual peccadilloes. Of course, she'd learn a lot.

'Mind you, Anna's got her revenge, scooped up Hugh Wyndham. She always did like a title.'

This was too good to miss. Diana settled down more comfortably on the seat, eased her skirts gingerly downwards. The small tin bin in the corner labelled *Napkins* rattled loudly. The two women paused; one of them called, 'You all right in there?'

'Yes, thank you.'

A silence ensued; they had obviously decided not to say any more. There was nothing for it but to tough it out. She stood up, knocking the napkin bin again trying to straighten her skirts, realised she couldn't do it in so small a space, and went out, her pants round her knees, her skirts held aloft.

'So sorry,' she said, smiling at them sweetly. 'Jolly small space, that. If you could just excuse me.' She pulled her pants up rather ostentatiously, re-fastened one of her suspenders, then started to rearrange her skirts. The women, clearly deciding the situation was irretrievable, smiled at her weakly and disappeared into the lavatories.

Diana washed her hands, powdered her nose, dabbed on generous dollops of Arpège, and left the room, calling out 'Bye' as she went.

Back with Leo, she smiled at him sweetly, accepted some more champagne and then said, 'So, tell me, are you really divorced now?'

'Not – not quite. Why?'

'Oh, I just heard two women talking about you in the ladies. Learned a lot. Poor Celia, she's still very upset, apparently. And as for Baba . . .'

'Look, Diana, I—'

'Oh dear –' she yawned ostentatiously – 'I'm rather tired, suddenly. I might like to go home. Is that all right?'

'Well – obviously I'd rather not. But if you're tired . . .'

'I really am. Oh, hello.' Her two new friends were walking back to their table; she waved at them. 'So – would you mind organising a taxi, sort of straight away? Thank you.'

He insisted on accompanying her in the taxi: sitting in silence beside her, clearly pondering his next move.

Just as they reached the mews, he said rather abruptly, 'Look – can I come in for a minute or two? I'd like to . . . well, explain.'

'I'm sorry, Leo. I really am awfully tired and it would take more than a minute or two, don't you think?'

'I'm surprised you're so upset,' he said after a moment's silence.

'Obviously, I have girlfriends. What do you expect, that I'm some kind of celibate, waiting for the next Mrs Bennett to come my way?'

'Only she wouldn't be Mrs Bennett. What would she be? Anyway, of course I don't mind the girlfriends. It's the wife I take exception to. Not that she exists, that's fine. But why did you tell me you were divorced? I don't like being lied to, Leo. Being taken for a fool. I don't like that one bit. Anyway, thank you for a very nice evening.'

And she got out of the taxi, tottered across the cobbles on her high heels, and went into the house.

Leo looked after her until she had shut the door behind her, trying to work out whether he minded never seeing her again or not. He decided he did mind, quite a lot.

# Chapter 61

Diana didn't take the *Sketch*, but she did take the *Daily News* and saw Josh's article, headed, *Principles or Politics? What would you choose?*

The piece was generally sympathetic, posing the age-old question about heart and head; but the journalist did finish by saying, *For most of us there would be no dilemma, and we would take any dangerously sick child to a private doctor if we could afford it and thought it was in the child's interests. It is unfortunate for him that Tom Knelston has hitched his wagon to Nye Bevan's star, and is known to be one of the most passionate disciples of the National Health Service.*

Poor Tom: that was the end of his political career, certainly for the foreseeable future.

Alice, who had crept out early to buy the papers, before Kit woke up, was sitting in the room surrounded by them, in a state of panicky misery. A third paper, the *Sunday Express*, had got the story, heaven knew how, and was thundering self-righteously about hypocrisy, clearly delighted to have caught another Labour man out: *Ironically, Tom Knelston was once described as the heir to Aneurin Bevan,* the paper stated. The headline, 'What Price Principles, Mr Knelston?', was only the beginning of a long tirade. This was illustrated with a picture of her – goodness knows how they'd got hold of it, she thought, taken years ago, looking very young and pretty in her St Thomas' uniform, Nightingale cap and all. *Alice Knelston,* the caption said, *trained at one of London's top teaching hospitals, where many of the girls are ex-debutantes.*

Somehow, in spite of all her angry, scornful words, Alice hadn't expected it to happen; hadn't thought Tom was important enough for his actions to merit such a lambasting, had seen it as all part of his arrogance. Now, staring at the headlines, she felt a pang of sympathy. Not remorse – to her the situation was still clear-cut, she had been acting for Kit, and had probably saved his life – but the whole business had probably seen off the political success that Tom had worked so hard for.

Josh had been right; Tom, looking cautiously out of the bedroom window at six o'clock, saw a gathering of about half a dozen men and one woman in front of his house. He pulled the curtains more closely together, and leaned against the wall. Now what did he do? It was all very well Josh telling him not to go out but he really must go down to Purbridge, do whatever troubleshooting he could. Besides, it looked cowardly and an admission of guilt.

He felt worried about Mrs Hartley, too, whether she would be nervous of the press: although it was hard to imagine Mrs Hartley being nervous of anyone. And he needed to ask her to have the children for the day if he was going to Purbridge. The Hartleys had no phone and the only way into the house, apart from the front door, was via the side passage to their back door. Charlie was now crying for a bottle. He would have to go down and the kitchen was in the front of the house; he could easily be seen.

Sure enough, one of the crowd saw him and there was a surge down the front path, and a steady press on the bell. Upstairs, Lucy woke up and started crying, and Charlie screamed more loudly still. Angry suddenly, Tom picked him up and opened the door. Several flashbulbs went off.

'Mr Knelston, how's your little boy this morning?' 'Mr Knelston, can I have a word?' 'Any idea what your constituents will have to say about this, Mr Knelston?'

'Would you all just go away, PLEASE!' shouted Tom, shaking

with rage and, he had to admit, fear as well. 'You've woken and frightened both my children. I would appreciate some peace and quiet while I settle them, and I have nothing to say to you, whatsoever.'

He slammed the front door shut, carried Charlie and his bottle upstairs to Lucy's room, and, having comforted her as best he could, wondered what on earth he was going to do. It was exactly like being under siege; he was trapped, well and truly.

He looked down into the back garden; the fence dividing it from the Hartleys was only waist-high. He could shin over that. They must be awake by now, poor things: on a Sunday morning, too, when Mr Hartley, who worked long shifts at the local canning factory, had his only lie-in of the week.

The bell-ringing had recommenced; and going to the top of the stairs, he saw a note being pushed through the letterbox. He went down, picked it off the mat; it was scrawled on a page of a reporters' notebook.

*Dear Mr Knelston,* it said. *Sorry about this. Given that you're going to have to talk to one of us, can I introduce myself? Fiona Jenkins,* Dispatch, *and may I suggest you talk to me exclusively? In return, the newspaper will make a generous donation to your favourite charity, and I'll try to persuade the others to go away.*

Tom, thinking things could hardly be worse, went down to open the door. More flashbulbs. God, it was relentless.

Fiona Jenkins – or so he presumed – was standing at the front nearest the door; she smiled at him, a rather irritating, self-satisfied smile.

'Come in. Quickly,' said Tom. He slammed the door shut again behind her.

'I'm sorry,' she said, and her voice was surprisingly posh. She was quite attractive altogether, he noticed now, mid-thirties, nice figure, dark red hair, good legs, wearing a fairly short skirt and tight sweater. It was obviously a uniform carefully designed for getting into people's homes; men's homes, anyway.

'Coffee?' said Tom. He wouldn't have offered it, but he was desperate for one himself.

'Yes, thanks. Black, please, plenty of sugar.'

'OK,' said Tom shortly, 'let's get this over. What sort of money are we talking about for charity, by the way?'

'Fifty pounds,' said Fiona Jenkins coolly.

Tom had expected something far less. But, 'Make it sixty,' he said. 'Pay it to the Great Ormond Street Hospital, and I'll answer your questions. Most of them, anyway.'

'Done,' she said, opening her notebook. 'First of all, how is your little boy?'

'Better. Thank you. At least, he was last night, I haven't had a chance to ring this morning.'

'And your wife's with him? Staying at the hospital.'

'Yes,' said Tom, ignoring the implied criticism. 'Now, just let me explain how he happens to be in a private hospital and then you can go.'

'Fine. Only I think your constituents will most want to know why you said it was nothing to do with them. I'd have thought everything an MP does was his constituents' business. I don't suppose many of them could afford a private hospital.'

'Listen,' said Tom, 'that was taken out of context. I was trying to explain to the reporter how it had happened. Kit was desperately ill. The GP was out on his rounds. He'd seen Kit before and diagnosed a grumbling appendix. My wife is a nurse and she wasn't satisfied. His temperature was almost a hundred and two and he was in dreadful pain, screaming and writhing about on the floor. She spoke to a family friend, a paediatric surgeon, who agreed to see him at once, and then, having seen him he diagnosed a problem with the gut, very rare, called intussusception. He said immediate surgery was essential or Kit could die, and he could operate that afternoon. What would you have done?'

'What you did, obviously,' said Fiona Jenkins.

'Exactly. My remark about the constituents was taken completely out of context. I was trying to make the point that this was a private, family matter. Although I admit it does sounds harsh. Lucy, not now, darling –'

The little girl was enthusiastically trying to show the reporter her treasured doll.

'She's all right. I like that doll's dress, Lucy, very pretty. Now, look, let me make us another coffee, I've just a couple more questions and then I'll be away.'

She sent the other reporters packing, got a message to the Hartleys, helped get Lucy dressed, and then left, having given Tom her card, with her direct line on it, so he could chase up the sixty pounds if necessary.

In another life, Tom thought, he would have married her.

Mr and Mrs Hartley had rather enjoyed the drama of the morning, particularly Fiona Jenkins's visit.

'Pretty girl,' Mr Hartley said, 'and well mannered too, you wouldn't think that was her job.'

'Well, and nor would we have thought Mr Knelston was a Labour politician,' said Mrs Hartley. 'Both so nicely spoken, specially Alice. I'd have put them down as Conservatives, both of them. Just goes to show.'

Mr Hartley agreed that it did, and drew her attention to the article in the *Dispatch*, delivered first thing by a now overexcited paper boy, telling anyone who cared to listen that the Hartleys had a great crowd of reporters on their doorstep.

Mr and Mrs Hartley read the article, which, as lifelong Tories themselves, they usually took as gospel.

'Well, I think that's most unpleasant of the paper, calling him a hypocrite,' said Mrs Hartley. 'I'd like to give them a piece of my mind. It seems to me the reporters didn't bother to check their facts.'

Mr Hartley said they never did, far as he could make out, otherwise how come all the papers always had different versions of the same stories.

'Yes, but if they had, they'd have known Kit was dangerously ill, poor little scrap. I blame that Dr Redmond, not knowing what he was doing. Remember when he said my friend Iris had bronchitis and it turned out to be pneumonia, and she ended up in hospital for weeks?'

Mr Hartley said he did.

'Yes, well, Alice being a nurse clearly knows better than him. And seeing she knew this Mr Welles, who's a specialist in kiddies' illnesses, of course she'd take a child to him – wouldn't you, if he was as ill as Kit – not mess about with any more GPs or even casualty, all that waiting, over two hours sometimes these days. I mean, little Kit could have died, it doesn't bear thinking about. Anyway, I'm going to pop next door, get Charlie and the little girl too, so poor Mr Knelston can do whatever he needs to do to put this rubbish straight. Fancy us living next door to a famous politician.'

Mr Hartley said Tom wasn't a politician, not yet, and he wasn't really famous either, but he always had a smile and a 'Good evening', which was good enough for him.

Colin Davidson, being Tom's political agent, was in despair; he sat at the breakfast table in Purbridge, staring at the papers, his jaw slack with disbelief. How in the name of heaven could Tom have been so stupid, so blind? Of all the idiotic things that he might have done, why choose the very one that went against all that he stood for? Well, it was the end of any hope of success for Tom, and the end of him, too, as an agent. Who would want such incompetence working for the party?

He knew he must go down to the office, try to put some positive interpretation on the whole miserable business; but it was with very low expectations that he drove there.

The last thing he expected to find when he got to the Labour Party office, actually sitting at his desk, was Tom Knelston.

'I've come to face the music,' he said. 'I'm very sorry.'

The long-suffering Christine Herbert feared that Donald might actually have his much-anticipated heart attack as he worked his way through the papers like some huge, clumsy beast, roaring with rage as he came upon each new headline, burying his head in his hands at some particularly damning detail, hurling each publication onto the floor as he finished reading it, dialling and redialling Tom's number, and cursing whatever malevolent fate had caused it to become unobtainable. Finally, through them all, he left the breakfast table and reappeared, a large glass of whisky in his hand.

'And don't tell me I shouldn't be drinking it at this time of day,' he said, glaring at her. 'Nothing else is going to get me through this. Stupid fucking young idiot. Now, where are my glasses?'

Christine said she had no idea; in fact, Donald had pushed them up onto the top of his head. It was a small but sweet piece of revenge, watching him continue to hunt for them.

Ned, who had visited the hospital early and talked to Alice, bought the papers on the way home and read them with great sadness. Josh's article, by far the most sympathetic, would only resonate with the *Daily News* readers, few of whom would be Tom's putative constituents. They would most likely be shaking their heads over the *Sketch* and wondering if they should vote Liberal by way of protest; and any waverers, who might have come down on the Labour side of the scales, would be stabbing at the paper with their forefingers and saying there you are, politicians were all the same, liars and hypocrites who, when push came to shove, were only interested in themselves and what they could get out of any situation. None of it was very good publicity for the hospital either, presenting it somehow as a symbol of class injustice. It was sad, too, to see the NHS presented as a kind of very poor relation to which no one would go if they had a choice.

Jillie only saw the *Daily News* and felt very sad and fearful for Alice, for Tom, and for their joint future, wondering if she should have directed Alice to take Kit to casualty, rather than to Ned. But no, he had been a very sick little boy, suffering from something extremely rare which only a paediatric specialist would recognise, and such beings were not always available at short notice in a large general hospital.

She was sure, however, that Alice was going through all sorts of tortuous hoops. She would ring her at the hospital, go and see her if she liked. She had nothing else to do, Patrick being away for the weekend, visiting his parents. But first she had some important news for Ned.

'So how are we going to handle this?' said Tom.

'What do you mean?'

In spite of hearing Tom's version of the story, Colin was still hostile. 'I can see there wasn't a lot you could do,' he said. 'But you could have at least given out a proper statement, about how ill Kit was, and how the surgeon was a personal friend, taken the edge off it a bit.'

'Colin,' said Tom patiently. 'You haven't even got any children, let alone a sick one, but if one of them was in real danger of dying I doubt you'd have made what you said to the press top priority. We were off our heads with worry, my only concern was Kit and whether he'd pull through. What we've got to do now is get across to the voters how it was. How can we do that? I don't mind addressing a few meetings, knocking on some doors.'

Colin smiled rather feebly. 'We haven't got any meetings until this afternoon, but we can go knocking on doors. You might get a few rotten eggs thrown at you, but it'll be a good way of testing the water. You had any breakfast? Because you're going to need it.'

The door knocking was as tedious and unproductive as usual, more people irritated at having their Sunday dinner disturbed than concerned about which sort of hospital their candidate had taken his small son to. Tom got a bit of a rough reception, mostly from men who'd spent an hour or two downing pints at the pub, telling him they'd read about him in the papers and thought he was a bloody hypocrite, although more often than not their wives would then appear and tell them off for swearing before assuring Tom that any parent would have done the same thing if they'd had the opportunity. The evening meeting, however, threatened to be more difficult, and Tom, most unusually, had a pint with a whisky chaser before going onto the platform.

His audience were mostly hostile; many of them were carrying one or more of the papers, and spoiling for a fight. There were also a couple of reporters.

Tom kept his speech short, then, his heart thumping, asked if there were any questions. A pugnacious-looking man, wearing a check shirt and denims slung under his large belly, stood up, waved the *Dispatch* at Tom, and said, 'So what's wrong with the Health Service then?'

'Nothing,' said Tom staunchly. 'Absolutely nothing.'

'So why not take your son there then, rather than some poncey place in the West End?'

'My son was dangerously ill, with something very rare that the GP hadn't recognised. It was literally a matter of life and death by Friday. The doctor at St Mary's was a family friend, he said he could see Kit immediately and having seen him, was able to operate that afternoon.'

'That's all well and good,' said the man, 'but suppose you hadn't had this convenient family friend? Then what?'

'Then I'd have had to take Kit to casualty where the long wait might have been just too long. Look, I admit it doesn't sound very fair but what would you have done? Can you honestly tell me you'd have risked your child's life?'

'Point is,' said another man, standing up, 'you happened to have the contacts and the means to save the kid. I'm happy for you, and I'm glad the little feller's pulled through, but I wonder if you're the sort of person to represent working people?'

There was a murmur of 'hear hear', growing louder,

'I believe I am,' said Tom, his voice steady. 'If I am elected, I can fight for the waiting times to come down, for more highly trained doctors in every local hospital. I can't do anything if I'm not elected. I believe passionately in the National Health Service, have done from the very beginning. I want it to work for everyone. But it's not perfect – it's short of funds. I want to see the money allotted to it doubled, and I shall fight for that if I get in, I promise you.'

'I'd probably have done the same as you,' said a rather earnest, well-spoken woman, standing up. 'Although I'd have felt very guilty.'

'I did,' said Tom. 'Believe me.'

'I do believe you,' said the woman. 'But what I didn't like was you saying that it was nothing to do with us. If you're our MP, then it is to do with us; you seem to regard your responsibilities to us rather lightly.'

'Which I most certainly don't,' said Tom. 'I was horrified when I read that. It was a remark taken out of context –'

'Oh, spare me,' said the plaid-shirted man. 'That old chestnut.'

The earnest woman ignored him.

'Even out of context, it shows a certain lack of concern for us. We need one hundred per cent support here. Life isn't easy, the schools are in need of investment, the housing lists are long . . .'

'I'd like to say something about schools and Mr Knelston's concern for them.' The voice came from the very back of the hall. 'Mr Knelston has been wonderfully supportive in that way. He's been to two prize-givings at my boy's school alone, and he's a governor at the grammar school, gives up a lot of his time. I'd say his commitment overall is impressive.'

And so it went on until they'd finished. The room emptied slowly; plaid shirt was one of the first to go, muttering under his breath. One of the reporters had left, but the other came and asked Tom if he would have done anything differently, faced with the same dilemma again.

'Yes, I would,' Tom said. 'With considerable misgivings, which I experienced anyway. But my son's life was at stake. I ask you, as I've asked so many people, what would you have done?'

The reporter said nothing.

They walked back to Labour HQ. 'That was very well done,' said Colin. 'Thank you. Sorry it was so tough.'

'Do you know,' said Tom, 'I rather enjoyed it.'

# Chapter 62

Julius always knew when he was seriously upset: he went off coffee. Instead of deliciously rich, it tasted bitter and heavy and nauseating. He sat and stared at the large cup of it he had just made, and after one sip, carried it over to the sink and poured it away, watching it, too miserable even to move.

What could he do? It was ridiculous, really, to overreact like this to Nell's increasingly high-handed, almost dismal behaviour. He had always known that Nell had her own life, and she would continue to do so. He couldn't imagine anything worse than having a wife who simply kept house and bought clothes and gave dinner parties. Jillie had an important career, of course – no, Julius, don't start thinking about Jillie. She belonged in the past – this awful, sickly, coffee-tainted misery was about Nell, not Jillie. Although exactly what about her was making him miserable, he couldn't quite work out.

He decided to go for a drive; driving always helped him to think. He climbed into the Bentley and set off southwards across London, down through Regent's Park; winding down his window as he always did, the better to hear the strange medley of noises coming from the zoo, the roars and high-pitched screeches.

It was a beautiful day and he had no idea where he was going, but found himself driving across Putney Bridge, and thence onto the A30, and eventually into Guildford and then out again up onto the Hog's Back: where he stopped with a lurch of his heart, for it was one of the Sunday drives he had done with Jillie, and he had managed to park in almost exactly the same place.

He suddenly saw Jillie absolutely clearly, her long straight brown hair, her green eyes, her narrow face with its high cheekbones, her slender body. He could hear her now too, her light, very clear voice, her delicious laugh. God, Julius, just stop it, you're hallucinating, get back to reality – you need to see Nell, actually see her, remind yourself about her. You're going to marry Nell, you want to marry Nell – yes, you do. He got back into the car, turned it round and retraced his steps, made for Nell's house in Kensington.

'Diana, it's me. Leo Bennett.'

'Ah! Would that be *the* Leo Bennett, three times divorced, no current girlfriend – married, devoted girlfriend presently sobbing into her lace-trimmed hanky?'

'Diana—'

'Because I have absolutely no interest in the latter, I'm so sorry.'

She put the phone down; it rang again immediately.

'Leo, you must be either deaf or very stupid.'

'I'm not deaf, but possibly – probably – very stupid. Look – could I come and see you later, say around six? I really can explain. And I so want to see you. Oh, and Celia doesn't have any lace-trimmed hankies. Just embroidered.'

It was that last that made her relent. He was funny and she liked funny men. Maybe there *was* some kind of satisfactory explanation – although it was hard to think what.

'All right. Make it six thirty, though, I'm going out for lunch.'

This was quite untrue, but what kind of girl had absolutely nothing to do on a Sunday? A boring one. And then she thought that if she was concerned that Leo might consider her boring, she must fancy him a little at least . . .

'I've had the most marvellous piece of news,' said Ned. His mother had phoned to say she was coming up to London the following week; having said that, there was a hopeful silence, which meant, he knew, that she was hoping to be invited to meet his new friend. And what an inadequate description that was for the person who had turned his life around, made him happier than he would ever have dreamed.

He determinedly ignored the silence, or rather its message. 'It's all through Jillie, really,' he said. 'We've managed to become friends again and her uncle is a chief consultant in obstetrics, as you know.'

'And . . . ?'

'Jillie saw him yesterday, and told him I'd resigned from St Luke's, and why, and about my campaign to have the mothers in the wards and he mentioned they had a vacancy for a consultant paediatrician, and he and various other doctors had been discussing the care of children in hospital and holding a conference on the subject. I've got to go and meet him, of course, but it looks as if there could be a happy ending to all this – including for the children.'

'Darling, I'm delighted for you,' said Persephone. 'Delighted and proud. Well, you deserve it, you've been so brave about everything. Let's hope that from now on everything's going to be much easier for you. Now, darling—'

'Mother, I'm sorry, I've got to go. I'm already late for my clinic . . .'

Persephone sighed as she put down the phone. She was so longing to meet this young man, whoever he was. Well, she supposed it would happen some time . . .

Patrick had arrived back in London earlier than he expected and decided that he really wanted to see Jillie. He felt that with increasing frequency. He rang from a call box on Euston Station to see if she was home; she wasn't, but her mother assured him she soon would be; she'd gone to see a friend in hospital, but had said she would be back in time for lunch. Patrick looked at the station clock and saw that it was half past three; Geraldine Curtis said half apologetically they always had lunch at four at the earliest on Sundays and asked if he would like to join them.

Patrick said that would be very nice and hurried to the taxi rank and a very long queue.

Julius felt better now, back in London, driving up Kensington High Street; the madness that had overtaken him on the Hog's Back had almost passed. What had he been thinking of? Dreaming of Jillie Curtis, who the last time he had spoken to her, begging her to meet him, had told him to go away and never come near her again, and then put the phone down on him.

'You can't marry him,' said Seth Gilbert, lying back contentedly in Nell's brass bed and reaching for his cigarettes. 'You don't love him, he irritates you to death, and besides, now you've got me.'

'Well,' said Nell briskly, 'I haven't exactly got you, have I? Except as a very thrilling lover.' She leaned over and kissed him. 'You're married, you've got children, and we hardly know one another. In three months' time we could loathe each other.'

'Unlikely, I'd say.'

'Be fun finding out, though.'

'But what I really meant was, you're not behaving too much like someone who's about to be married. And you must tell him, poor chap, that you don't want to marry him. I feel quite sorry for him.'

'Yes, I will tell him. Not about you – don't look so alarmed. Just that I can't marry him. But not just yet. I can't face it.'

'You're a funny girl,' said Seth, pulling her down onto him again. 'Wonderfully funny. Now look, how about one for the road? We've just about got time –' He looked at his watch. 'Half past three, come on, you know you want to . . . I can see it on your face . . .'

Julius let himself into Nell's house very quietly. If she was working, she got very cross if he made a noise. She would probably be cross anyway, but if he explained that he'd really had to see her and that he wasn't going to stay, she'd be perfectly happy.

He looked into her little study, which was a shambles as always, sheets of typescript all over the desk, and one half-typed sheet actually in the typewriter. Although it was strictly forbidden, he read what she was typing; it was set in an operating theatre, tracing the heroine's thoughts as she made her first incision into the patient's abdomen. He was a little surprised that it stopped mid-sentence; normally she hated not completing a chapter even. Something quite serious must have distracted her: a visitor perhaps, but no, she just wouldn't have opened the door; no one, not just he, was allowed to disturb her Sundays. Anyway, she wasn't reading in the little sitting room with the French windows open to the tiny terraced garden, or even the dining room, with its pretty round table covered in a lace cloth and the collection of blue and white china he had given her in a glass-fronted case.

Maybe she was having a rest; it was unlike her, but she had been very tired recently. He really must speak to her, he thought, about leaving doors and windows open, positively inviting burglars in. He unlaced his shoes and as silently as he could, which was very silently, for he knew every creak in every board of that house, he went up the stairs, tiptoed along the corridor, and very, very carefully opened Nell's bedroom door.

'Hello, darling, how are you? How was little Kit?'

'Oh – pretty good, considering.'

Jillie sat down suddenly; her legs were weary and achy.

'And Alice?'

'In a terrible state. Talking about divorcing Tom –'

'What! Whatever for?'

'Oh, I told you, he was very difficult about her taking Kit to a private hospital. You know how passionate he is about the National Health Service.'

'Oh, yes, I saw Josh's article. Hardly grounds for divorce,' said Geraldine. 'She'll get over it. They both will.'

'I'm not sure. I hope so. Anyway, sorry if I'm late for lunch –'

'You're not, and I hope you don't mind, but I've asked Patrick to join us.'

'Patrick! Oh, Mummy, why?'

'Well, he'd just got off the train from some godforsaken place, and he was so disappointed you weren't here –'

'I don't know why. Honestly, Mummy, I'm not feeling very sociable.'

'Well, it's too late now, he's on his way in a taxi.'

Jillie sighed. 'As long as he doesn't start talking about the latest gastroenteric virus –'

'Jillie, that's unfair. He has a very broad spectrum of conversation in my experience.'

'Well, perhaps you'd better start going out with him – no, sorry, I'm quite fond of him really, I'll go and brush my hair and make myself look a bit better.'

Actually, she thought it would be good to see Patrick; he was so nice and steady and normal, didn't have emotional crises every five minutes. And it had been quite a difficult few days, seeing Ned for the first time since – well, since. Yes, he definitely did have advantages. She not only brushed her hair but also put on a new dress, a blue cotton shirtwaister, and some lipstick, and sprayed herself with Guerlain's Jicky which was her current favourite and which Patrick had admired last time they went out.

She was just walking down the stairs when there was a crunch on the gravel as a taxi drove in. She ran down the last few steps, opened the front door and, rather to her own surprise, instead of shaking his hand, hugged Patrick and gave him a kiss.

Julius was halfway along Piccadilly when he realised he had left his shoes behind; his foot slipped on the brake and he only just avoided hitting a bus coming in the other direction.

It didn't seem to matter; nothing seemed to matter, except getting to Jillie's house. If she was working, he would drive out to Hackney and find her there. He had to find her, be with her; that emotion wiped out any anger or humiliation at the scene that had greeted him as he opened Nell's bedroom door, Nell pushing some man off her, and struggling to a sitting position, the sheet hugged to her chin.

Julius said nothing, nothing at all, nor did he wait to hear anything they might have to say; he just wanted to get away from them.

At Piccadilly Circus he pulled in to the side, just by Swan & Edgar's, and pulled off his socks, bare feet being indubitably safer, and proceeded up Regent Street, and then Portland Place, and thence Camden High Street, and on northwards, until at last he was in Highbury, and there, there on his right, at long last, number five. Number five, containing Jillie, happiness, safety. He had paused, wondering how he was going to get across the gravel in his bare feet, when a taxi came up behind him and drove into the drive. And as Julius watched, a man got out, the man he recognised from the other night at the restaurant – and walked up the steps to the front door, and before he had even raised his hand to the knocker, the door opened and Jillie appeared, hugged him – albeit briefly, and gave him a kiss and then shut the great door firmly. Julius sat there for at least half an hour, trying to establish which of his emotions was the most painful, and then turned the Bentley round and drove very slowly home.

# Chapter 63

'Oh – hello,' said Alice. 'I wasn't expecting you.'

'I don't suppose you were. But I wanted to see Kit. Where is he?'

'Playing with a new friend in the playroom. It's down the corridor, I'll show you.' She hesitated, struggling to get the words out, then, 'He'll be very pleased to see you. He's been asking where you were.'

Tom followed Alice to the playroom; it was big, the floor covered with toy trains, complete with railway lines, clockwork cars; a doll's house, filled with furniture, several doll's prams, a blackboard and chalks, a stack of jigsaws and a very well-filled bookcase, the bottom shelf packed with board games for older children. Kit had his back to the door and was engrossed in playing with a train.

'My God,' said Tom. 'Lucky little blighters.'

'Tom, don't start,' said Alice.

'I'm not starting anything.'

Kit heard his father's voice, turned from the train set, and sat on the floor, utterly still, looking up at him, his face sober and disbelieving; then he became one enormous engulfing smile, jumped up and stood hugging Tom's knees, with yells of 'Daddy, Daddy'. Tom picked him up and held him in silence for a while, repeatedly kissing the top of his blonde head; and then sat down, took him onto his knee, and held him very close. He looked up at Alice, and his eyes were brilliant with unshed tears.

'I'm – sorry,' he said, and she could hear the break in his voice. 'So very sorry.'

'It's all right,' she said.

A nurse appeared round the door. 'Kit, you should be in your room, having your wash, ready for bed. And then it's time for your favourite medicine.' She smiled at Tom. 'You must be Mr Knelston. How nice to see you. Kit's been missing you, hasn't he, Mrs Knelston?'

'Yes. Yes, he has.'

'He's been so brave. We haven't heard one single complaint.'

This wasn't quite true, Alice thought, but he had certainly complained very little, nor had there been any tears when the needle had to go into his small veins in order to take blood each day. He *was* brave, extremely brave. She wondered where that came from. Tom, she supposed; he had often told her of the agony of his leg wound in the desert, the nightmare journey to the field hospital and his absolute determination not to let go and yell.

It didn't occur to her that she was actually rather brave herself.

Tom stayed for an hour or so, reading to Kit until he fell asleep, and then said he'd better go and relieve Mrs Hartley, who had had the children since breakfast time.

'I swear Charlie's put on about five pounds! He drains his bottle, then bangs it to show he wants more. She's also got him guzzling Farex at bedtime, so he sleeps much later – till six this morning. Only time he cries is when I take him from her – I could murder the little sod.'

'Tom!' But something that might have been the beginning of a smile crossed Alice's face. 'And Lucy, is she all right?'

'Also very happy. She misses you,' he added hastily.

'Liar,' said Alice. This time the smile advanced a little further.

'No, she does. Right. Well, I've got to go down to Purbridge every day this week but I'll come back in the evening – we can't leave the kids with Mrs Hartley round the clock. So I won't be able to come over here again. When is Kit coming home?'

'Not sure. End of the week, I think.'

'Ah . . .'

'No, Tom, I can't.'

'Of course not. That's not what I meant at all. But this must be costing a pretty penny. Could you ask Ned to get some sort of account made up for us, please?'

'We have talked about it. He said he'd try to keep costs down, and if there's a real problem, we can pay in instalments.'

'Oh, no, I'm not having any favours, Alice. Kit's here, he's had –' He hesitated, then said quietly, 'He's had superb care, and we'll pay for it. There's some money in our savings account.'

He half smiled at her, and there was no rancour in his voice. She suddenly felt rather tearful without knowing why.

'All right. How – how is it, down there in Purbridge?'

'Oh – not exactly fun. Taken a bit of flak. But it could be a whole lot worse. It's pretty basic stuff now, we're down to just pounding the pavements, knocking on doors.'

'Still?'

He looked at her as if she had asked if she should keep on breathing.

'Of course. It's not over till it's over.'

'But I thought you said there was no hope.'

'I don't think there is, but we have to be seen to be hopeful still, working at it, otherwise all the people who've worked so hard, and indeed all the people who *are* going to vote for us, will feel betrayed.'

Alice met his eyes. 'I'm – well, I'm sorry,' she said quietly, as he had earlier. 'I'm sorry as well I can't come on Thursday, Tom. But I can't leave Kit.'

'Of course you can't. I understand. But now I must go. Goodnight, Alice.'


The week struggled on. Things got better than Tom had hoped, never as bad as he had feared. On Monday the *Daily Mail* picked up the story and in a double-page spread awarding vices and virtues to the candidates countrywide, labelled Tom *Greatest Hypocrite*. After that the story lost its legs and another victim was sought and indeed found.


Mrs Hartley decided to take Lucy and Charlie in to the hospital the next day. Charlie was fine, but Lucy was missing Alice badly. She let herself into the Knelston house to use their telephone, as Tom had told her to, and rang Alice at St Mary's; would that be all right?

Alice said it would be wonderful, and offered to pay for a taxi for her, but Mrs Hartley pooh-poohed the idea, and said it would be fun, they'd sit upstairs on the bus, Lucy would love it and Charlie would just sleep through it. Alice thanked her and wondered miserably if Charlie's normal behaviour was her fault as a mother, rather than some quirk of his genetic make-up. She feared the former.

They arrived just before lunchtime. Lucy hurled herself into her mother's arms and clung to her, kissing her rapturously; Charlie woke up, took one look at Alice, and started to cry.

'Well, I never,' said Mrs Hartley, 'we don't hear that very often. I'll give him a bottle, he's probably hungry. Unless you'd like to, Mrs Knelston,' she added hastily. Alice said equally hastily that she'd rather Mrs Hartley did it.

'And please call me Alice.'

A pretty nurse came in and offered them all lunch but Mrs Hartley had brought sandwiches; was there no end to her wonderfulness, Alice thought.

Kit, delighted by the reunion with his sister, bore her off to the playroom; Alice smiled at Mrs Hartley.

'I don't know what we'd have done without you,' she said. 'I just can't thank you enough.'

Mrs Hartley said there was no need to thank her, it had been nice to be of use, and anyway, what a time of it they'd had. 'So frightening for you. What an upheaval in Kit's little life, and Mr Knelston said at one stage that you could have lost him. Doesn't bear thinking about. And it doesn't say a lot for Dr Redmond, does it? Not spotting something so dangerous.'

'Well, it is very rare,' said Alice carefully.

'Even so. He could have died, poor little mite. He looks quite well today, though. There now, Charlie's gone to sleep, I thought he would. My goodness, what an upheaval – there's been a lot going on our end, as well, I can tell you.'

'Really?' said Alice.

'My word, yes. Reporters on the doorstep, one of them tried to interview me, I told him to mind his own business. The nerve! And half a dozen back in the morning. Mr Knelston dealt with them very well, they were all gone by ten. And then that very smart lady, arriving in a taxi, Saturday afternoon . . .'

'What smart lady was that?' said Alice, her voice determinedly steady.

'Well, might have been one of the reporters, but she didn't look like them. And she came on her own. I thought perhaps it was your mother at first, but I could see she was much younger when I got a better look at her,' she added hastily.

Alice felt as if she was falling into a deep abyss.

'It might have been Jillie,' she said. 'You know, the one who took us off to hospital on Friday morning.'

Mrs Hartley shook her head. 'No, this lady was very dark. Gorgeous dress, my goodness, bright red, and what looked like real diamond earrings, and the heels! I don't know how people walk in those heels, I really don't.'

Alice agreed that neither did she, and wondered how closely she could question Mrs Hartley without making her suspicious. Although suspicious of what? She felt breathless, disorientated, as if she was coming up for air from some deep, muddy water.

'Well, I can't think then,' she said brightly. 'Did she stay long?'

'Oh, over an hour at least. Mr Knelston brought Lucy in just after this lady arrived, asked me to look after her for a short while. And when she left – I heard the taxi arriving for her, you can't mistake that noise, can you, of a taxi – well, Mr Knelston came back for Lucy. He did seem very upset but I didn't like to ask –'

'No, of course not.'

Alice decided it was time to call a halt to her enquiries, and suggested they went to find the children.

She managed to banish all thoughts of the very smart lady for the rest of the day, but that night in bed the demons arrived in force. She had had this nightmare so often, about Tom and a mistress; had this been her, arriving at his house when they both knew she was out, Lucy banished – why, why else? – the description of her, dark, beautiful, clearly glamorous, in her high heels and red dress. Alice's mind raked over possibilities of who she could be – not many Labour Party workers wore high heels and diamonds. Or even travelled about in taxis.

542

She began to cry, with shock and despair; she fell asleep, and then woke up abruptly with the memory of Friday evening with Ned in the hospital absolutely fresh in her mind, when that woman had appeared, with her clearly expensive clothes, and just slightly condescending manner. 'She's a famous model,' Ned had said, apologising for her. 'Hide like a rhinoceros.'

Alice remembered her name now – 'I'm Diana Southcott,' she had said, and the whole thing fell into place: Diana Southcott, who had been photographed at Battersea Pleasure Gardens with Tom, long, long ago, the day that Tom had proposed. Now there was an irony; maybe her latest appearance in Alice's life might be followed by a divorce. He had obviously continued to see her; and while she had been obsessing with jealousy over Laura, it was Diana Southcott she should have been worrying about, watching for.

Bastard! Bastard, in bed with this appalling – and glamorous, and rich – woman when she had thought him trying to alleviate the plight of the working classes. It would have been almost funny, if it hadn't been so horribly sad and ugly. And bitch, knowing as she must have done, that Alice could hardly fight back, exhausted, permanently pregnant, tied to the home. God, she could have killed the pair of them, strung Tom up by his balls, stuffed Diana Southcott's diamond earrings down her throat until she choked. How was she going to bear this new awful pain? How could their marriage continue now?

By Wednesday afternoon, Tom was exhausted and so sick of it all that he scarcely knew what he was doing. Sick of shaking hands, of smiling at people who didn't smile back, of hearing complaints about things over which he had no control: not just the high rates, the lack of housing, the overcrowded schools, the uncleared bombsites, the neglected parks, the state of the roads – those were things which could, given that Purbridge had a Labour council, be laid at least partially at its door. But people also complained about their dripping taps, their neighbours' smelly dustbins, the noise their neighbours made, the Teddy Boys smoking and wolf-whistling on street corners. On and on it went, a non-stop, tedious, exhausting tirade. Some people, but fewer than he had feared, called him a bloody hypocrite for taking

Kit to a private hospital; some (a very few) said they'd have done the same if they'd had the means; most either hadn't taken in the report or didn't want to talk about it.

Tom was relieved by this, but at the same time, perversely disappointed that, for most people, all that mattered in a politician was that he provided higher wages, lower unemployment and better housing. The country at large was predisposed to approve of the Conservatives, who had delivered the end of food rationing, economic growth and a younger leader.

Tom's more thoughtful voters asked him what was going to happen about the H-bomb and why they couldn't have a younger leader too.

'Seventy-two, Attlee is,' said one man. 'Stands to reason he can't have that much energy – at least the old bulldog had the sense to stand down.'

He then went on to say that Eden was a bit of a toff, that his wife was pretty, and that he was impressed by his going on the television so much. 'I mean, it can't be easy, can it, not at first anyway, all those cameras poking in your face.'

After twenty minutes of politely and patiently listening to this, Tom said he really must get on, whereupon the man said yes, well, some people had work to do, and that he wasn't sure he was going to bother voting at all, but if he did he thought he might give the Liberals a go.

Tom decided he needed a break and made his way back to Labour Party HQ, where he was told there was a message from his wife.

'She said to ring her soon as you could.'

Fearing Kit had had a relapse, Tom dialled the hospital number; the relief of its being answered by a clearly enunciating, courteous voice, asking how its owner could help him, was enough for a moment to make him vote Tory.

When he got through to Alice, she sounded rather cool, but reassured him there was no problem with Kit; and then, rather as if offering a cup of tea, asked if he would like her to come to Purbridge the following day.

'I always said I would if I could,' she said, as he sank down, speechless with shock, onto a large box of pamphlets which promptly fell over, depositing him on the floor. 'Tom, Tom, are you there? Oh, good. Ned – rather conveniently, I must say – says Kit needs one more day in hospital. I'm a bit suspicious actually; I think Jillie might have had a word because she knew I wanted to come, and of course he couldn't be safer anywhere than here. My mother's coming up to visit him in hospital and to take over from Mrs Hartley at the end of the day, although I think they might actually come to blows over Charlie. Anyway, I'm at your disposal. I can be there by ten – I've looked up the trains – and I'm all ready to smile for the cameras, kiss other people's babies, and have eggs thrown at me, if required. Oh, and you can stay down there tonight, Mrs Hartley's dying to have both children to stay. I thought you could use the time. So where will you meet me? At the station?'

In that moment, Tom forgave her everything.

An icy calm had descended upon Alice. She felt cool, detached and quite, quite numb; she had decided that, until after the election, there would be no showdowns, no fights, no possibility of her being accused of wrecking his chances any further. She would go into battle afterwards, knowing no remorse, no guilt even, knowing she had done her best for him. It was surprisingly easy.

Now – what should she wear? She tried not to think of Diana Southcott's beautiful, elegant clothes. It was pointless – she couldn't compete – but she needed to go home and sort some clothes out. She might, if she hurried, be able to go to Freeman Hardy and Willis and buy the navy court shoes she had admired in *Woman's Own* that week. All her shoes were scuffed and down at heel, she couldn't go on stage as a political wife wearing those. And they would go with her pleated Terylene skirt, and perhaps that blue angora jumper she'd never worn – never an occasion more worthy of it.

'Friend Tom? Hello, darling. It's me, Diana.'

'What are you doing ringing me here?' Tom hissed into the telephone someone had just handed him. 'How did you get this number?'

'Well, that's not a very nice greeting. Really, Tom, I never know where I am with you. I got it from your office. And I only wanted to wish you luck for tomorrow. I do hope you get in.'

'Not very likely, I'm afraid,' said Tom, 'but thanks anyway. Alice is coming down in the morning, might help a bit.'

'Well, not if they know it was her idea to take your son to—'

'Diana, *please*. But thank you again for that –' he realised someone was hovering, threatening to take the phone from his hand – 'that information you gave me on Saturday night. It was extremely helpful.'

'OK, OK, I get the picture. I'll go. By the way, I might be moving to New York for a bit. Anyway, I'll let you go, you've got an election to win. Good luck, Friend Tom. I won't leave for New York without saying goodbye.'

'Bye. Thanks again.'

Tom rang off and then went outside and stared down Purbridge's main street. Against all odds, all the danger Diana represented, he didn't want her to go to New York, didn't like the prospect of a life quite without her. Perversely, she was one of the few people he actually trusted and how he would have got by that weekend without her, he could not imagine . . .

It was a long, hard day; Alice's new shoes had had a bad time of it.

Tom met her off the train, started her on a crash course of polling-day behaviour even before they had left the station.

'It will be like the by-election, only tougher. We're going to polling stations, all day long. The main thing is to smile. Smile at the voters, smile at the tellers, smile at the cameras. The local press will be about, may want an interview with you. Smile at them, smile at the party workers, smile at the press, smile at hostility, smile at compliments.'

'I think I get the idea. Smile.'

They had reached Labour Party HQ by now: Colin Davidson greeted her enthusiastically.

'My goodness, you do look smart. How's the little fellow? Must have been dreadful for you. But you being here today should make a big difference. You're a very popular lady down here, you know; we call you our secret weapon. Now, have a cup of tea, give you strength for the day ahead. And how about a buttered scone? Made by my wife.'

Had he not said that, Alice would have refused the scone, but she feared that would be taken as a slur on his wife's cooking. It proved to be both delicious and nourishing.

Her face ached from smiling by lunchtime, her feet ached from her new shoes well before that; there was no place for an aching heart as well. They progressed from polling station to polling station, both large and small; at one of the major ones, the *Purbridge Gazette* asked Alice for an interview.

The reporter was handsome, very young, a bit cocky, but polite. He asked Alice how she would feel about living in Purbridge if Tom won and she told him she couldn't wait. 'I especially love Sandbanks, of course, it's so beautiful, and we had a week's holiday there in a caravan.'

'Good. Of course, Sandbanks is the posh end of town.'

'Yes, but I like Purbridge itself too, and everyone's been so welcoming and kind, it feels like home already. And my little boy loves the quay.'

'Would that be the little boy who's been ill and in hospital? How is he now?'

'Much better, thank you. Otherwise I wouldn't be here?'

'How was it you and your husband took him to a private hospital, Mrs Knelston? I'd have thought Mr Knelston, with his devotion to Aneurin Bevan, would have chosen the National Health Service?'

'Ideally, we both would,' said Alice, without a breath of hesitation, 'but it was literally a crisis. Kit's life was in danger. We were lucky that we have a friend who is a paediatric surgeon, and he took Kit into his hospital and he was in the operating theatre in a couple of hours.'

'I see. And – don't you think a casualty department would have responded as quickly?'

'We would have hoped so, but we couldn't be sure, and believe me, if your child is that ill, you want certainties.'

'Of course. Lucky you to be able to afford such a certainty.'

'Well, it did take all our—' She was going to say, 'savings', but he had folded his notebook shut.

'Well, thanks for finding the time to talk to me, Mrs Knelston, and good luck with the vote.'

She was afraid she hadn't done very well. It must have shown in her face, for a woman came out of the small crowd which had gathered to watch the interview and the photographs being taken, and said, 'Don't you upset yourself, dear. We'd all do the same, if we could. He's too young to understand. You don't take risks with your child's life. Is he still in hospital?'

'My mother's looking after him today,' said Alice, half truthfully, 'and the other children too.'

'Yes, you've not long had a baby, have you? How's he doing?'

'Oh – fine, yes.' (When he's next door, she thought.)

'Well, I think it's very brave of you to come here today. Good luck with the vote. We're voting for Mr Knelston; we like the way he's been down so often, taken a real interest in the town. The other one,' she said darkly, 'we don't see his face from one month to the next. Great fat toff. Not that we'd vote Tory anyway. Oh, now look, your husband's coming over for you. Bye-bye, dear. Very nice to talk to you.'

'Very nice to talk to you,' said Alice. And she meant it.

They stopped at a pub for lunch, then whirled on. Alice was so exhausted she began to feel she was hallucinating.

Tom looked at her. 'Want a break?'

'No, of course not. Do I really have to go on drinking tea, though?'

'Yes, I'm sorry.'

'I never want to see a teapot again.'

The next polling station was a school; shabbily cheerful, with peeling paint and threadbare lino, but dozens of children's paintings and poems, carefully written out, were pinned on the wall. Alice stopped to admire them. The headmaster was there: he came over to them.

'We're looking to you to help us if you get in,' he said to Tom. 'Even with enough money for a few cans of paint.'

'We'll certainly try,' Tom said. 'Increasing the education budget is

right at the top of our manifesto, and that would include mainten-
ance of the buildings themselves, obviously.'

He and the headmaster moved on; Colin grinned at Alice.

'He's talking through his hat,' he said. 'It's the council who allot
spending, what goes on what and where. Still, does no harm to make
them think we can help.'

At six, they went back to HQ, and Alice phoned the hospital; her
mother was still with Kit.

'He's absolutely fine, dear, very happy. He's been up for most of the
day, far too long I'd have said for a child who's had major surgery less
than a week ago, but I suppose they know best.'

Her tone implied that the hospital knew nothing of the sort.

'I'll just wait till he's asleep and then I'll head over to Acton. Mrs
Hartley not being on the telephone is very inconvenient, I must say.
She's a curious woman. I popped in to introduce myself on the way in
to town – pleasant enough, I suppose, but she has a very odd attitude
to Charlie, almost as if *she* was his grandmother, not me. Still, it's
only for one night.'

The count was in the town hall, a huge Victorian building; they stayed
at the last polling station they had visited until it closed, and then
waited while the boxes were sealed and carried out to waiting cars. It
was a very emotional moment. Alice looked at them, thinking, in
those boxes lies my future and the future of my family. Whichever
way it goes. Possibly even of my marriage.

She looked at her watch: four hours at the very least to wait. It
seemed a very long time.

They didn't win, of course. It was close, but not as close as the by-
election. The nationwide swing was too big; there were no Labour
gains at all and twenty-three losses. Tom looked calmly cheerful and
made a short, simple speech, knowing he could never recapture the
drama of the last time. He thanked all the workers, particularly
Colin, 'And of course my wife, who has supported me throughout,

and enjoyed today so much she says she's thinking of entering parliament herself.'

'Tom,' said Alice suddenly as they drove home through the darkness, 'pull over, would you? I want to talk to you about something.'

'Can't it wait till we're home?' He sounded defensive.

'No. No, it can't.'

'Right. Well, let me find somewhere safer than this.'

They reached a bus stop; he pulled in.

'This sounds serious. Should I be nervous?'

'Yes,' she said, 'you should.'

She felt no nerves, just a cold confidence in herself which echoed in her voice.

'Tom,' she said, 'have you been having an affair with Diana Southcott?'

And without hesitation, although in a less steady voice, he said, 'Yes. I'm afraid I have. But it's over.'

'Oh, really. And why should I believe that? When all those evenings you told me you were at meetings and rallies and making speeches, you were in her bed?'

'I – don't know,' he said. 'I don't know why you should believe it.'

'Well, no. When you seem to be one of the most practised, skilful liars – probably the most – I have ever met.'

'But it is true. You must trust me on that, at least.'

'Trust you?' she said, and her voice was so filled with scorn that she saw him physically wince. 'Trust you? When you took advantage of me, when I was at my lowest ebb – pregnant, sick, exhausted, hideous—'

'No,' he said, 'not hideous. I never, ever found you that.'

'Tom, please don't lie. It's disgusting. Hideous – and completely unable to fight back. How could you do that, Tom, how could you? It makes a travesty of our marriage, of our family, of everything I thought we had. Tell me how it happened and I'll feel just a little less – shocked.'

'I don't know,' he said. 'I really don't know. I suppose because I'm a complete shit. Simple as that. It certainly had nothing to do with any – any comparison between you and her.'

'It must have had. Unless you just needed some sex – I admit there wasn't a lot on offer – but a prostitute could have done that for you.'

'Alice . . .'

'Come on, what was it? The fact that she's so beautiful? Which she certainly is. Famous? Does it tickle your vanity in some strange way, to have got your cock into some world-famous model?'

'Alice! I hate it when you talk like that.'

'Oh, I'm sorry. Not as much as I hate it when you act like that. Answer me, Tom, I need to know.'

'Well,' he said, after a long silence, 'and this reflects appallingly on me. It's what she could offer, that wasn't sex. Like a house that wasn't overrun with toys, a conversation peppered with other things than babies, a feeling that for a few hours I was free.'

'You are DISGUSTING.' It was a roar of pain and rage, that of a trapped animal. 'I hate you, I truly do hate you, loathe you for that. How could you throw that at me, the very things you had done to me?'

'Alice, Alice, you were extremely keen to have babies, you made not the slightest effort, as far as I could see, to offer me anything more.'

'I was TOO TIRED!' She was shouting now, beyond outrage.

'I know. And I'm sorry for that. But there was nothing else there for me. And, at the same time, you had the audacity to cling to this obsession about Laura. I couldn't stand it any longer, Alice. It was as simple as that. I'm sorry.'

'Laura!' she said, her voice heavy with despair. 'Yes, another rival for your affections. Or rather your love. I think, in a way, I still mind more about her. The way you keep her hidden, close to yourself, won't share that part of your life with me. Your whole life, for as many years as we've been together, was about Laura.'

'And what's so wrong with that? That's nothing to do with you. She was my past, incredibly precious to me.'

'Well, exactly,' she cried out, her voice cracking. 'But that's what stands between us, don't you see? She's so shadowy I feel I've only ever seen her outline. The basic facts, that she was twenty-nine years old, a teacher, a member of the bloody Labour Party, that she had curly hair and a nice smile, and I only know that because I found that picture of her that you keep in a drawer. I have no idea if she was good- or bad-tempered, clever or stupid, generous or mean, whether she could cook or sew. I have to fill in all those things for myself, imagining her. And of course I see someone absolutely perfect, who I can't possibly measure up to. I have longed – *longed* for you to say just once, "Would you like to go to West Hilton and to the churchyard where Laura is buried?" It makes me feel you don't want me there, you don't trust me with her. Trust is everything in a marriage, Tom, and I don't feel I can trust you. Less than ever now, of course, a hundred times less – but oh, this is unbearable. Let's go home, I've had enough.'

He remembered sharply the conversation with Diana, talking of this very thing, trust: and of how Alice had destroyed his in her, that dreadful day of Kit's surgery. And he felt a flare of anger that Alice was so blind to her own iniquities.

'No,' he said, 'not yet. I have things to say too, Alice. About the almost unbearable pain you inflicted on me, telling me that she and Hope might still have been alive without my obstinacy about the hospital. How do you think that makes me feel, Alice and—'

'Oh,' she said. 'That!'

'Yes, *that*, that revelation making me feel a murderer. How dared you do that? To leave me feeling for the rest of my life that Laura and Hope died because of me? The rest of it, the danger you put me in professionally, that was nothing, of course Kit should have come first – I feel ashamed even to have hesitated. But you did something else, that day – you stamped all over my most deeply held and precious convictions, without so much as a thought, a pause, simply to speak to me, however briefly, to tell me what you wanted to do. They mattered to me so much, those convictions, Alice, as dearly held as any religious ones – foolish as they may seem to you, they mattered desperately. I don't even mind that they seemed foolish to you, but I mind very deeply that you could swat them aside like some irritating fly. I find that very hard to bear.'

There was a long silence; then she said in quite a different voice, 'I'm – I'm sorry, Tom. Mostly for telling you about the harm you could have done to Laura, but the other too. It was – it was very wrong of me.'

'Well,' he said soberly, 'it seems to me we have done one another considerable wrong, almost unforgivable wrong. But I think, for what it is worth, and that may not be much, we should try to forgive them. For whatever you may think, Alice, I do love you very much. I would be lost without you, quite lost; you and the children. You are my life – not Laura, not Diana – and I would like you to allow me to spend the rest of my allotted span proving it. But it may be too much to ask; and I can see why.'

She sat there, considering all that he had said, all that he had done; and she knew that she must at least try. But could she? Was the gulf between them too huge, the rage too violent, the hurt too deep? Could she really behave as if it was some mild misdemeanour that had taken place between them, some trifling quarrel, when each of them had taken hold of their marriage and wrenched it so ruthlessly apart? It looked almost impossible, sitting there in the darkness; but as they drove on and she thought of the alternative, thought too of what they had had, it seemed worth at least an attempt. It would take a long time, it could not be accomplished in a day, or probably even a year, and indeed it would never be the same in a lifetime; but they had achieved much in this marriage of theirs, too much to abandon it without fighting for it first. And at least they would be on the same side.

'No,' she said. 'It's not too much to ask. I'm sorry, so sorry, for what I did. I love you too, Tom.' And then added, with a rather lopsided shadow of a smile, 'Although I can't for the life of me think why.'

# Chapter 64

'Well, that's all splendid, Mr Welles. We shall be delighted to have you on board. We're short on paediatric skills at the moment; Lionel Mainwaring has retired early, due to ill health, poor fellow, just as his research programme on childhood leukaemia was launched. But I believe that is one of your spheres of clinical interest.'

'It is indeed. I have been following Mr Mainwaring's work with great interest.'

'Good, good. And we are very much in agreement with you over children's hospitalisation, and the presence of mothers on the wards. There are considerable practical problems, but I don't think it is beyond the ingenuity of man to solve them. My only stricture would be that you proceed with any programme slowly and with great care.'

He really was a good man, Ned thought, Mr William Curtis, MD, BSc (Hons), FRCP, FRCS (Hons) and God knew how many more such letters, this uncle of Jillie: sitting there, smiling at him across his huge desk. To work under his enlightened aegis would not only be an honour, but a pleasure. He said so.

'The feelings are entirely mutual. Oh, Jillie did tell me, in the briefest possible terms, about the reasons for your engagement's cessation, and I would like to assure you my only feelings on that are sympathy. Such a lovely girl,' he added. 'One of my favourite people, not just in the family but beyond, and extremely clever too. She'll do very well, I'm sure.'

What he was saying, Ned knew, in the most sensitively expressed code, was that he felt no prejudice towards him for his sexuality, and moreover, given discretion, that he need have no fears of it from any-one else on the hospital staff.

Ned walked out of the hospital and over Westminster Bridge, smil-ing down at the water, the sun warm on his face. He could never remember feeling so happy, so fortunate. He had the job he had dreamed of, fear removed from his professional life, loneliness from his personal; he loved and was loved. It was a heady sensation.

He decided to walk down to St Luke's, rather than get a taxi; it would only take about half an hour along the river and he had plenty of time before his afternoon clinic. He would miss his patients there, he thought. He had made friends among them, and their mothers – their fathers were rarely to be seen. It was women's work, taking children to hospital. There was one little chap, Timmy Ford, the bravest and most cheerful nine-year-old; he had been born with one leg four inches shorter than the other, had had four operations, was in constant pain, and arthritis was already setting in. He had to wear calipers, and a heavily built-up shoe; his mother was always smiling, sometimes trailing one or more of her other four children into the clinic; and then there was Susan Mills, a cystic fibrosis case, also in leg irons, and with both bladder and bowel problems, a cheeky, curi-ous child who called him Dr Make-me-Welles. It was a splendid name that he tried to live up to.

As he walked along Chelsea Embankment, he looked up at the extremely handsome mansion blocks, and thought how much he would like to live there, with the fantastic view of the river and the space they offered – a huge reception room, more than decent kit-chen and some had three bedrooms. He could have a study and a proper guest room . . . And then thought, reckless with happiness, there would be room for a piano and he would be able to put his mother and other visitors up. One was for sale; he noted the name of the agent, and hurried on. It wouldn't do to be late for his clinic.

'Are you ready?'

Diana handed Leo Bennett a large gin and tonic, settled herself on the sofa on the opposite side of the fireplace from him, lit a cigarette.

She wanted a clear head, not remotely befuddled by alcohol. 'Go on, Leo, I'm all ears.'

It was Saturday; their assignation the previous week had been cancelled as he had been sent by the paper to Paris to attempt to interview Juliette Gréco about her affair with Miles Davis. He failed, but he did see her perform in Le Tabou, a music and poetry venue on the rue Dauphine, and wrote a rather amusing piece about the evening, the music, bohemian Paris, and hanging about for three hours hoping she would emerge, only to learn she had left quite early while he was in the gents.

'OK. First, Celia. The one who my friends in the ladies' lavatory said was still sobbing. It's her speciality, sobbing. And yes, we did have a fling, not a very long one, which is why I thought it would be all right to finish it.'

'That sounds a bit – harsh.'

'I agree. But she's an emotional girl, almost unstable I'd say –'

'That sounds harsher.'

'Sorry. I didn't realise at the outset. Nor did I realise something else.'

'What was that? She had some incurable disease?'

'Diana, that's hugely unfair. I really don't think I deserved that. I'm doing my utmost to be honest with you. I don't normally justify my behaviour in this rather pathetic way.'

'Well, stop doing it then. I don't mind. It was your idea. We can go our separate ways right now. Doesn't matter to me.'

'Fine.' He stood up and walked towards the door. Diana looked after him. Even from the back he was attractive, slim, quite broad shouldered, his thick blonde hair beautifully cut, exactly the right length; his Saturday clothes – dark blue jeans, brown Chelsea boots, open-necked white shirt, navy tweed jacket – exactly the style she most liked, and he had a very sexy walk. She suddenly very much wanted him to stay. And –

'I was being unfair,' she said. 'Hugely unfair. I'm sorry.'

She surprised herself with the thoroughness of her apology. She must really like him, she thought.

He turned; he still wasn't smiling, as she had thought he would be, but he looked less angry.

'Come back and at least finish your drink. I think I'll join you.'

He walked back rather slowly and sat down; while she was making her drink, the phone rang. It was Ned.

'Hello, Ned, darling. Lovely to hear from you. But I've got some-one here right now, can I ring you back? Um – no, not this afternoon, sorry. Why? Oh, I see. Oh, Ned, what a good idea, they're lovely those flats, and you are terribly squashed in your cottage, pretty as it is. Right. Well, see if you can arrange something for tomorrow or Monday and let me know.'

She put the phone down, went back to the sofa.

'Sorry.'

'Friend of yours?'

'Yes. Ned Welles, he's a doctor. You could say he's my best friend,' she added, determinedly banishing Tom Knelston from her thoughts.

'I see. And – is he married?'

'No. Couple of near-misses, but – no. Not yet.'

'Oh – hang on a minute. Isn't he a friend of the Bellingers? And Ludo Manners? I covered some wedding they all went to. And Michael Southcott and the delectable Betsey.'

'Michael's my brother.'

'Really? Nice chap.'

'Yes, well, I think so. Goodness, what a memory you've got.'

'Fearfully good-looking, your friend,' said Leo. 'I always thought he was probably queer. Or certainly swung both ways.'

'Ned! Heavens, no. I almost married him myself.'

'And why didn't you?'

'Because I met my husband.'

'From whom you're now divorced? Tell me, Diana, do you have a vast past?'

'Not really. Look, I thought we were going to discuss yours.'

'OK. What was next on the agenda? Oh, yes, Baba.'

'To whom you're still married?'

'Correct.'

'Why did you tell me you weren't?'

'I tell everyone that. It saves a lot of tedious explanations.'

'All right. Why do you deny your wife's existence? It's not the nicest thing to do.'

'She's not the nicest person.'

'Leo –' Diana was growing irritable now; she took a rather unlady-like slug of her gin and tonic.

'It suits her to be married to me. It goes like this. Marriage a big mistake. Soon dawned on us both. Anyway, we had no children, thank God, we agreed to divorce, and I was living in London anyway. She stayed in a house in the country we'd bought until it all went through. Only it didn't. She discovered she was very happy in the country without me; there wasn't anyone else, she just dug her heels in and wouldn't get on with it. And I had no grounds for divorcing her. I wouldn't anyway. Bad form.'

'Leo! Honestly.'

'Well, it is. No gentleman would divorce his wife.' Clearly he meant what he said. She was surprised and amused in equal measure.

'Anyway, the good news is she's met someone, who's rich, much richer than me, and good-looking and all the things that matter to her. So now she wants a divorce and quickly. I shall do the decent thing and provide grounds, you know, weekend in Brighton, and that will be that.'

'Goodness,' said Diana. She would have laid every kind of bad behaviour at Leo's door, but not this rather upright gentlemanly stuff. 'I didn't like the lying, Leo. Well, actually I don't mind lying when there's a reason for it, but that all seemed so pointless.'

'Like yours about Ned Welles?'

'I'm sorry?'

'My darling Diana, you're a rather bad liar. Ned Welles is as queer as a nine-bob note – I always thought so and just now you con-firmed it.'

Diana stood up. Her eyes were blazing. 'Get out,' she said. 'Just get out. How dare you insult and – and slander – my best friend.'

'Hey, did I say I disapproved in any way? Did I display any animos-ity, or prejudice? Of course I didn't. My little brother is homosexual. I love him most dearly. Together with our mother we conspire to keep it from our father. Who would treat it in the time-honoured way of a daily thrashing.'

'What does he do?'

'He's a landscape designer. He's currently working on a huge scheme at some pile in Warwickshire. Living in digs in Stratford. We could go up and see him, you'd love him, take in something at the RSC maybe. I'm a huge fan of the Bard. You?'

'Um – not really,' said Diana cautiously. Actually, there was nothing she hated more than an evening of the stuff.

'I shall convert you. I shall make that my Diana mission. I like to have a mission with every woman.'

Diana wasn't sure about being lumped together with the rest of womankind.

'Now, you can pour me another G and T, and then we can decide what to do about lunch. And then after lunch. I can think of a few things, but –'

All Diana could think of, and before rather than after lunch, was going to bed with him. She felt quite consumed by the idea, every part of her hungry, greedy, desire working at her like some restless animal, rampaging through her emotions.

'So,' he said, reading some of this in her dark eyes as she looked at him, in her shaking hand as she took his glass, in the smile trying to be cool as she handed it back again. 'So, would you like to go out to lunch or would you rather stay in? And you might as well be truthful, not fuss about being ladylike. Because –'

'I'd rather stay in,' she said.

# Chapter 65

Ned lay in bed, staring into the darkness. It was already half past two and he hadn't slept. He was worried, not seriously so, but enough to keep him awake. He had been so wonderfully, so joyfully happy, to have found love, and to feel so brave about it. But he was disappointed in being constantly held back from telling at least the people he loved about it – properly about it; in finding still a reluctance to go even to the theatre, or a restaurant, together, for fear of recognition, of reprisals. He understood, of course he did, he had felt like that himself for so long: but then he hadn't been in love. Perhaps this wasn't love, wasn't strong enough. It was a very frightening thought.

He decided to make himself a cup of tea and play some music; that would at least calm him down. And sitting, listening to Mahler, he began to feel better. He must be patient; he must understand. The judgement of society was a harsh one – despite the slow easing – and the fear of that judgement was hard to shake off. It would happen – with love and encouragement. That was all that was needed on his part: patience. He went back to bed and slept.

Jillie was working very hard at being in love with Patrick; without a great deal of success. She couldn't deceive herself (knowing so well what love felt like) and there were simply none of the essential ingredients. Her heart didn't lift at the sound of his voice on the phone, indeed it was more likely to turn irritably and then sink down again, and she didn't count the hours until they were to meet; she contemplated them calmly, often wondering why on earth she had agreed to see him at all when she could have done with some time to herself, to work, or to look for the little house that she was sure was waiting for her somewhere and which she now regarded as a near-necessity.

When she was actually with Patrick, she enjoyed herself; there was no doubt that he was more interesting than she had at first thought, and much funnier. They went to a lot of theatres and concerts, discussed their work with great enthusiasm – she couldn't imagine Julius sitting fascinated as she described a Caesarean section delivering non-identical twin boys. 'It was the two placentas, you see, it made it terribly complicated and then the second baby was a breech, not usually a problem with a C-section, but he was all tangled in the cord and I couldn't get a grip on him – and then the stupid nurse had given me the wrong clamps, and –'

'Nightmare,' said Patrick. 'Whatever did you do?'

'Well, just had to dig in deeper and turn him and –'

At this moment, they both realised the people at the next table were looking distinctly unhappy and had put their knives and forks down.

It was after evenings like that, when they got the giggles, that she thought well, maybe, after all, he was fun and so kind and generous. But it was the other evenings, like one last week when they had been to a concert, and he left his arms rather too tightly round her after helping her into her coat and she knew she should acquiesce to his hopeful suggestion that she went back to his flat for coffee and thought why not? Why not, because the thought of kissing him lengthily, and then him proceeding further simply gave her goosebumps of entirely the wrong kind – cold, crawling goosebumps.

No, it wasn't working; she should finish with him and soon. Only he would be so upset, and she couldn't face that either.

It was Josh who told her; Geraldine had invited him to one of her little soirées. Patrick couldn't come, but she'd found a couple of other young unmarried men . . . Actually, it was a nice evening, and one of the two young men, while being very dull, was also very handsome and clearly interested in Jillie, and she was about to agree to going to the cinema with him, when Josh arrived, late, full of apologies, gave her a huge hug, filled her glass up alongside his own, told her a bit of political gossip, and then said, oh, yes, he expected she'd heard Julius and Nell were no longer together.

'Wedding cancelled – Nell's having an affair with her editor – Julius is talking about moving to Paris for a couple of years.'

The room emptied for Jillie: or rather, everyone receded, the conversation became a distant buzz, she felt dizzy, disorientated, and stood staring at Josh, who too seemed to have moved far from her.

'You all right?' he said and, 'Yes,' she said, 'fine, you must excuse me a moment, Josh,' and fled to her room, where she sat on her bed, rigid and stupefied, trying to make sense of what he had just said.

For if Julius was no longer with Nell, why had he not at least contacted her? The last time they'd spoken, which was not more than a very few weeks ago, he had told her he had to see her, had to talk to her, that he could not stop thinking about her and she had put the phone down on him. How could he not therefore, now that he was free, at least have told her?

It hurt so much she could scarcely breathe; she sat down on the bed, her arms folded across her stomach, rocking backwards and forwards. How was she to bear it, this new betrayal, this fresh rejection?

There was a knock on the door – it was her mother, was she all right?

And she said, 'I'm all right. Well, not really, I've just been sick. Sorry, Mummy, I'm going to have to go to bed, you get back to your party.' Then she crawled into bed, pulled the eiderdown over her head and cried until the last guest had gone and the house was quiet again, and when her mother came up again to see how she was, she pretended to be asleep.


'Look,' said Freddie, 'I'm sorry to hassle you, but we need to make a decision soon. Very soon. By the end of this weekend, actually. Ottilie's on the phone to me hourly.'

'Freddie!'

They were having tea in the Soda Fountain at Fortnum's; it was very crowded, and half the customers were Freddie's compatriots. Diana, who had loved the American accent at first, wondered how she would feel about living with it twenty-four hours a day, seven days a week. Freddie's was all right, but then he was from the East Coast and a good family (which in America meant rich). But the Southern drawl, or worse the Midwestern roll, drove her mad.

'All right. She rings me daily. No, honestly, more than that, twice daily.'

'Well – gives her something to do,' said Diana.

'Diana! That wasn't worthy of you. We're talking serious business here.'

'Sorry. I don't know. I do want to go, it'd be heaven working with you all the time, we can do such amazing things –'

'I know. Did I tell you about my Schwarz idea?'

'No'

'F.A.O. Schwarz, that hugely famous toy shop at the top of Fifth. I thought we could do a shot in all the major departments, with you dressed to match. So something floaty and Ginger and Fred-ish on the piano floor and we'll have a Fred for you to dance with; sharpest suit we can find for the Lego room; something v v sporty for the life-size animals, I thought you could actually sit on one of the giraffes –'

'Oh, Freddie.' Diana set down her teacup, her face dreamy. Thinking about working with Freddie particularly, but really, simply work, creating photographs, always excited her, focused her mind. 'Maybe a picnic with the teddy bears, so a country afternoon dress, shirtwaister, I should think.'

'Marvellous. But I can't get them all worked up till you've made up your mind properly.'

'Miss Dickens and Ottilie worked up! I don't think so. I never saw a cooler pair in my life.'

'Not so sure. Remember them looking at the transparencies. Miss Dickens practically having an orgasm.'

'She wouldn't know an orgasm if she got hit in the eye with one.'

'Now there's an interesting thought. Flying orgasms. Like it.'

'Well, look, I'll let you know definitely on Monday. I mean, I'm sure I will come but –'

'But what?'

'Oh, nothing.'

'You've got your silly face on – you in love?'

'Of course not. No! No, I'm not –'

But she was.


'OK. Nearly there. Diana, wake up, you're not being very amusing.'

'Sorry. You shouldn't keep me awake all night. This is an amazing car. So comfortable.'

'It's been called many things, but not comfortable. Not sure the designers would approve.'

'Well, it's beautiful too, of course. I love it.'

She leaned back in her seat and smiled at Leo. It was hard to believe she could love anyone like this. She realised now she had never known love before. Ned had been a crush; Johnathan, at best, a fondness; Tom – well, who would believe her, but what he had been, and always would be, she hoped, was a friend, an odd, often awkward, truthful friend, the sex a very nice by-product. She was quite fond of Freddie, but she didn't love him. She hadn't loved any of them, hadn't been invaded by them, not found her entire being possessed by them, heart, head, soul, self. Taken, shaken, shocked: seeing differently, thinking differently; made to laugh, to cry, to fear, to hope; to be changed, absolutely, and yet to feel more herself than she had ever been.

How could she have suspected for one moment as she walked into that restaurant, her knees weakening, that this man, a journalist, for God's sake, and not even a respected kind of journalist, not a war correspondent, an arts critic, an essayist, a political pundit, but a gossip columnist; a lightweight, flighty creature, spinning and weaving gossip and scandal. This was what he did, all day and much of the night, this man she loved. But then she thought what was she, her career, but flighty and lightweight herself, so what could be more appropriate?

And he said he loved her. 'I have seldom said that,' he said, looking at her almost in awe one night, in bed, and she was consumed with jealousy, asking, demanding to know, to whom he had said it and why.

'No point in telling you, you'll be angry or upset, or both, and what does it matter, I love you now, more than I can ever remember loving anyone,' he'd said.

It was crazy really, it was only a week since that shining, dazzling Saturday, when they had gone to bed at lunchtime and not got up till morning when he had had to go to work, and returned a few hours later with champagne, a pot of caviar, and a bouquet of white roses so huge she could hardly see him behind it. And every night, and as much of every day as he could spare, they spent together, talking, laughing, she sometimes crying, he sometimes sad, telling stories, laying out their lives thus far for one another.

Diana told him everything. Her passion for Ned, her marriage on the rebound, her misery in Yorkshire, her adoration of Jamie, her hatred of her mother-in-law. She didn't tell him of her affair with Tom, for it was not her secret to tell, but she did tell him of her fling with Freddie, even of the baby, the lost baby, and what Johnathan had done.

'That is truly terrible behaviour,' said Leo, shocked for the first time.

'I know,' she said, 'but I did some terrible things to him, and besides, he's quite nice to me now he's happy with his plain, plump wife.'

Leo laughed. 'I love your malicious little asides.'

He talked too: of his disastrous schooling, of his tough war – first in Italy, then France. 'I did D-Day, the horrors will never leave me.' Of his first wife: 'She was only nineteen, madness it was, but so beautiful, I only love beautiful women –' he paused and kissed her – 'and I liked the idea of taking her virginity, of teaching her pleasure, it satisfied my vanity. But I was unfaithful to her in our first year, left her in the second – she had a lover of her own by then, a charming chap, professional soldier in the Hussars.' And then of Baba, and all the women before and after.

They drove up to the visitors' car park at Headleigh House, where Leo's brother was working.

A rather snooty girl said they might find him in the studio.

'Up the back stairs, first door on the right.'

They went up into a small room, with a huge desk. Its occupant, clearly engrossed in his task, didn't hear them come in.

Leo crept forward, put his hands over his eyes.

'Guess who?'

There was a shout of 'You bastard!' and Marcus, or so Diana presumed he was, turned, embraced Leo and then stared questioningly at Diana.

'This is Diana. She's a tourist. I picked her up in the drive.'

Marcus grinned at Diana, held out his hand.

'Tourists don't usually come as pretty as you. Hello. Marcus Bennett.'

'Hello, Marcus. What an amazing view.' She nodded at the window, at the grounds beyond; they were indeed amazing, broad rolling sweeps of meadowland, tree studded, set further from the house with what looked like toy sheep.

'Isn't it? The owners, frightfully nouveau, I'm afraid, but rich, want me to install a Greek temple – and a couple of little classical bridges.'

'Where's the water?' asked Diana curiously.

'There isn't any. But we can make a lake, that's no problem.'

'Sounds a tad naff to me,' said Leo.

'It is. But they're paying me zillions, and I can do tasteful naff. Shall we go and have coffee?'

They sat on an outside terrace, drinking coffee and eating shortbread biscuits, and Diana decided she liked Marcus very much. He was very like Leo both physically and in personality, but less abrasive. They were obviously very fond of one another, telling jokes in between more serious stories.

Diana left them to it and went in search of the ladies; when she came back, Leo was saying, 'I do actually want a divorce this time, you can see why.'

Hoping she could construe this in the best possible light, she smiled as she sat down, gave Leo a quick kiss. He took her hand and kissed that.

They were still at the stage of their relationship where any touch, any intimacy was still exciting; Marcus sat smiling at them benignly.

'He's a nice bloke,' he said to Diana, when Leo left them to see if the bar could provide anything in the way of alcohol. 'Not nearly as tough as he pretends.'

'Really?'

'Yes. Most women take him for a ride emotionally, if you get my point, use him as a provider of gossip and fun and possibly even a way into his column.'

'How horrible,' said Diana.

'Yes, but you're famous in your own right, so he knows he can trust you. He really likes you, I can tell.'

'Good,' said Diana lightly.

'But don't hurt him, Diana, he's had a hard time of it lately.'

'I'll try not to,' she said as Leo walked back towards them, smiling; her heart turned over and she vowed she never would.

# Chapter 66

'Anyway, show me the rest of this wonderful flat and then we'd better make for your vast Chelsea acreage. What are we having for lunch?'

'Salade Niçoise. Have you come across Elizabeth David?'

'Darling, of course I have. And her Mediterranean cooking. Wonderful. What a perfect day I'm having. Especially seeing you so happy.'

'Yes,' he said. 'Yes, I am so very happy. I can't quite believe how much.'

And Persephone, looking at him, thought this was how she would always remember him now, relaxed, smiling, totally at ease, his future set fair.

It made her very happy too.

'Oh, Diana, thank goodness you've rung. I don't know what's the matter with your phone – it just rings and rings, I've been trying all morning. I've even had it tested. You're usually so good at ringing in.'

'Sorry, Esmé. Been away.'

'You know you have to ring in first thing. Anyway, the *Evening Standard* rang an hour ago. Can you do a job on Wednesday? Rainwear?'

'Jolly short notice. Who's the photographer?'

'Some new young genius called Russell. Just that. Anyway, he's in the Bateman mould. Not as good, of course, but – think you'll like him.'

'OK. Yes, I'll do that. Sounds fun.'

'Good. Then *Harper's* are after you, two days next week, Wednesday and Thursday, and *Woman's Journal* are so thrilled with those pages they want to book you again, for their big autumn fashion issue. But that's not for a couple of weeks –'

'Esmé –'

'And how would you fancy a trip to Paris? Only a couple of days, but it's advertising, so the money's good.'

'Depends when. And what I decide to do.'

'About what?'

'New York, of course.'

'I thought you were going. That's why I'm cramming so much into the next two weeks for you.'

'And what's happening about Enchantée?'

Enchantée was a new perfume; they had approached Diana about signing her up exclusively not only in England, but France and the States as well. It was a big contract worth hundreds, possibly thousands, of pounds. It would take her right into the model stratosphere, one of a small exclusive band, but there hadn't been time for the lawyers to look at the contract.

'Diana . . .' Esmé hesitated, sounding more awkward than Diana had ever heard her. 'Enchantée have cancelled. I'm so sorry. They decided they wanted a blonde.'

'Ri–ight. When did this happen?'

'While you were in New York.'

'Bit sudden. I mean, I know we were dithering a bit, but they knew I was frightfully keen. It just seems – odd. So who?'

'The rumour is it's Jo Courtney.'

'Oh. Oh, I see. '

Jo Courtney was new on the scene, young, blonde, classically beautiful; she was clearly going to make it in a big way. And she could not have been more different from Diana.

'Bastards.'

'Yes, I agree. I did try, of course, fought very hard for you, but – well, it was no good. I'm sorry, Diana. But everyone else loves you.'

Diana was silent, then she said, 'Well, you win some and you lose some. Never mind. The exclusivity clause was a bore. Anyway, Esmé, you go ahead and call the *Standard* and *Harper's*; I need a bit of time to think about *Woman's Journal*. Sorry I didn't call in this morning.'

Waking, sleepy with love, in Leo's bed that morning, looking at him tenderly as he slept on, she wished – most unusually for her – she need never get up again, never work again, never go to another casting. She was in no mood for Monday, and especially this Monday, when she had to ring Freddie with her answer about New York. She and Leo had had a perfect Sunday, talking, talking, talking.

'Do you think we'll ever run out of things to say?'

'Not if you're there, Diana.'

They were walking in Kensington Gardens, saying 'Good morning' to Peter Pan, lunching at the Berkeley, and then back to Leo's flat for afternoon tea and the newspapers. 'I have to read them all, by mid-morning usually,' said Leo. 'Bath and bedtime,' he said firmly very shortly after that.

His bath was enormous; they sat in it together, she on his lap: with inevitable consequences. 'Oh,' she said, leaning back against him afterwards, 'that was *wonderful*. I never could see the sense when people went on about it, but I do now.'

Later, back in bed, drinking first tea for her, coffee for him, then the most poetically beautiful white burgundy; then more sex ('Where does it come from, all this – this wanting?' she asked) and then just as she was drifting off, he said, his voice blurred with sleep, 'Don't you dare agree to go to New York without discussing it with me first.'

That did it. She would not go, she decided, not if he didn't want her to, but then, in the morning, his phone started ringing, obviously with a lot of amusing gossip, and he sat up in bed, propped on his pillows, making notes and saying things like, 'She sounds a bit of a peach,' and 'I had a *huge* fling with her once, nympho really, but if that's what she's up to now, I'd love to see her,' until Diana began to feel irritated, and she got up and dressed and, blowing him a kiss from the doorway, which he returned without pausing in his conversation, went out into the street in search of a taxi home, feeling uncertain of herself: which was a most unusual emotion.

❖ ❖ ❖

Leaving the agency, she felt more uncertain still – and confused. It had all been wonderful at first, of course, being at the heart of it, admired, wanted, the centre of attention, soothing after the hour sitting beside Leo, very much the reverse. But the news about Enchantée had been a shock. As always when she was in emotional turmoil she phoned Wendelien and said she needed to see her.

'I don't know what to do,' she wailed. 'I love Leo, love love love him, and he loves me.'

'Well, that's wonderful,' said Wendelien. 'How perfect you must be together.'

'Well – maybe. But I have to make a decision about New York, whether I go or not, and I had decided to say no today. But now I'm not quite sure.'

'Why not, for heaven's sake?'

'Well – well, it's quite complicated.'

'Diana, it always is with you.'

'I know. Can I tell you? And then will you give me your advice?'

'Yes,' said Wendelien resignedly. 'As long as you don't take it.'

'Of course not.'

This was a running joke between them.

'Anyway, you know I thought I'd got that amazing perfume contract? Well, they've dropped me in favour of someone else, about fifteen years younger than me, the girl they want now. Esmé made a great thing of the reason being she's blonde, which she is, but that's not it. I'm thirty-five years old, Jo Courtney is twenty-one. She's making all sorts of waves and this is a huge campaign. All other things being equal, it's going to run for five years – and in five years I'll be in my forties. And however amazing the retouchers are at taking the years off and the lines away, far better that there aren't any years or lines to begin with. This is only the first time, Wendelien; it'll happen more and more, there'll be more gorgeous young girls, with beautiful faces and nimble, bendy, loose-limbed bodies. So I don't have very long left, however busy I am now, and I want to get out while I'm still at the top.'

Wendelien digested all this, then she said, 'Yes, I think you're being very brave and positive about it, and sensible. But I don't see what it's got to do with going to New York.'

'Well, it's a lot of money which I could quite do with at the moment. I've spent so much on my house. And it'll be fun. And they really, really want me, which is important to me, I've learned today. I rather like being the centre of attention. Wendelien, why are you looking at me in that funny way? I also like being independent, more so than ever now I'm involved with Leo. He's such a star, and I don't want to trail round being nothing but his girlfriend. I've got an idea about what I want to do next, but it'll take money to set it up.'

Wendelien listened politely, and when Diana had finally finished she said, 'I've listened very carefully, Diana, and if you really love Leo – and I must say it's rather early days to be sure – I still don't think you ought to go to New York. He's hardly a pipe and slippers man, waiting patiently for your return, and you could come back to find him gone. Metaphorically speaking. Sorry, not what you want to hear, I know . . .'

'No, but you're probably right,' said Diana. 'Anyway, thank you for your time and wisdom, as always. Can I have another sherry, please?'

She rang Leo's office when she finally got home but he was out to lunch; hourly calls after that yielded the same answer, right up to five o'clock. When, this being her deadline, and midday in New York, she rang first Freddie and then Miss Dickens and told them she had decided to make the move, and was looking forward to joining them in two weeks' time.

Leo Bennett, feeling that a five-hour lunch with a drunken (albeit wonderfully garrulous) peer of the realm, followed by a rather tough editors' conference, was enough for one day, was on his way to Diana's house as arranged, bearing a bottle of Perrier Jouet, with a suitably flashy diamond ring in his pocket, to tell her exactly why she shouldn't go to New York.

They had a rather ugly row, and Leo left half an hour later, the bottle of Perrier Jouet unopened on the dining-room table, and the diamond ring still in his pocket.

# Chapter 67

'Jillie, hello. I wondered if you'd care to come out for supper one night this week?'

'Oh, Ned. How lovely to hear from you. I'd like that very much.'

'Good. So – when?'

'Well, could it be Saturday? Week nights are hopeless – all my clinics run terribly late because half the women seem to have awful problems, quite apart from gynae ones, and I'm operating Tuesday and Thursday, terribly long lists.'

'No need to sound so apologetic, Saturday would be absolutely fine. Shall we say eight? And I'll think of somewhere nice where we can go. I've got something to tell you.'

'Oh – oh, goodness, yes. Ned, I'd love that. Thank you.'

She put the phone down, smiling.

She had ended the relationship with Patrick. It just didn't seem fair. He was getting increasingly keen, and – well, she felt she was using him, a bulwark against perceived spinsterhood. She was obviously destined to end up like Miss Moran, married to her work.

Diana spent the week in a frenzy of work. She was booked every day. Shopping – absurd, she knew, when she was moving to the shopping capital of the world, but it was a distraction – packing, arranging with Johnathan for Jamie to stay with her in the summer holidays, a few days in New York and then with Freddie's family in Maine. 'New York is vile in the summer, so hot. I'm spending a week in Sconsett

573

with my parents and a couple of my cousins, the family has a house there, and they'd all love you and Jamie.'

He had turned out to be a really good friend, Diana thought. Friends really were a much better idea than lovers, much more constant and far less trouble. Who needed lovers, for God's sake, she thought, crushing the thought of Leo and the terrible, devastating row they had had, saying the most appalling things to one another, dredged from defiance, from disbelief, from shock. After he had gone, assuring her he would never be back, she remained too angry to cry for over an hour. Then she wept, bitter, self-pitying tears; and when they had stopped, she became remorseful at the happiness she had so wantonly thrown away. Then, as the hours passed, she wondered if there might really have been happiness, if she could really have loved the man she now knew him to be, arrogant, egotistic, possessive. She half-expected him to return, to apologise, to say he understood; by the morning, she knew he never would; any more than she would go to him. It was over . . .

Tom and Alice had settled into a rather strained truce.

It was hard to make the reality live up to the wishful thinking of their future. Resolving to forgive, while utterly impossible to forget, was uncomfortable. They were polite, even nice to one another, but there it ended. As Alice said to Jillie, it needed some major event to bring them together again.

'The only bright spot in the sky is that Charlie's behaviour is improving. So life is a bit easier for me anyway. But Tom is quite depressed, more than I am; oddly, is talking about getting out of politics.'

'What?' said Jillie, genuinely horrified.

'Yes, really. He says he failed to win Purbridge twice and that the business over Kit has made him rather unpopular with certain sectors of the party. Donald Herbert isn't even speaking to him —'

'Great toad,' said Jillie.

'I know. So he's talking about going absolutely one hundred per cent into law, maybe even the bar —'

'Well, that would be exciting, wouldn't it?'

'I suppose so, yes.'

Thursday evening saw Tom summoned to Transport House – to be told the astonishing news that the Purbridge MP had had his long-predicted heart attack, and was not expected to live.

'So it's a by-election, dreadful thought so soon after the general election, but here it is, your last chance of getting hold of Purbridge. We thought of finding a new candidate, but frankly, you didn't do as badly as we all thought, that unfortunate business with your son considered. We'll postpone it as long as we can. He'll have to resign anyway, can't be more than a matter of weeks.'

Wendelien had never, in the nearly two decades of their friendship, interfered in Diana's life, beyond introducing her to Blanche Ellis Brown, which scarcely counted – and of course, trying and possibly suc-ceeding to stop her telling Leo Bennett about Tom. But she watched Diana's desperate, bright misery as she hurled happiness determinedly away and continued to pack and plan for her move to New York and knew she would never forgive herself if she didn't try to do something to help. No use her taking on the task – the only hope lay in Ned Welles, who Diana had always regarded with enormous respect, as well as great fondness. Her hand shaking as she picked up the telephone, Wendelien dialled Ned's number on the Thursday following Diana's decision. There was no time to be lost: Diana flew out in eight days' time.

Ned answered at once; she could hear music in the background, and when she began to stammer out her request, he asked if he could ring her back, he had a friend with him. Hating herself, Wendelien said yes, of course, but could it possibly be that evening, it was very important. Ned rather wearily agreed. It wasn't until after eleven that he rang, and said he couldn't be very long, he was very tired and he was operating all next day.

'I promise it won't take long. The conversation anyway. It's about Diana – I think she's making the most appalling mistake and I just terribly want to stop her.'

She kept it as brief as she could, horribly mindful of his weariness; when she had finished, he said, 'Well, I don't know,' and she could hear the laughter in his voice. 'Leo Bennett is a frightful bounder, she might be better off without him in the long run.'

'Ned,' said Wendelien. 'I really think Diana is a match for any number of bounders. The difference is, she loves this one, she really does, I've never seen her like this, ever, and she says he loves her –'

'And how many women do you think he's said that to?'

'Dozens, I daresay.'

'Modest estimate.'

'Well, anyway, I think this is different, for both of them, and if she wasn't going away, I'd think it was best to let it all take its course. But once she's gone, it really is over, and – oh, Ned, please talk to her.'

There was a silence, then he said, 'All right, I'll try. You know she'll be absolutely furious with me, probably never speak to me again.'

'I know she'll be furious,' said Wendelien, 'but of course she'll speak to you again. Thank you, Ned, very much. I'm so sorry to ask you.'


'That was a lovely evening,' said Jillie, 'thank you so much, Ned. And I am truly so thrilled by your news. He sounds perfect and it's lovely to see you so happy. I look forward to meeting him one day soon. And although it's frustrating, of course, not knowing a bit more, like who he is –' she grinned – 'I do understand. You want to take it very carefully. Especially as he wants that too. '

'Yes, he's nervous, of course. Afraid of losing his job . . . as might I be, without your wonderful Uncle William.'

'Of course. It's so hard, so wrong.' She sighed. 'Just the same, I wish I had someone to take it carefully with. '

'Oh Jillie, darling, darling Jillie, you'll find someone. I know you will.'

'Ned, I have found someone. Trouble is, he didn't seem to want to find me. Oh, well. One day, perhaps.'

'One day for sure.'

She looked at her watch. 'Goodness, it's late, I must go.'

'I'll get you a taxi.'

'No, I've got my car. It's just down the street.'

'Then I'll walk you to it.'

'Ned, you are such a gentleman.'

She took his arm as they walked along the road, and just before she climbed into her car, kissed him.

'Dear Ned,' she said.

'Thank you for that, Jillie. Thank you for everything. I still do love you, you know.'

She smiled. 'As well as him?'

'As well as him. You're two very special people.'

'Goodbye, Ned.'

'Goodbye, Jillie.'

As she neared the corner of the King's Road, she looked back at him in her driving mirror. He was walking down the middle of the street, clearly lost in deep, deep thought. And saw the next thing too: a car, coming round the corner too fast, carelessly confident in the silent late street, saw him, braked too late –

Neither Ned nor the car had a chance.

# Chapter 68

Persephone had taken upon herself the task of organising what they were calling not a funeral, but a celebration of Ned, Ned and his multi-faceted, brilliant, and often rather difficult life. She had called upon a diffident, sorrowful Jillie to help her. 'If I need it, darling, that is. It will be lovely to know you're there, and he did love you so – sometimes, I think, more than anyone. Even more than me,' she added, her great dark eyes spilling over with the ever-present tears.

Jillie, touched beyond anything, took upon herself the immediate task of compiling a list of possible attendants.

'I got to know so many of his friends and colleagues when we – we . . .' Her voice shook. 'I think that would be the most helpful thing I could do. And – it's going to be a long list,' she added, with a twisty, difficult smile.

They agreed the ceremony should be held in a church. 'I know he didn't quite believe,' said Persephone, 'any more than I do, but he loved church architecture and church music, and nothing can begin to uplift you like a stained-glass window, with the sun streaming through. I shall pray for sunshine,' she added. 'And if it works, we shall know, perhaps, that we were wrong, and there is a God. And then we will know that Ned is there, somewhere, approving of what we are doing. Or disapproving. Oh, dear, he was often quite critical of services he went to, funerals *and* weddings – we must get it right for him, Jillie.'

'We will,' said Jillie. 'Now, one thing I did think. His campaign was the children in hospital, so I think we should make a bit of a thing of that. He would have loved it. I'm sure Uncle William will talk. He was so impressed with it all.'

'Wonderful' said Persephone.

They chose St Mark's Chelsea, it being his local parish church. 'And, more important, the vicar, Christian Greenfell, has a beautiful voice,' said Persephone. 'Some of them these days are – well – not quite what you'd expect. And a perfect name – I mean, you'd more or less have to go into the Church being called Christian.'

Diana offered her house as a venue for afterwards, but agreed, as the list grew, it was simply not big enough.

'Number five is, but it's too far for everyone to go,' said Jillie. 'And we don't want to go to a hotel.'

'The Hurlingham,' Diana said, when Persephone invited her opinion over tea one day. 'It's a lovely house, the grounds are gorgeous, and it's on the river. Ned would approve,' she added firmly. 'So important.'

Persephone gave her a kiss and said she and Jillie had both been worrying about Ned's approval of everything.

'So silly,' she said, 'when we know he can't approve or disapprove of anything any more.'

'We may know it,' said Diana, 'but that's different from feeling it.' Her voice stumbled. 'Oh, dear. Here I go again. I've cried so much I'm totally parched.'

She had postponed her sojourn in the States until after the funeral. 'If it loses me the contract, I honestly don't care. And I want to bring Jamie. He adored Ned.'

Diana also organised the flowers: she had spent much of the past few years watching florists building displays for photographic sessions, and knew the very best of them. 'I know a marvellous girl, Harriet Jennings, she's terribly imaginative, makes flowers look extra graceful, extra perfect, don't ask me how. We can take her to the church, talk it all through with her. How lucky it's June – oh, what a dreadful thing to have said. So sorry, Persephone.'

'It's all right,' said Persephone, taking the proffered hanky. 'He died, that's unalterable, so much worse in November for all sorts of reasons.'

It was becoming real, this dreadful thing that none of them wanted, yet had to create. The music was chosen by a small committee, headed by Jillie, with Ludo Manners – perhaps Ned's closest male friend, and immensely musically sophisticated – William Curtis and the vicar, Greenfell. He had offered a full choir, but William Curtis said he thought a smaller group would be better. 'Maybe a dozen boys. We haven't chosen any of the big anthems, we're keeping this as an intimate tribute; he isn't – wasn't – some distant dignitary, and most of the people who come will have known him personally. And I think, Persephone, if you agree, a quartet or quintet to play the Mozart, a little unconventional perhaps, but again it would help capture the essential personality of the man.'

Persephone did agree; and also to Jillie's faltering request that they might for the recessional have 'Isn't This a Lovely Day to be Caught in the Rain?'

'I know it's very unconventional, but he so loved all that kind of music, as well as the classical, and that was his favourite song of all. I think he'd like it, but not, of course, if you'd find it wrong.'

'Not wrong at all. Very, very right,' Persephone said.

The obituaries had been almost elegiac: *The Times* pronounced Ned, *one of the most brilliant young surgeons of his generation*, and the *Telegraph, a visionary in the world of children's medicine.* The *Sunday Times* ran a short article, written by Josh, referring to his academic brilliance; his unfaltering courage in the war as commander of three torpedo ships, and his mention in dispatches; and then his skill as a distinguished paediatrician and a pioneer in the reform of pastoral care of children in hospital. The article was illustrated by a photograph of Ned in a hospital ward, looking absurdly handsome, holding a small blonde girl in his arms, her mother smiling beside them.

There had been a post-mortem and there would be an inquest, of course, but the coroner had released Ned's body early. The night before the service, Jillie asked Persephone very gently if she would like to go and see him before the coffin was closed.

'I would absolutely hate it, darling, thank you, not because I'm squeamish or anything, but because it won't be him so what would be the point?'

They both wondered, even to one another, about the man Ned had found so recently, and loved so briefly. Would he come forward, would he declare himself to them, or would he just come quietly and anonymously to the service? They hoped he knew about it. 'Of course, he'll have seen the obituaries,' Jillie said. 'There's no more we can do. Poor, poor man. Oh, it's so sad . . .'

They woke to rain on the day of the funeral; Persephone phoned Jillie.

'You see. No God. All those prayers . . .'

She arrived at the church an hour early; Harriet, the florist, was still working. The church was a great bower of flowers, everything white and pale blue – lilies, roses, stephanotis, scabious and love-in-a-mist – with huge urns, looking like seventeenth-century paintings, either side of the altar steps where the coffin would stand. Persephone winced at the supports, already in place. Small vases stood on every windowsill, with candles on either side of them, and at the end of each pew, a single lily, tied with a white ribbon.

'Oh,' said Persephone. 'Oh, Harriet, it's beautiful. So lovely. Thank you.'

'I do hope it's all right. I was afraid it was a bit – a bit happy, but the service is called a celebration and –'

'No, no, the happier the better. That's what we're trying to do, you're right. That's what we said. I can't thank you enough.'

'I didn't know Ned, of course,' said Harriet, weaving a thread of gypsophila through the pulpit garland. 'But I've built up such a picture of him, hearing you all talk, and he was obviously the most lovely man, very, very special.'

'Yes,' said Persephone. 'Yes, he was. Very special indeed.'

The organist arrived, came to speak to her, said how lovely the flowers were.

'Aren't they. Is it still raining?'

'No, it's stopped. Pretty grey, but not raining. Now, if you don't mind, I'm going to sit up there in my loft and just strum away for a bit.'

Glorious strains of Wagner and then Mozart filled the church; it didn't sound too much like strumming to Persephone.

She sat and looked at flowers, and thought about her beloved Ned, who she had loved so much and who had been taken from her by his father and the law when he was only four, a solemn brown-eyed little boy, his shining dark hair flopping over his brow, with a slow, cautious smile, and a laugh that bubbled and leapt out of him. But she could not entirely blame the law: most of the blame was her own; she should have stayed, not run away, kept him her own. Only – James had disliked her so much, disapproved of her so deeply. How had they got married, how could they have thought it was in any way a proper match? He had been handsome, of course, and rich, and she had been only seventeen and by the time she discovered her mistake there was Ned.

Persephone dropped her face into her hands and wept, as she had been weeping so many times over the past two weeks.

'Persephone, I'm here.' It was Jillie. 'Mummy and Daddy are just coming. We wanted to be early, we thought you might be here.'

Persephone looked at her through swimming brown eyes and said, 'Oh, Jillie, thank God for you. Please sit with me, you and your parents. Then I can be brave.'

'Of course. I just hope I can be too. And you know, it's stopped raining. So – there might be a God.'

Persephone looked at her and blew her nose, wiped her eyes.

'I want a bit better than that,' she said. And managed to smile.


Jillie sat next to Persephone and held her hand, very lightly; her father's hand she clung to rather more fervently. She was dreading more than anything the entry of the coffin; that would finalise it, make it real. Make their parting truly for always: that dreadful evening when he had told her he couldn't marry her and she had thought her heart would break was still, in part, the stuff that dreams were made of. While Ned was still alive, she could love him, even while at first she had hated him; he occupied the earth, he breathed the air, he moved, he laughed, he talked. Now that he was not alive, he was still, silent, solemn and she could love only his memory, fading with time as it must.

The church was filling up now, rows and rows of people, all come to say goodbye. She didn't recognise many of them: some powerful and important, some quite the reverse. There were the distinguished surgeons who had guided Ned's early career, two of his tutors from Cambridge, the dean of the medical school at St Bartholomew's, and Sir Digby Harrington from St Luke's, who, as she would have expected, was looking carefully sorrowful. A row of pretty young St Mary's nurses, and – how dare he come, how dare he – Sir Neil Lawson, who had threatened and virtually sacked Ned, made his life so wretched, looking painfully solemn.

There was another group, she had no idea who: three or four couples, the women all in tailored black, all wearing pearl chokers, the men in what were clearly Savile Row suits, with highly polished shoes, stern expressions. And then she saw that, pinned to the lapels of their suits, were rows of medals and realised: Ned's contemporaries in the navy. How nice that they came, after all that time. He had clearly made his mark even there.

Then there were several obviously poor families, sitting together in the pews at the back leaving those further forward empty, clearly feeling it was not their place to occupy them; the fathers stiffly awkward in seldom worn suits, the mothers in dark Sunday-best dresses, and their children: three or four in leg irons, a couple on crutches, a pale, huge-eyed little girl coughing intermittently, several looking completely healthy but overawed just the same.

'Jillie,' her father whispered urgently. 'Where is Josh? He should be here, we've held his seat.'

'I don't know,' she said, looking wildly round, wishing rather fervently that he was there, she didn't know quite why. 'He's just – just not here.'

'Odd. Very odd.'

It was.

And then, as the introit began from the organ loft, the glorious waterfall of Bach's Fugue in G Minor, she turned back to the front, to the flowers and the altar; thereby missing the arrival of a young man with wild dark hair, dressed in a black linen jacket and palest grey linen trousers, who had come to say goodbye to Ned who he had known a little, introduced by Josh, and perhaps see Jillie, risking the agony of her being there with the man she had clearly chosen to spend the rest of her life with.

Looking round helplessly for someone he knew, feeling dreadfully out of place, he saw Josh and, on the other side of the aisle, a wonderfully, gloriously familiar figure, her narrow coat in palest grey, with long straight brown hair, the sight of whom clutched at his heart and he stood, drinking her in for so long that a queue formed behind him, and one of the ushers came over and guided him very politely to a pew on the other side of the church, so that he could no longer see her. But it had been her, and the man beside her was most assuredly not The Man, for he was silver haired and far from thin. Comforted briefly, Julius settled to studying the order of service before wondering if The Man was sitting elsewhere. And then he read the order of service, delighted by the choice of music, the fact that Jillie was doing a reading, and especially the rather bold choice for the recessional.

Looking more furtively now at the people coming in, Julius saw a very beautiful woman he recognised from the pages of *Vogue*. She wore brilliant blue silk, and a wide-brimmed darker blue hat; huge dark glasses half obscured her lovely face, and she was holding the hand of a boy, aged about eight, with dark hair and huge brown eyes, followed closely by a heavily built man, with dark greying hair and the unmistakably, well-weathered looks of someone who spent his life outdoors. They were clearly important, inner circle, for they were being ushered right forward, near to where Jillie sat, and thus out of his sight. Following the usher also, another clearly important pair, she prettily dressed, but not fashionably so, with curly blonde hair and wide blue eyes, and he tall, extremely good-looking, with very dark auburn hair and wearing a dark suit, a little tight for his broad shoulders, but otherwise immaculate, apart from a small but distinct white stain on his left shoulder and down his back. Wendelien Bellinger, who was sitting behind him, caught the unmistakable whiff of baby sick.

Wendelien was sitting with the circle of friends that Ned had been part of from the very beginning – she and Ian, Ludo and Cecily, Michael Southcott and Betsey.

And once, when they were very young, Johnathan had been one of them as had Diana; but he belonged no more, removed from them both physically and emotionally. Wendelien had been fond of Johnathan, indeed they had had a very brief, summer-long fling when he was still a stockbroker and she had not yet met and fallen in love with Ian. She hadn't seen him at all since Jamie, who looked a nice boy, had been born. It was odd, seeing him with Diana: a study in incompatibility, she so showy and glamorous, he so introverted and – well, dull.

The church was almost full now; a few anxious-faced latecomers crowding in at the back, no seats left. Goodness, Ned had had a lot of friends; although he had often seemed lonely, or at any rate solitary. She supposed the crowd was as much made up of people who admired him and felt they wanted to celebrate his life, as ordinary friends.

There was a diversion then. One of the funeral directors bustled in, went up to Persephone and whispered in her ear; she looked startled, turned to Jillie for a whispered conference, then turned back to the man and nodded and smiled and he bustled out again.

'How strange,' was all she said to Jillie, who nodded, puzzled too.

Almost still now, the congregation; everyone there. Scanning the latecomers, standing at the now-crowded back of the church, Wendelien suddenly saw a half-remembered face: who was it? She knew him, with his thick blonde hair, his rather heavy eyebrows: he saw her looking at him, and smiled – and she remembered, at once. They had been on the same table at a couple of charity dinners and she had found him rather charming. Leo Bennett. Why was he here? To bid farewell to Ned or to find Diana under cover of that? Had Diana seen him? Probably not; she did look genuinely and deeply upset, and Wendelien knew she was dreading her reading, afraid she would break down and not get through. Few people, Wendelien thought, would believe Diana capable of such frail emotion.

Diana was indeed seldom fearful, but now, holding Jamie's hand, waiting trembling with anticipation, as Christian Greenfell's splendid voice rang through the suddenly silent church: 'I am the way, the truth and the life . . .' and the congregation stood, and the coffin, slowly and with infinite care, was borne down the aisle.

She looked at the coffin, and thought of what it contained and tried and failed to believe it. Ned, beautiful, charming, brilliant Ned, who she had danced and laughed and talked with, who she had known for so long, who had loved her she truly believed in the end, although not as she would once have wished, but who had become one of her dearest, most best-beloved friends. How could this have happened, how could he have changed into something cold and still and silent, gone from her, from all of them? It wasn't possible, it was a lie, a terrible, shocking, outrageous lie.

But – it seemed the truth; for the coffin had been set down, bearing its crown of white roses and trailing ivy. Only two of the coffin bearers were known to her – Ludo Manners and her brother, Michael Southcott. But then, two strangers, not William Curtis who she had expected, and who had come hurriedly, and taken his place with the family, but one a heavily built bruiser of a man, in an ill-fitting jacket, his face fierce with suppressed grief and pride: Jack Mills, father of the cheeky clever Susan, who had cystic fibrosis. And the fourth, a slight, dark young man, ashen pale, his eyes fixed straight ahead. And then – then she saw his grief-ravaged face, set determinedly, looking at no one, only the man before him, and she knew. It was Josh. Josh, as she had never seen him, white, stricken, his arm supporting the coffin trembling, but strong.

And at the same moment Jillie saw him, and in a huge, almost unbelievable moment of revelation, she understood it all, and stood there, staring, her eyes filled with tears of sympathy and love. How could they not have seen it, not understood; how hard for him it must have been, all of it, but especially her relationship with Ned, and how loving and how brave of him now to come, to have found the courage, to let them know, and to play his part in this farewell.

And now the first hymn, that well-worn, much-loved 'Lord of All Hopefulness', was announced and sung, and Diana, knowing she must, feeling she could not, was climbing the steps to the pulpit, to read.

She looked out over the congregation, her face quite calm now, and stood there, just for a moment, commanding their attention; and then half smiled and said, 'Death is nothing,' and her voice did tremble and she paused, clearly fighting for control. And then, more strongly, she read on: the lovely words of Henry Scott Holland, diminishing death, increasing hope:

'Death is nothing at all.

I have only slipped away to the next room.

I am I and you are you,

Whatever we were to each other,

That, we are still . . .'

Her voice was beautiful; low, musical, made more remarkable with just-suppressed grief.

Tom realised that he had never noticed it, being too taken up, or amused by, or angry with, or wondering at, what she was saying. He sat staring at her, at this woman who he knew really so extraordinarily and intimately, while so few people here were aware that he knew her at all, and then stopped looking and simply listened. And as he listened the day came back, the day when Ned had held, literally, his son's life in his surgeon's hands, how calm he had been and how patient, as the ugly war was waged before him, and how incredibly privileged they had been, Alice and he – and in that instant the last of the ice between them melted and a frail recovery began as he looked at Alice and smiled, and took her hand in his as they listened, in the utter stillness of the great church:

' . . . Wear no forced air of solemnity or sorrow.

Laugh as we always laughed

At the little jokes we enjoyed together

Play, smile, think of me, pray for me.
. . .
Somewhere. Very near.
Just around the corner.
All is well.
Nothing is hurt; nothing is lost
One brief moment and all will be as it was before.'
Diana paused there, clearly almost broken: but then she took a
deep breath and said, with a quick, bright smile,
'How we shall laugh at the trouble of parting when we meet again!'

Watching her, as she stayed in the pulpit for a moment, gazing out
over the congregation, Leo felt surprisingly moved: not for Ned, who
he had scarcely known, but for the cruelty of life, that it must end like
this, in death and sorrow; and for this remarkable woman whom he
had loved, albeit briefly, and whom he had so wantonly thrown away.
It had been madness, he thought, and must be set to rights: and
wondered if that was even possible. And suddenly, and almost miraculously, just as she placed her hand on the rail to come down the
steps, she saw him, their eyes met and all the bitterness and anger
between them was gone, flown from the church, shamed by this
greater, deeper emotion; and he smiled at her, and very, very briefly,
she smiled back at him and he knew that it was, after all, going to be
all right.

Music followed: 'Pie Jesu' from Fauré's Requiem, the soprano voice
flying, soaring; Tom felt deeply moved, his eyes filled with tears, staring at the now empty space that had held Diana; he wanted to go to
her, to thank her, for what he scarcely knew.

And then Jillie, looking very pale, very frail, went up to the pulpit,
looked over the church in silence. Then began, looking up.
'"Remember Me",' she read, her voice surprisingly strong, 'by
Christina Rossetti. Ned's favourite female poet.'
It was all Julius could do, staring at her, listening to her, to sit still,
and at the end, not to applaud.

'Better by far you should forget and smile,
Than that you should remember and be sad.'
'But,' she added, with her calm, sweet expression, 'I think we shall be able both to remember Ned *and* smile.' Then she returned to her seat and her composure left her, and she buried her head in her hands and wept.

Mozart then, the 'Benedictus' from the Requiem, enough for Jillie, and for Alice, suffering with her, to recover composure; and then William Curtis mounted the pulpit to give the eulogy.

He said he must begin with an apology, for he felt there were others, closer to Ned, with more right to speak of him, but he had admired him hugely, and when he had been asked, thought, 'I simply want to do it.'

He spoke of Ned's academic achievements, of his courage in the war, of his post-war student days at St Bartholomew's, where perhaps, for the only time in his life the words 'Could have done better' could have applied to Ned, and who could blame him, released from the horrors of war, and finding himself free?

'He spent much of his time, first learning, then playing, jazz piano, and those of us fortunate enough to have heard him will know that it was not time wasted.'

He spoke of Ned's early days as a junior doctor, his ability to carry on working for days on end with scarcely any sleep, 'learned, I suspect, during those years at sea', his unstinting giving of himself, his passionate longing to do good. He spoke of his pioneering work with children in hospital: his vision of a child frightened and in pain, able to be with the person it needed most, the mother, and his battle to accomplish that against considerable and extraordinary odds. 'As some of you know, he was about to join my own medical team. I cannot tell you for how many reasons I grieve that that will not be so.'

He spoke of Ned's love of music. 'I can only pray he will approve of today's offering. How we longed to have him with us to help us choose, but in his absence, we have done our poor best.' He looked at the coffin and smiled and said, 'Be tolerant of us, Ned, please,' and the whole church smiled, some laughed even.

He spoke of Ned's love of good food and wine, of the guarantee of the very best of both in his company, of his own talent for cooking and in unexpected ways. 'I tell you, if you have not tasted Ned Welles's marmalade, you have not lived.'

And then, finally, he moved on to his nature, his self:

'People always say what a lovely man he was, not just those closest to him, but his acquaintances, neighbours, colleagues, patients, and it was true; in all the time I have known Ned, I have never known him speak maliciously, behave shoddily. He was always courteous, gentle, tolerant of weakness, understanding of fear.'

And then he said, 'We have another speaker today, one who knew Ned very well indeed, one of his patients, a remarkable young person, Miss Susan Mills. Come and join me, Susan, and tell everyone what you wanted to say about Mr Welles.'

Susan, undaunted by the size of the church, the fact that it was packed from wall to wall, that she had heard more wonderful words and music than she had ever done in her short life, scrambled past her mother, marched to the pulpit, climbed the steps, coughed a few times and then beamed round the church.

'Mr Welles was a very special doctor. I called him Dr Make-me-Welles. He was always kind, he always had time to listen to us, sometimes he read us stories, and he never minded if any of us children was noisy, or cried, or wetted our beds.' Laughter at that, but gentle, tolerant laughter. 'He didn't just make us better, he made us *feel* better.' She looked down towards the coffin. 'I would just like to say, thank you, Mr Welles, for all you did for all of us. We shall miss you very much.'

At which moment, the sun shone suddenly and determinedly through the stained-glass window above the altar; and Jillie and Persephone looked at one another and smiled, and embraced, and Jillie whispered, 'Phew! He liked it,' and Persephone whispered back, 'And, maybe, there is a God.'

And William Curtis climbed down the steps back to his seat.

✳ ✳ ✳

'We will now have the anthem,' said Christian Greenwell, into the silence, 'and make no apologies for more Fauré. Ned loved Fauré, and he would not mind – I hope – "In Paradisum", from the Requiem.'

And so, Edward Welles, MD, FRCS, was borne to whatever heaven he might have wished, and they sang a last hymn, and then he was lifted by the pallbearers, for the start of his journey towards his earthly resting place, a graveyard in Cornwall, found by Persephone and near the sea.

And Julius, pushing determinedly against the flow, reached Jillie finally; and she saw him, and was briefly and entirely lifted from her sorrow, and smiled at him in pure joy as he took her hand and they made their way slowly out of the church together.

Even the most sternly faced members of the congregation looked around at one another, tear-stained and smiling at the same time, as they were assured it was a lovely day to be caught in the rain. Which was just as well, as the sun had already relinquished its place in the sky, and the clouds had rolled in once more.

# Epilogue

It was a beautiful day, in the end. The sun had finally won its battle with the clouds, and shone determinedly through the afternoon. People were able to leave the marquee and walk on the lawn, exclaiming at the garden and its beauty; a little faded, to be sure, now that autumn was almost come, but still offering roses. And besides, with so charming a service behind them, what promised to be a banquet to come, and the most perfectly chilled, vintage champagne to drink now, who would criticise anything, anything at all?

A few eyebrows had been raised at the bridegroom's variation upon his morning dress, namely a striped coat and black trousers; mercifully, no one had seen his choice of top hat, which had been white, rather than black, and vetoed by the bride only the evening before in extremely certain terms.

The bride, however, looked wonderfully and conventionally bride-like, her dress white silk, with a slightly elongated bodice, long tight sleeves and a skirt that billowed into almost exaggerated fullness, becoming a train at the back. Her grandmother's tiara held her veil, and her bouquet, passed to her matron of honour for the service – she had no bridesmaids – was of white and yellow roses. The only criticism, voiced by perhaps only a very few after she had gone away, was that her hair was not teased into conventional bridal curls, or bound into a stiff chignon, but hung, die-straight, down her back.

That was how the bridegroom liked it, and indeed, he had told her it was one of the first things about her he had noticed, and therefore fell in love with; and since it was the sort of hair that did not take kindly to teasing or binding, it was a decision easily taken.

Not that any of them had been difficult: for who else would she want as her matron of honour, but her best friend from her school-days, with whom she had shared and suffered and rejoiced so much? And who was looking quite absurdly pretty in a long, narrow dress, made of blue taffeta in a shade that exactly matched her eyes: her hair at least she wore in the statutory curls, but then it had a mind of its own, and she never wore it otherwise. Her husband, watching her as she walked down the aisle behind the bride, thought how much he loved her, and how incredible it was that that slender body had borne three children, the eldest of whom sat on his knee, bribed into silence with a new *Thomas the Tank Engine* book, which he studied intently throughout, the younger two being in the care of their next-door neighbours for the day.

The easiest decision of all for the bride had been saying yes to the bridegroom, despite his proposal following rather swiftly, and some might have thought unsuitably, upon another ceremony, namely the funeral of one of the bride's best friends. But a few misunderstand-ings safely explained, there seemed little point to him in waiting any further, and fortunately the bride had agreed.

And how extremely appropriate for the best man today to have been best man at the wedding of the matron of honour and her husband: another piece of felicity, and even more so as it was he who had intro-duced the bride and groom. It had been his wish, most forcibly voiced, and the bride, touched beyond anything, had most happily agreed.

The speeches were all splendid; the groom's a little short, for he said he had nothing to say except that he adored the bride, considered himself the luckiest man alive, and couldn't wait to embark upon married life, and asked them to toast the very beautiful matron of honour, 'And while you are about it, could we also raise our glasses to her husband who has recently – very recently – been elected as a Member of Parliament. I'm sure we all wish him well.'

The Member of Parliament, who was, at the behest of his wife, dressed rather more grandly than he felt appropriate to his new calling – but he was anxious to please her in as many ways as he possibly could – stood up and bowed and thanked him graciously.

Later, as the guests began to drift away, and the late summer dusk was thickening to darkness, Tom walked round the garden, thinking how, in spite of its sorrows, his life had been extremely blessed. He travelled back in time, to the very beginning, to his childhood in Hampshire, and to Diana, who recently, he had read, having retired rather publicly from modelling, was now turned society photographer, working closely with the gossip columnist Leo Bennett.

An unlikely liaison theirs had been, and hugely dangerous, but she had been a good and wise friend to him, and he would not have been in as happy a situation as he was today without her. For her advice that dreadful day, to set the tragedy of Laura finally behind him, whatever the circumstances and in whichever hospital they had occurred, and to concentrate on what he could do with his future, rather than what he could not with his past, had saved, he truly felt, his marriage and his career.

And then he thought of Laura and the tiny Hope, lying in the churchyard, and decided that the very next day, before they returned to Sandbanks, he would take not just Alice, but the children, to visit them; and he resolved in some strange and wonderful way to make them all one family.

# Acknowledgements

Acknowledgements are really thank you letters – a record of extremely heartfelt gratitude to all the people who have helped to create a book, to give it interest and colour, and to make the characters creatures of substance, with ambitions and passions beyond the personal. And writing them is to travel through the book again, from beginning to end, and realise what a journey of discovery it has been.

In writing *A Question of Trust*, I have relied hugely on many people, kind, generous people, all hugely knowledgeable in their fields, who gave me their time and attention and I really do thank them from the bottom of my heart.

From the very outset, I was lucky enough to have a brilliant and fascinating ally in Barbara Hosking, former Whitehall 'Spin Doctor' with an encyclopaedic memory, an ongoing passion for politics and, as a very welcome bonus, a brisk sense of humour about the political scene. She worked for such mighty legends from the forties and fifties as Harold Wilson, Nye Bevan, and Barbara Castle and the hours I spent either with her or reading her emails were both awesome and immense fun. She was also very helpful in creating situations for me that my hero, Tom Knelston, might find himself in, thus extending the plot neatly more than once. I quite simply could not have written the book without her.

I was led to Barbara by the redoubtable Sue Stapely – no stranger to my acknowledgement pages! – who also contributed on the political front, having not only been a political candidate in the eighties, but Head of PR at the law society. She proved as always a rich source of knowledge on both political and legal procedures and on the divorce process in the fifties – astonishingly different from today.

And Lorraine Lindsay-Gale, County Councillor for many years, who gave me a nail-biting description of the tension of polling day – and The Count!

For information on the medical front, I was incredibly fortunate to find one Professor Harold Ellis, (still lecturing on anatomy as he marches briskly through his nineties – he says it keeps him young) who was actually working for the NHS on the day it was launched. His memories of that day and indeed those preceding it, and his life as a young surgeon, were totally fascinating.

I was introduced to him by another doctor, Anthony Rossi, retired consultant plastic surgeon and lifelong personal friend; he dredged his considerable memory and introduced me to a medical condition, absolutely crucial to the plot, of which I had never heard, patiently explaining it to me in all its complexity at least three times.

I met Dr Herbert Barrie, a paediatrician in the fifties, working at Great Ormond Street among other places and whose stories of caring for sick children then were both moving and fascinating. He has, very sadly, now died; but the morning I spent with him, hearing of his work and the passion he felt for it, is still a most vivid and happy memory.

Professor Ray Powles CBE, the distinguished Head of Heamato-Oncology at the Cancer Centre London, gave me a most hilarious account of his days as a medical student in the fifties and a slightly more sober one of his early days as a doctor; I could have listened all day, and actually did for several hours.

I must also thank most profoundly Alexandra Annand, who hostessed a wonderful tea party for me and two ladies who had trained at St Thomas's Hospital from 1947 onwards. Their stories were absolutely riveting, right from their very first day, under the iron rule of Sister, (prayers in the ward at eight sharp, probationers having cleaned polished and 'hot dusted' first). Alexandra herself trained at Thomas's in the sixties, rising in rank to Night Sister in the seventies. Her stories were equally fascinating; I might have to write another book, just to accommodate them! This one would have been much the poorer without her help.

Then huge thanks also to Walter Merricks CBE, former Chief Ombudsman, who was so helpful in giving me background into the life and training of a young solicitor taking his articles in those far-off days, as he lunched me most generously in the splendid Law Society building in Chancery Lane.

And many thanks to Sheila Sharp, old friend from the same girls' grammar school as me in Totnes, South Devon, who provided invaluable background information on grammar school entry, in those far-off days.

Immense help on the military front; Christopher White-Thomson, another lifelong friend, recounted wonderfully vivid stories from his military family archives of the taking of Monte Casino, and the events surrounding it.

Two of the old soldiers I met wished to remain anonymous, but I am able to thank one beloved old friend, Neil Mills, who recounted in enormous detail and with great relish, tales of his war experiences in a series of torpedo boats in both the Atlantic and the Med, two of which he commanded. Neil has, very sadly, died now, and I miss him a lot; and deeply regret that he will never know of my gratitude for what was a crucial chapter in the book.

The stories from these men, boys really, straight from school, of the horrors they endured, and the courage that was called upon them to show, all recounted with cheery dismissiveness, were exceedingly humbling.

On the glamour front, as you might call it, fascinating stuff from Liz Smith, one of the great Fashion Editors of my own era, who had worked with some of the legendary photographers of an earlier age, as did my heroine; and from Felicity Green, OBE, Grande Dame of fashion and fashion journalism in newspapers from the fifties onwards, a true visionary and pioneer of some of the new trends in fashion photography and presentation.

Closer to home, and in the here and now, I have so much to be grateful for.

Especially at Headline, my publishers; I have a wise and wonderful editor, Imogen Taylor, patient and appreciative, who never seems to pressure or hurry me in any way, while somehow miraculously getting me to deliver copy when she wants it, and then to reassure me that it is not the load of rubbish I had convinced myself I'd produced. She is also given to sudden lightning flashes of inspiration herself which add to the story considerably. Truly an editorial magician.

Immense thanks to Jo Liddiard, Head of Marketing, who has picked up the book and run with it, ensuring its image is perfectly honed and recognised in all manner of brilliant ways; to Becky Bader, Sales Director, who has, quite simply, ensured *A Question of Trust* is to be found in every shopping outlet in the land and indeed in space, if you count the internet; and Georgina Moore, Communications Director, who has sprinkled news of the book like fairy dust, in her inimitable way, into just about every facet of the media it could possibly be.

If you can judge a book by its cover, then *A Question of Trust* is the most glamorous, dazzling and beautiful ever; huge gratitude to Yeti Lambregts who designed it. It has left everyone who has seen it gasping.

I don't think we'd have seen the book on the shelves for many a long moon, and certainly well past its proper date, without the calm, tireless efficiency of Amy Perkins, Editorial Assistant, who has somehow managed to see the manuscript in its various stages is always on time, wherever it's supposed to be, when it's supposed to be there.

A thousand thanks to my brilliant agent, Clare Alexander, who, apart from the more obvious agent-y gifts which she possesses in spades, has a kind of eighth sense that has her ringing me when I am a despairing, limp heap, and leaves me feeling lit up, freshly inspired and like a million dollars.

And finally, my four lovely, lovely daughters, Polly, Sophie, Emily and Claudia, who even after all these years and all these books, know how much I need cossetting and encouraging from time to time and in spite of all the other calls on their time and attention, like husbands, children and careers, never ever fail me.